FALLING
WITH
FOLDED
WINGS

Falling with Folded Wings

 BOOK 1

Plum Parrot

For Clay
Thanks for being my first reader
and for pushing me to keep writing

All rights reserved. No part of this publication may be reproduced, stored in a retrieval system, or transmitted in any form or by any means electronic, mechanical, photocopying, recording, or otherwise without prior written permission from Podium Publishing.

This is a work of fiction. Names, characters, places, and incidents are either products of the author's imagination or used fictitiously. Any resemblance to actual events, locales, or persons, living, dead, or undead, is entirely coincidental.

Copyright © 2022 by Miles C. Gallup

Cover design by Podium Publishing

ISBN: 978-1-0394-1714-4

Published in 2022 by Podium Publishing, ULC
www.podiumaudio.com

FALLING
WITH
FOLDED
WINGS

ᑭ MORGAN ᑐ

The massive ship shuddered from a blast of the Bussard drive as it steadily decelerated on approach to the Tau Ceti system. Sifting through the long-range sensor array data, Noah-9 dedicated a tiny fraction of his processing power to simulate a nearly perfect approximation of a human frown. There had to be an error—physics generally wouldn't allow for a non-gaseous planet this size. Almost the size of Jupiter in the Sol system, but with terrestrial formations that resembled Earth. Mountains, rivers, oceans of apparent H2O? Not only impossible, but this sort of planet was not what was supposed to be waiting for them.

Before the ship's departure, two hundred forty Earth years ago, the orbital telescope, Raleigh 2, had confirmed four super-Earth planets, two in the Goldilocks zone. Additionally, the system was supposed to have one gas giant and six other icy planets and planetoids. Now, on approach, the long-range sensors showed just this one giant, impossible world. Noah deliberated, calculating thousands of scenarios, and finally decided to wake one of the colony technicians.

Five thousand humans were in cryo-stasis on the *Pilgrim 9*. Ensign Hall would not be happy to be awakened seventeen months before orbit was established, but Noah-9 could not carry out the required troubleshooting of the long-range sensors on his own. He quickly initiated life support, flooding the habitation area with oxygen and raising the ambient temperature to 21 degrees Celsius. Noah-9 moved from the Data Bridge to the central elevator and "descended" to Stasis Bay 4. Therein slept the hundreds of engineers and technicians chosen to create a new human colony. Ensign Hall had scored the highest on the applied troubleshooting simulations, so he would be the lucky human first to lay eyes on their new home. He would have to stay awake after repairing the sensors, because his body wouldn't be ready to re-enter cryo-stasis before their arrival.

Morgan wasn't sure what he'd been dreaming about, but he knew he was having a good time. He had a sense he'd been laughing. Now, as reality crashed in, he was choking to death. Morgan heaved, over and over, and with each contraction of his diaphragm, clear cryo-gel flooded out of his lungs. He noted the circular drain in the metal floor and realized he was on his hands and knees in front of his cryo-pod. After he heaved and coughed for a few minutes, he began to breathe in the rather cold air without sputtering, and he blearily looked up. He was in a circular cryo-pod bay, and all the other pods were closed, covered in a thin sheen of frost, displaying green LEDs. Morgan nearly jumped out of his skin when he realized a figure was silently standing just to his right. He relaxed when he realized it was just one of those creepy Noah units, its human shape and *almost* human skin making it rather nightmare-inducing in the dark, quiet cryo-pod bay.

"Ensign Hall, you've just woken from cryo-stasis on board the *Pilgrim 9* en route to the Tau Ceti system," the Noah unit said, with a passably human note of emotion. It continued, "I am Noah-9, the ship's physicalized AI unit. I've woken you 17.34 months prior to our scheduled arrival because I need your assistance with the troubleshooting and repair of our long-range telemetric and photometric scanners."

Morgan coughed out one last hunk of cryo-gel, and then sputtered, "What? Seventeen months? Scanners?"

"That's right, Ensign. You'll note the showers are through the archway to your left, and a clean ship's uniform has been prepared for you." Morgan squinted at the Noah unit, noting the utter lack of emotion on its face, then struggled to his feet. He stumbled into the shower room and shoved the curtain aside on the first stall. As Morgan stepped under the showerhead, he punched the single chrome button, and a steamy deluge sprayed over his bare scalp and down his back, making him feel immensely more alive. He noted the digital countdown above the shower button and realized he only had twenty-seven more seconds to rinse off. Groaning, he quickly scrubbed his arms and legs, urging his blood to circulate. At the same time, he watched the cryo-gel that had been clinging to him circle the drain and descend to God knows where to be recycled into some necessary component chemicals for the ship to utilize. As the timer ticked down to zero, the water stopped as suddenly as it began. Morgan sighed and punched the button again to no avail.

"Stingy bastards," he muttered as he turned around and opened the curtain. A towel and a silvery jumpsuit hung above the bench opposite the stall. He quickly dried off and pulled on the jumpsuit. It was baggy until he pulled the zipper to the top, then it constricted to fit his form perfectly. Warm, flexible, and utterly devoid of any discretion, the silvery jumpsuit was standard for Pilgrim class ship crews. "All right, Noah unit. Tell me, what's the problem?"

"Ensign Hall, I need you to spacewalk to the aft sensor arrays and see if you can troubleshoot the problem I'm having. I have exhaustively examined the software and internal circuitry—there are no anomalies."

"What's the actual problem?" Morgan pressed with another long-suffering sigh.

"Upon system entry, the sensors indicated there is only one planet orbiting Tau Ceti. A Jupiter-size Earth analog," Noah-9 reported, completely deadpan.

"That doesn't make sense. A planet that size would have to be a gas giant."

"Not necessarily, there have been giant rocky planets observed, but they are, indeed, anomalies. I'm more concerned with the fact that our sensors are not properly reading the system at all—there should, obviously, be at least fourteen planets and planetoids in the system."

"Do I detect some snark, Noah-9? I thought you guys didn't have emotions?" Morgan grinned as he started walking through the cryo-pod bay to the elevator.

"Pardon me, Ensign, but all Noah units are capable of approximating human emotion at nearly eighty-seven percent homogeneity!" Noah-9 huffed as it followed Morgan into the elevator.

"Yeah, but there's no way a human would ever say something like that." Morgan chuckled as he punched the button for the Data Bridge.

"Why are you going to the Data Bridge? I need you to debark the ship at Bay 12 and examine the aft sensor array."

"Before I go spacewalking, I'm going to verify the readings you are reporting—what if you are the source of the error and not the sensors?"

"An insightful point, Ensign. If I were the source of the error, I might not notice it. It seems I chose the correct technician for this job." Noah-9 smiled in an almost human way, and Morgan shuddered slightly. He preferred the previous generation of androids that didn't try so hard to look human. When it's fake, it's fake, but when it's almost but not quite human, it comes off as creepy.

Ninety minutes later, Morgan was resignedly stuffing himself into an extravehicular activity, or EVA, suit. He hadn't been able to find any flaws with the Noah unit or with the way it was reading the data coming through the sensor array. Something had to be off. Navigation systems all indicated they were in the right place, but the readings coming out of Tau Ceti were just not right. The star's spectral signature matched Tau Ceti, but the planetary information was just wrong. One giant planet? With rivers; oceans; green, fertile areas? It sounded great if it really could exist, except that it would have to have gravity that would be instantly lethal to humans. Morgan checked the magnetic locks on his boots, then sealed his helmet. He walked into the EVA bay and spoke into his helmet's communicator: "Alright, Noah, cycle this airlock, and I'll go see what I can see."

It took Morgan nearly an hour to walk from EVA Bay 12 along the hull to the aft sensor array. The ship was "falling" into the Tau Ceti system—the engine pointed at their destination so that the Bussard drive could decelerate the ship. It had been decelerating for 118 years. The problem Morgan was having now was that the sensor array looked perfectly fine. No debris, no broken bits, no exposed wiring. All diagnostics processed in the green. What the hell was going on? "Noah, I'm not finding any problem out here. I'm going to walk farther aft and up onto the starboard h-mass container to check if I can see anything beyond the Bussard cone with my own eyes. When's the Bussard supposed to fire next?"

"The next Bussard mass ejection will occur in three hours and fourteen minutes," Noah responded with his precise diction.

"Alright." Morgan started hiking along the ship's hull, and within a few minutes, he was scaling the long steep slope of one of the ship's massive hydrogen tanks. He was hoping he'd be able to see around the big Bussard drive cone and get a view of their eventual destination. Yeah, he knew there was no way to see the planet or planets yet, tens of thousands of miles away, but something made him want to lay his eyes on the center of the system anyway.

When he finally crested the slope of the tank, and the light from Tau's sun caused his visor to darken automatically, he was breathing heavily from the exertion. "Ensign Hall, your oxygen is at sixty-five percent. At your current burn rate, you will run out in one hundred seventeen minutes."

"No worries, Noah. Are you seeing what I'm seeing? Is that yellow haze an artifact from my visor or . . . ?" Tau's light held a slightly more orange tint than Sol's, but it otherwise felt very familiar. What wasn't familiar was the yellow haze that seemed to fill the entirety of Morgan's field of view. It was almost like the ship was falling into a yellowish fog.

"I see your feed, and I do not see any sort of visual artifact." Noah's voice was clinical, as always.

"There's something there. It must be a video processing artifact. It's so weird, though. If it's a camera artifact, why does it seem like we're getting closer to it." Morgan's imagination started to wander toward thoughts he'd rather it didn't: solar flares, radiation, ion storms. Nothing that made sense with what he was seeing, but he couldn't help feeling a slight twinge of panic as he stood out on the hull, exposed to the void.

Morgan grunted as he started to move as quickly as he could in the magnetic boots, back down the side of the h-mass container. The boots made movement a lot slower than a natural walk because the failsafe wouldn't allow one to come unclamped until the other was secured. He wasn't sure why he was hurrying back toward the EVA bay—no matter what, he'd be outside when the ship entered that yellow haze . . . if it was real. Still, he moved as quickly as he could and was about ten feet past the sensor array when Noah's voice cut into the silence: "Ensign Hall, I've lost contact with the systems in the Bussard drive."

"Excuse me?" Morgan hissed, his lungs heaving from the exertion of his pace.

"The diagnostic nodes and all controls to the Bussard engine have stopped responding. I appear to be losing contact with engineering now. I . . ." Noah's precise diction cut out. Morgan suddenly felt very strange. For a moment, his vision got brighter, and he felt like he'd been dosed with a strong euphoric drug, then everything was black. He couldn't feel or see anything. He tried to take a step, and he couldn't be sure his leg moved. He couldn't even tell if his boot was clamped down or not. Panic surged through his mind. Had the ship exploded? Was he drifting in the void? Was he dead?

Integrating non-System entities.

What? "Noah, was that you?" Morgan tried to say, but he wasn't sure any sound came out of his mouth. Was he even breathing? The voice hadn't sounded like Noah. It was emotionless, almost like a discordant mesh of several voices at once.

Calculating: 5,000 species individuals.

Scanning: Human civilization added to System database.

Species average Energy affinity rating: 4.9

Species integration zone D-1.4—Ardent Vale.

1 non-living entity.

Non-living entity Energy affinity rating: 0.0

Non-living entity deleted.

Ice cold calm settled on Morgan's mind. If he could yell or run, he might be doing that, but now he just listened with rapt attention. What the hell was going on, and where was that voice coming from? Non-living entity deleted? Was the voice talking about Noah-9? Energy affinity?

Human Individual, you are separate from the other 4,999 human individuals

Morgan suddenly felt like he had taken a breath, and he could speak: "Yes, I was awake . . ." The voice cut him off:

Champion status assigned. Your Energy affinity rating is 9.2. Individual integration zone D-1.16—Crucible

MORGAN

Morgan felt like he'd been on a week-long bender. His head was throbbing, and his stomach groaned like an angry abyss. Blearily, he pried open his dry, crusty eyelids and looked around. For a few moments, he was stricken with confusion—was he on the floor of his bathroom? Wait, that wasn't right; he was on board the *Pilgrim 9*. No, that wasn't right, either—there weren't tiles on the spacecraft, even in the officer suites. What? Suddenly it rushed back to him, and Morgan sat up with a jolt of adrenaline. He'd been on an EVA, the golden mist, the darkness, the strange voice in his head. Morgan rubbed his eyes quickly and looked around. Yes, the floor was some sort of dark ceramic tilework and, in the dim shadows, he could make out gray walls in front of him and to his left. The light was faint, but it had a golden hue. Morgan looked to his right and then behind him and gasped. There was the source of the glow. It was a small golden ball, about the size of a marble, seemingly hovering in the air about two feet off the ground and about a yard away.

"What the fuck . . .?" Morgan struggled to his knees and realized they were bare; he wasn't wearing his EVA suit or the silver jumper he'd had on underneath. He was wearing a simple pair of brown cloth shorts, and that was it. "Seriously, what the fuck?" He wasn't cold, and he realized that the glowing, floating marble gave off a bit of heat. Behind the light source, the tile floor stretched into yawning shadows. Morgan couldn't hear a sound, but as he strained to see past the marble, he started to notice that the light felt *good*. Like stepping into the summer sunshine after sitting in a dark, cold movie theater sort of good. He hesitantly stretched his hand toward the marble, and it steadily glowed, not moving, not blasting him with heat—just a warm, comfortable radiance. He stopped his fingers about an inch from the marble and pulled back his hand. Just what the hell was going on?

Morgan stood up and stretched his aching joints, peering into the shadows. He could see that the ceiling was average height and looked to be gray in the dim light, just like the wall he'd been lying near. He took a step toward the nearby wall and placed a hand on it. Cool stone. Definitely stone. Solid and thick. Morgan walked along the wall and came to a corner. Another stone wall. As he moved away from the glowing marble, his eyes adjusted gradually to the dark, and he realized he was in a rectangular room about fifteen by thirty feet. He'd been lying near one corner. Morgan walked the perimeter until he was in the corner opposite where he'd been lying and furthest from the glowing marble, and he saw that there was a wooden door with large metal hinges. The door was smooth, and the boards it was crafted from were a rich, deep brown. It fit almost perfectly into the stone doorway, with just the tiniest of cracks between the wood and stone. There was no handle.

Morgan gingerly felt around the wood, gently pressing and trying to pull at the edge with his fingernails. He couldn't get it to move at all. So he continued his circuit around the room and found absolutely nothing but the tile floor and the stone walls. He felt he'd be hard-pressed to even come up with some dust. He walked over the cool, hard tiles back to the glowing marble. "I guess it comes down to you, eh?" Once again, Morgan stretched his right hand out to the marble, noting that the warmth was not at all unpleasant, even less than an inch from his fingers. Very gingerly, he stretched his fingers out the last little bit and felt the smooth, warm surface of the glowing ball.

There was a bit of a flare, and Morgan pulled his hand back, but the light moved with it. He realized his hand felt very warm and the light was moving through his finger and into his skin. The warmth spread through his hand and up his arm. He held his arm out and saw that the light was spreading through his body, almost like it was traveling in his veins. At first, his hand and arm were glowing, but as the warmth spread through his body, Morgan felt like he'd been dropped into a warm, luxurious bath, and the glow faded.

Congratulations! You have achieved level 1 base human.

The message was floating in front of Morgan's eyes. White text on a gray, semi-opaque background. Morgan reached up to his face, wondering if he'd had augmented reality glasses on this whole time, but there was nothing there. He closed his eyes, and the screen was still there! He opened his eyes and realized the room wasn't completely dark, despite the disappearance of the glowing marble—there was a diffuse dim light emanating from the ceiling. He reached out and tried to feel the screen in front of his face. To his surprise, he could feel it. It was pliable and stretchy and moved with this hand. Morgan swiped the screen like he would dismiss a notification on a workstation, and it worked—it zipped away, shrinking into nothing. Only to be replaced with another one:

Status		
Name:	Morgan Hall	
Race:	Human - Base 1	
Class:	—	
Level:	1	
Energy Affinity:	9.2	Energy: 20/0
Strength:	6	Vitality: 8
Dexterity:	8	Agility: 7
Intelligence:	12	Will: 10
Titles & Feats:	Human Champion	
Skills:	System Language Integration - Not Upgradeable	

"Uh, what the hell is this? Am I in a game?" Morgan's mind was spinning. Though he spoke out loud, he was surprised when another screen popped up in front of the status screen.

*****You have been integrated into a System controlled domain.*****

Morgan grunted in thought and then swiped the message aside, looking more closely at the status screen. "Let's see. Race, class, level, stats—a lot like a VR RPG back home." Morgan wondered about his stats. What was the maximum stat? Was there a maximum? It seemed his intelligence was much higher than his strength. It made sense—he wasn't a weakling, but he wasn't exactly a bodybuilder. He'd always been smart, though, and good with puzzles—it's how he'd gotten his position on the colony ship. What was Energy affinity? He suddenly had a thought and spoke out loud, "What is the System?"

*****The System is a term used to describe the autonomous collective of benevolent entities that collaboratively manage the Energy infused portions of the known universes to create better harmony between sapient species and Energy and to push those sapient species to greater heights of understanding and advancement.*****

Morgan swiped away the screen and said, "What is energy?"

*****Energy is the living force that infuses all beings and materials in System-controlled portions of the known universes.*****

Morgan sighed and pushed away the screen. That seemed a little circular. "What does Energy do?" No response. "Who are the entities that make up the System?" No response. "Am I speaking to the System now?" No response. He decided to take another tack: "What is a class?"

A Class is a System-curated set of skills and attributes.

Interesting. "How do I get a class?"

The System has determined that Humans will be eligible for a class selection at the tenth level.

"What are attributes?" Nothing. "What is strength?"

Strength is the measure of your physical power relative to other Energy infused beings.

That was basically what Morgan had figured. "What is will?"

Will is the measure of your ability to impose or resist Energy-based influences. It is one of the determining factors in the calculation of your maximum Energy potential.

Morgan rubbed his head in thought. "What is an Energy-based influence?" No response. "Uh, why do I have twenty out of zero Energy?" Nothing. "What is vitality?"

Vitality is the measure of your physical and mental durability relative to other Energy infused beings.

So far, he hadn't heard anything surprising. "What are dexterity, intelligence, and agility?"

Dexterity is the measure of your fine motor skills relative to other Energy infused beings.

Intelligence is the measure of your ability to manipulate Energy in novel and complex ways and how quickly you do so. It is the main factor in the calculation of your maximum Energy potential.

Agility is the measure of your physical prowess and speed relative to other Energy infused beings.

So, intelligence didn't automatically make you a super genius, but was more about how fast you could think and use this so-called Energy. "What is a title?"

Titles and Feats are System generated packages of perks that are reflective of individual merit.

Morgan chuckled to himself at the idea that the system had marked him out as some kind of champion based on the "merit" that he was awake, and everyone else was in cryo-sleep. Clearly, the System was not flawless. "How do I see what my title does?"

Human Champion: Transient title. Energy efficacy enhanced 1.5x. More frequent access to System generated Opportunities for Refinement.

"What the hell is an opportunity for refinement?" No window popped up to answer his frustrated query. "What is a transient title?" No answer. Morgan could only assume that it meant that the title was literally transient—it moved around. He guessed it made sense—whoever the "champion" of a civilization was would have the title, and that wouldn't always be the same person. Surely, whenever the rest of the colonists were awake, the system would realize its mistake and move the title to Arthur Ballard, the leader of the Colonial Senate. "What is system language integration?"

All sapient beings in System controlled space are enhanced with the ability to communicate via a common dialect.

Well, that solidified a fear Morgan was starting to develop—the System could monkey with him in any number of ways, including planting a language in his mind. He didn't even know if he was speaking English or "System" right now. He spent the next several minutes trying to get more information out of the strange System UI, but he couldn't pull any more help screens up. Apparently, he wasn't talking to the System, but just accessing some very minimal help files that were built into whatever interface the System had provided him. "Well, what now?"

Quest: Survive the Crucible. Reward(s): Commensurate with achievements. Continued existence. Location of other Human entities. Accept? YES/NO

❦ MORGAN ᴆ

"What the fuck?" Morgan groaned as an unseen lock on the door clicked, and it silently swung open. There was evidently more light outside the room than in, because Morgan could see a flickering amber glow outlining the gap between the door and the wall. He wanted to look through the opening and see what was beyond, but he also wanted to know just what the hell was going on with himself. Something was up with his mind. Morgan's entire world had been turned upside down here; he was in a stone room in some boxer shorts and was seeing and hearing shit that should only exist in a VR game. Yet, he was taking things in stride. He hadn't always had a cushy life; he'd seen his share of problems on Earth during the collapse, but he sure as hell shouldn't be feeling so fine about things. Had the System screwed with his mind? Like more than just putting in a UI and changing his language? Did it pump him with dopamine or something? What else had the System changed about him?

Morgan examined his thoughts for a few minutes. He thought about his childhood, his schooling, the competition to join the Arkship colony. Everything seemed to be there, but would he know if something wasn't? He thought back to his sister and how she had died during the Great Lakes conflict. Yeah, he still felt shitty about that. He still could imagine crawling into a ball and giving up. Okay, so his emotions weren't all smoothed over, but for some reason, he just wasn't freaking out about his current situation. "Huh, survive the Crucible, eh?" He stepped over to the doorway.

Tiptoeing, barefoot on the cool tile floor, he felt like he was nearly silent. Gingerly, he pulled the door just a bit wider and peered into the space beyond. He saw a hallway with walls and a floor much like the room in which he stood. It stretched to his left and right, and about forty feet to the right, he could make out a corner because there appeared to be a lantern mounted there. It was glowing with an actual flame dancing behind a glass panel. Morgan stepped out of the room and began to creep toward the lantern. He'd made it about halfway to the corner when he heard feet slapping rapidly on the stone floor and wheezing, grunting inhalations behind him. Morgan spun around in time to see a short, gray, totally nude, and hairless man charging at him with a sharpened stick pointed right at his stomach. By the time Morgan recovered from his shock, the makeshift spear was almost upon him. He twisted to his left, and instead of running him through, the jagged wooden tip left a painful scratch along his stomach. The momentum of the little man carried him in front of Morgan, and Morgan reflexively shoved him as he went by.

The gray man stumbled and fell to the hard floor, tangling with the haft of his spear. He turned and looked at Morgan from the ground, and that was when Morgan realized the man's eyes were bright yellow. He spread his lips and hissed at him, and Morgan saw that the man had teeth more fitting a wildcat than a person, and his tongue was long and forked.

"Yo, settle down, man!" Morgan yelled, holding out his hands and crouching into a defensive pose. He'd been trained in self-defense techniques like all prospective colonists, and before that, he'd served in one of the Resistance militias, though he spent that time mostly pulling a trigger, not fighting hand to hand. The man, or creature, as Morgan was now starting to think of it, hissed again and struggled to its feet, leveling the spear once more at Morgan and advancing. "I'm serious, guy. Back off!"

"Hssssssssss!" The creature burst into a run, once more trying to skewer Morgan. This time Morgan was ready, and he sidestepped, grabbing the haft of the spear and wrenching it in a half-circle while thrusting his weight into the creature's forward momentum. It lost its grip on the spear and sprawled onto the hard floor. Morgan could see dark blood smearing the creature's knees and the tiles. This time it was Morgan's turn to level the spear at the little beast.

"Back off," he said, once again. The creature struggled to its feet, and Morgan could see that it was weak; its stomach was hollow, and its ribs protruded. It looked at Morgan, hissed, gnashed its many sharp teeth, and charged him, hands with black claws outstretched. Morgan lowered his center of gravity and thrust the spear directly into the creature's stomach. He felt a moment of resistance, and the spear burst through, dark blood splattering onto the floor. The creature wailed piteously, gripping at the haft of the spear weakly. Morgan pushed the little monster backward and held it pinned to the ground. Soon, its wails turned to gurgles, and foamy blood dripped from its mouth as its chest stopped heaving, and its arms fell limply to the ground.

Morgan didn't have time to think about what he'd just done before something strange happened to the corpse. A shimmering layer of gold-colored dust sparkled around it, and surged into a stream that flowed straight at Morgan. He was startled and tried to dodge to the side, but it was impossible to avoid. The stream of tiny golden motes hit him square in the chest, and it felt just like when he'd touched the glowing marble earlier—warmth spread from his chest into his limbs and head, then faded to a general feeling of warm satisfaction.

"Goddamn! What the hell was that?" Morgan ran his hands along his body and couldn't find anything amiss. Surprisingly, he felt pretty good. The scratch along his abdomen wasn't as bad as he'd thought it was, just a raised welt with a thin line of blood in the middle.

Morgan had killed plenty of people in the various conflicts that ravaged the North American continent over the decade or so before he'd been selected to join the *Pilgrim 9* mission. It haunted him at first, but survival was survival, and he'd created a hard place in his mind to put those feelings, especially when his sister died. He definitely wasn't the same guy he'd been before that. He didn't like that he'd had to kill this creature, but if it wanted to stab him, he was plenty happy to turn the tables rather than the alternative. "Status." The only difference he could see is that he now had twenty-four out of zero energy. What the hell? It was a mystery he'd have to unravel sooner rather than later, if his gut feeling was correct.

Morgan looked up and down the hall and at the corpse at his feet. He wondered if this guy was alone. The fight certainly hadn't been quiet with the thing screeching and Morgan yelling at it. So far, nothing else seemed to be coming. He reached down and grabbed the body by the ankle and dragged it back to his doorway and into the room he'd started in. There wasn't much he could do about the blood smears, though. He took a good look at the spear he'd taken from the creature. It was made of tough wood, and the carved point was black like it had been hardened in a fire. Morgan felt immeasurably less naked with the spear in his hand.

Once again, Morgan was stealthily creeping toward the lantern at the corner of the hallway. This time he managed to get there without being attacked, and his eyes had become so adjusted to the darkness that he found it difficult to look directly at the little flame in the brass-colored lantern. It was hung from an iron bracket by a long brass handle, and Morgan decided to take it with him, lifting it off the bracket without any trouble. It was heavy with oil or whatever it used for fuel, and he had to assume someone or something had filled it fairly recently. The hallway that stretched in front of him continued for about fifty feet and, there, highlighted by the glow of another lantern, was a second wooden door.

Morgan kept the lantern in his left hand while holding the spear, like he was ready to stab it forward, as you might hold it if you were going to throw it, in his other hand. He advanced at a slow, careful pace toward the door. When he was about eight feet or so from the door, Morgan noticed a sound coming from within. It was sort of a mewling, crying sound. As he crept closer, more noises started to leak through the door—grunting and guttural laughter. This door wasn't so perfectly fit into the frame, and the wooden slats didn't mesh without a gap like the door to his room. Holding his breath, Morgan leaned forward, peering with one eye through a wide crack. If he hadn't been holding his breath, he would have found himself frozen with shock, and unable to breathe anyway, by the sight that confronted him.

The door separated the hallway from a much more crudely wrought room. The walls weren't uniform to the point of almost looking like natural cavern walls. The room had a stone floor covered in debris and bits of rock and dirt. Lying on the floor, with her hands and feet bound with a rough hemp rope, was a humanoid female. The woman had long, bright-yellow hair and pale blue skin. Her eyes and mouth were covered with strips of cloth, and Morgan could see she was the source of the keening, muffled cries. There were two of those gray creatures hunched over the lower part of her body, and as Morgan realized what they were doing, he started to hyperventilate: they were eating her. Alive.

Something snapped in Morgan, and his vision narrowed to a tunnel. He set the lantern down and yanked the door open. The door wasn't held in place by any sort of a latch, and it scraped along the tiles as he pulled, but he was through it and jamming a spear, with two hands, into the back of the first creature before it could turn around. He kicked the creature off the spear and swung the haft around, smashing the face of the second creature before it could finish standing up. The butt of the spear crunched into its nose and left eye socket, and it dropped to the ground with a thud. The first creature was writhing on its stomach away from Morgan, leaving a broad, slippery streak of blood behind it. Morgan stepped forward and drove the spear into its lower back, and it stopped moving. He looked around in the dark room, but nothing else moved. The woman was still crying, and Morgan started to walk over to her when two streams of golden motes slammed into his chest.

Congratulations! You have achieved level 2 base human and have 5 attribute points to allocate.

The brief euphoria from the Energy, at least that's what Morgan suspected it was, flooding into him broke through his murderous rage, and he took a deep breath, steadying himself before he knelt next to the woman. She was wearing a tan-colored close-fitting cloth shift, her legs and feet bare. The beasts had horrifically mutilated her right leg, the thigh chewed to the bone. Although she'd bled a great deal, Morgan could see she was still taking shallow breaths and softly whimpering. He carefully pulled the blindfold away from her eyes and said, "Easy, easy. They're dead."

◈ MORGAN ◈

The woman's large, amber eyes widened in fear as Morgan pulled the cloth away, and she struggled to writhe away from him. He held his hands out and, keeping his voice low and calm, said, "Easy, I'm not going to hurt you. I just want to help you get out of those ropes." Her eyes darted around, but she seemed to stop panicking as she nodded quickly. Morgan reached forward. "I'm going to remove the gag first. Don't yell, 'cause I don't know how many more of these creeps are around." He reached up and pulled the cloth away from the woman's mouth, letting it settle around her neck. He was startled to see that, while her facial features were similar to a human's, her teeth were not—overly large canines descended from her top gums and most of her other visible teeth were pointy as well.

"Thank you, but you're right—there are many more of the Yeksa in this area. You should run." Her voice was sharp and tinged with repressed pain. Morgan could only imagine how badly her leg hurt. He was also a little surprised he could understand her. He'd been speaking soothingly, hoping for her to at least comprehend his intentions, if not his words, but he understood her perfectly, and apparently, it went the same way for her.

"I guess we're both speaking System, eh?" Morgan said as he started to work on the bindings around her wrists.

"Ancestors damn the System!" The woman hissed.

"Yeah, I'm not much of a fan, either. By the way, my name's Morgan. I think I'm going to have to use this rope to tourniquet that leg. Jesus, those fuckers did a number on you."

"My name is Issa. I think you should leave me. I'll die soon without proper healing, anyway." She grimaced in pain as Morgan jostled her leg, trying to get at the knot of the ropes binding her ankles.

"Nah, I'm not leaving you like this. We'll figure something out."

"We're far too deep in this damned Crucible to find help, and I won't be much use to you if we meet more of the Yeksa, or worse. I damaged my Core fighting beyond my means when I was captured." Issa winced and bit off her last words in pain as the knot finally came loose, and Morgan gingerly unwound the tightly wrapped rope.

"Look, these Yeksa are dumb assholes, and we'll cross that bridge when we come to it, but, yeah, we need to do something about your leg. I'm going to stop the bleeding, and it's going to hurt like a bitch," Morgan said as he started to slip the rope gently around Issa's upper right thigh. He could see her eyes widening in fear, but she just gripped her lavender-colored fists and stared past him at the ceiling. Morgan grimaced as he double wrapped the rope around Issa's thigh. She wasn't a big person, and he didn't doubt his ability to staunch the blood seeping out of her mutilated thigh, but he knew it was going to hurt, and it was different hurting someone in the heat of a fight and hurting someone as they lay helplessly at your feet. "Hey, I'm about to tighten this thing. You want something to bite on?" Morgan looked around for something he could give her.

"Just do it, please, Morgan. My vision grows darker by the second." Morgan nodded and pulled the rope as tight as he could. Issa hissed in pain but didn't make any other sound.

"All right, let's get you on your feet. Just a second," Morgan said as he hurried back to the door and fetched the lantern he had set down in the hallway. When he brought the lantern back to Issa, his field of vision in the rough-hewn room was much more expansive, and he could see that some objects were lying around and against the wall. Some ratty furs were piled off to one side, and Morgan thought maybe it was a bed for the Yeksa. Leaning against one wall were two more rough spears. Neither was as long or straight as his but would serve as a crutch. He fetched one for Issa to use while he supported her other side.

She was light, and Morgan easily helped her get to her feet. She couldn't have been much more than five feet tall and was very slight. Other than her odd coloring and predatory teeth, she looked much like a human. Her features were sharp, with a slightly upturned elfin nose and yellow eyebrows framing bright amber eyes. "Sorry, I'm kinda staring; you don't look like the people where I come from."

"I could say the same about you, Morgan." Issa grunted, obviously more focused on her plight than her strange-looking new companion.

"Right, sorry," Morgan said, as he tried to support as much of her weight as he could. "Which way should we go?"

"I was hoping you'd know more than I. I was unconscious when they dragged me in here. Maybe we should explore this cave a bit further," Issa said, gesturing deeper into the darkness. Morgan nodded, and they began to slowly and carefully shuffle deeper. Morgan couldn't hold the lantern and his spear while holding Issa, so she insisted on just holding his shoulder with one hand and the spear with the other as she hobbled along at his side.

"You're tougher than you look, Issa." Morgan smiled as they advanced. She just grunted in response. The lantern light slowly revealed that the carved stone walls grew ever narrower as they moved, and soon the room was more of a corridor. Bits of stone and dirt were strewn about the floor. They proceeded this way for quite a while, with the tunnel becoming rougher the whole time as it began to wind in different directions, seemingly at random. Morgan couldn't help noticing that it seemed to have a slight downward slope. "I dunno about you, but I was kinda hoping we'd be going up rather than down."

"Yes, but the Crucible is not so easily departed, I'm afraid," Issa whispered hoarsely.

"Just what the fuck is the Crucible, anyway?"

"It's funny, Morgan, I can understand most of your words, but it seems you're also using some vestiges of your old tongue. How do you not know what the Crucible is? You're in it."

"Huh, I guess the System didn't translate some of my curse words. Oddly, that makes me feel better. Well, I don't know what the Crucible is because my people are from another world, and the System decided to throw me in here without an explanation!"

"This star system? I don't quite understand you, Morgan. The idea that the System is testing you is no surprise, though. We are insects to it, and it loves to toy with us, offering dreams of power to keep us playing along. We should be quiet, though—I find it harder and harder to speak, and we should not alert potential enemies to our presence." Issa's final few words were almost a hiss as she took a pained breath.

"Right, sorry! Hang in there—you're going to make it."

*****Quest: Don't let Issa die within 1 week. Reward: Energy Core Cultivation Manual, Improved Relations with Ardeni faction. Penalty for failure: Diminished Will efficacy—permanent. Accept? YES/NO*****

So, the System was making him put his money where his mouth was, eh? Morgan almost smashed the YES out of sheer stubbornness, but he suddenly had a thought: "Issa, how long is a day on this world?"

"Um, that's a strange question. A day is as long as it takes for the sun to rise and set, but, as I'm sure you know, the System measures days in twenty standard hours."

"Well, actually, I didn't know that. Much like I'm new to this world, I'm new to the System. How long is a 'standard hour'?"

"A standard hour is seventy-five minutes. I suppose you want to know that a minute is seventy-five seconds. If you're new to the System, I can see why this might be confusing. My grandfather had to relearn a lot when the System came to our world."

"Ah, thanks for the explanation. So, is a second kind of like one-Mississippi, two-Mississippi, three-Mississippi?"

"I don't know what a missy sippy is, but yes, that's about how long a second is."

"Right, right, thanks." Morgan didn't think about it long. It sounded like a week to the System was longer than a week on Earth, but not by a huge amount. He didn't fully understand the reward or penalty being offered, but he didn't care. "Fuck you, System. Accept."

"What did you just do, Morgan?" Issa hissed. Before Morgan could reply, he heard the guttural sounds of some Yeksa talking or laughing or who knows what the hell they were doing; it all sounded the same to Morgan. He held his finger to his lips and pointed into the darkness. Issa nodded, and Morgan helped her lean against the tunnel wall, setting the lantern on the ground. He gripped his spear and moved to take a step into the darkness, but Issa grabbed his arm.

"Wait," she whispered in a barely audible breath. She scrunched up her face in a grimace of concentration, then lifted her hand, two fingers extended, the others folded. She pressed her fingers to Morgan's forehead and a few seconds passed while she concentrated, clearly trying to do something. Morgan was about to step away, worried the Yeksa would come around the corner at any second, when he felt a tingling warmth spread from Issa's fingers into his forehead and down into his eyes. She pulled her hand away, panting, and he blinked rapidly. The once dark tunnel was now much brighter, highlighted in bright whites and grays; the lantern looked like a blooming white nova rather than a flickering yellow flame. "Dark vision!" Issa smiled and said with a weary sigh, "I can't make it last long with my Core the way it is, but it should be long enough."

Morgan nodded, gripped his spear, and advanced into the darkness. Well, not really darkness anymore. He still needed the light from the lantern behind him, but it was like the lantern was a sun. All the rocks and rough edges of the tunnel wall stood out in stark contrast to the shadows thrown by the light. He could see at least fifty feet into the tunnel and could see that it curved slightly to the left at first and then, at the extremity of his view, sharply. He quietly padded forward to the curve, listening to the guttural sounds of the Yeksa growing steadily nearer. He saw a bit of a crevice near the corner and jammed himself into it, quieting his breaths, willing himself to be invisible. In just a few seconds, the first Yeksa stepped around the corner. It was probably five feet tall, with the same pale gray skin as the first ones Morgan had encountered. It didn't even glance to the side where Morgan hid as it caught sight of the lantern light coming from up the hallway. It crouched and brandished a rough-looking club, motioning forward and hissing something in that rough, animalistic tongue. It started to creep forward as three more Yeksa came around the corner. They were all hyper-focused on the light coming from down the tunnel and passed by Morgan's crevice without a glance.

Of the three Yeksa that joined the first, two wielded spears, and one had a dark, heavy-looking knife. Morgan waited for them to get a few yards up the tunnel before he slithered out of the crevice, and, before he could have second thoughts, he blasted his spear into the lower back of the knife-wielding Yeksa. It screamed, mortally wounded and flailing about, impaled on the spear. Morgan stepped forward, kicking out while pulling back on the spear, and launched the wounded creature sprawling into one of the spear wielders. The next few minutes were a blur of nightmare images: red-yellow eyes, sharp fangs, spears, and claws, and above all of it, Morgan roaring in rage and pain as he accumulated wounds and dished out devastating blows to the smaller creatures. When it was over, Morgan was smeared with blood, much of it his own, but the Yeksa were dead. He'd been gored through his left bicep by the second spear wielder, he'd been bitten at least four times, and it felt like his left hand had a couple of broken bones from when he'd blocked a flurry of blows from a club.

He bent over his knees, panting and taking stock of his injuries, as the familiar rush of golden motes rose from the five dead creatures and slammed into his chest. He could feel the Energy rushing through his body, and suddenly his exhaustion was forgotten. His throbbing injuries subsided to a dull ache, and he confirmed what he'd only suspected before—his wounds actually began to close, even the horrible puncture wound on his arm scabbed over and shrank to half its size like it had been healing for a week or more.

*****Congratulations! You have achieved level 3 base human and have 10 attribute points to allocate. You have learned the skill Spear Mastery—Basic.*****

As Morgan quietly walked back to Issa and the lantern, he called up his status sheet, noting that his Energy level had gone up to fifty-two over zero.

BRONWYN

As the sputtering, twirling glob of fire popped into the straw dummy, Bronwyn snorted a huff of air out her nose. "Bleh, this is the longest tutorial I've ever had to do." She called it a tutorial because that's what it reminded her of. The "System" called it an orientation. The past two days had been worse; today at least, she'd gotten to mess with some simple spells, which had given her some hope. But roman candles? Come on.

Three days ago, Bronwyn and the other five thousand passengers that had been on the *Pilgrim 9* had awoken in a large meadow. They had not awoken retching out cryo-gel on a cold plasteel floor but in soft beds of grass, which was a pleasant surprise. The meadow was roughly six miles across; Bronwyn knew this because she had run its diameter during her first day. It was bordered to the east, west, and south by a dense forest of tall, alien trees. The northern edge was peppered with sparse trees and opened up into a much larger grassland extending as far as the horizon, where tall, purple mountains rose against the cobalt sky.

Upon waking, none of the colonists knew where they were; this planet did not match the description of any they were traveling to, and they had seen no sign of their ship or belongings. However, every single one of them shared the same dream of being enveloped in glowing golden light. They shared a sensation of traveling through space in the cloud of light and being deposited on a new world. Nobody seemed panicked about the situation. In fact, many people refused to believe that any of this was real—they insisted they were still in cryo-sleep, living through some sort of a lucid dream as a side effect of being in the gel for hundreds of years. Those that seemed to accept the situation, like Bronwyn, couldn't explain their lack of concern; perhaps the "System" drugged them with the fruits it had supplied upon their waking.

When Bronwyn woke, she was greeted by the "System," a seemingly benevolent entity that would help her learn the ropes of this new world. It gave her access to many of the same commands and interface screens that she was used to in the VR games she was famous for on Earth. However, the UI was far more limited; information about stats was sparse, and there were no chat options nor, and this had been the first clue that she really was awake, any sign of a log-out button.

As soon as she realized how the System worked, she knew she would have to sprint ahead of everyone else. There were five thousand people in this meadow, and there was no way she would be stuck in queues and fall behind. She'd played countless VR MMOs and knew that being ahead of the pack on launch day was the best way to get exclusive rewards and the best gear. This world might not be VR, but that didn't mean she wouldn't compete.

The first two days of the "orientation" were lessons on building simple shelters, crafting various wooden trinkets and stone tools, and cooking simple recipes. The meadow had no resources other than the soft, feathery blue grass and occasional clumps of purple-green shrubs; the forest was inaccessible, simply blocked by an invisible wall. Whenever something was needed for the next lesson, the System would somehow manifest small, yellow chests that contained whatever ingredients were required. The first time Bronwyn saw one of those chests disappear in a smokey, yellow haze after being emptied, a nearby colonist had lost his shit, screaming about cryo-madness and running off across the meadow.

As it voiced the orientation, the System often cautioned about an overdependence on technology. It explained that Energy use and cultivation were hindered by it and that, as beings new to the use of Energy, they should avoid higher forms of technology. It warned that, as they grew in this new world, explored new territories, they might run into other "cultivating species," and could be threatened by beings whose Energy use would eclipse any perceived technological advantage. For that reason, the System refused to provide any weapons that Energy didn't easily enhance. In other words, no projectile or beam weapons were offered in the weapons and combat training, and there were no stimulants or personal electronics provided in any of the supply boxes.

The third day was all about combat training, at least for Bronwyn. As far as she could see, no one else in the meadow had training dummies spawning around them yet. The morning had been filled with hand-to-hand combat training, and Bronwyn found it quite rudimentary, just some short punching combos. The afternoon had been weapons training. The System had provided swords, maces, axes, and bows that unfortunately disappeared when the training ended. After that was lessons on using Energy, essentially one's ability to cast magic spells. Bronwyn had never been a fan of spellcasting classes, occasionally playing some sort of spellsword, but never a full caster. She preferred fast-paced melee combat. To her, it was more fun, and she liked putting on a good show for her fans. Who wants to watch some nerd stand a hundred yards away and spam firebolts?

The Energy training took the better part of five hours, and it mainly consisted of hurling around various elements. Bronwyn believed before, but at this point, she truly became convinced that the colonists weren't all hallucinating or sharing some kind of VR experience in the cryo-pods. She'd played every VR game there was. She owned the best immersion pod that money could buy. Nothing came close to what this felt like. She was here. Unbelievably, she was channeling magic and creating fire out of thin air.

Bowing to her inclinations to avoid spellcasting classes, she focused the most on the spell tutorial that involved using earth magic to shield parts of her body from impact. The System was quick to inform her that her access to these powers was "borrowed"—she'd have to gather Energy and form her own "Core" before she could wield Energy in skills or spells.

Now, as the night grew dark, she stood watching her last dummy smolder, a thin line of smoke wafting up from the burn mark she'd made. She hoped to be done with this drawn-out "orientation" and move on to whatever was next. "I guess the magic is cool, but fighting straw dummies is kinda garbage, Mr. System. What nonsense are you going to make me do next?"

The soft voice of the System entered Bronwyn's head.

*****Congratulations! Orientation sequence complete.*****

*****Rewards: Level 2 base human, Title: First Colonist, First Colonist Reward Box, Ardent Vale borders: unlocked. You have 5 attribute points to allocate.*****

A swirl of yellow-blue, crackling smoke appeared on the ground near her feet and coalesced into the shape of a large, yellow box with blue runic symbols all over it. "FUCK YEAH!!" Bronwyn shouted. "It always pays to be in the lead; let's see what these rewards are all about. Character sheet."

Status			
Name:	Bronwyn Tallow		
Race:	Human - Base 1		
Class:	—		
Level:	2		
Energy Affinity:	6.1	Energy:	30/0
Strength:	13	Vitality:	11
Dexterity:	9	Agility:	11

Intelligence:	9	Will:	11
Points Available:	5		
Titles & Feats:	First Colonist		
Skills:	System Language Integration - Not Upgradeable		

"What are the benefits of the First Colonist title?"

First Colonist: +1 to all Attributes and + 10 percent Energy gain from vanquishing other Energy users.

Bronwyn pondered for a moment. Having +1 to all stats didn't sound like a lot, but 10 percent Energy gain would undoubtedly help her keep her momentum, especially since none of the other colonists, as far as she knew, were even working on combat training yet. The unspent stat points were a more significant concern for her; her natural strength was reasonably high, but she didn't have a clear choice for secondaries.

Her stat choices made her think about what kind of skills she wanted to learn. Unarmed combat seemed somewhat overpowered—her strikes were doing as much damage as the orientation weapons, but when she practiced on multiple dummies, it seemed to lack any kind of cleave. Magic was an option, but her energy affinity, while good, wasn't exceptional compared to some of the other colonists she'd spoken to. Her intelligence was a bit low; she wished she would've paid more attention to math. Maybe she'd just focus on some low-level spells to amplify her strengths a bit.

Not wanting to remain indecisive for too long, she settled on mastering unarmed combat. After all, her first international championship had been in VR mixed martial arts; she was no stranger to punching in a few teeth. Might as well focus on her strengths, she laughed inwardly, as she spent three of her five points. Her other two points she put into agility. "Can't get hurt if they can't hit you," she muttered, still smiling as she punched one fist into her open palm.

"Now, let's see about those rewards!" Bronwyn knelt and lifted the lid of the yellow, footlocker-shaped box. Inside was a leather pouch about the size of her two fists, a leather-bound book, a folded set of leather armor, two heavy-looking gauntlets, a backpack that looked to be full of equipment, and an obelisk-shaped stone, about the size of her forearm.

She picked up the leather pouch and looked inside. Three smooth, amber-colored gems rested inside the pouch, one of them about twice the size of the others. She held the largest one in her hand and allowed some Energy to trickle into it, the way the System had taught her during the orientation, and was rewarded with an information screen:

Energy Core rank 2, type: tri-node.

These stones appeared to be related to the Energy Core that the System had mentioned earlier. Judging from the description, the Core would be a slightly advanced one at that. She wondered how long it would take any of the other colonists to acquire any rank 2 item, let alone something seemingly so important. She was pleased to see that it came with a manual, as the orientation had been pretty brief concerning forming and building a Core. She picked up the small leather book and repeated the process. Nothing happened, so she assumed it wasn't magical or bondable. Was that a word? Instead, she opened the book and saw a title page: Amber Class Energy Core Manual. That would make things easier!

Next, she picked up the folded leather armor and tried to bond with it in the same fashion. Nothing happened. "Must just be normal leather armor, I guess." She set it aside and looked at the gauntlets. They weren't just armor for her hands, she could tell. They were weighted gauntlets. On the one hand, Bronwyn was ecstatic—if she could pick weapons to start with, these would be them. She was familiar with a fighting style that worked perfectly with them, and she'd enjoyed using Energy to complement that kind of fighting during the combat lessons. On the other hand, it was creepy as fuck that the System seemed to know what she wanted. There was no way this was a coincidence.

She picked up the backpack and rifled through it. It seemed to contain everything one needed to start a life in the woods: a bedroll, hatchet, shovel, flint and steel, a simple mess kit, fifty feet of rope, four torches, and a boot knife. Finally, she picked up the obelisk and examined it. It was about a foot tall and had four flat sides angled to a sharp point at the top. All along its sides, seeming to move around in the dark stone, were gold-colored runes. She took a minute to bond with the item and was rewarded with a prompt:

Settlement Stone, activate at the present location? YES/NO

Bronwyn quickly said, "No!" and the prompt went away. She carefully packed the stone in the backpack for now; there'd be time to deal with that later.

MORGAN

It dawned on Morgan that he had more points available than some of his total abilities. He should probably allocate those soon, but he wasn't sure he knew the best way to do so. He was thinking about it when he realized his night vision was fading, and he was closing in on the lantern and Issa. "Morgan, are you all right?" Issa was leaning against the tunnel just as he'd left her, and her brows were furrowed in concern.

"Yeah, mostly flesh wounds at this point. It seems I heal quite a bit when I absorb the Energy of those bastards when they die."

"You must have a high Energy Affinity. I'd hardly notice it if I killed such a lowly beast. You're covered in blood, though. Are you sure you're alright?"

"Yeah, I'm good. We should keep moving before more of them come along. So, Energy Affinity has to do with how much Energy you get for killing monsters and whether it heals you?" Morgan paused while Issa picked up her spear and grabbed his shoulder, and they continued walking.

"Not just monsters, but any creature that channels Energy. Yeksa are lowly beings that don't have much base Energy. The fact that you healed so much from slaying some of them means your affinity must be high. Affinity does more than that, though. Energy Affinity determines how easily and how much you can channel Energy into skills, spells, and abilities. It determines how much you can draw on ambient Energy. Probably more than that, but our world is relatively new to the System, and my people are still learning."

"So, yeah, my Energy Affinity is 9.2. Is that pretty high?" Issa's hand tightened on his shoulder, and she stopped moving. She looked into Morgan's eyes.

"Do you tell the truth?" Morgan nodded. "My Energy Affinity is 2.3, and that's considered high among my people. What type of Core do you have?"

"Eh, Core? You mentioned that before, and I didn't get a chance to ask you about it. I don't really know what a Core is, to be honest."

"You joke!" When Issa saw that Morgan was serious, she continued, "How much Energy do you have?"

"Ummm, fifty-two out of zero? It doesn't make sense to me."

"Ancestors! You haven't formed a Core yet! That fifty-two Energy is vestigial Energy that resides in your body, leftover from what you've absorbed. You can't make use of it or add it to your Core because you don't have one! I'll think about how to help you, but for now, I need to stop talking and focus on walking quietly." Issa looked, pointedly, into the dark tunnel and nudged Morgan with the hand on his shoulder to keep moving. Morgan nodded, and soon, they were passing the scene of his battle. Issa inhaled sharply. "Five of them? You're either very lucky or a stronger fighter than I thought."

"Maybe a little of both? I found a lucky ambush site. I really didn't think there'd be five; I was more hoping for two. Guess I'm lucky for my quick healing, too, 'cause they fucked me up pretty good before it was over." Morgan shrugged as he nudged the bodies with his foot, looking for the knife that one of the Yeksa had held. He found it under one of the bodies and realized it hadn't been metal but rather obsidian, and it had broken when the creature fell on it.

"This word 'fucked'—you use it a lot. Does it mean the same as turjaa?" Issa was smiling faintly.

"Uh, I don't know that word, and since the System didn't translate it, I'll guess maybe it's similar!" Morgan laughed before he caught himself and slapped his hand over his mouth. Issa smiled, wanly, and held her finger to her lips. Morgan looked at her drawn face and the dark hollows forming around her eyes and knew they had to do something about her leg soon, or she'd collapse.

They continued on their downward sloping trek, through the dark tunnel, for another few minutes before the ambient light began to change. Morgan frowned and lowered the wick on the lantern until it just emitted a faint amber glow. With the lantern dimmed, they could see that a soft, sporadically flaring, green-tinged light came from farther down the tunnel, where it opened into a larger space. They crept, as carefully and quietly as they could, with Issa hobbling along with the spear haft, making faint wooden clicking noises with each step. As they neared the opening, they could hear a strange, keening wail. Morgan looked at Issa with a raised eyebrow. She leaned very close to his ear and breathed the words "Yeksa shaman."

Morgan frowned and motioned for Issa to back up to the tunnel wall. He set the lantern down and crouched low, carefully creeping up to the edge of the tunnel. As his eyes adjusted and he drew closer to the opening, Morgan could see that the space's ceiling was very high, and the light was coming from below the tunnel opening. He crouched even lower and advanced. As he exited the tunnel, he could see that a rocky, sloping pathway led off to his left and downward, and just ahead of the opening was a ledge. Morgan very carefully crept to the edge and peered over. The source of the green light was a brazier that burned in the center of a cavern. The cavern was fairly large, about the size of a handball court onboard the *Pilgrim*. It looked to be about twenty feet below the level of the ledge on which Morgan crouched. Standing with its back to Morgan, at the brazier, was a Yeksa that had to be two or three times the size of any he'd met so far. It was probably just a bit over six feet tall, but it had to weigh close to three hundred pounds. Loose folds of pale skin layered its back, and its naked haunches were the size of ham hocks. It wore some sort of iron or dark-wood crown affixed with a fat, white candle that burned with a red, sparkling flame.

Periodically the shaman, as Issa had named it, would reach into a pouch that it held in its left hand and throw something into the brazier while making that high, keening wail. Morgan noted that the Yeksa had a crude, wooden trunk next to it. He carefully and methodically studied the rest of the cavern and couldn't find any sign of other Yeksa nearby. "All right, fucker." Barefoot, covered in dark bloodstains, Morgan quietly snuck down the ramp, spear in a two-handed grip. The spear felt good in his hands; while Morgan carefully advanced, he could imagine several different thrusts that he could use to great effect on the back of that creature. He almost stumbled when he realized what he was thinking about. How did he *know* those movements? It was more than just being familiar with the spear after having fought with it—the motions felt natural to him like he'd practiced them as many times as he had the hip throw that he'd learned in basic defense training, and their instructor had made his unit do that throw many, many times. It must be the basic spear mastery the System message had mentioned. He didn't know how he felt about having knowledge dropped into his mind, but Morgan couldn't dwell on it—he'd reached the bottom of the rocky ramp.

There wasn't much cover, but the Yeksa shaman hadn't turned around yet, and Morgan still couldn't see any other creatures around. He had about twenty-five feet of dusty, rocky ground between him and the creature. Once more, he crept forward, spear raised over his right shoulder, ready to stab. Patience was the key here, and Morgan was determined not to blow it, each step as slow and steady as a glacier inexorably inching its way toward civilization. Twenty feet, fifteen, ten. The creature reached into its pouch to throw a handful of some kind of dust into the brazier. This close, Morgan could see the green flames flare as the shaman wailed into the darkness. Three more steps and he was close enough—he bunched the muscles in his shoulders and sprang with his legs, driving with the full power of his body.

Morgan had envisioned this strike in his mind over and over as he approached, and he couldn't imagine it going any better. The spear tip exploded into the Yeksa's fat broad back, right beneath its left shoulder blade. Morgan roared as he drove the spear forward, and he felt it sink at least a foot into the creature's thick body. The shaman shrieked, flinging both its arms wide. The pouch flew from its grasp, and it spun its body, ripping the spear from Morgan's hands. Stumbling drunkenly, the huge Yeksa roared in pain and shock as it caught sight of Morgan. It reached a hand up to its neck and gripped a huge crudely carved gemstone that hung from a chain there. The fist that held the stone started to glow red, and the candle on the Yeksa's crown began to flare like a Roman candle. Morgan's eyes widened with panic, and he leaped forward, kicking the Yeksa in its fat belly and knocking it back into the flaming, green brazier. The Yeksa shrieked in agony as it stumbled backward, its huge, bare ass landing square in the center of the flames. Its hands flailed for purchase, trying to stand up. Having let go of the gem and lost its concentration, the flaring candle on its crown died down.

The green flames were quickly crawling over the shaman's body, and its shrieks turned more and more desperate. It managed to flail enough to roll to the side, but the Yeksa only made it a few feet before it collapsed. Either the wound from the spear or the flames had finally sapped it of the strength to keep fighting. Morgan moved around the brazier that was still sputtering with green, glowing coals and pulled his spear from the shaman's back. It twitched slightly, so he drove the spear into it again. This time golden motes began to coalesce on the body, and Morgan braced himself. The layer of motes grew denser for several seconds before they streamed into his chest. Morgan couldn't help smiling as the warm energy flowed into him. He watched as the last of his scabs and bruises cleared up.

Congratulations! You have achieved level 4 base human and have 15 attribute points to allocate. You have learned the skill Stealthy Maneuvers—Basic.

That was easy. Maybe that shaman wasn't supposed to go down so quickly? Morgan smiled and said, "Status." His Energy level had risen seventy-seven over zero. "Yeah, that fucker gave me 25 Energy all by himself."

"Who are you talking to?" Morgan jumped when Issa spoke up from the foot of the sloping path. "Sorry to startle you. I heard the screaming and yelling and figured I should come to see what happened rather than wait to die alone in a dark tunnel."

"Yeah, I, uh, was just about to come to get you. Well, I managed to sneak up and stab him in the back; the fight was quick and dirty after that—feels like I got lucky." Morgan gestured at the corpse. "You're not looking good, Issa; I think we need to rest for a while."

"I haven't looked good since you found me, but yes, I'm feeling more faint." She looked down at the corpse. "Ancestors! He was a big one." She slowly hobbled over to the brazier and trunk that was next to it. "Shaman Yeksa have much more control of their Energy than the scavengers you've dealt with up to now. You *are* lucky to have caught it by surprise. Well, maybe lucky isn't the right word—I think it's more than that." She shrugged and smiled weakly at Morgan as she nudged the crude wooden trunk. "I wonder if there's anything useful in there."

"Yeah, I hope so, but give me a minute to make sure we're not going to have company imminently," Morgan replied, as he began to look around the perimeter of the room. It looked like the tunnel they had come through was one of two entrances to the room. The other was a heavy wooden door that was in the opposite wall. Morgan moved over to the door and could see that it was barred from inside the room. Apparently, the Yeksa shaman hadn't wanted to be bothered. Morgan couldn't see any light coming under the door, so he placed his ear to the wood. He listened for several long, slow breaths but couldn't make out any noise. "Good news—looks like this guy enjoyed his privacy."

When he made his way back to the brazier, the big corpse, and Issa, he found her sitting in front of the wooden trunk with her bad leg stretched out in front of her. Morgan inwardly winced when he saw her leg. It was a much darker shade of bluish-purple than the rest of her, and the wound looked angry, swollen, and just as life-threatening as when he'd found her. He knew that if the chewed-up area weren't filled with dark, clotting blood, he'd still be able to see her bone. "Let's see if there's anything in the trunk we can use to bandage that leg up. I wish we could take that tourniquet off; I'm afraid you're going to lose that leg if we don't figure something out soon."

"My grandfather would tell you that before Energy came to our world, I would not only lose this leg but die from this wound. If we were back in my village, though, there are several Energy healers who could mend this wound without any trouble. If we can find a good Energy source here, I could absorb it and begin the process of mending my leg; I can't absorb Energy as well as you, but with enough, that won't matter." Morgan nodded and lifted the trunk's lid. Issa flinched back, holding her hands up, but sheepishly lowered them when nothing happened. "You should be more careful; that shaman might have trapped that trunk."

"Uh, yeah, I didn't think of that." Morgan couldn't help grinning as he started lifting out various jars and burlap style bags and pouches from the trunk. He also found multiple bundles of herbs tied with string. At the bottom was a small leather pouch that was heavier than the others and made a clinking, tinkling sound as he jostled it. He opened it, and inside were maybe fifty little beads that looked like they were made of glass. They had a green luster and almost seemed to be glowing. "What are these?"

Issa looked up from one of the burlap bags, her hand cupping some sort of grain. When she saw the beads in Morgan's hand, she smiled. "Those are Energy beads, attuned to nature. They're valuable to Energy users, but especially those that use nature magic. I know this is your treasure, but I might be able to absorb enough Energy from a few of those beads to mend my Core and start my leg healing!"

"Seriously? That's great!" Morgan tossed her the leather pouch. Issa smiled and turned away from the sack she'd been rummaging through. She scooted her back to the trunk and took one of the Energy beads from the pouch, resting it on the palm of her hand. Issa held it out in front of her and closed her eyes. Morgan watched, waiting for something miraculous to happen, but it seemed like she was meditating or something. After a few moments, he got bored with watching her and moved over to the corpse of the shaman.

The shaman's crown with the candle had fallen off its head when it collapsed, and Morgan wanted to check it out. The fat, white candle had gone out, and upon closer inspection, Morgan could see that the crown was made of dark metal. Morgan reached out a hand toward it, but before he could touch it, he felt a wave of nausea come over him, and he pulled his hand back. Once his hand was away from the metal, the nausea passed. He decided to leave the crown alone. He moved instead to the silvery chain around the shaman's neck. He found the clasp on the back and unscrewed it, allowing him to pull the chain away from the shaman. Affixed to the chain was a fist-size red and black gem. It was crudely cut, but when Morgan held it, warmth spread into his hand, and it throbbed with a dim orange-red light. He let go of the gem but held onto the necklace by the chain.

"Morgan, can you help me?" Morgan looked over at Issa and saw that she was still sitting against the trunk, but her face was less wan, and her eyes were brighter.

"You look better already!" He walked over to her and saw that she still held a green Energy bead in her hand and that there was a small pile of clear, empty-looking beads next to her.

"Yes, I'm sorry to use so many of your Energy beads, but once I gathered and solidified my core, I started to draw the Energy into my leg faster than I thought I would. I think it's ready for me to take the tourniquet off. Would you help?" Morgan looked at her leg and was astonished to see that much of the flesh and muscle had filled in, and now there was a large, dark scab over the remaining wound. He nodded and walked over.

"This will probably hurt," he said, as he started to untie the knotted rope. Issa closed her eyes and seemed to focus on her breathing while he slowly unwound the tightly cinched rope. She gasped, and her breathing faltered for a moment when he finally pulled loose the last wind of the cord, and the blood rushed into her leg. Slowly, Issa managed to get her breathing steady, and Morgan marveled as the green energy in the bead drained into her outstretched palm. She exhaled one last time, opening her eyes with a smile.

"Thank you very much, Morgan. Without your help, I'd have suffered a terrible fate. I hope that I can repay you someday."

MORGAN

"I don't need you to repay me, Issa. I don't know what kind of a person could leave someone to be eaten alive by some cannibalistic freaks." Morgan smiled as he stood up, the red gemstone hanging from his wrist on the chain. Huh, did he wrap the chain around his wrist like that?

"That necklace has a strong aura, Morgan. Be careful with it until you learn more about it. Anyway, you'd be surprised at how many cultivators would have not only left me but perhaps taken the opportunity to kill me while I was bound. I hold a lot more Energy in my Core than these Yeksa vermin."

"What do you mean by 'cultivator'?"

"Cultivation is the act of gathering Energy to increase your own power. One way to do so, as you've learned, is to slay other beings that use Energy."

"Hmm, and people on this world would just kill another person to gain Energy?" Morgan frowned.

"Unfortunately, the System encourages cultivation by any means. People from my village wouldn't do that, but someone that didn't know me? I would not be surprised if they never took my blindfold off and just ended me. What an opportunity! Maybe they'd find it harder if they had to look into my eyes while they did it." She smiled fatalistically.

"Well, I'm not like that. I don't think most humans are like that, though we've never had to deal with the System before. I hope it doesn't bring the worst out in us."

"Human? Is that your race, Morgan? I've never met a person that looked like you. Brown hair, pale skin, pale eyes? And you're very tall. No, I've definitely never seen or heard of your kind before." Morgan self-consciously rubbed his hand over the short, brown buzzcut; it was the easiest haircut to deal with when it came to cryo-sleep, and he'd never much cared about hairstyles.

"Yeah, well, you're a lot more colorful than most humans, but we do have a pretty wide variety, ourselves. I'm not surprised you've never seen us. Remember I mentioned that I was new to your star system? My world is around twelve light-years from here. Like seventy trillion miles or so."

"Trillion . . ." Issa stared into space, trying to wrap her head around the number.

"Well, what's next? We've gotta get out of here, and I need to find where the System put my people."

"Morgan, this is the first level of the Crucible. We can work together to get out, but I feel the System will make things harder for us if we do."

"Okay, I remember the System saying it was sending me to the Crucible, and you've mentioned it a couple of times, but just what the fuck is it?"

"The System is, indeed, cruel to send you here with no knowledge, though in its twisted way it probably thinks it's giving you an opportunity. The Crucible is a testing ground. A place to prove your potential, to have a chance to find rare rewards and gain in power."

"So, the System chose you to come here, also?"

"No, my situation is different. There's a temple near my village. Once every moon cycle, a portal opens, and one person can step through into the Crucible. I won a lottery to come here."

"Uh." Morgan almost said that she might have made a mistake, as he'd found her, literally, being eaten alive, but he caught himself. Her pale, lavender cheeks reddened, though, and she looked away, probably guessing what he'd been about to say. "Anyway, I think we should work together. In fact, I have an incentive to do so—a quest."

"You have a quest to work with me?" Issa arched an eyebrow, looking at Morgan intently.

"Well, actually, when I found you, I got a quest not to let you die. For a week."

"And you accepted? Well, in that case, I will be glad to have a companion, at least for a week." Issa smiled and grunted as she pushed herself to her feet. "We should figure out where to go next."

"What about this stuff? Anything worth taking?" Morgan gestured to the burlap sacks and jars of various liquids.

"Actually, yes, many of those herbs are Energy-dense and would be useful to an alchemist. I don't know what's in those jars, but, again, an alchemist might find them valuable." Morgan nodded and started sifting through the burlap bags, looking for the largest one. He then took the smaller bags, pouches, and bundled herbs and stuffed them inside.

"I don't think I can carry these jars. I hate just to leave them, but this sack is almost full, and I want to keep my hand free for my spear."

"I'll carry a few of the most Energy-dense jars in one of the sacks. I'll wrap them in burlap to keep them from clinking," Issa said, bending to the task, and Morgan nodded. It took Issa a couple of minutes to examine the jars, and she ended up wrapping four of them in torn burlap and stuffing them into a sack.

"Right, then," Morgan said, as he stepped over to the shaman corpse and yanked his spear out of its back. The hard, wooden tip was holding up surprisingly well, though it was duller than when he'd first acquired it. He was walking over to the door, getting ready to see what lay beyond, when he heard a gasp from Issa. "What is it?" He asked, looking back over his shoulder.

"This crown, it's cursed, and it's steeped in death magic."

"Yeah, it made me nauseous when I got close, so I backed off."

"What?" Issa shook her hand like it had been burned and quickly walked his way, her spear in the other hand. "It must be nice to have such affinity! I didn't feel anything until it started to pass necrosis into my hand. It'll take me an hour to push this foul Energy out."

"Sorry. I should have said something," Morgan replied softly. He stepped up to the door and put his ear to it, listening. Issa silently moved to his side, still wringing her hand in front of her. When he couldn't hear anything for several long moments, he carefully lifted the bar from the door and set it down against the wall next to the door. He pulled the door open just an inch and peered through the gap.

Beyond the door was a short stone hallway that opened into a large, circular room, brightly lit with two lanterns. A circular stone stairway led upward in the center of the room. "Huh, looks like we found the way to the next level." Morgan pulled open the door, and Issa peered around his shoulder.

"I think you're right, Morgan! That doesn't look like the same sort of stone as in the Yeksa area."

"So, you think the System will make things harder for us if we're together. Does that mean this area, these encounters, are tailor-made for each participant of the Crucible?"

Issa shrugged. "My people have speculated that the System takes a heavy hand in the Crucible, but I don't know for sure. I surely wasn't ready for my first encounter."

"Well, before we go up, can you give me some advice? I have fifteen attribute points to allocate."

"Oh, that's a lot to ask of me. I don't want to point you on the wrong path. I wish I knew you better before I tried to give you advice like that."

"Look, you know a lot more about this System than I do. I can tell you right now that my highest stat is intelligence, but I don't even know what would happen if I dumped more points into it. I can guess what strength or agility or vitality would do."

"Intelligence helps you to process your thoughts faster. It helps you to manipulate Energy and apply it more effectively."

"Which I can't do until I have a 'Core,' right?" Morgan frowned.

"Yes, that's right. Though, when you form your Core, having a high intelligence will help you to do it more perfectly and perhaps improve its initial grade."

"Oh, great, so there are different grades of cores?"

"That's right."

"Okay, give me a minute. Status."

Morgan liked the idea of having high intelligence, so he "thought" of putting five points into intelligence and the number on his status screen updated. Until he could use Energy actively, though, he figured he should add some points to his physical stats as well. He applied two points to vitality, four points to strength, and four points to agility.

Morgan smiled as he felt his body changing. It wasn't a huge change, but he felt more sure-footed, the spear felt lighter, and he felt more confident in its control. He started to flex his bicep and touch it with his other hand when he realized Issa was watching him. He blushed and cleared his throat. "Ahem, uh there. I'm done. Should be a little more fit for whatever is waiting up those stairs." Issa grinned, exposing her sharp teeth while raising one bright, yellow eyebrow.

"If you had a Core, I'd feel more confident, but you didn't have any trouble on this floor, and, now that I'm on the mend, I can be of some help."

Morgan smiled back at her. "Yeah, well, I'm not gonna lie; it made it easier creeping through those dark tunnels with your hand on my shoulder, so don't sell yourself short. With regard to a Core, you know the quest the System gave me? The one about keeping you from dying? It offered me an Energy Core cultivation manual. Will that help?"

"Yes, that will help a lot! My tribe has a cultivation manual that we share and teach to the young. It teaches meditation techniques to help focus the Energy in your body into the act of forming a Core," Issa said, nodding.

"Wait, so you could show me how to make a Core now?" Morgan stepped back from the doorway and pushed it closed.

"I'm not sure that's the best idea, Morgan. What if our technique isn't compatible with your race or with the cultivation manual the System is offering you?" Issa frowned, backing away a step and scratching the side of her head.

"Does that happen? Do some methods not work for some races?"

"I really don't know. The Ardeni, my people, are allied with another race, the Ilyathi, and we share our cultivation method with certain promising prospects as part of our treaty. There are many other peoples that we don't share with, though, and I'm not sure they would cultivate like us. Take the Onaghi, for instance. They don't even have a body like us, so I can't imagine they circulate Energy in the same way that we do."

"Well, you and I seem pretty similar in our physiology! I mean, you're a lot more colorful and have sharper teeth"—Morgan smiled, tapping a finger on his teeth—"but we both have ten fingers and toes, and we both bleed red blood."

"Well, we could try it, I suppose. Our manual has three stages, and since we are working together, and you've already saved my life once, I could show you the first stage. It will allow you to form a basic Core. To do more than that might be risking too much at this point, and it would take longer than we want to spend in this place, anyway." Issa relented, and Morgan smiled at her.

"Alright, let's put this bar back over this door, and you can show me what this is all about." Morgan lifted the heavy wooden beam and secured the door. "Let's go over here"—he gestured to the left side of the cavern where the ground was clear of rubble—"away from that dead shaman." Issa nodded and followed him. She instructed him to sit, legs folded and hands open, palms up, on his knees. Morgan was pretty sure this was called a lotus position among yoga aficionados back home. Back when people had time to do yoga. She took a similar position in front of him.

"Morgan, I'm going to try to tell you what to do, but I'll be infusing some of my own Energy into you so that I can feel what you're doing. Just a trickle. Try not to fight it," Issa said as she, very lightly, placed her small hands, palms down against his own. Her hands were warm, and Morgan took a moment to appreciate the connection to another living being among the horrors he'd been through in the last few hours. When that thought struck him, he felt a wave of emotion and shuddered with an unexpected deep sigh. "Are you alright, Morgan?"

"Yeah." Morgan nodded, sighing out another big breath, feeling a wave of pent-up pressure flowing out of him. "I think I was holding a lot of stress in, and sitting here like this, with you, opened up the valve."

Issa smiled gently and said, "It's good to let that go before we attempt to form your Core. Take a few more deep breaths and exhale them slowly, then close your eyes, and listen to my voice." Morgan did as she instructed, inhaling deeply and slowly exhaling, willing his stress, anger, and fear to go out with each breath. By the time he'd done this five times, he was feeling a lot more relaxed. He kept his eyes closed and just concentrated on the feeling of Issa's hands in his and the sound of her voice as she spoke. "Now, concentrate on where my fingertips rest against your palms; feel the Energy I'm sending out and pull it into your body. Imagine it flowing up your arms, down through your chest, and into the center of your body."

Morgan, feeling very relaxed, felt his consciousness drift to the point of Issa's fingers, where they met his palms, just as she instructed. He immediately felt a tingling, warm pressure building at the point where their skin met. He concentrated on that tingling pressure and *pulled* on it, urging it into his hand. How he did it, he couldn't describe if pressed to do so; it felt almost like he had another set of muscles in his body that he'd never used before. He continued to direct the warm, tingling energy up, along his arms, and down into the center of his torso, just as Issa had instructed him. When the two streams met, he could feel them coalesce into a loose, diffuse cloud of warmth there in the center of his being.

"Good, Morgan! That was fast! Now take that Energy and push it together; try to imagine it condensing."

Once again, Morgan listened, and, with his inner eye turned toward his center, he didn't feel like he had to imagine the Energy doing his will; he could feel it so clearly. It was like he could see it—a slowly spinning cloud of golden motes, just above and behind his navel. He willed it to move faster, to funnel tighter and tighter toward the center. As the energy spiraled into a vortex, he became aware of more Energy in his body. The residual Energy he had absorbed from the glowing marble and from the enemies he'd killed. He imagined that Energy was flowing through his limbs, from his head, all toward his center. He pushed and gathered that Energy in the already spinning vortex, exerting his will against it, making a ball out of the spinning point of Energy as it collected. Soon, all the Energy he had absorbed was swirling at his center, and he continued to push his will against it, and it spun ever faster. He pressed and condensed the spinning ball of Energy until he felt it snap into place somehow, maintaining its shape and momentum yet attaining a state of equilibrium. Smiling, he opened his eyes.

Issa was standing a few feet away from him, breathing heavily. "Morgan, are you alright?" Her voice sounded winded and strained.

"Yeah, I think I'm great! What happened?"

"I think, once again, I underestimated your affinity. I could sense you starting to form your Core, and then I noticed the pull on the Energy I was sending into you increased, to the point I struggled to resist it! I had to break contact and step away from you! In just seconds, you pulled half the Energy out of my Core!"

"God! I'm sorry! I didn't know I was doing that! It felt like I was just gathering all the Energy in my body and pulling it into my Core as I formed it. I'm sorry, Issa!" Morgan hurried over to Issa and put his hand on her shoulder. To her credit, she didn't shy away from his touch.

"It's alright, Morgan; I'll recover in a few hours. The ambient Energy here is high. Well? How did it go? Did you make a strong Core?"

Morgan said, "I'm not sure. It feels good. Hang on. Status." He focused on the lines that described his Core and Energy levels.

Core:	Vortex Class - Base 1		
Energy Affinity:	9.2	Energy:	97/204

"Huh, Vortex Class, base one?" Morgan said, looking at Issa quizzically.

"Um, base 1 means that it's in its earliest stage. That's normal for a new Core. I haven't learned about a Vortex Class Core, though. It sounds good, I think. My Core is a Pearl Class. It's pretty common among my people. Some of our Energy masters, those with strong spellcasting classes, have Cores named after gemstones. My teacher had a Sapphire Class Core."

"Thanks for showing me what to do, Issa. I feel better knowing I'm on the right track here. I think we've sat around in this room long enough, though. Probably asking for trouble if we stick around much longer. Besides, if this Crucible is going to take a week or more, we need to get ahold of some food and water." Morgan gestured toward the barred door and started walking over to it.

Issa nodded and replied, "You're right; we will need to find some provisions, but don't worry too much. Energy users don't require food and water as much as creatures without any Energy affinity. Besides, the System will provide an opportunity, and we just have to make sure we don't miss it. Well, we also need to avoid dying while we try to get it!"

MORGAN

The spiral stairway's stonework was different from that in the tunnels or even the area where Morgan first came into the Crucible. The blocks were uniform and fit together closely, with no apparent mortar. The lanterns gave off enough light to see the steps clearly and quite a way up the stairwell. The stairwell itself was a pretty impressive feat of engineering. The steps were uniform, the outer wall seemed very nearly a perfect circle, and the central spire of steps rose in a tight spiral. There was no handrail, and the gap between the steps and the outer wall was several feet, meaning that a tumble off the steps would be pretty devastating. Still, Morgan and Issa made steady progress, Morgan in the lead with his left hand tracing along the central column, his right hand gripping his spear. Issa held her spear and a lantern.

Every twenty feet or so, another lantern burned, and the steps went on this way for a long time. Soon, Morgan realized they had to be hundreds of feet above the bottom landing. "Just how deep is this fucking place?"

"No one really knows. No one knows where the Crucible actually is. People always travel to and from here through System portals." Issa's voice was barely louder than a whisper, and Morgan realized she was, rightly, worried about alerting potential enemies to their presence. He looked back at her and nodded, continuing the climb in silence.

A good fifteen minutes later, he became aware of a change in the ambient light. Looking out and up, he could see that there was a lot more light up ahead than they'd grown accustomed to. He looked back at Issa and motioned for her to follow a bit farther back, and then he started to climb as quietly as he could. He felt he knew how to place his feet just right not to make any noise, and he seemed to naturally move within the shadows cast by the central stairway spire. He figured it was his new Stealthy Maneuvers skill at work. After just a few minutes of quietly climbing, Morgan found himself looking up at the end of the stairway. It ended at a landing that opened into another circular room, much like the one at the bottom of the stairs. He crept up slowly and silently but soon could see that the entire room was empty, other than having four lanterns spaced around the outer wall. A solid-looking wooden door was placed in the wall opposite the top of the stairway. He crouched there at the top of the stairs, waiting for Issa.

Her whisper came up from behind him: "Nothing here?"

"Doesn't look like it. There's a door, though." Morgan nodded toward the door and then started to pad his way over to it quietly. He was halfway across the room to the door when it slammed open. A huge, hulking figure stalked into the room.

"Some little piggies for Rotger?" It had the voice of a drill sergeant gargling gravel. Morgan froze in place, taking in the sight of Rotger. He was at least seven feet tall, with maroon-colored skin and bristling black fur covering most of his body. He was clad in leather straps and bits of cured leather and held the haft of an axe in one hand while slapping the heavy axe head into his other. "I been wanting some meat!"

"Filthy Urghat!" Issa hissed, sidestepping around to Rotger's flank, keeping her spear pointed at him.

Rotger licked his lips, running his tongue along yellow teeth and tusks. "I'm gonna enjoy you, little blueberry." He lowered his body into a crouch and made a wet, snorting bark sound, then chortled obscenely.

"So, I take it we can't just all go our own way?" Morgan also started to sidestep, in the opposite direction of Issa, trying to ensure that one of them would have the beastman's flank.

"Haha, little piggy wants to go his own way? Don't worry, piggy. You'll be going your way into my cookfire," Rotger chortled, continuing to slap his axe into his big, meaty palm. While Morgan fixated on the axe, Rotger leaped with ferocious, explosive energy at him. Morgan was so startled by the sudden movement that he didn't even get his spear up to intervene. His arm started the motion to jab the spear forward, but the next thing he knew, he was crashing into the stone wall.

It was so disorienting that, for a second, he thought his mind was playing tricks on him. Then he realized his left arm didn't work, and blood was quickly pooling on the stone around him. He glanced at his left arm and saw that it was bloodied and crooked, and as he struggled to get his breath, his ribs screamed in protest. Blood was flowing freely from a massive gash in his side. Rotger looked at him from about ten feet away, brandishing the bloody axe and laughing in that sick, wet, gravelly chortle. Morgan struggled to breathe while using his spear to pull himself up into a standing position. Rotger took one step toward him, and that's when Issa struck.

Morgan wasn't sure if it was the injury, the lighting, or what, but it seemed that Issa was lurking in the shadow by the stairwell one second, and the next instant, she was screaming and jamming her spear deep into Rotger's back. Rotger roared, spinning so fast that he ripped Issa's spear from her hands. He swung his axe at her, but she dodged back, escaping by a hair's breadth. Before she could recover her balance, though, Rotger stomped forward and kicked her. She flew backward, crashing into the wall above the stairway and falling out of sight.

Morgan knew he had seconds to act, so he shut the agony of his left side out of his mind, lifted his spear in an overhead strike, and lunged. He just *knew* that if he hit Rotger to the right side of his spine, a few inches down from his shoulder, he'd rupture a vital organ and cripple him. His aim was true, and his spear tore through Rotger's flesh and muscle. The spear moved deep into Rotger's chest cavity, coming to a stop when it hit the underside of his sternum. Rotger screamed hoarsely, stumbling forward, and Morgan kept the pressure on, pushing on the spear until Rotger fell to his knees, coughing up huge gouts of blood.

As he stood over him, Morgan could feel the Energy start to coalesce around Rotger, getting ready to leave his dying form. Morgan leaned forward and placed his hand on the back of Rotger's neck. He could feel the Energy coursing under his hand. It was the simplest thing to just *pull* on it. Rotger squealed hoarsely, thrashing weakly, as a torrent of Energy entered Morgan's hand, and he *pulled* it up along his arm and down into his Core. As he pulled more and more Energy from Rotger, some flowed around his Core and over to his wounded left side and arm. He could feel the wounds partially mending. Soon the flow halted, and Morgan could see that Rotger was a drained husk—clearly dead and strangely washed out in color.

"Did you pull his Energy out while he was still alive?" Issa asked in a shaky voice from the stairwell. Morgan looked over his shoulder and saw her standing there, staring at him warily.

"He was dying, and I held him down with the spear. I could feel his Energy, so I reached out for it. Are you okay?" Morgan straightened and looked around. Nothing else seemed to be coming from the doorway, and he couldn't hear anything.

"That's not something I've seen before, Morgan. It must have something to do with your Vortex Core. Please never do something like that to me. It looked horrific."

Morgan frowned. "I wouldn't! Why would I hurt you at all? Please don't think of me like that."

Issa sighed and shook her head. "I'm sorry, Morgan. You're right. You've done nothing but help me. I just . . . I just haven't met someone like you before, and in this world, people are suspicious because many Energy users are looking for a path to power regardless of the cost."

Morgan nodded and pointed at the body. "What the fuck is this guy? He swatted me across the room like I was a fly." He flexed his left arm, shaking it out. It was still very sore and black and blue, but the bone seemed to have knitted together. His ribs, while stiff, seemed to have mostly healed, also.

"That is an Urghat. My people have been at war with them for as long as anyone remembers. They eat us. Filthy, disgusting creatures. The Yeksa are little more than animals, but the Urghat have speech, and still, they choose to be such savages." Issa walked over to the Urghat and pulled her spear out. It was bent near the middle with cracks and splinters along the shaft. "Damn. Broken!"

"Why don't you take his axe? You'll need to use two hands, but at least it has a metal head. Sharp, too, let me tell you." Morgan grinned sheepishly, rubbing the scab over his ribs.

Issa nodded and hefted the Urghat's hatchet in two hands, resting the haft on her right shoulder.

Morgan pulled his own spear out of the corpse and pushed the corpse over with his foot, looking at its gear. The leather straps didn't seem to offer much protection, and they were filthy. Of course, so was he, but at least it was his filth. The Urghat did wear a wide girdle-like belt. A thick leather satchel was attached to the girdle hanging off a decorative, gilt-metal hook. "Well, that's something," he said, as he bent to unfasten the belt and pull it out from under the creature's back.

The belt truly was a girdle when he put it on, covering most of his abdomen and lower back. He had to pull the clasp's teeth through the very last set of holes, making the girdle nearly wrap double around his waist. He tucked the overlapping leather under the belt. It wasn't pretty, but it fit. The satchel, when Morgan lifted the top flap, seemed to be empty, just a dark space inside. Morgan frowned and reached his hand into it, feeling nothing but air as he waved his hand around. "What the fuck?"

"It's a dimensional container," Issa said matter-of-factly.

"What do you mean, 'dimensional container'?"

"Energy users that have an Artificer-type Class can create items like this. It's a bag that opens onto another dimensional space, larger than the inside of the bag would be."

"How do I see what's in it?" Morgan asked, trying to keep his bewilderment under control. Imagine what the scientists back on the Arkship could do if they got their hands on something like this; think what they could do with drive technology, cargo capacity, or even food storage. He shook his head—it wasn't really science, was it? Energy seemed more like magic than science to him; would it even be compatible with electricity or microchips?

"Its owner is dead, so you should be able to bond with it. Just trickle a bit of your Energy out and into the bag."

"Trickle my Energy out?" Morgan thought about it. He'd pulled Energy in, easily enough; could he move it out of himself? He concentrated on his core and willed some of the Energy in there to flow out and up toward his left arm. At first, he felt a burning sensation and he pulled back, reducing the amount of Energy to a small "trickle" as Issa had said. It moved swiftly out along his arm and down to his fingertip. He touched the satchel, pushing the Energy the last little bit out of his finger and into the leather. He instantly felt a connection in his mind to the satchel, and while he was touching it, he could see in his mind's eye everything that was inside it.

"How do I take things out?"

"Just put your hand into the opening and think about grabbing the item. You should be able to see what's in there now, right?"

"Yeah, hang on a sec." Morgan grunted as he pulled the corpse of a rather large, brightly furred wolf-like creature from the sack and tossed it to the ground. "Jesus, he had three of these things in there."

Morgan ended up leaving most of Rotger's possessions on the ground near his corpse: the corpses of three wolf-like creatures that Issa called "boyii" hounds, a pile of mystery meat that he and Issa agreed they would not eat for fear that it was the flesh of sentient beings, a small pile of broken, random masonry and furniture, and a crudely carved effigy of a bipedal bear-like creature that Issa thought might be a religious artifact to the Urghat. What they did keep from the Urghat's belongings were three paper-wrapped loaves of dry bread and a large tin canteen full of water. Morgan easily stowed the hemp sacks full of herbs and jars from the shaman's chest in the bag, along with three extra lanterns from the stairwell. When he was finished, he closed up the satchel and made sure to fasten the cords to his girdle securely.

"That girdle looks like it might have some special properties, too. Probably the work of an Artificer. Try bonding with it, also," Issa said, running a finger along some of the strange symbols worked into the leather of the girdle. Morgan did as she suggested, and after trickling a bit of Energy into the girdle, he sensed a strong aura of health and well-being from it.

"Does it make sense that I feel more healthy?" Morgan asked.

"Well, you can check your status to see if it has affected you, and that's the best we'll be able to do until we find some way to identify it fully."

"There are skills to identify items?"

"Yes, you can learn spells and skills that do that. I don't have any," Issa replied, shrugging.

"Don't worry about it. We'll figure it out sooner or later. Status." He concentrated on the lines that described his attributes:

Strength:	10	Vitality:	10 (12)
Dexterity:	8	Agility:	11
Intelligence:	17	Will:	10

It looked like the girdle did, indeed, alter his vitality stat. "Well, that's cool. I think it's giving me two more vitality." He smiled at Issa. "Are items like this rare?"

"No, not really. After gaining a few levels, most Energy cultivators manage to acquire a magical item or two, especially low-level dimensional containers like that bag. Artificers learn to make those very early, as they are, obviously, very useful."

"Um, not to be rude, but why didn't you come into the Crucible with some items like this?"

"I'm sure you noticed the shift I'm wearing is made from the same material as your shorts? The System doesn't allow entrants to bring items from the outside. Stepping through the portal strips you of belongings," Issa replied, gesturing at her blood-stained, knee-length, tunic-like garment.

Morgan nodded. "All right, let's get going. See where this big asshole came from," he growled as he started advancing on the open doorway, spear leveled in front of him. "I won't be letting one of them get the jump on me like that again."

BRONWYN

After about five minutes, Bronwyn had the leather armor equipped. It wasn't anything too fancy, just a leather vest, pants, and boots. The leather was a dark brown, and the buckles were made of a sturdy gray-green metal she didn't recognize. It fit her perfectly and was fairly light. She felt like she hadn't lost any range of motion. "One slight issue." She sighed as she tied her curly red hair back into a loose ponytail. "No head protection."

Bronwyn knelt to lift the first gauntlet, and it was lighter than she expected it to be, significantly so. She'd always been strong; she lifted weights regularly and practiced various MMA fighting styles several times a week; her only off day was Saturday. Still, though, there was something different. She looked the same as she had on Earth, but Bronwyn could *feel* that she was stronger. She slipped the gauntlets on, noticing they were made of heavy plates of lobstered metal, the same gray-green metal as the buckles on her armor. The metal plates were attached to a mail glove lined with soft leather. The gauntlets fit all the way up to about an inch below her elbow and had leather straps on the underside to secure them onto her arms. Once strapped on, they weren't exactly weightless, but she could move her arms easily.

Satisfied with her choice of weaponry, she took the gauntlets off for now and sat down to examine the small pouch of gems and the book titled "Energy Core Manual." The book was a rather dense piece of literature detailing how energy flows through the body, how nodes help gather your energy in certain areas, and the effects of intelligence and will on your energy storage and expenditure. The Core the System awarded her was tier two and had three nodes. The central core was the first node, meant to be placed near her solar plexus. The other two nodes were smaller and could be placed anywhere in her body; the placement was up to her. Bronwyn decided that she would put one in each hand. Her eventual hope was that the increased storage of Energy in her fists would help her channel energy into her punches. The process of merging an Energy Core with oneself was not overly complicated. She simply had to place the Core directly on her skin in the correct area and meditate on the image of it slowly pressing through, embedding itself within her.

Bronwyn lay on her back in the grassy field; the soft light blue stalks of grass were almost as comfortable as her bed back on Earth. She placed the largest of the three crystals directly over her solar plexus; it was bright orange, about the size of her fist, and seemed to thrum with potential. She closed her eyes and imagined it slowly sinking into her abdomen. The process took a while, maybe twenty minutes. The core felt hot as it phased through her skin. It was not quite hot enough to hurt but just enough to be slightly uncomfortable. It left her with a sheen of sweat on her forehead as she tried not to become distracted by the heat and focused intently on the image of the Core forming in her center. When it was fully absorbed, she lay there for a moment, staring up at the sky. It was a sunny day with a few bright white clouds. She noticed birds for the first time above her, small, many-colored avians. They ranged in color from white to red to pastel green, and they had long ribbon-like feathers trailing from their tails as they soared through the sky. She wondered if removing the barrier around the meadow had allowed them to start flying overhead.

When she finally sat up, she could no longer feel the Core. Well, that is to say, she could no longer feel a large rock in the center of her body. She could feel warmth there when she focused intently, charged with potential Energy. She remembered one of the earth spells she practiced earlier in the tutorial and attempted to call upon it to shield her torso. A rough stone shell encased her chest, stomach, and back as she did. This effect was much stronger than the jumble of gravel-like rock that the tutorial spell summoned; she surmised that the improved Core must have enhanced the spell somehow. It didn't last very long, about a minute, before it shimmered away into a silvery gray mist.

Amazed by the power of the Core, she hurried to read about how to connect the smaller nodes to it. Reading the manual, she learned the process was much the same as with the Core. She was to place each node on the part of her body she wanted it to phase into and meditate on the image of it doing so. However, a second step was required: she'd need to create a pathway or channel from the Core to the node. According to the manual, the pathway could be imagined and designed in many different ways, but these nodes were earth attuned, and the connection would literally be burned into her. She didn't think that sounded very fun.

Bronwyn studied the diagrams in the manual and thought of her options: she could just have a direct line from the core to the node, have a path that followed her veins, or even one that was more on the surface level, flowing along her skin. After some consideration, she decided she would attempt to form a path that was more like a thick ribbon than a straight line. It would travel up to and fill her entire pectoralis, climb up to her shoulder and deltoid muscles, and spiral down her arm, passing through every muscle. According to the manual, such a long pathway would slow down the Energy; however, it would, hopefully, allow her to channel more of it at once.

She sat in the meadow with her legs crossed, her right hand in her lap, holding the first of the nodes. The node was a perfect sphere and looked identical to the core, only much smaller at about one inch in diameter. Phasing it into her hand only took a few minutes, faster than the Core, and it didn't feel nearly as hot, just a slight comforting warmth. Then came the process of connecting the two. Bronwyn took a deep breath and started to imagine the pathway she thought of earlier, the bright orange glow of the Core traveling up from her solar plexus to her right pectoral. As soon as she imagined the pathway exiting the Core, she felt a burning heat in her chest that caused her to gasp in pain. The raw energy was burning this new path into her body. It was excruciating, but she could feel it working. She knew she couldn't stop—she feared she would have to start all over if she did.

Bronwyn could barely handle the pain. As it coursed past her chest, it engulfed her shoulder in agony as if she had dislocated it and torn the muscles apart in the process. Forcing the thick ribbon of energy past her shoulder and spiraling down her arm nearly caused her to black out. As she fell forward, she slammed her right fist down into the ground and forced herself to finish. She sat there for a moment, fist planted, as the pain slowly subsided to a low burning, and the final tears of pain ran down her face and landed in the grass.

Eventually, after a long rest, she felt strong enough to move. She lifted her head, holding her arm out in front of her, startled by what she saw. She had been squeezing her eyes shut, focusing on the path the Energy was taking through her body, so she hadn't noticed that the Energy had burned not only through her muscle and inner tissue but left a dark charcoal black marking across her skin. It looked almost like a tattoo and traveled as a two-inch-thick ribbon across the path the energy followed. It wasn't the worst look; honestly, she usually gave most of her VR avatars tattoos.

Though she dreaded it, she set to work on the second node right away. The brief respite she enjoyed while the warm node sank into her flesh was quickly overshadowed by the agony of creating her pathway. Knowing what was coming didn't lessen the burning; in fact, the anticipation might have made it worse.

When all was said and done, she had completed connecting the node in each hand to her Core. She was exhausted, the muscles in her arms ached, and her skin felt like she had the worst sunburn of her life. The markings on her upper body mirrored each other perfectly, making a circuit from her Core to the palm of each hand. She was glad to be done and glad it worked out so well, but she certainly hadn't made things easy on herself. Several times during the process, she cursed her need always to try to be the best—it would have been a lot less painful to just run a straight pathway from the nodes to her Core.

Despite being extremely curious about the settlement stone, Bronwyn was exhausted physically and mentally. She looked around the meadow; it was getting later in the evening, and most of the other colonists were sitting around campfires cooking the foods the System had provided. During the cooking portion of the orientation, each person was supplied with enough food for about seven days. Bronwyn's camp was on the outskirts of the meadow, closer to the eastern trees than most of the other colonists. She had wanted enough space to try and rush through the tutorial as quickly as possible without any of the other settlers perhaps recognizing her and bothering her for help and advice.

She noticed that many of the colonists had formed into groups over the past few days, clustering their tents together based on either past friendships, family ties, or perhaps just common interests and the desire to not be alone in this strange new world. She wasn't sure how she felt. She was lonely, maybe, as she sat by her small tent and started the fire under her cooking pot. She knew there would be plenty of time in the coming days to make friendships, though, and right now, keeping her lead was what was most important.

Bronwyn sat and stared at the flames, her stew slowly cooking. She missed her home, her friends, her family. Her mission had been critical; she and everyone else knew that. Every person aboard the *Pilgrim 9* had a purpose, a reason to be there. Bronwyn was one of the best, if not the best, VR players and pilots in settled space. She had been recruited by Arthur Ballard himself to pilot the Titan-9, a forty-foot tall mech with two purposes: initially, she was to use it to help build the settlement on the new planet, and when construction was complete, she'd use it for combat and scouting. However, their ship never landed, and the Titan-9 didn't seem to have made the journey, either. If she were going to protect these people, she'd have to do it herself.

With a renewed sense of purpose, Bronwyn finished off her bowl of stew and crawled into her tent. She was quick to fall into a dreamless sleep.

BRONWYN

Adrenaline and pain jerked Bronwyn out of a murky, formless dream—something about swimming. She was startled awake to realize she was being physically pulled out of her tent by the ankle. In the dim morning light, she could see a large, orange-furred, wolf-like creature. Her left foot was wholly engulfed inside of its jaw as it pulled. She lashed out with her right heel, trying to stomp it down on the creature's snout. Her kick connected, and it yelped out in pain, dropping her.

Bronwyn frantically grasped around the entrance to her tent, managing to grab hold of one of her gauntlets. She kept kicking at the wolf, keeping it from grabbing her again while pulling the gauntlet onto her right hand. Wasting no time, she pulled herself into a crouched position, favoring her gored and bloodied ankle, and lunged at the beast, bringing her fist up into its throat. The strike landed, and she could feel its windpipe crunch as the weighted gauntlet slammed into it. She saw a burst of movement in the corner of her eye and barely dodged as another one of the wolves lunged from the shadows. The world almost seemed to slow, and without thinking, she willed energy from her core into the pathway to the node in her fist. She launched it toward the side of the beast, and stone formed around her hand as it connected. The sickening sound of snapping bone erupted into the night as her hand sank into the creature, breaking bone and rupturing organs. It flew to the side with an unnatural flop and lay motionless. She knelt next to the first, asphyxiating wolf as it struggled to crawl away and slammed her stone-covered fist into its head, ending the suffering.

Standing there, breathing heavily, she saw a third beast slink off into the forest's edge. It disappeared quickly into the foliage, choosing to retreat rather than face the fate of its packmates. As Bronwyn waited to see if any more of the beasts would come from the forest, glowing motes of golden light coalesced on the bodies of the dead animals. They formed into a kind of mist and suddenly shot forth in a stream of light into her chest before she could react. As the light streamed into her, she could feel her exhaustion and the throbbing pain of her ankle wounds fade away.

Congratulations! You have achieved level 3 base human and have 5 attribute points to allocate.

Bronwyn saw the System message and remembered from the orientation that defeated enemies would reward the victor with Energy. Still unsure if more of the creatures stalked her in the woods, she stood there, silent and waiting. Many minutes passed before she heard a shrill shriek from the north and then another farther west. She quickly ducked into her tent and strapped on her other gauntlet. Not wanting to spend precious time putting on her armor, she sprinted toward the nearest scream, hoping she wouldn't need it.

While she ran toward the conflict, Bronwyn contemplated how to spend her five attribute points. She decided to spend them the same way she had before, three in strength and two in agility. After mentally allocating the points, Bronwyn thought she could feel herself running just a bit faster than she could've before, but she wondered if that was just in her head.

When she arrived at the first cluster of tents, the scene laid out in front of her was grisly. Five of the beasts had made their way into the camp and were tearing apart the corpses of a dozen dead colonists. She sprinted headlong into the fray; the first wolf's back was to her, and with a roar, she leaped into the air and brought her gauntlet down on the back of its skull, caving it in with ease. The rest of the battle was a blur of motion, Bronwyn a terrible maelstrom. With each swing of her gauntlets, she unhinged jaws and shattered limbs, ribs, and spines. Twice, the wolves almost outflanked her, leaping at her back and side while she was dealing with an attack from the front. She used the stone shielding spell that she'd practiced in the orientation and stopped most of the wolves' bites long enough for her to lash out with a gauntlet. After just a few seconds of furious combat, all five lay dead and mangled at her feet.

She quickly checked to see if any colonists in this camp had survived the attack. They hadn't, or at least any that did had already run away. She shoved back the growing realization that this was all her fault and sprinted into the dark; there were still screams from the west.

Golden motes of light flowed into her back as she was running, and she saw a System message:

Congratulations! You have learned the skill Unarmed Mastery—Basic.

Congratulations! You have learned the spell Stone Warding—Basic.

She'd have to figure out what all that meant when this crisis was over.

The scene on the western side of the meadow was much different than what she had encountered earlier. She saw an older man waving his hands placatingly toward a panicked crowd. "Calm yourselves, stop shouting! They're gone and there's nothing we can do for them. Hells, we haven't got any weapons. We need to stay put, keep guard, and watch for more attacks!" There was a general murmuring and a few loud voices of dissent, but everyone seemed to defer to him, though Bronwyn didn't recognize him at all.

Jogging up to the crowd, she studied the man; he looked like he was probably in his early sixties. He had a bald head and a closely cropped white beard, with a longer, slightly twirled mustache. Shoving her way through the crowd to get to him, she called out, "Sir, what's your name and what happened here?"

He let out a long sigh and, before looking at her, spoke: "Girl, I haven't got the time to explain to everyone . . ." It was then that his head turned, and he caught sight of her in the firelight. Bronwyn's entire upper body was covered in blood and gore. "Hells bells!" he sputtered. "Is that your blood, girl, or have you been fighting these little fuckers?"

Bronwyn, looking down, attempted, unsuccessfully, to wipe some of the blood from herself. "Not mine, at least not most of it." She shrugged and asked, "What happened here? Did the wolves attack here, also? Who can't you save?"

Somewhere between being aghast and awestruck, the old man quickly replied, "Well, not wolves, little gray men; they took some of ours. Kicking and screaming! Took 'em alive into the forest, to the west."

"Fuck!" Bronwyn yelled. "This isn't good." She had no idea who or what the gray men might be, but she had to try and stop them. "Stay here," she commanded. "Spread the word through the camp—all colonists need to set a watch with torches on the perimeter. I'm going to get our people back."

As she started running toward the forest, the old man called out from behind her, "What's your name, girl?" She turned quickly, jogging backward for a moment.

"Name's Bronwyn, but most people call me Blodwyn."

She turned her back to the crowd and, before she disappeared into the forest, heard one of them ask incredulously, "Wait, does she mean THE Blodwyn? No way!" She chuckled to herself and smiled. She didn't know how many years they'd been in cryo, but to her, it seemed like her last tournament was only a month ago. Hundreds of thousands of people had filled the virtual stands, chanting her name. It felt good to be recognized again.

She quickly picked up the abductors' trail; she saw noticeable drag marks and splotches of blood. The prints were a strange story: some were about the size and shape of a human foot, others much smaller, with thin, sharp claw marks. She painstakingly followed the footprints for what felt like hours, tagging trees with big, clear X marks whenever the path turned. She occasionally lost sight of the prints and had to backtrack to find a trace of them. She was doing so for what felt like the tenth time when something happened: as she focused intently on the tracks, the prints' outer edges began to glow with a faint red light. Bronwyn paused for a moment, puzzled, and suddenly some yellow motes coalesced on the trail she'd been following, gathering up into a stream and flooded into her.

Congratulations! You have achieved level 4 base human and have 5 attribute points to allocate. You have learned the skill Tracking—Basic.

"What the fuck?" She wasn't complaining, but these levels were coming fast. Was the System still treating this like part of the "orientation?" Strength and agility had been doing well for her so far, so she spent her points once again, three and two. She pulled up her status sheet to see if her new skill was listed:

| Skills: | System Language Integration - Not Upgradeable, Unarmed Mastery - Basic, Stone Warding - Basic, Tracking - Basic |

She spoke aloud, asking the System, "What is Unarmed Mastery?"

Unarmed Mastery—Basic: You are learning the most efficient way to strike at your opponent. You know the basics of grappling and how to escape being held.

"Pretty evident by the name, but how are you giving me a skill to do something I already knew how to do?" No answer came, but she hadn't really expected one. She decided to check the other two before continuing:

Stone Warding—Basic: You are learning how to bend stone and earth to defend yourself against attacks. Amber Class Core Enhancement: Your armoring spells have twice the duration and cost half the energy. Energy cost: 5 per second.

Tracking—Basic: Tracks that have not been concealed in any way glow faintly with the traces of your prey's Energy.

System Language Integration: All sentient beings in System controlled space are enhanced with the ability to communicate via a common dialect.

Bronwyn focused more intently on the tracks laid out on her path. She noticed that when she selectively looked at the small-clawed tracks, a small text window appeared to the side of her vision that just said Yeksa. When she focused on the larger footprints, it changed to Human. She was on the right path, and these abductors were evidently another sentient race in the world. Perhaps she could try to reason with them with her System Language Integration. As she was traveling along the path, a System window popped up in front of her:

Quest: Rescue the captured colonists from the Yeksa village. Reward: Energy-rich natural material. Penalty for failure: None. Accept? YES/NO

The System had mentioned quests in the orientation, but this was Bronwyn's first. She accepted it without hesitation, considering it was what she planned on accomplishing anyway. She hadn't even thought of the captives being held in a village; in fact, she hadn't thought about what she might find at all. Whatever she encountered, though, it didn't matter; people were in danger, people she was supposed to be protecting. These colonists didn't even have a security detail. *She* was the security detail. She was supposed to have selected security personnel from among the general laborers after the colony was established. Of course, she hadn't had time during the System "orientation," and everyone had been busy, but she still felt like this was all her fault; if she hadn't rushed through orientation and given the System an excuse to drop the barrier, maybe these people never would have been taken. She continued down the path.

It wasn't too long before she heard the sounds of struggle from up ahead. She burst through the underbrush without any thought of stealth or self-preservation, surprising two of the Yeksa trying to get an unruly captive under control. The Yeksa had pale gray skin and spindly limbs, and both were wielding short wooden spears. Distracted by their captive, they hadn't heard her run up behind them. Bronwyn slammed her gauntlet into the back of the first one's neck, shattering his vertebra. He slumped down instantly. The second barely had time to react; he attempted a hurried, inaccurate stab toward Bronwyn's head that she easily ducked to avoid. She launched a lightning-fast right hook at him in retaliation, and the impact crunched in the left side of his head, dropping him to the ground with a thud.

The man on the ground had his feet tied and started to scramble away from her in fear before recognizing her face. In an uncharacteristically shaky voice, Arthur Ballard spoke, "Bronwyn, is that you? Dear God, you looked like a nightmare, crashing in here covered in blood."

"Ballard!" Bronwyn leaned over to get her breath. "Here, let me take those ropes off of you." She pulled a small knife off the belt of one of the Yeksa and began sawing away at the thick bindings. "Look, I know a lot is going on, and you probably have a million questions, but I don't have many answers. All I know is that the System removed the barrier when I finished the tutorial, and evidently, there's more than just us on this . . ."

"You did what?" Arthur shouted. "None of us were prepared for this! The barrier was the only thing keeping us safe! Hell, most of us have barely figured out how to cook, let alone defend ourselves! You didn't even think to let anyone know it was gone?" He was furious, and rightfully so, in Bronwyn's opinion.

"I know! Listen. I know. I was just trying to get ahead so I could protect the people here. I made a mistake, and I should've told everyone the barrier was down; I just didn't think of it. I was so tired and . . ." She trailed off, realizing she was just making excuses. "This isn't the world we envisioned, and there's no Titan-9 here for me to pilot. Someone has to become strong and protect our people. I know I fucked up, but I'm going to make it right. I'm going to save the rest of the people that were taken. You have to get back to the colony and set up some sort of perimeter. Torches, knives, hell, sharpen some sticks and make spears. Just stay safe until I get back. Whatever you do, don't go into the forest."

Tiny motes of golden light streamed into Bronwyn from the Yeksa as she helped Arthur to his feet and handed him the two Yeksa spears. "Go. The way back is clear; it's not a straight line, but I've marked the path with big X marks on the trees. Get back and make sure the rest of our people stay safe. I'll be back soon." He started to make a reply, but she was already tearing off into the forest.

MORGAN

Morgan led the way through the doorway, which opened into a wide, stone hallway. This tunnel was made from tight-fitting stone blocks rather than the carved stone of the level below. Just a few feet from the doorway was an alcove illuminated with flickering lantern light. In the alcove were a small wooden table and a crude wooden chair. As they grew nearer, Morgan could see that the table held a short rusty knife and a block of cheese with prodigious mold growths colonizing its rind. He shrugged and put them both into his pouch. The pouch seemed to be able to hold a lot, considering the wolf corpses he'd pulled out of it, so he was determined to pick up anything that might be of use down the road. He looked at Issa, and she nodded, and they both continued on their way down the tunnel.

The tunnel continued for a good thirty feet, then branched to the left. Unlike the tunnel on the first floor, there weren't regularly spaced lanterns, and it was very dark. Issa cast her night vision spell on Morgan again, assuring him that she could keep it going for a long time, now that her Core was back in one piece. The spell required some level of light to work, but even the bit of light coming from the lantern back in the alcove lit the hallway like daylight. Peering around the corner, Morgan could see another fifty feet of hallway ending in a door similar to the one leading to the stairwell. "Seems pretty straightforward."

"Yes, but go quietly," Issa whispered. Morgan nodded and proceeded toward the door. When he was about five feet from it, with Issa right behind him, he started to make out sounds. Deep, grinding voices, words indistinct through the wooden door, and the sounds of wood scraping on stone conjured visions of large men scooting around in chairs. Morgan studied the latch on the door and saw an iron lever that lifted a bolt out of a similar iron bracket mounted to the stone wall. He felt he could depress it quietly if he were careful, so he motioned Issa to back up a bit and then carefully pushed on the latch. It scraped ever so slightly, but the minute noise was lost amongst the racket coming from the other side of the door. Centimeter by centimeter, Morgan pulled the door slowly open until he could see through the crack with one eye.

The room beyond the door was brightly lit with lanterns, once again. Three Urghat were in the room. Two of them were sitting at a crude, wooden table throwing carved stones and arguing about the results. They were drinking mugs of something—beer or some other alcohol if Morgan had to guess. The third Urghat, shorter than the others Morgan had seen, but half again as wide and with bright orange fur, was wrestling with a barrel, trying to pry the top off it with a bent and rusty knife. Morgan gently closed the door but held the latch open. He leaned close to Issa's ear and whispered, "Three Urghat. I think they might be drunk, though, and we might be able to get the jump on them."

"One second," Issa whispered back, her breath hot on his ear, "I can hasten your attacks for a few seconds. When you feel it, strike fast; it won't last long." Morgan nodded, and Issa reached her hand to his shoulder and very quietly started muttering something that he couldn't make out. A moment later, he felt a flare of Energy enter his shoulder from her hand, and it seemed to flood into his heart. He felt his eyes dilate, and taking that as a signal the spell had worked, he yanked the door open and burst through, spear poised to strike.

The Urghat reacted to his entry, but it was like they were moving through thick syrup. By the time the brindle-coated Urghat with his back to Morgan had started to stand up, Morgan had speared his back three times. Brindle's attempt to stand was cut short, and he fell to the ground bleeding out. Morgan moved past the falling body, driving his spear at the other seated Urghat, a hulking, gray-furred fellow with two prodigious lower tusks.

Tusks roared and managed to lift his big, wooden mug, knocking Morgan's spear aside and splashing some kind of watery alcohol all over him. Meanwhile, Issa breached the door and flashed forward, trying to hit Orange-fur with her axe. Orange-fur howled, ducking the blow, and counterattacked with his big, iron knife, but he stumbled over the barrel he'd been trying to open and sprawled on the stone floor in front of her. For just a beat, everyone breathed and looked around the fight scene. Still under the effects of the haste spell, Morgan recovered first and stepped to the side and back, giving himself a little room to maneuver. He thrust at Tusks. The big Urghat didn't dodge, but he had on a thick, leather vest, and Morgan's fire-hardened spear finally met its match; it failed to pierce the armor and skidded past the Urghat's side. Tusks grabbed the spear and shoved it down with all his might, snapping it against the tabletop.

Issa took advantage of her downed foe and brought the axe around from her initial swing and up over her head, chopping down with a grunt. Orange-fur tried to scamper out of the way, and he partially succeeded, but not enough— the heavy axe cleaved into the back of his knee with a grinding, wet crunch. Orange-fur howled and frantically rolled to his back, brandishing his knife to keep Issa away. At the same time, Tusks finally launched himself out of his chair, diving straight at Morgan. Morgan felt like his perception of time was returning to normal because Tusks was on him before he could get out of the way. The Urghat crushed him against the wall, and Morgan was trying to shove him off when Tusks bit down hard on his right shoulder, sinking his teeth into Morgan's flesh and growling with a wet, savage delight.

"FUCK!" was all Morgan could think to shout when he felt those tusks enter his shoulder. He groped around with his left hand, trying to find something to hit the Urghat with, but there was nothing. He felt helpless. The brute was at least twice his weight and much stronger than he was. Tusks growled and shook his head back and forth like a terrier killing a rat, and Morgan felt his vision going dark from the pain. He reached his left hand up in desperation and gripped the Urghat's thick, furry neck. Meanwhile, the Urghat drove its fists into Morgan's body, punching while it bit deeper and deeper into his shoulder.

Morgan dug his fingers through the fur on Tusk's neck, and desperately he *pulled*. He could feel the strength leaving him, his breath strained and ragged, his arm like lead, his whole body screamed in agony; but through it all, he felt something enter his hand from the Urghat's neck—Energy. Once he felt that first trickle, he grabbed onto it and *pulled* harder. It was like a dam broke, and Energy flooded into his arm and down to his core. He kept pulling, and the Urghat stopped shaking him and opened its mouth. Suddenly, the Urghat wasn't trying to pummel him; it pushed against the wall, tried to get away from him. Morgan dug his fingers in with renewed strength and *pulled*. In a desperate panic, the Urghat managed to shove away from Morgan and fell, sprawled into the table, and knocked it over.

Morgan pushed away from the wall and stretched. He rubbed his shoulder, noting that the punctured, shredded skin was already mending and scabbing over. He took a step toward the big Urghat as it struggled to get up, but an axe sprouted from its head, and it collapsed. Morgan looked at the other end of the axe and saw Issa grimly yank it out and prepare another strike. The Urghat didn't move, though, and Morgan took several deep breaths, noting the silence. Golden motes collected on the corpses, and this time, Morgan saw a stream of them flowing not only to him but also to Issa.

Congratulations! You have achieved level 5 base human and have 5 attribute points to allocate. You have learned the skill Backstab—Basic. You have learned the spell Energy Drain—Basic.

Morgan grunted and said, "Status." He wanted to see how his new skills were listed.

Skills:	System Language Integration - Not Upgradeable, Spear Mastery - Basic, Stealthy Maneuvers - Basic, Backstab - Basic, Energy Drain - Basic

"I leveled!" Issa said, smiling brightly, her sharp teeth on full display.

"Hah, great! I did, too. Fuck me, though; that was harrowing. That bastard was ripping me apart like a rottweiler with a rabbit," Morgan groaned as he rubbed at his tender shoulder. "Hey, is there any way to see what exactly my skills do?"

"Yes! I can't believe you didn't know this, but just look at the skill on your status screen and ask what it does in your head," Issa said, while she wiped the blood off her hands and axe on the orange fur of the Urghat she'd killed.

"Hey, it's been, like, a day since I learned about the System. Cut me some slack. Can you make sure nothing sneaks up on us through that other door while I try to figure this out real quick?" Morgan replied, once again studying his status screen.

Issa nodded. "Yes. Better that you know what you're doing before we meet more like this." Morgan didn't reply because he'd studied his spear mastery skill and "asked" what it did, and now he had a new window in front of his eyes:

Spear Mastery—Basic: You are learning the forms and movements needed to kill things in the most efficient way possible. You know the basics about keeping enemies at bay and piercing their vitals.

Not anything he didn't already suspect, but it was good to see his suspicions confirmed. The System was actually putting knowledge in his head beyond what he figured out through his actions. Just like with the System language. He concentrated on his other skills:

Stealthy Maneuvers—Basic: You are on your way to becoming one with the shadows. Moving without tripping on twigs or debris, you could inspire a cat with your sure-footedness.

Backstab—Basic: Woe to the foe that lets you approach from behind unnoticed. You know just where to strike to cause the most damage, and, as you advance your skill, you gain the ability to land devastating combinations of strikes before your enemy can react. Energy cost: 25, Cooldown: Short.

Energy Drain—Basic: Prerequisite: Vortex Class Core. You expend some Energy to forcefully pull the Energy from a foe you have made physical contact with, using that Energy to restore your health and vitality. Energy cost: 50, Cooldown: Long.

"Issa, what's a cooldown?" Morgan asked, after reading about his skills.

"Using skills is taxing on your mind, Core, and body. The System limits how often you can use some skills to balance those factors. At least that's how my mentor explained it to me," Issa quietly replied, as she held her ear to the other door.

"Why is it so vague? Short? Long? What's the difference?"

"I really don't know. I learned how often I could use my skills through trial and error, but if you improve your skills beyond basic, the cooldown will change, even if it still says 'short' or whatever," Issa answered.

"One more question: according to the System description, some of my skills use Energy, but I always seem to be at full Energy when I check, even after a fight. What gives?"

"Well, you're looking at your status after you've consolidated the gains from your vanquished foes. You must have expended less than you gained. Not surprising, as these three were not trivial foes."

"Hmm, give me a couple more minutes; I'm going to spend my attribute points," Morgan said as he studied his status sheet again. He looked at Dexterity and Agility and "asked" in his mind what they did, wanting to clarify something.

*****Dexterity is the measure of your fine motor skills relative to other Energy infused beings.*****

*****Agility is the measure of your physical prowess and speed relative to other Energy infused beings.*****

Right, so agility seemed like the skill he would need for fighting and moving around, while dexterity was more about doing things with his hands like, what, watchmaking? Morgan shrugged and put three points into intelligence to bring it to an even twenty and two points into agility, bringing it to thirteen. He figured being able to sneak around and move quickly during combat had served him well so far, so he might as well keep pushing his agility. While looking at his status sheet, he noticed that his maximum Energy had gone up to 240 with his stat increase, and he assumed it was from the intelligence gain. Good to know. "All right, Issa, you keep listening for a minute, and I'll check this room for loot."

WHITESTAR

Whitestar sniffed the air. She smelled smoke, so much smoke and burning, cooking things. She crouched low in the tall grass, her reddish-brown fur and soft blue leather clothes blending in with the shadows of the blue stalks. Her only spot of bright color was the star-shaped patch of fur around her right eye for which she'd been named. She hated that she still had to use her cub name; she was eager to earn her true name, her warrior's name. She didn't know what would be making so much smoke, but she would find out, and she'd be the first to report it. That would get Goretusk's attention.

She unslung her long plains bow and carefully strung it with the string she'd kept in the oiled pouch at her belt; no sign of rain, and it would pay to be ready. Whitestar didn't nock an arrow, trusting in her ability to pull one from the quiver at her side and fire it quickly enough. Crouching in a predator's stalking gait, she advanced through the grassland toward the source of the fires. She knew it wasn't a singular, big fire like a lightning strike caused last spring. No, it was many small fires. The horizon wasn't orange and filled with smoke, there were just wisps climbing into the air, and the smells were so varied that she knew something odd was going on.

The Gresh Woods were in this direction, and she hoped she'd find the source of the fires before she had to go in there; uncle Bladefist had told her about Yovashi lurking in those woods. She'd never seen a Yovashi, and she didn't want to. The smells were starting to make her crazy—they were so good, sizzling fat with herbs like the warriors took from Ardeni raids. Whitestar's mouth was watering and her belly rumbling by the time she crested a slight rise and could look out over the last stretch of plains to the edge of the Gresh Woods. She dropped flat to her belly when she took in the sight. What in the world was going on? Was this an invading army? Maybe the Ardeni, she mused while stroking the soft, blue leather vest her grandfather, Bluebiter, had made for her. Laying on her belly, she advanced through the grass, watchful for the blue-skinned devils that hid so well in the tall, blue stalks.

After long minutes of slow, careful crawling, she drew close enough to see the people walking among the tents and campfires in the meadow. They weren't Ardeni; they were taller than Ardeni, not as tall as her people, but definitely bigger than Ghelli or Cadwalli. They had coloring like the Ghelli, with their furless pale, brown, and black skin, not like the blue of the Ardeni, who, at least, were good at hiding. These people stood out like flowers on the blue grass with their bright clothes and chaotic meandering. Did they even have weapons?

Whitestar watched the strange people for a long time, never seeing any guards. Now and then, she'd see one or two of them wielding a weapon at a straw dummy or even casting spells with Energy, but they were baby spells, and as she watched, the ones with weapons would sit down after a while, and the weapons would fade away in a yellow mist. What was going on? She inched closer and closer, her curiosity making her brave. Soon, she was among the sparse trees that shielded the strangers' meadow from the greater grassland. She crouched next to a red and white-barked Tigroi tree. She watched a group of the odd people sitting around one of the little white tents.

The more she watched them, the more Whitestar thought she had stumbled on an opportunity for real glory—the Ur-clan could easily overwhelm these soft creatures. They'd make good slaves and food. She had to hurry, though, before another hunter found them and brought word back to the clan. But, would Goretusk even listen to her? Forget Goretusk; what about one of the Underclaws? Could she bring this news to Demonkiller or Thistleback? No, their Fists would laugh at her and wouldn't even let her close. They'd make her give them the information, and they'd take the glory. No, she'd need to bring one of these soft creatures back as proof. If she came into camp with a captive, things would be different. Whitestar smiled, slowly exposing the rows of crooked fangs in her wide, red mouth.

She leaned her bow against the tree, away from the meadow, then spent some time among the deadwood accumulated around the tall trees until she found a stout hard branch about as wide around as her forearm. She quietly dragged it back to her tree and began to cut the small twigs away, shaping the branch into a sturdy club. She smiled, sheathing her knife and smacking the branch's solid weight into the palm of her hand.

The little group of invaders that she'd been watching was sitting around their fire now, eating something out of a pot; she could smell meat and spices. She didn't know which spices because her clan rarely had anything other than salt. Around the Ur-clan, though, she'd smelled things like this, especially after a good raid. These people might not look like warriors, but their food smelled amazing. There were three of them; two were smallish, probably half of Whitestar's weight. The third one was bigger and would probably be hard for her to carry. She watched patiently, waiting for the right moment, just like her uncle had taught her when stalking prey. As the shadows lengthened and the sister moons filled the sky, one of the small strangers and the bigger one went into the tent together. Trusting her nose and the dim light of the moons, Whitestar began to creep forward, silently padding over the grass toward the side of the lone, furless invader. As she got closer, she could see that the stranger was only wearing pants, and she guessed from its build that it was a male. She had learned a bit about Ardeni and other races, and she felt confident in her assessment; after all, even Urghat had breasts, but they had the decency to cover them with hair.

He was sitting in the grass, feet toward the embers of the fire and staring up at the moon and stars. He had a blissful expression on his face, and the only reaction he had when Whitestar came looming out of the shadows, swinging her club at the back of his neck, was to open his eyes a bit wider. The club connected, and he slumped noiselessly into the grass. Whitestar froze for a second to listen for any sign that she'd been discovered, but she only heard soft murmurs and rustling from within the tent. She dropped her club in the grass and scooped up her captive, throwing him easily over her broad shoulder and sprinting across the grassy meadow back into the tree line to the north.

As soon as she hit a full sprint, Whitestar activated her Plainsrunner skill, and her steps suddenly started carrying her twice as far. The trees passed in a blur, and she was back into the plains, moving like a dark shadow through the tall grass. Anyone watching her run past in the shadows would have seen a dark form with a bright star on her head and an enormous, white fang-filled grin. She could only keep her Plainsrunner ability going for a few minutes, but by the time she had to let it drop, she'd run a couple of miles north of the invaders' meadow. She slowed to a trot, her burden bouncing and flopping against the pack on her back.

"Umf, unh, hargh, hey! Hey! What the fuck is happening? Let me down!" Her captive had woken, and Whitestar slowed her run further to drop him into the grass at her feet. She promptly began to kick and beat him until he rolled over and stopped talking.

"You will be silent!" she growled. He cautiously peeked around his hands at her, and his eyes widened. He nodded. She grabbed his wrist and yanked him to his feet. "Walk beside me. Silently. I will beat you if you run." Again, he nodded, and, when she started to walk, he limped beside her. Whitestar frowned at him; he was weak but obeyed her order and wasn't crying. She had an urge to beat him, but she didn't know why. She snorted and continued to walk.

MORGAN

The first thing Morgan checked was whether any of the dead Urghat in the room had a dimensional bag similar to the one he was wearing. He struck out on the first two, but the third guy, the one that had mauled his shoulder, had a leather case, longer and narrower than his, with a strap, kind of like an old leather book bag. It was worked with runes that looked similar to the ones on his belt pouch. "Issa, check this out. See what's in there," he said, tossing the leather case over to Issa.

"You don't mind if I bond with this item?" Issa asked, picking it up, still keeping her eyes trained on the closed door that led from the room.

"Hey, you did just as much during this fight as I did. Besides, I already have this bag," Morgan replied as he rolled the Urghat over, checking it for other belongings. This Urghat had a hard leather vest held closed by straps and brass-colored buckles. Morgan spent a few seconds undoing the clasps and then rolled the Urghat over, yanking the vest off as the corpse turned. Holding up the vest, he could see it was too large for him, but he could shorten the straps on the sides if he had something to cut them. Morgan took a few minutes rummaging through the other bodies, kicking broken furniture around. He came up with a couple of rusty knives, a few wooden mugs, a barrel of some kind of mystery drink, and various scraps of leather clothing that were either too filthy or too large to wear.

Morgan was using one of the iron knives to shorten the straps on the side of the leather vest when Issa started dumping items out of her new bag. Two more barrels of some kind of oily alcohol, a partially cooked hunk of meat, the furs of several large animals, some more loaves of the hard, dry bread, a club with large iron nails driven through the heavy end of it, and another knife, this one longer and sharper than the ones Morgan had found. Morgan smiled at Issa. "Hey, we should keep most of that stuff, except maybe the mystery meat. Can I use that big knife since my spear broke?"

"Of course," Issa replied, flipping the knife and holding the handle out to Morgan. He stepped over to her and took it. The knife was about eight inches of blade with a leather-wrapped hilt and a round, metal guard. It was heavy, sturdy, and sharp but not fancy at all. Morgan smiled and gestured to the door.

"Shall we?"

"Yes, we should keep going, but I hope we find a good place to rest soon," Issa said, though she gripped her axe and stood, crouched and ready, just behind Morgan.

"Yeah, me too; seems like ages ago I woke up with a floating, glowing marble next to my head." Morgan gingerly depressed the iron latch on the door and slowly pulled it open.

Congratulations! You have achieved level 6 base human and have 5 attribute points to allocate. You have learned the skill Dagger Mastery—Basic.

Morgan received this latest message from the System as he retrieved his knife from the back of an Urghat that he'd surprised. It had been looking through an iron grating on a closed, wooden door at the end of another long corridor. Morgan and Issa had been wandering through stone-block passages for what had to be nearly a day. They'd fought several more Urghat, though never more than two at a time, and had to backtrack and try different corridors and doors many times. Morgan indicated that Issa should search the corpse while he stealthily sidled up to the door and looked out through the grating.

The room beyond held another circular stairwell. This one was much larger than the previous one, though, and instead of a central spire with stairs around it, some stairs climbed along the outer circular wall. Morgan guessed that the stairwell was a good fifty feet across. In the center of the room was an iron stand about five feet tall. It held a metal basin at the top of it, and the basin contained some sort of liquid that was burning with a red-orange flame. It lit the stairwell in an amber glow that created dancing shadows. Curled around the iron stand was some sort of creature. The first animal that came to mind when Morgan saw it was a rat. He wasn't sure why because it was about the size of a horse, and it didn't have any fur. Something about its sleeping face reminded him of a rodent, though. Its flesh was pale pink and was folded in many places from its thick neck all the way to its long, whip-like tail. Fangs that had to be six inches long jutted out of its upper and lower jaws, making the wrinkled, pale skin pucker around its lips. It was clear that this was the guardian to the next level.

Morgan held his finger to his lips and gestured for Issa to look through the iron grating in the door. While she studied the creature, he called up his status sheet. Once again, Morgan wished he had a better idea of what to do with his attribute points. He felt like his intelligence was starting to outstrip his other attributes by maybe too significant a margin, and he hadn't felt like he was ever running low on Energy yet. He decided that no matter what, it couldn't hurt to have more vitality, especially considering how badly he'd been injured in a couple of encounters already. He decided to put all five of his free points into vitality, bringing it to seventeen with the bonus from his belt. He wasn't sure exactly how it helped; he didn't *think* he felt any different.

Issa put her mouth right next to his ear and, barely louder than a breath, whispered, "I don't know what that creature is."

Morgan whispered back, "Do you think we can sneak past it?"

"Maybe. I don't have any stealth skills, but we can try." Issa shrugged. "You go first," she said, backing up a step and holding her axe in two hands.

"Can you cast that haste spell on us?" He whispered.

She shook her head, whispering, "Not and be sneaky."

Morgan nodded, and with the utmost care, millimeter by millimeter, he pushed on the latch to the door and carefully inched it open. He could tell that the door wanted to squeak, but he moved it so slowly that he managed to get it open a full two feet without making a sound. Ever so carefully, he edged, sideways, through the opening and padded on his still-bare feet toward the start of the stairway. He passed within twenty feet of the tail end of the creature, and he could feel cold sweat spring up along his neck and head. He held his breath and kept moving, along the perimeter of the room, until he reached the first step. He silently crept up a few steps, then looked back at the door.

Issa was standing in the shadows, her bright yellow eyes pointed his way, clearly waiting for a signal to move. Morgan motioned with one hand for her to come, and she carefully stepped through the opening. She was almost through when the handle of her axe just barely bumped and slid along the wooden door. In the silence, it sounded like a train crashing to Morgan. Issa froze, and, for a moment, Morgan thought it would be all right, but then he heard the papery, susurrous scraping of dry flesh unwinding. He looked at the center of the room and saw that the long, naked, rat-like creature had uncurled and was standing on its short, thick legs. Its eyes no longer closed, Morgan could see their baleful red glow as it stared at Issa.

Before Morgan could react, Issa started running. He didn't know why she would run forward instead of back through the door, but she did. Simultaneously, the rat creature lunged toward her, screeching in a discordant blast of oversized vocal cords. Issa shrank back, turning the axe toward the monster, but she seemed to freeze as the screech enveloped her. Morgan leapt from the fourth step of the staircase, took two lunging steps, and then jumped toward the monster's exposed back. Just as he had with the Urghat earlier, he concentrated on activating his Backstab skill. He felt Energy pulled out of his core, and he knew just how and where to thrust his knife. He grabbed ahold of a loose fold of the creature's skin with his left hand, hauling himself up the side of the beast. With his right hand, he hammered the knife home, next to its spine.

With a shriek, the monster stopped moving forward and rolled over its right shoulder, smashed Morgan into the stone floor and sent him sprawling. His knife was left stuck in the rat beast's back. Having wholly forgotten Issa, the monster listed sideways, clearly hurt with blood streaming down its back and side, but it focused its enraged glare on Morgan and stalked forward, gnashing its dagger-like teeth. Morgan, limping and aching all over, edged away from the beast, reaching a hand into his pouch and thinking about the spiked club he'd stored earlier. He hefted it, just in time to thrust it into the monster's gnashing teeth as it lunged at him. He might have been able to hold it back, but the teeth were just the first attack. The monster feinted to the side, bringing its thick, six-foot-long tail around in a cracking whiplash that snapped across Morgan's left side and back. Searing pain shot through him as his skin parted, and the force of the blow smashed him into the stone steps.

Morgan struggled to his feet, the club with two hands, and braced for another attack. He heard the creature shriek again, this time in a higher, more strident tone. He blearily looked around and saw half the monster's tail flapping on the ground while the stump sprayed a mist of blood around the room. Issa held her bloody axe before her, feinting at the beast while backing away in a circle. Morgan grimly smiled and hefted the big club onto his shoulder; then, he started climbing the stone steps around the perimeter of the room. By the time he'd gained enough height to look down on the combatants, Issa had been backed around the room almost a full circle, and she was sporting a few claw marks on her arms and legs. Morgan crouched on the steps above and waited for them to circle beneath him; then, holding the spiked club high above his head, he activated Backstab and jumped.

He wasn't sure the skill would work with a club, but it did have huge spikes on it and he was performing a sneak attack, so he was hopeful. Morgan zeroed in on the spot he should strike, signaling the skill's success, and he smiled, bringing the club down with all his might as he fell. He landed on the beast's back, much as he would have if he were trying to ride it, but at the same time, the spiked end of the club crashed into the base of its skull. Two of the long, thick iron spikes buried themselves, and he heard a cracking noise like a board snapping, and the beast fell to the stone floor like a wet sack of laundry. Morgan rode the beast to the ground, keeping his balance by holding on to the club. He looked around and saw Issa collapse to her knees a few feet in front of the creature's corpse, breathing heavily. He started to climb off the beast's back when the usual golden motes began to coalesce all around it. He was just stepping to the ground when a massive torrent of Energy slammed into him and Issa.

Congratulations! You have achieved level 7 base human and have 5 attribute points to allocate.

He staggered back, swiping the notification away in time to see Issa also transfixed by the torrent of Energy. Soon she stopped glowing, and he could see her wave her hand in front of her face. "I got a full level from that thing!" Morgan said, walking toward her.

"I did as well! It must have been an evolved beast. We're lucky to have lived."

"It didn't seem that bad." Morgan grunted, stretching out his newly healed, slightly bruised side and back. He was dismayed to see the creature's tail had ripped right through his leather vest. "What do you mean, evolved?"

"Its race must have been higher than Base 1. Maybe Base 2 or 3." Issa shrugged. Morgan wanted to ask her more about races and evolving, but she exclaimed, "Look! Did you see that chest earlier?"

WHITESTAR

Whitestar pushed on for another few hours until she saw a jumble of ruins off to the northeast. She veered that way with her captive, intending to make camp among the spirits of the old ones. She looked down at her prisoner. "What are you?" The creature stumbled in alarm, jerking his head away from her while looking up at her with wide eyes. "Answer me!" She growled.

"I'm uh, I'm a human." The man cringed as he spoke, expecting to be struck. Whitestar snorted a short laugh.

"Human. Hyoooman. Hmm, never heard of this. Why are you here? Are you invading?" She lowered her head and snarled at him with the last question.

"No, uh, we're um, we're starting a new colony. The uh, the uh System put us here? You know about the System?"

"Har, System. Yes, the System has decided to gift the Ur-clan with fresh meat and Energy! The ancestors must bless me to find you first."

"Um, we don't have to fight; I'm sure my leaders would want to talk to you. You'd probably get a big reward for returning me safely!"

"Har, human is funny. What's your name, human?" As she asked the question, Whitestar scaled a pile of rubble and crawled through a gap in some ruined walls. There wasn't any roof, but the walls gave them cover from three and a half directions. As she looked around the ruined structure, she could hear the human hesitating outside. "I said, what's your name, human? Go ahead. Run. See what happens." She heard him sigh and then begin to climb up the rubble.

"I'm Cal. Cal Jennings," he said, as he crawled through the gap and into the ruin.

"So, humans have weak names, too. How will you strike fear with that name?" She sat down with her back to a stone wall and gestured for Cal to sit.

"Well, I don't think our parents name us with that in mind," Cal said, sitting down on the hard stone in front of her.

"Can you at least earn a better name in battle?"

"Um, I suppose. There's a process for changing your name in my society, and someone could, I suppose, pick a scarier name." Cal rubbed at his bare feet, massaging the soles with his thumbs.

"You should wear better clothes and armor, especially with your soft, furless skin." Whitestar grabbed one side of her beautiful blue leather vest as an example. The vest was worked with dark amber beads hung on little tassels and dark metal rings stitched in neat rows.

"Right, I should work on that." Cal nodded, not making eye contact with her.

"Are all your people so soft, Cal? Do you have any warriors?"

"Hey, I'm not that soft!" He cringed as Whitestar bared her fangs and jerked toward him. She laughed, leaning back against the wall. "Uh, anyway, yes, we have warriors, well, I mean we will. We're still figuring stuff out with the System and everything." Whitestar grinned when she heard his words; they truly were ripe for the picking. "Well, what about you? What's your name?"

"Hmm." She stared at him a moment. "Alright, human, you can know me as Whitestar, but I'll be taking my warrior name soon. Don't get used to it."

Whitestar pulled off her pack and rummaged through it, pulling out a heavy skin filled with watery wine. She pulled the cork and drank half the skin in a single, long pull. She pulled it away from her mouth with a gasp. She wiped the droplets from her hairy chin with the back of her hand. Holding out the skin, she said, "Drink, Cal. We walk far tomorrow." He took the skin and drank a mouthful. To his credit, he didn't sputter or hesitate; he swallowed it down. He took another, longer pull, and then he actually smiled.

"First booze I've had in a long time. Maybe hundreds of years!" he grinned and took another long pull, and Whitestar reached out and yanked the skin away from him.

"You want more, you earn it."

"Earn it? What do you want me to do?" He clearly wanted to drink more of her wine, weak as it was.

"You sing for it, human." She sought to tease him. Her uncle, Bladefist, used to make her sing for lessons. It had always humiliated her, but she did it anyway because she was desperate to learn to fight like the warriors. To her surprise, Cal smiled and began to hum. After a moment, he burst into song:

"Twinkle, twinkle, dear Whitestar,
   Please don't drag me very far,
Through the wilderness at night,
   After you woke me with a fright,
Twinkle, Twinkle, dear Whitestar,
   Please don't drag me very far."

He stretched out the notes in a lovely, smooth tenor, and Whitestar found herself savoring the music as he finished, not even bothering to take offense at his lyrics. Urghat warriors didn't sing like that! "Ha, human, you have a pretty voice, like a maiden cub. No, better; I don't know an Urghat that can sing so pretty." She tossed him her wineskin, and he proceeded to take several long pulls, nearly emptying it. "Slow down, human. You have to leave some in there for me to make more, idiot."

"Oh, er, sorry," he said, handing her the skin and slumping to the side. Soon his eyes were closed, and he was taking deep, regular breaths. When she looked at his face, Whitestar could see that he had a bit of fur starting to grow on his cheeks and neck.

"That's more like it, human. Maybe you won't be so ugly when that fur grows in." Whitestar scooted out from the wall and laid back, using her pack as a pillow. She was tired, and they still had two days of hard travel ahead of them.

When Whitestar slept, she very rarely remembered her dreams. That night, in the ruins with the human, though, she had a vivid dream that she kept waking from and then going back to as her eyes grew heavy again. In the dream, she wasn't living with her clan but in a small house on a hillside, tending to a flock of holbyis. While dreaming, she alternated between worrying about boyii hounds attacking the holbyis to being inside the little house and arranging the rooms in preparation for visitors. She was confused and frustrated each time she woke, not knowing why she'd be dreaming about a house and being some kind of herder. She was a warrior! Each time she fitfully rolled over, she determined to dream about slaughter and feasts, and each time her traitor spirit-self would take her to the hillside with the flock.

Whitestar woke with the first light of dawn, unrested and feeling irritated. She dug some dried meat and flatbread from her pack, kicked the human awake, and then sat down to eat while he struggled, stiffly to a sitting position. "You look tired and weak, human."

"Yeah, I had a bad night; turns out I was kidnapped, beaten, and . . ."

"You want more beating?" Whitestar cut him off.

"No," Cal replied, cradling his head in his hands and moaning. "Damn, but that booze of yours did a number on me."

"Har, this?" She lifted the nearly empty skin. "Mostly water, human." She stared at the skin, concentrating on her Replenish Water spell, and felt her Energy draining out of her and into the skin, and then it swelled and got heavier. "Now it's even weaker. Hardly any wine left." She wolfed down the last of her breakfast and drank several long swallows of the considerably weaker wine. She tossed the skin to the human, looked at him as he drank it, then nodded and dug out a bit of dried meat for him. When she handed it to him, he sniffed it, glanced at her, and then shrugged, stuffing it in his mouth.

"That's an interesting spell you have there, creating water out of nothing. The System hasn't taught me anything like that yet."

"Get up, human; you can talk while we walk. Don't be a fool and expect the System to teach you everything. You need to learn from masters." She looked at him for a long moment, then continued, "Probably doesn't matter—you won't be learning much in this life." Without waiting for a response, she ducked through the broken wall and scrambled down the loose stones to the grass. Cal followed after, a dour expression on his face. "Cheer up, human; you can sing while we walk today. It will keep the wild boyii away and make time go faster."

MORGAN

At the base of the iron brazier, nearly obscured by the shadows cast by the flickering red flames above it, sat a small, dark, metal chest. Morgan whistled and walked over to it. "That rat bastard must have been curled around it when we first came in."

Issa nodded, walking closer to Morgan. "Thank you for not leaving me with that thing, Morgan. You could have escaped while it was chasing me."

"Huh?" Morgan looked at Issa. "The thought didn't cross my mind. You should know me better than that by now. Besides, you could have done the same after it whipped me against the wall. Instead, you chopped its damn tail off!"

Issa smiled hugely, her grinning, fang-filled mouth looking truly, sinisterly, happy. "It *really* didn't like that, did it?" She laughed, and Morgan did, too, reveling in the moment. After they'd collected themselves, the two of them knelt by the chest, studying it closely. It had a metal latch but no lock. "I don't see anything dangerous about it. I'm not an expert on traps, though," Issa said.

"I'm not either," Morgan said. "Stand back a bit; I have an idea." To be honest, he hadn't thought about the chest being trapped, but he figured it made sense that it might be. Morgan pulled a long leather cord from his pouch. One of the many scraps that he'd collected from dead Urghats. He carefully tied the end of the cord into a loop and slipped it over the latch to the chest, then he moved around to the back of the chest, stretching the cord as far as he could—about four feet. When he saw Issa standing back by the stairs, he pulled, and the top of the chest flipped open. At the same time, the brazier tipped, pouring burning fluid onto the stone floor in front of the chest. "Well, that would have hurt!"

Issa nodded, gingerly walking around the flames to join Morgan looking into the chest. The inside of the metal chest was lined with dark, soft fabric. Nestled in the folds of the material were a red leather pouch, a folded, silky, blue garment, and a dark stone ring with a thin silvery band of metal running through the center of it. Morgan whistled again. "A lot different from the stuff we've been finding on these Urghats.

"This chest, with these fine-looking items, feels like a System-generated treasure. I think we're being rewarded for making it this far in the Crucible." Issa leaned down and picked up the blue cloth. It unfolded as she lifted it, and he could see it was a deeper blue color on the reverse side, and it had a white wood or bone clasp, carved in the shape of a serpent's head, meant to fasten it around a person's neck. "This is beautiful." She sighed.

"You take it," Morgan said, smiling. "It's a little fancy for my taste. Besides, it looks like it will be a proper cloak on you but would look more like a cape on me, and that strikes me as kind of funny."

Issa smiled again, this time emitting a tiny laugh that *almost* sounded like purring. She swung the cloak around behind her and fastened the clasp around her neck. She pulled the sides close in front of her and did a little spin, preening in front of Morgan. "Hah, it looks great! Perfect fit!" Morgan crowed and clapped. He didn't know why he felt so giddy; it didn't make sense, considering the hell they'd been through over the last day or so. He supposed it had to do with many factors: the thrill of victory, the actual euphoria of absorbing Energy, and, of course, the System could be messing with their heads. He shrugged inwardly and decided it was better to enjoy small moments when he could than to debate whether he should be smiling or sobbing constantly. "Does it do anything?"

"Let me bond with it, one second," Issa replied, grabbing ahold of the cloth and concentrating. "Oh, this is great!" she said, walking over to the stone wall near the base of the stairs. As she got close to the wall, the cloak shimmered almost imperceptibly, and Morgan took a second to realize it was a dark gray color, perfectly matching the wall.

"Wow, that's cool! Pull the hood up and stand still," Morgan said. Issa complied, and she almost disappeared from sight. If Morgan didn't know to look for her there, he'd have a hard time spotting her. "Really cool! You aren't invisible, but it's damn good camouflage!"

"Okay, your turn; see what that ring does!" Issa was still smiling as she pulled the hood down and walked back over to the chest, sidestepping the puddle of oil that was smoldering on the stone floor.

"Alright," Morgan said, bending over to pick up the stone band. It was a big ring, maybe half an inch wide, carved from some kind of dark stone. The silvery river running along the center of the band looked almost like a natural vein in the stone. He looked at the inside of the ring and could make out thousands of tiny markings, letters from an alphabet that he didn't know. "Should I bond with it before I put it on?"

"It wouldn't hurt. I think these items are System generated, not made by an Artificer. When I bonded with the cloak, I had a System message tell me what it was, almost like I'd cast an Identify spell," Issa replied. Morgan nodded and sent a trickle of Energy forth into the cold, stone ring.

Ring of Shielding—This item will absorb damage intended to hit the wearer up to a certain threshold. After use, it will regenerate its potential over one day.

"Oh, nice! It's a ring of shielding; it will absorb some damage that comes my way." Morgan slipped the ring over his middle finger, and the cool stone contracted to fit snugly. "It says it's 'Base 2.' What does that mean?"

"The System categorizes everything on a scale. Base 1 is the lowest; Base 2 is next, then Base 3, etcetera, up to Base 9. Then, after some kind of breakthrough, the next tier is reached, which is Improved 1," Issa explained.

"How many tiers are there?"

"I don't know. The highest I've seen is the Town Stone in my village, which is Improved 5."

"I have so many questions, but let's see what this last thing is first," Morgan said, reaching into the chest and picking up the red leather pouch. It weighed about a pound and clinked familiarly. "I think it's more of those beads like the shaman had."

Issa moved closer, watching as Morgan undid the drawstring and poured some of the pouch contents into his other hand. Sure enough, small, glimmering beads flowed out into his palm, but these were shining with a deep red luster, not the green of the other ones. "Fire attuned," Issa said.

"Is that good?"

"Well, it would be very good to certain Energy users who are attuned to fire, but for you and me, they're just as useful as any other Energy source. Best to hold on to these, for trading, or until you can use their full potential." Morgan nodded and closed the beads back up in the pouch.

"How about I hold on to these, and you keep the green ones from the shaman?"

"Thank you, Morgan." Issa smiled, and Morgan nodded.

"The System indicated I'd get to choose a 'class' at level ten. Is that normal?" Morgan asked.

"I don't know how normal it is, but my people also get to choose a class at level ten," Issa replied.

"What exactly does that mean? I mean, I know the System definition for a class, but how many choices are there? Does it affect a person's abilities a lot?"

"Well, your choices are dependent on many factors. I know some of them, but remember, the System is also fairly new to our people, so I don't know everything. My teachers explained that my abilities, skills, Core, and experiences could all be factored into what classes the System offers. Some people believe that a large part of it is just random luck." Issa shrugged, then stared into space, and Morgan assumed she was also looking over her status sheet.

Morgan thought about it and decided to hold onto his extra ability points for now. He felt it would be nice to reserve points to spend when he hit level ten and had a better idea about classes. While he was thinking about classes and advancement, he decided he'd review his current System generated quests, so he thought about them, and a screen appeared in his vision:

Quest: Survive the Crucible. Reward(s): Commensurate with achievements. Continued existence. Location of other Human entities.

Quest: Don't let Issa die within 1 week (2/7). Reward: Energy Core Cultivation Manual (Improved), Improved Relations with Ardeni faction. Penalty for failure: Diminished Will efficacy—permanent.

Morgan did a double take when he read through the second quest. It looked like he'd already made it into the second day of his week of keeping Issa alive. If only the System knew Issa had saved him as much as he'd saved her by now. He also noticed that the reward had changed. He was sure that the (Improved) part of the cultivation manual reward was new.

The two of them spent a few more minutes catching their breath and going through their belongings. Morgan had to work for a few minutes to dig his dagger out of the dead rat monster, but he finally pulled it free. "How do you feel about getting some sleep here? I know it's kind of risky with the open staircase, but we could drag this guy's corpse in front of the door at least and then take turns getting some shuteye. I feel dead on my feet."

"It's not a bad idea, and this oil burning here hasn't given any signs of slowing down. The light is good, and it's warm enough," Issa replied. The two of them took a few minutes to drag the enormous corpse in front of the door, blocking it and holding it shut. The rat-beast had seemed a lot bigger when alive; in death, with its skinny limbs pulled in and its long tail chopped off, it seemed much smaller, almost pitifully so. It couldn't have weighed more than a few hundred pounds. Still, anything trying to come through the door would be very noticeable. After blocking the door, they moved to the farthest point of the room and took turns sleeping at the edge of the curving, stone stairway. Morgan let Issa sleep first. He didn't know how long, exactly, he watched her sleep, but he tried to give her as much time as he could, only waking her when he absolutely couldn't keep his eyes open any longer. When she was awake, he took his turn laying his head on the rolled-up, thick, gray animal fur that they'd taken from an Urghat just hours earlier, though it felt like a month ago in Morgan's mind.

In his dreams, Morgan was once again back on Earth, taking the computer exam to join the Arkship expedition force. However, this time, he couldn't think of the answer to a question that seemed very basic, he couldn't even make sense of the words. It was like they were written in another language. He sat and stared at the screen, panic making his heart race, and a cold, uncomfortable sheen of sweat started to soak his pale blue dress shirt, the only dress shirt that he owned. He frantically tried to think of an excuse to get out of the test and try again at another date, but he feared he wouldn't make it past the psych eval a second time and be allowed to test again. He clicked a random answer on the screen and read the following question:

*****What formula is used to calculate a person's maximum Energy?*****

Morgan woke up with a start. His eyes were wide and panicked as they glanced around the unfamiliar room. Slowly things came back to him, and he realized where he was. He groaned and sat up from the hard stone floor. Issa was sitting nearby, leaning her back against the stone staircase, her eyes were closed, and her chest was rising and falling in slow, steady breaths. She'd fallen asleep. Morgan looked around the room. Nothing seemed different, except that maybe the strange oil that burned with the red flames was a little dimmer. He had a thought and pulled up his quest again:

*****Quest: Don't let Issa die within 1 week (3/7). Reward: Energy Core Cultivation Manual (Improved), Improved Relations with Ardeni faction. Penalty for failure: Diminished Will efficacy—permanent.*****

Well, that settled that—they'd slept into the next day. He fished some bread and a canteen of water out of his pouch and was eating it quietly when Issa woke up. "Good morning!" He'd decided to make light of her falling asleep rather than throw a fit about it. What was done was done, and clearly she'd been exhausted.

"Oh!" Issa's pale blue cheeks reddened with embarrassment. "I can't believe I fell asleep! I'm so sorry, Morgan; I was just watching the flames burning in the oil, and the next thing I knew, you were saying 'Good morning'!"

"Don't beat yourself up about it. We've both been through hell the last couple of days, and nothing bad seems to have come from it. Here, have some bread." Morgan tossed her the loaf of bread he'd been breaking pieces off to eat. After they'd both had as much of the dry, hard bread as they could stomach, they gathered their things and began their trek up the steps toward the next level of the Crucible.

WHITESTAR

They made good time in the morning; Cal did as he was told and sang while they walked. He said he wasn't really good at making up lyrics, so he sang songs from his homeworld. They were different from any kind of songs that the Urghat sang, and Whitestar had to hide her pleasure by forcing a scowl to her face while they walked. It seemed to intimidate the human even more, and he apologized for his singing after each song. Whitestar, ever sparing with her praise, only grunted and told him to keep singing.

By the time the sun was high in the sky, and the Sisters were starting to rise in the west, the human was limping badly, and their progress had slowed. "I won't carry you all the way to the Ur-clan. Why do you falter?"

"My feet; they're blistering, and I've got some sharp pebbles or twigs stuck in them."

"Sit." Whitestar looked around slowly, making sure nothing moved in the grass nearby. She took several long, deep sniffs of the air and then removed her pack and sat down. She pulled a large swatch of soft leather from her backpack and took her leather knife from her belt pouch. She proceeded to shave long thin strips from the leather swatch, then she cut the swatch in half and, using her tool, poked holes along the edges. She ran the leather strips through the holes and pulled them tight, fashioning crude leather shoes.

While she'd been working, Cal had been digging at the soles of his feet, pulling out splinters. Whitestart tsked and said, "Such soft skin. I could walk these plains for days with no discomfort, even without boots!" She slipped the makeshift shoes over the human's feet and pulled the drawstrings tight, tying them off. "There, now you can walk faster."

"Um, thank you, Whitestar." Cal smiled at her as he struggled to his feet.

"Don't thank me, fool. I'm your doom." Whitestar snorted and continued to walk, listening for the human to catch up. "Sing something, Cal," she commanded when his footsteps caught up to hers. Cal coughed, clearing his throat.

"I think you'll like this one—it's about a famous farmer in my world called Old MacDonald." He proceeded to sing a lively tune about a farmer with many strange-sounding animals. Whitestar especially enjoyed the parts when Cal would make sounds like the animals. She found herself wanting to sing along but kept a straight face and surveyed the surroundings while they marched.

They continued this way until late in the afternoon and they had marched deep into the heart of the plains. The Great-fang Mountains were still purple on the horizon, but they filled more of the sky. Whitestar was sure that they'd reach the Ur-clan encampment by the end of the next day, so she looked for shelter for the night. These plains were pockmarked with ruins of the old ones. Most had been explored or closed off, so that the surface buildings were reasonably safe to use as shelter. She was confident that if they turned east a bit, they'd come upon some ruins with intact buildings to use as a shelter. Usually, Whitestar wouldn't worry about making a fire and sleeping under the stars, but she was hoping not to be noticed by other Urghat hunters before she returned with her prize. "Time to be quiet now, little human. Follow me closely."

They turned east, and, as the sun began to set, and the Sisters were high in the sky, their destination came into view: jumbled broken stone walls, overgrown with grass and lichen spread out in front of them for several miles. This was one of the great cities of the old ones millennia ago. They had been ancient history even before the System came and crushed the worlds together. Whitestar led Cal among the broken walls and buildings, looking for a structure with four walls still standing. After a short search, she found what she was looking for. It might have been a temple or meeting hall in another life. Now, it was just a large stone structure with four walls. It had no doors in the openings, and the windows were empty of glass. The inside was filled with dirt, broken stone, and decayed piles of wood. Maybe the wood had been furnishings or roofing material once upon a time, but now it was mostly dust and jumbled rot.

"Who lived in these ruins?" Cal asked, following her into the building.

"Old ones." Whitestar shrugged, putting an end to the discussion. She piled some dried grass and bits of wood into a cleared area in the center of the building and used her fire striker to get a flame going. "Gather a pile of dry wood, human. We'll sleep warmly tonight." As Cal moved to obey her, she brought out her wineskin and refilled it with her Replenish Water spell. She didn't make a big deal out of it, but she was quite proud of that spell; very few Urghat had the Energy affinity required for creation magic. Even so, it exhausted her Energy to cast it, and she sat down to rest while the human finished stacking the dry wood.

They sat for a while, neither speaking, as they ate more dried meat and drank the water from her skin. Whitestar could see that Cal was disappointed by the strength of the mostly-diluted wine, and she laughed inwardly—he must have been hoping to drink himself into oblivion again. After eating and sitting in silence for a while, Cal asked, "Are your people going to kill me?"

"That will be up to the Overclaw. I imagine he will want to question you for a while before he eats you, though." She looked at him closely as she spoke, and she could see the pale skin beneath his new, black face-fur grow paler.

"Eat me?"

"Yes, human. What did you imagine we'd do with your kind?"

"I don't know, couldn't we trade with each other? You know, become friends? Make an alliance?"

"Cal, human, the Urghat don't need alliances to be strong. We grow stronger by conquering and eating our enemies. I'll promise you this: I won't eat you, Cal. I can't speak for the whole Ur-Clan, though."

"Listen, Whitestar; you seem like a nice, lovely lady. Don't you think you could let me go?" Cal reached forward and tried to hold one of Whitestar's furry hands with his two pale, furless hands. She pulled back.

"Are you trying for another beating, human?" Whitestar's voice had a dangerous growl to it. "Sing something relaxing, and maybe I'll sleep before thinking of how I want to punish you." Cal pulled his hands back and sighed, his face a study in dejection.

"All right, Whitestar. This is a song about a place called Alabama and a man wanting to go home to it." The human began to sing a song that had a lovely tune, and Whitestar could almost picture the blue skies he sang about. Some of the words didn't make sense to her, but she thought it might be her favorite song that Cal had sung.

"Well, well. Aren't this some pretty singing?" The rough, nasally growl came from the doorway to the old building, and when she heard it, Whitestar leaped to her feet, pulling out her hunting knife. Cal sputtered and stopped singing, backing away from the fire. "Calm down, missy. It's just old Thornpaw. What clan is you from?" The shadow in the doorway moved forward into the light, and Whitestar saw another Urghat, an old, lean one. He was tall but stooped, and his long, thin arms hung down past his knees with his stooped posture. His face-fur was gray, and he was marked with many scars. As he walked closer, waiting for her answer, his grin widened, exposing yellow fangs and two tusks, both broken and cracked.

"I'm part of Goretusk's clan," she replied, still holding the hilt of her knife.

"Ah, Goretusk, is it? Kind of a pissant clan, isn't it?" His grin continued to widen as he walked toward the fire.

"Try saying that to Goretusk's face. You're lucky I'm a hunter and not yet a warrior-named, or I'd lay you out for that." Whitestar bristled.

"Oh? Gonna lay old Thornpaw out, are you?" He stepped closer to the fire, and Cal began to scoot backward like he might jump to his feet and run.

"Stay still, Cal," Whitestar growled, stepping forward toward Thornpaw.

"What's this, then? It has a pretty voice and a pretty smell. Shouldn't you offer to share your meal with a fellow hunter?" Thornpaw stepped closer, a long stream of saliva starting to drip from his lower tusk where it protruded from his mouth.

"This isn't for us! I'm bringing him to the Underclaws, and they'll let me in to see the Overclaw after they hear my report!" Whitestar stepped forward, trying to make herself bigger. Even with his stooped posture and wiry build, the old hunter was more physically imposing than she was.

"Oh, the Underclaws, is it?" Thornpaw stepped closer and reached out a clawed hand toward Cal. "Look how soft it is. Let's just have a taste, then. We can still get a reward for bringing him in with some parts missing."

"There's no we!" Whitestar slapped his hand away from Cal and continued, "I have the information. I captured him." Suddenly Thornpaw's demeanor changed—he stopped stooping and rose to his full height, slapped Whitestar's hunting knife from her hand, and grabbed the fur at her neck, driving her back against a wall.

"You'll need to show respect for your betters, welp!" he growled, squeezing his fist full of her fur and driving his knuckles against her throat. "I could use a little warm company and a delicious snack. I've been out on the hunt for weeks." Whitestar was having trouble breathing, and she could feel the wiry strength in the old Urghat's grip, but she didn't reply. She reached behind her, groping along the top of her belt for one of her other knives. She'd just gotten her hand around the hilt and was ready to yank it free and give this old bastard a mark to remember her by when he howled, let go of her, and spun around.

"You dare?" Thornpaw screamed at Cal, who was scrambling backward, Whitestar's hunting knife gripped in his hand, blade drenched in blood. Thornpaw reached for the hatchet he had slung on his belt, and, without thinking, Whitestar drew her knife and buried it to the hilt in his kidney. He coughed out a terrible cry of agony and stumbled forward into the fire. He howled again as his hands fell into the coals, and Whitestar jumped on his back, driving him down into them, stabbing him repeatedly on the side of his neck and shoulder. Arterial blood pumped forth, and his struggles soon subsided.

"Why? Why? You stupid idiot." Whitestar looked up from the bloody mess at Cal, and it wasn't clear if she was talking to him, the dead Urghat, or herself.

BRONWYN

The Yeksa were not difficult to follow; they made no attempts to cover their tracks. Bronwyn found she could easily spot the winding path ahead of her, glowing red with their residual energy. She headed deeper and deeper into the forest. She ran along the trail for about a mile and didn't see any sign of the other captives. However, it was clear that she was on the right path, and it had to lead somewhere.

She followed the trail for a few hundred more until it led her straight into a stream. It was only about ten feet across and no more than a few feet deep at the center. She looked around and found a shallow ford so as not to get water into her boots. She was able to pick the trail up again quickly, but she almost didn't need it; once she was on the other side of the river, she could easily smell the smoke of campfires.

Bronwyn was never one for stealth, but she wanted to get a layout of the village and find where they were holding the captives before she started anything. She slowly crept forward in the thick underbrush until she could make out the first buildings. They weren't so much buildings as crudely constructed tents made out of a light-yellowish hide she didn't recognize. The Yeksa lacked an actual social structure, and the village looked more like a gathering of individuals than any sort of community or town. However, the raid on the colonists did prove that they were at least willing to work together toward a common goal.

She crept around the edges of the forest, and it seemed to her like twenty to thirty Yeksa were living in this small community. She didn't feel entirely comfortable taking them on all at once, but given how disorganized they seemed to be, she figured she might be able to attack them in smaller clusters. After sneaking most of the way around the camp, she finally found the other nine colonists. They were tied to poles, in groups of three, on the southern side of the clearing. She decided that starting her assault on the northern tents would draw some attention away from them and maybe keep them safe for longer.

After quietly making her way back to the northern dwellings, she found what looked like a good place to start. There were two tents, a little bit spread apart from the others, with four Yeksa in the vicinity. She waited until the seated one was about to take a bite of some foul-looking gruel he was slopping around in a wooden bowl. As he lifted the bowl to drink from it, she wordlessly sprang out of the forest and slammed her fist into the back of his head. She kept the momentum of the punch going, following the collapsing Yeksa to the ground, burying his face in the dirt. Before any of the Yeksa could react, she wrenched her gauntlet from the back of the first one's skull and threw her whole body into an uppercut against the Yeksa standing adjacent to her. Her gauntlet squarely made contact with the bottom of his sternum, and she could feel a multitude of bones snapping as she lifted him three feet in the air with the force of the impact. The third Yeksa let out a screeching battle cry as it lunged with a spear toward her. She caught the head of the spear with her right gauntlet and yanked it past her side, pulling the Yeksa into her. Bronwyn shoulder-checked his face as he flew into her, knocking him to the ground. Taking the spear from his weakened grasp, she plunged it into his stomach, pinning him to the ground. The final Yeksa attempted to run into the camp, crying in alarm, but Bronwyn was significantly faster than he. She caught him almost instantly and grabbed the back of his neck, pulling him to the ground. She brought her gauntlet down on his face, but not before he could let out another loud shriek. She could hear the other Yeksa coming.

Not wanting to become surrounded, she sprinted toward the western voices. Bronwyn left a trail of blood in her wake. Careening around ratty lean-tos made of hides and leaping over fire pits, she felled a dozen Yeksa before they had any chance to gather together. When she reached the southern side of the village, she turned, not wanting to get too close to the captives. She rounded a corner to be confronted by a small mob the remaining ten or so Yeksa had formed. Bronwyn braced herself and readied the energy in her Core. She let them get within ten yards of her before she launched herself into a charge. Just as the first Yeksa was about to skewer her with its spear, she released the stored Energy in her Core, letting it flow out toward her fists. Her skin turned to stone, and the tip of the spear exploded against her, not even leaving a scratch. She flew into a rapid assault, always sprinting toward her next opponent as soon as she felled the last. When there was nothing around her but broken bodies, Bronwyn yelled out in triumph and dropped to her knees, breathing heavily. She realized she had received a few minor cuts on her legs during the fight as she knelt there. None of them were much of a threat to her health, though, and, in fact, the incoming stream of energy from her defeated foes was causing them to close right before her eyes.

Congratulations! You have achieved level 5 base human and have 5 attribute points to allocate.

She contemplated putting some points into Intelligence to use her earth magic better, or maybe into Vitality in case she started to take some bigger hits. However, she did notice that, at least at the moment, she was significantly faster than any of the opponents she had fought. She reasoned that there was no real use in spending points in Vitality if she never got hit, and she had her stone armor to shore up that weakness to some degree. "Well, three strength and two agility it is," she said, spending the points and checking her status screen to see her attributes:

Strength:	25	Vitality:	11
Dexterity:	9	Agility:	19
Intelligence:	9	Will:	11

As she was heading back to free the captives, she heard a rumbling, angry roar erupt from the central, largest tent behind her.

Bonus objective added to Quest: Rescue the captured colonists from the Yeksa village: Defeat Gristle Snot, the Yeksa shaman, before freeing the captives. Bonus Reward: One Basic Treasure Box.

Bronwyn felt torn: on the one hand, she was the reason these people were in trouble in the first place; on the other, if she didn't take risks, how would she ever grow? "Ugh!" She tightened the straps on her gauntlets and stomped off toward the source of the roar. When they'd first arrived here, she'd felt that the kind, nurturing voice of the System was genuine. It even described itself as a "benevolent entity," but she was starting to wonder. First of all, if it was genuinely benevolent, would it have to tell people that? Why would it drop the barrier with no warning? Why would it put quests like this in front of her when people were waiting to be rescued. She supposed the shaman's arrival could be outside the System's control and that it was just taking advantage of the situation, but she had her doubts.

She rounded the side of a ramshackle tent, and directly in front of her, not fifteen feet away, she saw the creature. Gristle Snot was much larger than the other Yeksa she had fought earlier; he was nearly seven feet tall and had to weigh five hundred pounds or more. His gigantic rolls of fat jostled around as he spun to look at her. He shouted something in a grotesque phlegmy voice, spit dribbling down his chins and thick mucus running freely from his drooping, troll-like nose. She had no idea what he was saying, but it sounded like an insult.

"Well, come and get it then, lard ass!" She raised her gauntlets and beckoned him forward. The Yeksa took one giant, lumbering step forward, and, as his foot touched the ground, Bronwyn lunged toward him. Except, she didn't lunge. She didn't move at all. Looking down, Bronwyn realized her feet had been encased in ice and were frozen to the ground. Gristle Snot let out a gurgling laugh as she panicked and tried to wrench her feet free. He raised one of his thick slimy hands and conjured a massive ice spike in the air above his head. He let it sit there for a moment, hovering in place, before hurling it down at her.

The spike reached her almost instantly; she barely had time to activate her Core and cover herself in stone. Her gauntlets took most of the impact of the five-foot spike, blocking as it crashed into her. The impact was enough to break the ice beneath her and send her tumbling backward a half dozen feet. If she hadn't conjured her armor, she was sure she'd be dead. Even with the stone armor and blocking the spike with her gauntlets, she had numerous tiny shards of ice puncturing her arms, shoulders, and chest; she was bleeding from a dozen wounds.

Gristle laughed again as Bronwyn crawled to her feet, and he started conjuring another spike above his head. However, her feet were free this time, and Bronwyn, even wounded badly, was much faster than he presumed. She sent herself into a full sprint, closing the distance between them before he could finish his spell. She dove forward, and her right fist made solid contact with Gristle's kneecap. A sickening popping and snapping sound erupted from the Yeksa's knee as it bent backward, and he toppled to the side. Bronwyn ended her dive with a roll and stood behind Gristle as he writhed on the floor, his bloated body too heavy to stand on one leg. Gristle rolled onto his back and tried a last attempt to shoot a smaller icicle at Bronwyn, but she darted forward and caught it in her gauntleted hand before it could take flight. Spinning the icicle in her hand, so it was pointed downward, she knelt, slamming it down into Gristle's bulging right eye. His eye popped and froze against the ice as she shoved it through the socket and into his brain.

Bronwyn flopped down onto her butt, breathing heavily and taking stock of her injuries. She was pulling shards of ice from her shoulders and upper arms when the stream of golden motes flew out from Gristle to her.

Congratulations! You have achieved level 6 base human and have 5 attribute points to allocate.

"A whole level from just one creature?" Bronwyn felt like she was leveling fast, but then, she had no idea what the level cap was. Was there even a level cap? True, the shaman had rewarded her a whole level, but he had been a dangerous opponent; if she hadn't reacted as quickly as she did, that icicle would have skewered her. Gristle's magic had been much more potent than anything she had seen so far; she hadn't even realized he froze her feet to the ground until it had already happened. "Well, you slimy fuck, you almost did me in, but you were just a touch slow." She slapped Gristle's belly as she stood up and noticed two things. One, a small, blue box had, at some point, appeared to her right, and two, Gristle was wearing a belt with about a dozen small pouches tied to little brass hooks.

The little blue box was very similar to those given to her during the tutorial that contained food and basic materials to build her tent. The primary difference was that it was much more ornate, covered in fine filagree, and engraved with silver runes she didn't recognize. She picked the box up and sat it down in front of her, gently lifting the lid. Inside was a ten-inch long scroll with golden caps on each end. She unraveled the scroll and, written in flowing dark green calligraphy, were the words "Blacksmithy Requisition." The detailing text explained that the scroll would instantaneously build a fully supplied, rank one smithy upon activation near a settlement stone. Bronwyn figured she better finish up here soon and get back to the colony to sort out this whole settlement business. She hoped this smithy would let them make weapons to defend themselves better from whatever threat came next.

She knelt next to Gristle and removed the belt from around his waist. Rummaging through the pouches, she found they were mostly filled with various herbs and some dried meats she couldn't quite identify. There were two pouches, however, that were of interest. One held about thirty light blue spheres, slightly smaller than a marble. The other seemed to open into a lightless void. She reached her hand into the darkness all the way up to her elbow, an impressive feat, given the bag was the size of a coin purse. She presumed it was much like the bags of holding that were prevalent in VR games. She focused her intent on the bag, allowing Energy to flow into it, attempting to bond with it as she had earlier with her orientation rewards. The System had explained that directing your energy into magical objects would often give you a greater insight into their uses, and that proved true with the bag: in her mind's eye, she found herself looking into a cube, it was thirty feet in every direction, and had a random assortment of objects left by the previous owner. Inside was, unfortunately, mostly a bunch of trash. There were a few maggot-ridden animal hides with chunks of meat still stuck to them, various bits of uneaten food, and myriad bones. Bronwyn unceremoniously dumped the contents out next to Gristle's body. The bag would come in handy, but she certainly did not want to keep its contents. She wasn't interested in wearing the filthy belt, so she took the two pouches off their hooks and slipped them into her pockets.

Having retrieved everything she wanted from Gristle, she ran back to where the colonists were being held captive. When she arrived, they were right where she'd seen them last, tied to poles on the southern end of camp. Most of them were squirming and trying to get out of their bindings; a couple seemed resigned to their fate and were just silently weeping. Seeing her return, they started shouting for joy and begging her to free them. She took some kind of a flint knife off of a nearby Yeksa corpse and started sawing away at the ropes binding the captives to the poles.

Once they were all free, she convinced them to look around the tents and take weapons off the dead Yeksa. After about twenty minutes, they had gathered a couple of dozen spears, even more of the flint knives, and an assortment of other makeshift clubs and shivs. They decided to leave most of the other stuff the Yeksa had in their tents, most of it being ragged furs and soiled garments. With their newly found weaponry, Bronwyn led them back toward the colony.

The sun was just starting to rise when she had left the colony in search of survivors, and the path back was clear and easy to follow in the golden light of late morning. Bronwyn didn't even need to use her tracking skill to retrace her footsteps. She looked around at the forest, partially watching for any danger but also noticing how alien and beautiful it was. The trees were similar to Earth's, but there were at least forty different varieties just along the route back to the meadow. Some had leaves that glowed a vibrant green in the sunlight. Some had bark that looked like rusted iron, and many had various fruits or brightly colored flowers growing from their branches.

Bronwyn also noticed many small creatures scurrying away from their path. One particularly curious beast, about the size of a robin, caught her attention. It had a body like a squirrel with pristine white fur, a large fluffy tail, and a golden turtle-like shell speckled with dark green splotches. It hopped down from a nearby branch, startling Bronwyn, and she nearly swatted it out of the air as it took a seat on her shoulder. It didn't seem to have any interest in leaving, and when Bronwyn reached to pick it up, it deftly hopped to her other shoulder and plopped down once again. After a few capture attempts, Bronwyn decided that the creature seemed harmless enough and simply let it be.

She and the colonists could hear the human encampment before they could see it; there were no sounds of alarm, just the sounds of a large number of people getting ready to start their day. Soon the forest gave way, and they walked, once again, into the familiar meadow.

Congratulations! You have completed a Quest: Rescue the captured colonists from the Yeksa village. Reward: Energy-rich natural material.

Another blue box with golden runes shimmered into view at Bronwyn's feet. Not wanting to make the people she rescued wait any longer, she quickly flipped the lid. She didn't know what to expect exactly, but she certainly didn't think she was going to open it to find, what seemed to be, a perfectly ripe, purple plum. As confused as she was, she felt the instant desire, the uncontrollable need, to consume it. She plucked the plum from the box and sank her teeth into it without even thinking. The next thing she knew, she was lying flat on her back, the little squirrel-turtle nibbling gently on her nose, and one of the colonists she was escorting kneeling next to her.

Feeling groggy, like she just slept for far too long, she mumbled, "What in the hells just happened to me?"

"Well, I couldn't really tell you, ma'am; you picked up that fruit from the box and devoured it like you were starving to death, then your hair started to shimmer, you swelled all up, and you fell flat on your back. That was all a couple of minutes ago; we've been trying to wake you up since."

Bronwyn looked down at herself—things looked alright. "What the hell do you mean I swelled all up?"

"Honestly, ma'am, I don't know how to explain it. It was like you were growing, or you were just *more* than before, do you know what I mean?" The man emphasized the word more. Bronwyn frowned and pushed herself to her feet, her small companion hopping back onto her shoulder as she did. Standing next to the man, he did seem smallish to her, but she didn't remember exactly how he'd looked before. It was something to figure out later, maybe. As it was, she felt fantastic. She called up her status sheet to see what was different, and there it was next to her race.

Race:	Human - Base 2

Bronwyn hadn't had any idea you could upgrade your race or what that descriptor even meant. She didn't exactly know how to describe the changes she felt, but the colonist was right; she did, somehow, feel more substantial. Her muscles had better definition, her skin on her arms and hands seemed smoother, and she could almost swear her sight was better than before. Bronwyn took the tie out of her hair and let it fall, hanging just past her shoulders. Lifting it into view, she noticed that the bright red shock of curls had an almost metallic quality that shimmered in the sunlight.

Seeing her status screen also reminded her that she had forgotten to spend her latest five points in her haste to return the colonists. Strength and agility had treated her well so far; she won the fight with the shaman because of her speed. *Three and two it is,* she thought, spending the points and bringing her strength and agility up to 28 and 21, respectively.

Realizing she had been standing there for a few minutes, she motioned toward the colonists. "I'm not entirely sure what just happened, but come on, we need to report back to Mr. Ballard."

WHITESTAR

Cal looked at Whitestar, at the corpse, and back to Whitestar. "Well, he was choking you, and . . ."

"Enough. Let me think," Whitestar snapped, rubbing her bloody hands along the back of Thornpaw's cloak while she stood up. Golden motes collected around the body, and streams of Energy flooded into her and Cal.

Congratulations! You have achieved level 12 Plains Hunter and have gained 3 Agility, 2 Strength, 2 Vitality, and 1 Dexterity.

"Hey, it says I just gained a level," Cal stammered.

"Well, you shared the kill. It is fitting." Whitestar saw that Thornpaw had been wearing a storage pouch, and it looked like a good one. She took it off his belt and bonded with it, inspecting the contents. He had over a dozen good hides and lots of meat—enough for her to get paid more for this outing than in her last five hunts. Still, it was risky going back to camp with this haul; she'd have to sell off the goods bit by bit. She stuffed the pouch deep into her backpack—too many of her clanmates knew she didn't have one. "Help me drag the body outside, and we'll stack stones over it. Hopefully, rain will wash this blood away before another hunter comes along."

"We could spread dirt and soot from the fire over the blood," Cal said, as he grabbed the dead Urghat's feet. Whitestar grunted in agreement, and together they hauled the body outside and several dozen yards away. They stopped by a collapsed wall and moved away much of the rubble, creating a depression. Whitestar dragged the body into the space and piled the stones back on top. She backed away from the pile of scree and rocks, then reached into her belt pouch and took out her little folded packet of blackvine tea. She carefully unwrapped the waxed paper and took a pinch of the powdery tea, gently sprinkling it over the unmarked grave.

"Something precious to help you pay your way to the next hunt, old man. You were a scoundrel, but you were Urghat, and I hope you find your way." She folded up her packet and tucked it away, walking back to their campsite, Cal quietly following behind. When they were back in the ruined building,

Whitestar piled the rest of their gathered wood onto the bloody ashes and got the fire going again. Without a word to Cal, she put her pack a few feet farther from the bloody soil and stretched out, going to sleep.

When she opened her eyes in the gray light of dawn, she was surprised to see Cal curled up and sleeping on the other side of the firepit; she'd half expected him to run off in the night. The fire was down to embers, and the pool of blood from the night before had blackened and congealed as it sank into the soil. When Whitestar saw the blood, she had a surge of emotion, but she couldn't put her finger on what it was—not regret, or fear, or sorrow. It was more like guilt. She felt guilty, she decided, because she'd killed an Urghat, and she couldn't exactly brag about it, like if she'd won a duel. She'd killed him because he wanted to eat a human. No, it was more than that—he'd wanted to steal her glory. She growled in frustration at her unusual feelings and stood up. She started to kick the ashes and soot from the firepit all over the bloodstain. The cloud of ash and hot embers flying around woke Cal, who scrambled away from her in a mild panic. "Get up, get ready to march," she barked at him. After spreading the ash around, she picked up her pack and walked outside, where she found Cal standing around, rubbing his hands together in the morning chill. She turned to the northwest and started to walk, not saying a word.

"Are you really just going to take me to my death, then?" Cal asked, scrambling after her.

"Why wouldn't I? My kind makes war. We eat our enemies. I'll gain honor and standing when I am the one to deliver you and your people to the Underclaws." She felt a strange constriction in her throat as she spoke and realized it was much like how she felt when her uncles and father teased her or when one of the older hunters made her give tribute. She felt upset, wrong, and she didn't know how to deal with it. Part of her wanted to turn around and beat Cal to a pulp.

"You're more than that, though! You like good music! You like wine! You said a prayer for that dead hunter, even though he was awful." Cal's voice had a pleading edge to it.

"Those are stupid things. We take those things. The only important thing is strength. I can't grow stronger listening to you sing. I have to train and fight, and I need to earn opportunities for that. You're going to earn me a good opportunity, Cal." She didn't look back at him while she spoke, and she could hear his steps slow and stop.

"I think you're wrong! There're ways to gain strength, or at least Energy without fighting. The System told us that during the orientation! It said you could cultivate Energy and learn to do things that don't involve fighting with it. When I leveled just now, I learned some kind of singing skill. That's not fighting!" Whitestar stopped walking and turned around, staring at Cal.

"The System is a liar. Urghat don't have much Energy affinity. To try to level without killing would be thousands of times slower for us. Our enemies would crush us. You learned a singing skill? That's very great, but you got the Energy to improve yourself from the death of an Urghat. An Urghat who was much greater than you."

"Greater how? Because he was an Urghat? Because he was stronger than me? I bet he couldn't sing as well as I do! I bet he doesn't know about Bussard cone dynamics, I bet . . ."

"Quiet! I meant he was higher level than you! But, yes, he was greater because he was an Urghat!" Whitestar walked up to Cal, grabbed his shoulder, and shoved him in front of her. "Now, walk in that direction until I tell you to stop!" He obeyed, fiercely scowling but not daring a retort. Whitestar followed him, silently fuming, unable to take any joy from his compliance.

They walked in silence for hours, and the sun was nearing its zenith when she heard the first baying of some boyii hounds. Cal stopped walking and looked back at her, his eyes wide. She held a finger to her lips and looked around. The grass here was more sparse and not as tall as in the southern end of the plains. She kicked around in a bit of a circle until she found what she was looking for: an old feyris hole. She pulled her knife and started clawing at the soft dirt around the hole, pulling up piles of loose, grassy soil. While she was digging, the sounds of the boyii got louder and closer. She finally judged the hole big enough and said, "Cal, climb in there and curl up really small. I'm going to bury you and try to hide your scent. Those boyii sound like a hunting pack, so other Urghat will be here soon."

"You're going to bury me?"

"Not deep! Get in, hurry!" Cal groaned and crawled into the loose soil. Whitestar quickly started shoving the grass and dirt over him, then she broke some branches from nearby shrubs and laid them atop his hiding area. She took off her pack and pulled out the storage pouch she'd stolen from Thornpaw. Then she took out two large, uncured huldii hides from the storage pouch. The brown leather was still freshly bloody, having been preserved in the storage pouch. She laid the hides over the broken shrubs, and then she commenced to build a small fire nearby.

She'd gotten the fire going and was throwing green shrub branches and grass onto it to make a lot of smoke when the first boyii hounds came barking around her. Whitestar whistled loudly in the hunter's call, and the dogs calmed a bit, circling her and sniffing. After another few minutes, she could hear the lumbering steps of several large Urghat coming her way. She whistled again, making sure there was no question of her being an Urghat hunter.

Three oversized Urghat warriors came into her makeshift camp, coughing and waving away the smoke from her fire. "What you doing, girl?"

"I'm trying to cure these hides a bit. Who's asking?" Whitestar snarled.

"Dumb place to cure hides. Go to Ur-clan. Use rack," he growled, stepping closer to her and sniffing deeply.

"You smell funny, girl. Who are you?" His two friends began to walk, widely, around the smokey fire, flanking her.

"I'm Whitestar, daughter of Goretusk. I hunt. Who you?" She growled, stepping closer to the big, brindle-coated Urghat. He wore a heavy metal breastplate and was clearly not a hunter.

"Har, I be Eyesnatcher! You smell good, Whitestar. Come find me at Thickneck's clan. I give you taste of Ardeni wine!" He smiled and whistled, motioning for his comrades to follow him, and then they were off, moving west in whatever patrol pattern they were following. The boyii hounds' baying slowly faded. Whitestar listened, sniffing the air. She made sure to keep feeding her fire green branches, and by now, there was quite a plume of white smoke climbing into the sky. Finally, judging it safe, she ripped away the animal hides and branches and scrabbled the loose dirt off Cal's hiding spot. She couldn't explain her relief when she saw his dirt-covered face emerge and his eyes pop open. At first, she tried to tell herself that she just didn't want him to die before she could give him over to one of the Underclaws. She knew she was lying, though—she hadn't wanted to see him harmed.

BRONWYN

Arthur Ballard was not a difficult man to find. Bronwyn only had to ask a few colonists, each time being pointed in the same direction. She found him delegating tasks not far from where the attack had been on the eastern side of the camp. As Bronwyn approached his camp, she realized that, while she had been busy rushing to gain the lead, Arthur had been organizing the colony. What she thought had been just a massive jumble of tents actually had a very well-thought-out and utilitarian pattern. From the viewpoint of Arthur's tent, a dozen roads were going off in every direction across the meadow; should anyone need to, they could easily reach him. Bronwyn walked up behind him as he sent two men off on an unknown task. Clearing her throat, she spoke, "Ballard, sir, I've returned with the captives."

Spinning around with a look of shock on his face, he stammered, "B-Bronwyn, you're back already? How? There had to be a dozen of those bastards!"

"Closer to two, actually," Bronwyn said with a satisfied grin. "They had a big fucker leading 'em, too. He knew some pretty fancy ice magic but didn't seem any smarter than the rest." She paused for a moment, letting her pride fall to the side. "Look, I know I fucked I up, but they're back safe, every one of them. We got some basic weapons, too. I think maybe it's time to set up the security detail, especially once people start finishing the orientation and know how to fight a bit."

"It's true, sir," one of the colonists spoke up from behind her. "We saw it with our own eyes; she was a damn machine—wiped out the whole camp!"

Arthur Ballard held up a hand, silencing him. "That may be so, but we still had losses, Bronwyn. We had fifteen people die last night, fifteen people that were not yet ready for this world. What you did to save these men was brave, heroic, even, but it's just one step toward making up for the trouble you've caused. I don't know who you thought you were or what you expected to accomplish. There are five thousand people in this meadow; what were you going to do, single-handedly defend each and every one of them?"

Bronwyn clenched her fists and turned toward the formerly captive colonists. "I'm sorry for what you've been through, but please, leave the weapons we gathered and go; Ballard and I need to speak." She turned back to Arthur Ballard, awkwardly staring while she waited for the sounds of the colonists to fade. Looking at his self-righteous face, she grew more and more offended by the second. When they were finally alone, she spoke through gritted teeth: "Who do I think I am? I'm your fucking champion! You hired me to fight, and that's what I'm doing! I tried being penitent, but I'm done. I'm tired of your chastisement." Her voice rose to a shout now: "How the fuck was I supposed to know the System would bring the barrier down when one person finished? Yes, this world is fucked, but some people will push themselves, take risks, and fight for every inch! Those are the people that will be rewarded, and I'm going to be on top of that list!"

She walked up until she was an inch away from him, realizing now that she really *had* grown taller. She was always tall, but Arthur was around six feet, and she now found herself looking straight into his eyes. Her height was compounded by her points in strength which had caused her muscles to define and her shoulders to widen, making her physical presence a lot more intimidating than it used to be. "I suggest you and all your lackeys start making some progress with the System before your names are forgotten." She checked her shoulder into his, causing him to stumble back as he was forming a response, and stalked off toward the center of the meadow.

She was fuming as she walked through the camp. Who the fuck was Arthur to criticize her actions? She obviously had no idea what would happen when she finished the tutorial. How did he get off criticizing her for thinking she could protect everyone and then blaming her in the next breath for everything that happened? Her silent brooding was broken by a sudden crunching and grinding sound in her right ear. Her hand shot up, and she grabbed hold of the little squirrel-turtle perched on her shoulder. Finally having caught it, she pulled it into view in front of her and saw it happily munching on a lock of her hair. "You're lucky you're cute, you little shit." She chuckled and let out a long sigh. "What do you think? Did I overreact?" It stared at her blankly, still chewing on the clump of hair it held in its tiny hands. "Yeah, I don't think so either; fuck that guy. Anyway, enough thinking about him; we need a name for you if you're gonna stick around. Have a preference?" It finished chewing and started struggling in her grasp, attempting to climb up her arm and back onto her shoulder.

Bronwyn had an idea: she walked over to a muddy patch near the path and set the little creature down in the mud. It immediately, upon being released, scrambled up her pant leg, up her back, and onto her shoulder, leaving muddy little footprints as it went. She smiled and patted it on the head; it cautiously allowed the touch without trying to jump around. "Let's see what you're called then," she murmured as she activated her Tracking skill on the footprints it left on her pants. To her delight, a small window did pop up in the corner of her vision. Unfortunately, when she tried to read the name, it said, "Skill level insufficient." She noted that the footprints left behind emitted an almost blinding light, even in the midday sun, when viewed by her tracking skill. What in the hell was this little guy? The Tracking skill worked by detecting trace amounts of Energy left behind by creatures; if the Yeksa tracks were a candle, then these were like a bonfire.

"Well, that'll be a mystery to solve at a later date. How about for now I just call you . . ." Bronwyn paused for a moment, thinking. "Hops?" The little critter let out a satisfied sounding chirp and nuzzled into the crook of her neck. Closing its eyes, Hops started to doze off, evidently tired from an adventurous day of nose nibbling and hair eating. Bronwyn smiled at the little creature and continued down the path.

She'd been walking for a little over a mile and passed hundreds of tents, noticing that most of the people she walked by were in surprisingly good spirits, given the situation. Over the last few days, she'd been constantly amazed by how well the average person seemed to handle everything going on. They were all initially hired to colonize a new planet, so some amount of mental fortitude had to be present, she supposed. Bronwyn noted that most of the people she passed were still working on the orientation, and many of them had begun the combat training today. One group of ten or so had realized the intro to ice magic spell could be used like a paintball gun, leaving a small frosty circle wherever it hit someone. They were sprinting around tents, laughing and zapping little bolts of ice at each other.

After about fifteen or twenty minutes of walking, she found the area in the meadow she had been thinking of. She was standing on a slightly raised hill, with a fairly large, spring-fed pond nested on the western edge of it. The pond was large enough to have some small fish swimming about in it, and occasionally one of the brightly colored ribbon birds would swoop down and grab one in its beak. The colonists had left this central portion of the meadow open for use as a community area, and Bronwyn thought it would be the perfect area to place the Settlement Stone.

"Well, Hops, what do you say we find out what this Settlement Stone is all about?" Earlier, on the walk back to the meadow, she had placed all of her belongings into the magic pouch she took from the Yeksa shaman. She reached her hand into the pouch now and thought of the stone, calling it to her hand. She sat down in the soft blue grass and crossed her legs, placing the dark-gray, obelisk-shaped stone in front of her. The foot-tall stone nestled down into the grass, almost as if it wanted to be in contact with the ground. She placed her hand on its surface and willed her Energy into it. Immediately, a System UI screen appeared in front of her:

Settlement Stone, activate at the present location? YES/NO

"Yes," Bronwyn spoke aloud, but she didn't think she had to. In a way, she hoped that people were watching her and wondering what she was doing.

Who is the leader of this settlement?

Bronwyn hung up on this question for quite some time. Arthur Ballard would be the responsible answer. The more she thought about him, his stupid smug face, and his accusations, the less reasonable she felt. Her brash anger toward him from before resurfaced. Fuck being reasonable and fuck Arthur Ballard; she'd put in the work. They weren't at his colony on Tau Ceti anyway; this was a different world, and there was no way the old settlement structure would stand once everyone started learning what they could do with Energy. She answered the prompt: "Bronwyn Tallow."

What is the name of your settlement?

Bronwyn inwardly grinned at this question; Ballard was going to throw a fit at not being the one to name the first human colony on this world. She thought about all the possibilities. She could be selfish and call it something after herself like "Tallow" or "Bronwyn's Place." She laughed at that. No, that wouldn't do. She could name it after a famous Earth city like "New Boston" or "Paris 2." Again, she laughed. She thought about how they were pioneers on a new world and how they'd come from space on a ship. She thought about how the System had robbed them of the accomplishment of landing and setting up a town on their own terms. She decided that future generations would remember that they came here in a spaceship—one of humanity's greatest achievements. She said, out loud so the System could hear her, "First Landing."

The prompt disappeared from her view, and she heard the sound of thousands of tiny cracks splitting the stone in front of her. Heat and steam burst forth from the cracks, and she scrambled backward, hurriedly clambering to her feet. In seemingly random order, segments of the stone split apart, stretched, and then re-fused with the whole. This occurred over and over, hundreds or thousands of times; all the while, steam lit with golden highlights burst forth from the seams of stone. With each cracking and fusing of the stone, the obelisk grew, and Bronwyn found herself backing up several times during the process. She watched, mouth agape, as the stone grew to immense proportions; after a minute or two, there was so much steam flowing down the sides of the hilltop that she was standing knee-deep in it, even at the top. It was hard to take her eyes off of the incredible process, but she did look around once when she heard excited voices, noticing that a large crowd was gathering at the base of the hill.

The stone continued to grow, cracking, fusing, and emitting gouts of dense steam the whole time. After what must have been fifteen or twenty minutes, it finally started to slow and gradually settled into its final, solid shape. The little obelisk-shaped stone was now a true monolith, towering thirty feet into the air, and each of its four sides was six feet wide at the base. It was still a dense gray-colored stone, and Bronwyn noticed that the golden-colored symbols and runes still seemed to float, somehow, beneath the surface of the stone. As the steam settled and dissipated, a System message appeared in front of her eyes, and from the gasps, everyone else's:

 *****Colony: First Landing established. Area of influence: 25 square kilometers. Leader: Bronwyn Tallow.*****

⪻ WHITESTAR ⪼

Whitestar was pushing Cal to his limits, she could tell. He stumbled every few steps, and his breath was coming in sharp wheezing sounds. Still, she urged him on, maintaining her easy, loping, hunting pace. "Hurry, Cal. We need to clear this stretch of plains and get into those foothills if we want to avoid another patrol." The human didn't respond, only doggedly kept plodding forward, concentrating on not tripping on the scrub-brush predominant in the northern extremes of the plains.

They were moving northeast now. Whitestar was aware that something had changed, that she wasn't leading Cal directly to the Ur-clan. She knew she wanted to avoid other Urghat, but she hadn't put her decisions into conscious thought yet; she was avoiding it. Instead, she concentrated on the next step to get Cal into the eastern foothills before another clan patrol swept through. She was feeling good about their odds—the foothills were within sight now, and she couldn't hear any boyii hounds. She kept her focus and urged Cal to hurry, and soon they were moving among the twisted, dried out trees, the sparse, dried grass, and the crumbling slopes of scree. Black yakkaw birds kept them company, watching from dead branches and making their characteristic, questioning sound. Whitestar sighed, slowing their pace and reluctantly turning her mind to what came next.

"Something's changed," Cal said, leaning over his knees and taking deep breaths.

"Hrm." Whitestar paced in a circle, flexing her hands, so her claws stretched out and retracted in a slow rhythm.

"Back before that patrol came, when you hid me, we were making a fast pace straight to the mountains. Now you've had me running mostly east. What happened? Are you in trouble?"

"Ha. Me in trouble? Worry about your own skin, human. Now, drink some water, and we'll get moving." She tossed him her wineskin, turned, and started to slowly walk to the northeast, following a gully that skirted along the base of the foothills. The human was right. Sometime during that encounter with the patrol, Whitestar had made a decision. She wasn't going to bring Cal to the Ur-clan. She wasn't going to let him go home, though. No, she might have gotten soft where he was concerned, but she was still Urghat. She'd still tell Goretusk about the human settlement. Let him go to the Underclaws. Let them do what they would with the news, but first, she'd get Cal out of the area. She felt something nudging her elbow and looked down to see Cal was handing her back the wineskin. She sniffed and took it from his hand.

"Human, I made a mistake with you."

"What do you mean?" Cal asked, gamely, scrambling after her long strides.

"I should never have learned your name; I should have kept a rag in your mouth. I shouldn't have let you sing to me. I shouldn't have shared my wine with you. Now I don't want to see other Urghat eat you. You are my shame, Cal."

"Hey, that's not a thing to be ashamed of, Whitestar. You're learning something that a lot of people struggle with: just because someone looks different doesn't mean they're your enemy. As far as I'm concerned, that makes you the best Urghat I've ever met. Of course, I've only really met two." Cal's voice was light with relief like he'd just been granted a pardon.

"Bah, what do you know. You're a weakness to me, and I'm going to wash my hands of you." Cal's face blanched a bit at those words.

"Um, wait. Are you going to let me go?" Whitestar looked over her shoulder at him, studying his face for a long moment.

"Yes, Cal, I'm going to let you go." She turned and kept plodding on.

"Oh, great, 'cause I thought you were going to kill me for a moment there."

"Hmm, that would certainly be *easier*." Whitestar let a bit of a grin show and glanced sidelong at Cal again.

"Hey! Not funny!" Cal's mock indignation brought a wider grin to Whitestar's face.

"Har, don't worry, Cal. If we go through these foothills, there is a Ghelli wood on the other side. They are soft people like you. They'll probably take you in. You'll like them; they don't even eat their enemies."

"Oh? That sounds great, Whitestar, but couldn't we just, like, take me back to the other humans? I mean, you could even just point me in the right direction, and I'll make a run for it."

"You would not make it, Cal. You think you can travel fast for three more days? You think you can avoid Urghat patrols and hunters? What about wild boyii packs? There will be many more Urghat in the plains once news of the humans spreads. Better for you to make a home with the Ghelli for now." Cal didn't respond to her words, just looked at the ground and kept following her.

"I feel like a coward if I can really be safe with the Ghelli. Shouldn't I try to warn my people about the Urghat? About your clan? Do you really think they'll attack?"

"You have a good spirit, Cal. I think I would want to warn my people, too. Maybe the Ghelli can help with that. Meet them, talk to them, maybe one of their scouts can make the journey and bring a warning." Cal didn't respond, just following, clearly lost in thought. Whitestar didn't worry about whether he could get a warning to the humans or not—her people would crush them, regardless.

They hiked through the foothills for another few hours until the sun was halfway down toward the western horizon. Whitestar wanted to push on, knowing that the woods where the Ghelli lived were just on the other side of the foothills, and they had to be more than halfway through by now. "Keep pushing just a few more hours, Cal. I want to drop you off before nightfall."

"Okay, I think I should tell you . . ." The shriek of a howler cat cut off his voice. Whitestar frantically pulled her bow from her back and dug the string from the pouch at her belt.

"Put your back to mine, Cal, that's a howler cat, and it will not hesitate to try to turn us into its dinner." She hooked the string to one end of her bow and bent the bow against her knee, trying to secure the second loop when she heard scrabbling and a grunt of pain from behind her. She just managed to finish stringing the bow as she spun around. The howler cat had struck; Cal's entire head and upper torso were in its mouth, and it was dragging him away, up the loose dirt on the side of the gully. The cat had to weigh close to a thousand pounds. Its brightly striped orange, red, and black fur stood out in stark contrast to the shadowed gully. Its saucer-size yellow eyes glared at Whitestar, almost daring her to do something as it pulled Cal's kicking body backward up the slope.

Whitestar didn't hesitate: in one smooth motion, she pulled an arrow from her quiver, nocked it, and activated her True Aim skill, drawing on most of her meager pool of Energy to fire an arrow directly into the big cat's eye. Whitestar might not have been as strong as most of the warriors in the clan, but she was undoubtedly a better shot than most. Her arrow flew true and buried itself deep into the eye of the cat, which didn't even have time for death throes; it simply collapsed in a twitching heap. Whitestar ran forward, thrilled with her perfect shot and enjoying the influx of Energy from the dead beast. She put one foot on the cat's lower jaw and yanked the top up with her hands. Cal was still weakly struggling as she reached in, grabbed him above his shoulder, and pulled him out of the beast's maw.

Cal moaned and thrashed weakly, barely conscious. He had terrible puncture wounds on the upper parts of his chest and back. Whitestar dug into her pack and pulled out her folded packet of toril-root powder. She unfolded it with bloodstained fingers and hastily sprinkled it into Cal's wounds. Sizzling steam erupted from the punctures, and Cal suddenly opened his eyes and screamed until his voice went hoarse. The bleeding halted, Whitestar used her stolen pouch of storage to stow away the valuable corpse of the howler cat; what a story she'd have to tell when she showed her clan the corpse with the arrow through its eye! Then, she hoisted Cal onto her shoulder and set off through the last stretch of hills.

"Oh, it burns! God! What was that thing? What was that stuff you put on me?" Cal weakly whined while he flopped against her back.

"Hush, Cal. That was a fated encounter! A million times, that cat would have eaten you for dinner, but on this lucky occasion, I landed a perfect shot in time to save you. You're going to have some memorable scars. Toril-root powder stops bleeding, but you'll bear your marks of courage, don't worry."

"Uhnn," Cal mumbled as his consciousness slipped away. Whitestar grinned. She was happy. She was happy that Cal had lived through the encounter, happy that she had made such an amazing shot, and happy that she'd have hides to trade back at the Ur-clan. She was even happy that she was about to set Cal free with the Ghelli. Let someone else take the glory for capturing humans. She didn't care.

ᘓ MORGAN ᘔ

The stairs seemed interminable. Morgan and Issa had to stop and rest after climbing for a couple of hours. There were no lanterns, and the stone steps and wall seemed the same, no matter how high they climbed. After the first twenty minutes or so, the light down the middle of the stairwell from the burning oil faded into darkness, and then it truly became impossible to mark their progress. Morgan started to wonder if they were in some kind of evil loop created by the System. As Issa sat on a step, resting her legs, he walked toward the edge and reached into his dimensional pouch, pulling out a cracked wooden mug. He dropped it, and the darkness quickly swallowed it. He strained his ears but never heard it hit bottom.

Another hour of climbing brought a change to the stairwell: the stone blocks gradually became smaller, and rather than being fit together with neat, straight angles, they were less regularly shaped and mortared together. The change in scenery renewed the duo's vigor, and they climbed more rapidly for a few minutes and soon noticed that a dim flickering light came from up ahead. Issa pulled the hood on her cloak up, and the two of them slowed their pace, creeping up the stairs with as little noise as possible. As they rounded the final turn, they became aware of a haze of smoke in the air, then they saw the source—a large, crackling torch was mounted in the wall next to a sturdy-looking door. The door was built from wide, well-worn wooden planks and had iron fittings. Morgan continued up to the door and planted his eye against it, peering through one of the wider gaps in the wooden boards.

Morgan could make out a square room through the crack, perhaps twenty feet on a side. The floor of the room was made up of rough wooden slats, and the walls were paneled in similar-looking wood. Light filled the room from an iron fixture holding five big candles that hung in the middle of the ceiling. A heavy-looking, maroon drape obscured the only exit from the room in the opposite wall. Morgan looked down at Issa and whispered, "Looks empty." Issa shrugged, and Morgan carefully opened the door. He immediately noticed that the air was warmer on this level. He stepped onto the wooden slats carefully, but they creaked nonetheless. He froze for a few seconds, but nothing seemed to have been alerted. He and Issa carefully moved into the room, and Morgan advanced toward the curtained doorway on the opposite side. He pulled one edge aside, just a bit, and looked through. What he saw caused him to drop the curtain immediately. He leaned close to Issa's ear and whispered, "There's a body in the hallway."

"Well, we can't stay here," Issa whispered back. Morgan nodded and pulled the curtain aside again. A long, wood-paneled hallway stretched into the distance, and, about ten paces from the room, a humanoid corpse lay spread eagle on the floor. Morgan knew it was a corpse because the head was about three feet separate from the rest of the body. Morgan slowly approached the body, and, at first, he thought it was a human. On closer inspection, though, he saw some differences: this man was ebony-skinned with a long white beard, but his nails were also black and pointed, not like the flat nails of a human. The most striking difference, though, was that the man had hooves rather than feet, and his exposed legs were hirsute. "He's a Cadwalli," Issa whispered.

"Huh, he looks almost like a mythological being from my world. A satyr." Morgan walked closer to the body and saw that it was nearly bereft of belongings, other than a pair of short, knee-length pants and a ripped and bloody tunic. Morgan thought the pants looked like they'd cover him better than the little shorts the System gave him, but he couldn't bring himself to strip them off the corpse. He was still contemplating the body, noticing how cleanly the head had been removed, and how it seemed to be wet, a thick gobbet of some sort of clear liquid coating one side of the bearded face, when he heard a sound, like wood clicking against the wood of the hallway. He looked up, down the direction they'd yet to explore. The clicking grew louder and more rapid, and a horror appeared out of the shadows.

The monster resembled a gray-skinned man, but instead of legs, his lower abdomen ended in a writhing mass of long, thin tentacles. The clicking sound came from his arms and legs. They were long, thin, and multi-jointed like a huge spider's legs. It had two sets coming out of its back and a set coming out of its shoulders where a person's arms would be. As he laid eyes on its face, Morgan felt transfixed by the horrific creature. Its lower jaw hung down to make room for teeth that resembled butcher's knives, and its eyes were large, black ovals that seemed to exude darkness. With its long legs and writhing tentacles, it filled the entirety of the corridor, and it was approaching fast. "Yovashi! RUN!" Issa shouted, turning and running back the way they had come without a backward glance.

Morgan broke from his trance in time to turn and start running, but the monster was just too fast. He'd only taken two steps when he felt a crushing blow on his shoulder and stumbled forward. The Yovashi had driven one of its hard, chitin-covered leg tips into him, and it felt like getting hit by a missile. Morgan scrambled onto his hands and knees, gripping his knife in one fist. He could feel the creature looming over him, so he turned and stabbed in an upward motion. His knife and hand drove into the mass of writhing tentacles. He thought he could feel the blade pierce something. Before he could savor that small victory, several of the tentacles wrapped around his forearm with a vise-like grip, and he suddenly found himself being flung back and forth in the hallway, smashing into one wall and then another. He barely had time to think about trying to use Energy Drain on the creature before he felt his shoulder joint give way and his arm dislocate. He screamed in agony, but then the back of his head made contact with the wall, and things went dark.

Morgan woke to darkness and agony. He couldn't take a full breath, and he came to realize that he was somewhat upside down, his head and shoulders bearing the brunt of his weight. He tried to flail his arms about to right himself, but his right arm flared with searing pain, and his left arm was pinned beneath him. He began to panic and jerk his body around, but then he heard a moaning sound, and he froze. His eyes darted around, looking for any kind of clue, but it was pitch-black. He listened, taking shallow, painful breaths. Another moan came from what sounded like above and behind him. It was a male voice. Morgan couldn't help himself, and he hoarsely whispered, "Hello? Who's there?"

"Help!" The voice said, followed by another long, pained moan.

Suddenly another voice, this one feminine, came from below and from the opposite direction of the moaning man: "Quiet, fools! Unless you want to be eaten alive." Morgan was about to ignore her advice and ask for help when he heard a wet thunking sound, and the original voice screamed in a blood-curdling cry, "My foot! My foot!" Then there was a crunching sound, and he fell silent. Morgan grew very still, cold sweat sheathing his exposed body parts.

After nothing came for him for several minutes, he started to breathe more deeply and then concentrated on freeing himself. He realized he could move both his legs, and so Morgan began to swing them, building momentum until he threw them in front of him, forcing his top half to roll out of its cramped position. Blood rushed back into his left arm and neck as his body's weight was removed from them. Morgan rolled to his back. The ground felt lumpy and covered with hard and soft objects. The air was frigid, to the extent that it felt like it burned his lungs as he took his first full breath since waking. Despite the cold, there was a tinge of rot in the air, and Morgan's stomach threatened to revolt. Luckily, it was pretty much empty. He gingerly pulled his right arm up to his chest in an attempt to keep from jostling it while he sat up.

The room was still pitch-black, but he could now make out a very faint orange glow perhaps twenty feet above and slightly to his left. He patted around with his left hand, trying to get an idea of where he was, and that's when he felt the unmistakable squish of cold, torn flesh. He froze for a second, but then he let his hand explore some more, feeling various shapes that made him think of different body parts, body parts of people, maybe not human, but definitely arms and hands with fingers and faces that felt somewhat familiar. Morgan had a thought and felt around his waist. Sure enough, he still had the girdle on, and the dimensional pouch was still attached to it. He grimly smiled and reached his hand into the pouch, calling forth the pouch of fire attuned Energy beads. As gently and quietly as he could, he set the pouch in his lap and fumbled open the drawstring with his good hand. Red light, once a dull luster, flared out like a search beacon to his deprived eyes, and he slapped his hand over the top of the pouch, holding his breath. He heard something big stirring a ways off behind him, and he hunched over and froze.

The thing rustled around a bit more, but eventually it stopped, and Morgan slowly started to breathe again. Keeping his body hunched over the pouch of beads, he wormed two fingers into it and pulled one out, clenched tightly in his fist. He concentrated and *pulled* the Energy out of the bead, and he felt it flow into him and down into his Core. From there, he felt warmth and relief flood outward. Minor injuries he hadn't seen or realized he had felt better, and the tendons and muscles around his right shoulder contracted. With an audible *pop*, his shoulder reset. Morgan clenched his teeth and stifled a howl of agony; instead, he gripped his fists and very slowly breathed out through the pain. Careful to stay hunched over the pouch of beads, he pulled the drawstrings tight and put it back into his dimensional container.

Morgan carefully stretched out both his hands, now that his arm was mobile, and gently felt around with his fingertips. He was sitting among the bodies and pieces of bodies of other people. In the pitch-black, it wasn't as horrific as it could be, partly because it was so cold. There were some sticky, thick pools of liquid, but the flesh he felt was stiff and rigid, and the smell of rot wasn't as pervasive as it would have been had the area been warm. Still, he felt weak with fear, stress, and disgust as he, ever so slowly, expanded his search area, patting around himself in a circle, all the while trying to silently scoot in the direction away from where he'd heard whatever creature had been moving behind him. He'd traveled about a foot and a half when he heard an almost silent "Shh" coming from what seemed like a short distance to his left. Morgan looked in the direction from where he'd heard the sound, then opened his mouth to ask something. Before he could speak, the whisper came again: "Shh." Morgan nodded and very carefully lay back and waited.

MORGAN

Morgan lay, staring into the darkness for a long time. Once he stirred, doubting he had ever heard a voice, and it came again, just a soft breath saying, "Shh." He couldn't be sure, but he thought he recognized a hint of Issa's voice in the admonishment, so he lay back down and he continued to wait. He let his mind drift and he thought of his ring. He could feel it resting, heavy and cool, on his finger. Had it even worked? He thought back to when the Yovashi first hit him, knocking him to the ground. It had hurt, and he'd gone sprawling, but he'd been fine to bring his knife around for an attack immediately. That ring might have saved him being speared through by that bastard's pointy leg. He wondered if it was recharged yet. Now that he thought about it, he had no idea how long he'd been unconscious.

After what felt like hours, he heard something large stirring behind him, and he listened to the wet crunching and snapping sounds of what he could only imagine was the Yovashi feasting on some poor soul that happened to be closer to its resting spot than Morgan. After the slurping, crunching sounds died down, he heard the rustling noises of it moving away, and the distinct *click-clack*ing sound of its insectile legs receding through a wooden tunnel, farther and farther away behind him. He started to sit up, and he felt a warm, small hand rest on his cheek, and he frantically reached up and held it with his own.

"It's gone hunting or something; we should move quickly," Issa whispered. Morgan nodded, and he felt a warmth flow out of Issa's hand and, the next thing he knew, his surroundings lit up in shades of gray. He stifled a gasp as he took in his surroundings. Steep dirt and stone walls rose on three sides of a veritable charnel pit. Bones, bodies, and pieces of bodies were strewn in piles. Morgan recognized many bodies that had to be of the same race as Issa. He also saw more of the strange goat-like people, as well as Yeksa and Urghat bodies. He looked around, in a horrified fascination, trying to see if any of the corpses were human, but he didn't see any. He did see a few types of people that he hadn't seen before, including a fair-haired, pale-skinned woman that he thought was human, at first, but he saw that she had a pair of ripped, gossamer-thin wings on her back and long, delicate antennae sprouting from her forehead. Issa was pulling on his arm to get him moving when he noticed that the winged lady had opened her eyes and was looking their way.

"Hold on! That fairy lady is alive!" Morgan whispered to Issa and pointed.

"Fairy lady?" Issa looked where he was pointing and nodded. "Ah, yes, the Ghelli. I saw her moving around a little while I hid against the wall with my cloak. Morgan, there are a few people alive down here, but if we linger, we'll all end up dead." Issa's voice sounded pained, but she shook her head regretfully.

Quest: Don't let the Yovashi eat the surviving people in its larder. Reward: Commensurate with achievement 0/4. Penalty for failure: None. Accept? YES/NO

Issa hissed and swiped at the air in front of her face. "You got it, too?" Morgan asked.

"Yes, but Morgan, the Yovashi is a terror, as you well know! Among my people, even the higher level Hunters with Improved Cores avoid them." Morgan thought about what Issa was saying, and he knew she was speaking reasonably. That thing had treated him like a rag doll. Still, he didn't like the idea of leaving four thinking and feeling people down here to be eaten bit by bit by that damn thing. He looked around, up the slope of carnage to where the Yovashi had been resting, and he could see in the highlighted grays of Issa's spell, the broken wooden paneling of the tunnel the Yovashi had left through. Something caught his eye, and he stood up, walking carefully up the slope, and that's when he saw the second survivor: a stocky man with brightly colored hair laying at the base of a pile of bones. He lay on his side, holding the stump of his right foot elevated. He'd tied a belt around his calf, right where the limb ended. He looked in Morgan's direction as he moved up the slope, but Morgan could tell that the man couldn't see him; his eyes kept darting around, trying to pinpoint the source of the scuffling sounds Morgan and Issa were making. Morgan noted that his hair and skin looked similar to Issa's in the gray light and whispered, "Is he one of your people?"

"Yes. Oh, Morgan, I have to try to help them. I won't be able to live with myself."

"Yeah," Morgan whispered, "I'm feeling the same way. Let me get a good look around. How long do you think that thing will be gone?"

"The first time I watched it leave, to sneak in, it was gone for quite a while, maybe an hour," Issa whispered.

"Hello? Who's there? Help me!" The Ardeni man croaked hoarsely.

"Quiet, friend, I'm trying to think of a way to help," Morgan whispered back. He nodded to Issa then looked around the upper area of the slope that led out of the charnel pit. The slope was about fifty feet long, and they were halfway up when they passed the man. Morgan looked closely at the body parts and piles of bones that were strewn around, wondering if there were other survivors. The quest had indicated four, but had it been including him and Issa? He didn't feel like it made sense for him and Issa to save themselves, but then, what did he know?

He and Issa were almost up the slope to the flat area where the Yovashi had been feasting. The floor here was more stone than dirt, and it was stained dark with old blood and other fluids. The piles up here were different. Morgan could see that the Yovashi had been saving belongings from the people and creatures it ate, throwing them into sloppily sorted stacks of weapons, ragged clothing, armor, ripped backpacks, broken and whole tools, and supplies like ropes and even a cast-iron pan. Morgan's eye was immediately pulled to a cluster of long staves, spears, and polearms leaning against one wall. "Oh, *fuck* yes!"

Morgan hurried over to the weapons and picked out the spear that had caught his eye. It was about seven feet of smooth, dark wood that stood out in pitch-black in his dark vision against the lighter grays of the other weapons and surroundings. Its blade added another foot to its length, and it was a hell of a blade—four inches wide at the base, with two curving half-moons that converged on a gradually tapering point. He felt the edge, and it was like a razor. "Oh, come here, my lovely. You and I are going to do some damage!"

Issa sucked air in with a gasp, and Morgan looked over at her; she'd pulled a long, slender rapier out of a stack of other swords, some broken and rusted, a few looking to be in decent repair. The rapier she whipped back and forth gleamed brightly in his vision, though, almost like it gave off its own light rather than just reflecting the dim lantern light coming from down the tunnel. "It's a beauty!" Morgan said.

"Better than that axe, and better than any sword I trained with, that's for sure," Issa said.

"Okay, that's half the plan—we have some weapons, but we've gotta hurry up," Morgan said, looking to what had first given him a sliver of a plan earlier. When he'd first looked at the area at the top of the ramp, he'd seen that the Yovashi's lair was a natural cavern, one part deeper, where he had been flung, unconscious, and the other part up higher, where the Yovashi rested, ate and stored its belongings. What he'd seen was that the natural cavern wall near the wooden tunnel entrance had some clefts and even a large boulder jutting out of it. The boulder was about eight or ten feet from the tunnel, and Morgan could see that if he climbed it, he'd be able to crouch there in the shadows, prepping a potentially devastating sneak attack.

The only problem was that the top of the boulder was too far from the tunnel for him to be sure he'd be able to jump onto the Yovashi. It would have to be lured closer. "Issa, let me explain my plan," Morgan whispered and then proceeded to do so.

"I'll do it," Issa said.

"I knew you'd say that, but I have a better idea. I want you up on the boulder with me. You can cast Haste on me before I jump."

"Who will bait the beast?" Issa's eyes opened wide, and she looked over to the man with the missing foot. "No, Morgan!"

"Hear me out," Morgan said as he looked around the piles of equipment. He saw what he was looking for, and hurried over to a pile of discarded armor and clothing and picked up a large, round shield made of wood and metal. He nodded and walked over to the man holding his tourniqueted leg up. "Hey man, we're gonna get you outta here, but I need your help to make it happen."

The man introduced himself as Darran. He wasn't pleased with Morgan's plan, but he couldn't really argue. He knew he was dead if Morgan and Issa couldn't get him out of the pit, and he knew they had to deal with the Yovashi for that to happen. In the end, Morgan only had to press a little before he allowed himself to be dragged over next to the wall, about five feet past the boulder. Morgan gave him the shield. "Listen, just turtle up behind this after it starts coming your way. We'll handle the rest." Darran nodded, mouthing the word turtle with a quizzical expression, and held the shield in front of his chest.

Morgan boosted Issa up onto the boulder, leaned his spear against the rock, then reached up, taking Issa's hand and clambering up beside her. He grabbed his spear and shrank back into the shadows to wait. Issa crouched beside him, one hand on his shoulder, concentrating. She'd said she'd prep the Haste spell so she could cast it nearly instantly. The minutes ticked by, and both he and Issa grew uncomfortable, but they knew they had to stay still. After what felt like hours but was probably more like twenty minutes, they heard the *click-clack* of the creature's spider legs moving through the wooden hallway. It was nearly time.

Morgan raised his spear in a two-handed, stabbing pose and drew in a slow deep breath. Issa's hand tightened on his shoulder. The *click-clack*ing stopped right at the edge of the hallway, followed by long moments of silence. Morgan started to sweat; something was wrong. A deep, sibilant voice poured out of the hallway: "Where's my snack?" *Click-scrape*, and the first few legs poked into the cavern. The Yovashi's head became visible as it leaned into the cave. "I know I had a fresh one just over there," it said in that same deep hiss. Darran played his part flawlessly as he scooted and scraped along the wall, reaching one hand toward a pile of rusty knives and daggers. The Yovashi finished stepping into the room and swiveled to stare at Darran. "Ah, there we are," it hissed, stepping quickly toward him.

Morgan looked into Issa's bright eyes and nodded. He instantly felt a surge of Energy flow out of her hand, and he felt his heart start to race, his mind breaking free from its fetters. Before he could contemplate his actions, he stood and leaped, driving the spear forward and activating his Backstab skill. He had to adjust his stab mid-flight because Backstab was guiding his blow into a more vertical angle. He dared not scream a war cry, but he cursed the Yovashi in his mind. He drove the vicious spearhead down through its torso from just behind its left collarbone all the way into its creepy abdomen. For a second, the spear hung up when the spearhead was fully embedded into the creature, and then it punched through something, and Morgan kept pushing as the shaft sank in. Resistance broke once more as the razor-sharp spearhead ripped through the bottom of the Yovashi's torso, slicing through several flailing tentacles on its way out. Morgan kicked off the Yovashi's back, managing to land on his feet. He quickly backpedaled away from the screaming creature's flailing rear legs and tentacles.

Issa was standing on the boulder watching the death throes of the sadistic creature, and she shouted, "Fuck you!" The Yovashi, convulsing and coughing black ichor, managed to turn around and look at Issa. It took two steps toward her and then collapsed.

"Hey, you used that word perfectly!" Morgan laughed.

MORGAN

Golden motes began to coalesce on the corpse of the Yovashi. Morgan could see that they were larger than the motes on other creatures he'd killed and more numerous. They swirled around, forming three distinct streams, the widest flooding toward Morgan, another nearly as large flowing to Issa, and a final, thin stream swirling toward Darran. Morgan braced himself as the influx of Energy slammed into him, much more than he'd felt before, even from the huge, naked rat creature.

*****Congratulations! You have achieved level 8 base human and have 10 attribute points to allocate.*****

*****Congratulations! You have completed a Quest: Don't let the Yovashi eat the surviving people in its larder—4/4. Reward: Four escape talismans, two Energy-rich natural materials, two Advancement Orbs.*****

Morgan blinked rapidly, reigning in the Energy euphoria as he read the messages. Wiping the screen away, he saw that swirling blue light was coalescing at his and Issa's feet. He stepped back, watching, and the lights condensed and faded, leaving behind a blue, wooden box, inlaid with complex, silver lettering that he couldn't read. The box was about a foot square, its lid clasped with a silver latch.

"A System treasure box. I've only heard my elders talk about these, never seen one myself," Issa said, leaning close. Darran had put the shield aside and was scooting himself over. Morgan could see that his stump had scabbed up quite a lot, clearly healed a bit from the Energy he'd absorbed.

"Did you two have a quest?" Darran asked.

"Yeah, we did," Morgan replied, gesturing to the box. "Issa, why don't you do the honors." Issa smiled and leaned over, flipping open the silver latch and lifting the lid. The inside of the box was lined in a silky, blue material. The first things Morgan noticed were the two glowing, golden marbles hovering near the center of the box. They looked exactly like the one that he'd woken next to. "Those must be 'Advancement Orbs'?" he asked, looking at Issa.

"Yes, they are!" Darran was the one who spoke up, not Issa. "Each one will grant a level's worth of Energy to the person that touches it. Too bad you can't store or carry them without activating them. Imagine what a high-level cultivator would pay for one!" Darran sighed wistfully, scooting into a sitting position and adjusting the belt he had tied around his stump. Issa looked at Darran with narrowed eyes.

"Don't get any ideas, Darran. Morgan and I will decide what to do with these rewards," she said, edging herself sideways between the man and the box.

"I'm not a fool! I know you both saved my life, and I know you could kill me if I tried to grasp at your rewards. I just wanted to see, that's all!" Darran looked genuinely offended, and Issa relaxed.

"All right, just give us a little space," Morgan said, trying to soothe the tension a little. He leaned over and closed the box. "Listen, we need to go over this a little later. Right now, there's at least one other survivor down there that is probably terrified, hurting, and wondering what the hell is going on up here." Morgan pulled Issa to the side a little and whispered in her ear, "You watch the box; I'll go down there and get the fairy lady."

"Fairy . . . oh you mean the Ghelli." Issa's cheeks reddened. "Yes, Morgan! I'm sorry! I can't believe I was so focused on our rewards. Go help her!" Issa sat down on the box, grinning savagely at Darran.

Morgan started walking down the slope into the darker, colder, charnel pit portion of the Yovashi's lair. He could surmise that their reward box was worth a lot, and he figured he was risking losing it by leaving it with Issa, but he also felt he could trust her by now; they'd both saved each other's lives several times. When he was near the pile of old bones and corpses that he'd woken up near, he looked to where he remembered the Ghelli woman to be but didn't see her. He called out, "Hello? It's safe to answer. The Yovashi is dead."

"It is?" A blonde-haired head poked out from behind a pile of bones, antennae quivering. "Thank the gods!" She nearly sobbed with released tension. Morgan hurried over to her and held out his hand but stopped himself.

"I'm going to grasp your hand to lead you out of this dark pit, okay?" he said, remembering that this woman might not be able to see in the dark as clearly as he currently could.

"Yes, thank you! But, please, my two sisters are in here somewhere, also. I know they aren't dead, but I don't think they're conscious."

"Well, that explains the four out of four," Morgan muttered, leaning forward to hold her hand and pull her to her feet. She was exceedingly light, to the point that Morgan could barely feel her weight when she stood, though he could tell from the tension on his fingers that she was pulling herself up. She was tall, maybe close to six feet, but extremely thin. She had many bruises and scrapes, but her only real injury appeared to be her mangled wing. "Come, I'll lead you up near my friend, then I'll look for your sisters."

She nodded, and Morgan started to walk with her, but then he had a thought. Why was he still creeping around in the darkness? The Yovashi was dead. "Actually, hold on a minute." He reached into his dimensional pouch and pulled forth a lantern, then pulled out a piece of rough flint that he and Issa had been using to make sparks. He set the lantern down, opened the glass, and dragged one of the rusty daggers he'd looted along the flint to spark the wick to life. Glorious light bloomed in the dark, horrible pit.

"Oh, Gods of the Wood!" the woman whispered, looking around. Her already pale skin blanched further as she took in the bones and cold, dead bodies.

"C'mon, let's head up; there's less of this up there. My name's Morgan, by the way."

"Thank you, Morgan. My name is Tiala," she said, and Morgan noticed she didn't let go of his hand, even though she could see now. With the lantern making his Nightvision almost painful, Morgan smiled and led the way up the slope to the flat area where Issa was waiting.

"Issa, this is Tiala. She says she has two sisters still unconscious down there. I'm going to go look for them," Morgan said while he rustled in his pouch for another lantern.

"Hi, Tiala, I'm Issa and this is Darran. Sit down here, and I'll give you some water." Issa smiled at the Ghelli and laid out one of the furs she and Morgan had looted from the Urghat. Darran nodded to Tiala but didn't speak. Morgan lit the other lantern and headed back down the slope to conduct the unsavory task of looking through the charnel for the surviving Ghelli sisters.

Morgan searched the pit, going from pile to pile. Before he found Tiala's sisters, he found the source of the cold. There was a pool of water near the farthest wall, almost obscured by bones and offal, but it gave off waves of cold air. Morgan stretched a hand out toward it, but the cold became painful, and he decided he'd rather not have a finger frozen off. Continuing his search, he looked around the edge of the pool, seeing a pile of fresher-looking corpses. There were seven bodies, most were Ardeni, like Issa, but two had the gossamer wings of the Ghelli, and Morgan carefully extricated them. Both appeared to be dead, but Morgan could detect a faint pulse in each of the female Ghelli's necks upon closer inspection. Neither looked good, though. One was missing a hand, and the other had severely broken legs. Their faces and exposed body parts were purple with bruises.

Morgan carefully carried the Ghelli sisters up to Tiala one by one. When they were both lying on a fur near their sister, he sat down heavily near Issa, happy to be done with that unpleasant task.

"Now, what are we going to do?" Darran asked.

"What do you mean?" Issa replied.

"I'm crippled, those two are nearly dead, and their sister is too distraught to be of any use," Darran huffed, indicating Tiala, who was weeping and gently stroking the face of one of her sisters.

"Don't be so cold!" Issa hissed.

"I'm not trying to be, but we're stuck in the depths of the Crucible, and I don't know how we'll get out in this condition!"

"Well, I think the System had a plan for that," Morgan replied. Darran shut his mouth and looked at him, hope in his eyes. "Part of our reward for killing the Yovashi were some 'escape talismans.' I'm assuming those will get you out of here."

"Truly?" Tiala said, wiping at her eyes. "You'll give them to us?"

"Well, I will. We got four, and so two are Issa's to use or give away."

Issa looked at him and smiled. "I wouldn't leave you here alone with one of these people, Morgan! Not after all we've been through."

"I was hoping you'd say that!" Morgan grinned. He stood up and motioned for Issa to stand up from the box and then opened it. Light flooded out from the two Advancement Orbs. Nestled around the orbs, in the blue cloth, were four silver-colored amulets, each the size of a small coin and containing the same pattern of strange writing. There was also a small square of orange-red metal and a fruit the shape and size of a plum but shaded in blue and bright greens, its stem still protruding with a pointy green leaf hanging off it. Morgan carefully extracted the four amulets, being sure not to touch the Advancement Orbs.

He knew what he was doing would be viewed as foolish by many. He was in a dangerous place, having already nearly died several times. He held in his hands a literal opportunity to "escape," and he was going to give it away. Not only that, but he was allowing Issa to risk her life as well. Looking at the pathetic survivors, though, he knew what he was doing was right. The System might seem like an emotionless, all-powerful entity, but Morgan felt like it had an agenda. Why would it give them four amulets and not six? Because it wanted Morgan to have to make a tough choice. Just like when it gave him the quest to help Issa. It tied a penalty for failure to him accepting the quest. It was like it was trying to get him to be selfish, and he didn't want to give in. It was becoming a point of pride for him. Still, he handed two amulets to Issa, then handed one to Darran and one to Tiala.

Issa didn't hesitate, carefully clasping her two amulets around the necks of the two unconscious Ghelli. Morgan was about to ask how to activate them when the air shimmered, and the two women were simply gone. He closed his mouth with a click.

"Thank you so much, Morgan and Issa! I will never forget what you've done for my sisters and me! My people live in the Umbertide Woods. If you're familiar with the area, seek me out, and my family will repay you!" Tiala wiped tears from her eyes, slipped the necklace over her head, and three seconds later, she was gone.

"I also will take my leave. Thank you very much for not taking advantage of my, our, weakness. You both showed honor in this hellish place. Issa, I am from the Evundi clan. I hope to repay you and Morgan if you ever make your way out of here." Issa smiled and nodded.

"Good luck, Darran," Morgan said, reaching out a hand. Darran clasped it and smiled, and Morgan felt good knowing that a handshake wasn't just a human thing. Darran put the necklace on, waved one more time, and then he, too, was gone. Morgan sighed and then spoke: "What a nightmare. I wish we were on our way out of here, too."

"I know, Morgan, I also do. At least I chose to come to this place. I can only imagine how you must feel, being thrust into it the way you were." Issa laid a hand on his arm. Reflexively, Morgan reached an arm around her and pulled her into a hug. She didn't resist and put her arms around his waist, and they stood that way, taking comfort in each other's presence for several moments.

"You know, Issa, I never thanked you for coming to help me when I was down in that pit. I have never felt so alone and lost. When you whispered for me to 'shh,' it was like hope came to life in me. I'll never be able to repay you."

"Don't be silly, Morgan. How do you think I felt when I was being eaten alive, and you saved me? I'll make you this promise: you'll never owe me anything, but you can always depend on me!"

Morgan smiled and squeezed Issa tighter. "I'm lucky I ran into you, Issa. You can always depend on me, too." Reluctantly, Morgan stepped away and gestured to the blue box. "We still have some rewards to deal with. What level are you, Issa? Is that rude to ask?"

"It's not rude among friends, but, yes, don't ask that of everyone you meet!" Issa laughed. "I'm level six now."

"Alright, I'm eight. Let's each take one of the Advancement Orbs?"

"Well, if you took them both, you'd get your class choice. It might be beneficial for us both if you gained a strong class. Though, if you wait and get some other gains before you hit level ten, you might get different or better class choices. It's the classic dilemma about advancing quickly or advancing thoroughly." Morgan thought about what Issa said and then nodded.

"Yeah, I'd feel better if we shared the reward, anyway. I'll get to ten soon enough." Issa nodded, and they both stretched out their hands to one of the Advancement Orbs. Warmth flooded through his fingers and rushed up into his body.

Congratulations! You have achieved level 9 base human and have 15 attribute points to allocate.

"Now for the last rewards. 'Energy-rich natural materials'?"

"Yes, when Energy is very dense in a place, certain minerals and living things take on the Energy, evolving into more powerful variants of their original form," Issa replied. Morgan nodded and reached into the box to lift out the strange, orange metal. It was about the size of a deck of cards but many times heavier. He could feel a humming potential in the metal, but he didn't know how to describe the feeling more than that. Issa looked at it in his hand and said, "That looks like Amber Ore. I don't know much about it, but Artificers greatly value it. My father is an Artificer, and I think I remember him crafting a small bit of ore like this into an arrowhead for our Grand Hunter."

"Okay, what about the fruit?" Morgan asked, reaching in and lifting out the blue and green fruit. It was soft, and a rich, sugary scent wafted into his nostrils. He started to salivate involuntarily. Issa sniffed it, licking her lips.

"You eat it, Morgan. I don't know what it does, but it must be beneficial to come in a System treasure box."

Morgan hesitated, but then he decided to go with his urges. He handed the Amber Ore to Issa, and then he bit into the fruit; in two bites, it was gone. "I'm sorry, Issa, I couldn't resist . . ." he started to say, but then he was transfixed by a warm, almost hot wave that rolled out from his stomach through his whole body. He felt like someone was pouring hot water on him, methodically moving from his stomach to his extremities, over and over. His vision became obscured by a dark curtain and kaleidoscopic lights. When the feeling subsided, he realized he was lying on his back, breathing heavily. "What the hell . . .?"

"I think you upgraded your race!" Issa said, kneeling next to him.

"Uh. Status," Morgan croaked, studying the descriptor for his race:

Race:	Human - Base 2

"Yeah, base two," Morgan said. "I'm sorry, Issa, I feel greedy."

"Don't be! This Amber Ore will be very valuable. My father will be able to make big gains in his Artificer class using it, and the wealth he accrues will allow me to buy other treasures that can help me in similar ways."

"Oh, okay, good. So, what does improving one's race do for a person?" Morgan asked, trying to note any differences.

"Oh, it was amazing to watch! If you could see yourself, I think you'd notice a difference! I think you're a little taller, your hair has more luster, your eyes, too! I'm not joking," she said, as Morgan looked at her like he thought she was making fun of him. "In my village, there's a Hunter with a Base 9 race, and he's nearly six inches taller than anyone else, and his features are amazing! His eyes could pierce your soul, his hair is the yellow-white of the sun, and his skin . . ." she trailed off, her cheeks starting to blush.

"Easy there"—Morgan laughed—"don't need you to start spouting poetry or something."

Issa growled and punched his shoulder, saying, "Well, the important thing about advancing your race is that it lets you continue to level. There are points where you'll reach a cap and be unable to level because your body can't contain the Energy required."

"Gotcha, thanks for explaining," Morgan said as he clambered to his feet. "Well, what now?"

"I know where the stairs are to the next level," Issa replied, grinning widely.

BRONWYN

When Bronwyn stepped away from the monolithic Colony Stone, she saw Arthur Ballard and two others walking up the hill from the gathered crowd. They were obviously coming to talk to her; she had known he'd come when she realized how large the obelisk was growing and when it started making such a spectacle with the steam and golden lights, but she hadn't known there'd be a System announcement. She was dreading this conversation, but she steeled herself and got ready to defend her actions. She stood up straight, the obelisk behind her, and planted her fists on her hips, staring at the trio as they approached.

As Arthur and his companions got about halfway up the hill, she recognized one of them as the older man from the night before who had been trying to calm the crowds. The other was a woman whom Bronwyn knew immediately. Her name was Olivia Bennet; she was a celebrity genius back on Earth. Olivia was the sole reason they could even travel to Tau Ceti; the cryo technology that kept them all alive and free from aging during the centuries-long flight was her crowning achievement. She had straight raven-colored hair running down past her shoulders, framing a pale, oval face. She walked slightly apart from Arthur and his other companion, and Bronwyn noticed, as she got closer, that in the palm of her hand, she was spinning around four different colored orbs of Energy, each the size of a grape. If Bronwyn were to guess, she had an orb for each base element: fire, water, earth, and air. She was causing them to spin and interact with each other in dozens of confusing patterns, all without seeming to concentrate much at all.

"Bronwyn," Arthur said flatly, and the three of them came to the top of the hill and stood before her.

"Yes, Arthur, before you ask, I set up the Colony Stone here. It was one of my rewards for finishing the tutorial." Bronwyn sighed, already weary of this conversation before it started.

"Don't you think some sort of discussion would have been in order? Aren't you at all concerned . . ." He abruptly stopped speaking as Olivia put her hand on his shoulder.

"Arthur, let's give Bronwyn a chance to explain what she's done. I think it's clear that she has good intentions, considering the heroics she pulled off this morning, don't you?" Olivia's voice was soothing and not a little patronizing. Ballard frowned but nodded.

"All right, Bronwyn, do you mind explaining this stone to us? Do you mind explaining why the System just said you are the 'leader'?"

"Okay, but first, let's make introductions. I know you, Arthur; you're the one who hired me. Ms. Bennet, I know you by reputation. Sir, I recognize you from the attack, but I don't know your name. I am assuming you all know my name? Bronwyn Tallow? I was hired to pilot the Titan mech and provide security for the colony, longterm." Bronwyn had decided to take this slowly and create the illusion of a formal meeting. Why should she let Ballard bluster his way through, keeping her on her back foot?

"Oh yes, I remember you, Ms. Tallow. Thank you again for your heroics. My name is Dr. Kerns, and I'm the chief medical officer for the *Pilgrim-9* mission," the white-bearded man replied with a smile. Bronwyn could see that she'd hit the right nerve by keeping things formal.

"Very good; I can see that we have three high-ranking members of the colony mission here. Arthur, you're the nominal mission leader, and we have the Chief Science Officer and Chief Medical Officer. Is there anyone else we should have in this discussion before I go into what I know? Because I'm not someone who likes to repeat herself a lot." As Bronwyn made the last statement, her eyebrows drew together, and she practiced her "very serious" expression.

"Just what do you mean by 'nominal' leader?" Arthur spluttered.

"Arthur, relax; I'm sure she didn't mean any offense. What about her question?" Again, Olivia used a placating tone, and Arthur stiffened but listened to her, actually responding to Bronwyn's question.

"Chief Engineer Durant is missing. Several people from the area where he was camping seem to have been dragged off by the wolves. Because the wolves don't seem to keep prisoners, we're counting them among the casualties." He paused for breath, and Bronwyn nodded for him to continue. "Well, we're still taking stock of where everyone is in the meadow and at what stage of this absurd orientation they're on. I really don't know which of his lieutenants should take his place in a meeting like this, and none of them have come forward." For the first time, Bronwyn could see the frustration and fear beneath Arthur's bluster. She actually started to feel a bit sorry for him.

"Yeah, I know, Arthur. It's a clusterfuck." Bronwyn began to pace slightly. "Well, what about agriculture? Husbandry? Anyone else?"

"Yes. I'm sure many department heads should be here, but Bronwyn, we don't have any of our tools or supplies or embryos; people are just trying to figure out how to adapt right now. I think we should keep it to this small group for now, and if you are loath to repeat yourself, I'm sure the three of us could help with that."

"All right. Well, here's the deal. I was awarded the Colony Stone from the System. The System doesn't give a fuck about what Ivy League schools we all went to. It doesn't care what the people on Earth said we should do when we got here. The System seems to care about Energy and how well we use it, and that seems to be about it. Based on what happened this morning with the attack, I decided we couldn't sit around and debate things for days on end, so I made a decision: I planted the Colony Stone, and the System assigned me as the leader. Now, I'm pretty sure that can be changed down the road, so don't start hand-wringing and calling me a dictator. After we get things secure and people find their roles, maybe we can have an election or something, and I'll be willing to adjust the settings. Assuming I can do so." Bronwyn took a deep breath and paused. It was the most she'd spoken at once since they left Earth.

Before Arthur could respond, Dr. Kerns cleared his throat and spoke: "Arthur, dear man, you must be able to see that things are different than we planned? You can't expect things to just go according to plan when we don't know what planet we're on, we don't have any of our supplies, we don't know what hostilities we face, and we're dealing with some sort of omnipotent entity? For Christ's sake, man, people are performing magic!" As he spoke, his tone continued to rise until his exasperation came through as a near shout. Arthur looked to Kerns and then to Bennet and then back to Bronwyn.

"You're willing to relinquish leadership if people wish it? When things are settled?" Bronwyn stared at him for a moment, then nodded. "Very well." He sighed. "Bronwyn, just what can this monolith do?" He stepped to the side and gestured to the stone. It stood there, unmoving save for the dim runic symbols that seemed to be inches beneath the stone's surface, its immense shadow stretching down the hill and across the blue meadow to the east in the waning sunlight.

"Well, I haven't had a chance to look it over," Bronwyn said, following his gaze. She walked over to the stone and placed her palm upon it. It felt solid and cool, but she could sense the Energy within thrumming with potential. "Let me check it out. Be patient." She could feel them draw closer to watch as she pushed forth a trickle of Energy into the obelisk.

The periphery of her vision seemed to darken slightly, and a System window, larger and with much greater complexity than she'd seen before, filled her vision. It was much like a user interface for any high-end business software back on Earth. There were menus and, within some menus, even three-dimensional renderings of buildings and the local landscape. When she explored some menus like "Optional Upgrades to Colony Stone," she found dozens of subcategories. Within those subcategories were hundreds of menu items. It would, quite literally, take her days to explore all of the functionality of the Colony Stone.

One of the first things, she noticed, was that most of the optional upgrades to the stone, and then, in further menus, upgrades to the Colony itself, cost something called "System Credits." Bronwyn noted that First Landing had a whopping zero System Credits. She explored some more until she found the submenu she was looking for: System Credit Exchange. Reading through the menu and the options, she learned that Energy users could exchange "Energy rich" treasures and items for System Credits at any Colony Stone or the upgraded versions, Town, City, Nation, or World Stones.

Reading over the interface for exchanging System Credits, Bronwyn had a thought and reached into her pouch, calling to mind the little sack of green-colored beads she'd gotten from the Yeksa shaman. Holding it near the smooth surface of the monolith, she noticed that a green menu item had filled in on the menu, asking if she wanted to exchange fifty-six Nature Attuned Energy Beads for 1120 System Credits. Bronwyn selected the "yes" prompt and wasn't surprised at all when the pouch in her hand was suddenly a lot lighter and quite empty. "Well, that was fast," she muttered.

"What was?" Olivia Bennett's voice was hushed, almost a whisper, but it still startled Bronwyn; she'd nearly forgotten she had an audience.

Not taking her eyes off the menu, she explained, "If you want to buy anything from the System, you need to have System Credits. I just traded some Energy beads I got from a monster I killed for some System Credits."

"Huh, almost exactly as I had postulated to Arthur earlier."

"What? You guessed there'd be something like this?" Bronwyn was distracted by the conversation, but she was also curious.

"Not exactly, but I've theorized that the System is something of a parasite," Olivia responded and didn't elaborate.

"Uh, can you explain what you mean?" Bronwyn wanted to keep exploring the menu, but the subject of just who or what the System was had been on the back of her mind since day one.

"Well, clearly, it wants to nurture Energy users and encourages growth and strength. I've assumed that it somehow gains in power as we do. This stone is the first concrete evidence I've seen, though. It wants people to exchange Energy for goods. Do you think it is benevolent, as it claims, and only asks for enough Energy to create the goods? Or do you think it keeps a percentage and grows in power?"

"Damn. A fucking parasite, huh?"

"Apparently, a very large one. The "tutorial" spoke of many worlds and even multiple universes. Imagine!" Olivia sounded almost excited by the prospect. Bronwyn could see how a scientist would be giddy at the idea of multiple universes and some kind of inter-dimensional parasite, but she just felt creeped out. She snorted and continued looking through the interface.

"I'm checking out defensive options, and there are a lot of them, but, most basically, we can purchase walls. It looks like we can buy wooden palisades for five thousand Credits plus the required building material. For a four-square-mile area, it wants eight hundred fucking tons of lumber. There are other options, though: stone, living wood, marble, steel. Fuck, the menu goes on and on. They all require materials, but up near the top, there's an option for a packed-earth bulwark that only requires 8k Energy. Nothing else."

"Interesting," Arthur said from her right side. "Why did you select a four-square-mile area? Is eight thousand a lot of Credits? How many did you get for that pouch of beads?"

"I was just looking at the prices, and it seems to climb exponentially. I figured that was plenty of space for us until we get a foothold. The System gave me eleven hundred credits for those. Gimme a couple of minutes, please. I'm trying to figure something out." Bronwyn cut off his follow-up question. She'd realized that they didn't have enough Credits to do much of anything, so she was looking for ways to make them. She'd found a submenu called "Contribution Store System" and was reading through it. It looked like she'd be able to set up a semi-autonomous process for the people in the colony to contribute to the bank of Credits she could draw on. The System would create a Contribution Store, and people could turn in Energy bearing items or perform tasks or "quests" in exchange for Credits. Bronwyn looked at the basic Contribution Store item list and was amazed at its depth. Anything from food, to alcohol, to clothing, to weapons, to potions, all the way up to "conscious" items and "natural treasures" that could improve your body in numerous ways. It was mind-boggling.

One item stood out to her, though, because it was the first thing on the item list and was offered for zero contribution points. It was a manual on how to refine raw Energy into Energy beads. At that moment, what Olivia had said earlier finally clicked for Bronwyn. The System was giving them, Energy cultivators, a manual that taught them how to harvest Energy so that they could feed it to the System through this stone. Sure, it was offering them prizes and treasures, but Bronwyn just didn't believe that it wasn't keeping more than it needed to provide the items on the list. Out loud, she said, "Fuck. I think you're right, Olivia, but I don't see a way around it. We're going to have to play this game if we want to survive. For now."

Bronwyn spent the next several minutes setting up a Contribution Store for the colony. There was an option to increase the cost of the items, thereby receiving a larger amount of Credits in the colony bank. *Just like fucking taxes*, she thought. She decided to leave the slider at the baseline Credit cost for now.

She could customize the item rewards but couldn't think why anyone would do that. She assumed that maybe some communities wouldn't want people to buy alcohol or drugs, or certain kinds of clothing. She decided not to worry about that unless it became a problem, and she would rather that be an issue that was voted on later, not a mandate from her.

Finally, she turned away from the menu and looked at the three patient observers. "I set up a Contribution Store. Anyone in the colony can use the menu here to complete tasks, earn rewards, and thereby earn the colony System Credits."

"Now I see why you said I was right!" Olivia was beaming, obviously pleased with herself for her guess about the System's nature.

"Also, it looks like anyone who can channel Energy can create those Energy beads. There's a manual in the Contribution Store for free. I think everyone should be told about that; it's a way to earn points without risking your life in the forest."

"Yes, we'll spread the word. Also, if you don't mind, we three will begin canvassing the population for ideas on what should be a priority after the wall. Does the System sell buildings?" Arthur was clearly trying to have a deferring tone with her, and Bronwyn saw the strain it was causing him.

"Yes. Everything from gazebos to libraries. I also earned a certificate for a blacksmithy doing a quest this morning. I'll take your advice on where to place that tomorrow. In the meantime, I need to get something to eat and then shout for volunteers to keep watch tonight. It's clear we won't have walls up before dark." Arthur blanched at the mention of darkness and nodded to her.

"See you later, okay, Bronwyn?" Olivia said as she started to walk past and down the hill.

"Yeah, for sure. We have a lot to do and talk about." Bronwyn turned to smile, but Olivia had already turned to the obelisk, resting her hand on the stone. Stepping away, Bronwyn rubbed her dry and bleary eyes. She felt like she had been reading through lists and looking at graphs for hours. She stretched and looked out at the scene before her. Tents were sprawled out for acres in every direction in the short blue grass. People were congregating in groups; the largest was here, at the base of the hill where the Colony Stone rose above like a thick, dark finger. She walked down the hill toward the biggest crowd and mentally prepared to exhort them about the need to keep watch with a fire burning all night.

BRONWYN

Bronwyn stretched her neck, feeling it crack and smiling at the release of tension. The conversation with the crowd that had gathered while the Colony Stone established itself went better than she had anticipated. People were generally in a rather good mood, even with the attack that happened last night. They'd received her explanation of why she was announced as the "leader" of the colony without much argument and had seemed excited about the Contribution Store she'd set up. She explained how it worked and then asked for volunteers to stand watch at night and spread the word about the need for more people to do so. Almost the entire group had stepped forward.

The general euphoria in the face of a life-altering circumstance was puzzling to her, but she was starting to develop ideas. Could it be the Energy? When Bronwyn had received Energy influxes from the System or from fighting the attackers that morning, she'd felt an extreme rush of vitality and positive emotions, almost like an intense dopamine infusion. Could living in an Energy saturated environment have a more subtle effect on one's mood?

It was hard not to wonder that something was going on. People were standing around cookfires, laughing, some even singing old-Earth camping songs. Younger adults were playing games, practicing with the tutorial spells. The game of frost tag that she'd seen earlier seemed to have spread, and several groups were doing something similar. As she passed by a cluster of tents, she saw several older women and men standing around a kettle and talking about the right way to use Energy to enhance certain flavors. Curiosity got the better of her, and she walked up to the group. "Hey, how'd you guys get a kettle? That wasn't in my tutorial."

"Oh, hello there. I'm not sure why you didn't get a kettle. After I completed the third cooking tutorial, the System generated it as a reward and offered me a quest to teach five others how to prepare something called ithiak stew," a woman with steel gray hair tied up in a bun replied, stepping forward. "Would you like to learn?"

"Wait, third cooking tutorial? I only had one!" Bronwyn scoured her memory of the orientation experience. Had she skipped something?

"Oh, really? That doesn't surprise me. It seems the System adjusts the orientation to a person's talents. Harold, there, got several lessons on how to shape living wood. It seems, with practice, he can make dwellings or other structures out of trees. Anyway, would you like to learn the recipe?" The woman gestured to an older man standing over the cookpot, concentrating on something; Bronwyn wasn't sure what.

"Uh, no, thank you. I'm going to sleep a few hours so I can wake up and keep watch for part of the night. Do me a favor and spread the word. One person should be awake at all times near each cluster of tents." Bronwyn started walking again as the woman nodded in agreement and turned back to her cooking lesson. Apparently, she hadn't finished the orientation quickly just because she was more talented than everyone else. She'd just focused on getting it done quickly. Or had the System steered her that way? She doubted any colonist could perform better in martial skills than she had. Maybe the System had seen that as her main aptitude and pushed her through it? She was starting to feel more and more paranoid about the System. There was no denying that her main goal during the whole orientation was to get done with it. Maybe the System just picked up on that and didn't try to bog her down with extra cooking tutorials or whatever. Regardless, she was dead tired and ready for some sleep as she made her way to her little tent, standing off from any others. She felt a slight pang of loneliness but pushed it down. There'd be time for making friends when they had some security and a sense of what was coming next. She crawled into her tent, making sure her gauntlets were close to hand and closed her eyes. She knew her body would sleep for about six hours, which should have her waking up right around midnight.

Bronwyn opened her eyes to darkness and silence. She sat up, noticing that she'd kicked her boots off at some point. She listened for any noise while she felt around for her boots, tugging them on and fastening the buckles. Then she slipped her gauntlets on and crawled out of the tent. She stood up in the cool darkness, and as her eyes adjusted, she realized there was quite a lot of light. There was a fat, orange-yellow moon about two-thirds toward the western horizon, and she could see the edge of the giant, ringed moon starting to rise in the east. It was bizarre seeing those alien bodies in the sky and facing them as a constant reminder that they were not on Earth anymore. She was pretty sure that there were just three moons: the nighttime orange-yellow moon that seemed about twice the size of Earth's moon, and then the two other moons that were mainly in the sky during the daytime. One was huge with rings, and the other followed in its wake—a small pale reflection.

In addition to the moonlight, Bronwyn was pleased to see many campfires still lit up around the colony. She could also discern people with torches moving around the perimeter and through the encampment. They'd heeded her advice and maintained a watch! Bronwyn stretched, then dug one of her own torches out of her pack and used the fire starter that had been included in her pack to light it. The fire starter was a fascinating tool—it was a heavy metallic rod, just a bit bigger than her pointer finger, with tiny runes lining its length. When she'd first noticed it in her pack, she'd bonded with it and learned that she just had to channel a tiny bit of Energy into it to cause sparks to flare out one end, almost like a Fourth of July sparkler back on Earth. Torch grasped in one gauntleted hand, she began her rounds.

The night was uneventful. Bronwyn patrolled the camp's perimeter, making several circuits throughout the dark morning into the gray light of dawn. The air was crisp but not too cold, and she rather enjoyed the pleasant exercise. She had several whispered conversations with other watch people and felt a sense of camaraderie in their shared duty that she hadn't felt since waking on this strange planet. As the sky grew light and more and more people woke, starting their morning routines, she made her way to the center of the campground and climbed the hill to the Colony Stone. It was time for her to earn some contribution points.

Suddenly aware of the lack of a presence she'd grown accustomed to on her shoulder, she spun around, eyes darting back and forth. "Hops! Hops! Where are you?" she called out like she was calling her dog from back on Earth. She heard a slight chirping sound from a nearby bush, and Hops came bounding out toward her, the white fur of his face splattered in purple. He also had managed to dye his little hands, and he was carrying what looked like a half dozen tiny berries. "Well, it looks like you eat more than hair after all. You had me worried for a minute there, cutie; I thought you'd left." Hops stopped next to her feet and looked up at her expectantly, his arms full of berries. Bronwyn knelt and scooped the little critter up in her hands, depositing him back up on her shoulder. Once he was situated, Bronwyn watched as he started packing the berries away into his shell; evidently, it was more spacious than it looked. Afterward, he proceeded to lick his little hands clean and wipe them off on Bronwyn's hair. "Hey! That's not a towel! If you dye my hair purple, I swear, I'll make you ride in my backpack." She awkwardly pointed her finger back at Hops as she made her faux threat. He chirped back at her in response and pulled her hair around himself, needing another nap after that strenuous eating session. She chuckled at the bizarre and adorable little creature and proceeded to make her way up the hill and up to the Colony Stone.

Resting her hand on the Colony Stone, Bronwyn accessed the Contribution Store and then selected the Quests and Tasks menu:

Contribution Activities for Bronwyn Tallow:		
Forge earth attuned Energy beads.	20 contribution points per bead.	Accept? YES/NO
Quest: Track the invading Yeksa to their origin and scout the vicinity.	1500 contribution points.	Accept? YES/NO
Quest: Explore the northern plains and find points of interest.	200 contribution points per POI.	Accept? YES/NO
Quest: Return Energy-rich natural materials to the Colony Stone	Contribution points awarded based on material value.	Accept? YES/NO

Bronwyn had spoken with several volunteer guards through the night and learned that many people had already picked up the manual for creating Energy beads and were hard at work. The rumor going around was that people without an affinity for a particular type of Energy were being paid ten contribution points per bead, and those with an affinity were making twenty. That seemed to be confirmed by this menu. The menu didn't mention that it took people almost a full day of channeling to form one bead. She imagined that it got faster as a person gained in strength or aptitude, but it was a pretty slow way to earn points.

Judging from the menu's title, the System was personalizing contribution activities for individuals. She looked at her three options for "quests" and accepted them all. She had in mind scouting anyway, and they needed as many contribution points as possible. As she stepped away from the stone, a notification appeared in her vision:

*** **Quest accepted: Track the invading Yeksa to their origin and scout the vicinity.***

*** **Quest accepted: Explore the northern plains and find points of interest.***

Quest accepted: Return Energy-rich natural materials to the Colony Stone.

When she cleared the notification, she saw that Arthur Ballard had made his way up the hill and was standing to the side, waiting for her to finish her business with the stone. "Good morning, Arthur," she said flatly.

"Good morning, Bronwyn. I was hoping to speak to you about some logistics." Bronwyn didn't know why he was being so agreeable, but she decided not to look a gift horse in the mouth.

"Oh, alright. I have some quests to work on to earn contribution points and thereby some System credits for the colony, but we can talk before I head out."

"Yes, of course. I'm glad you're taking such an active role. I'll be here to help oversee things while you're out. In the meantime, I spoke with some of our Engineering staff, and we've decided that we should build our town center with the pond and this hill at the center. With that in mind, we thought your blacksmithy should be placed just to the north there, about fifty yards from the base of the hill. Do you mind trying to get it started before you leave?" Truthfully, Bronwyn had forgotten about the blacksmith building reward. She had planned to put it down before leaving, but a night of sleep had placed that thought a bit too far in the back of her mind.

"Oh, yes, I was going to do that before I left. Glad I didn't have to hunt you down to ask about a building site." Inwardly she grimaced at her dishonesty, but she just had a hard time letting her guard down around Ballard. "Right, right, let's see here . . ." She dug the scroll for the blacksmith building out of her pouch and unfurled it. Nothing happened, so she stepped over to the Colony Stone and placed one hand upon it. As the UI appeared in her vision, a new screen was already open, prompting her to select the location for the blacksmith building. She reached out to touch the three-dimensional, topographical map and found she could highlight appropriate building sites. She chose a spot just a bit north of the hill she was standing on and clicked the "accept" button. The scroll flashed in her hand, dissolving into white steam and yellow streaming fractals that flooded into the Colony Stone's surface.

Bronwyn felt a rumbling sensation and could hear yells and people clamoring about to the north of the hill, so she ran around the stone to the edge of the hilltop to see what she'd done. Several people scrambled away from an area of about two thousand square feet of ground that was shifting like something was digging just beneath the surface. Bronwyn watched in amazement as a building slowly rose out of the earth, fully intact. It was a square, tan-colored, brick building with brown clay tiles for a roof. The building was a single-story and had a set of three massive chimneys along the eastern edge of the roof. Bronwyn was looking at the south side of the building, and she could see that it had a red-brick patio and a solid set of double doors facing the hillside. As the building settled, the displaced soil seemed to sink into the ground, and a smooth, grassless area of packed earth surrounded the building and the red brick deck.

"Wow, that is pretty damn cool," Bronwyn said softly.

She was surprised when Arthur answered her, "Yes, it surely is."

"Well, let's see what we're dealing with." Bronwyn started striding down the hill with Arthur in tow, a frazzled look on his face.

MORGAN

It turned out, Issa had explored quite a few of the nearby tunnels while looking for the Yovashi's lair. It had taken her the better part of a day to find her way, having to stop, pull the cloak up and freeze in a corner whenever she heard the Yovashi or some other sound. It had been harrowing, wondering all the while if she'd be discovered and killed. She'd stumbled upon the stairwell leading up just a short distance from where she'd ended up hiding and waiting for the Yovashi to leave its lair. She explained all this to Morgan while sorting through the equipment piles the creature had scavenged from its victims.

Of the weapons, Morgan ended up storing an extra spear, not nearly as nice as the one he was using, but it still had a sharp, steel blade. He also took a black metal mace and a broadsword that wasn't rusted too badly. He still marveled at how all those items fit into his dimensional pouch along with all his other loot, and he could see that he'd only used about half its space. Sifting through the clothes and armor, Morgan found a pair of soft leather boots that fit him reasonably well. Most of the clothes were too small, too torn, or too filthy for him to wear, but he found a set of black, tattered robes that seemed relatively clean, and they fit him very well. The robe's inner layer fit his body snuggly, while an outer cloak-like layer, tattered and stripped but largely whole, covered his shoulders and hung around him. He wore his girdle over the inner robe and smiled; it felt good not to be wandering around nearly naked for once.

Issa also found some gray trousers and a light blue blouse, with only one large stain on the back, near the neckline. Her cloak covered it up. While she stepped over behind the boulder to change into her new clothes, Morgan dug out a pair of small leather boots and threw them her way, saying, "See if these fit." She stepped out a few moments later with her foot in one boot and smiling.

"They fit!"

"Great! Anything else you want? If not, let's get moving." Issa nodded and moved through the nearby piles one more time, and Morgan saw her slip a couple more small items into her pouch.

"I don't think anything else here is very valuable. I wish we could bury this place," Issa said as she walked back.

"Yeah, this place is terrible. I've been meaning to ask, does the System make these places to put in the Crucible? Is it always the same?"

"No! No one has ever reported having the same Crucible experience unless they went in together or met up inside, like you and I have. My teachers think the System puts invisible portals in the stairwell rooms and connects many places around the world together in a design to challenge each person differently," Issa explained.

"So, your teachers didn't really know, then?"

"Well, no. My village is pretty small and only has an improved Town Stone. That means we only have communication and trade through the System with other similarly leveled settlements."

"So?"

"So, the people we communicate with regularly have a similar level of knowledge about the System, and none of us know exactly how things like the Crucible work." Issa shrugged.

"Oh, so there aren't more advanced towns or cities you could travel to physically? You only have access through this 'Town Stone'?" Morgan scratched his head.

"Oh, good question! Yes, there are bigger towns and cities we could travel to, but not easily, and it's rare. Our world is huge and dangerous. It's much larger than it was before the System came here, at least that's what my grandfather tells me."

"Uh-huh," Morgan said, taking it in. "Hmm, well, now that you mention it, when our ship arrived near your planet, we thought the sensors were broken because of the size of your planet."

"Sensors? It sounds like your people are pretty advanced. I didn't even know one could travel between planets and stars without the System."

"Well, we had more advanced technology than lanterns and spears, that's for sure, but we didn't have any magic or magical items. Wait. Did you say the System allows travel between planets and stars?" Morgan asked.

"Yes! Town Stones can be upgraded to allow travel to other Town or City Stones, even on different worlds. It costs System Credits, though." Issa frowned and continued, "You can trade treasures like the Energy beads for System Credits at a Town Stone."

"All right, my head's spinning. Let's get walking while I mull these facts over." Morgan chuckled, and they advanced, armed and clothed and feeling a lot better about their prospects, into the hallway and toward the stairs.

This time the stairwell was a rickety mishmash of wooden planks. The steps were flat and sturdy, but they were cut in all sorts of different sizes, and the railing was of varying heights. The walls were boards and planks that were unevenly matched together, and the gaps in the panels seemed to lead into endless shadow. It was nerve-wracking climbing those steps, and they seemed to go on forever. Their lanterns made islands of light in the dark, creaking stairwell as they climbed. Morgan kept track of the time with his quest tracker. When they started the climb, he was on four out of seven days in his quest to help Issa stay alive.

As they climbed, Morgan and Issa spoke in quiet voices, telling each other about their lives before the Crucible. Issa told Morgan about her father and how she was an only child. She told him about losing her mother to raiders when she was a little girl and how her father had begged her not to enter the lottery to come to the Crucible. According to Issa, less than half the Hunters, the most common class of Energy cultivators among her people, that entered the Crucible ever came back. However, those who did usually returned with significant gains in both personal power and wealth. Issa wanted to be able to stand on her own, and she accepted that the world was dangerous. She wanted to face danger on her terms and not be a victim like her mother had been.

"I lost my parents when I was young, also," Morgan quietly said after Issa had stopped talking for a while. Issa looked at him, inviting him to continue. "Things were pretty bad on my home world when I was young; lots of wars. Well, most of the media called them 'conflicts,' but they were wars. Water was a problem, which is crazy because our world was rich with water. I guess clean freshwater was the problem. We still had lots of water, but not enough was usable to sustain the megacities that started to sprout up in the last century."

Issa looked a little confused. "Megacities?"

"Yeah, that's what they called them because they grew to the size of small countries or states. Like the New Detroit Megacity, where my parents were born, was thousands of square miles of concrete." He saw Issa's confusion again and clarified: "Uh, concrete is a building material that looks like stone. Anyway, over a hundred million people were living in New Detroit when the Great Lakes conflict started. By the time it was over, everyone was dead or had fled, leaving just a couple hundred thousand scraping by in the rubble. My parents were on the run when some biological agent caught up to their caravan. It was carried on the wind, a kind of poison. This is according to my big sister, who was nine at the time. The caravan didn't have enough gas masks for everyone, so they gave them to the children and a couple of lucky adults. I was only four, so I don't remember it, but it really messed up my sister."

"That sounds horrible, Morgan," Issa said, reaching out a hand. Morgan took the offered hand in his, and they walked quietly for a while.

"Anyway, things were starting to get better on Earth when I left. I'd been a part of a few conflicts, but it was at the tail end of the global violence. Some breakthroughs in tech allowed us to start cleaning our atmosphere and terraforming some of the other planets and moons nearby. It gave us a purpose other than fighting with each other. That's why I was on my way here; in fact, I was on a ship full of settlers, hoping to start a new human colony. We didn't know other people were here already."

"Is your sister here, also?" Issa asked after they'd walked quietly for a while.

"Oh. No, she died a few years ago. Actually, it's more than two hundred years now, but it feels like a few years to me," Morgan said with a sigh. He could see Issa had more questions, but she didn't ask them, and he didn't feel like saying any more.

When the tracker said five of seven, they stopped mid-climb and rested. Issa slept first, and Morgan was able to stay awake until she woke on her own. This time, when he slept, she didn't doze off. Their precautions proved unnecessary, though; nothing happened while they were resting, and after they'd eaten some of their spartan rations, they began the climb again. By the time a small wooden door appeared around the paneled curve of the stairwell, Morgan was on day six of seven in his quest.

As was becoming their usual practice, Issa fell in behind Morgan while he crept up to the door. He placed his ear to the wood and thought he heard the sound of the wind, but nothing else. Morgan studied the door for a crack or hole he could spy through, but it seemed to be too well made for that. He checked the handle and saw that there wasn't a latch—it looked like the door would swing open if he just pulled it. He gently pulled on the handle, and it didn't move. He applied more force, and it still didn't move. "I'm going to have to pull hard. It might make some noise, so be ready," he whispered. He gripped the wooden handle in two hands and pulled hard, slowly increasing the force. After straining for a few seconds, he felt the door budge just the smallest amount. He took a deep breath and jerked the door. It scraped along the jam about an inch but still wasn't free. He yanked on it again, and it popped out of the frame, causing him to stumble backward.

Hot air flowed into the stairwell, and dim red light revealed a stone platform beyond the doorway. Morgan gathered himself and carefully crept through the opening. Once again, he found himself in a stone-walled, high ceilinged, natural-looking cavern. The floor was unnaturally flat, though, and just ahead, he could see carved stone steps leading down a slope. Looking down, along the steps, he saw the cavern opened into a larger space. The red glow was coming from that area. He motioned for Issa to follow and softly padded down the stone steps.

When Morgan reached the cavern opening with Issa close behind, he took in his breath at the sight that unfolded in front of him. The opening was about twenty feet across, and looking through it, Morgan could see another cavern that dwarfed any indoor space he had ever seen. The cavern ceiling had to be hundreds of feet in the air, and he could see all the way across to the other end, which must have been more than a kilometer. The entire, massive space was suffused with a red glow from a literal river of red-orange magma that flowed horizontally across the cavern. More steps led down to the bottom of the enormous cavern from where they stood. From there, a cobblestone road traversed the length of the cavern. It crossed the magma river via a stone bridge. It then continued to another set of steps leading up and out the other end of the cavern through an opening like Morgan and Issa were standing in.

"Incredible," Issa whispered from just behind Morgan.

"Yeah, it is. Who made this road? Are we in some kind of underground kingdom, or did the System just put a piece of an old civilization here, or . . . Bah! There are a million possibilities. I wish the System would just answer my damn questions." Morgan ground his teeth in frustration, studying the cavern carefully, trying to see if something moved. He could tell Issa was doing the same. After a few minutes of watching the sluggish flow of the magma and seeing nothing else moving, they decided to venture forth.

"This feels like a trap." Morgan groaned as they set foot on the cobbled roadway. Issa nodded, gripping her rapier and looking around. There were lots of places for something to hide: boulders littered the cavern floor as well as hundreds, maybe thousands, of stalagmites, while long stalactites hung from the vaulted ceiling. "Well, we can't go back." Morgan shrugged, and they started walking down the road.

The roadway was similar in width to an old, two-lane road on Earth. The cobbles were irregular in size and rough, but Morgan could imagine that it was a pretty impressive feat of engineering, the way they were mortared together and flush with the stone of the cavern floor. After a few minutes of walking, they came in sight of the bridge that crossed the lava. The road narrowed and smoothly continued up onto the stone support arches. They stopped at the foot of the upward slope and took in the sight of the magma river flowing sluggishly through the cavern. The magma was in some sort of a natural channel or crevasse and was a good fifteen feet down from the edge, but even so, it gave off a very uncomfortable amount of heat. Morgan had been to the Sonoran Desert a few times, and this billowing heat felt similar to how the dry wind would blow off the asphalt in those little desert towns. Issa gestured at the bridge, and Morgan nodded. He was ready to get over this lava and put some distance between him and that heat.

The stone bridge had a gentle arc and narrowed to about ten feet at the apex. It was constructed with rather graceful stone railings, and Morgan realized that concrete and stone were quite different. He wondered if he'd ever seen something actually built from stone before. He was musing about that when they heard the horn. It was a loud, brassy, BAAAAAROOOOO, and it seemed to come from off to their right. Morgan looked over the railing, trying to find the source, when he heard a loud clanking and crash from back the way they had come. An identical sound came from the direction of the other end of the cavern. Standing at the midpoint of the bridge, Morgan could just make out the cavern openings atop their respective sets of stone steps, and he saw that a broad, metal portcullis had somehow been erected in front of each. "Oh fuck."

MORGAN

"I knew this felt like a trap, dammit!" Morgan growled, adjusting his stance and holding his spear in a way that he just "knew" was a ready stance. Issa readied her rapier and looked around warily.

"Well, that was obvious, though," she said, inadvertently showing her teeth. Seconds later, she pointed toward the rock field through which the road they'd traversed cut. Morgan saw it immediately—dark figures were pouring toward the road, coming, seemingly from nowhere. Morgan could see that they moved in a bipedal gait that was forward-leaning. They carried clubs and sharpened sticks, and some just hoisted large rocks. They appeared to be bereft of clothing and armor, though it wasn't clear that they needed any, because as they got closer, Morgan could see that they were some kind of lizard men. No, they looked more like salamanders. They had smooth-looking black skin with rough ridges and irregular orange and yellow spots, but they had lizard-like heads and long tongues. Their collective hiss drowned out the sound of the lava flow.

Morgan looked around and realized they were coming from the other side of the bridge as well. "Holy shit, there's gotta be more than a hundred! They don't look interested in talking, either!"

"Put your back to mine, Morgan, we have to fight—the System is challenging us, as always." Issa whipped her rapier back and forth and faced one direction while Morgan leveled his spear and faced the other. As the salamander creatures reached the bridge and started swarming up toward them, Morgan could see that they were smaller than he thought at first, maybe four feet tall, but what they lacked in size, they seemed to make up in intensity and numbers.

"Here they come! Get ready!" Morgan felt adrenaline start to pump through him, and as the hissing, slithering mob crossed the halfway point up the bridge toward him and Issa, he realized he was yelling, stabbing, and swinging the big, razor-sharp spear in a complicated dance. Some of the creatures leading the group coming toward him hesitated and were careened into by the ones behind. It messed up their charge, and Morgan roared again. Just as the battle was nearly upon them, he felt Issa's hand on his back, and warmth spread through him. His pulse quickened even more, and thoughts narrowed in on the topic at hand—killing. With the Haste spell making him look like a blur, Morgan stabbed into the crowd of salamander men or women; he had no way of telling. He whipped the spear around in slashing arcs and thrusts and brought the haft around to knock the little creatures away. The long, slicing blade of the spear left sprays of blood in its wake, and when Morgan stabbed, he'd often have to kick the corpses off the spear as he hurriedly whipped the haft around to crunch into a skull or ribs.

Issa was like liquid death with her rapier, unleashing days of pent-up fear and aggression on the creatures. She moved with deadly grace, keeping her back to Morgan's general direction while slashing out and opening wounds on the salamanders with each strike. She may not kill with every strike, but she could move the rapier so quickly that she wasn't having much trouble keeping the creatures at bay as she slowly piled the wounds on them.

Morgan reveled in the euphoria of battle and victory and was confident that they'd pull through, and that's when the Haste spell wore off. It felt like he slowed to a crawl, even though he was only crashing back to normal speed. Morgan was suddenly aware of the burning in his lungs and the leaden weight of his limbs. He swung his spear in a wide arc and backed into Issa. He urged her to the edge of the bridge near the railing to reduce the angles from which they could be attacked. With a few seconds of breathing room, he took stock of the situation: his back to the railing, he could see about fifteen salamander corpses to his right, sprawled around the bridge and down the slope, he could see another five or so to his left where Issa had been fighting. There had to be at least thirty or forty more of the creatures closing in a semi-circle around them, glancing warily at their weapons and the corpses of their erstwhile comrades. Panting for breath, he asked, "Haste. Gone. Can you do it again?"

"Not so soon; I'd pass out." Issa wheezed.

"Alright, watch my flank. I have an idea." Morgan grunted, then gripped his spear, looking for his next target. The salamanders could only approach them about five at a time without tripping over themselves, and Morgan and Issa seemed to be able to feint with enough of a credible threat to keep them at bay. Morgan waited for one of the braver ones to lunge with its pointed wooden spear. He used his spear to push down on the other's spear, twirling and flicking it up and to the side, then he stepped inside its reach to grab the tacky skin of its shoulder with his left hand. As soon as Morgan had a grip, he concentrated on his Energy Drain skill and *pulled*. He could sense Issa behind him and to the left, fighting to keep the salamanders at bay. As soon as he felt the energy coming out of the salamander, he redoubled his efforts, willing his Vortex Core to spin faster and *pull* harder. He felt a torrent of Energy flood into him, and he immediately felt his exhaustion ebb. As soon as the Energy stopped coming, he dropped the lifeless, gray salamander to the ground. With wide eyes, he realized he was about to be gored by another spear-wielding salamander, and another one was pounding on his back with a club.

His vigor renewed, Morgan dodged aside from the stab and swung the haft of his spear around to crack the skull of the little club-wielding salamander. He launched into another deadly dance with his spear, killing several more salamanders and wounding just as many. When Morgan thought about his Energy Drain skill, he could feel a sense of whether it was ready or not, and when it felt like he could use it again, he did so, grabbing a salamander by the arm and pulling the Energy out of it. After he'd repeated this three times, he could see that he was having a demoralizing effect on the salamanders. They were more reluctant to launch attacks, and he found that he could more easily single them out and dominate them with his longer, more deadly spear and his repeatedly refreshed endurance. Issa had to work less hard to keep his flank clear as well; he'd frequently dart in front of her to swing his long spear in a blinding arc, driving the salamanders back.

The salamander bodies were stacking up, and the pale stonework of the bridge was painted with blood and bits of gore. Morgan and Issa fought, and what had seemed a hopeless battle began to turn in their favor. Once the salamanders' morale began to break, and Morgan had to hunt them out for a conflict, he knew they had won. No longer worried about his flank, he began to rampage after the creatures, chasing them around the top of the bridge, spinning and catching them as they tried to slink around him to make a move at Issa. Eventually, he found himself standing atop the arch of the bridge, leaning on his spear, breathing heavily, and looking fruitlessly for the next opponent. Issa walked over to him, cleaning the blade of her rapier with a piece of leather she'd taken from her dimensional pouch. Morgan could see she had some bruises and a few gashes here and there, but her smile belied her mood; they'd won, and it felt glorious. Suddenly the bridge grew bright, and it took Morgan a minute to realize all of the corpses were gathering a mist of tiny golden motes. The motes coalesced into two churning streams as they flew into him and Issa.

Congratulations! You have achieved level 10 base human and have 20 attribute points to allocate. Your first Class selection is available to you.

"We did it, Issa! It was a bit hairy, but we fucking did it." Morgan laughed and gripped Issa's shoulder, giving her a little shake. She returned his smile, looking into his eyes. They stayed that way for a minute, and Morgan was about to say something when, BAAAAAAROOOOOO—the horn blew again. "Oh, goddammit!"

Quest: You have slain the children; now put the mother to rest. Reward: Improved Treasure Box. Penalty for failure: Death. Accept? YES/NO

"I want to know who's blowing that horn!" Issa growled.

"Yeah, no shit!" Morgan looked around, wondering just what the "mother" was. He looked over the side of the bridge and saw a large, dark shape pushing out of the lava river about a hundred yards from the bridge. Awestruck, he watched as an actual four-legged salamander crawled out of the lava and began to scale the broken slope. It was at least twenty feet from nose to tail and had to weigh thousands of pounds. "Oh, man. Look at that, Issa."

"Gods, it's huge," Issa whispered.

"Do you have a spear or some kind of ranged weapon? You don't wanna get close enough to that thing to hit it with your rapier." Issa nodded and reached into her pouch, stashing her rapier and pulling out a spear. It didn't have the reach of Morgan's, but it wasn't bad, and it had a shiny metal tip. Morgan looked up to see where the salamander was and couldn't spot it. Where the hell? Then he heard a screech and scrabbling claws and realized it was already at the bridge and charging their way. He leveled his spear and moved to the center of the arch.

Morgan knew he couldn't brute force this fight—this creature was aware of him and had a great deal more weight and strength. He'd have to wear it down. The beast seemed enraged, charging headlong toward him, and as it approached, Morgan was dismayed to see that it had left smoldering black footprints in its wake. Once again, just before the giant salamander got in range, he felt Issa's hand on his back, pushing Energy and her Haste spell into him. He gained focus and speed and saw an opening. He lunged forward and to the left, feinting to the creature's face with his spear while sidestepping, then brought the spear down and around in a loop, jamming it into the salamander's massive torso, right behind its left front leg. The spear bit deeply, and the salamander shrieked, rolling away from him and spinning, bringing its tail around in a vicious sweep. If Morgan hadn't been affected by the Haste spell, he was sure it would have hit him and sent him flying off the bridge into the lava. Luckily, he was able to react and hopped over the tail, putting him in a perfect position to activate Backstab and drive the spear twice into the soft flesh to either side of the salamander's lower spine.

Once again, the salamander matron shrieked in rage and pain, spinning to snap at Morgan, but he danced back, avoiding the vast maw. He feinted at the salamander's face with his spear, backpedaling to keep its attention. Just as he'd hoped, Issa used that moment to dart forward and spear the salamander in the soft, fleshy side of its belly. She'd see what its tail could do and was ready, dancing back before the whip-like appendage could slap into her. When the salamander swiped its tail at Issa, its head had turned away from Morgan. He stepped forward and drove the entire length of his spearhead into its neck, just behind its jawline. He immediately ripped the spear free and rolled backward, avoiding a retaliatory claw swipe. By now, the salamander was pouring blood out of several very severe wounds. Its movements were growing more sluggish, and Morgan thought it was over for a moment.

Then, the salamander stopped moving altogether and started to heave. Morgan thought it was about to throw up and die or something, but then he saw that its black skin was beginning to glow brightly in certain areas, and he could see smoke rising from it. It continued to heave and convulse, and the bright glowing spots grew larger. "Run!" he shouted, grabbing Issa's hand and running over the crest of the bridge. They'd made it about halfway down the far slope of the bridge when a tremendous roar tore through the air, and a gust of hot air knocked them to the ground. Morgan and Issa scrambled to their feet and kept running; when they'd cleared the bridge and made it another fifty yards, Morgan looked over his shoulder. He could see a geyser of lava shooting into the air on the far side of the bridge, and droplets of magma were starting to splatter down all over the stonework. He and Issa had narrowly escaped being immolated by the salamander's death throes.

Congratulations! You have completed a Quest: You have slain the children; now put the mother to rest. Reward: Improved Treasure Box.

Morgan and Issa collapsed to the cobbled street, breathing heavily with fatigue and relief. Just like before, a glowing, blue mist started to gather nearby, swirling together into the form of a blue box. This one was smaller, about eight inches square. After a moment, Morgan looked up with a puzzled expression. "Huh, no Energy from that big salamander?"

"Maybe because it blew itself up?" Issa pondered, rubbing at a red welt on her blue-tinted forehead.

Morgan grunted, struggling to his feet, and helped Issa stand, and together they walked over to the box. "You open this one," Issa said.

"Alright." Morgan shrugged and bent over, flipping open the lid of the box. The inside was lined with the familiar silky blue cloth, but this time there weren't any bright orbs floating inside, just what looked like two sticks with paper wrapped around them. It took Morgan a minute to realize he was looking at two scrolls. They looked identical. "Any idea what these are?"

"They're scrolls, but I don't know what might be on them. A skill? A title? I've heard the System conveys rewards through scrolls sometimes." Issa shrugged, and Morgan nodded, reaching into the box and picking up one of the scrolls. Issa grabbed the other.

"Nothing ventured, nothing gained," Morgan said, unrolling the scroll. The page was about a foot long and covered with symbols that didn't mean anything to him. He was staring at them, trying to figure them out when they started to move around on the page. Then they were flowing off the page and streaming into his eyes. It felt similar to when Energy entered his body, a sensation of warmth and a feeling like he understood something, and then he had a notification screen in his vision:

Congratulations! You have gained an upgrade to your level 10 Class selection.

MORGAN

"Did your scroll give you an upgrade to your class selection?" Morgan asked Issa after he'd waved the notification away.

"It did! I'm only level eight, but I'm very excited. All the fighting we've done and challenges we've overcome, plus this upgrade reward? I should have some interesting selection options! At least a lot more than most of my people who just level up to ten by hunting or training with masters." Issa was practically hopping with enthusiasm. "What about you? You must be ten by now! What options do you have?"

"I'll check it out in a minute," Morgan said. "Let's make sure we aren't going to get attacked again anytime soon, first." They were about a quarter of a mile from the unexplored end of the cavern, and Morgan wanted to check it out before he settled in to go over his status sheet and notifications. Issa agreed that it was a smart idea, and they continued up the cobbled road and its gradual rise to the second set of wide, smooth, stone steps. When they got to the base of the steps, the incline made it hard to see the cavern exit, but Morgan could just see the top of it and confirm that the portcullis that had appeared during the ambush was gone. "I don't remember hearing that portcullis open, did you?"

"No, but there was a lot of noise with the mother salamander exploding into a fountain of lava," Issa said with that unique growling, purr of a giggle that she made when she thought she said something funny.

Morgan laughed. "Good point!"

They hiked up the steps, frequently looking behind them at the enormous cavern but never seeing any other movement than the sluggish flow of the lava river and the bubbling pops of steaming gasses. When they got to the top of the steps, the cavern opening was clear, and they could see another smaller cavern with a spiral staircase situated at its back. These stairs were carved in stone and ascended into an opening in the rocky ceiling. Morgan looked around and listened to the silence, only occasionally hearing a distant hissing sound as a magma bubble burst in the river. "This looks like a good spot to rest and take stock of things." Issa nodded, sitting down and taking her usual meditation pose. She closed her eyes, and Morgan knew she was going over her attributes and using her cultivation technique to work on her Core. He knew he had to be close to finishing his quest to help her survive for a week, and he'd hopefully gain some sort of cultivation method to practice as well. He thought about it, and the System UI showed it to him again:

Quest: Don't let Issa die within 1 week (6/7). Reward: Energy Core Cultivation Manual (Improved), Improved Relations with Ardeni faction. Penalty for failure: Diminished Will efficacy—permanent.

Morgan smiled, dismissed the quest page, and called up his status sheet, just concentrating on his attributes:

Energy Affinity:	9.2	Energy:	240/240
Strength:	10	Vitality:	15 (17)
Dexterity:	8	Agility:	13
Intelligence:	20	Will:	10
Points Available:	20		

All right, time to see what he'd been working for over the last nightmarish week. He thought about Class selection, and a UI window with an arrow to page forward appeared, filled with information:

Level 10 Class selection. Class selection is permanent. Human Energy cultivators will next be offered a Class refinement selection at level 20. To view your options and make your selection, use the arrows to page through this interface.

That seemed straightforward enough—he'd be sort of stuck with whatever decision he made but could refine his class in a certain direction at level 20. Morgan wondered if there would be more "refinement" opportunities at even higher levels. He tapped the arrow, and the screen changed:

Class selection option 1: Scout—Basic. You use stealth and wit to maneuver through dangerous areas, able to spot danger and overcome challenging obstacles. Class attributes: Agility and Intelligence.

Morgan read the first selection and felt a little underwhelmed. On the one hand, he could see why the System was offering it to him; he'd been "scouting" from the moment he arrived in this world. On the other hand, it seemed pretty plain. He hit the arrow to move to the next screen:

Class selection option 2: Fighter—Basic. You use physical prowess to best your foes with remarkable feats of combat skill. Master weapons and your body to become a force that can change the tide of a battle. Class attributes: Strength, Agility, and Vitality.

He had to admit, "changing the tide of a battle" sounded great, but Morgan wasn't sure he liked pigeonholing himself into the role of something as mundane sounding as "Fighter." Maybe he was being shallow, though. Still, the arrow indicated more options, so he touched it again:

Class selection option 3: Spearmaster—Improved. Unparalleled grace with the spear is your hallmark; using the reach and versatility of the spear, you control the pace and tempo of the battle while perfecting your movements and strikes to deliver devastating strikes. Class attributes: Agility, Strength, and Dexterity.

Morgan noticed a couple of things about this option. It was the first that was classified as improved and, though it had the same class attributes as Fighter, it had them in a different order. Did that mean that these classes awarded differing values of their class attributes? He still had an arrow, indicating at least one more option, but he wanted to understand this better before he kept looking. "Hey, Issa, sorry to interrupt you, but can you answer a couple of questions?"

"I can try, but I've never picked a class." She smiled. "My instructors gave me some tips, though."

"One of my options, so far, is 'improved' and the others are 'basic.' What's the difference?"

"Oh, nice, an improved Class at level 10 isn't very common. The System curates classes for people based on many factors, and most people think that the different rarity of the classes has to do with meeting certain, unknown prerequisites. At least, they're unknown to us. I'm sure that on worlds with more experience with Energy and the System, there are factions that know what they need to do to be offered certain classes. Like, even my people know exactly how to get offered the Hunter class. Anyway, your improved Class probably has higher prerequisites than the Basic ones. I've heard that more highly ranked Classes offer you more skills and attributes, or maybe just better skills, but I've also heard that they are slower to advance."

"And what about the 'class attributes'? Does that have something to do with where I should put my points?"

"Not exactly. When you have a Class and gain a level, you might not get any, or as many, free attribute points to distribute. Your Class will determine where and how many points you get per level. Like how, every level, Hunters get three points of agility, one point in Intelligence, one point in Vitality, and two points in Dexterity." Morgan nodded. "Oh, one more thing; you know how you have some skills, and they say that they are 'basic'?"

"Yeah, like my Backstab skill."

"Right, well, skills can only move past basic if you have a Class that supports them and the Class is higher than basic."

"So, if I wanted to get better at Backstab, I'd need a Class that supports the skill, and it would need to be higher than basic?"

"Right, but keep in mind that even if you pick a basic Class now, you can refine it at level 20, and it will almost certainly become an improved class. You'll also get chances to refine your class at higher level thresholds as well."

"Huh, complicated. Alright, thanks," Morgan muttered, thinking. He reached up and pushed the arrow:

Class selection option 4: Assassin—Improved. You use stealth and deadly combat abilities to end fights before they can begin. Class attributes: Agility, Intelligence, and Dexterity.

Speak of the devil, Morgan thought. He was pretty sure this was the Class to choose if he wanted to keep working on his Backstab. He liked the Class description, but he didn't know how he felt about himself being an "Assassin"—something about it seemed out of character for him. Though he had to admit, he had made a habit of using his Backstab skill on a fairly regular basis. The arrow was still there, so he touched it:

Class selection option 5: Vortex Mage—Advanced. You work on perfecting and cultivating your Vortex Core to develop understanding and control over Energy and Space. Class attributes: Intelligence, Will, and Vitality.

Morgan couldn't help thinking that this Class choice seemed tailored to him. The System must have offered it because of his Vortex Core. When he read the description, his interest in the earlier options waned, and he almost selected it, but then he noticed that the arrow indicating another screen was still present. He touched the arrow:

Class selection option 6: Hollow Guard—Advanced. Protecting those weaker than you comes as second nature. You use your unique abilities to siphon the Energy of your foes while dominating them with your superior martial prowess. Class attributes: Strength, Will, Vitality, Intelligence, and Agility.

Morgan's mind raced with the possibilities he imagined after reading that description. The lack of an arrow indicated this was his final choice, making his decision a lot more difficult. He'd been sure that the Vortex Mage Class was the one for him, but now he was torn. Hollow Guard sounded very powerful, as well, and it seemed to award a lot more attribute points. He didn't know that, though—just because it listed more class attributes didn't mean it awarded more points overall. What if Vortex Mage gave twice as many points for its three attributes as Hollow Guard gave for its five. "Um, Issa, I need some advice."

"Oh? You must have some good choices, don't you? How exciting! That reward we just got must have really helped! I can't wait for my choices!" Issa blushed when she realized she was babbling. "Well, tell me about it!"

"Well, the System gave me two Advanced options, on top of the other ones, and they both seem great."

"What?" Issa jumped up. "Two Advanced Classes!" She walked around in a little circle, then plopped down in front of Morgan, smiling hugely. "This is great, Morgan! Only one person in my village has an Advanced Class, and she didn't get it until she completed her second refinement! Well, tell me about the options!"

"Well, they both seem to be pretty tailored to me. There's a Vortex Mage that focuses on utilizing my Vortex Core to 'understand and control Energy and Space.' Then there's the Hollow Guard, which says I can use my 'unique abilities to siphon Energy from my foes while dominating them with martial prowess,' but that's not what really excites me about it. It also says that protecting those weaker than me comes naturally."

"What are their Class attributes?" Issa asked, and Morgan told her. "Hmm, well, that is a tough choice."

"That's all you got for me?" Morgan laughed.

"No, no, hah, give me a chance. So, think about the names of the two Classes. One is a 'mage' type, and one is a 'guard' type. I'm pretty sure if you want to keep getting better with weapons, like that lovely spear, you will want to choose the 'guard' type Class. On the other hand, if you want to learn a lot more spells, the 'mage' type is the way to go. Not that the Hollow Guard Class won't come with interesting skills and spells, but I just know from the few 'mage' type cultivators in my village that they have a larger repertoire of spells than the Hunters and Soldiers, for instance."

"That's interesting," Morgan said, "but it doesn't mean I won't still be able to use my spear, right? I just won't be able to take my skill past basic."

"That's right, but it won't be your focus. There's no way your basic spear skill will ever hold up against a weapon user with improved, advanced, or even higher skill."

"There's higher than advanced?"

"Oh yes, if the rumors or legends are true. I've never met anyone like that, but the universe is a big place."

"Damn, tough choice," Morgan said, standing up and pacing around. What finally clinched it for him was the line about protecting others. He liked that idea. He liked it for lots of reasons, but the main one was that he'd always wished he'd been able to protect his sister when she got killed. Thinking about it, he realized it had become a part of his personality. He hadn't hesitated to accept the quest to help Issa, and he hadn't wanted to leave those people in the pit. It was the kind of person he was, and it might not always be wise, but he wanted to be that kind of person, regardless. Mind made up, he called up the Class selection menu again and scrolled to the Hollow Guard page, tapping on the "accept" button.

Congratulations! You have gained your first Class: Hollow Guard. Class skill gained: Energy Drain—Improved. Class skill gained: Guard Ally.

Congratulations! World-first Hollow Guard! Feat awarded.

Morgan laughed and shouted, "Yes!" Issa looked at him quizzically, and he explained, "I guess I'm the first Hollow Guard on this world."

"Well, that doesn't surprise me! I have never heard of your kind of Core, let alone a Hollow Guard." Morgan smiled and pulled up the information for his new skills:

Energy Drain—Improved: Prerequisite: Vortex Class Core. You expend some Energy to forcefully pull the Energy from a foe you or your weapon is in physical contact with, using that Energy to restore your health and vitality. Energy cost: 75, Cooldown: Medium.

Guard Ally—Basic: You expend some Energy to create a barrier around a nearby ally for up to five minutes, transferring damage they take to yourself at a ratio of 2:1. Energy cost: 100, Cooldown: Long.

Morgan was happy with those new skills. His Energy Drain skill had gone up in cost, but now he could use his weapon to initiate the drain, and he could do it more often. Guard Ally seemed great, also; he'd be able to protect Issa or anyone else and only receive half the damage they would have taken. Thinking about taking damage for someone else made Morgan realize he hadn't been focusing on his vitality enough. He also needed more Energy to use his skills, and with that in mind, he took another look at his status screen, scanning for changes. His new class was listed, and he saw his new feat listed under "Titles and Feats," so he pulled up that page to see what it did:

Human Champion: Transient title. Energy efficacy enhanced 1.5x. More frequent access to System generated Opportunities for Refinement.

First Hollow Guard: Feat granted: Guardian's Senses—concentrate on an ally or ward to have an innate understanding of their direction and distance from you, so long as they are on the same world.

Morgan could imagine endless possibilities for that ability to come in use, and, though he doubted the benevolence of the System, he once again silently celebrated being the first to get this Class. Looking over his stats, he decided to put three points into intelligence, five points into vitality, five points into will, two points into agility, and five points into strength. Feeling the almost imperceptible sensation of wellness flow through his body, he took a look at his newly updated status page.

He felt a real sense of progress and was glad to see that his maximum Energy had improved when he increased his intelligence and will. "Well, do I look different?" Morgan laughed, striking a combat pose in front of Issa.

"Yes! You look like that big lizard hit you in the head one too many times!" She laughed, throwing a hunk of dry bread at him. "Let's take a rest before we see what's up those stairs."

Status			
Name:	Morgan Hall		
Race:	Human - Base 2		
Class:	Hollow Guard – Advanced		
Level:	10		
Core:	Vortex Class - Base 1		
Energy Affinity:	9.2	Energy:	240/299
Strength:	15	Vitality:	20 (22)
Dexterity:	8	Agility:	15
Intelligence:	23	Will:	15
Points Available:	0		
Titles & Feats:	Human Champion, First Hollow Guard		
Skills:	System Language Integration - Not Upgradeable, Spear Mastery - Basic, Dagger Mastery - Basic, Stealthy Maneuvers - Basic, Backstab - Basic, Energy Drain - Improved, Guard Ally - Basic		

BRONWYN

Needless to say, the forge's construction, or rather unearthing, caused quite a stir and drew a large crowd. Bronwyn and Arthur were the first to enter, though they didn't try to stop the curious onlookers who followed them into the structure to see what was going on. The building was a proper blacksmithing forge, complete with a massive, open furnace along one wall with a chain and pulley-operated bellows system. In front of the furnace were three separate forging stations with large and small anvils, racks of variously sized hammers, and quenching barrels. The back half of the shop was a storeroom, and it was stocked with dozens of bags of coal and several large crates of iron ingots. It seemed the System didn't deem this reward worthy of any more rare metals than that. Near the forges, and sharing their chimney system, was a big, round kiln-looking thing that Arthur guessed was a smelter; it seemed the System really had provided a full-service forge, or at least enough of one to get the colony started in the right direction.

"Well, do you think you can find some engineers with the background to make heads or tails of this stuff?" Bronwyn asked Arthur after they'd looked around for a few minutes.

"I think so. It's not exactly modern technology, but the principles aren't foreign to engineers chosen for the Pioneer missions. Not to mention the System seems to like to put information into people's heads as they learn new things. Have you noticed that?"

"Yeah, I sure have. I learned how to track and read the Energy in footprints by following around those Yeksa yesterday." Bronwyn was beginning to warm up to Arthur now that he wasn't trying to pin all their troubles on her.

"Yeksa?"

"Yeah, those little gray men. The System labeled their tracks, so I learned what they're called." Bronwyn shrugged.

"Interesting. That could be very useful. Do you think others can learn that skill?" Arthur frowned in thought, scratching at his chin.

"I don't know why not. Hey, can you take care of things for a while? Speaking of Yeksa, I have a pretty lucrative 'quest' to find out where they came from. I guess the encampment I wiped out wasn't their source."

"Yes, yes. Of course. Perhaps you should take someone with you?"

"Well, I had planned to go alone. Let me think about it." Bronwyn reached up to her shoulder to scratch the little furry head of Hops. He'd nestled under her hair, which she hadn't tied up yet. He nudged into her hand with his head, obviously enjoying the scratch. Arthur saw what she was doing and recoiled slightly. "Relax. It's just a friendly little squirrel-type animal. Anyway, I don't think I'll take anyone right now. It's just a scouting mission. I'll be back before night, whether I figure it out or not.

"Very well. We should have a meeting upon your return."

"Ugh, another meeting, huh? Alright, but you're doing a good job at convincing me that we need to have an election sooner rather than later." Arthur just smiled at that, and Bronwyn walked out of the building, noting that the crowd had grown. She waved as a few people called out her name or just said hello, and then she started to jog toward the western tree line.

When she was clear of the grassy meadow and into the first few trees, she ran a bit north until she picked up the trail she'd used to hunt the Yeksa the day before. As she started running along the path following her own prints because the older Yeksa prints had lost their Energy luminosity, she felt Hops leap off her shoulder and into a nearby tree. "Hey! Well, see you later, I guess!" Hops squeaked, and she imagined he was reassuring her that he'd be back soon; she chuckled at that idea.

The rest of the morning and into the afternoon, she retraced her steps to the ruined Yeksa camp and followed various, faint Yeksa tracks through poorly defined paths and game trails in the nearby woods. The camp itself hadn't changed since she had last been there, other than the smell—it had gotten immeasurably worse as the corpses began to rot, forcing Bronwyn to hold a sleeve over her nose and mouth as she hunted for trails leading out of the area. She noted that many of the corpses were far less complete than she left them, apparently being used as a pantry of sorts by the local wildlife. She pondered piling the bodies and trying to burn them but felt that the camp was far enough away from the meadow that she could let nature take its course.

It wasn't until the sun was well on its way toward the western horizon that Bronwyn found a clear, heavily traversed trail several miles north and west of the Yeksa camp. The prints were still quite faint, but there were a lot of them, and the underbrush was well-trampled and even cleared away from the path in many areas. She noted an occasional primitive talisman hanging from branches along the trail. They looked like little rodent skulls hung from leather cords and decorated with colorful beads and stones. She detached one and slipped it into her pouch for later study. She felt a slight chill and wondered if she was being superstitious but suddenly regretted taking the little charm. The trees were very dense here, and she occasionally heard rustling sounds, but they sounded like small animals or birds hopping among the leaves, or so she reasoned in order to keep her sanity.

She followed the trail for about twenty minutes, and then she noticed that she was climbing a bit of a rocky slope. Looking ahead, she could see more and larger rocks and outcroppings, and she realized this was some sort of large hillock in the midst of the forest. She began to move more carefully, flitting from tree trunk to tree trunk and not walking in the middle of the path. After a time, she saw that the path curved to the left around a large, jutting spar of rock. She stopped for a while and listened. Mostly, she heard the wind rustling the leaves high up in the boughs of the big trees nearby. She heard birds making song and the far-off tinkling melody of a stream splashing down its stony path. Bronwyn felt surprisingly at ease, and, rather than being nervous about nearby enemies, she reveled in the unadulterated beauty of the forest she was surrounded by. Shaking herself out of her reverie, she carefully crept up to the rocky spar and then peered around the side, holding herself close to the stone. The faintly glowing footprints led around the rock and straight into the hillside, where the dark maw of an apparently natural cave opened into darkness.

*****Congratulations! You have completed a Quest: Track the invading Yeksa to their origin and scout the vicinity. Return to the Colony Stone to claim your reward.*****

"Well, that wasn't so hard," Bronwyn said, moving back around the spar of rock and using a dead branch to carve a large X into the hillside. She briefly contemplated exploring the cave but decided that she should wait for a couple of reasons: one, she wanted to make sure she had the time and supplies for a protracted cave delve, and, two, she wondered if the System would offer her a quest involving the cave. She saw no sense doing things for free if the System would foot the bill. She wanted to make sure that if something happened to her, the other colonists would be able to find this cave. Keeping that in mind, Bronwyn retraced her steps back toward the colony, marking trees with X marks, visible from two directions, the entire way. Even knowing the path and making good time, it was starting to get dark when she finally trotted into the meadow.

Bronwyn kept her head down and didn't talk to anyone, trying to hurry to the Colony Stone before she got bogged down in another conversation or crisis. Perhaps it was the waning light, or perhaps it was because everyone was busy, but she got to the stone without anyone bothering her. She hustled up the hill and slapped her hand against the stone, ignoring the other two people who were standing nearby, staring into space with their hands also on the flat, cool surface.

The System automatically awarded her the promised contribution points, and she checked the colony menus to see that her contribution points were mirrored as System Credits in the colony bank. She was surprised to see that the colony already had over six thousand System Credits. Apparently, she wasn't the only one to complete a task that day. She supposed it made sense—if a significant number of the thousands of colonists spent the day forging Energy beads, the numbers would add up quickly. More and more colonists were finishing the orientation lessons and learning how to channel Energy. True, they were extremely limited until they learned to form a Core and pathways, but Bronwyn knew she wasn't the only one the System had awarded with a Core stone. If rumors were to be believed, Olivia Bennet had been given some kind of rare multi-element Core.

If all went well, they'd have their walls tomorrow, and then they could start thinking about some housing structures, storage facilities, and maybe a bathhouse. Bronwyn stopped that train of thought before she began to spiral into musings of sewage systems, irrigation, and greenhouses. Enough time to worry about those things as the colony became more secure and people started to fill roles that would lessen the need for executive decisions. She sighed, feeling a weight lifting that she hadn't realized had been there the whole time. She turned her back to the stone and allowed herself to slide down until she was sitting on the soft grass, leaning back against it. She shut her eyes, relaxing and waiting for the inevitable moment when the three ersatz council members would find her.

She hadn't intended to doze off, and she probably wasn't really asleep so much as just barely awake when she heard Olivia's voice: "Bronwyn. Bronwyn, are you awake?" She had a gentle way of speaking that was easy on the ears, and for a minute, Bronwyn thought she was somewhere else, but then her eyes snapped open, and she remembered herself. She smiled up at Olivia and was happy to see that she was unaccompanied.

"Oh, hey Olivia. I was just resting my eyes while I waited for you guys."

"Mmhmm, I don't blame you. You've had a wild couple of days. Dr. Kerns filled me in on your little escapade into the forest yesterday morning."

Bronwyn didn't quite understand why, but she felt her cheeks start to flush, so she looked down and grunted something noncommittal while she clambered to her feet. "Uh, well, where are the old guys?"

"Oh dear, I hope they don't hear you labeling them that way!" Olivia laughed, and her blue eyes scrunched up, giving truth to the emotion.

Bronwyn laughed in turn, and the relief of the small nap and the laughter did wonders for her mood. She didn't even frown when Arthur strode up the hill. "Hey, Arthur. How are things?"

"Oh, hello, ladies. I'm glad to see you sharing a moment of levity. Perhaps it's something you could share?" The two young women looked at each other, and Bronwyn raised an eyebrow. Olivia stifled a laugh and looked down, shaking her head.

"No, no. It's nothing, really . . ." Olivia started to say, but then Bronwyn stepped in:

"Actually, I was telling Olivia about how we almost have enough System Credits for the wall already. I don't think most new settlements in the System-controlled worlds start out with five thousand members. We should be able to start accumulating credits pretty quickly as more and more people finish the tutorial."

"Ah, that's wonderful news! Yes, I have located a few of our civil engineers, and they are currently using a plot of cleared soil near the forge to draw a potential layout for upcoming town structures. Most agree that after the wall is constructed, we need to see to immediate survival needs: water, food, shelter." As Arthur spoke, Kerns nodded along.

"Yes, Arthur, I wanted to bring up shelter. I think, depending on the options available, we should award homes to individuals and groups that earn the most points in the Contribution Store," Kerns said, clearing his throat.

"What? Surely everyone should be housed!"

"Yes, of course, but we won't be able to build individual houses for everyone right away. I mean to say, as we can afford them, the priority should be to house the largest contributors. It will incentivize productivity!"

"Actually, that makes sense," Bronwyn interjected. "I had wondered what the point of a leaderboard was when I noticed it in the store menu."

"You know, I was never a fan of utilitarian styles of governance, but with the contribution system in place, it's hard for people to slack off and advance in this society without merit, one of the shortcomings of governing systems in the past," Arthur mused.

"Well, it doesn't solve everything. Just because we have a merit system does not mean we'll be able to be completely hands-off in our leadership. I foresee something of a hybrid governing style, with some elected council making large community decisions and the contribution system handling day-to-day recompense and incentives," Olivia interjected.

"I'll agree that the System isn't going to make life easy for slackers, but let's not get ahead of ourselves debating about governing ideologies right now," Bronwyn said, trying to head off a lengthy academic debate. "Anyway, I found the source of the Yeksa. There's some kind of a cave system a few miles into the forest to the east. I think we should explore it and maybe head off a future invasion. I'd like to spend a couple of days here, first, getting the town secured and establishing a standing guard for the wall once it's up."

"Yes, actually, I was going to ask you, Bronwyn, have you forged any Energy beads yet?" Olivia asked.

"Uh, no, not yet. I was pretty busy today finding that cave," Bronwyn said flatly.

"Relax, I'm not casting aspersions. I asked because I noticed those marks on your arms—you've developed channels already, haven't you?" The two men looked at Bronwyn's arms as Olivia spoke, and Bronwyn folded them across her chest self-consciously.

"Yeah, I have. It hurt like hell, too." She glanced down at her arms as she spoke.

"Oh, well, that's exciting! I can tell you have very wide channels! I bet you can form Energy beads a lot faster than most of us. You should give it a try." Olivia reached out a hand to lightly trace one of the dark channel marks on Bronwyn's left arm. Bronwyn suppressed an urge to pull away, not seeing any malice in Olivia's facial expression. She shrugged and nodded at Olivia.

"Alright, I'll give that a try tomorrow; I'm sure with everyone contributing, we should be able to get things started with the wall."

"Excuse me?" A new voice spoke up from just a few feet away. Bronwyn looked to her right and saw the woman who had offered to teach her a recipe the night before. "My name is Maria Rios. My friends and I would like to invite you four to our fire for dinner tonight."

BRONWYN

Bronwyn spent the next few days alternating between exhausted, amazed, and feeling anxiety-ridden. She was exhausted because she worked hard every day from pitch-dark-morning until late in the evening. She was amazed because of how things were taking shape: they'd constructed the wall and several dozen housing units that looked to Bronwyn like the base housing she'd lived in with her dad as a little girl. She was anxiety-ridden because, in the back of her mind, she was aware of the quest the System had given her to clear out the Yeksa cave, and she knew she needed to get going on it.

Quest: Explore the cavern from which the Yeksa emerged. Contend with the evil that lies within. Accept? YES/NO

Something about the wording really bothered Bronwyn: the System was labeling something as "evil," and it didn't seem to be referring directly to the Yeksa. It was ominous, foreboding; she could think of a dozen more adjectives, but it didn't change the fact that it worried her, and she'd put off going for three days now.

Just like with the forge, the wall and the houses had taken shape directly out of the ground. Unlike the forge, though, they were made from packed earth or clay bricks. The wall hadn't required any additional materials—its entire structure was made from the bricks, from the ramparts to the stairs leading up to them. Yes, the wall had ramparts; it was positively huge, ten feet wide, with an open archway leading in each cardinal direction, and it was imposingly high, rising just past thirty feet at the crenellations. The packed clay bricks seemed very sturdy, and at such a depth, the wall would take a tremendous amount of punishment before coming down. For now, they didn't have any sort of gates in the archways, but two people could easily maintain a watch at each one.

The houses had required lumber before the System would allow for their purchase. Luckily, the contribution store sold axes and saws and offered quests to many colonists to cut trees and gather wood into stacks. Once the colonists had collected enough lumber, Bronwyn had made the purchase for the first twenty houses, and they'd risen in the designated area along the southern wall of the colony. They'd stacked lumber in the plots beforehand, and when the buildings rose, clouds of yellow Energy and smoke erupted around the lumber, and as the pyrotechnics cleared, square dwellings built from clay bricks and roofed and shuttered in wood were standing, ready to be lived in. Each home boasted a living area with arched wooden beams, a small kitchen with wooden cabinets and countertops, and three bedrooms. They were not furnished, but budding artisans were helping to remedy that, and people were free to spend contribution points on furnishings purchased from the System.

Since that first housing purchase, they'd constructed two more rows of twenty homes. Doing the math, Bronwyn knew it would take a long time, and they'd probably run out of space before they housed every colonist this way. She'd spoken with Olivia and Arthur about the situation, and they'd agreed that the next purchase would have to be larger dormitory-style buildings. They required thousands more System Credits and a lot more lumber, but they each could house five hundred individuals. There were also larger, more sophisticated housing options, which they would surely strive for down the road, awarding the best houses to the highest contributors on the leaderboard.

As the days had passed, nearly everyone had finished the tutorial and contributed to the pool of System Credits the colony had. Aside from a few sour grapes, everyone felt incentivized to participate because, after the orientation, there were no free meals. If you wanted something fresh to eat, you had to buy it from the Contribution Store or find it in the wilderness. In addition to that, people wanted to buy weapons, and clothing, and tools, and supplies. Bronwyn wondered how difficult it would have been to get started without the Colony Stone, but following that thought was a recollection of what Olivia had said: the System was a parasite. It wanted them to live and gather Energy for it. It wanted them to become stronger so that they could generate more Energy. It made sense to Bronwyn, and she no longer thought of the System as benevolent. Still, they'd have to use it until they got their footing. That last thought made Bronwyn think of what an addict might say, and she worried that they'd never break free from the System.

During any downtime she'd had, partially to keep her mind off of her looming quest, she'd taken Olivia's advice and learned to channel Energy into physical beads. Olivia had been correct: she was able to make an attuned earth Energy bead in just about two hours. Someone without pathways took closer to twelve. Olivia had a "base 2" Core, but it was unique among the colonists—a "Prisma Core." She'd also developed pathways in her body but had gone through a much different process than Bronwyn. She hadn't been awarded any nodes, so she had to create her pathways from scratch, following a manual she bought from the Contribution Store. It had taken her a couple of full days of work. Even so, with her specialty Core and new pathways, she couldn't channel as much direct Energy as Bronwyn; it took her almost three hours to make a bead. However, one thing that she had over Bronwyn was her ability to choose to make attuned beads for fire, water, air, or earth.

As the third day of building wound down, Bronwyn found herself standing on the hill next to the Colony Stone, looking out over the settlement. The walls were truly impressive; immense earthen bulwarks that encompassed four square miles of grassland. The forge was still the only building near the hilltop, but, off in the distance to the south, she could see the neat rows of housing taking shape in the southwest corner of the walled-in meadow. Tents still dominated the central portion of the field, and Bronwyn could see that dirt paths were forming along major thoroughfares. If there was a rainy season, and with so much plant life nearby, she imagined there must be, they'd have a real mud problem. She sighed, mentally adding roads to her checklist.

"Penny, or Credit for your thoughts?" Olivia had walked up behind her, smiling at her attempt at humor.

"Yeah, I guess we'll have to explain mythical pennies to our children someday, huh?"

"Children? Getting a bit ahead of yourself, aren't you?" Olivia teased, arching an eyebrow.

"Yeah, I suppose. Lord knows if I'll be alive long enough for kids, let alone breakfast tomorrow." She realized how grouchy she sounded and tried to soften the words with a bit of a smile.

"Oh, my! Come now, it hasn't been that bad since that first attack. If you go by percentages, we've got an outstanding survival rate these last few days. We have the wall now, too." Olivia gestured to the imposing structure.

"Yeah, but there's more to this world than what we've seen so far. Don't you remember, during the tutorial, when the System warned us not to 'grow dependent on tech,' how it mentioned hostile Energy users, multiple universes, strength through conflict, and a hundred other rather foreboding hints?" Bronwyn kicked one foot along the ground, scuffing her leather boot heel along some rough gravel.

"Hmm, yes. I understand you have a quest that you've been putting off, also." Olivia moved around in front of Bronwyn, so she had to look at her.

"What the hell? Arthur is talking about my quests and whether I'm doing them behind my back? I knew I shouldn't have mentioned it to him!" Bronwyn's feigned outrage didn't fool Olivia.

"Come on. You know Arthur. He's doing his level best to keep a finger in every pot in the entire colony. What's the deal with the quest? I can see you're bothered about it." Olivia stretched out her arm, reaching for Bronwyn's wrist.

"Fuck yeah, I'm bothered. The System has asked me to climb into a deep-ass cave in the middle of the forest and 'contend with the evil that lies within.'

What the fuck?" Bronwyn hadn't meant to get so worked up, but she felt the pressure that she'd put on hold for days starting to boil over. She yanked her arm back from Olivia and began to turn.

"Woah, hang on, Bronwyn! I can see why that bothers you. Think about it—the System implies that it has some kind of moral code by calling whatever is in that cave 'evil.' It's also scary as hell sounding. We'll need to bring a few people with us, don't you think?"

"What? Fuck no, Olivia! Do you even know how to fight? You're a scientist!" Bronwyn had turned around, startled out of her intent to storm off by Olivia's statement.

"Well, not per se, but I have purchased a couple of offensive spells from the Contribution Store. They seemed rather devastating to the shrub I attacked," Olivia replied, again stepping close to Bronwyn and looking up to her face, forcing eye contact. "You aren't alone. You don't need to take on the burden of defending the colony single-handedly. No one signed up for what we're dealing with, not even you."

Bronwyn let out an explosive sigh and said, "I don't want to risk other people's lives." Her words were true, she knew that, but she could tell that a sliver of doubt had entered her mind—she *wanted* help.

"I know you don't, Bronwyn. You can't stop people from doing what they feel a duty to do, right? I can't stop you, and you can't stop me. And other people want to help. It would be wrong to stop them, right?"

"I guess so," Bronwyn replied quietly. She felt like tearing up suddenly, and she wasn't sure why. Maybe it was because Olivia was being kind to her, or maybe it was because she felt relief at not holding onto the dread of this quest by herself. Maybe it was because she still felt guilty about the people who had died when the barrier around the meadow came down. She blew out a breath and turned to rub the back of her hand at her eyes. Olivia smiled and rested a hand on her shoulder, gently urging her down the hill.

"C'mon, Bron, there are a few people I'd like to introduce you to." Bronwyn allowed herself to be led around to various campsites, where Olivia introduced her to some people who had expressed an interest in exploring and defending the colony. Bronwyn wasn't surprised that Olivia knew so many people. She was extremely outgoing and very famous among the colonists. However, she was surprised that so many people were eager to delve into the Yeksa cave with her.

After meeting with a baker's dozen possible recruits, they settled on three people to bring with them into the cave the next day. The first was a large man named Martin Hoyle, who demonstrated an astonishing ability to smash the ground with a large club, causing a fissure six inches wide to split the earth for several strides. He claimed he could elicit a similar response in anything he struck with his skill which he said was called "Earth Cracker." Their next recruit was a tall, very dark-skinned woman named Maya Hollister. She had spent the last few days completing gathering quests for the Contribution Store and had used her points to buy a broad-bladed hatchet and a round shield. She was an imposing woman, taller even than Bronwyn, and insisted she knew what to do in a fight. Their final teammate was a thin, bald Bostonian named Emmet O'Brien. They chose him because he claimed to have a skill that allowed him to see in the dark and because he wasn't dissuaded when Bronwyn described the Yeksa Shaman she'd fought.

The five companions agreed to meet by the western gateway at first light. Bronwyn said goodnight to Olivia and then began walking to her tent to sleep. She could have easily claimed one of the houses, but then she'd have to share it with other people, and she didn't mind sleeping under the stars, especially now that they had a wall and an established guard rotation. She was off for the night, so she intended to get plenty of sleep before heading into the cave the next day.

She made a quick detour to visit the latrines that some of the engineering personnel had constructed. They were mainly just holes in the ground near the eastern wall, over which they'd built crude wooden benches and outhouses. The volunteers had built them with green lumber and rough iron nails that the new forge workers had made in the last couple of days; the whole affair was decidedly temporary. Bronwyn mentally moved bathhouses and sewage infrastructure up the checklist of colony upgrades as she finished up and continued to her tent.

For the first time in days, she took off her armor, boots, and gauntlets before crawling into the little nest of wool-like blankets the System had provided during the orientation. She stretched out on her back and listened to the sounds of the colony falling asleep around her: low murmurs and laughter coming from a nearby campfire, the occasional steps of someone walking nearby through the grass, and the strange chirps of cricket-like insects. The omnipresent smell of woodsmoke was becoming somehow comforting to her, and she found her eyelids heavy before she could even begin to worry about what the next day would bring.

MORGAN

Morgan pulled some animal skins out of his pouch and sat down on them. As he choked down some of the dry bread with generous amounts of water, he looked at Issa. She was sitting cross-legged in front of him, also crunching on the bread. It looked funny how she crunched the bread in the back of her mouth because she had a lot more sharp teeth than a human. He couldn't help smiling, watching her scrunched-up face. She saw him smiling and stopped chewing. "What?"

"Nothing, nothing." Morgan laughed.

"Seriously, what? Are you laughing at me?" Issa narrowed her eyes, her amber irises becoming yellow slits as she started to growl.

"Hey, take it easy; I was just smiling because you looked cute eating that bread!"

"I looked CUTE?" Issa howled.

"Oh man"—Morgan laughed again, scooting away from her as she kicked a foot out like she was aiming at his knee—"c'mon, I didn't mean anything bad. I'm sure my face looks funny, choking this bread down, too."

"Oh! So now I look funny?" Issa huffed, her pale blue cheeks gaining a red hue as she stared.

"Ugh, no! Let's forget it, okay? Hey, I have a serious question: just how long is this damn Crucible? You'd think I would have asked that before, but I think the System is messing with my mind; I feel way too good considering the hell we've been through."

Issa's face relaxed, and she took on a thoughtful expression. "You might be feeling what my grandfather calls Energy euphoria. He said people noticed it a lot when Energy and the System first came to our world. As you make gains in Energy, you feel better, physically and mentally. If you don't make gains and start to stagnate, that feeling will slowly decline."

"Oh, so it might not be the System messing with my mind?"

"Maybe not. I'm not sure. I've never lived without Energy, so I don't know what that's like. Anyway, your other question: I don't know how long the

Crucible is. Some people say it depends on your level when you enter it. Some people who've made it out didn't think they were at the end—they came upon escape talismans or a reward that offered an exit." Issa shrugged, then took a bite of hard bread, staring at Morgan, daring him to laugh.

"I'm glad I found you, Issa," Morgan said, a genuine smile on his face. She harrumphed and chewed her bread, but Morgan could see a smile in her eyes. They decided to rest, and, as before, Morgan took first watch. Issa didn't sleep as long this time, and soon Morgan closed his eyes for his turn. He was pretty sure he was dreaming about swimming in the ocean when he was woken by a System message appearing in his vision.

Congratulations! You have completed a Quest: Don't let Issa die within 1 week (7/7). Reward: Energy Core Cultivation Manual (Improved), Improved Relations with Ardeni faction.

Seeing the screen while dreaming had jarred him awake, and he felt a bit grumpy as he wiped it aside, even though it was good news.

"Hey, you finished a quest? That box just formed next to you!" Issa said, excitedly pointing at a blue, rectangular box next to his furs. Morgan sat up and looked at it. The box had the same blue shade and silver writing on it as the others, but it was smaller—only about three inches high and about the shape and size of an old school textbook.

"I sure did. I finished my quest to save you and keep you alive for a week. You're welcome!" Morgan grinned at Issa, knowing he was about to set her off.

"Oh, sure! Sure, you did! Where's MY reward for saving your hide fifteen different times?" Issa growled.

"Hey, I'm not the System! I don't make the rules." Morgan laughed. "But seriously, I know it was a team effort so far, and if this reward is shareable, I'll share it!" Issa, seemingly placated, nodded and sat down by the box to watch. Morgan lifted the box and flipped open the thin lid. Inside, resting on the usual silky lining, were two scrolls. One was more than two inches thick. The other was very thin, almost like an old pencil. "Well, one of these will be my cultivation manual."

"Ah, that's right, you told me about that. Lucky! Hopefully, the scroll will remain after you learn it so that you can share it with your clan."

"Well, I don't know what the other scroll might be, so I'll look at the smaller one first," Morgan said, reaching into the box. Issa intently watched while he unrolled the thin scroll. The page was only about six inches long, and it had the usual, weird, System symbols all over it. Morgan stared at the characters, and, as before, they started to move around and then flood into his eyes.

Congratulations! You have earned the title: Ardeni Friend.

"What the . . ." Morgan started to say, then called up his Titles and Feats page, selecting the new title:

Ardeni Friend: Members of the Ardeni race will initially view you with less hostility, feeling a familiarity with you as they would a member of the Ardeni people.

"Issa, do I seem any different to you?" Morgan asked, concern in his tone.

"What? Not this again. No, Morgan, you didn't get taller or more handsome!"

"No! I'm serious! Really look at me. Do I seem different? Do you *feel* different when you see me?" Issa narrowed her eyes, but she did as he asked, really looking at him for a minute.

"No. You seem the same to me, sorry," was Issa's eventual response.

"Well, that's good. I got a new title, and its effect creeps me out. It says I'm an "Ardeni Friend" and that your people will view me with less hostility when we meet. I don't like the idea of the System messing with people's thoughts. I hate it," Morgan growled.

"The System uses Energy. It's more powerful than any cultivator I've ever heard of, by an immeasurable amount. The only thing we can do is accept it and hope that it is just. From my teachers, I've heard that philosophers believe the System works on Karmic principles, and fairness is its goal. I'd like to hope that if you meant harm to the Ardeni, the System would balance things by taking your title or changing it or giving you a different one." Morgan frowned, but he nodded. "In any case, Morgan, I consider that title earned, and it didn't affect me because I already see you as a friend." Issa smiled.

"Alright, well, as you said, it doesn't seem I can do anything about it." Morgan reached into the box and picked up the much larger, heavier scroll. He started to unroll it and realized it had a second scroll rod embedded in the larger, central scroll rod. As he pulled it out, the page expanded. It only opened about a foot, then stopped. Morgan could see that there was more scroll material but assumed there was a trick to unrolling it that he might learn when he studied this section, so he did just that; he stared at the page. He stared, and he stared. The minutes began to tick by, and Morgan noticed Issa shift her position, but he didn't look at her. He didn't want to break his concentration.

After what must have been five or ten minutes, Morgan saw the first of the symbols start to move. At first, he wasn't sure; he thought maybe his vision was blurring and that he was going cross-eyed. Soon, all of the symbols were swimming around, though, and a stream of them, railing silver-gold dust, began to flow toward his eyes. Shortly, a flood of them was pouring into his eyes, and he felt immense pressure and heat start to build up in his head, concepts flooded into his mind, and as he tried to think about each one, another would take its place, leaving him confused and grasping. The pressure continued to build, to the point where he thought he might be in danger, and just as he was starting to feel real panic, it began to subside. The flow of characters slowed to a crawl and then came to a stop, and he once again could see his surroundings. He realized he was on his back, staring up into Issa's grinning face. "That looked like a really big one!"

Congratulations! You have learned the skill Vortex Core Cultivation Drill—Basic.

Morgan thought about it and realized he did have a greater understanding of his Vortex Core now. He knew how to improve it through meditation and by focusing on absorbing and building specific pathways for Energy in his body. He realized he was still holding the scroll. The symbols that had flown off the page and into his eyes were back on the page, though they seemed slightly faded. He tried to pull more of the scroll out, but it wouldn't move. Issa was watching him closely and said, "It looks like this scroll can be used again, but I'm not sure how many more times—the symbols are fading. I bet when you master this first page, it will let you open more of the scroll."

Morgan grunted, sitting back up. "Uh, yeah, that makes sense. Man, I feel like I just woke up after drinking too much of cheap vodka," he groaned, cradling his head in his hands.

"That will fade; we can take an early break after we climb some steps," Issa said, reaching over and gently scratching Morgan's head. Her sharp nails felt nice on his stubble, where his cryo-sleep haircut was finally growing out. After a moment, Morgan and Issa got to their feet, stowed their furs and grabbed their weapons and lantern, and began the hike up the spiraling stone steps.

Soon, the warmth of the volcanic cavern was behind them, and they were climbing up dark, cool steps. These steps were of higher quality craftsmanship than the previous stairs they'd climbed. They had smooth marble pavers on the treads and were of perfectly regular height and size. The stairway itself was narrow, barely allowing the two of them to traverse it side by side, but the walls were constructed of uniformly sized, smooth grayish white marble bricks. Morgan assumed it was marble, anyway; it was smooth and cool to the touch.

Their climb ended much more quickly and abruptly than when they'd climbed to a new level previously. One minute they were rounding a turn in the stairwell, and the next, Morgan was setting his foot onto a smooth marble landing that opened up into a small, dark room, also walled in the same marble stone. Before he could react, he'd taken a step into the room, and a System message appeared:

Quest: Survive four challenges in the Marble Halls 0/4. Reward: One Improved Treasure Box, egress from the Crucible. Accept? YES/NO

"Oh, hell yes! Did you see that, Issa?" Morgan asked, trying to keep his voice down.

"Yes!" Issa replied happily, stepping up beside him.

"Starting to see some light at the end of the tunnel!"

"Where?" Issa asked, looking around the dark room.

"Doh! I guess not all idioms translate. I didn't mean it literally. Like, imagine being lost in the dark and seeing some light—you feel the end of your problem is coming up."

"Oh, sure! Like when we say 'the vine was long, but the branch is near.'" Morgan pondered her words, then nodded, smiling.

"Yeah, just like that." The room they were in was about ten square feet. The ceiling was a foot higher than Morgan's head, and all of it, walls, ceiling, floor, was made from the same white-gray marble. "I don't see a door, do you?"

"I was just about to say that," Issa said, walking toward a wall and running her fingers along it. Morgan did the same, going in the opposite direction. They met halfway along the wall farthest from the stairwell. "I didn't feel any seams, did you?"

"Nope." Morgan shook his head. They spent the next several minutes walking around the room again, knocking gently on the marble blocks with their knuckles. They didn't find any that sounded different than the others. "Maybe the floor," Morgan said, dropping to his hands and knees and crawling around, tapping on each marble tile. Issa nodded and followed suit. After a minute, even Morgan could hear it when Issa knocked on a hollow tile.

"Here!" They'd long since given up on any pretense of stealth, and she practically shouted with excitement. Morgan scrambled over to her and tapped on the big marble tile with one of his rusty daggers. It sounded hollow. The tile was about eighteen inches square, and Morgan and Issa tried pressing all along the edge. They even tried to jam daggers into the tiny gap around the edge, but they couldn't budge it. Finally, Morgan told Issa to stand back, and he pulled the mace he'd taken from the Yovashi lair out of his pouch. Lifting the heavy weapon high over his head, he brought it down with a crash onto the hollow-sounding tile. It shattered into hundreds of pieces, revealing a hollow space underneath it. In the tile-lined cavity was a brass-colored lever, just big enough that Morgan could wrap one hand around it.

"Nice job, Issa! Should we pull this lever?"

"I don't know, but I don't know what else we can do. Like you've said before, we can't go back the way we came."

"Alright, brace yourself. Morgan grasped the cool brass lever and pulled. It lifted easily, without much resistance, and a rumbling, scraping sound came from the far wall of the little room. They both looked up, just in time to see the entire wall was sinking into the floor. It revealed a long hallway, the same width as the room, lined in the same marble and lit from above by softly glowing white orbs every ten feet or so. The hallway stretched hundreds of feet into the distance. Standing about fifty feet into the hallway, a huge bipedal bear-like creature hunched to avoid hitting its head on the ceiling. Sideways in both clawed hands, the bear-man grasped a giant axe and wore bronze-colored greaves and vambraces. Otherwise, it was clad only in its thick, black fur.

Morgan scrambled to his feet, getting his spear ready, and the bear-man's dark eyes zeroed in on him. It lowered its head, opened its bearlike snout, and roared. The sound of the roar was deafening as it echoed in the marble hallway, and it went on for several seconds, saliva stringing out from the creature's mouth with the force of the bellow.

Morgan leveled his spear and walked to the hallway entrance. "Here we go again."

⚜ REGGIE ⚜

Reggie Arnold Gandry-Thule was a big man, and he liked having a big name. He stretched his big, thick arms over his head and yawned, kicking his legs to throw off the annoyingly scratchy blankets that the dumbass System had given him. He sat up and scooted, on his butt, out of his little tent. The morning was cool, dew was in the air, and he once again cursed the lack of showers in this place. So, the bigwigs had made a wall, yippee. What about a nice, hot damn shower? Reggie yawned, hugely, again, scratching his bushy red beard, then stood up in the grass. It was cold and squishy between his toes, and he frowned. "We should have a house by now." He pulled up the leaderboard for the Contribution Store:

Name:	Points:
1. Bronwyn Tallow	4230
2. Olivia Bennet	2120
3. Oscar Sandoval	1940
4. Maria Rios	1700
5. Boris Saltzki	1380
6. Tanya Delgado	1340
7. Alec Green	1100
8. Rene Bisset	900
9. Tina Bensen	880
10. Reggie Gandry-Thule	760

"Goddamn right! Top ten, baby." Reggie had gotten onto the top ten last night, and he was glad to see no one had usurped his position while he'd been asleep. He was still pissed that the System didn't put his full name on the list, though. "Get up, dipshits!" He yelled at the three tents sharing the firepit with him. Muffled grumbles accompanied by the shaking of the cloth tents informed him that they'd heard him and were moving. Good old Sam, Tony, and Robbie; they'd been working together for years, long before they got selected for the Arkship. What a joke—they were in-vitro technicians, and none of the fucking cryo-storage units or the damn eggs they contained had made it to the surface. "So, we're fucking useless, eh? Nah, we gonna get me to the top of the leaderboard. Wake the fuck up, you lazy bums!"

After a minute, Sam crawled out of his tent, bleary-eyed and frowning. Soon all four of them were sitting around the fire, Reggie having gotten it started back up. They had a good-size stack of wood; all of them had done "quests" to collect wood, and, after they deposited it for credit, they'd gone and taken a bunch of it for themselves, stacking it near their tents. "All right, boys; I have a plan for how we are gonna get me up that list. You heard the bigwig, Ballard—first place gets awarded the first big house. I'm gonna pick up all the quests I can; then we'll work as a team to get them done. After I get first place, we can take turns helping the rest of us to get up on the list. Make sense?"

"Aw, man. I really need some new shoes, and I'm sick of eating bread," Sam grumbled.

"Chill, brother! I'm going to get points for turning in these quests. I'll buy you guys the shit you need 'til we're done pumping up my score." No one else spoke up. Reggie wasn't sure it was because they agreed with him, or if they were afraid of him, or if they were just too tired and dumb to put up a fuss. "Get dressed and eat something. I'm going to pick up my quests."

Their tents were close to the hill with the Colony Stone, just about a hundred yards north of it. Not many people were on this side, and Reggie liked it like that. After he slipped his boots on, he stomped toward the hill and quickly climbed up, slapping his hand on the stone. He called up the Contribution Store and then the Quests menu:

Contribution Activities for Reggie Gandry-Thule:		
Task: Forge Energy beads.	10 contribution points per bead.	Accept? YES/NO
Task: Collect 1000 lbs of lumber	250 contribution points.	Accept? YES/NO

Task: Gather 100 mushrooms from surrounding woods.	100 contribution points.	Accept? YES/NO
Quest: Find an animal den west of the colony.	500 contribution points.	Accept? YES/NO

"Interesting!" Reggie hadn't seen a quest to find an animal den before. He accepted all of his tasks, except the dumbass Energy bead one, and then walked back to his buddies. "Alright, buds, we got some work to do."

Reggie split the jobs among his buddies: he would find the animal den, Sam and Tony would chop wood, and Robbie would pick mushrooms. Haha, what a goof; he laughed to himself every time he thought of Robbie rooting around under bushes and fallen logs looking for mushrooms. He wasn't fooling himself—their job had been easy enough that a twelve-year-old could do it. They each had been assigned to monitor a bank of cryo units that held five thousand fertilized eggs. The only tricky part of the job was making sure you didn't fall asleep and miss any sort of alert. Alerts that never happened as far as his experience in the business had gone. That being said, his buddies weren't exactly on the level of Olivia Bennet. That fucking babe was like Einstein compared to Robbie, so picking mushrooms was probably a good job for him.

Reggie strolled out the west gate while his boys worked on the grunt work. He'd bought a big wood-cutting axe the day before, so he walked with it resting on one shoulder, and he couldn't help the swagger that entered his stride. Reggie was a big man, and he had a big axe, and this was a world where that mattered. He smiled at the two dipshits guarding the gate, nodding his head as he strolled by into the woods. "So, some kind of animal den, eh?" He wandered around, wondering how he was supposed to find a den in a forest that seemed to spread out for dozens or hundreds of miles. He figured the System wouldn't give him a wild goose chase, so he started looking closely at the ground while he wandered, hoping to find some sign of an animal.

Congratulations! You have learned the skill Tracking—Basic.

"Oh sweet!" He called up his status sheet, admiring his beefy strength stat, much higher than any of his friends'. His fifteen vitality also left them in the dust. He flexed a couple of times, and almost dropped down to throw out some pushups to really get his pump on. Looking around the woods, though, he decided to leave it for later. His new tracking skill was listed along with his basic axe skill.

"Looking good, brother." He grunted and started to look at the ground using the new skill the System had given him. As he pushed himself through the underbrush, staring at the ground, he occasionally saw little glowing tracks with labels. He saw tiny tracks that said, "feyris." He followed those for a while, but then he saw bigger tracks that looked like glowing hoofmarks, and they said, "huldii." So, he started to follow those because he figured bigger was always better.

Reggie plodded along through the woods for nearly another hour, following the huldii tracks, then they crossed with some other hoofmarks that were even bigger, and the system just said, "Cadwalli." Reggie followed both sets of tracks for a few minutes, and then they seemed to spread out, crossing all over each other, and it was a bit of an anticlimactic surprise when a System message appeared:

Congratulations! You have completed the Quest: Find an animal den west of the colony. Return to the Colony Stone for your reward.

"Huh, what the hell?" The "Cadwalli" tracks he'd been following continued into a dense section of undergrowth, so he pressed forward, pulling the thorny bushes apart and peering within the hedge-like growth. He was startled to see a red-furred deer-like animal's corpse hanging from a tree branch by a rope.

"That'd be my lunch," a gruff voice said from right behind him. Reggie turned and just about shat himself when he saw the speaker. A wiry little man with brown skin and gray hair stood not three feet behind him. He wore a fringed leather vest and short pants, but what startled Reggie were his horns and the fact that his legs were furry and ended in hooves.

"What the fuck?" Reggie stepped back, holding his axe in front of his chest.

"You're feeling tired, sit down," the man said in his rough voice, and Reggie suddenly *did* feel tired. Wouldn't it be nice to sit down right here? He plopped down on his butt, his axe resting on his lap, entirely forgotten. "That's better, boyo; we've got some things to talk about."

⚔ MORGAN ⚔

Morgan had a reason for feeling some confidence facing the bearlike creature. Even though it was a lot larger than he and had a wicked-looking battleaxe to boot, Morgan looked at the creature's size and the axe and couldn't imagine it being able to swing it very effectively in the marble corridor. He turned to say something to Issa but couldn't see her. Hopefully, she was hiding in an attempt to catch the beast by surprise. Morgan strode forward toward the challenge, and as he took his second step into the corridor, the creature roared again and charged.

Morgan fell, instinctively, into a stance that he knew was best for receiving an enemy charge. He turned his hips sideways, with wide footing, and couched the spear lengthwise in front of him, with two hands, lowering his center of gravity. The enraged bear-man charged right into the spear, and to Morgan's dismay, it didn't bite very deeply. Instead, the barrel-chested charging creature drove it back, almost causing Morgan to lose his grip, and the beast swung his axe sideways with such force that Morgan swore he could see the air parting before the blade. He tried to dodge, but it was too fast. He pulled his body back, bending at the waist, and the axe tangled slightly in his loose black robes, before the blade connected with his chest, ripping an inch-deep channel through his pectorals and furrowing into his sternum. At the same time, he felt a sharp stinging sensation in his right hand and realized the stone ring of shielding had snapped, apparently taking more damage than it was capable of withstanding. Morgan cried out in pain, flung backward, and tumbled into the small room that housed the stairwell.

Morgan's chest was agony incarnate, but adrenaline allowed him to push the pain aside. He scrambled to his feet, rushing forward to grab up his spear, which he'd dropped in his tumble. Luckily the beast had stopped to roar again, clearly proud of its devastating attack. As he picked up his spear, he heard Issa's voice coming from his left-hand side: "Step closer, and I'll Haste you!" Morgan quickly sidestepped, keeping his spear pointed toward the bear-man. He glanced to the side and could just make out Issa's face from within the folds of her camouflage cloak. He moved slightly in front of her to shield her from the creature's view, and he felt her hand grab his arm above the elbow, and then his heart raced, his vision focused, and he was sprinting forward toward the beast.

He was a blur of movement, rushing side to side toward the bear-man, and as he came within range, he feinted with the spear toward its face. It instinctively brought its axe up high to block, but Morgan had already pulled the spear back and jammed it into the bear's waist, just above the greave on its right leg. Once again, the bear-man's thick fur and hide slowed the spear, so only a couple of inches bit in, but it was enough for Morgan to activate Energy Drain, and he did so as he rushed past the bear, trying to outflank it. He kept the spear planted while he ran past, pulling the handle sideways, opening the rip further while pulling Energy through the weapon and into himself. He felt a surge of primal Energy enter his body, forcing his ripped chest to begin to knit and his muscles to respond with greater speed and power.

As the bear roared in anger and pain, he yanked the spear out and punched it forward again, into the bear's side as it tried to turn to face him. The bear whipped its axe around, sideways, in a bid to remove Morgan's head, but Morgan, still hasted, was able to duck the blow, and using his low angle, drove the spear up inside the bear's guard and into its throat. The bear jerked backward, pulling free of the spear, and tried to roar in rage, but it came out more like a thunderous cough, spraying blood all over the marble hallway and Morgan. As the bear coughed and sputtered, its murderous eyes refocused on Morgan, and it lifted its axe. Just then, a shiny, thin blade sprouted from the bear-man's stomach. It looked startled for a second but then took a step and started to swing its axe. Morgan's first thought was that the swing was a bad one; it would miss him completely, but then he saw the bear's left leg pivot, and he knew it was going to spin with the axe and cut Issa in half. Morgan cried out and quickly focused on activating his Guard Ally ability.

He instantly felt a connection to Issa—it was hard to explain, but it was almost like he had a phantom arm wrapped around her. The bear-man spun with his axe, leaking blood from several terrible wounds, and the blade ripped into Issa's side. Or it would have, but a bright blue flash erupted from the point of impact and, instead of Issa being hit, Morgan felt a terrible pressure on his own side, and he was knocked into the corridor wall. The phantom blade had hit him right where his girdle covered his waist. The blade had bitten into the leather and cut him slightly, but most of the impact had been mitigated by his Guard Ally ability and the sturdy leather. In fact, it hurt more hitting the marble wall than being hit by the axe.

Issa had a shocked look on her face like she didn't know why she was still breathing, but she recovered quickly and danced backward away from the bearman. Morgan took the opportunity to jump forward, jamming his spear into the creature's back. Instinctively he activated Backstab, and he felt the tip bite much more deeply than any of his other attacks, and the bear creature moaned its last, foamy breath and collapsed in a heap.

Issa walked around the big corpse, over to Morgan, and hugged him as the motes of golden Energy coalesced and surged into them both. Issa pushed back from him and smiled, saying, "I leveled!"

"I didn't, but you have some catching up to do anyway. What level is that for you?"

"Nine! One more to select my class!" Issa walked over to the bear and extricated her rapier from its back. "What a tough beast! I've never seen its like. How did you save me from that blow? I was sure I was dead!"

"It's one of my class abilities. I can guard an ally and take the damage intended for them. It seems pretty great."

"That's a fantastic skill, and it suits you! I'm glad you chose the class you did, Morgan."

"Yeah, but you never know, that other class might have had a similarly great skill."

"Yes, but better to count the feyris in your larder than the ones in the branches." Issa grinned.

"Feyris?"

"You don't have feyris on your world? Small game animals? Tasty in a stew?" Issa licked her lips.

"Huh, I guess not. We have a similar idiom, though: a bird in the hand is worth two in the bush," Morgan said, while he walked over to the corpse.

"Oh, we have one just like that; most of my people are hunters." She stepped to the side while Morgan struggled to pull the greaves and vambraces off the big bear-man. "I don't think those will fit you, Morgan."

"Well, maybe not, but they're the first decent-looking armor I've found in this place. I'm going to take them."

"Actually, Morgan, look, they have Artificer marks on them. Try bonding with one of the bracers." Morgan dropped the greave he was trying to pull off the corpse and picked up one of the vambraces. Sure enough, some strange marks were lining the outer edge of the bronze-colored metal. He pulled it on, over his left arm. The vambraces were solid metal cones with soft fur lining meant to cover the entire forearm. On him, it engulfed his whole arm, leaving far too much space inside. It was like a little kid trying to wear his dad's shoes. Still, Morgan held it in place while he trickled some of his Energy into the metal. The bronze piece of armor flashed briefly then quickly constricted to fit his arm perfectly.

"Oh, hell yes!" Morgan enthusiastically repeated the process with the other vambrace, then went back to work on the greaves with Issa lending a hand.

After a few minutes, Morgan was walking around with his arms and legs armored in very sturdy, apparently magical armor. The greaves covered the tops of his feet, his shins and had hinged pieces that extended over his knees. Whatever Artificer magic allowed them to adjust to his size made them fit better than Morgan could imagine any mundane armor would. Though the metal was thick, it wasn't much of a hindrance to his movement. He figured his much-improved strength was part of that equation. "Not bad, eh?" He grinned at Issa.

"It looks very sturdy, and I'd much rather for you to have it than that beastman!" Issa shuddered.

"Well, you take that axe. It looks good, but I like my spear. Maybe you can trade it when you get home." Issa walked over to the axe and lifted its handle. It was nearly as tall as she was with the head resting on the ground. She shrugged and gestured toward her dimensional pouch with the handle, and it disappeared.

"Got it!"

"Well, shall we see what's down this hallway? I definitely underestimated that bear guy's ability to swing that axe in here, so if you think I'm doing something stupid, please speak up!"

"I will, but I didn't think he'd be that fast, either." Issa and Morgan began to walk down the marble hallway, and after just a minute of walking, an end came into view. The hallway continued smoothly, with no interruptions, up to a smooth wall. In front of the wall was a statue of a person, but not a human. From where they stood, Morgan couldn't make out its features, but it had a head that was too large for its body and very short arms and legs. Morgan was pretty sure it was a statue because it looked like it was made from the same marble as the hallway, affixed to a pedestal about three feet high.

"That's a statue, right?" Morgan arched an eyebrow as he asked, shrugging at the need to confirm something seemingly obvious.

"It looks like one." Issa dragged out the word "looks," casting doubt on her certainty. The two of them continued cautiously, and as they got within ten feet or so, they stopped. The marble statue was very finely carved, with many little details. The creature depicted was about three feet tall, so the whole thing, including the pedestal, was nearly as tall as Morgan. The little marble man had very short legs and arms, a short, rotund body, and had a head almost as large as his body, with fat, cherubic cheeks, and curly marble hair, modeled in exquisitely fine detail. The little man was clad only in a skirt of finely carved marble leaves. "Such detail!" Issa exclaimed quietly, walking forward another step.

"Thank you!" The little cherubic man tilted his head toward Morgan and Issa and spoke with a high, slightly unnatural voice, almost like how a person sounded on an intercom back on the Arkship. Other than his head tilting and his lips moving, nothing about the man moved.

"Oh, hello," Issa said, glancing at Morgan and raising her bright yellow eyebrow.

"Hello, indeed!" The man said cheerily.

Morgan stepped forward. "Ahem, I'm Morgan, and this is Issa. We're trying to get through the Crucible. Can you offer any aid?"

"Oh my! We've only just met, and you are asking for help? My name is Takamennion, and I have a job to do. As it so happens, my job involves helping you, to some degree." The statue came to life, briefly, to bow as it spoke, but then it straightened up and was completely still.

"Thank you, uh, sir?" Morgan said, moving up in front of the statue with Issa.

"You are quite welcome; however, the appropriate honorific for me is Magus," the little marble man said, affecting a bit of a long-suffering smile while widening its marble eyes. The rest of the statue was utterly motionless.

"My apologies, Magus. Might I inquire as to how you are meant to aid us?" Morgan decided to play it safe and be polite, having been attacked by nearly every being he'd met in the Crucible.

"Of course, of course. As part of my debt to the System, I am bound to help administer the challenges on this floor. It seems you passed the combat challenge, or you'd not be standing here."

"Can you answer any questions? What do you mean by a debt to the System? Is this floor the same for everyone? Does everyone who comes to the Crucible have the same challenge? Where, exactly, are we?" Morgan had about ten other questions lined up, but he was interrupted by the statue.

"Ahem! Before you rattle off more questions, let me answer your first one: I can answer questions, but I will not." Takamennion's eyes narrowed sternly, then froze in that position.

"Oh, but, sir Magus," Morgan began, trying not to sound too obsequious, "I just got thrust into this place, and I have no idea what's going on."

"Well, I must admit, I've not seen your kind before. Your friend there, though, I've seen her people plenty of times! Surely, she's told you a thing or two. Not to mention, you've made it this far! Why should I give you free education?" For the first time, the statue's arms moved and settled into a pose with the little fists resting on Takamennion's plump hips.

"Sir! Aren't you bored sitting here waiting for people to arrive? Surely a little civilized conversation isn't so much to ask?" Issa spoke, a scolding tone in her voice.

"How dare you question my civility? I'll have you know; I was quite well known for entertaining the greatest minds on my planet!"

"So, you aren't from this planet?" Morgan asked.

"Well, no, of course not. My planet, Toralax, reached Advanced status long ago and is a regular crossroads and trading hub for even Epic ranked cultivators."

The statue, remarkably, managed a haughty sniff, though its expression became frozen in the sniffing pose, which almost made Morgan start to laugh.

"That sounds impressive, sir. Issa, here, has only ever met Improved cultivators. I didn't even know cultivators or Energy existed a little more than a week ago." Issa nodded along with Morgan's words.

"Truly? How is it you climb the Crucible on a world that the System has curated for over a century if you've never known of Energy?" Morgan smiled and began to answer, explaining how humans were from far away and had traveled here via a spacecraft. Takamennion listened raptly, then said, "Fascinating. I knew that some races could traverse the stars before Energy reached their worlds, but I've not met anyone from a society like that. Perhaps I could answer a few questions in exchange for a bit more about your people and your world. I must warn you, though, my time here is limited. The System moves me from Crucible to Crucible in order to serve out my sentence."

"Well, then, you've already answered one of my questions: the Crucible is different for different people?"

"That's correct. The System curates countless worlds where Energy reaches, and on each of those worlds creates opportunities for cultivators to refine their abilities and selves."

"What do you mean by 'where Energy reaches?' Why wasn't there any Energy on my world?"

"Now you're asking questions beyond even my great understanding. I know the System is working on expanding the reach of Energy, but I don't know how or why. If one were to believe the System, its motivations are altruistic—it simply wants to bring the benefit of Energy to everyone." Takamennion rolled his eyes and held a finger to his lips with a smirk. Morgan got the impression that he didn't accept the System's charitable claims, but he couldn't openly say so. "Now, I've answered some of your questions. Tell me more about your world!"

"Well, what do you want to know?" Morgan asked. Surprisingly it was Issa who spoke up.

"Tell us about how you travel among the stars." Takamennion nodded, so Morgan spent the next few minutes talking about the shipyards on the moon, about Bussard drives and nuclear fusion, about cryo-sleep, and even started talking about the Noah AI units, but then Takamennion interrupted him.

"Oh no, I've lost track of time. I'm going to be moved soon. We have to commence your trial! Quickly, which one of you will take the Energy manipulation challenge?"

REGGIE

"So, tell me again about this Bronwyn person? The leader of your village?" Thun asked. He'd introduced himself to Reggie and begun dressing his dead deer creature with a big, wickedly sharp knife. Thun had told Reggie that he was interested in the human colony and asked him a bunch of questions, most of which Reggie couldn't even remember. He just felt so tired and wanted to get done here.

"Bronwyn? She's a fucking solid ten, that's for sure. Kind of a bitch, I hear, though." Reggie shrugged lethargically.

"She's level ten?" Thun asked, slicing another long strip of meat off the hanging corpse.

"Oh, no. I don't know what level she is; I meant she's a knockout, a real babe."

"Are you trying to tell me she's beautiful? Words are important, Reggie. Try to be precise." Thun flicked his big, sharp knife toward Reggie, and some blood splattered onto his cheek. Reggie wasn't sure why, but that act scared the fuck out of him.

"Yeah, she's fucking beautiful, alright? She seems tough, too, but I dunno, I've never talked to her."

"And she's running things there? With the help of some others?" Thun began to carve meat again, taking his eyes off Reggie. Reggie thought about running briefly, but he was so tired, and why was he running again? It all seemed a bit foggy.

"That's right. There are some other bigwigs. Arthur Ballard, Olivia Bennet, a few others."

"Mmhmm. There are five thousand humans? That's the right word, yes? Humans?"

"Yes, like I already told you, ten goddamn times, there are five thousand." Reggie flinched when Thun turned to him, and those fucking creepy vertically slit eyes focused on him. "Sorry, yes, five thousand."

"And none of them are children? Or the elderly?"

"Uh, no kids. I mean, Arthur and some others might be considered seniors, but they get around fine."

"Mmhmm. What level is your Colony Stone?" Thun began hacking at the joints of the deer or huldii's tendons, separating one of the rear legs from the carcass. He held the skinned haunch up and smiled, and, for a goat-man, he had fucking sharp teeth. "This will make a lovely roast."

"I think you already asked me that. I don't know what level it is. I don't even know how to tell. I'm just trying to collect wood and shit so I can earn contribution points." Reggie didn't know why, but he was feeling very fucking stressed, like meet your girlfriend's parents and let them know she's knocked up stressed.

"Ah, so there's a Contribution Store established. Excellent, Reggie. Thank you. Now, Reggie, this is important: how many people have access to the Colony's Stone's controls?" Thun turned back to the carcass while he waited for an answer. Reggie's eyes drifted to the pile of entrails and other innards that Thun had let fall out of the dead animal when he started cleaning it.

"Umm, I really don't know. Maybe just Bronwyn? When she set it up, we all got a notification that she was the leader."

"You're doing better, Reggie. Now, how would you like to learn a new skill? Something powerful?" After Thun spoke, Reggie perked up. A powerful new skill? Fuck yes, he'd like to learn that.

"Yes, that sounds great!" He started to stand up, but Thun looked at him sternly with those eyes again, and he slumped, too tired to bother standing.

"Good, Reggie. You and I are going to be good friends. I'm going to teach you something new right now. If you keep helping me out, I'll teach you more. Does that sound like a good deal?"

"That sounds like a great fucking deal!" Reggie's fear had been replaced with excitement. None of those other dipshits had a scary-ass goat-man teaching them secret skills.

"Be calm, Reggie. Now, first, a couple of things. You must agree to keep my existence a secret. Secondly, you must agree to return to me, here, each evening to give me a report."

"Uh, every night?" Reggie's eyes narrowed slightly, some of the fog lifting from his mind.

"Only until I have the answers I need. It shouldn't take more than a week." Thun smiled, his long canines and creepy fucking eyes making it more threatening than comforting.

"Okay, I agree." Reggie shivered. Thun's smile grew more expansive, and he somehow produced a sheet of paper and a long quill. He gestured for Reggie to sit still and then walked around smoothing the paper out on Reggie's broad back. Then Reggie heard the sound of scribbling, and he felt the tickle of the quill moving around on the parchment. This went on for several minutes, and then Thun straightened, walked around to face Reggie, and produced the parchment with a flourish. Reggie took the parchment and looked at it; it was covered with scribbles that didn't mean shit to him.

"What the fuck do I do with this?" Reggie flinched as Thun frowned at him.

"Stare at it for a moment. Will yourself to understand." He frowned further, some annoyance leaking into his words. Reggie did as Thun asked, staring at the strange writing, and then something fucking weird started to happen: the squiggly characters began to move around, and then they flew off the paper and started to fly into Reggie's eyes. At first, he freaked out and almost threw the scroll away, but he knew Thun would be pissed, so he held still and let it happen. When it ended, a System message appeared:

*****You have been offered a contract: Become Thun's agent, obeying his directives in exchange for the skill Enrage—Basic. Accept? YES/NO.*****

Enrage sounded pretty fucking cool, but the contract seemed more severe than Thun had made out. "Hey, it says I have to obey your directives, and it doesn't say for how long."

"Excellent! Your discernment is striking! Yes, it would take me hours to craft a contract with such specific contingencies. You'll have to trust that all I need is information for a few days. Why would I lie, Reggie? I could easily force you to comply rather than offer you this valuable skill." Thun absently used his large, razor-bladed knife to carve one of his dark, pointy nails into an even sharper point. Reggie's mind raced for a moment, but, again, lethargy took hold, and he wondered what he was so worried about. He selected the "yes" option, and suddenly warmth spread out through his scalp, almost like someone cracked a warm egg over his head.

*****Congratulations! You have learned the skill Enrage—Basic.*****

*****You have gained a new title: Thun's Agent.*****

Reggie couldn't resist and accessed the part of his status sheet that showed what his new abilities would do:

*****Enrage—Basic—Using Energy, you are able to enter into a state of rage, canceling fear effects and increasing your physical power by 20 percent. While in this state, you have reduced sensitivity to pain. Energy Cost: 50 activation + 1 per second.*****

*****Thun's Agent: Thun's will holds authority over you. You must follow Thun's directives or suffer Energy deprivation.*****

"Good, I can see by your expression that you understand our new relationship," Thun said, a crooked grin spreading on his face.

MORGAN

Morgan couldn't help feeling like he'd been cheated. Takamennion had answered hardly any questions, and now he was saying he was out of time. Still, he spoke up: "I'll take the Energy challenge. What is it?"

Takamennion studied him and looked at Issa, then he said, "Probably a wise decision; I can see your affinity is very high." The statue made a smooth, barely audible grinding sound as it turned, lifted an arm, and waved at the marble wall to Morgan's left. A section of the marble wall slid down into the ground. Now, an identical corridor led a short distance to a set of marble steps that led downward. "The challenge is that way, and only you may proceed, Morgan. Your companion will have to face the agility challenge while you progress. Time is short; please get moving!" The statue turned and opened another doorway in the opposite wall as it spoke.

"Wait! Is it dangerous?" Morgan asked, resting a hand on Issa's shoulder.

"Of course! Though, probably not fatally so. Usually, failure for these two challenges results in expulsion from the Crucible sans reward. Now, please make haste. Provided you succeed, you'll be reunited for your final challenge."

"I'll be fine, Morgan. Besides, I think I'm better suited for a test of agility than you are," Issa said, giving Morgan a quick hug and then pushing him gently toward his doorway. Morgan nodded, stepped through his exit, and then turned to ask Takamennion for clarification on their challenges, but a solid wall of marble was already in place, blocking his view.

"That was sudden." Morgan was fuming inside. He was certain that the little statue-man had been willing to talk to them more. The way he had abruptly cut Morgan off made him wonder if the System had interfered as if it didn't want Morgan getting more answers to his questions. Then there was the whole thing of splitting him and Issa up. He didn't like it. What if one of them failed and was ejected. Would they ever see each other again? He didn't like the idea that he might have just said his final goodbye to her.

Frustrated and angry, he turned and looked to the steps that led down from the short hallway. Like everything else on this level, they were made from smooth white-gray marble. The room below was much darker than the hallway. Where he stood, the light was reminiscent of a fluorescent bulb back on Earth, the source being a softly glowing white orb near the ceiling. Looking down the steps, Morgan saw a definite blue tinge to the light, and it was dimmer, though still plenty bright enough to see. He sighed and started descending the steps.

The air was cool, almost chilly, and the blue light that illuminated the steps had a calming effect on his mind. By the time he reached the bottom, Morgan was feeling more relaxed. He was in a large, open space; he could tell by the echoes of his steps, but the light only illuminated the immediate area at the base of the steps. He realized why when he saw the source of the blue glow. A pool of softly glowing blue water was about ten paces from the foot of the steps. It was about ten feet wide and on the far side was another marble wall. This wall had a pattern, though; it looked like someone had carved a complicated swirl that branched into five other, increasingly complex designs.

Morgan assumed that his challenge had something to do with the pool and the marble wall with the patterns, but he didn't immediately understand what to do. He paced around the room and found that the shadows around it were quite deep but didn't contain any clues. In each direction from the pool, he could take twenty steps, and then he'd meet another smooth marble wall. The only exit was back up the steps. Having exhausted the other possibilities, he approached the pool and saw that three shallow steps led down into the water. Was he meant to go in?

Morgan looked more closely at the pool, trying to discern where the light source was. He couldn't see any glowing orbs or anything, and after he leaned close to the water, he could see that the light seemed to come from the water itself. Maybe water was the wrong word to use. He knelt at the edge of the pool and held a hand about an inch above the liquid. He could feel the Energy in it, thrumming with potential. He didn't feel any heat or cold coming from the liquid, so he decided to take a chance, and he dipped the tip of his little finger into it. The fluid had the consistency of water, but the Energy teaming within it was immediately apparent in how it tingled and how his mind craved it. He could feel his Core start to spin faster like it wanted to absorb the Energy, and he almost gave in, just managing to break his connection and sprawl back away from the pool at the last second.

He wasn't sure why he didn't absorb the Energy in the water. Surely it would be good to cultivate that Energy and use it to enhance his Core. He thought about the Vortex Core Cultivation Drill he'd learned from the scroll the System had provided. He knew that if he performed the meditations involved in that technique while in contact with the water, he'd surely make some significant gains. Still, he felt that this might be part of the challenge. Takamennion had called this challenge an "Energy manipulation challenge." The water was steeped in Energy; was he supposed to manipulate it somehow? If he tried to absorb the Energy and cultivate his Core, would that be sufficient to pass the challenge? He felt like there was more to it.

Once again, Morgan studied the wall with the complicated patterns, and this time he noticed something else. The central, spiraling pattern had a stem that extended from the marble wall and down along the pool's edge and then over the edge and into the pool itself. Morgan walked around the perimeter of the pool and looked more closely at the patterned wall. The patterns were fairly deep grooves; he could easily fit the tip of a finger into them. An idea started to take place in his mind. He could imagine the water flowing up the groove that extended into the pool, filling the big spiral pattern, and then taking the little branching lines from the spiral into the five other, smaller but more complicated patterns. How would he get the water to flow into the grooves, though? Energy manipulation. The test was called Energy manipulation, and the water was saturated with Energy. He had to push the Energy somehow.

Once again, Morgan prepared to submerge a finger into the water. This time he braced himself to resist the desire to pull the water in, and instead, he prepared to send a trickle of his own Energy into the pool. Just as he would to bond with an item, he started a trickle of Energy into his finger, and then he touched the water, pushing the Energy out. It felt like his mind expanded suddenly; he was aware of much more than himself, like he was suddenly a part of the pool. He could feel the Energy all around, and he *understood* how he could manipulate it, move it, the way he wanted to, by exerting pressure with his own Energy. He tried to move the Energy infused water toward the narrow channel that led to the patterned wall, and at first, nothing happened, then a tiny bit of Energy infused water started to climb up the channel and out of the pool. Morgan pushed with all his might, but he couldn't get it to move more than a few inches. He needed more of his Energy in the pool. He tried to push more out of his body and into the water, but he felt a terrible burning sensation anytime he tried to channel more than a thin trickle. Finally, exhausted, he collapsed backward, staring at the pale, blue-tinted ceiling.

Morgan needed to channel more Energy, but when he did, it felt like he was burning a pathway through his body, and it didn't feel like it was something he should be doing; it felt like he was damaging himself. Something about the word "pathway" clicked a memory in his mind, and he thought about the cultivation drill that he'd learned from the scroll just hours (a day?) ago. The whole point of the cultivation drill was to improve his Core by teaching his body to channel Energy more efficiently, allowing him to gather more Energy and push it into his Core. The point of which was to increase its density and power gradually. Morgan sighed at how stupid he'd been. Literally, the answer was right there in his mind the whole time.

He backed a bit farther away from the pool and took up the lotus position that Issa had shown him. He concentrated on his "knowledge" of the cultivation drill that the System had taught him and the various steps came into his mind. First, Morgan cleared his mind by turning his eye inward toward his Core. He imagined he could see it, spinning, almost like a nebula in space, or a whirlpool in the ocean. As he imagined it, it became more and more vivid until he was sure he actually saw his Core, and it brought back the memory of when he'd formed it. There, in the center of his being, a maelstrom of golden energy was spinning, and from its outer edges, Morgan could discern tiny, thin pathways that led out to the rest of his body.

Having cleared his mind and established his Core firmly in his consciousness, he moved to the next step. The Vortex Core Cultivation Drill was tailored to help him build pathways that worked with his Core. Morgan began to follow it, moving painstakingly small amounts of Energy out of his Core and into the specific patterns of the drill, over and over. At first, he could only complete the patterns closest to his Core. Still, as Morgan gradually learned the feel for them and increased the Energy he put into them, they became wider and allowed him to continue the pattern farther from his Core, moving ever so slowly outward into his body. By the time he collapsed, utterly exhausted, he'd managed to complete the patterns branching out from his Core into, if he had to guess, about 5 percent of his body; this was going to take a while.

Morgan chewed on some rough bread and drank some of the watery wine he and Issa had looted from the Urghat. It seemed like years ago, but Morgan knew it was less than a week since they had taken those barrels of questionable alcohol. He'd never have tasted it, if not for the fact that, a couple of days ago, they'd run out of the plain water in the canteens. Thinking of Issa, Morgan began to worry. He'd be at this for days at this rate, and how was she doing? He decided to try out his Guardian's Senses ability. Laying there on the cool marble floor, he thought of Issa and concentrated on activating the ability. Suddenly he was aware of Issa's presence. She was behind him and a couple of hundred feet away to the right. Morgan knew he couldn't get to her but feeling her and knowing she wasn't that far away, brought him immeasurable comfort. He closed his eyes and rested.

REGGIE

Reggie stumbled through the gate; he was tired as hell. Man, who knew finding a little animal den would be such a slog. Then there was that fucking guy, Thun. Yeah, he'd given him a cool skill, but he didn't like that dude. He reminded Reggie of his uncle Paul, and Paul was a scary asshole who broke a guy's teeth out for looking at his girlfriend wrong. Well, he'd have to live with it; he didn't have to do much, anyway. Plus, the guy had promised Reggie he'd get a new skill if he finished all the tasks he gave him.

He wandered over to the Colony Stone, where he'd told the other knuckleheads to meet him. All three of them were sitting on the grass eating some kind of mushy-looking blue melon. "Hey, dudes, you could always go collect more of this stuff. The System might repeat tasks."

"Bro, we just got here, anyway. Been fucking cutting wood all day." Tony tossed a hunk of melon rind at Reggie as he drew the last word out in a whine.

"Whatever, man. I've had a fucking nightmare of a day out in the woods, so don't even complain. Where'd you guys stack the shit you brought in?" Reggie couldn't see any sign of a pile of mushrooms or wood. Tony held up a crude-looking leather bag with all kinds of funny-looking runes burned into the leather. The runes reminded him a little of the squiggly words on Thun's contract, and he suppressed an involuntary shudder.

"The fuck is that?"

"It's a damn bag of holding; some dude named Boris sold it to me. I had to give him half our wood, but it fucking holds a lot." He tossed it to Reggie, who pulled the leather drawstring, opening it. The inside looked like a window into space, but with no stars. He reached his hand in and felt nothing. He kept moving his arm in, and soon it was up to his shoulder. He waved his arm around, reaching in different directions, not touching anything. He strained a bit further, but then his hand started to get cold, and he realized he couldn't feel anything. In a panic, he yanked it out and saw that his skin had taken on a gray tinge. Slowly it regained its pink tone.

"What the fuck, dude?" Reggie's voice was shrill with outrage.

"Goddamn, man; I didn't know it would do that. I had to bind with it to use it, but when I put my hand in there, I can grab any item I want out."

Reggie tossed the bag back and said, "So all the shit's in there? But you gave up half the wood?"

"Yeah, man, all of it. We gave up the wood, but we cut more; it was twice as fast since we didn't have to carry it around and stack it up. I'll go dump it by the Colony Stone." Tony started walking up the hill, and Robbie and Sam stood up. Reggie gestured for them to follow and walked up to the stone. A few other people were around, but they weren't using the stone at the moment, so Tony just dumped the contents at the base. Reggie called up the menu for the Contribution Store and collected his rewards. He started laughing when the stone offered him another task to stack his goods down the hill by the pond. It was only fifty points, but he wouldn't turn his nose up at easy money.

Reggie passed out his new tasks to his crew after they'd collected the easy reward for moving all the wood and mushrooms down the hill. Sam and Robbie had to find berries in the eastern woods, and Robbie, having no other task, was going to sit by the tent and learn how to make Energy beads. "What about you, Reggie?" he asked when Reggie put an end to his grousing about not wanting to study some "dumb manual."

"You think I'm not pulling my weight? I have a bigger quest I'm working on, which will pay big dividends. Don't worry, boys; we work as a team, we'll share rewards like a team. Last one for the day, then we chill by the tents, and I'll buy us some booze with the contribution points we earned today." Reggie waved the three of them off; then, he turned back to the Colony Stone and the small crowd of people starting to mill about now that the day was winding down and they were ready to turn in their tasks. He walked over to a group of four people. He looked at the better looking of the two women, a dark-skinned beauty with extremely short hair, almost shaved. "Hey, any of you guys seen Olivia Bennet or Arthur Ballard or any of the other bigwigs?" When he spoke, he looked right at the woman, even though his words were for all of them.

"Uh, no, I haven't," the short-haired babe said, backing up a step from him.

"I saw Arthur. He was just over by the west gate, talking to some people plotting building locations," a little Asian guy said from behind the woman. Reggie looked at him and nodded.

"Alright, thanks. Hey, if you guys wanna party later, visit us a bit north of here in the meadow. Look for a group of four tents and a bonfire. Later." He offered a smile to the woman and walked off; she had her eyebrow arched and a weird look on her face, but it seemed like she was into him.

He asked around a bit by the west gate and eventually found Arthur talking to a guy who had a leather-bound notebook and a pencil, scratching notes and diagrams as they walked and talked. Reggie stepped up and said, "Arthur, uh, Mr. Ballard."

"Yes?" the old guy replied.

"Yeah, uh, the name's Reggie. Reggie Arnold Gandry-Thule." Reggie reached a hand out to shake, and Arthur took it in a surprisingly firm grip. "Hey, I had a few questions for you, if you don't mind?"

"Well, sure. Brian, go pencil in the area for the bathhouse, and I'll catch up." The man that had been walking with Ballard nodded and kept moving while he scribbled in his book. "Well, what can I do for you, Reggie?"

"What's the deal with the leadership of the colony? Why'd we all get that message about that Bronwyn chick? It doesn't seem like she should be our leader; I thought she was just some VR pilot."

"Oh, well, that's a good question. I'm happy to help. The System awarded her leadership because she finished the orientation first, but she's agreed to share responsibilities with a council of sorts. We have some people acting as council members, but we'll have an election soon. I'd appreciate it if you'd help to spread the word about this; I'm sure you're not the only one with questions."

"Oh, alright. And who can run for council member?" Finally, Reggie had gotten to the question that Thun had told him to ask. He hated all this diplomacy bullshit.

"Well, I don't think there will be any restrictions. Anyone can throw their hat in the ring. Was there anything else?"

"Yeah, when's the election?"

"Oh, not too long. We want to get things settled a bit and feel secure here."

"Alright, and what about the leaderboard? When will you start building the nice houses for the leaders?"

"It's on our list! We know we need to keep people incentivized, so look for the first leaderboard award within a few days." Arthur started to turn away. "If there's nothing else?"

"Alright, thanks, Ballard." Reggie also turned away, walking up the hill. That was easy as hell; he'd already gotten the answer that Thun wanted, and now he could party with his friends, not needing to report back to Thun until tomorrow afternoon. Reggie stopped by the stone and bought a small cask of hard cider from the contribution store. He had planned to buy more than one because it only cost twenty contribution points, but when the first one appeared, it was the size of a pony keg. He lifted it and realized it wasn't pressurized like a keg, so maybe he would need two. He bought another and then walked to his campsite, one cask hanging heavily from each hand; it was party time.

MORGAN

Morgan continued working on his pathways for the next several days. After waking from that first rest, he was at a loss for how long he had slept. Morgan could only judge the time by how hungry or thirsty he was, and since he'd come to this world, his usual reference for that was skewed; now that Energy infused his body, more and more, as he gained in levels, he didn't need to eat or even drink as much as he once had. He reached out with this Guardian's Senses and, once again, felt Issa in the same general area as he had before. She was either still working on her trial or had finished and was waiting for him. How would she know he hadn't failed and wasn't dead? All he could do was continue as quickly as he could, but he was limited by his body's endurance and the painstaking process that his cultivation drill called for. He settled into a routine of waking, taking a few bites of bread with some watered wine, stretching, taking his lotus position, and working on his pathways until exhaustion forced him to rest again.

As he expanded his pathways, his cultivation drill took longer and was more exhausting with each repetition. The first day he got through the routine eight times, resting between each cycle. Now that he had been at it for three days or, really, three periods of sleep, his pathways extended through more than half of his body, and each drill repetition took him hours and left him feeling drained and weak. From the imparted knowledge of his cultivation manual, he knew that once his pathways were complete, he'd be able to passively draw excess Energy into his Core with the drill, gradually increasing his Core's density and thereby his power.

He estimated he was nearly three-fourths of the way finished at the end of the fourth "day" of building his pathways. He lay back, exhausted, and thought about all that he'd seen and done in the short time he'd been thrust into this strange, new world. Things that he would have considered the ravings of a lunatic back in his old life seemed completely normal to him now. The idea that he was meditating for days on end, focusing on guiding a mystical force through his body, seemed crazy when he examined it. Still, he couldn't deny what he had seen and what he felt: Energy was real, and the things that it could help people or "cultivators" do were real, however fantastical the idea might seem. Though he'd been forced to fight for his life, almost from the first moment he was here, been forced to do horrific acts of violence, been forced to see and hear and smell gut-wrenching acts of savagery, Morgan felt a sense of calm as he lay back, reflecting on his cultivation. How strange his life had become!

A big part of it was his connection to Issa. He shuddered to think how alone and lost he'd feel right now if he hadn't found her so quickly. Thinking of her, Morgan reached out with his Guardian's Senses again and was startled to feel her in a different direction and a bit farther away from him than she had been for the last few days. Now she was somewhere, maybe a hundred yards or so beyond and slightly above the far end of the pool chamber. Hopefully, this meant she'd passed her trial. Thinking about how relieved he was to know Issa was close by, Morgan had to come to terms with the fact that he was developing strong feelings for her. He'd noticed his attraction to her quite a while ago, feeling a closeness and a fondness for her starting back when they'd first needed to rely on each other to battle the Urghat.

There was no denying how pretty Issa was, but Morgan didn't know how to feel about being attracted to someone not, well, not human. He knew that feeling was stupid, and it wasn't fair; he was the alien here. He sighed wistfully; really, it was foolish to think like that—they were both people, and they clearly had compatible thoughts and emotions. What really mattered was how she felt about him, though; she wasn't the one lost on an alien planet. She had a village, and her people were there waiting for her. For all Morgan knew, she had someone she loved back home. As his thoughts started to spiral, Morgan determined that it didn't matter—he cared for her, and he felt lucky to have her with him, and he needed to hurry the fuck up and get through this trial, so she didn't leave without him. Thinking of finishing his quest, Morgan realized that he had a way to see if Issa had completed her challenge. He called up his quest interface and looked at the status of the most recent quest.

*****Quest: Survive four challenges in the Marble Halls 2/4. Reward: One Improved Treasure Box, egress from the Crucible.*****

Two of four? The battle with the bear-man was one; this Energy challenge was incomplete, which meant Issa must have completed her Agility challenge. That also meant that they could hopefully face the fourth one together if he could hurry up and finish this challenge. Those thoughts in mind, Morgan closed his eyes and allowed himself to drift into sleep.

When he woke, Morgan immediately checked on Issa and could feel her in the same general area as before he fell asleep. He ate some bread, drank some weak wine, and assumed his meditative pose. He was determined to get three complete cycles of his cultivation drill before he had to call it a day. He was exhausted by the time he finished and allowed himself to rest, but he'd been successful; he was almost certain that he'd be able to finish his pathways with one more cycle. He checked on Issa, ate a pitiful meal, and then fell asleep, hopefully for the last time in this room.

The next day, Morgan didn't have the patience to eat before settling down to finish his pathways. He settled into his meditation pose and focused on his Core. It came into his mind much more quickly now that he'd been practicing for days on end. He could sense his Energy swirling around in a bright vortex right at the center of his being. He traced the pathways he'd painstakingly created over the last several days, marveling at their complexity of purpose. Morgan had pushed pathways most of the way through his body, following the intricate pattern of his manual. They stretched into his arms and hands, down his legs, and into his feet. All that was left was the final push through the distant extremities of his fingers. He began his drill, carefully and methodically repeating the patterns of Energy into each final swirl that ended in the pads of his fingers and thumbs. As he finished the first complete cycle of his cultivation drill for the day, he forced the last bit of Energy necessary to open his pathways out of the ends of his fingers.

Congratulations! You have improved your Vortex Core to Base 2.

Morgan sighed with relief that everything had gone the way he had hoped. He could feel the Energy in the room much more palpably now; it felt like he could pull it into his body through the open channels at his extremities. Now that he'd built his channels, he could move on to the next step of his cultivation drill—actually cultivating Energy. Morgan moved through his drill; this time, as he cycled Energy from his core through his body, he also pulled Energy from the room into the flow as he channeled it back to his Core. The difference was minuscule, but he felt his Core flared more brightly in his mind's eye and spun just a bit faster as he finished the cycle.

However, he didn't want to waste more time cultivating and decided to put off practicing his drill. He ate a small meal and then gathered himself for another attempt at controlling the Energy in the pool. Now that he could feel the Energy around him more clearly, the pool beckoned even more invitingly than before. However, he knew that he could resist the urge to pull that Energy in as long as he was expelling his own Energy into the water to control it. He sat at the edge of the pool and focused, cycling his Energy out through his channels until it was just at the end of his fingers, ready to flow forth. Then, he submerged his hands into the water and *pushed*. Where before it had burned like he was branding himself when he tried to send forth more than a trickle of Energy, now it was painless as he allowed his Energy to surge from his Core, through his pathways, and into the pool.

He was instantly more aware of the water and its strange Energy than he had been during his first attempt. After a few seconds of pushing Energy into the water, he knew he could control it, so he did. He urged the blue water to flow up the channel and into the complicated, large, central spiral on the wall. Before, he had run out of steam after a few inches, but now the water surged up the channel into the spiral and tore through it like ocean water coming in with the tide into a child's sand pattern. Morgan smiled as the first pattern filled with water, and a pleasant chime sounded. He instinctively knew that he'd passed the test and could stop, but why should he? He felt he had plenty of strength left, so he continued pushing the water out of the central spiral and into the first of the outer spirals. This spiral filled even more quickly, and Morgan heard another chime. Still, he continued, and the water flowed at nearly the same pace as when he started. Within moments, he'd filled the second and third outer patterns, each time hearing another chime.

Morgan pushed on into the fourth pattern, but then he noticed something that alarmed him enough that he almost lost his concentration: the water had lost much of its blue tint and was now shining with a golden aura. It was the color that Morgan saw in his mind's eye when he looked at his Core. Doing his best to maintain his concentration, Morgan called up his status display focusing on his Core and Energy:

Core:	Vortex Class - Base 2		
Energy Affinity:	9.2	**Energy:**	65/399

He'd poured almost all of his Energy into the pool. He wasn't even sure what would happen to him if he allowed his Energy to hit zero. Would he pass out? Die? He wasn't sure he wanted to find out the hard way. Morgan concentrated on his drill, taking up the meditation at the point where he usually would start to cycle Energy back to his Core. He didn't know if he could still control the water while cycling Energy to his Core, but Morgan did his best, and he soon realized he could split his attention. Perhaps it was an effect of his high intelligence or Energy affinity, but he found it almost effortless. He continued to push the water into the final two spirals, rewarded with a chime for each completion. At that point, he stopped pushing the water and instead completed an entire cycle of his cultivation drill, replenishing most of his Energy. It felt glorious as it coursed from the water, intermingled with his own, surged into his channels and his rapidly spinning Vortex Core.

Morgan didn't stop there, however. Knowing he'd finished the challenge, he decided to take advantage of this opportunity and continued his cultivation drill, completing two more cycles. When he finished and opened his eyes, Morgan was surprised to see that the water was still infused into the patterns on the short marble wall. More than that, the water was no longer vibrantly blue but sparkled in a more subdued shimmer. He looked inward to his Core, and it seemed a good deal wilder and denser than before. He'd taken a lot of Energy from the water, and if he had to guess, his Core was close to ranking up again. That was fast, but Morgan couldn't imagine that opportunities like this were common outside the Crucible.

Morgan stood, taking a deep breath and steadying himself. As he looked around, he realized the room was no longer as dark beyond the pool and behind the short, patterned wall. Light flowed into the room through an open doorway, where a section of the marble wall had disappeared. Next to the exit were five green lights, about the size and shape of a finger. Below the lights, a shelf had appeared from the wall. On the shelf was a small, blue chest with silver filagree. Morgan walked up to the doorway, noting that brightly lit stairs climbed upward beyond the opening. The chest, upon closer inspection, looked much like the treasure chests that the System had rewarded them for completing quests. Morgan could only assume that the five green lights had something to do with the five patterns on the wall that he'd filled with Energy. Perhaps the chest was meant as a reward for those able to push the Energy infused water farther than just the central pattern.

"One way to find out," Morgan said out loud, flipping the chest open. He felt sure that it was a reward because of the styling of the chest and so didn't think it was likely to be trapped. Luckily, he was correct, as the lid flopped open revealing a glass vial, about twice the size of his thumb, cushioned by a silky, blue lining. Morgan could see that the vial was filled with a thick orange liquid and that it had a label affixed to it by a length of blue ribbon. Morgan picked up the vial and found it warm to the touch. Morgan held up the label and saw, in what he figured was standard System script, but what looked like English to his brain:

Distilled Argent Emperor Fruit Sap—known for permanently enhancing the intelligence of those who imbibe.

"Bottom's up!" Morgan grinned as he popped the cork and drank the extremely sweet syrup. He felt a rush, almost like a burst of adrenaline, and found his scalp tingling in a strange, electrical itch. As his heart rate normalized, he took a look at his attributes, immediately noting that his intelligence had gained five points, and his maximum Energy had gotten a nice bump. He wondered at the idea that to get this reward, one needed to already be good at manipulating Energy, which almost surely meant high intelligence. In other words, the strong got stronger. In a way, it didn't seem fair, but Morgan was used to life not being fair, and for once, he was glad to have things going his way. He pulled up his current quest log:

Quest: Survive four challenges in the Marble Halls 3/4. Reward: One Improved Treasure Box, egress from the Crucible.

Then he used Guardian's Senses to locate Issa and saw that she was roughly in the same area as before and the stairs that opened up for him ought to take him in the right direction. He smiled at that, turned to look one last time at the pool that had been his home for what felt like almost a week, and started to climb the steps.

REGGIE

"Wake up, dipshits!" Once again, Reggie found himself standing in the damp grass, trying to wake up his boys. His head throbbed slightly from the excess of the previous night, but he felt alright, and it was time to get moving on the leaderboard. He picked up a half-full mug of cider and chugged it down. "Hair of the dog!" He laughed and shook Robbie's tent. "Get up, get up!"

"Jesus, man, chill. My head feels like it's about to split open." Robbie's head poked out of the tent, and his eyes were swollen, puffy, and red as hell.

"Damn, dude. You should put more points into vitality." Reggie laughed again. "Come on, boys! I'm fucking third on the leaderboard. Time to get moving if you want that first house!" Reggie pulled up the leaderboard one more time, just to see that glorious sight:

Name:	Points:
1. Bronwyn Tallow	4330
2. Olivia Bennet	2420
3. Reggie Gandry-Thule	2260
4. Maria Rios	2140
5. Oscar Sandoval	1940
6. Boris Saltzki	1480
7. Tanya Delgado	1340
8. Alec Green	1140
9. Rene Bisset	960
10. Tina Bensen	910

"I dunno what the others were up to yesterday, but they hardly moved. We can win this thing! C'mon!" Reggie started walking around the firepit, lifting his knees high and thrusting his fists alternately into the air, making sounds like a train: "Chug-a, chug-a, choo, choo!" He felt pumped up today. They'd climb the leaderboard, he'd go talk to Thun and give him his dopey information, and then they could party again. What a fucking life!

The morning went as planned; he got another job to cut wood, and two other gathering jobs, so they split it all up, went to work, and met back by the stone at noon. Once again, Reggie collected all the rewards, but when he checked for new jobs, the only thing available was making Energy beads. "Maybe we're finishing them faster than it can refresh? Hmm, alright, boys, it looks like you're making beads for the afternoon. I gotta go finish up another task I got." He turned and started walking toward the west gate.

"Hold up, dude," Tony called. "I hate making those fucking beads; it takes hours. Let me come with you."

"Nah, bro, this is a solo quest. Sorry you hate it, but we need all the points we can get. I've heard some people make them faster—maybe try to trade for other people's beads? Then I can turn them all in together? Whatever works for you, but don't dick around." Reggie kept walking, ignoring the stormy looks from Tony and Sam. They'd get over it after he invited them all into their new house. Before that, even, he'd get back on their good sides with another party. Reggie kept his eyes open for any babes as he walked to the gate, calling out invites to party later that night.

Reggie meandered down to the west gate, smiling and waving at all the women he passed, letting them know there'd be a party at his tents again tonight. He was surprised that most of them didn't know what he was talking about or who he was; that was when Reggie would remind them to check the leaderboard and look at number three. When he walked past the guards, he saw one of them eating what looked like a pulled-pork sandwich wrapped in a paper towel. "Yo, where'd you get that sandwich?"

"Oh, one of the cooking enthusiasts on the south end. Someone killed a boar-like animal, and they've been trying to make a good barbeque sauce all day. This one tastes pretty damn good; I think they got the buns from the Contribution Guild."

"Huh, south end, you say? I'll have to check it out, maybe grab some grub for my party tonight."

"Oh, a party?" the other guard asked.

"Yeah, bring your girlfriends. Come to the tents just north of the hill; look for the big campfire. Oh, and bring some of that pork." Reggie sauntered out through the meadow and into the woods, walking to where he met Thun the day before. A few people were out and about, but after he'd walked for about thirty minutes, he stopped hearing other people moving around. Reggie practiced using his new tracking ability, noticing the highlighted names of a few new little woodland animals and even seeing some human tracks, though they seemed faint and old. He wondered if they could be his. He realized he was walking slower and slower, and he knew it was because he dreaded meeting with Thun; Reggie didn't like that guy's attitude one bit. The dude had a superiority complex.

"Good, you're back, Reggie." Thun's voice nearly made Reggie jump out of his skin. He jumped and whirled around.

"Jesus, dude."

"No, no, I am Thun, Reggie. Well? Have you gleaned the details of the leadership in your village?"

"Yes, man. I talked to Arthur Ballard himself, and he told me that the council isn't official, and they'll be having elections."

"Oh?" Thun scratched his thick, gray goatee. "Is there some law among your people determining who can be in elections? What is your social status, Reggie? Could you be elected to the council?"

"Anyone can run for council, man. I'm not that kind of guy, though. I'm more of a go and do A, then B, then C, kinda guy."

"Nonsense! What about this leaderboard you were telling me about? Aren't you highly regarded among the people?" Now it was Reggie's turn to scratch the orange hair on his chin.

"I mean, yeah, I'm getting famous already. I bet I'll get the first big house awarded at this rate, too. The people seem to love me—I throw a party almost every night."

"So, you see," Thun said, stepping closer to Reggie. "It only makes sense for you to be on the council. Who is better suited than the man who won the top prize on the leaderboard? Who has helped the community more than you?" Thun leaned in, ever closer as he spoke. Reggie felt a little fuzzy again and had to sit down on a mossy log.

"Yeah, who fuckin' better?" he asked quietly.

"Yes, good, Reggie," Thun said, as he produced another sheet of paper and his long, black quill. He scribbled on the paper, holding a thin, smooth black book underneath it. "Now, Reggie, I'm going to give you another skill, one that will prove very valuable to you. Using this skill, you'll be able to sway others to see things your way. Use caution, however: if you use this ability on the wrong person, someone more powerful than you or with a very high will, they'll see what you're doing, and it may provoke them."

"Alright, man." Reggie accepted the paper that Thun passed to him, turning the writing side up and staring at it. Just as before, the squiggly runes started moving around and then flowed off the sheet and into his eyes.

*****Congratulations! You have learned the skill Rabble-rouse—Basic.*****

*****Rabble-rouse—Basic—Using Energy, you are able to inspire emotion in people listening to your words, causing them to view you more favorably**

and making them more receptive to your arguments. While maintaining this effect, you are especially susceptible to mental attacks, reducing your will-based resistance by 50 percent. Energy Cost: 50 activation + 1 per second.***

"Good, Reggie, good. Use this at the end of your conversations with people. Urge them to vote for you. Remind them that they deserve a voice on the council, and that voice will be you!" Thun smiled his creepy fucking smile at Reggie and gently massaged his shoulder with one dark-taloned hand. Reggie felt like he was going to crawl out of his own skin, but he forced himself to maintain a neutral expression.

BRONWYN

In the early light of the rising moons, with just a sliver of the sun's light brightening the eastern horizon, Bronwyn and Olivia waited near the western archway that led to the forest where the Yeksa cave was hidden. Olivia shivered slightly, her breath steaming in the shadows at the base of the wall. Bronwyn stamped her feet, knocking some feeling into her cold toes, and looked to the nearest cluster of colonist tents. "Well, where are they?"

"I'm sure they're coming! Look, I can see a torch weaving this way," Olivia said, gesturing toward the sputtering spot of flame that was moving between some tents toward them. As it got closer, Bronwyn could see that two people were walking together under the smoking brand.

"Hey, Maya and Martin!" she called. "Seen Emmett?"

"I'm here," a quiet voice said from the shadows of the archway. "I was outside the wall looking around while I waited."

"Dammit! You scared the shit outta me!" Bronwyn whirled around as he spoke. He just grinned and walked over to bump fists in greeting. Bronwyn didn't exactly feel friendly toward the guy, having just met him the night before, but she bumped knuckles out of reflex. At that point, the other two walked up with cheery "Hellos," and Bronwyn grumbled, "Alright, put that torch out, it's bright enough, and you're wrecking my night vision."

"Sheesh, who pissed in your cereal?" Maya huffed, as she ground the torch out in the damp grass.

"Sorry, this mission or 'quest' has me on edge. You guys ready to head out?"

Everyone muttered their readiness, and the group began their trek. They nodded to the guards on their way out of the wall, and one of them called out, "Goodluck, Bronwyn!" She didn't recognize him, but maybe he'd seen her compete back home. She mustered a smile and waved, leading the way across the grass, and into the forest. By the time they crossed the mile or so of meadow, the sky had lightened considerably, and she could make out her trail of X marks in the woods.

"If something happens to me, you can follow those X marks to the cave or back home." Olivia, who was walking close behind her, reached forward and gave her a little shove on the back of her shoulder.

"Nothing's going to happen to you. Have you ever heard of manifesting reality?"

"What? Uh, yeah. Not really a believer." Bronwyn scoffed.

"Well, I do, and I'd appreciate it if you could be more positive. For me?" Olivia's voice took on a petulant note, and Bronwyn laughed despite herself.

"Yeah, okay. For you." Bronwyn smiled with half her mouth and kept walking.

The other three were mostly walking in silence behind them, but occasionally Maya would exclaim at an interesting-looking tree or the flash of a small animal jumping through branches. Martin didn't utter a word, but Emmet would sometimes respond to Maya's exclamations.

"You haven't been in the woods yet, Maya?" Bronwyn asked, after the woman stopped to admire a wide, oak-shaped tree sporting white bark with spots of red sap seeping out here and there.

"No, I've been helping with some digging and path making around the colony. I've been sparring with some of the other colonists in my spare time—we've made something of a club. You should check it out, Bronwyn. People would love to get some practice in with you." Bronwyn grunted in reply, but she walked up to the big, white tree and stuck her finger in the red sap, pulling it to her nose and sniffing. It smelled kind of like maple, so she tasted it.

"Hey, it's sweet!" Maya held a hand over her mouth, but Olivia was openly laughing. "What?"

Emmet peered around from behind Olivia and said, "Your teeth and lips are stained bright red."

"Ah, dammit," Bronwyn said, looking at her finger, which was also stained crimson. "Alright, alright, laugh it up." They all took her up on the offer and laughed as they followed her, stomping up the trail.

A couple of hours later, Bronwyn and her four companions sidled up next to the cave. Bronwyn held her finger to her lips, gesturing for them to be quiet as she crept toward the opening. She crouched there, silently waiting, listening for any sounds of life from the inside. After a few minutes of silence, she waved for the rest of the party to follow her in. She swiftly swung herself into the cave, her gauntlets raised to protect her face. No sounds of alarm rang out, nor were any spears eminently rushing toward her. Her eyes slowly adjusted to the low light, and she saw that they were in a low-ceilinged, natural tunnel that ran steeply down into the hill. The light was still good enough to see by this close to the opening, so she gestured for the troop to follow her and began to slowly, softly advance into the tunnel.

After just a couple dozen feet, Bronwyn could see that the tunnel opened up into a larger space. She motioned Emmet forward and whispered to him, "Can you sneak forward and scout things out?" He nodded, a serious expression on his face, and slinked off, quickly scuttling behind an outcrop of stone and peering around it. She could see his shadow there, still as stone as he stared into the opening. After a few moments, he silently crept back to her and reported.

"There's a big open area down there, with huts and stuff. I don't see anything moving, though, and there ain't no lights or fires or anything." His rough whisper had a hint of a Boston accent, hiding the r's in his speech in a way that made Bronwyn smile. She nodded and motioned for everyone to follow, and they made their way through the tunnel and into the cavern.

There were small dwellings tucked against every wall and piles of refuse strewn about the cafeteria-size cavern, but Bronwyn saw no movement, no signs of recent life. The party searched the large room and found nothing except heavily rotted meats and cold campfires near the entrance. Bronwyn realized that nothing had been here for quite some time, perhaps even before she had cleared out the camp a few days ago. After some minutes of silent searching, Emmet walked up to Bronwyn and whispered, "I think I found something on the far wall; it's dark over there, so the rest of you may need torches, follow me."

Bronwyn tapped her metal gauntlets together softly, the sound echoing in the still silence in an effort to garner everyone's attention, and motioned for them to follow her. Emmet led them to the far corner, where the ceiling dipped to about seven feet. It was a lot darker there, Bronwyn thought as she pulled a torch out of her storage pouch. However, before she could go about lighting it, Olivia summoned her spinning orbs of magic and caused the small marble of fire to grow and held it in her hand like a miniature little sun.

"Why don't you keep those hands of yours free in case it comes to violence." Olivia grinned and gave Bronwyn a slight wink.

"Handy trick, but are you sure that won't drain your Energy? We'll need you if it comes to a fight as well." Bronwyn spoke in a hushed tone.

"This little parlor trick? Oh Bron, are your expectations of me so low?" She gave a mock frown. "That almost hurts, but have no fear; I could float twenty of these around before I started to outpace my regeneration."

Bronwyn raised an eyebrow; she could hardly keep her armor up for more than a couple of minutes before completely depleting herself. "Well, if you're sure." She shrugged and put the torch away. "What is this anyway, Emmet?" She asked as she started to inspect a large tapestry that he had led them to. It ran from ceiling to floor and was about five feet wide. The tapestry was a faded depiction of a dozen circles interconnected into a maze-like knot, with tiny squiggly runes interconnected within the rings.

"Couldn't really tell ya what's on it, but I think you'll be more interested in what's behind. I felt a cold draft from back here and noticed the corner there drifting away from the wall a bit. Watch." He knelt and pulled the tapestry back about a foot and revealed a tunnel leading down at a slight angle farther into the earth. "Even with my dark vision, it extends past what I can see."

Bronwyn inspected the tunnel with the aid of Olivia's light. "Well, it looks like we can fit two of us side by side. I'll take the lead with Martin and Maya behind me and Olivia and Emmet in the back. Sound good to everyone?"

The group all nodded their assent and got into formation. Before Bronwyn stepped into the tunnel, she unpinned the tapestry from the wall and folded it up, placing it in her pouch. She wasn't sure why, but the symbol seemed significant.

Immediately upon entering the tunnel, the climate changed drastically: the air temperature dropped by about ten degrees, and the stench of rotten meat grew thicker with every step. They traveled for a couple of hundred yards, the light of Olivia's orb illuminating the passage thirty feet in front and behind them before Emmet whispered for them to halt. "Hold up. I see something up ahead. It looks like the passage widens into a larger cavern or room. How should we approach this? I haven't seen any movement, but there's gotta be something down here, right?"

Bronwyn was honestly stumped; whether something was down there or not, they would all need light except Emmet. She didn't feel comfortable sending him to scout alone; whatever did live down in these tunnels probably didn't need light either. She was about to speak up when Emmet spoke again.

"Why don't you all just wait here? I'll go check it out and report back. Besides, I'm better at keeping quiet than you guys, and I can see down here without glowing like a Christmas tree." He chuckled. "Oh, and don't worry, if anything down there sees me, I'll give 'em the ol' one-two sucker punch and come running straight back. That's a promise. Go ahead and put that light out, though, so I'm not backlit on my way." He pointed toward the orb.

Olivia tossed Bronwyn a questioning look. "If you're sure, Emmet. It would be our best chance not to get caught off guard. You really up for this?" Bronwyn asked him

"Yeah, yeah, I'm sure, I'm sure." His Boston accent was getting thicker, and Bronwyn thought it might be because of false bravado.

Bronwyn paused for a moment. "Alright. Olivia, put out the light. Maya, Martin, get ready in case something spots him." Martin hefted his massive club up onto his shoulder, and Maya tightened the straps on her shield. Olivia caused the marble of earth to flatten out into a disk and then envelope the orb of fire, casting the tunnel into complete darkness.

"Be back before you know it," Emmet whispered as he slunk off down the tunnel. After just a couple of feet, Bronwyn lost track of his slightly darker shadow. She felt a hand exploring down her shoulder and arm, and then a cool, small hand grasped her left wrist above her gauntlet.

"Sorry, I'm just freaking out a little here," Olivia whispered from right beside her.

"No worries. Maya, Martin, you guys good?" Bronwyn whispered just a little louder.

"Yeah, I . . ." Maya was cut off by a panicked shriek from down the tunnel, followed shortly by hundreds of bare feet slapping on stone, rushing toward the four companions. Before Bronwyn could ask her to, Olivia uncovered her light, and the fiery orb blazed with Energy, lighting the tunnel as if it were midday. Dozens of pale gray Yeksa were rushing toward them from the bottom chamber where Emmet had gone. They advanced at a dead run, but they didn't yell or vocalize at all; the only sounds were their bare feet and rustling clothes as they pushed and bumped into each other. It was unnerving.

Bronwyn shouted something, perhaps a command to fight or run; she was aware she called forth her stone armor and slammed into the front wave of Yeksa, and her gauntlets left devastation in their wake. She rolled and dodged among them, lashed out with fists and occasionally knees and elbows. She knew that the Yeksa weren't a match for her, but there were so many. Dimly, Bronwyn knew Maya and Martin were also embroiled in combat. She could hear the thunderous crack of Martin's club connecting with the stone walls and floor as he punishingly smashed it through the masses of the little monsters. Maya yelled with each swing of her axe like it was some sort of kiai, and Bronwyn could feel its effectiveness with each spray of cold dark blood that showered the tunnel.

Wait, why was their blood cold? Bronwyn's red-tinged battle rage subsided as she scrambled for an answer to that thought. She looked around and realized that they were still swarmed with Yeksa—hardly any of them lay unmoving on the tunnel floor. She shouted, "They aren't fucking dying!" She looked, wide-eyed, back up the tunnel and saw that Olivia was repeatedly throwing razor-sharp icicles, seemingly out of the palm of her hand, into the swarm of Yeksa. She started to fight her way back toward Olivia and the others.

"They're like zombies!" Martin bellowed.

"He's right! They aren't alive!" Maya yelled, also fighting to retreat out of the horde.

"Well, cut their fucking heads off, then!" Bronwyn shouted, kicking a Yeksa in the back and sending it sprawling as she finally forced her way, panting and bleeding, to the rear of the fight with the other three.

"I have a better idea. Everyone get down on the count of three!" Olivia screamed. "One, two, three!" Trusting the shrill panic in Olivia's voice, Bronwyn dove to the floor. Martin and Maya followed suit, and then the tunnel was filled with the heat of a furnace blast. Looking over her shoulder, Bronwyn saw Olivia standing with both palms outstretched and her fire orb spinning in a blazing figure eight around her wrists. Thin streams of flame were pouring forth from her hands, liberally coating the horde of Yeksa with fire. They thrashed and bumped into each other, and, as the fire engulfed them, they started running in every direction, having lost sight of their purpose.

As the Yeksa faltered, congregating in a blazing mass, the four companions ran up the tunnel out of the heat and smoke. They stopped after a couple of dozen feet and looked back, panting. Olivia was white in the orange light of the flames below, and Bronwyn knew she was spent. Only a handful of burned and mangled Yeksa made it through the knot of burning bodies, and Bronwyn, Maya, and Martin dispatched them by crushing or removing their heads. After a few minutes, the flames began to die down, and the occasionally thrashing Yeksa finally stilled.

"That was insane," Bronwyn gasped, and her comrades grunted in agreement. As they recovered their breath, Bronwyn thought about finding Emmet, wanting badly for him to be okay, but dreading that he wasn't. Energy coalesced around the mass of dead Yeksa and coursed in a thick stream toward the group. Most of the Energy flew straight into Olivia, but a sizable amount hit the rest of them also.

Congratulations! You have achieved level 7 base human and have 5 attribute points to allocate.

"I leveled twice!" Olivia said, noticeably refreshed from the Energy infusion.

"I think we all leveled," Bronwyn said, "but we need to get down there and see what happened to Emmet." She stood up and quickly allocated her attribute points, putting three points in strength and two into agility, bringing them to 31 and 23 respectively.

"I hope Emmet managed to run somewhere safe!" Martin said, kicking aside some of the burnt Yeksa corpses and trying to clear a path. Maya stepped forward to help Martin, wiping soot from her eyes.

"Yeah, I hope so. At least they're dead." Maya grunted, shoving aside a few smoldering bodies.

"Well, I wouldn't be so sure," Bronwyn said. "My quest didn't update."

THUN

Thun watched Reggie's back as he walked away, slowly becoming lost in the dappled shadows of the forest. He snorted, pulling his walking stick from his dimensional storage ring. Reggie would be a decent tool, though Thun wished he'd time to cultivate another. Still, Reggie had proved to be a decent candidate; he had just the right amount of inflated self-worth and ambition coupled with a feeble will and lack of critical thinking. By all indications, though, it seemed these humans were of a universally low level; Thun might well have made an agent out of any one of them. Thun knew he was risking a backlash, but as long as he didn't push things too far directly, he was reasonably sure he'd avoid notice from any rivals in the area.

He set off, using his Steps of the Dark Maiden to accelerate his pace. Soon Thun was miles from the human settlement, in the very shadowy, ancient heart of the Gresh Woods. He could feel the presence of beings even older than he nearby, but they were slumbering, not yet aware of the new developments in the area. "Good, let them sleep away, oblivious." Thun grinned and produced a thin pipe, stuffing a crinkled blue weed in the bowl and lighting it with a flaming fingertip. He inhaled, pulling the sweet, gray-blue smoke through the stem and filling his lungs. Thun felt his senses expand, and Energy flowed out from his lungs into his Core. It was just the boost he needed.

Thun placed his hand on the ancient bark of the Umbrilak tree, reciting the words he'd learned from the Weave Dancer among the Ghelli Corpse Dreamers so many years ago. He felt the Energy being pulled out of him, into the bark, and then a seam appeared, and the trunk started to pull apart from itself, revealing a shadowy tunnel leading down into the roots of the ancient tree. Thun stepped into the tunnel and calmly descended, whistling a tune as he went; the lines of Energy were so thick here, he could feel it humming through the roots around him. After a short spiral wind of tunnel, Thun came to the chamber he'd prepared.

He'd carved a perfectly round room here, nestled among the roots of the Umbrilak. The walls were smooth, hardened dirt, with lengths of gnarled, dark roots extending through them at seemingly random angles. More important, Thun had compressed the soil of the floor and etched it with an immensely intricate pattern. He stood at the center of the design, removed his knife from his belt, and slashed his palm. Thun dripped blood into the bowl-shaped depression near the edge of the pattern, channeling Energy along with the fluid. Slowly at first, but then more quickly, the blood propagated all the lines of the pattern. He gave a final push of Energy, and then his vision faded.

Thun's vision slowly returned to him, and he saw that he was standing on the pattern, but it was in a different room. Now he was in a dark stone chamber, and he knew he was high in the Blue Spine Mountains. He again called flame to his finger and walked over to the sconce he knew was on the wall opposite him. As the sconce flared to life, Thun took in the small, round, stone room—another place of power that he'd found. Veins of Amber Ore extended beneath him, gathering Energy and creating a natural focal point for it here. He counted three paces from the flaming sconce, and then he turned to the wall, tracing some faint runic symbols etched in the stone. With a little push of Energy, the wall split, sliding open with a soft rumbling grind.

Thun walked up the sloping stone tunnel toward the hazy gray daylight in the distance. Soon he was standing on the ledge of his little mountain getaway, looking out over the diagonal folds of mountain ridges, and watching the sun turn the sky a million shades of gold and crimson with its setting. He pulled lazily on his pipe and sat down on a smooth boulder that had born his weight hundreds of times on evenings just like this. Thun didn't have to wait long before he heard what he'd been waiting for—the scrabbling sound of someone making the ascent up the narrow, gravel-strewn path from the valley below.

Soon, the bobbing head and shoulders of his visitor came into view. The trail was difficult, and the visitor's eyes were on the ground, taking each step with care; a fall from this height would prove fatal to most. Thun waited patiently, refilling his pipe and savoring the cool moonlight as the sun finally gave up the fight, slipping away behind the world. He closed his eyes, reveling in the heady smoke from his pipe. The scrape of gravel and the heavy sigh one makes after completing a difficult task signaled his visitor's arrival. Thun opened his eyes. "Greetings, lordling."

"Huh, hello, Thun. You have news for my father?" The red-furred Urghat was a dark shadow in the dim light. Only his teeth and parts of his eyes reflected the pale light of the moons.

"Guts, you may bring this news to your father: I have an agent in place within the human colony. I anticipate being able to hamper their defenses severely. Tell Spineripper that he'd best prepare the artifact for delivery. I'll continue my plans, but I won't have my agent act before I've received the payment."

"You should use more respect when talking about the Overclaw." The Urghat took a step, his looming bulk meant to be threatening.

"Sit down, Guts. You're feeling tired." With just a bit of Energy, Thun pushed the Suggestion. The Urghat immediately yawned and sat down on another smooth boulder, conveniently situated across from Thun's. "Now, your father wouldn't have lied, would he? He has the Calamity Shrike's heart?"

"Yar, he has it. Was part of his System reward for completing a clan challenge." The Urghat yawned.

"Imagine that. The System loves to sow strife, that's for certain, giving out a reward that your 'Overclaw' couldn't possibly be ready to use. Still, I suppose it makes for a sound bargaining chip. So, as I said, I have my agent in place. I'll continue to make preparations. When your people are ready, send someone with the artifact to the heart of the Gresh Woods."

"Gresh Woods? Isn't that place crawling with Yovashi?"

"No, not crawling with them. Don't worry, my eyes will be open, and your courier need not fear, so long as your father doesn't deviate from our bargain. Now, sleep here until the sun rises, then scurry down, back to your father." Thun stood and left the Urghat there, stifling another yawn. Guts didn't attempt to stop him or even speak again; he was busy rolling out a bedroll and getting ready to follow Thun's instructions. Thun shook his head; here was another creature with entirely too weak a will for its level.

Thun walked back down the sloping tunnel to his hideaway. He closed the seam in the wall and opened another on the pattern room's opposite side. A short hallway led him to a much cozier room: here, he had a luxurious rug laid over the stone floor, and a short set of steps led to a natural hot spring, vented out through a stone chimney. The sulfur smell was strong in the air, and Thun reveled in it. He doffed his leather gear, stowed it directly into his ring, climbed the steps, and sank into the hot, Energy-rich water. He'd cultivate here for a few hours before making the portal back to the Gresh Woods.

MORGAN

The pristine, white marble steps led up a relatively short flight of stairs into another marble chamber that was, again, lit with a soft white glow emanating from an orb that hovered near the ceiling. Morgan noted that the room was circular and about twenty paces across. In the center of the room was another statue, this one of a giant humanoid. The statue loomed over Morgan's head, and as he approached, Morgan could see that the figure depicted in the marble stone was bedecked in heavy armor and wore an eyeless mask shaped like a turtle's beak. Morgan continued his approach cautiously, holding his spear in front of him. Was this another challenge so soon? Where was Issa?

"Hello, Challenger," a gravely, basso voice issued forth from the beaked mask.

"Hello," Morgan replied cautiously.

"You stand upon the threshold to your final challenge. The Challenge of Virtue," the statue announced grandiosely, its booming voice echoing in the marble chamber.

"Virtue? What virtue are you testing? Where is my companion?"

"Concern yourself not. The System has determined a fitting Challenge of Virtue for you and each other Challenger to set foot in these halls."

"I was told that Issa and I would be reunited for the fourth challenge." Morgan's voice had gained an edge.

"I know not of this Issa. I know not what you were promised. Only the administrators of the Challenge of Virtue know what it entails. Any information you were given prior to coming here cannot be relied upon." The statue spoke firmly and for the first time moved; it uncrossed its arms and punched one marble gauntlet into the palm of the other. The resultant crack of stone on stone reverberated off the marble walls, causing Morgan to wince and hold his hands up to his ears.

"So, is Issa facing this challenge on her own?"

"If your comrade has entered the Marble Halls with you and progressed apace, then yes, your comrade is now facing a similar challenge."

"Alright, what's the challenge, then?"

"At last, down to the business at hand." The statue relaxed its arms, allowing them to fall to its side with a smooth grinding sound. "The System has contrived a choice for you to make. Your choice will reveal an aspect of your character. You are fortunate to have this challenge as your fourth; there is no failing it."

"There's no failing it? So, either choice will allow me to pass?" Morgan felt like there must be some sort of a catch—the System hadn't really given him anything for free. Actually, he reasoned, that wasn't entirely true; he'd woken up in this place with an Advancement Orb floating next to him.

"That is correct. The System values all virtues, or even the lack thereof. The System understands that all sorts of individuals are needed in the great tapestry of existence."

"So, if there is no correct choice, what's the point of the challenge?"

"Ah, this challenge is an opportunity for you to display your character and earn a reward that will facilitate your progression." The statue's deep, gravelly voice took on a higher tone, and Morgan felt it was almost like hearing a sand mixer trying to be coy.

"All right, anything else I need to know?" Morgan was tired, and he wanted to get through this and reunite with Issa.

"Yes. After completing this challenge, you will remember that it involved a choice, but you will not remember the choice you were given or the choice you made."

"What? Why?" Morgan backed up a step.

"Simply because people who finish this challenge are not meant to share their experience and choices with others who might enter the Crucible. It wouldn't do for others to make plans for such eventualities."

"Well, I hate the idea that the System can just mess around in my head, removing memories."

"A frivolous fear! You should know that such a feat is not merely the province of the System; many billions of individuals have achieved sufficient skill to alter the memories of a welp such as yourself." The statue once again crossed its arms, and its voice rumbled like boulders clashing.

"It would seem I don't have a choice, then. Let's proceed." Morgan gestured with his arm toward the empty walls of the room, assuming that the challenge would appear behind another disappearing wall.

"Very good." The statue spread its arms, and two pedestals rose from the floor in front of Morgan, one to his left and one to his right. Atop the marble pedestals, different colored lights began to coalesce as he watched. Atop the left-hand pedestal, red motes gathered into a spinning orb and condensed to form a round crystalline sphere with swirls of inky black moving inside the predominantly red crystal. A similar crystal orb had formed on the right-hand pedestal, but it was primarily silver, shot through with azure.

"What? I thought this was a test of virtue. Am I just supposed to pick the color I like best?"

"Patience." The statue's voice was clipped, and for the first time, Morgan realized that it was concentrating. "Look into each sphere, but do not touch until you've made your choice. The only way to fail this test is by not viewing both of your choices," it said after several moments of silence. Morgan followed its instruction, stepping forward to peer into the red and black sphere.

Morgan seemed to be flying over a vast forest. He saw trees unlike any from Earth filling the horizon: tall white trunks with blue leaves, massive, fern-like red canopies that resembled fall foliage, blooms like multi-colored orchids, sunflower-shaped blossoms of every hue sprinkled among green boughs. The wild chaos of the alien forest nearly overwhelmed his senses, but soon he was nearing the edge, and he could see a vast grassland opening up. The grass was the color of robin's eggs and short and feathery. From his perspective, Morgan could see that the plains continued for many miles, all the way to the foothills of massive purple mountains that rose in the distance. Looking over his shoulder, he realized more mountains rose on the other side of the forest he'd just flown over; this was a valley, teeming with vibrant life.

Not in control of his flight, Morgan was forced to observe as he veered to the right, swooping lower over the grassland. In moments objects came into view: thousands of small tents and just as many small fires. As he drew nearer, he could see the people milling around the tents, and his heart lurched when he realized they were humans. These were his people. This verdant valley was where the rest of the colonists had been placed. His joy turned to frustration as his flight veered to the left, leaving the human encampment behind, soon he was soaring toward the distant, purple mountains. They rose, massive crags, into the sky as he approached, and he realized just how big they were. The sunlight grew dim, and as the yellow-orange light faded, twin moons rose above the mountains. One moon was massive, with a ring orbiting it, and it filled a quarter of the sky. The other was smaller, more reminiscent of Earth's moon.

Morgan became aware of small yellow lights all along hills leading up to the mountainside. Thousands, tens of thousands of them. He wondered what they were. Were they some kind of insect or natural crystal formations reflecting the moonlight? His flight brought him ever closer, and he realized that they were fires. Soon, he could make out that they were big, like bonfires, and then he saw the tents around them. He flew even closer, and then he could make out the figures dancing around the fires and banging on drums. He could hear the drums now and the guttural chanting. Finally, his flight slowed, and he was hovering over one of the bonfires, and he saw the dancing figures more closely—Urghat, thousands upon thousands of Urghat.

Suddenly, Morgan was back in the marble chamber in front of the statue. Somehow he knew that if he grasped the black and red sphere, he'd aid his people in some way against the impending Urghat invasion. Morgan was tempted to touch it right away, but the statue's words still rang in his mind—he had to view both of his choices. He took a step to his right and looked into the silver and blue orb.

Once again, Morgan had a bird's eye view of a scene. This time he wasn't flying over an alien forest, but he was hovering near the ceiling of an immense cavern. He was instantly sweltering in the dry air of the hot cavern. A gibbet was hanging from a black iron chain in the cavern's center. Beneath it, bubbling with green light and exuding toxic vapors, was a pool of green, viscous fluid. The iron cage was just big enough to hold a person, and it was swinging, slowly, back and forth about fifty feet over the acidic-looking pool. Morgan's heart lurched when he saw that a person was struggling with the door to the cage. Just as in his last vision, he didn't have control of his flight, but soon enough, he found himself floating gently down toward the gibbet. When he was just a dozen feet away, he finally was low enough to see directly into the cage, and nausea struck him like a tidal wave when he saw it was Issa.

How could this be? His quest showed that she had passed her Agility challenge. She should be making her own choice right now, not swinging from a gibbet over a lake of acid. Morgan tried to call out to her, but she couldn't seem to see or hear him. As his mind spun, trying to think of a solution, he suddenly found himself back in the round, marble room with the statue.

"What the fuck, man? Are these visions true?" Morgan could feel the heat building in the back of his neck, rage threatening to overtake his good sense.

"I don't believe they would create much of a dilemma if they weren't true, but I cannot be sure. I'm simply an administrator." Morgan thought he saw a hint of a shrug in the stony shoulders, which further enraged him.

"This is bullshit." Morgan paced back and forth. Just as with the first, when he finished the second vision, he'd known that if he grasped the orb, it would somehow aid Issa in her predicament. So, what was the System's game? Clearly, it wanted to rile up his emotions. Did it want him to pick the Utilitarian choice and help the most people? Did it want him to value the individual and go with his gut instinct to help Issa? Did the System even care? The statue had said that the System valued all virtues. Morgan knew that a general or captain would choose the option to help the most people. They would weigh the lives of all the people who might die fighting the Urghat against Issa's life, and they would say, "I had to go with the greater good." Morgan also knew that he wasn't a politician or a ship captain. Would he be able to live happily knowing he had sealed Issa's fate?

A thought occurred to him: he wouldn't have to live with it. The System was going to remove the memory of his choice from him. He could save his people, sacrificing Issa, and he'd never have to remember he did it. "Fuck that," he said, and reached out to grasp the blue and silver orb. He knew it was impulsive and probably not the "smart" move, but he didn't care. Yes, he valued the colonists' lives, but he honestly didn't feel invested in them at all. He also felt like they weren't under the imminent threat of death, and maybe they'd be able to mount a good defense against whatever the Urghat were planning. Deep down, Morgan knew he was simply justifying his decision; he cared about Issa and wanted to save her. He hated being manipulated, though.

These thoughts raced through his mind as his hand made contact with the cold, glassy surface of the orb. As he gripped the baseball-size ball of glass, he felt it become pliable, and then it was like it had turned into liquid as it splashed over his fist. A sensation, like ice water entering his veins, rushed up his arm, and then his vision narrowed to a pinprick, and he lost consciousness.

MORGAN

Morgan opened his eyes and was immediately disoriented, and as he looked around at the white marble walls lining the circular room, he was stricken with a strong sense of déjà vu. He'd been here before. Memories rushed back to him, and he began to understand what was happening; he had taken the fourth challenge. It had involved him making a choice, and the statue had told him that he'd forget about what choice he'd made. Angrily, Morgan clambered to his feet and wracked his brain for some kind of memory of the challenge. All he could recall was walking into a circular room just like this one, except it had held a tall statue. He remembered the statue's deep, gravelly voice and how it told him he'd forget about the choices. That was all. "Goddamn, it sucks having your mind fucked with."

"Uh," said a soft voice, grunting with the effort of sitting up, "it sure does." Morgan whirled around to look behind him and saw Issa sitting on the marble floor behind where he'd woken.

"Issa!" Morgan rushed over to her and knelt, pulling her into a hug.

"Morgan, I'm glad to see you! I was beginning to wonder if you'd ever finish your challenge. Oh, my head is aching!" Issa rubbed at her head, tousling her bright yellow locks.

"Yeah, sorry about that. I had to use my cultivation drill to create channels before I could complete the Energy manipulation trial." Morgan sat back and looked at Issa. He felt so relieved to see her. The last he recalled, he'd been hoping to meet her during the fourth challenge, but then the statue had spoken to him, and . . . damn it! He couldn't really remember anything after that. Still, here she was, and he couldn't complain about that. "What about you? Was the Agility challenge hard?"

"Not really. I had to climb some stalagmites and leap over some acid pits, swinging on chains. I finished the main challenge, but there were further optional challenges that awarded chests. I only felt confident finishing one of those." She smiled suddenly. "I got a fruit that gave me two permanent agility!"

"Oh, that's great! I got something similar for intelligence." Morgan smiled, happy not to try to overshadow her enthusiasm by mentioning the details of his reward. "Did you also have to . . . wait, what the fuck? What was the fourth challenge again?"

Issa scratched her head and frowned, saying, "Um, I can't recall! I swear, just a minute ago, I had some memory of it!" She scrunched up her face in concentration and looked into space just in front of her. Morgan could tell she was looking at a System screen. "Morgan, do you have a new title?"

"Let me see." Morgan pulled up his tiles and feats page and saw:

__Human Champion, First Hollow Guard, Ardeni Friend, Mark of Loyalty__

There was a new entry. He concentrated on the Mark of Loyalty, and a description appeared:

__Mark of Loyalty: You have proven yourself an exemplar of the Virtue of Loyalty. This Mark will serve to improve and focus the choices you are offered for Class Refinement opportunities in the future.__

"Yeah, I do. I have something called the Mark of Loyalty." Morgan stared thoughtfully at a blank spot on the wall, wracking his brain for some memory.

"I have the same one!" Issa excitedly punched Morgan in the arm. "I wish I could remember what I did to earn it!"

"Me, too. I guess the System is serious about keeping it a secret. Wait, that's right, somebody told me I'd forget it because it was meant to stay a secret." Morgan stood, rubbing a knuckle between his eyes, and looked around.

"That sounds right," Issa replied, also standing up. "Do you think it's an actual mark?" She started examining her limbs. "Is there anything on my face?"

"No, what about mine?" Morgan, too, began to look at his arms, even pulling his vambraces off. He was in the process of putting them back on when Issa made an excited yelping sound. He looked at her and saw she was looking down the front of her blouse.

"I have a tattoo. Or something like a tattoo; it's silvery and right over my heart. And, no, I'm not showing you!" Morgan grinned at her words and started shrugging his robe off, wondering if he also had a mark on his chest. When he pulled the inner, close-fitting robe aside, he saw that he did. It was a silvery sigil about the size of his palm. He didn't recognize it, but he felt a sense of calm when he looked at it, and it brought up memories of his childhood home and friends. It also made him think of Issa, and he looked up at her, smiling.

"It looks just like mine," she whispered, smiling back at him. She reached out a hand and rested it on his chest, over the mark. She closed her eyes and stood that way for a minute, and Morgan stayed quiet, enjoying her touch. After a few long breaths, she pulled her hand away. "It makes me feel safe, like when I'm at home with friends and family," she said.

"Yeah, I got that impression from just looking at it," Morgan said. He pulled his robes back tight and shrugged on the outer layer, still feeling relaxed and at peace.

"Let's see what's through that archway," Issa said. Morgan looked where she was pointing and saw that there was an arch-shaped opening in the marble wall to his left. Had that been there before?

"Yeah, alright." He retrieved his spear from his dimensional bag and walked toward the opening with Issa right behind him, her hand on her rapier hilt. As he stepped through, he found himself in a gently curving and slightly upward sloping tunnel made from the same gray-white marble as he'd grown accustomed to over the last several days. Morgan couldn't see any of the glowing orbs that had lit much of the Marble Halls, but there was some sort of soft, diffuse white lighting, nonetheless. He couldn't tell if the light was coming from the marble itself or if it was just some kind of magically lit space. The tunnel continued for several hundred feet, constantly climbing and gradually curving to the right.

After several minutes of walking, an ornate marble archway came into view. It was easy to guess that it was the tunnel's endpoint, and Morgan could just make out a natural-looking cavern beyond the archway. It seemed to be lit with natural light—he could see a thick beam of sunlight with motes of dust lazily drifting in it just beyond the archway. Subconsciously, the two quickened their pace, and as they passed beneath the filigreed archway, exquisitely carved with marble vines and flower petals, System messages popped up in Morgan's view:

*****Congratulations! You have completed a Quest: Survive four challenges in the Marble Halls 4/4. Reward: One Improved Treasure Box, egress from the Crucible.*****

*****Congratulations! You have completed a Quest: Survive the Crucible. Reward(s): Commensurate with achievements—84th percentile—One Advanced Treasure Box, continued existence, Token of Travel.*****

Morgan wiped the messages away and looked around. He was standing in a small cave with a natural, rocky slope leading up to an opening about the size of a garage door. Sunlight was streaming in through the opening, and he could see, from this angle, a glimpse of deep blue sky. They'd made it.

Morgan looked down to see four System treasure chests forming out of swirling silver and blue Energy, two in front of him and two in front of Issa. Morgan smiled, anticipation brightening his mood even more, and reached an arm around Issa's shoulders. She smiled back and leaned into him as they watched the chests finish forming. Three of the boxes were of similar size and design, but one of Morgan's was smaller with more silver than blue in its design. The silver made up most of the box, and the ornate designs were blue, the opposite of the other three. "Did you get two improved rewards?" he asked Issa.

"Yes, the System said I was in the 58th percentile and gave me an improved treasure box." Issa shrugged, stepping over to her boxes. "I suppose your little silver box is higher rank?"

"Hey, don't blame me!" Morgan laughed, kneeling to open his Improved box, but then he stopped, deciding to watch Issa open hers first. She noticed him sit back from his chest and watch her, and she performed a small, mocking curtsey. She knelt before her first box and opened it. Inside, nestled in the usual silky cloth, were three small vials, all labeled. Issa picked them up, one by one, and read the labels, her smile growing the whole time.

"One elixir that will advance my race, and two healing potions! The label says they can gradually heal even a grievous injury," she explained, holding each little vial up as she spoke.

"Those sound great! Are you going to drink the one for your race?"

"Maybe in a bit, let's see what else we got, first!" Issa leaned forward and opened the second one as the first chest dissipated in wisps of blue smoke. When she flipped the lid open, Morgan noticed the golden glow of an Advancement Orb right away. Next to the orb was a silver, coin-shaped object about two inches in diameter, and next to that was a stoppered wooden flask about the size of a typical plastic soda bottle back on Earth. Issa excitedly clapped when she saw the Advancement Orb. "This will get me to ten, and then I'll be able to see my class choices!"

"Yeah! That's great, Issa. What are the other things, though? Issa picked up the silver coin and concentrated. Morgan guessed she was bonding with it. After a moment, she looked up, and understanding lit her eyes.

"It's the Token of Travel. Morgan, it's reusable! Once per month, it will transport me back to my home Settlement Stone!" She tucked the token into a pocket and picked up the wooden flask. Once again, she concentrated and then looked up at Morgan. "It's like a dimensional bag, except for liquids. It's much higher quality than the bags we found, though—it can hold a lot and is very durable."

"Pretty awesome rewards, Issa. I hope my Token of Travel is like that," Morgan said, then gestured to the orb. "Use your orb real quick, and then I'll open my boxes." Issa nodded and touched the glowing yellow ball of light. Morgan watched the Energy flash into her hand and advance through to her Core. He even noticed her eyes glowing for a brief moment. "That's cool to watch!"

Issa laughed and said, "I'm not going to look at my classes yet! Open your boxes!"

"Alright, here goes," Morgan said, reaching for the blue, larger box. Issa waved away the smokey blue remnants of her treasure box dissipating and sat down to watch him. He opened the lid and saw that he had also been awarded three vials. "I wonder if mine are the same as yours." He picked up the first one, a glass container just a bit larger than his thumb filled with a sparkling green syrup. He read the label:

Refined extract of Tundra Bee Royal Jelly—known for pushing the advancement of one's racial lineage.

"I think I did get the same reward as you—that one is for racial advancement." Morgan picked up the other two vials. They were smaller than the first one, and each contained a clear liquid. Suspended in the fluid were tiny, pink bubbles. Morgan looked at the labels:

Botnor's Tincture of Superior Mending—imbibe this tincture to heal even grievous injuries over time.

"Yeah, my box was the same as yours. Still, it's pretty nice having these for emergencies." Morgan carefully set the Tundra Bee Royal Jelly aside and put the two healing tinctures into his bag. As the Improved Treasure Box sublimated into wisps of blue smoke, Morgan pulled the silver Advanced Treasure Box over to him. "Well, here goes!" He opened the lid.

The first thing he noticed was the Advancement Orb—it wasn't like the ones he and Issa had gotten before. This one was smaller, but it had a denser appearance, and the aura of Energy that smoldered off of it was palpable. Next to the orb was a silver token, just like Issa's. The last object nestled in the folds of silvery cloth was a dark gray metallic polyhedron with twelve sides. It was a little smaller than his fist, and when Morgan lifted it out, he was startled by the weight. It was easily the heaviest object of that size that he'd ever held; he guessed it must weigh fifty pounds.

Lifting the polyhedron with two hands, he looked closely at it. He could see, moving on hidden currents within the metal, bronze-colored symbols and runes that reminded Morgan of the characters he'd seen on scrolls he'd received from the System in other rewards. "What the hell is this thing? It's damn heavy!"

"I don't know! Bond with it!" Issa leaned closer, peering at the many-sided ball in Morgan's hands. "It has runes floating around in the metal!" Morgan nodded and sent a thin stream of Energy into the polyhedron.

Dwelling Seed: Vormendion's Iron Tower. One use, permanent dwelling construct.

"It's a dwelling seed, whatever that is," Morgan said.

"Really? I think that's a scarce reward, Morgan. I've heard the System sometimes awards buildings for new colonies and towns, but they aren't common, and something tells me the one you got is rarer still."

"Yeah, it feels pretty exceptional—I can get a sense of the Energy potential in it, now that I'm bonded, and it feels almost like I'm holding a bomb." Morgan tried to put the seed into his bag, but it wouldn't work. He tried to push it in physically, and it was like trying to put two powerful magnets together on opposing poles.

"Morgan! Imagine the dimensional magic involved if that is a seed that turns into a building! It can't go into another dimensional container!" Issa grabbed onto his wrists and pulled his hands away from his pouch.

"Oh! I guess that makes sense. I'm glad I didn't get it in there, 'cause now I'm imagining a black hole or something!"

"I don't know about a black hole, but you could perhaps tear reality," Issa said flatly. Morgan stopped grinning and blanched. He took a leather bag from his dimensional satchel and put the seed into it, pulling the leather drawstring tight. He wrapped the neck of the bag around his leather girdle and used the drawstrings to hold it in place.

Next, Morgan picked up his Token of Travel and bonded with it:

Token of Travel: Activate to travel to your home Settlement Stone. Recharges over one month.

Popping the Token of Travel into his pouch, Morgan reached for the Advancement Orb. The surge of Energy that rushed into him was unlike anything he'd felt before. It was like he was getting a massage and taking a hot shower simultaneously. When his vision cleared, he noted the System message:

Congratulations! You have achieved level 12 Hollow Guard and have gained 10 Strength, 10 Will, 8 Vitality, 8 Intelligence, and 6 Agility.

"Holy shit! I just gained two levels, and my class apparently gives out a lot of stats per level!" Morgan looked at Issa, eyes wide with surprise and excitement. "I just gained forty-two stat points for two levels!"

"Yes, I saw the effect! Your aura is more palpable now. You remind me of some of the older hunters in my village already. You're going to be a real monster someday!"

"A monster?" Morgan frowned.

"I don't mean that in a bad way! According to my elders, in our world and in others rich in Energy, some of the strongest Energy users are creatures that have evolved many times. Powerful people like to compare their strength to these 'monsters,' so if someone calls you a real monster, it's a compliment!"

"Oh well, on my world, the only real monsters were people, and we called them that for doing terrible things. I saw the handiwork of some 'monsters,' so I feel a bit negative about the term." Morgan tried to shake it off, standing up to stretch.

"Well, don't worry, Morgan, I only think good things about you," Issa said, also standing up. Morgan felt a slight lurch in his stomach when she said that, and he realized he was feeling some dread about being done with the Crucible—didn't finishing mean they'd soon be parting ways?

MORGAN

Morgan pushed his dread of parting with Issa aside and said, "Hey, what about your class choices?"

"I looked briefly, and I have a lot of options! Most of them are Improved!" Issa was beaming. "I'm not going to choose a class yet, though, since we're at the end of the Crucible. I'll get some advice from my elders back home."

"Sounds smart, but what about our racial upgrades? Let's drink those before we leave." Morgan paused for a moment and looked at Issa. "If you had taken the racial upgrade first, would you have had better options with your class choices?"

"Um"—Issa's face lost some of its color—"oh, Morgan! I don't know! Did I make a big mistake?"

"Well, nah, I doubt it. I wouldn't worry, Issa; it's nothing you can control anyway." Morgan picked up the vial of refined royal jelly. "Have you ever heard of a Tundra Bee?"

"Hah, no, but the world is huge, and since the reward came from the System, there's a good chance it's not even from this world."

"Ah, yeah, good point. Well, we should sit down for this. The last time, when I ate that fruit, it knocked me on my ass." Issa nodded, and they sat down, facing each other. They each removed the cork stoppers from their vials and then tipped the contents into their mouths. The thick jelly slid from the vials like water on wax, and the explosion of taste made both of them gasp in pleasure. From the moment Morgan swallowed the jelly, he could feel it doing something. His throat tingled, then his stomach, and then the tingling spread through his body. Before he knew it, his eyes were closed, and he felt like he was flying through swirls of colorful fog. Surprisingly, he felt like Issa was flying with him, and he could hear her laughing as they swooped in circles through the mists. Morgan reached out and held her hand and her purring laugh intensified.

Sometime later, it could have been minutes or years for all Morgan could tell, he sat up from the stone floor. He had Issa's hand in his, and he looked over at her. She was still lying on her back with her eyes closed. Blue steam was rising from her body in a thick haze. Morgan realized he was similarly steaming. Issa looked different: her bright yellow hair had a new sheen to it, almost like it was made of impossibly fine metal strands. Her skin was a lighter, more luminous shade of blue, and she was bigger. Morgan was sure of this because her scavenged pants, which had almost fit her perfectly, now ended a good two or three inches from her feet. More than that, though, she just felt more present, more significant. Was this the aura she had spoken about with regard to him gaining stats?

"What are you staring at?" Issa's voice was soft and purring, and her lips were turned up in a smile.

"You look incredible!"

"You're not so bad yourself! Your hair is shining like bronze, and you look even bigger." She sat up and openly stared at him. "Your eyes look like icy diamonds. Look at the steam coming off you! Think of all the impurities leaving your body and the improvements to your biology. That jelly was amazing!" She focused her bright yellow eyes in front of her for a second, then exclaimed, "Base 3! I gained two racial ranks! Think, Morgan, our lifespans just increased by a hundred years or more!" She laughed, leaning forward to grab Morgan in a quick hug, then stood up and bounced around, stretching her improved body.

Morgan was content to sit and watch her with a big, stupid smile on his face. Eventually, curiosity got the better of him, and he pulled up his status sheet:

Status			
Name:	Morgan Hall		
Race:	Human - Base 4		
Class:	Hollow Guard - Advanced		
Level:	12		
Core:	Vortex Class - Base 2		
Energy Affinity:	9.2	Energy:	640/640
Strength:	25	Vitality:	28 (30)
Dexterity:	8	Agility:	21
Intelligence:	36	Will:	25

Titles & Feats:	Human Champion, First Hollow Guard, Ardeni Friend, Mark of Loyalty
Skills:	System Language Integration - Not Upgradeable, Spear Mastery - Basic, Dagger Mastery - Basic, Stealthy Maneuvers - Basic, Backstab - Basic, Energy Drain - Improved, Guard Ally - Basic, Vortex Core Cultivation Drill - Basic

He'd made a lot of improvements since he had arrived on this planet. Well, since he'd been kidnapped and thrust into this world was a better way of putting it. If the Crucible was truly a place designed to give advancement opportunities, then it seemed to have worked. The problem Morgan had with it was that it had nearly killed him and Issa many times in the process. He'd seen evidence of many people dying in this place, and he and Issa had been through hell. Despite his gains, Morgan didn't feel like a big fan of the Crucible or the System that had sent him here without his consent.

"Issa, I'm going to miss you," he said suddenly, standing up. Issa stopped stretching, and her face became serious.

"I'll miss you, too, Morgan. I've even been thinking of maybe not using my Token of Travel. Maybe we are in a place near my village. Let's go out of the cave and have a look!" Issa gestured to the sunlit opening a couple of dozen yards up the slope of the cave.

"I hadn't thought of that. Alright, let's see!" Morgan reached out, and Issa took his hand, and together they walked toward the sunlight. As they advanced up the slope, Morgan could see more and more of the sky, and a massive moon started to come into view. The daylight was still fairly bright, so the moon wasn't well defined, but he could see that it filled a considerable portion of the sky and had giant, arcing rings around it. "Woah, I didn't realize this planet had such a big moon."

"Yes, that's Thivia, the biggest moon, and it's visible at night for half the year and during the day for the other half." They continued to walk, and another, much smaller, moon came into view.

"What's that moon's name?"

"Galia, Thivia's little sister. She moves through the sky, always right behind Thivia." Issa's voice was relaxed, almost dreamy sounding, and Morgan realized she was feeling the release of a lot of pent-up stress and emotional turmoil.

"You're happy to see them again, aren't you?" He squeezed her hand. Issa nodded, and he could see she was holding back even more emotion. When they stepped through the cave opening, Morgan knew Issa's idea of walking back to her people wasn't going to work. The cave opened onto a short ledge on the side of a mountain, an incredibly big mountain, judging by the vista that stretched before them.

Smaller, snow-capped mountains stretched away from them into the horizon. To their left, more mountains extended, but there was a green haze near the horizon that might be an ocean or forest; it was too hard to tell. To their right, foothills extended for dozens of miles into a dense forest that continued as far as they could see. The trees were similar to pines or evergreens back on Earth, but Morgan could tell that they were immense even from this height and distance. They looked something like the Redwoods that had been starting to make a comeback in California when they'd left, onboard the *Pilgrim-9*.

Morgan and Issa stood for a long while, taking in the incredible view. The air was brisk but not freezing, and Issa's hand felt warm in his. After a time, he looked down and saw that she had tears in her eyes. "Hey, don't worry, Issa. I'm going to find you." He squeezed her hand.

"How, Morgan? Our world is huge, and I have no idea where your Token of Travel will take you. What if you're on the other side of the planet?" Her voice cracked, and she angrily reached up and rubbed the tears from her eyes.

"I have an ability to sense my friends, Issa. As long as we're on the same world, I'll be able to feel you, and I promise: I'm going to find you." Morgan put his hands on her shoulders and looked into her eyes while he spoke. Issa reached up to his neck and pulled his face to hers, kissing him gently.

"My village is called Tarn's Crossing. You better find me, Morgan," she said softly. Then, she reached into her pocket, closed her eyes in concentration, and disappeared.

Morgan jerked in surprise, taking a step back, and then it clicked in his head—she'd used her Token of Travel. "Not one for long goodbyes, I see," he said wryly. He felt like he should be upset at the prospect that she was gone, but he couldn't stop grinning at the warm feeling of her lips that still lingered on his. Just to be sure, he activated Guardian's Senses while thinking of Issa, and he had a very faint impression of her in front of where he was standing and off to the right, thousands of miles away. Hopefully, his Token of Travel would deposit him closer than that, but if not, he'd still find a way to get to her.

Morgan took one last look around, drinking in the view of the mountains, the forest, the cobalt sky, and the moons. He inhaled a deep breath of the crisp, cold, impossibly clean air. Then, he took his Token of Travel and his spear from his pouch. He grasped the token in his left hand and the spear in his right and activated the token. His vision spiraled like he was inside a massive kaleidoscope, and then a new scene came into focus.

BRONWYN

"What do you mean? How can there be more? There were so many..." A short fit of coughing cut off Olivia's voice.

"We need to get out of this smoke; let's push up and find Emmet," Bronwyn said as she put an arm around Olivia and half carried her down the hall past the smoldering corpses. "I don't suppose you have enough Energy for some light, do you?"

"Oh! Yes, of course, just one second; I got quite a bit back after the fight." Olivia summoned her array of energy marbles and forced the fire mote to grow until it shone bright light down the hallway. Nothing else was coming toward them, at least not at the moment. The smoke was drifting up toward the cave's exit, so they could breathe more easily after pushing past the pile of smoldering bodies. They could see the end of the tunnel and the opening into the cave where Emmet had gone just a dozen or so feet ahead. Nothing moved in their line of vision, but Bronwyn thought she heard something. It was some kind of crunching sound.

"Shh. Stop for a minute," she said, straining to hear. It was definitely a wet crunching sound and a muffled grunting sound. Heat rose in her neck as she imagined Emmet being tortured or something, and she pounded her right gauntleted fist into the other and strode purposefully down the tunnel and into the cave. She could hear the others scrambling to follow her, but she was several seconds ahead of them through the opening.

The chamber she walked into wasn't entirely devoid of light, but it took her a moment to see the shape of the cave. She was aware of open space and could hear the grunting and cracking sound coming from off to her right, but it wasn't until Olivia caught up and her fiery, baseball-size orb drove the shadows back that she could clearly see the horrors before her. The cave was oval in general shape, with the longer side going off to Bronwyn's right. About twenty feet in front of her, she could see a pile of rotting, dismembered Yeksa corpses halfway submerged in a pool of frigid-looking, blue liquid. She could see ice crystals forming on the bottom corpses, and a sheen of thin ice covered the cavern floor near the pool. The air itself was cold, and with the light shining behind her, she noticed her breath pluming forth. Before she could take in the rest of the scene, Olivia choked out a gasp, and Martin's deep voice rang out, "Holy Fuck!"

Bronwyn jerked her head to the right, looking down the length of the cave, and saw what had caused the reaction. A horrific creature lurked there among the long shadows cast by rubble and stalagmites. It had a humanoid body, supported by six huge spider-like legs. From the base of its torso, where a human's legs would be, a nest of writhing tentacles sprouted, and in the tentacles, gripped around the neck and waist was Emmet's corpse. His legs were gone, and, as Bronwyn stared aghast, a vicious beak like you might imagine on a giant bird or turtle lunged out of the nest of tentacles and ripped away a considerable portion of Emmet's pelvis. Bones crunched. The face on the top of the humanoid body was nightmarish: an elongated, widely hinged lower jaw, black eyes that seemed to absorb the light, a flat nose with long slits for nostrils, all in a smooth dark gray skin that belied no emotion.

"Huh, huh, huh," the creature said in a deep mocking laugh. "Some more delicious System cattle for me? I'm not that hungry, so some of you will serve me after death. Rejoice." While it spoke, the beak shot forth and took a crunching bite out of Emmet's side.

"You mother fucker!" Bronwyn called forth her stone armor and charged at the monstrosity, channeling as much Energy as she could into her fist as she jumped over some loose rubble, swinging a wild haymaker at its writhing tentacles where she had seen the beak withdraw. Bronwyn was fast. She knew she was miles faster than anyone she'd ever met, now that she'd leveled up a few times in this Energy-rich world and applied her gains to her agility. She still wasn't fast enough to react when the monster lashed out with one of its long, carapace-covered legs and slammed her into the ground, shattering her layer of stone armor and driving the breath from her lungs.

"No!" Olivia shouted, stepping forward and starting to form a large, needle-pointed fragment of ice. She was just about to launch her attack at the creature when it carelessly flung Emmet's corpse at her, as fast as a professional might throw a baseball. The corpse slammed into Olivia, sending her careening into a nearby wall with a *crunch*. She slid to the ground, unmoving, and her four little orbs, including the one providing most of the light, disappeared with little audible pops.

Bronwyn struggled to get her breath and push the creature's spidery leg off her chest when Maya and Martin entered the fray. The two advanced much more cautiously than Bronwyn had, especially now, in the deeper darkness. Each circled the monster in a different direction. To her left, Maya approached, her shield held high and her axe up and ready to swing. To her right, Martin circled, his club held like a baseball bat waiting for a pitch. Bronwyn could hear them and see faint outlines of their shadows. As she lay on her back, she could see that the faint light was coming from a high, natural chimney in the cavern that opened in a small crack a hundred feet above their heads. Bronwyn gripped the spidery leg with both gauntleted fists and squeezed, lifting with all her might.

"Come now, cattle. You only prolong the suffering. Lie before me that I might end your feeble existence and add you to my legion." The creature's humanoid head spoke, but Bronwyn could see, among the twisting tentacles, a glinting pair of red eyes betrayed the beak, beginning to move forth. Panic flooded her, and adrenaline compounded with Energy poured into her veins, and she heaved with all her might. She rolled to her left as the leg lifted just an inch and she scrambled away.

Before the Lovecraftian horror could pursue her, Maya shouted, "Now, Martin!" and the two of them attacked from opposite directions. Holding her shield up, Maya stepped forward and swung a wide arc with her axe, hoping to cleave through some of the tentacles. Martin roared and brought his club down, using his Earth Cracker skill to shatter the carapace covering one of the monster's rear legs. Maya's attack proved ineffectual, as the speed of the tentacles outmatched her; they wrapped around her arm and drew her close, and the beak shot forth to snap a section away from her throat. She didn't even get a chance to scream as gouts of blood sprayed out from the gaping wound, and the tentacles flung her away. As Martin lifted his club for another blow, the monster almost lazily spun around and smacked him to the ground with one of its legs, just as it had to Bronwyn earlier. This time, though, it spoke in its deep, rumbling voice in a language that sounded discordant and chaotic in the humans' ears. Greenish black smoke spread from the tip of the leg that held Martin pinned, flowing over him and into his lungs as he inhaled.

Martin shrieked as he started to wither. His flesh began to desiccate as thick black steam rose from his body, making the already dim chamber darker still. The whole exchange between her two companions and the monster only took a couple of seconds, and by the time Bronwyn was back to her feet and facing the creature, Martin had withered to a dried-out husk, his mouth open in a rictus howl. Bronwyn glanced at the monster, then at Olivia's crumpled form, her white blouse the only part of her that stood out in the dark, near the tunnel. Maya and Martin were gone, and the creature had treated her like a rag doll.

Frustration, rage, fear, despair all together nearly overwhelmed her. It was all Bronwyn could do to choke back a sob as she turned and ran to Olivia's bloodied and broken form, lifting her into a fireman's carry and sprinting for the tunnel. The monster took one step after Bronwyn, but it faltered on its broken leg and stopped. Instead, it let out that sickening, guttural laugh and called after her, "Run then, cattle. I'll come to collect you soon."

Bronwyn ran, tears streaming down her cheeks, unbidden. Olivia flopped lifelessly on her shoulder, her arms dripping blood down the backs of Bronwyn's legs as she ran past the pile of burnt Yeksa. She sprinted with all her might, her lungs working like a bellows and the hallway flashing past her in a blur. She ran past the old Yeksa dwellings and into the tunnel leading to the surface. She ran out of the cave, and she didn't stop until she was halfway back to the settlement.

When she finally stopped, Bronwyn wasn't far from where she'd tasted the red sap. Not far from where everyone had laughed at her red-stained teeth—before they had died. She angrily wiped the tears streaking the soot and blood on her cheeks and gently knelt, cupping a hand behind Olivia's head as she laid her down in a patch of grass. Bronwyn gently straightened her friend's arms, feeling for broken bones and finding several. She felt along her legs but couldn't tell if they had any breaks. Last, because she'd been dreading it, she inspected her face and head. Olivia's face and scalp were a bloody mess. Bronwyn could tell that her left orbital bone had broken, and a terrible, bloody gash ran from her forehead, through her eye, and down her cheek. Her face had been the main point of impact with the rough cave wall. "Oh God, Olivia, this looks bad," she whispered while holding her fingers to her neck. She had a pulse, but it was weak and slow.

Bronwyn dug in her pouch for one of the blankets she'd stowed within and cut a long, wide strip. She used it to gently bind and cover the cut on Olivia's eye and face. Then she cut more strips of cloth and some green branches to make splints for Olivia's arms. That done, she picked her up, cradling her in her arms, and walked back to the settlement. Her mind was a thundercloud of guilt, anger, and regret. She berated herself for running so far with Olivia's wounded head hanging down her back. She cursed herself for being too weak to hurt the monster. She hated herself for letting Olivia and the others come with and leading them to their deaths.

Even with her improved strength, she was wrung dry and stumbling by the time she made it out of the forest. She hurried across the grass, refusing to allow herself to slow. The colonists on watch by the archway ran up to her, offering to help with Olivia, but Bronwyn shrugged them off, walking with Olivia straight up the cleared pathway that led to the Colony Stone. She gathered quite a crowd, with many people asking what happened. She just shook her head, not trusting herself to speak. When she began the hike up the easy grade of the hill, she noticed Arthur was standing by the stone. She tried to ignore him, but before she was halfway up the slope, he was in front of her asking, "What happened, Bronwyn? Is that Olivia? Is she okay?"

"Just wait, Arthur." Bronwyn pushed past him, climbed the rest of the way to the stone, and then slapped her hand on it, opening the Contribution Store. She'd spent the last few days earning System Credits with her quest to find the Yeksa cave and by creating Energy beads, but she hadn't spent any of her store points; she had just over four thousand. She searched through the menus until she found the one titled Healing Items and was rewarded with a long list, ranging from cloth bandages for two contribution points to something called the Dew of Absolution for 580,000. Not wanting to waste time, she scrolled to items listed for around four thousand and found something called an unguent of major healing for 3,800. The description said it would vastly improve an individual's natural healing rate and efficacy. Bronwyn touched the menu button to purchase the ointment. A swirl of golden motes streamed out of the stone and coalesced on the ground by Bronwyn's feet. Steam rose from the spot, and when it cleared, a small glass jar with a silver lid was resting on the ground.

Bronwyn gently laid Olivia on the grass near the stone and then picked up the jar. By this time, a fairly large crowd had gathered, and she could hear people asking each other what was going on, but she ignored everyone. Focusing intently on her task, she picked up the jar and knelt next to Olivia. She looked at the simple label on the side of the jar: "Gently spread topically near the injured area." Bronwyn unscrewed the lid and saw that the cream was an ivory-white and of a consistency not unlike the expensive night cream she'd left behind in her apartment. She was getting ready to apply it when she looked up suddenly at the circle of inquiring faces. "Hey, can you give me some space? I doubt Olivia would want you all staring at her when I put this stuff on her ribs and stomach!"

Some people looked away, ashamed, but many refused to budge. Surprisingly it was Arthur who took up her cause and exhorted them all to back up and "Give her some space!" Bronwyn scooped some of the cream onto a finger, noticing that her own hand was covered in soot and blood, and her nails were torn. When had that happened? She shoved the thought aside and gently tested the cream on some of the more superficial cuts on Olivia's arm, spreading it on the purple, swollen area where it was broken. The cream spread like melted butter and was absorbed immediately into Olivia's skin. The cuts on her arm closed instantly, leaving thin, white scars as if the wound had been healed for years. The bruise over her broken forearm faded immediately, and most of the swelling went down. Bronwyn took another dab of cream and gently rubbed it into the same spot. The swelling continued to subside, and she felt the bone shift. The arm was straight and smooth, and Bronwyn couldn't feel any sign of a break, even when she pressed along the bone with her thumb.

That test done, she set the jar down and gently unwrapped the cloth from around Olivia's face. She winced and again felt tears welling in her eyes, but she fought them back; time for self-pity later. Olivia's left brow was misshapen and swollen, and the deep cut that traversed it had been enough to rip her eyelid and probably her eye; Bronwyn couldn't see the eye through all the scabbed blood. Her cheek was cut to the bone as well. She liberally spread the unguent on Olivia's face, from her forehead to her eyebrow, then carefully applied it over her bloodied eye socket and her cheek. She breathed a sigh of relief when Olivia's swelling immediately receded, and the little bones around her eye shifted back into place. Her eyelid mended, and the skin and muscle in her cheek knitted neatly.

Bronwyn delicately felt Olivia's face, ensuring that all the bones were where they should be and that there wasn't any leftover swelling. Olivia hadn't escaped unscathed; she had a white scar about a centimeter wide that ran from just above her eyebrow to halfway down her cheek. Bronwyn was terrified that her eye hadn't healed, so she gently peeled open her eyelids and looked. Olivia's eye was in one piece, but the iris wasn't pale blue anymore; it was a silvery-white. "Oh, dammit! I hope you can still see when you wake up," Bronwyn whispered.

After Bronwyn used the rest of the cream to clear up the bruises and cuts on the rest of Olivia's body, particularly on her ribs and abdomen, she lifted her and made to carry her to her tent. Arthur tried to follow, and when she brushed past him, he said, "Bronwyn! What happened? We have to know what's going on!"

Bronwyn sighed heavily and said, "Thank you for helping with the crowd, Arthur. When Olivia wakes, we'll explain everything, but I just can't right now. Put extra guards on the gateways. Like twenty."

BRONWYN

Bronwyn walked to the edge of the camp, near the western wall. Her tent was still situated there, apart from any other tents. She cradled Olivia in her arms as she walked; she was still unconscious but breathing more normally. Bronwyn pulled open the tent flap and laid Olivia down on her pile of blankets, saving aside her favorite blue one to pull over her and bundling another under Olivia's head to keep it slightly elevated. As she began to pull her thick navy blue blanket over her friend, she was startled to find a very sleepy Hops curled up under it. "Well, hey there, little buddy, sorry to wake you, but I'm gonna need this blanket." She laid it over Olivia and reached out her hand to pick up Hops, who nuzzled into it, but then let out the smallest yawn and scrambled over to sleep on top of Olivia's chest, tucking everything but his big fluffy tail into his shell. His tail he curled around to block the front of his shell and was soon letting out a faint, purring snore. Bronwyn sat there for a minute at the tent opening. "Glad to have you back, Hops; watch over her for me, just for a bit." She closed the tent flap and stood up.

Bronwyn walked around to the side of her tent, where she had a large barrel of water collected from the nearby stream. She sniffed the water, wondering how long it would be potable, but it seemed fine after a couple of days. She put a few ladles-full in her cooking pot and ignited the fire underneath. Her hands and arms were covered in blood, soot, and grime. She wanted to be rid of it. When the water was hot but not quite boiling, she dipped a mostly clean cloth into the pot and began scrubbing her arms and face. It wasn't a hot bath, but it'd do for now. She repeated the process until her hands and arms were pink from the hot water and the scrubbing. She rinsed the cloth and laid it over the pot's lip once more.

She stretched back in the soft grass, but she couldn't close her eyes; her vision swam with inky black tentacles, glowing red eyes, and that hideous beak every time she did. She heard footsteps coming from behind her. "Arthur, I told you I'd come to tell you everything as soon as I was ready and she was awake."

"Well, I do believe that's the first time I've been mistaken for a man," said Maria Rios in her soft motherly voice, chuckling. "Don't worry, dear I'm not here to pry or even ask you any questions. I heard you may have had a rough go of things on your recent outing, and as my mother always said, 'soup warms the heart as much as it does the body.' I've got two bowls of my new favorite recipe here; it's an egg drop soup with some mushrooms from the forest. The eggs are from those bright ribbon-tailed birds we have flying all over the place. Would you believe they keep their nests in the little purple-green shrubs? Not the trees? Well, anyway, I won't talk your ear off. There's a bowl for each of you here, and if Olivia isn't up to eating, why don't you just have two and feel extra warm." She placed the bowls on a log Bronwyn had pulled over to her fire on the second day of the orientation. Maria walked up to her, kneeling and placing her hand on Bronwyn's shoulder. "If you need anything, dear, I'm here to help, even if you just need someone to listen." She stood up and started to walk away.

Bronwyn sat up. "Maria, wait." She stood up all the way and turned toward the older woman. "I . . . oh never mind; it's stupid anyway." Bronwyn sighed.

"Spit it out, dear, or it'll eat you up from the inside. There's no point holding things in." Her voice was firm but caring.

"I—" Bronwyn's voice caught in her throat. "Well, I was just wondering if I could maybe have a hug?" The faintest tears welled up in her eyes, and she tried to will them away, to no success. "I don't know what's wrong with me! I'm so damn weepy and emotional . . ."

"Shh." Maria didn't hesitate, interrupting Bronwyn and immediately striding over to her with arms wide. She embraced her as if she had known her for her whole life. "Well, that's not stupid at all!"

Bronwyn rested her head on Maria's shoulder, not quite crying but taking big, gasping breaths, her throat feeling constricted with emotion. "I don't know what to do, and it's all my fault. I led them out there. I wanted to go on my own; I knew I should've gone alone! I watched them die! There was nothing I could do; I was too slow, too weak. I watched them die, and I ran!" She had tears streaming down her face now. "What if Olivia never wakes up? What if her brain was damaged, and that ointment didn't help? I carried her upside down for over a mile! I'm such an idiot!"

Maria held onto Bronwyn tightly, listening to her vent her frustration. "Come now, dear, you're hardly being fair with yourself. I'm sure you can be very persuasive, but all those who went with you didn't go just because you asked them to. They went because they believed it was what the colony needed, and they were right. You found something terrible out there, didn't you? Now we know we need to put a stop to it. What if you had never gone, and it came in the night? I don't know what it was, girl, but it had to be bad. Do you think two guards would have slowed it down? How many people could it have taken or killed while we felt safe behind our wall?" Bronwyn limply let go of Maria and slumped down to the grass.

"I've never felt so helpless. It was like we were children, and one minute they were alive and becoming my friends, and the next they were gone," she said quietly, looking down at the grass.

"Oh, Bronwyn. I'm so sorry. Loss is something a lot of us had to get used to back during the conflicts, but you're young, and, from your reputation, you're used to winning, aren't you?"

Bronwyn looked up, eyes narrowing. "This isn't about me losing. It's about my friends dying. It's about being helpless. He was fucking taunting us while he *ate* Emmet."

Maria blanched a little, but she pressed on: "Still, Bronwyn, it's not on you. They were all adults and, they knew the risk they were taking. As for Olivia, give it time; the body needs time to heal, and some wounds are more than skin deep. She may be fighting a battle in her mind right this moment."

Maria squatted in front of her and held Bronwyn by her shoulders. "Be strong and stay by her side. That's what she needs right now. Don't dwell on the fact that she got hurt or that you ran; rather, think about how she'd be a hell of a lot worse off right now if you hadn't carried her out of there. There'll be time to figure out what's next after you've rested."

Bronwyn wiped the final tears from her eyes and took a deep breath. "Thank you, Maria. I needed to hear that more than I realized." She smiled for a moment but let it drop slightly. "But listen to me: no one else is going into that cave. I know what I need to do, and I need to do it on my own. I'll finish what we started."

"You do whatever you think is right, dear, but remember, there's no shame in accepting help. Now eat that soup before it gets cold." She squeezed Bronwyn's shoulders one last time and gave her a warm smile before turning around and walking back the way she'd come.

Bronwyn took a quick look in the tent to see if Olivia had stirred, but she and Hops were still soundly asleep. She scooped up both the bowls of soup and sat down by her fire. She hadn't even realized how hungry and tired she was, but after a couple of minutes, she found herself leaning back against her log, two empty bowls beside her, slowly drifting off to sleep.

In her dreams, she felt herself being pinned down by huge spider-like legs, slimy tentacles constricting her throat so tightly she couldn't breathe. She woke with a start, gasping for air, eyes wide, head spinning around, looking for a threat that wasn't there. She took a deep breath. "It was just a dream, just a dream."

Judging by the light, it was near or slightly after midnight, which meant she had slept for the better part of a day. She lifted the tent flap and found the two still sleeping, just as she'd left them. She crouched inside and sat down at Olivia's side. Her pulse seemed stronger, and she was breathing normally. Bronwyn put her hand over Olivia's and let out a strained breath she didn't even realize she was holding as she leaned back against the support post of the tent.

"Bronwyn. Bron, wake up." Olivia's voice was soft and crackly, and she gently squeezed Bronwyn's hand as she spoke.

Bronwyn's eyes shot open "Olivia! Oh, thank God you're awake. What do you need? What, what can I get for you?" She stammered.

"Water, please." Olivia was barely able to speak; her voice sounded so dry. Bronwyn immediately scrambled out of the tent returning swiftly with a mug of water from her barrel.

"Here, let me help you sit up." She set down the mug and put an arm under Olivia, slowly lifting her into a seated position. She winced slightly but seemed okay for the most part. Bronwyn handed her the mug and helped her hold it as she lifted it to drink. "How do you feel? Does it hurt anywhere in particular? There's a little bit of healing cream left, I tried to put it on all your injuries, but I'm not sure if I missed any. There were so many. I, I'm so sorry, Olivia." Bronwyn's voice trailed off as she looked down.

Olivia placed the mug in her lap, lifting her hand up to Bronwyn's cheek. "What do you mean you're sorry? I thought I was dead! You must have saved me, silly." She lifted Bronwyn's head, looking her in the eyes. "Without you, I never would have made it out of that nightmare, right?" She dropped her hand down onto Bronwyn's arm and smiled at her. "I owe you my life, Bronwyn Tallow."

"Olivia, I'm the whole reason you were . . ." Bronwyn started before Olivia shushed her.

"Stop. None of that matters. You risked your life to save mine." Olivia finished the water in her mug and laid her head back down on the makeshift pillow. "You're a hero, Bronwyn. You're my hero." She closed her eyes. "Thank you for watching over me, but I can't take up all of your time, even if I want to. I can see on your face that you have something in mind."

"Yeah, I need to get some levels, get my class. Then I'm going back in there, and I'm going to handle that thing. We need to fill in Arthur and the others about what happened, though."

"I can do that, Bronwyn; I'll tell them everything. You get out there and do what you need to do. I'll be fine; just promise me you'll come back before you go to that cave again."

Bronwyn placed her hand over Olivia's and smiled. "I promise."

She stood up outside of the tent and closed the leather flap. Sitting down on the log by her fire pit, she started to strap on her gauntlets. As she tightened the last strap, she felt Hops's familiar weight climb up her side and onto her shoulder. "Hey, little buddy, I've missed you." She nudged him with her head. "Ready to do some hunting?" Hops gave a small chirp in reply and nestled down into her hair as she started to jog toward the northern gates.

MORGAN

When the wild, shifting colors began to settle, Morgan could see a vastly different scene in front of him. He was standing on a low hillock, covered in short, feathery blue grass. People were milling around not far from him, talking, laughing, sitting on blankets in the sunlight, and eating. It looked almost like a day at a big park. For the most part, the people were wearing loose-fitting cottony trousers and shirts in various muted colors. Many of them were barefoot. Where the hell was he? At the base of the hill, the grassland extended for a mile or so, and then a huge, earth-colored wall rose out of the meadow. Hundreds of nearly identical little canvas tents were spread out in a quasi-orderly fashion between the hill and the wall.

"Jesus, who are you, man?" a startled-sounding voice came from behind Morgan.

"Ahem," Morgan cleared his throat as he turned around. He looked down upon a soft-looking man in his middle years. He had smooth brown hair and a round face, and he wore a pair of loose, pale drawstring pants with a similar-looking shirt tucked in. The outfit looked very comfortable. "Hello. I'm Morgan Hall. Ensign Hall. From the Arkship? Are you guys the colonists?"

"What do you mean, man? Hell yes, we're the colonists. Haven't you been here? Jesus, you're a big guy. Fuckin' A, where'd you get that spear?" The man walked closer to Morgan, and a few other people seemed to have taken notice of him now and were drawing close. Morgan could see a monolithic dark stone standing about a dozen yards back from the man talking to him. It seemed to be situated right in the center of the hilltop, and several people were standing around it, holding their hands against its surface.

"Yeah, that's a long story. What's your name? Who's in charge? Is Arthur Ballard here?" Morgan took a moment to stow his Token of Travel in his dimensional pouch, then reached a hand out to shake the guy's hand.

"Oh, uh, sorry about that. My name's Nels Gibson," he stammered, reaching out a hand to shake Morgan's. Nels's hand felt small and soft, and Morgan had to concentrate on not squeezing too hard. Had his improved stats changed him that much?

"Hey, how tall are you, if you don't mind the strange question?" Morgan asked, letting the guy's hand go and stepping back a pace. More people were starting to gather.

"Um, five foot nine. Why?"

"I got some racial upgrades. You guys are aware of the System, right? You know your stats? Where it gives you the "race" stat? Yeah, I got some upgrades to that. I think I grew more than I realized. Well, that's awkward." Morgan positively towered over the guy. He felt like an adult around some middle schoolers as more people gathered around. A few people might have been close to his height, but he'd been five foot eleven in his old life; there was no way that was still the case. That was a weird way of thinking about it—his old life. He supposed it was accurate, though. Things had changed a lot, even before the System; Earth was hundreds of years behind him. He shook himself out of his musings and looked at the crowd of colonists. "Hey, all. I'm Morgan Hall. I know I don't look like it, but I came here on the *Pilgrim-9* with the rest of you. Is Arthur Ballard around? Or is someone else in charge?"

"Hello there." A striking woman stepped forward, speaking in a smooth, clear voice. She had long, dark hair and pale skin. What struck Morgan was that her eyes were heterochromatic—one was pale blue and the other was a silvery color. A narrow white scar bisected her silvery eye from brow to cheek. "My name's Olivia Bennett. Arthur is around, and he's helping to run things, but we have sort of a small, informal council for the time being. Where did you come from, Mr. Hall?"

"Oh, hello, Ms. Bennett. I'm familiar with your work. I was a tech specialist on the *Pilgrim-9*. Um, I came here from a place the System calls the Crucible." Morgan reached out to shake Olivia's hand, and she coolly grasped his hand, her grip noticeably firmer than Nels's.

"Interesting. We knew people were missing from our counts, but we thought they'd been taken by wolves or Yeksa before we got the walls up."

"You guys built these walls? Jesus, that's an accomplishment. Do we still have the landers? What about the mech and other rigs?" Morgan looked around but couldn't see any sign of heavy equipment.

"No, no, Morgan. We were able to purchase the walls and a few other buildings with the help of the System. I'm sure it's getting more out of the bargain than we are, but we work with what we have. So, you were in some place called the Crucible, hmm? And how did you get here?" She stood back, clearly eyeing Morgan's strange garb—his frayed black robes, his bronze-colored vambraces and greaves, his wide belt with sacks and pouches hanging from it, and his wicked-looking black spear.

"Let's back up," Morgan said, noting the suspicion behind Olivia's gaze. "First of all, I'm not a threat to you. I've been busting my ass trying to get out of the Crucible and get to you all. I don't know what you all have been through or what you know about the System, but I've been through some shit in the last couple of weeks."

"Why you?" another voice queried before Olivia could respond. Morgan turned and saw the older, gray-bearded man and knew it was Arthur Ballard. "Why were you in this Crucible? Why were you not with the rest of us?"

"Great question. When the Noah unit woke me up to do a systems analysis . . ."

Ballard cut Morgan off: "What? Noah woke you up? Why? Where was the ship? Why didn't you wake any other crew?"

"Easy, let me start from the beginning. It's not a very long story: the Noah unit thought the sensors were messing up when we arrived at Tau Ceti because they only displayed one large planet. He woke me up to check on the sensor arrays, and while I was outside doing a physical check, the ship entered what I'm assuming was the border of the System's controlled space." Several conversations started up, and the noise became too much for Arthur.

"Everyone, calm down! I want to hear the rest of this!"

"Anyway, when the System noticed us, everything went dark for me, but I could hear it in my head. It was taking stock of us; it counted how many of us there were, it noticed Noah-9 and said it 'deleted' him. I think it said something about Noah having zero Energy affinity. The System addressed me and said I was separate from the rest of you, and I tried to explain why I was the only one awake, but it cut me off and tossed me in the Crucible. That's it. That's the whole story." Morgan folded his arms, starting to feel a bit defensive.

"I *knew* it!" Olivia interjected. "I knew the System wanted us for our access to Energy. It's parasitic! Why else would it discard Noah-9? He was of no value to the System!"

"Ahem, alright. Well, as I was saying, after that, I don't have any idea what happened with you all. I woke up in the Crucible and have been fighting and running for my life ever since. If it weren't for. . . ."

Morgan suddenly stopped talking and activated his Guardian's Senses ability, thinking of Issa. There she was! Faint, but much closer than when she'd disappeared from the mountain top. She felt like she was, judging by where the sun was sinking toward the horizon, to the southeast and less than a hundred miles away. "Uh, sorry about that. I just remembered something. Anyway, if it weren't for a friend I met in there, I don't know if I would've made it out alive."

"A friend? Another colonist?" Arthur's eyes widened, and he leaned forward.

"No. I'm pretty sure she's a native of this world."

"Sapient?" Olivia stepped closer.

"Yes, and damn smart, in fact. You guys haven't met any sapient natives? Wait, you met Yeksa. I think they're primitive, but I'm pretty sure they have a society." Morgan looked around while he spoke, once again marveling at the tall earthen walls.

"Well, we never got a chance to talk to the Yeksa—it was straight to fighting for our lives with them. Tell us about this friend of yours—do you think her people will want to ally with us?" Olivia pressed.

"Yes, and what about this planet? You were awake to see it from the ship's sensors. Which one are we on? E? F?" Arthur spoke almost simultaneously with Olivia. Other people were beginning to encroach closer to their conversation, and Morgan was starting to feel a little claustrophobic.

"Alright, alright, I'll answer all I can, but then I want a tour of this place, and I'd like a spot where I can place my tower. Yes, before you ask, I said tower. I got an award from the System while in the Crucible—I have an item that will, supposedly, become a tower when I activate it." The next few minutes stretched into an hour as Morgan answered as many questions as possible about the planet, the Crucible, Issa and her people, and even everything he'd learned about gaining levels and improving his race. The way he saw it, for all he knew, these were the last humans in the universe, and they needed to work together.

Later, after Morgan had talked himself out and people had wandered off, Arthur left Morgan in Olivia's hands to tour the colony. The two of them were strolling down the side of the hillock toward the forge building. "So, Bronwyn, the actual VR champ from Earth, built this forge?"

"That's right!" Olivia smiled and began to speak animatedly. "She rescued some colonists from the Yeksa, and the System rewarded her with the building. I bet it works similarly to your tower. She just read some scroll by the Colony Stone, and this building grew out of the ground. It was pretty amazing."

"Well, that's great. Yeah, the System seems to enjoy incentivizing people to do things with 'quests.' So far, it hasn't tried to get me to do anything I didn't want to do. Well, not directly, at least. Sometimes I feel like its quests are passive-aggressive, or like it's testing me or something. I fucking felt constantly manipulated while I was in the Crucible."

"Can you elaborate on that? What do you mean by passive-aggressive?" Oliva stopped, and her face grew serious, and Morgan suddenly remembered that she'd been a world-renowned research scientist back on Earth.

"Maybe I'm using the wrong term, but I'll give you an example: when I first met my friend Issa, she was badly wounded. I was trying to encourage her and said something like, 'we'll get you out of here,' and the System popped up a quest for me to keep her alive for a week. The kicker was that there was a penalty for failure, and it gave me a yes or no option to accept. Like it wanted to make me put some skin in the game, so to speak."

"Interesting. Interesting," Olivia said, nodding and rubbing at her chin. They talked about the System and how it had changed its tone since the "orientation" the colonists had gone through. Olivia told Morgan about Bronwyn and her quest to clear the cave in the woods. About how the System had labeled what lurked within as evil.

"Oh, really? That's a first for me. What did it end up being?" Morgan asked, almost offhandedly.

"Um," Olivia started, but she had gone sort of white, and she self-consciously reached up to touch the scar on her face.

"Oh, uh, are you okay? You don't have to talk about it. Believe me, there's some shit that went down in the Crucible that I never want to think about again."

Olivia shook her head and said, "It was bad, I won't dwell on it, but some of us died, some got hurt"—she gestured to her face—"and we ran. It really messed with Bronwyn. She's out trying to level up to face that thing again." She shuddered a little bit, then shook her head and started walking again. "We haven't built anything along the northern wall yet, and if your building is a tower, I think the northeast corner would be great; you'd have a view out over the plains and of the mountains in the distance.

"Oh, mountain views, eh?" Morgan took the hint and changed the subject.

"I'd think so. Do you know how tall the tower is? The ground slopes slightly downward as you approach the northern wall, so you'll have a view if you pick a spot a couple of hundred yards back from the wall. Unless it's a really short tower." She grinned.

"Well, to be honest, I'm not sure. It just might be positively squat." Morgan laughed, and Olivia joined in.

"You seem all right, Morgan Hall; I think Bronwyn will like you." Once again, Olivia's face grew somber, and they kept walking in silence for a while. Eventually, she broke the silence: "You know, she's pretty important to me. When she gets back, I know she'll go after the thing in that cave again. Do you think you'd consider going with her? You're the only person I know that's higher level than she is."

"You worry about her, huh?"

"Very much, Morgan. Very much."

"Well, I'd have to be a real creep to say no to that, wouldn't I?" He smiled, and it was easy because he didn't know what was waiting for him in that cave, but he knew that he liked Olivia, and he couldn't abide that haunted look on her face every time this subject came up. "Hey, did I tell you what my class is called? I'm known as a Hollow Guard, and it's my job to get between my friends and trouble."

᚛ MORGAN ᚜

Morgan looked over the area that Olivia had led him to—the grass was unblemished, no tents having been in the area, and it had a very gentle downward slope leading to the northern wall of the settlement about two hundred yards away. Because of the grade and the distance, the wall seemed less imposing than it was, and Morgan could see sprawling plains out past the sparse trees. Beyond the plains, tall, purple mountains rose against the horizon. The sky was tinged orange in the fading light, and the jagged, bruised peaks had highlights of amber and ochre. "You weren't kidding about having a view."

"Yeah, when we have enough System Credits, we're going to start building nicer homes around here to offer as an incentive for top contributors to the colony." Olivia looked around, taking in a deep breath of the fresh air.

"The Contribution Store seems like a great tool to get people motivated. It practically runs the colony for you," Morgan commented, while fumbling with the heavy sack tied to his wide belt. He finally untied the leather cord and lifted it free. "This dwelling seed is heavy as hell. Was the forge seed heavy, too?"

"I don't think so, Bronwyn described it as a scroll, and she activated it by the Colony Stone, not where she wanted the forge to be."

"Different things, I guess," Morgan said, pulling the dense polyhedron from the sack. "So, again, I don't know how big this thing will be. You're sure people are okay with me putting a tower here?"

"Yes, the civil engineers from among the colonists have created a layout for the initial colony, and as I said, this area was designated for higher-tier homes. Right now, we're still building high occupancy dwellings to get people out of tents."

"Alright, well, you reckon this thing will account for the slope? I don't want the tower to be leaning." Morgan scratched his head, contemplating the heavy lump of rune-infused metal. Olivia just shrugged in response. "Well, let's give it a go," he said, channeling some Energy into the polyhedron.

*****Dwelling Seed: Vormendion's Iron Tower. One use, permanent dwelling construct.*****

Morgan pushed a little more Energy into the seed, and a new prompt appeared:

Dwelling Seed: Vormendion's Iron Tower. One use, permanent dwelling construct. Activate? YES/NO

Morgan selected "YES," and the prompt disappeared. The seed grew warm and emitted a clanging sound, like a large, metal bell ringing just one time. He kept hold of the seed, and it continued to grow warmer and warmer. After a few seconds, it clanged again. The seed continued to heat up, becoming uncomfortable, and it clanged again, this time jumping in his hand a bit. A few more seconds passed, the seed was growing painfully hot, and the dark bronze-colored runes in the depths of the gray metal started to glow brighter. Morgan set it down on the grass, and it steamed, turning the grass beneath it brown and then black. It clanged every few seconds, and the sound seemed to be getting louder and more frequent. Olivia looked at Morgan and then the seed, and she began to back up. Morgan understood the wisdom of her action and also began to back away from the smoking, jumping, clanging seed.

After about five minutes, the seed was glowing orange and emitting copious amounts of smoke. The clangs were coming every two or three seconds, and with each clang, the seed jumped several feet in the air, always landing exactly in the blackened grass where Morgan had first set it. Morgan was starting to wonder if he was supposed to do something else when something different happened: the seed jumped, clanged, and then expanded, falling back to the grass, nearly twice as large as it had been. Things calmed down for a few minutes after that, the seed having lost much of its heat. It sat in the grass, smoking still but visibly less agitated. Then it clanged, and the sound was much deeper and louder than before. The process began again, with the clangs slowly coming faster and the seed slowly growing hotter. By the time the seed jumped and expanded again, a crowd had started to form on the grassy meadow.

The sun had nearly set, and the sky was growing dark. The seed looked especially bright as the shadows elongated, though many people were carrying lanterns and a few had little glowing balls of light. Morgan wondered if they knew how to create those with some skill or spell or if they'd bought them from the Contribution Store. As they watched the seed heat up, clang, and expand, Morgan fielded questions about what was happening. After thirty minutes or so, the seed was the size of a beach ball, and the sonorous clangs sounded like a church bell. Morgan was beginning to wonder if this would continue until the seed was the size of a tower, but then something changed: the seed started to spin in place, glowing and smoldering like a fallen meteorite.

As the seed spun faster and faster, a glowing disc extruded from its center. People were making sounds like they were watching a fireworks show: "Oooh, aaah!" Morgan smiled, happy to be among a community again. The disc had expanded to about ten feet out from the ball in just a few seconds. People saw the expansion of the spinning, glowing disc and began to back away. The disc continued to expand until it was a good forty or fifty feet across, then it flashed, and with a flare like a bomb going off, it expanded up into the sky and down into the ground, forming a glowing orange cylinder. The structure was forty feet at the base and stretched almost a hundred feet into the air, where it tapered to about half the diameter. Morgan could see crenelations formed at the top of the tower, though they became indistinct in the darkness as the orange glow faded from the metal tower.

Morgan couldn't stop the grin on his face as he watched the immense metal construct slowly cool, ticking as the metal contracted in the night air. A short set of dark metal stairs, complete with a handrail, led to a heavy pair of solid-looking double doors made from the same metal as the rest of the tower. A peaked metal gable extended from the tower's surface to protect the doors from the elements. Morgan was eager to explore the building, but, like the rest of the crowd that had gathered, he was wary of the heat. He looked to Olivia and said, "Hey, thanks for the company, but I think it's gonna be a little while before I can open the door. You don't have to hang around."

"Oh? Don't want to invite me in, I see," Olivia said, a teasing note in her voice. "Don't worry, I'm just joking. I do have a few things to do before I turn in. I'll check on you in the morning, or someone will. It was nice to get to know you a bit today, Morgan." She stood up from where she'd been sitting in the grass and waved, starting back up the slope to the main colony encampment.

"Thanks for everything!" Morgan called after her. She waved, again, over her shoulder. As the tower cooled and the shadows lengthened, most of the crowd dispersed. When Morgan finally decided to go up and give the door a try, a few people stood around expectantly, but he turned to them and said, "I'm going in alone for now. Happy to give tours another time. Nice to meet you all." There were a few disappointed grumbles, but he tuned them out and climbed the steps, gingerly placing a hand on the ornate door handle.

Quest: Defeat the guardians of Vormendion's Iron Tower 0/8. Reward: Access to each guardian's level and Vormendion's Reliquary. Accept? YES/NO

"There's a quest to access my quest reward. Of course." Morgan sighed and selected the "YES" prompt. An audible click vibrated through the door, and he was able to pull it open. It swung smoothly and easily, with almost no friction. Looking through the doorway, Morgan could see a foyer before him. The lighting was warm, provided by a wrought-metal chandelier with some sort of flame spouts filling orange and yellow glass globes. The flames gave off no smoke and seemed entirely contained within the globes. Metal benches lined the short entry hall, and beyond the entry, an elaborate metal staircase rose in a graceful spiral into the shadows. Three sets of double doors led out of the central room, one behind the stairs and one to either side. The doors were made from dark wood, like mahogany. The floor and walls of the interior were, likewise, paneled in a dark hardwood. It was warm and rather pleasant in the glow of the bright chandelier.

Morgan gripped his spear and advanced toward the spiral stairs. He could see that the metal of the railings was carved into myriad shapes of animals, leaves, and flowers. He marveled at the craftsmanship, all the while wondering when the first guardian would jump out of the shadows. As he walked around the central spiral, he concentrated on being stealthy, hoping his skill would serve him well. He noted that the tower seemed to be larger inside than on the outside. The central room alone was easily as wide as the building appeared from the outside. After completing a circuit of the chamber, he looked up the staircase and could just make out a dim landing about twenty feet above. He decided he should deal with one floor at a time and approached the doors to the right of the entryway first.

Morgan found himself wishing Issa were there. He could use the companionship for one, and for two, she could open the door while he burst through with the spear ready. As it was, he'd have to let go of the spear to open the door with one hand. He did so, adrenaline pumping, senses hyper-alert as the door creaked open. He winced at the sound and backed up, leveling the spear in front of him. Nothing happened. He pushed the door farther open with the tip of his spear and slowly advanced into the room. He just about lost control of his bodily functions when another chandelier flamed into life, shedding light on a new scene. A long dark table filled the center of this room, directly beneath the chandelier, and it was lined with ten chairs of similar make. Faded tapestries hung on the paneled walls.

Morgan wanted to study the scenes on those tapestries but didn't allow himself to be distracted. The dining hall was rectangular and large, with an outer wall curved like the tower wall. He could see no exit to his left, so he turned to his right and steadily advanced through the room. He was walking to the right side of the table and could see that a few feet from the end of the table, a set of swinging double doors led out of the room. He guessed they led to a kitchen and was proven right when he poked his spear into one of the dark doors and pushed.

The kitchen was shaped similarly to the dining room but was appointed much differently. Once again, it was lit with flaming glass orbs, but these were in six sconces attached to the walls. The walls were bare metal, like the outside of the tower. Lining both long walls were butcher-block counters with cabinets beneath. A sizeable cast-iron oven and stovetop dominated the far wall. To the left of the oven was a metal door secured with a rune-inscribed padlock. After making sure nothing was hiding in the corners, Morgan tried to pull open the padlock, but it wouldn't budge. A mystery for later, he supposed.

Back in the central chamber, Morgan repeated the process of opening the next set of doors. This time, he was prepared when the room flared with light. Another chandelier hung from wood-paneled ceilings, illuminating a room lined with built-in bookcases. They were, tragically, entirely bare. Comfortable-looking chairs and couches were placed in conversational groupings. Some of the chairs were upholstered in soft brown leather, and some in a faded, age-worn printed fabric. Morgan counted the chairs and sofas and realized thirty people could comfortably sit in this room. The tower's layout didn't make sense; a room this large shouldn't be here, but he had long since stopped trying to make sense of things that employed dimensional magic. There were no other exits from the room, so he went back to the central chamber to open the last doors.

The lack of confrontation thus far had Morgan feeling a little careless, and he shoved the last set of doors open, then grasped his spear in both hands. Nothing came for him, so he stepped into the room. Sconces along the walls flared to life, and he was rewarded with a poshly appointed study. A colossal desk filled one wall with a deep leather chair behind it. Behind the chair were more empty bookcases. This was the first room to be carpeted, and the carpet was a thick, unworn, deep burgundy with a plush pile. There were a couple of polished wooden chairs with leather seats in front of the desk, and off to the left was a large square table covered with an ornately carved, wooden, topographical map. Morgan was instantly transfixed by the site of the map table and walked over to look at it.

The map was incredibly detailed with ornate carvings and vibrant paints, but Morgan couldn't make heads or tails of what it was depicting. There were mountain ranges and bodies of water and forests, but he had no way of knowing where they were or if they were even on this world. Who knew where Vormendion had initially built this tower? He supposed the System knew. Those were his thoughts when he saw the shadow move on the table, just to the right of his own.

Morgan didn't think; he just dropped and rolled to his left, dragging his spear with him. He almost got it tangled with a table leg but managed to shift and roll farther away from the table, springing to his feet. He'd been vaguely aware of something moving behind him, and he looked around now, furiously scanning the room, but couldn't see what it had been.

He slowly turned in a circle, looking for any sign of an aggressor, but found nothing. He was starting to doubt himself, wondering if he'd been, literally, jumping at shadows. Just as he began to relax, though, he felt an icy stab of pain in his left shoulder, and out of reflex, he spun and swung his spear in a wide arc.

He was just barely fast enough to see a shadowy entity break apart as his spear tore through it. He wondered if he'd killed it or hurt it, but the shadows came together again in the corner of his eye, and he felt another icy cut rip into his right bicep. Once again, he whirled and stabbed with his spear only to be met with air as the shadowy being dispersed around the tip.

Morgan growled in frustration and pain and began to channel Energy Drain through his spear, bracing himself for another attack, trying to move in erratic directions to throw his tormentor off. He made a lucky feint to his right, spinning to his left, and caught the shadow mid-swing. It looked like a tall, skeletally-thin person entirely made of dark smoke, the only color coming from cobalt eyes. Morgan thrust his spear into the being and *pulled*. This time, when the shadowy creature started to disperse, Morgan's drain resisted it, forcing it back into form. Morgan saw the panic in its eyes as they widened, and he grinned angrily, continuing to channel his Energy Drain. He felt the foreign Energy enter his body like a splash of cold water, but he kept pulling as the blue light faded in the shadow visage's eyes. When they finally winked out, Morgan felt stronger and knew that his wounds had healed. The shadows fell away into nothing, and he looked around, making sure it had been a lone attacker.

"Congratulations, Lord, on vanquishing the first guardian," a voice like tinkling glass said from right behind him.

⚔ MORGAN ⚜

Morgan whirled around, his spear in a guard position, and took a step back. Hovering in the air before him was what he could only describe as a bundle of oscillating silvery lights and mist. The voice tinkled forth from the lights, and they seemed to flare in time with the words. "Don't be alarmed, Lord. I am here to serve at your pleasure. My name is Tiladia."

"You're a servant?" he asked, lifting the tip of his spear and relaxing his guard a bit.

"Of a sort, Lord. I was bound to this tower by its creator. When Lord Vormendion ascended, he instructed me to serve the one who defeated the first guardian." Several things about that sentence piqued Morgan's interest.

"What do you mean ascended?"

"Departed this plane, Lord."

"Uh-huh, and what do you mean he bound you to this tower?"

"When Lord Vormendion vanquished my physical form, he bound my soul here." Morgan wasn't sure if he imagined it, but it seemed the tinkling voice took on a note of sorrow.

"Your physical form?" he pressed.

"Yes, Lord. I was a dragon." The silvery lights and mist pulled together and refined into the shape of a winged serpent that did a lazy flip in the air and then broke apart, back into the previous formless cluster.

"Wow, so he stole your soul? Can I release you?"

"Lord, that wouldn't be wise at this juncture, even if you were able. I possess keen evaluation skills, and you cannot free me. Not with your present abilities."

"Well, let's focus on matters at hand, then. First, please don't refer to me as 'lord'—my name is Morgan, and I'm fine with you using it. Second, I have a quest to clear eight guardians from this tower. Am I in danger of being attacked by the other guardians?"

"No, Morgan. Not until you venture onto their respective floors of the tower; they are bound, much like I am, though not so completely."

"Alright, well, can you help me deal with them?" Despite his better judgment, Morgan found himself trusting the spirit, and he relaxed his posture, placing the butt of his spear on the ground and leaning on it.

"Only so much as to warn you off if I feel your chances of success are too small. I'm sorry, Lord Morgan, but I'm bound by myriad esoteric rules that Vormendion etched into my soulstone."

"Well, what are my odds? Can I take them?" Morgan sighed deeply. Things never seemed to go easily, and he was starting to realize that the System liked it that way.

"Morgan, I feel you stand a great chance of success against the next guardian. I think you would be wise to gather more strength before you attempt to face the third." The lights flashed and did a quick circuit around him as it spoke.

"All right, um, I'm sorry, what was your name again?"

"I am Tiladia."

"Okay, Tiladia, are there any other threats on this floor of the tower?"

"No, Lord Morgan. This floor is clear of danger."

"Well, in that case, I'm going to go over to that library area and get some sleep on one of those couches. I'm beat. I'll look into facing the second guardian tomorrow." Morgan walked past the spirit to the central hall and back into the empty library with all the comfortable-looking couches and chairs. Tiladia followed behind him, emitting a faint tinkling sound as it moved.

"Tiladia, is that a feminine name? I'm sorry for the personal question, but I don't want to think of you as 'it' in my mind."

"Yes, Morgan, I was a female dragon. I was so beautiful, Morgan! I had dozens of suitors, from Red to Gold. Morgan, my children would have filled the skies of Aradnue. Alas, Vormendion came to our world and took many of our lives in his quest for power. I was the only soul he kept, though, and I know it was because of the beauty of my scales and the ferocity of my breath. He became enamored with me, you see."

"Well, I'm glad to meet you, Tiladia, and if it's possible, I'll do my best to find a way to set you free if that's what you want." Morgan loosened the buckles on his armor and his girdle and set his belongings on the floor next to a particularly puffy-looking leather sofa. "Tiladia, do you know how to dim these lights?"

"Yes, Morgan. I will do that for you. Sleep well, and thank you for offering to free me. You've given me a lot to think about." The tinkling voice faded as Tiladia floated from the room and the orange and yellow orbs of fire in the chandelier dimmed to just a faint glimmer. Morgan sighed, stretched out with his robes wrapped tightly around himself, and slept more soundly than he had in many long days.

Morgan stirred, hearing the sound of tinkling bells. As reality intruded on his sleeping mind, he realized he wasn't hearing someone jingling bells nearby but Tiladia speaking to him. Her voice was musical but very strange, having the quality of crystal or glass breaking and falling on a hard surface. "Morgan. Lord Morgan!" Her voice rose in volume, and he opened his eyes.

"Hello, Tiladia," he muttered.

"Good morning, Morgan. I am sorry to disturb your rest, but you have a visitor pounding on the door to the tower." Morgan grunted and immediately leaned over to pull on his boots and greaves.

"How long did I sleep?"

"Just a bit more than ten hours, Morgan." Tiladia flashed and swirled as she spoke, and Morgan got the impression she was agitated.

"Is something wrong, Tiladia?" he asked, as he fastened his vambraces and stood up to put on his girdle and pouches.

"I'm worried about the intruder, Morgan. Friendly people very seldom visit this tower."

"Oh, well, that was during Vormendion's time. I think things will be different while I live here. Don't worry, that's probably just one of the colonists coming to see if I'm alive or whatever." Morgan stretched hugely; he felt good if a bit hungry. "Tiladia, is there a bathroom, you know, a toilet, on this floor?"

"Morgan, the baths are on the fifth floor with the bedrooms. There is a toilet for guests on this floor, though, on the left-hand wall of the entry hall."

"What? I can't believe I missed a door; I walked around that central staircase room three times." Morgan started walking out of the library and into the central chamber.

"The door is discrete, Morgan, and it's not in this room, but just at the end of the entry hall. I'll show you," Tiladia tinkled as she floated ahead of him toward the tower entrance. Morgan followed and, now that he was looking, quickly spotted the paneled door just inside the short hallway leading to the front door. He depressed the little brass handle, and it opened inward into a little bathroom complete with a marble sink and toilet. It was paneled in the same wood as the entry hall and had a decorative tile floor that was an off-white color with black designs, sort of like paisley.

"Running water?" Morgan asked, pushing the little handle to the sink faucet. He marveled as warm water immediately came out of the brass-colored tap.

"Yes, Vormendion liked his creature comforts. He built an Energy-based steam engine in the basement."

"There's a basement? Hold on. Answer that when I come out, give me a minute alone in here, please." Tiladia made a high-pitched tinkling sound as she hurriedly floated out of the bathroom. Morgan closed the door, took care of his business, and returned to the hallway.

"Yes, there's a basement. It's through the door in the kitchens, though I'm afraid the key to the lock is in the master bedchamber," Tiladia responded as soon as he stepped back into the hallway.

"Ugh, and that's on the fifth floor?"

"No, the guest rooms, seldom-used, by the way, are on the fifth floor. The master bed-chamber is on the sixth floor."

"Ugh!" Morgan huffed, more loudly this time. Truthfully, he didn't care that much; he was happy to sleep on a couch for a while, so long as he wasn't forced to keep watch and wonder what the System might send to interrupt his sleep. He figured it would take him a while to take full ownership of this tower, and he didn't know how long he'd stick around to mess with it: he wanted to find Issa and her people. With that in mind, he stepped over to one of the front doors and was just reaching to open it when someone banged on it vigorously, four times. When Morgan put his hand on the handle, the door loudly clicked as it unlocked. He pushed it open and was greeted with a familiar face.

"Hey, Boris! Long time no fuckin' see!" Morgan reached out a hand to shake, but Boris backed up a step.

"Morgan, that's you? Shit, man, you've changed a lot since training." Morgan and Boris had been in the same training group as they prepared for the Pilgrim mission. They'd both been assigned as technicians and had many of the same classes together.

"Yeah, man, but what hasn't changed?" Morgan kept his hand out, and Boris snapped out of his stupor and reached forward to shake. "How are you? Are you adjusting to things?"

"Oh, yeah, better than most. I'm pretty good at this Energy shit. Been learning to use it to improve mundane items. Like I learned to enchant an axe, so it doesn't need to be sharpened so often while cutting trees. People have been trading me all kinds of shit to work on their tools. Arthur says I'm up high on the list to get one of the bigger houses when they start building them." Boris shrugged and backed up to the edge of the stoop, and gestured to the tower. "Nothing like this, though. This tower is insane, man. Where'd you get it? Oh, by the way, Olivia sent me to get you; they're having a meeting soon and want you to attend."

Morgan stepped out, closed the door behind him, then said, "Yeah, this tower was a reward for completing a fairly difficult quest. I'll tell you the whole story sometime. Where are we headed?"

"Over to the forge. They like to meet there 'cause it has big worktables they can stand around and talk." Boris turned, walked down the steps, and waited for Morgan, who followed. Morgan took a breath of the crisp morning air, letting Boris lead the way as they walked up the slight incline to the main encampment. They made small talk, Morgan feeling awkward because of the deference with which Boris treated him. Boris kept surreptitiously looking at him from the side of his eyes, and Morgan could feel the gulf that had sprung up between them—another side effect of sleeping for hundreds of years and then waking up in a magical reality, he supposed.

Soon, they were walking into the warm air of the forge, and Morgan saw several people, including Olivia and Arthur, standing around a big work table. The table was littered with large sheets of paper covered with diagrams, maps, and notes. Morgan walked up to the table with Boris, and the conversation halted. Olivia smiled and said, "Good morning, Morgan. Let me introduce our temporary council. You already met Arthur Ballard. This gentleman on my left is Dr. Kerns. He's our Chief Medical Officer. You know Boris; he's representing the technical groups, and next to Arthur, there, is Tanya Delgado. She's our Chief Civil Engineer."

"Hello everyone," Morgan said, as he moved to stand in an empty spot to Olivia's left.

"Yes, everyone, this is Morgan Hall. I won't pretend that we haven't already been talking about him all morning. Morgan, we wanted you here because you've experienced a lot more of this world than we have and obviously had some success. We're also keen to hear about your plans to contact your friend's community."

"Well, I've already debriefed you and Arthur about nearly everything. I'm happy to answer specific questions, though. As far as my friend, Issa, goes, I'm going to start scouting toward her settlement as soon as possible. I'm not sure what lies between here and there, so I may or may not have to improve my abilities prior to trying to make the journey."

"How do you know where she is? Did she help you to make a map?" Tanya Delgado asked.

"No. Neither Issa nor I knew where in the world the Crucible was. We weren't even sure it was on this planet until we got to the top and saw the moons. She didn't recognize the landscape. Not only that, but she had no idea where in the world the System put the humans. So, yeah, no map. I have an ability, though, granted by my class, that allows me to kind of feel where an ally is."

"Is that why you've grown? Because of your class?" Boris interrupted.

"No, Boris, that's because of his racial improvements. He's already been over this with us; let's stay on topic," Olivia answered for Morgan.

"Well, what about your class, then? Can you tell us about it? I don't know anyone else that's made it to level ten," Boris pressed.

"Ahem," Arthur spoke up, "Boris, please be patient, and one of us can fill you in. Morgan already talked to us about his class advancement and even gave us some tips on how to earn better options. Olivia and I will draft a manual to spread among the colonists in the next day or two."

"Right, well, anyway, I can feel Issa about a hundred miles or so to the southeast." Morgan shrugged. "I'll be exploring in that direction for the next little while."

"But you'll be basing your explorations from here, right? You meant what you said about helping Bronwyn with the creature in the cave when she returns?" Olivia asked, a note of worry in her voice.

"Yeah, of course, unless she takes forever to get back here. I do want to get to Issa before the seasons change. If they do. Does anyone have any idea about that?"

"Yes. We've determined there's a definite tilt to this planet's axis, and, in the short time we've been here, the days have increased in length by fourteen minutes." Dr. Kerns spoke up for the first time.

"That's right; we think we're moving into summer. Though we don't know how long each season will last, we think it'll be some time before winter," Olivia added.

Morgan nodded, and the meeting continued. It ended up dragging on for another hour. The group covered many topics, like where they should put the first roads, how many colonists still needed housing, who led the contribution lists, and which colonists were struggling and required assistance obtaining food. Morgan listened politely and tried to contribute where he could, but he honestly just wanted to get back to the tower and see about dealing with the second guardian.

As the meeting started to break up, Morgan remembered that he had quite a few weapons and scraps in his pouch that he'd scavenged from the many Urghat he and Issa had slain and from the lair of the Yovashi. He started to remove them, one by one, and created a pile in the middle of the forge. The temporary council members marveled as he pulled one item after another from his pouch, dropping spears, daggers, swords, furs, leather scraps, hammers, and axes. He kept a backup spear for himself and a couple of sharp daggers; otherwise, he unloaded most of the rusty and mundane items he and Issa had acquired. "I don't think these will do me much good, and maybe the people working in the forge can practice with them. You know, melt them down, sharpen them, whatever."

"That's generous, Morgan. You're going to have to give me the whole story about the Crucible someday," Olivia said.

"That will require a lot of good bourbon, and, so far, I haven't seen any in this world." He laughed, gave Olivia a short wave, and made his way back to his tower; it was time to see what was on the second floor.

BRONWYN

Bronwyn jogged out the northern gate headed toward the plains. Before she left, she'd accessed the Colony Stone to give Olivia permissions to purchase and place structures. She hadn't wanted them to be unable to keep working on the settlement while she was gone. Surprisingly, very few arguments had come up about whether or not she should be heading out to "gain levels," as she had put it. People were beginning to understand this world, and when Olivia made a report about the creature in the cave, even the non-violent types understood the need for people to grow in strength. She tried to clear her mind and think about only the task at hand; the rest could wait. Some of the hunters from the colony had reported seeing some ruins a few miles to the northwest; she figured it would be a good place to start.

There were no roads through the plains, but the grass was short, slightly below her knee at the highest. Occasionally a flash of movement and the sound of feet would sound from the nearby grass, and Bronwyn caught sight of a white-furred little animal that reminded her of a rabbit as it bounded away. Birds were plentiful, and the long ribbons of their tails would stream up into the air as she startled them away from their nests. Once, she stopped to investigate a clump of high grass where two ribbon-birds had erupted, and she found a nest, about the size of a picnic basket, and it had cradled four pale-blue eggs speckled with yellow. They were about half again as big as a chicken egg. She left the nest and continued on her way.

Bronwyn found herself lost in thought as she ran. She knew she wanted to be at least level ten before she went after that demon in the cave again. She hoped that obtaining a class would give her some sort of power jump. The problem was, she couldn't plan too much; she had no idea what a class did for you exactly; none of the colonists had leveled up enough yet. She assumed it would give her special abilities and maybe a stat boost if she was lucky. She started to imagine what kinds of classes she'd be able to choose from and what they might do. She was so zoned out she hardly even noticed when something whizzed past her face, lightly grazing her cheek.

The tinge of pain as the small cut opened across her cheekbone thrust her back into the present. She dove to the ground; the ruins were roughly thirty yards off to her left; had she run so far already? A low stone wall surrounded a dozen or so small buildings. She could hear whoever had thrown something at her somewhere ahead and a bit toward the ruins; a low, growling voice called out, and she presumed there were multiple attackers. She wasn't sure if they could see her in the grass, but she certainly didn't want to provide them with target practice. She brought her right leg up underneath herself and launched forward toward the western-most portion of the wall. She heard a dull thud behind her and assumed they'd missed her with another projectile but didn't turn around to check. She reached the wall and crouched low, using it for cover from one direction and hoping the grass would hide her from the other. She could hear loud footsteps approaching among the ruined structures; whatever they were, they definitely weren't the diminutive Yeksa.

She braced herself to fight her unknown assailants as she heard the footsteps grow closer and closer. She was hoping to surprise them by vaulting over the wall. She quietly summoned her stone armor, covering her arms and chest in a second layer of rough, gray skin. She listened intently and heard a heavy foot crunch into the grass about ten feet away on the other side of the wall. Bronwyn took a deep breath and, in one smooth motion, reached up and pulled herself over the wall toward her quarry. The sight that met her was monstrous: a giant fur-covered humanoid wearing leather armor studded with black metal spikes and wielding a massive, hook-shaped, rusty blade with a jagged, notched edge. He was cautiously approaching the wall, but Bronwyn's head-on assault caught him by surprise. The bestial man fumbled, swinging his blade up and snagging the tip on the corner of a crumbled wall. Panic opened his eyes as he tried to jerk it free. Bronwyn saw her opening and threw a wild haymaker at her opponent's right temple, the impact letting out a thunderous crack. He fell in a boneless heap to the ground as his eyes rolled into the back of his head. Bronwyn shook her hand, wincing and glad for the protection of the heavy gauntlet. Wanting to keep her advantage of surprise, she ducked behind a collapsed stone building that vines and dark blue moss had long overtaken.

She wasn't sure how many of them there were, but there was at least one more sprinting toward the sound of conflict. Bronwyn edged her way around the outside of the building, hoping to sneak up behind him as he came upon his downed companion. She heard the thudding of his heavy steps as he ran past the building, and she turned the corner, fists raised. Immediately in front of her was a large, round, wooden shield held together with thick metal bands.

"Thought you was sneaky, didn't you, littl' rat?" He let out a hoarse laugh as he spoke. "Could smell yer coming a mile away. You and yer little fairy pet have the sweetest scent I've smelled in years. But I'll bet you taste even sweeter." He was practically drooling, eyeing Bronwyn from behind the shield. He raised his axe and pointed it toward her shoulder. "I'll even cut yer a deal, ya hand over that fae of yers, and I'll let ya walk on home. Ya 'ave my word." He shot her a toothy grin full of yellowed fangs. "Ol' Grimjowl hain't tasted fae in far, far ter long." He howled with laughter as he spoke.

"I don't know what you're talking about, you prick, but no one here's getting eaten tonight." She heard a soft chirp and some rustling from her backpack and knew Hops had climbed in there when the fighting had started. "Stay in there, buddy; I'll keep you safe." Hops let out another nervous chirp and scrabbled deeper into the pack. "You scared to fight me, Grime Face? You talk a big game, but your eyes look scared. I can't blame you, I suppose. I mean, just look at your friend on the ground there. Barely even had a chance to move." Bronwyn gestured at the ground behind him.

"Grimjowl!" He shrieked. "Not Grime Face, you little rat!" His eyes bulged with fury, darting left and right. "Ripfang was a fool anyway, deserved to die." His scowl deepened, and he briefly turned his gaze back toward his fallen compatriot.

Bronwyn lunged into action, willing raw Energy into her fist until the node there started to burn physically, and she slammed her gauntlet into the bear-like man's shield. The wood exploded into a dozen pieces, and the metal band snapped away like springs being let loose. The beast-man howled in pain as his arm hung limply at his side, his forearm bent at a grotesque angle. He furiously swung his axe down at her head, but Bronwyn deflected the blade with the armored back of her gauntlet. She grabbed his fur-covered arm with her other hand and pulled it toward her, slamming her shoulder into his face. He reared backward, dropping his axe as blood gushed from his shattered nose. Scrambling away from her and wiping his face with the back of his good hand, his eyes darted about for a place to run. Bronwyn slowly closed in on him, backing him into the corner of a ruined stone wall. "You're gonna tell me who your people are and what you know about Hops. If you're lucky, I might even let you leave." She tried her best to sound threatening, though she didn't really like the idea of executing an unarmed foe.

She was closing the final distance between them when a searing pain erupted from her lower back. She spun around and locked eyes with a leaner, slightly shorter beast-man, the tip of his spear dripping with blood. Grimjowl, who had been cowering before Bronwyn, took his opportunity to lunge forward and wrap his good arm around her neck, attempting to choke her. As she struggled to release his grip, the spear wielder leveled his weapon at her stomach and charged forward. Bronwyn shoved herself backward toward the wall, slamming Grimjowl's spine into the stone and eliciting a howl. His grip loosened, and she spun to her left, burying her face in his chest fur while punching up at his elbow. She created just enough of a gap to yank her head free, her ears burning at the friction. The smaller beast-man's spear grazed along her leather armor and sank deep into Grimjowl's stomach.

Grimjowl's heavy body slumped forward and pinned the spear to the ground. The last beast-man frantically pulled at the spear haft but gave up as Bronwyn circled him. He roared and charged forward, tackling Bronwyn. His sudden charge was enough to catch her off guard, and he pulled her to the ground. She found herself pinned beneath him while he sat on her stomach, both hands wrapped around her neck, shouting in fury, spittle dripping out of his grimacing mouth down onto her face. Instincts from all the jiujitsu classes she'd taken kicked in, and she thrust her left fist up between his outstretched arms, popped her hips up to make a space, and then rotated out from under him while looping his arm up with hers. She forgot all safety sparring rules and dropped the full weight of her body onto his elbow joint, distending it with a loud *pop*. He screamed in pain.

She didn't waste any time and began to alternate blows, left then right, onto the back of his head with her gauntlets. Panic and fury at feeling helpless, even for just a moment, fueled her barrage, and the creature was long dead before she stopped punching.

Bronwyn sagged her shoulders down, relaxing her posture. She sat there over the body of the beast-man for a minute, too tired to move. Her breath was ragged and heavy, her throat hoarse from where he had held it. She took a deep breath and held it briefly. "Fuck!" She let out an explosive breath of air with her shout. "First other people to talk to on this fucking planet, and I killed all three of them." She grumbled in a ragged croak. "God damn it!" She knew she should have left the last one alive to question, but her temper had gotten the better of her again.

Stiffly, she planted one of her feet and stood; the Energy was just starting to coalesce around the three bodies and fly toward her in heavy streams of light. She took a few deep breaths as she could feel the Energy closing the puncture wound in her back and restoring a portion of what she'd used during the encounter.

Congratulations! You have achieved level 8 base human and have 5 attribute points to allocate.

Almost without thinking about it, Bronwyn focused inward and spent her points, three in strength and two in agility. Just like every time before. She thought of her character sheet, checking out her attributes:

Strength:	34	Vitality:	11
Dexterity:	9	Agility:	25
Intelligence:	9	Will:	11

She knew it would be a while before her Energy recovered again; it didn't recharge as quickly for her as it did for people like Olivia. She raised her arms above her head and took a few deep breaths before checking the bodies for anything of note.

The weapons they carried were weighty and pockmarked with rust. Bronwyn threw them in her pouch just to drop them off in the colony; maybe some of the aspiring smiths could attempt to improve them. The armor the first had worn, on the other hand, was masterfully crafted. It was treated dark brown leather with black metal spikes on the front, and the back was covered in small metal discs, about an inch wide. She unbuckled the straps on the side of the vest and pulled it away from the beast-man, noticing faint golden runes sewn into the edges. She held it in front of her and let a small trickle of her Energy flow into it.

*****Breastplate of the Berserker: +2 strength.*****

Bronwyn set her backpack down and practically ripped her old leather chest piece off. She lifted the spiked breastplate to her nose and gave it a good sniff. It had a musty odor, but it also smelled like oiled leather, like it had been treated well and cleaned regularly. An unbidden memory of a catcher's mitt and her dad showing her how to rub oil into the leather came to her. She shrugged, slipping the new armor down over her head. As she tightened the straps, the armor melded itself to her body like it had been made for her. She was moving her arms around, making sure none of the half-inch-long spikes on the armor impeded her movement when Hops poked his head out of her backpack, cocking it to the side quizzically as he stared at her.

Bronwyn noticed her audience and let out a small chuckle. "Don't worry, little buddy; there're no spikes on the shoulders." She patted it for emphasis. "You might have to be a little more careful climbing up, though." She smiled and reached down her hand so he could climb up her arm. After he was situated and done inspecting the armor for himself, she slung her backpack on.

Bronwyn moved to pull the spear out of the impaled Grimjowl. He let out a soft burbling chuckle as she reached for it, blood spilling from his mouth. "More are coming, more than you can imagine; they'll burn all you have to the ground. Run while you can, littl' rat." He coughed up a stream of blood, and the light left his eyes, his last bit of Energy flowing into Bronwyn. She wrenched the spear from his gut, and his body collapsed onto the floor.

Bronwyn's thoughts raced. *It could be an empty threat, but why would he lie with his last breath?* She had to follow their tracks and see where they came from. If there were more of them out there and they knew about the human colony, it could be a threat to all of them. She activated her tracking skill and quickly found their stomping footprints glowing faintly red in the grass. A gray text window appeared next to them: Urghat.

BRONWYN

Bronwyn settled into a small stone building after spending an hour clearing the ruins of threats and getting an idea of where the Urghat tracks led. The sun was starting to get low in the sky, and she decided it would be best to wait until morning before following the tracks to wherever they might lead. She hunkered down behind a fallen stone pillar in what was once probably someone's home. Bronwyn withdrew a bedroll and a thick, dark blue blanket from her pouch. She thought about making a small fire but decided there might be other Urghat in the area and didn't want them to see the light or smoke. Unable to cook, she just ate some dried meat and berries that she had purchased from the Contribution Store. Hops looked at her expectantly when she pulled out the berries, and she placed a few on the ground for him, most of which he gobbled up quickly, leaving just a couple to store in his shell for later.

After her cold dinner, she lay on her back, staring up at the stars of this strange new world through a hole in the long ruined rooftop. Hops nudged the side of her neck and then curled up in his shell right above her shoulder, his soft, purring snore starting up almost immediately. Despite being worried about the coming days and the possible implications of what Grimjowl had said, Bronwyn quickly found her eyes getting heavy as a deep sleep took hold of her.

Bronwyn's eyes shot open as she heard the howling and braying barks of multiple hounds. The sky was painted red from the morning sun, and she could just make out her surroundings in the ruined building. She silently got to her feet and started packing up her camp when she heard a gruff voice out in the ruins. "Hah! I knew there'd be something left behind. Give the boyii that vest; they'll find the scent in no time."

"Right, right, smart as eva', Underclaw Bloodfang," another wheedling voice responded.

"Shit!" Bronwyn whispered. She hadn't even thought of taking her old armor with her and had just left it lying next to the bodies. Trying to move without a sound, Bronwyn slipped all of her belongings into the pouch. She scooped up the still sleeping Hops and gently deposited him into her backpack. She finished strapping on her gauntlets as she edged toward the empty doorframe.

The ruined house she had taken refuge in for the evening was across from the small square where she had left the bodies. Looking out the door frame, Bronwyn saw there was a large crumbling fountain, long dry, between her and the Urghat she had heard talking. The one she assumed to be Bloodfang was massive, even by Urghat standards, probably more than seven feet tall. He was wearing heavy metal armor and had no visible weapons. The smaller Urghat wore leather armor and held two leashed, brightly colored wolves. They were the same type she had fought the night the colony had been attacked. As she watched, he picked up her old leather vest and held it out for the hounds to sniff.

Bronwyn ducked down into a crouch and hurriedly stepped around the side of the building; she knew the hounds would catch her scent in no time. As soon as she rounded the corner and was out of sight, she took off into a dead sprint, trying to make as much distance as possible. It was only moments before she heard the excited barking of dogs that had found their quarry. She glanced over her shoulder and could see their brightly colored backs racing through the tall grass toward her, their handler just seconds behind.

She spotted a lone pillar of stone about fifty yards away to her left. Pushing herself to the limit, she sprinted toward it, hoping to reach it before the hounds caught her. She slid to a stop at the stone monolith and slipped behind it. One of the dogs raced past her left side, and as it did, she slammed her fist down onto it, the impact shattering its spine. It slid to a stop a few yards away from her, unmoving. The other hound rounded the right side of the pillar and lunged toward her just as she finished her first attack. The large canine's teeth latched onto her gauntlet as she brought it up in front of her face. The beast didn't let go and tried to pull Bronwyn down to the ground. It was no match for her strength, though, and she lifted it into the air and slammed its body against the stone pillar; the sound of crunching bone filled the air as its ribcage impacted. The hound released its grip on her and growled, trying to stand, wobbling for a second before it fell to the ground.

The hound master, seconds behind his beasts, roared in fury at the sight before him and charged Bronwyn with two wickedly sharp knives. He was fast, faster than Bronwyn, nearly as fast as the creature in the cave; she felt like molasses as he assailed her with a flurry of stabs and slashes. While trying to block his cuts, she activated her Stone Skin, saving her from several deep cuts that got past her guard. One powerful stab got through and punctured even her Stone Skin, though; she could feel it sink an inch into her left side. She was sure that, without her magic, he would've buried that knife to the hilt.

Over the next few moments, Bronwyn accumulated a dozen small slashes and puncture wounds on her upper arms, legs, and torso. She was growing tired and more frustrated by the second; every time she let up her defense to swing at the Urghat, he would dodge out of the way and land another strike. She was back peddling, on the defensive, doing everything she could to keep the daggers at bay when an idea struck her.

She took a few quick steps backward, gaining some space from the Urghat, and focused her Energy into the palms of her hands. She hadn't done much spell casting, especially to affect other people, but she had seen Olivia practicing on multiple occasions, and she still remembered her lessons from the orientation. She concentrated on her Stone Warding spell, but instead of willing it to activate on her skin, she pushed Energy out of the node on her palm toward the Urghat. She willed her Stone Warding to form on the Urghat's legs, conjuring it over and over. Streams of light gray sand shot out of her hands and started to solidify on his legs. The effect wasn't immediate, and he closed the distance on her, giving her another handful of deeper cuts now that her stone skin was gone. She clenched her teeth and focused on the spell and on blocking his blades with her gauntleted forearms.

After a few seconds, the stone was thickly coating the Urghat's legs and feet. His strikes and twisting dodges were still fast, but his footwork couldn't keep up. Bronwyn could see that his slower legs were throwing off his entire combat style, and he started to slow and stumble, to the point where he was no longer landing any strikes on her as she danced around his swings. He roared with frustration and tried to charge her again, and, as he did, Bronwyn stopped channeling the stone and swatted his hands down, causing his face to jut forward from the motion. She was bleeding profusely now and nearly exhausted; she knew she had used up most of her Energy. Reaching deep, she pulled what little reserves she had left and swung an uppercut at his exposed chin. The Energy infused strike connected with a *crunch* as his head snapped back and his eyes rolled to reveal white, dead orbs. He fell backward, and Bronwyn sank to a knee. The Energy that flowed into her started to mend her most dangerous wounds, but it wasn't enough; she could still feel many of them open and bleeding.

Congratulations! You have learned the spell Fetters of Stone—Basic.

It seemed that experimenting with her skill had paid off. Bronwyn turned and looked toward the ruins she had run from and saw the huge Urghat called Bloodfang slowly walking through the plains toward her, maybe a hundred yards away. She inspected her wounds. "Fuck," she quietly cursed to herself; there was no way she could win a fight in her current state. She had to get away and make it back to the colony to warn them. She turned and began to run southward, letting out a frustrated scream.

The wounds in her legs burned as she sprinted through the fields. There was a tree line a mile to the southeast, and she beelined toward it, never looking back. When Bronwyn reached the stand of trees that separated the greater grasslands from the colony, she finally turned and found an empty field behind her. She scanned the horizon, searching for any movement, but it seemed that the big Urghat hadn't chased after her. She breathed a sigh of relief.

Quest: Defeat Underclaw Bloodfang and retrieve Ur-clan missives. Time limit: 24 hours. Reward: Energy-rich natural material. Accept? YES/NO

"Fuck." She stared into the distance as she let out a long breath and pressed her finger against the "Yes" button on the pale gray window. "Guess I won't be going home after all," she groaned, pulling the last remaining bit of healing cream from her pouch.

By the time Bronwyn finished dabbing the cream on a dozen different wounds, she'd used every last molecule of it. She had been hesitant to use the last bit of it in case she received some kind of mortal injury, but she knew she'd need to be in perfect condition for this fight. She had never been closer than fifty yards from Bloodfang, but she could see his presence, his aura, surrounding him even from that distance. It was nothing like the demon they fought in the cave, but he projected a raw power. Fighting him wouldn't be easy, and she would need to get him alone somehow, but she wasn't going to back down. Not again.

She rested for an hour, eating some more of her travel rations and allowing her Energy to refill slowly. During her rest, Hops finally woke from his slumber; she had no idea how he slept through the fighting and running. He scrambled out of the pack pulling a few berries of his own out from his shell, and perched atop her shoulder to share breakfast. "This fight I'm heading into is gonna be a little rough; I'm pretty sure I can take him, though. You sure you wanna stick around? They seem pretty fond of eating, well, whatever you are. Might be dangerous." In response, Hops finished off his last berry, wiping his hands and face on Bronwyn's hair, eliciting a slight sigh and chuckle from her. He wrapped himself in her long red curls and chirped happily, nuzzling into her neck. "Alrighty cutie, I'm glad to hear it." She finished her jerky and stood up, stretching her freshly healed muscles before taking off in a light jog, back toward the stone obelisk.

The sight that greeted her upon her arrival was confusing. She was about fifty yards out when she realized Bloodfang had not left the area. He was sitting on a small stool in the shade of the obelisk where she'd fought the hounds and their master. He saw her jog into view and beckoned her closer, making no move to stand. Bronwyn carefully approached and saw that he was eating some kind of charred meat, and a small fire was smoldering next to him. He chewed his latest bite and looked up toward her. "Hope you don't mind, but I'll be finishing this meat before we get this over with. I'd offer you a piece, but this is the last of it." He gestured with the remainder of what looked like a turkey drumstick. Seeing Bronwyn's blank stare of confusion, he continued, pointing one of his clawed fingers toward the sky: "Seems as though they want one of us to die today, and well, I planned on killing you anyway." He gave her a toothy smile and tore off another bite of meat.

"You got a quest to defeat me, too?" Bronwyn was struggling with the scene—with the surreal sight of him sitting on a stool and waiting for her, with the way he spoke to her in a cultured, precise diction. She hadn't really intended on talking to him at all.

"Defeat you?" Bloodfang let out a harsh laugh. "I'm supposed to take your head and capture that little fairy of yours, Blodwyn. Strong name, much better than the other Humans we've heard of. Let's see if you can live up to it; I'd like to sound proud tonight when I boast around the fire." He tore off the last chunk of meat and tossed the bone behind him. He stood up to his full, towering height; he was clad in metal armor from neck to shins. "Well then, shall we?" He pulled a dagger from his belt and sank the blade into his own hand. He ripped it away and chanted some strange words as the blood arced into the air. The droplets shimmered brightly and came together, forming a shining, bright red cutlass that thrummed with power. He stared Bronwyn down, a smile carving itself across his face.

MORGAN

In the daylight, Morgan's tower was quite a sight to behold. It was like a dark gray finger pointing up out of the blue grass. It had lost the bronze-colored runes that had swum in the polyhedron, and Morgan wondered if they had been responsible for the tower being packaged into such a small container. The metal was smooth and free of any rust, and it had a density and weight to it that belied the hollow interior. He walked around the circumference, finding that the only door was the main entrance. He saw a balcony about two-thirds of the way up, but other than that, the sides were smooth and bare. He briefly contemplated trying to scale the tower to see if he could reach that balcony, but he had no grapple, and he also didn't think whatever door or window was up there would be trivial to circumvent. Instead, he walked through the front door, mentally preparing for the promised confrontation.

He was immediately greeted by Tiladia: "Morgan, welcome home. Has it been long since you were here? I lose track of the passage of time when I'm alone."

"No, no. I've only been gone an hour or so." Morgan walked in, closing the door, and he noted that it locked as soon as he removed his hand from the handle. "Tiladia, what's on the second floor?"

"The second-floor houses a music room, a reception hall, and an atrium."

"An atrium? I didn't see any windows or balconies low enough to be on the second floor." Morgan began striding toward the central stair.

"The atrium is quite extensive and is warmed and lit with a sunstone. Lord, be careful if you intend to climb those stairs; space moves differently on them—two or three steps, and you'll be on the second floor."

"Oh"—Morgan stopped in his tracks—"that's quite handy. Thanks for the warning. So, you think I have a good chance against the next guardian?"

"Yes, I believe your raw stats and power to be a match." Tiladia's lights bobbed up and down in a way that made Morgan think of a nod.

"What about the third?"

"I'm not as confident, Morgan. I think you'd be in grave peril."

"Alright. I had another thought. You said you have keen evaluation abilities. Can you identify items? Items made by an Artificer, for instance?"

"Yes, Morgan! Unless something is beyond the Advanced stage, I should be able to discern its properties." Tiladia spun around him in an upward spiral.

"That's great! Speaking of the Advanced stage, I'd love to pick your brain about different aspects of the way the System categorizes things like race and classes and skills." Morgan said, as he reached into his dimensional pouch and pulled out the necklace he'd taken from the Yeksa shaman. The silver chain glinted dully in the chandelier's light, but the red gem pulsed with a deep ruby glow of its own.

"Oh, that's a power-stone. I can see it's infused with fire attuned Energy."

"A power-stone?" Morgan held the necklace up, noting the warmth emanating from the gem.

"Yes, you should be able to store a certain amount of Energy within it and draw upon that Energy to power skills or spells, even if your own Energy is spent."

"So, it's like a battery. Do I have to bond with it or something? Will I have trouble with the fire attuned Energy? I don't have a fire affinity."

"Yes, you should bond with it; that will allow you to sense how much Energy is within and access it. As far as your affinity goes, you simply will feel some heat as you access this Energy, but it will work just like any other Energy for you. To take advantage of its fire properties, you would need a fire affinity." Morgan nodded and bonded with the necklace—he was immediately aware of the Energy within and knew that he could pull it out or even spend time adding more of his Energy to it. It felt like it held enough to activate his Guard Ally skill once with a little leftover. He slipped the chain over his head.

"Thanks, Tiladia. I hadn't wanted to mess with that necklace because I got it from a rather nasty fellow, and it looked kind of ominous to me."

"Caution is always well advised when dealing with strange artifacts, Morgan," Tiladia replied with her usual tinkling voice.

"Yeah, I suppose. I sure wish this tower had some items in it. The rooms seem pretty bare, at least on this floor."

"Vormendion sealed most of the belongings he left behind in his reliquary. It's a large vault on the eighth floor. Most of his library is contained therein, which is why your shelves are bare."

"It doesn't seem like there'd be enough space for a vault up that high—the tower narrows. I suppose dimensional magic is at play?" Morgan arched an eyebrow.

"That's correct, Morgan."

"Alright, well, here goes." Morgan called forth his spear, lowered his center of gravity, and started to climb the steps, ready for anything. Or so he thought—he took one step, then two, then a third, and his stomach lurched a little, and he was stumbling onto the second floor's landing. As his senses oriented, a chandelier much like the one below flared to life. He heard a sibilant shriek and a dark, lean form came flying out of the shadows at him.

Morgan had just enough time to twist and push the haft of his spear between him and the attacker. As he halted its forward momentum, it shrieked again, this time in Morgan's face, and he got a good look at it: the only way he could describe it was to call it a lizard-man. Tall, wiry, covered in dark green scales. It had yellow eyes slit vertically and a snout full of pointy teeth in at least two rows. As it shrieked, it clawed viciously, adding to the shredded and frayed look of Morgan's robes. He felt a few claws strike home, giving him long, deep gashes on his shoulders and upper ribs.

Morgan kicked out while pushing on the horizontal spear and managed to dislodge the creature. He swung the sharp end of the spear around, keeping it between him and the attacker. "Can you speak?" he asked sharply, anger tinting the words. The creature hissed again, lunging to swing a clawed hand at him. Morgan struck with the spear, punching a deep wound in the lizard-man's stomach. It screamed, twisted, and launched itself at him. The sudden leap caught Morgan unprepared, and while he tried to bring the spear-tip up, he was a hair too slow. The lizard-man landed on him, feet first, and its long sharp toe-claws raked his chest from breast to navel, only stopping because his thick leather girdle caught the claws. The creature's weight pushed Morgan to his knees, and he nearly toppled backward.

Agony flared, and Morgan's vision went red with pain and rage, adrenaline flooding his system. He let go of his spear, grabbed hold of the lizard's waist, and hurled it to the side, stumbling to his feet. His inner robes were utterly shredded and soaked in blood, and he knew his skin wasn't in much better shape. He tried to lean over to pick up his spear, but the lizard-man was back on its feet and hissed, darting forward to rake at him as he reached down. Morgan winced in pain, backing up a step. He reached into his pouch, frantically calling forth his spare spear. It came into his hand just in time for him to jab it forward, fending off another swipe of claws.

Each move Morgan took was agony. His pectorals were a mess, and he knew the creature's claws had torn deep into his abdomen. He was leaving a broad swatch of blood everywhere he moved. He cursed himself for not going for the kill with his first stab of the spear. He'd half-assed the shot, trying to talk to the fucking lizard-man. Now he was bleeding out, scrambling for an opening while feeling weaker with each second. The creature was also clearly hurting, blood running freely from the stab wound in its abdomen.

The landing was well-lit now, and the dark smears of blood drew Morgan's peripheral attention to the patterned marble floor. It was really quite lovely, he thought. Another swipe jerked his attention back to the fight, and he realized he was losing it. He tightened his grip on the spear and urged himself into an offensive stance, taking several quick feints at the lizard-man. He kept jabbing, using his spear's length like he knew he should have from the beginning. He pushed and feinted, all the while waiting for the lizard-man to grow frustrated and leap again. Morgan started to worry that his opponent wouldn't do it, that it knew he was running out of blood and strength, and that it would wear him down. He tried one last ploy, faking a stumble and dropping the spear's tip. The lizard-man pounced on the opportunity, literally; it jumped, but Morgan was ready this time, and the spear was waiting. The creature's weight pushed the spearhead deep into its chest, and Morgan drove it to the ground while he activated Energy Drain.

A blood-curdling shriek accompanied the Energy that flooded into Morgan, binding his wounds and adding to the long list of scars he'd earned since his arrival in this world. The Energy wasn't enough to fully heal him, but he could live with being stiff and sore while the scabs held him together.

Congratulations! You have achieved level 13 Hollow Guard and have gained 5 Strength, 5 Will, 4 Vitality, 4 Intelligence, and 3 Agility.

"Congratulations, Morgan, on mastering the tower's second floor." Tiladia's voice came from the landing, near the stairs. Morgan turned to her and smiled, sketching a bow, though it made his head rush, and he felt faint afterward.

"It was closer than I would've wanted it to be."

"I admit that I grew worried for a moment as your life's blood was being used to wash the floors."

"Was that a joke, Tiladia? At my expense, no less?" Morgan had to smile; he was coming off a post-victory high, and the rush of Energy always put him in a good mood.

"No Morgan, I was being serious! Such a blood-letting usually signals imminent defeat! I was quite relieved to see you begin to take the battle seriously. In the future, I think you should be ferocious like a dragon from the beginning!"

"Noted," Morgan said as he called up his status sheet, ignoring sections that hadn't changed recently:

Race:	Human - Base 4		
Class:	Hollow Guard - Advanced		
Level:	13		
Energy Affinity:	9.2	Energy:	547/740

Strength:	30	Vitality:	32 (34)
Dexterity:	8	Agility:	24
Intelligence:	40	Will:	30
Titles & Feats:	Human Champion, First Hollow Guard, Ardeni Friend, Mark of Loyalty		

Morgan was happy at his improvements, but he was starting to get worried about his dexterity. Would it matter that he had one stat lagging so far behind his others? "Hey, Tiladia, I want to explore this floor, but first, can you answer me a question? I have an advanced class that gives me quite a few stat points at level, but my dexterity is falling behind all my other stats. Is that going to be a problem for me?"

"It could be a problem for you, yes. If you continue to push forward your other physical attributes and have a deficit in dexterity, you will find that you will be unable to take advantage of the full potential of your strength or agility. This wouldn't be such a factor if you were focusing more on spell casting. Some wizards only ever improve their intelligence and their will. There are as many theories about the best way to improve yourself as there are people, though. I'm sorry I'm not more help, Morgan."

"Well, if that's the case, why would the System create this class that pumps up my physical stats, but not dexterity?"

"There are ways to improve ability scores other than leveling. You might want to seek methods to increase your dexterity. Another thing to remember is that as you gain levels within the System, there will be opportunities to refine or change your class. You might open different doors at those times."

"Alright, yeah, I kinda knew that was coming, but it's good to get confirmation." Morgan looked around the landing. Aside from the blood-smeared floor, he hadn't taken in his surroundings. It was a large circular room, the stairs in the middle. Sets of wooden doors led off the room to the left and straight on from the stairs. On the right-hand side, windows and glass-paneled French doors opened onto a brightly lit room overgrown with plant life. "That's the atrium, I guess."

"Yes, Morgan." Tiladia whirled in the air, briefly taking on her dragon form and flitting back and forth before the glass leading to the atrium.

"Tiladia! I just had a thought; why do I know what a dragon is? There were creatures from fantasy stories on my homeworld, but when you change your shape, you look like dragons from our stories. It's strange, though, because there's no Energy or System there."

Tiladia flashed over to him before answering: "Morgan, Energy isn't always present in an ocean, like around this world. Sometimes it's a river, a stream, or even just a trickle. Perhaps Energy touched your world at some point, and some elder beings like dragons visited. The flow of Energy in the universe, especially where the System hasn't exerted an influence, can shift."

"What? The System isn't everywhere that Energy is?"

"No, Morgan. The System is ever-expanding its influence, but it hasn't spread over more than a fraction of this universe, let alone the myriad others." Tiladia's pulsing lights slowed for a long moment, and then she continued, "I forget myself, Morgan. I'm giving you information that might be terribly outdated. Time moves differently for me when I'm alone in this tower, and I don't know how accurate what I just said was."

"It's still good information, Tiladia. Thank you." Morgan moved over to the doors on the left side of the landing. He pushed them open, trusting that the only threat on the second floor had been dealt with. They opened smoothly like the hinges had been oiled regularly, and light fixtures flared to life around a large, empty gallery room. The ceiling had to be twenty feet high and was plastered with filigreed crown molding. The walls were a matching plaster, and the floor was covered in marble tiles with a pattern just like on the landing outside. Overall, it was a big, empty room that echoed as Morgan stepped around. He could imagine balls or parties taking place in this room. He stepped out and opened the next doors.

The second room was similarly designed, but it was smaller in scale, and the walls were lined with empty, glass-doored cabinets. However, one item remained in the room, a beautiful black piano-like instrument. Morgan whistled and walked over to it. "Is this a piano?"

"I believe Vormendion called it an angeliphone, but perhaps it's known by other names." Tiladia performed a loop over and under the piano—Morgan had decided he'd call it a piano. He smiled, running a finger along the silky black wood of the instrument, then made his way out and over to the atrium.

When he opened the doors to the atrium, he found his path blocked by verdant plant life. The plants within seemed to have grown unchecked for a very long time. "Tiladia, how are they still alive? Did you water them?"

"No, Morgan, the Atrium has a stream flowing through that keeps the soil enriched. As you can see, the sunstone provides plenty of light and warmth."

"Are there any valuable plants growing in there?"

"Oh, most definitely! Vormendion was quite an alchemist, and he grew many of his own reagents. I'm sure that, if enough time has passed, many of the plants within this atrium will have developed into natural treasures."

"I don't feel like fighting my way through these plants at the moment. Is there any chance you could catalog what's in there, and I can get to it a bit later?"

"Of course, Morgan. I'll be happy to do that."

"Thanks; right now, I want to head into the colony and see about getting some clean, unripped clothes." Morgan gestured to his shredded, blood-soaked black robes.

"An excellent idea, Morgan! I think you should try to get some armor to protect your vitals, as well! I'm glad to see you value your limbs, but your body is important too!" The lights flared quickly, and Morgan was starting to think Tiladia was laughing at him.

ॐ MORGAN ॐ

Morgan climbed the hill to the monolithic Colony Stone, ignoring the many sidelong looks he got from the people he walked by. By now, most people knew who he was, so he didn't get confronted by anyone, but he knew he looked a sight: halfway between six and seven feet tall, heavy bronze-colored armor on his wrists and shins, and tattered, bloodied black robes hanging in strips from his body. At least Morgan had put his spear away while he walked through the colony. He knew it was more than his height and attire that drew looks, though. He had a presence now that he hadn't before. Issa had referred to it as an aura, and Morgan knew that with each improvement to his being, his aura increased in weight. Morgan didn't know what increased the aura the most. It could be his increased stats, higher total Energy, or racial improvements. He felt like it was a combination of all those things. Whatever the cause, it had an impact: people noticed him coming, and they got out of his way.

He laid his hand on the stone, noting his minimal permissions. He selected the Contribution Store and looked through the various lists of items. He found some simple clothes like most colonists were wearing and saw that they were reasonably cheap—only twenty points for an outfit. Thinking about how cheap they were, he looked at his zero balance and realized he needed to sell some things.

Morgan dug the Energy beads from his pouch that he'd hoarded in the Crucible. He thought of keeping some to absorb in a pinch but decided that he had his healing potion and could buy others that would serve him better in an emergency. He placed his hand back on the stone and noticed a new menu for exchanging the beads he was holding for contribution points. Altogether, the System was offering him 3,200 points for his beads. He touched the "Accept" button, and he was suddenly holding empty pouches in his hand.

Morgan bought a couple of the soft, linen-like pants and shirts in a simple unstained cream color and two other sets in black. He figured he'd want to wear black under his armor to hide stains. Then he turned to a list of armor;

the store had everything from leather bracers for one hundred points to something called Gatallion Empire Battle Plate for 317,000. Morgan narrowed his search to items for the torso and scrolled until he got to items costing one thousand points. He saw an Artificed leather vest and a steel chain hauberk at that price point. He kept scrolling to two thousand points and saw what he was looking for, an Artificed bronze breastplate. He pushed the "Purchase" button, and a stream of yellow and blue smokey Energy flowed out of the Stone and coalesced into a silk-wrapped bundle on the ground by his feet.

Morgan picked up the bundle, noting the significant weight, and pulled the pale silk wrapping off. Before he looked at the contents, he marveled at the nice swatch of silk about the size of a bath towel that he'd gotten as a bonus. Smiling, he stowed it in his dimensional satchel. The breastplate looked similar to his greaves and vambraces, but it was a slightly lighter color of bronze and had quite a few more runes etched around it. The straps that fastened it to his shoulders and waist were made of soft, oily leather and also had runes burned into them. Morgan put his arms through the leather loops and tightened all the straps. Then, he attempted to bond with the item, and the breastplate shifted slightly, stretching and changing shape to fit him perfectly.

*****Artificed Bronze Breastplate: enchanted to match its owner's size and to repair damage gradually.*****

That was interesting; he hadn't gotten a description like that when he bonded to his greaves and vambraces. He imagined it was because the System had provided this, so its properties were fully known.

He spent the next several minutes buying many different kinds of food, from apples, to rye bread, to elk jerky. He was intrigued to see that the contribution store had foods familiar to him. Apples and elk? Was it simply because the System had access to millions or billions of worlds? The more Morgan thought he was getting a handle on this new world and the System, the more questions he seemed to come up with.

After stocking his satchel with spare clothes and provisions, Morgan spent a bit of time shopping through the miscellaneous sections of the store and bought some blankets, towels, a bucket, gardening tools, and a couple of bars of soap. He walked away with about nine hundred points remaining that he'd decided to save for future purchases. Morgan had just finished stowing all his goods in his satchel and was stepping away from the Colony Stone when he saw that a group of four men was standing quite close and staring at him.

"Can I help you?" he asked, not liking the expressions on their faces.

"Yeah, what's your name? Morton, ain't it?"

"No, Morgan. You are?"

"Right, right, Morgan. Hey, why don't I see you on the leaderboard?" The man speaking was a big fellow with a bushy reddish-blonde beard. He looked

Morgan straight in the eyes and stepped forward. His mouth was straight, and his posture leaned forward like he was trying to intimidate him. His three friends, all wearing scowls and clenching their fists, stood in a semi-circle around him and stared at Morgan.

"Leaderboard? Is there a problem here, guys?" Morgan didn't like their threatening posture, and he stood up straight, scowling at the big guy.

"Yeah, the Contribution Store leaderboard. I don't see you on it, Morgan, and I want to know how you got the first luxury home."

"You mean my tower? I got that from killing a bunch of shit that was a lot scarier than you, so back the fuck off, and don't ever get in my face again." Morgan wasn't sure how he did it, but he somehow pushed his aura out, almost like he was flexing a muscle. The weight of his accomplishments bore down on the man and his friends, and they blanched a little, backing off a step. Morgan nodded and walked right through them, bumping shoulders with the ginger-bearded guy. They didn't follow him or even say anything as he strode away. Morgan wasn't sure why he'd reacted so strongly to their bullying tactics. He wasn't sure if it had been smart, but something about some colonists, who hadn't even faced a life or death battle, talking down to him had really pushed the wrong buttons.

It was afternoon by the time he stepped back into his tower. Once again, he was greeted by Tiladia asking him how long he'd been gone. "Just a little while, Tiladia. I'm going to spend some time cleaning up my mess upstairs, and then I'd like to hear what you learned about the plants in the atrium while I was gone."

"Of course, Morgan."

"By the way," Morgan continued as he stepped onto the stairs, "what would happen if I got a few people to come to help me kill the guardians on the other floors?"

"I'm afraid that wouldn't work. Just as the stairs manipulate space to allow you to climb them quickly, they can do the opposite, making an ascent interminable."

"Let me guess, anyone else trying to climb the stairs with me would take a step and not move while I quickly ascend without them?"

"Yes, Morgan, guests you bring into the tower can only ascend to the floors you control. Once you've mastered the tower, you will also gain control of the stairway."

"All right, thanks, Tiladia." Morgan spent the next hour or so cleaning up the blood he'd spilled all over the second-floor landing. He made several trips to the sink in the kitchen to fill and rinse his bucket. Tiladia assured him that he'd never run out of water. Apparently, the enchanted equipment in the tower's basement drew water from a dimensional rift with access to a space with billions of gallons of fresh water. Tiladia showed him a well-hidden set of chutes in the tower wall where he could drop his towels for laundry and his robe to the incinerator. Of course, he wouldn't be able to get to the laundry until he'd opened the basement, but he figured he'd worry about crossing that bridge later.

Once he had cleaned up his mess, he started to work on the atrium. As he cut back the growth that blocked the door, Tiladia gave him pointers on what was valuable and what were just overgrown plants and branches that he could toss down to the incinerator. Morgan removed his armor and got to work in just his loose black outfit and his boots. Soon, he lost himself in the good honest work of gardening. Hours later, he was standing in the middle of the atrium. He could see why it was called an atrium and not a greenhouse. It really looked like the ceiling led up to an open sky. He couldn't discern any sort of roof, instead seeing a pale blue expanse and a bright sun directly overhead. "That's a sunstone, you say? What about that sky? It looks real."

"The ceiling is quite high, thanks to some dimensional magic, and the blue expanse is a trick of illusion. The sunstone is mounted a hundred feet up. Vormendion was quite proud of this room."

"I can see why!" Morgan stood on a stone bench situated in a square with three others at the atrium's center. He could see the glass windows leading out to the landing about fifty feet from the center, but he just saw trees and plants in every other direction. He could see that the stone pathway he was on continued in every direction, but he'd have to spend some time clearing the way through the whole atrium. A bit farther from where he was standing, he could hear running water and knew it was the stream Tiladia had told him about earlier.

While clearing the path to the center, he'd amassed a sizeable stack of leaves, flowers, and fruits that Tiladia said would be valuable to an alchemist. "Tiladia, does it hurt things like fruit to put them into a dimensional container?"

"Things like that are preserved in most dimensional storage containers. Anything that needs to breathe will surely be harmed, though. Never try to put a pet into a standard dimensional container, Morgan!" Tiladia flashed rapidly and spun around, and Morgan interpreted her behavior as agitation—like she was trying to get him to take her seriously.

"Alright, Tiladia, thank you! I won't put any furry friends into my pouch!" Morgan stowed the cuttings into his pouch, hoping to either meet an alchemist or learn about it himself at some point. After that, he went downstairs and, with the help of his new blankets, made a cozy bed out of one of the couches in the library. He was beat, and though he wasn't sure what time it was, he wanted to get some sleep. "Tiladia, please wake me if someone beats on the door, and please dim the lights."

Morgan woke on his own, feeling rested. He sat up in the dimmed light of the chandelier, yawning and stretching. He was just pulling his boots on when Tiladia floated through the doorway. "Good morning, Morgan."

"Is it morning? Thanks, Tiladia. What can you tell me about the third-level guardian?" Morgan ate some bread, some dried meat, and a piece of fruit called a yulanox; it was sort of like a banana, but it was tinted red and had a more savory flavor that was less sweet.

"I think the third-level guardian will be a dangerous challenge for you, Morgan. I can't tell you more than that. I'm so sorry! I wish I could give you clues about it being an elemental creature or. . . ." Tiladia suddenly emitted a high-pitched shriek that sounded like a thousand crystal bowls shattering on a marble floor and spun around rapidly.

"Tiladia, are you okay?" Morgan stood up and tried to reach out to her misty form, but she spun away from him, and a moment later, the shrieking sound stopped.

"Oh, oh, I shouldn't have done that, Morgan. I knew better, but I so wanted to help you. I'm sorry I can't help you more."

"Don't mention it, Tiladia! I don't want you to do anything that causes you harm. Are you okay?"

"I'll be fine, Morgan, but I don't want to go through that again. I felt like Vormendion's fingers were wiggling around in my brain."

"Jesus." Morgan shook his head and, though he liked this home he'd been granted, quietly cursed the faceless mage who had created it. So, the next guardian was some kind of elemental creature? He'd need to prepare for that, and he was pretty sure Olivia could help; she'd mentioned that she was learning to cast elemental spells.

❧ MORGAN ❧

"Morgan! I'm glad to see you; it's been a busy couple of days, and I'd meant to talk to you sooner. Wait 'til you see what we're having built next!" Olivia waved to Morgan as he approached the Colony Stone.

"Oh, something other than housing?" he asked as he walked up to her. She had a hand on the stone and seemed to be concentrating on something in the air in front of her face. He chuckled at her blank stare as she navigated the System UI screens.

"That's right! We put up the last mass housing unit yesterday. Now we have enough beds for every colonist. We'll start building nicer homes soon, but first, we want to get some infrastructure and important buildings in, starting with a brewery and tavern! We all agreed that a gathering place should take precedence, and Arthur, of all people, suggested a bar to help with morale." Olivia was chuckling as her eyes darted back and forth over the menus.

"You won't get any arguments from me." Morgan felt a rumbling in the ground and heard some yelling and cheering from off to his left. He walked over the crown of the hilltop to see what was happening, Olivia following close behind. Down the western slope of the hill, Morgan could see a crowd gathered but held back by several people who had staked off a large rectangular section of ground. Within the rectangle, the colonists had piled large stacks of cut trees. A cloud of yellow, sparkling fog grew out of the grass around the timber. Soon, nothing was visible within the sparkling mist, and the ground started churning. As Morgan watched, a large two-story building rose out of the earth. "Goddamn, that's what I call fast construction!"

"Yeah, the System certainly makes construction painless," Olivia replied, coming to stand next to him. The building was settling into place, the ground smoothing out into packed earth around it. The sides of the building were made from the same dark earth-colored bricks as the smithy. It had large windows framed in wooden shutters. The roof was peaked and made from heavy-looking timbers and slats.

"So, you only had to supply the wood? Does the System pull everything else out of the earth? Glass? Metals? Brick? Pretty damn convenient." Morgan had thought his tower construction was novel, but it seemed that building structures out of nothing was fairly commonplace, with Energy use being the new normal.

"Yeah, I guess so." Olivia's frown belied her agreement.

"Judging by the vents on the roof, I bet the brewery portion is on the second floor? You think it comes with supplies to make beer?"

"No, the description indicated we'd need to grow our own or purchase ingredients from the Contribution Store."

"Huh, well, that's pretty cool, anyway. You already have people picked out to work in there?" Morgan looked around at the crowd, wondering if any of the onlookers would soon be making beer and serving customers.

"Actually, yes. Some colonists with agricultural backgrounds were assigned to create this industry in the planned settlement, so they'll be stepping in."

"Well, I wasn't just happening by; I was looking for you to pick your brain about something," Morgan said, turning away from the new building and looking at Olivia.

"Oh?" Olivia turned to him, arching an eyebrow.

"Yeah. So, you know my new tower?" He paused while Olivia nodded. "Well, I don't actually have control of all of it yet. I guess the previous owner was kind of a prick, and he's set up these guardians on each floor. I can't do anything on the floors they're guarding until I defeat them. So far, I've beaten the first two guardians."

"You need help with the others?" Olivia asked, her voice rising in excitement.

"Not exactly. The guy made it so only I can climb the stairs to the uncleared levels, so I have to defeat them by myself. There's this spirit, though, that kind of manages the tower. She's friendly and is allowed to give me an idea of my chance of success with each guardian. She said I could maybe, barely beat the third guardian, and she let it slip that it's some kind of 'elemental creature' whatever that is. I thought you might have some idea?"

"Elemental?" Olivia pursed her lips and tapped her pointer finger on her chin while contemplating. "I take it you came to me because I told you about my elemental magic?" Morgan nodded. "Well, I've learned a basic spell for four different elements and a couple of stronger ones for fire and ice. Unfortunately, those spells would be no help to you if I can't go with you to the fight."

"Right, I figured that, but I was hoping you'd have some insight into what I could do to prepare."

"Oh, well, as far as I know, the four main elemental attunements are fire, earth, water, and air. You know there are potions in the Contribution Store—maybe you could buy some to help resist those elements."

"Ah, I hadn't thought of that! I knew you were the person to talk to!" Morgan turned back toward the stone.

"Well, you're welcome!" Olivia called, laughing, as he walked away.

"Thank you!" Morgan laughed as he slapped his hand on the stone. He shopped through the menus, finding the one labeled "Consumables," where he'd bought his food earlier, and then noticed a sub-category called "Potions." He selected it and saw quite a lengthy list. The cheapest item was a potion of minor stamina that was supposed to give you a quick boost of endurance. It only cost five points, and Morgan wondered if it was any better than a cup of coffee. He bought one to try it out. He scrolled down the list until he found a section called resistance potions. Minor elemental resistance potions were sold for fifty points each. The next tier was a standard resistance potion, and they sold for one hundred. Morgan bought one for each element and one for poison, reasoning that it sounded like a good thing to have on hand. He turned away from the stone, five hundred points poorer.

Olivia was gone when he looked up, presumably to check out the new construction. Morgan figured he'd wait for things to settle down. Maybe they'd have a grand opening when there was some beer, ale, or perhaps cider to share. He turned, instead, to the north and started walking toward the dark gray spire of his tower. As he walked, he thought about his actions. Why didn't he want to go and hang out with people as they celebrated a new building? They were clearly in a festive mood down there. Maybe he just wanted to make more progress in his tower before something else called him away? He knew that he'd be obligated to help Olivia's friend, Bronwyn, when she came back, and he had a feeling it would be any time now. Then he had to start pathfinding toward Issa's village. He missed her already, and maybe that was the real reason he wasn't interested in hanging out with a bunch of colonists that he really had no connection to other than that they were from the same planet. He and Issa had been through hell together, and he didn't want to spend time away from her frivolously.

He stepped into his tower and exchanged his usual greeting with Tiladia. "No, I haven't been gone long, just thirty minutes or so."

"Excellent! Morgan, I've been cataloging the plants and fruits that have grown in the atrium, and I should finish by the end of the day. There's one fruit, in particular, that might interest you, though. The old master had a Heesporian plum tree that he carefully cultivated from a seedling. They only bear fruit once every seventy to ninety years, and it has produced a very ripe plum. The Energy in it is quite dense."

"Uh, what's this plum supposed to do?" Morgan started walking to the stairs.

"If I recall correctly, it's supposed to be of great use when someone is trying to evolve their Core."

"Ah"—Morgan stopped walking and looked at Tiladia—"I don't think I'm ready to try to do that yet. I don't know what it means. How and why does one 'evolve' their Core?"

"Morgan, I can sense that you have a base 2 Core—if you want to improve your Core's capacity and power, you'll need to evolve it. The Heesporian plum would probably help you gain several stages on your Core, but such a valuable item might be better used when you are at a plateau rather than just starting."

"Right. So, I should save it until I get stuck. I've never tried to improve my Core, and I've already gained a rank, so I'm assuming that my cultivation drill will help me gradually improve it? So far, I've only practiced it in order to open my pathways."

"That's right, Morgan. I'm glad that you have a suitable drill for your Core. I've never learned anything about a Vortex Core."

"You can see what kind of Core I have?"

"Yes, scrying and evaluation are my specialties! I told you I was good at that!" Tiladia flared and whirled around him.

"Alright, changing subjects: What's on the third floor?"

"The third floor is the gallery level. It houses the art gallery and the dueling gallery."

"Interesting fellow, Vormendion, keeping his art and duels on equal footing." Morgan snorted. "Hey, I don't suppose you can tell me if it's particularly warm, cold, or windy on the third floor?"

"Morgan, I—" Tiladia pulsed for a few seconds, then continued, "I want to reply, Morgan, but I know what you are asking, and my knowing means that the bindings on me apply. I'm sorry, I don't want to go through that torment again." Her lights dimmed, and she positively drooped.

"Relax, Tiladia, it was just a long shot. Don't worry; I don't want you to do anything to hurt yourself." Morgan put one hand into his pouch, clearly picturing his four elemental resistance potions. He gripped his spear firmly in his other hand and stepped onto the stairs. Two steps later, he was on the second-floor landing. He turned and stepped onto the ascending curve of the stairway, and two more steps saw him on a new landing.

The third-floor landing was much like the one below. A similar fixture flared to life, illuminating similar tiles, though the pattern was different—pale porcelain split by two burgundy half circles with the open ends pointing away from each other. The walls were paneled in a warm, lightly stained wood, and two sets of doors led off the landing to the left and the right. Nothing jumped out of the shadows to attack him. Morgan turned to his left and quickly opened one of the doors with his left hand, then put it back in his pouch, ready to pull out a potion.

The room that came into view as three big chandeliers flared to life was much like the big reception hall below, but this one was narrower and longer and had obviously once housed dozens of large paintings; they were gone, but the plaster was lighter where they used to rest. In the bright light, Morgan was sure nothing was hiding in the gallery, so he left, crossed over to the other side of the landing, and pushed the door open.

This room was a mirror to the art gallery, but instead of tile floors, it had a blonde-colored wood slat floor, and low benches lined the hallway, presumably for spectators. Empty weapons racks lined the far, short ends of the room. Morgan pulled out his potion of fire resistance when he looked to the end of the room on his left: a figure stood down there, about forty feet away from him. The figure looked like a man, but he appeared to be made of smoldering coal. He wore no clothes, and most of his body was pitch black, but some spots were glowing red, and white ash seemed to follow in his wake as he paced back and forth, whipping a slender, shiny sword back and forth. Two red embers filled his eye sockets, and, as they locked onto Morgan's eyes, the man's mouth parted in a red, smoking grin.

Morgan quaffed the small potion of fire resistance, grimacing at the bitter flavor; it was like a mixture of tart cranberries and vinegar. He put the empty vial in his pouch and gripped his spear with both hands while a chill ran over his body, and a thin rime of ice spread over his bronze vambraces and hands. He stepped into the gallery and faced the smoldering man. The man stepped forward and silently bowed, straightened, and looked at Morgan. Morgan figured he knew what the man was waiting for, so he reciprocated the bow. The man's smoking grin widened, and he stepped forward, lashing out with the rapier. Morgan was ready, though, and used his longer weapon to menace the attacker, keeping him at bay.

The smoldering swordsman shortly grew frustrated, his grin turning into a frown. He scowled, backed up a step, then spun in a circle, whipping his sword in a flat arc toward Morgan. Morgan knew the man was too far away for the sword to hit him, but alarm bells rang in his mind anyway. He was alarmed for good reason—the smoking duelist's sword flared bright red, like steel about to melt, and an arc of liquid fire whipped away from the blade and flew toward Morgan. Morgan frantically raised his spear to "block" the stream of fire, and it only managed to interrupt a tiny portion of the wave of flame. His spear's haft smoldered, and the rest of the fire slammed into Morgan's chest and upper arms. Where it hit his breastplate, he didn't feel any pain, but his upper arms screamed in agony, and Morgan knew that if he hadn't had that potion of resistance, he'd probably have been charred to the bone. As it was, his breastplate was uncomfortably warm, and his sleeves were smoldering over blistered skin.

The potion was helpful but not enough for Morgan to ignore the fiery attack, and he knew that he couldn't win a battle of attrition with this guy. The blistering pain in his arms was incentive for him to try to end this fight quickly, so he started channeling his Energy Drain ability and pushed himself into an offensive flurry. He used every feint and flourish that came to mind from his Spear Mastery skill, but his basic level was starting to show its limitations; the smoldering duelist was clearly on another level. He sidestepped, parried, and neatly riposted several of Morgan's stabs. Morgan kept up the attack, but the duelist suddenly started smoking, glowing like an ember all over, and then opened his mouth and coughed a huge ball of fire at Morgan. Morgan rolled to the side, but the flames half engulfed him, and he screamed in agony. He rolled away from the charcoal man, extinguishing his smoldering clothes. As he rolled, the duelist followed him, stabbing at him with his rapier. He pierced Morgan in the back of his left thigh and again in his upper back. Morgan screamed in rage and pain, rolling frantically away and using the momentum to spring to his feet.

Morgan was starting to feel his wounds and exertions and knew that he'd have collapsed a while ago if he hadn't improved his vitality so much. He knew that he couldn't beat this guardian with skill. He also knew that his fire resistance potion would wear off soon. He contemplated making a run for the stairwell and getting out while he could for a brief moment, but a streak of stubbornness wouldn't allow that. Instead, he slowly circled and backstepped, keeping the man at bay while he worked his way to a corner of the gallery. Once he had his back to a corner, he slowly started to sidestep while stabbing at the man until they'd switched positions—now the smoldering duelist had his back to the corner. "Dodge this, cigar face!" Morgan grunted as he charged, the point of his spear leading the way.

The duelist grinned, using his superior skill to redirect the point of Morgan's spear to the side, then driving his rapier toward Morgan's stomach. Morgan didn't slow, though, and the rapier's point didn't quite get to his gut, instead impacting the top of his left thigh, grinding into the bone of Morgan's hip. Morgan's growl turned into a roar as he kept charging, driving the man into the corner of the room. When they impacted the wall, Morgan dropped his grip on the spear and grabbed hold of the man's head with both hands, activating Energy Drain. Through the burning in his hands, he felt torrents of fiery Energy flow into him. He pulled it with all his ability, willing his Vortex Core to vacuum in as much as possible.

The duelist's mouth opened in a silent scream. Flames started to coalesce in his throat, and Morgan knew that he would fire another gout of flame at him, but the flames never gathered, instead slowly fading down to embers as Morgan pulled the Energy out of the duelist. Finally, Morgan's spell had run its course, and he stepped away from the charcoal man, taking up his spear, which had fallen against the wall. The smoldering man wasn't dead, and he weakly held onto his rapier as Morgan stepped back, but it was lodged in Morgan's hip bone. Though it was agonizing, Morgan kept pulling away, and the duelist's grip wasn't strong enough to hold on. As his hand slipped away from the sword's hilt, Morgan leveled his spear, resting the point on the man's chest where a normal person's heart would be. "Yield?" he croaked, spittle and blood spraying out with the word.

The man just stared at Morgan, then slowly shook his head, weakly pushing against Morgan's spear. Morgan growled and said louder, "Yield!" The man jerked his head in a vehement negation and then shoved against the spear, nodding.

"He can't yield, Morgan; he's bound." Tiladia's voice tinkled sadly from behind him.

"Well, that's fucked," Morgan said, but he shoved with all his might, driving his spear through the duelist's chest and into the wall behind him. The man's mouth opened again, but, like before, no sound came out. The fire in his eyes dimmed, and then he slowly started to crumble. As he fell into a pile of ash, a stream of dense silvery-gold motes rushed into Morgan.

Congratulations! You have achieved level 14 Hollow Guard and have gained 5 Strength, 5 Will, 4 Vitality, 4 Intelligence, and 3 Agility. You have learned the skill Hollow Charge—Basic.

"Tiladia, I feel dirty. That guy was a better fighter." Morgan sighed as he looked down at the state of his clothes and body.

"He was a better duelist, Morgan, but your Energy Drain ability is quite effective against Energy-based beings. You were fighting for your life, not for a sporting competition. It's good that you found a way to vanquish him."

Morgan still had some pink skin where he'd been burned, but he'd mostly healed from the massive influx of Energy he'd gotten from the smoldering man. He still had a rapier stuck in his hip, though. He reached into his pouch and pulled out a scrap of leather that he gingerly wrapped around the rapier's blade, close to where it had entered his body. He gripped the leather tightly and jerked the blade out quickly with all his strength. "Ouch! Jesus!" He limped around in a circle, cursing for several moments.

"I wish I could help you, Morgan; alas, I cannot physically interact."

"It's the thought that counts." Morgan grunted, stowing the rapier in his dimensional satchel. He noticed that his hip had already stopped bleeding, and though it was tender, he could see that he wouldn't need surgery or anything. His high vitality was starting to show its benefits. He called up his status sheet to see the progress of his attributes and Energy:

Energy Affinity:	9.2	Energy:	669/848
Strength:	35	Vitality:	36 (38)
Dexterity:	8	Agility:	27
Intelligence:	44	Will:	35

He focused on his new skill and read the information screen that appeared:

Hollow Charge—Basic: Prerequisite: Vortex Class Core. You expend some Energy to sheath yourself in the currents of your Vortex Core and move with great alacrity up to 25 feet. Energy-based attacks that hit you during this charge will be absorbed by your Core. Energy cost: 100, Cooldown: Medium.

"Well, that's pretty badass," he murmured.

"What's that, Morgan?" Tiladia queried, pulsing and spinning around him.

"Oh, I got a new skill," Morgan replied, walking out of the room. He was feeling the need for some fresh air.

"Oh yes, I saw that. Congratulations on your level, and belated congratulations on conquering the third level of the tower. I estimate you have roughly a fifty percent chance to conquer the fourth guardian."

"Hah, thanks, Tiladia. I think I'll put that off for now."

BRONWYN

"How do you, uh, wanna start this?" Bronwyn set her backpack down on the ground and shook her arms out, hopping from foot to foot.

"Hah! Have you never had a duel to the death before, Human Blodwyn?" Bloodfang crossed his sword over his chest and gave her a deep mocking bow. "It's my pleasure to be both your first and your last. Now, come fight me!" He roared the last few words and charged at her.

Bronwyn was about twenty yards from the charging Urghat. She saw his cutlass held low at his right side as he ran and took a few seconds to channel her stone skin. Bloodfang spun to the right at the end of the charge, bringing his sword up and slamming it down toward her left clavicle. She quickly adjusted her guard and blocked the strike with the hard metal backing of her gauntlets. A thunderous echo blasted across the clearing, and Bronwyn, even as braced as she was, was sent tumbling backward from the force of the blow. She caught herself and rolled to her feet, feeling a bit dizzy. Her ears were ringing, and her arms felt slightly numb; in fact, her whole body felt like it just got hit with a sonic blast.

She shook her head, bringing things into focus just in time for her to evade Bloodfang's sword, ripping down toward her head. She slid to the left as it carved through the air at her side, shaving so close that bits of leather peeled away at the blade's passage. Almost without thinking, she reached out and grabbed the wrist of his sword arm with both hands. Using his momentum, she twisted it behind his back and ripped it upwards toward the back of his neck, straining until she heard a loud *pop* from his right shoulder. The Urghat dropped his sword and roared out in pain, slamming his head backward into Bronwyn's face. "Fuck!" She yelled and grabbed her bloodied nose, dropping his wrist and stepping back.

Bloodfang lunged toward the ground, picking up his sword with his left hand as his right arm hung uselessly at his side. He made a sweeping strike at Bronwyn's midsection, and she leaped backward; the tip of the sword barely touched her stomach. It erupted with thunder, throwing her onto her back and knocking the wind from her lungs. On the ground, gasping for breath, Bronwyn focused on Bloodfang's legs and activated her Fetters of Stone skill. The earth erupted at his feet as his lower legs became encased in stone up to his shins. He struggled for a moment, grunting in frustration as he tried to rip them free. It was all the time Bronwyn needed: she caught a couple of deep breaths and charged the Urghat, ducking under his off-balance swing and tackling him to the ground. His good arm windmilled, but he couldn't keep his balance with his feet still encased in stone. He fell backward, unable to twist or get any footing to try to push Bronwyn off. She used her left arm and all her body weight to pin his good arm to the ground and pummeled his face with her gauntlet.

Bronwyn kept swinging until she was sure it was over. When Bloodfang stopped breathing and struggling, she fell to her side and rolled onto her back, still trying to catch her breath fully. Her whole body was one giant bruise from the impacts of that cutlass, her ears were still ringing, and her vision felt a little blurry as she lay there, looking up at the sky. She closed her eyes and breathed deeply until the motes of Energy from Bloodfang funneled into her, relieving much of her pain and clearing her vision. Her ears were still ringing slightly, and she worried for a moment, as she wiggled a finger in her ear, that it would be permanent.

Congratulations! You have achieved level 9 base human and have 5 attribute points to allocate.

Grunting, she sat up and kneeled over the body of Bloodfang. His sword had melted into a pool of blood, and the stone around his legs had turned to sand. She started inspecting his other items. His armor was inscribed with very faint runes, and he wore two golden armbands, one of which was inscribed with simple, jagged runes that glowed faintly. He also carried a small dimensional pouch, similar to the one she already owned. She attempted to bond with both armbands; the first one had no effect, meaning it was probably just a simple gold band. The second, with the red inscription, immediately slid up over her gauntlet and fit itself directly on the upper third of her right bicep. As she stared in shock, the text shifted, and it read "Underclaw Blodwyn."

Congratulations! You have earned the title "Underclaw" this is a transient title. Relations with the Ur-clan increased. +4 Strength +4 Vitality.

"What the fuck . . ." she muttered, trailing off to silence as the implications hit her. She tried to unbind the armband from herself and found that she couldn't move it physically or by taking her Energy out of it like she could with her pouch and armor. "Shit." She didn't want to dwell on all the possible outcomes this might cause and moved on to her examination of the pouch. Somewhat hesitant now, she bonded with it and found that it only contained some rations, a couple of daggers, and a rolled-up scroll. She pulled the scroll from the pouch.

***Congratulations! You have completed a Quest: Defeat Underclaw Bloodfang and retrieve Ur-clan missives.**

A medium-size blue chest apparated into existence to her right. She flipped the lid and found two rewards inside: a brightly glowing golden orb and a slice of what looked like a blood orange. She felt the desire to eat the fruit immediately and shoved it into her mouth without thinking. It tasted like an orange chocolate lava cake, and it warmed her whole body as she ate it. She felt a surge of Energy flooding into the muscles of her arms. She was almost sad when the fruit was gone and slightly frowned as she reached her hand forward to touch the golden orb. As she wrapped her palm around it, Energy coursed through her arm and her remaining aches and pains left her.

Congratulations! You have achieved level 10 base human and have 10 attribute points to allocate. Your first Class selection is available to you.*

Bronwyn thought about it for a moment and decided to allocate her points before looking at her class choices. She had a feeling that her stats might influence what kind of class she was offered. That decided, she put six points into strength and four into agility. She looked at her updated attributes on her status sheet:

Strength:	48	Vitality:	15
Dexterity:	9	Agility:	29
Intelligence:	9	Will:	11

She noticed that her strength was slightly higher than she thought it should be and surmised that the fruit she'd been awarded had improved that attribute. Happy with her progress, she decided to take a look at her class options. She saw a new prompt labeled "Class selection" on her status screen and touched it:

Level 10 Class selection. Class selection is permanent. Human Energy cultivators will next be offered a Class refinement selection at level 20. To view your options and make your selection, use the arrows to page through this interface.*

Class selection option 1: Brawler—Basic. You use your honed physique to pummel your foes into submission while nimbly avoiding damage. Class attributes: Agility, Strength, and Vitality.*

Bronwyn stopped to consider this class for a moment but decided to look at the rest of her options first. She touched the arrow to advance the screen several times, reading through each option:

Class selection option 2: Fighter—Basic. You use physical prowess to best your foes with remarkable feats of combat skill. Master weapons and your body to become a force that can change the tide of a battle. Class attributes: Strength, Agility, and Vitality.

Class selection option 3: Berserker—Improved. Fury and overwhelming force guide you on the battlefield. With little concern for your safety, you put the domination of your foes first. Class attributes: Strength, Vitality, Agility, and Will.

Class selection option 4: Stone Warden—Improved. Prerequisite—Affinity to Earth Energy. You work to master your manipulation of Earth magic to become a moving fortress on which your enemies will break. Class attributes: Vitality, Strength, and Will.

Class selection option 5: Stone Pugilist—Improved. Prerequisite—Affinity to Earth Energy. You work to master your manipulation of Earth magic to enhance your physical presence and combat prowess. Class attributes: Strength, Agility, Will, Vitality, Dexterity.

She dismissed the idea of Fighter and Brawler out of hand—no way would she be choosing a "basic" class. That decided, she looked long and hard at the three "improved" options. She liked how fierce and brutal the berserker sounded, but she felt like her temper had already gotten her in enough trouble. She didn't know exactly how things would work in this world, but berserkers in pretty much every game she'd ever played tended to lose control of themselves while raging or whatever.

That brought her choices down to Stone Warden and Stone Pugilist. She'd like to say it was a hard decision, and if she ever talked about this with anyone, she might play it up to have been, but the fact that Stone Warden didn't focus on agility at all pushed her in the direction of Stone Pugilist. Stone Warden sounded like a tank, and she didn't tend to play tanks. Taking a few deep breaths and thoroughly clearing her mind, she thought about her decision. Finding no second thoughts lingering, she double-checked that she was on the right screen, hit the "accept" button, and was rewarded with a new screen:

Congratulations! You have gained your first Class: Stone Pugilist. Class skill gained: Stone Fists—Basic. Class skill gained: Stone Warding—Improved.

Bronwyn whooped loudly, pumping a fist in the air. She called up her skills page and read the descriptions of her new abilities:

Stone Warding—Improved: Your ability to bend stone and earth to defend yourself against attacks has increased. You can now stop larger and more deadly blows. Amber Class Core Enhancement: Your armoring spells have twice the duration and cost half the energy. Energy cost: 10 per second.

Stone Fists—Basic: Your fists are becoming natural weapons. You are able to enhance your unarmed strikes with added weight and power. Energy cost: 10 per minute.

Bronwyn was thrilled with her new abilities. It seemed like she picked the perfect class to keep advancing on her current path. Filled with the euphoria of victory and achievement, she bent to the task of unbuckling the heavy, scaled armor that the Urghat had been wearing, stuffing it into her storage pouch. Before heading to town, she contemplated burying or burning the body of the Urghat. She'd never fought an actual duel before and didn't know if some show of respect was in order. Finally, deciding that his people would want to recover the corpse, she folded his arms over his chest and spread his cloak over him. Bronwyn knelt, picked up her backpack, and then turned back toward the settlement. She'd only made it a few steps before she felt a familiar nuzzle on the back of her neck and a comfortable weight on her shoulder.

MORGAN

Morgan spent the rest of the morning making more progress in the atrium. He cut away excess branches, vines, and sprawling undergrowth in an ever-widening pattern out from the central benches. Just before he was ready to quit for the day, he uncovered the little stream that flowed through the room and found that it had a delicately carved, arched marble bridge crossing it along the northern path. He stood on the span, looking down at the slowly flowing stream of water, and marveled at the myriad colorful fish that made it their home. Say what you would about Vormendion; he certainly knew how to design an amazing tower.

While he was watching the fish swimming by, a glint of something caught his eye, and he realized there was something metallic in the sandy bed of the stream. He walked to the edge of the stream, climbed down the piled, mossy stones to the water's edge, and took off his boots. After rolling up his black trousers, he waded out into the cold water and dug around in the silty sand until he felt the hard, cold metal in his hand. He pulled forth a decidedly feminine and fancy-looking tiara. It was crafted from silvery metal, but it wasn't in the least bit tarnished. A large sapphire sat at the top center of the filigreed metal, and several dozen diamonds, or diamond-looking stones, lined the rest of the peaks and whorls of metal. Morgan let out a low whistle at the sight of the obviously valuable item.

"That belonged to Lady Ymreesa Canst. Vormendion would often, after drinking copious amounts of brandy, loudly proclaim her as the only woman he ever loved." Tiladia had approached while he was digging around in the streambed.

"Oh? Why's it in the water?"

"They had a falling out. I knew Vormendion had the diadem crafted for her, but I didn't know what became of it."

"Is it magical?" Morgan asked, still admiring the beauty of the tiara.

"Oh, very. I wouldn't recommend you try to bond with it yet. I'm fairly sure there is a conscious spirit bound to it, and I'm not sure you could dominate it."

"Would I have to dominate it?"

"Either that or risk being dominated. Bound spirits often seek to experience life through a vessel like you." Tiladia's tinkling sounds took on a lower note, and Morgan felt a somber emotion coming from her.

"Aren't you a bound spirit?"

"Oh, yes. My bindings are far more intricate than those in an item like that, though. At least I have the freedom to roam this tower and to interact with people."

"You don't sound happy, Tiladia. I'd love it if we could find a way to make your life better. Keep that in mind, okay? That's one of my primary goals. In the meantime, I better stow this tiara, or diadem as you put it, away for now." Morgan did just that, putting the diadem into his pouch.

"No, Morgan, please don't put that into your dimensional container! The conscious spirit within could go mad if you leave it in there for any length of time!" Tiladia whirled in agitation until Morgan nodded and pulled the diadem from his pouch.

"I'll put it in the desk in the study, then." He climbed out of the water, got his shoes back on, left the atrium, and went to do just that. Afterward, he made his way to the library.

He was on his third day out of the Crucible, and it didn't seem like he'd taken any time to reflect on what he'd learned and how he should progress. He knew he had to continue to gain strength. If the Crucible had taught him anything, it was that he didn't want to be helpless before more powerful Energy users. It would be one thing if there were laws and people to enforce them, but, as far as Morgan could tell, the humans were on their own here. There were clearly some hostile entities in this world, and some had shown their faces already. He even had doubts about the System's motivations; its idea of evaluating him and helping him improve himself was to throw him into a deadly proving ground. The System seemed to like conflict as a means for growth. If Olivia was correct, its overall goal was to get the Energy users under its influence to become stronger Energy users, all as some means to siphon more Energy from them.

These were big picture problems, though, and Morgan knew that he had to make some short-term gains for more immediate reasons: he wanted to clear more of the guardians in the tower, and he needed to help defend the colony from hostiles. Speaking with Tiladia earlier had reminded him that he hadn't touched his cultivation drill since he had opened his pathways in the Crucible. He resolved to make a habit of it, spending some time each day practicing the drill to improve his Core and, theoretically, his level. He had only been able to access the first part of the cultivation manual so far and hoped that if he continued to improve his Core, he'd gain access to more of it.

With new motivation, Morgan assumed the lotus position in front of the couch where he had been sleeping and commenced cultivating Energy. He closely followed the methods the scroll had imprinted into his mind. With each deep breath, he focused on his Core spinning and drawing Energy in through his pathways. With each exhalation, he pushed that Energy out along his pathways. Each time, he concentrated on trying to draw more Energy, and each time he exhaled, he tried to push the Energy out slightly faster. The goal was to improve his Core's capacity as well as the pathways'. At one point, Morgan realized he was only breathing about five times per minute. He marveled, momentarily, at the fact that he wasn't struggling for air or even uncomfortable. Either the Energy was supplementing the oxygen he took in, or his improved attributes were having an effect. Perhaps it was a combination of the two.

He was just winding down after a couple of hours of cultivating, trying to see if he could notice any improvements when Tiladia shimmered into the room. "Morgan! A woman is knocking on the front door."

"You can see who's knocking?"

"Oh, yes. Being bound to the tower, I experience occurrences like people pounding on the door quite viscerally." She shimmered brightly, and the tinkling glass quality of her voice rose slightly in pitch.

"Alright, I'll go see what's going on." Morgan stood and walked to the front door, opening it just as someone began to rap on the door. Midday sun came into his eyes and, as they adjusted, he saw Olivia stepping back away from the swinging door. "Oh, hi, Olivia."

"Morgan, I'm glad you're home. Speaking of, you're going to have to give me a tour someday soon. I'm here for something else, though; Bronwyn's back." She spoke rapidly, and though she had a calm expression, Morgan could detect some anxiety in her voice.

"Oh, alright, you want me to meet with her? Everything alright?" He stepped out of the tower and swung the big door closed behind him, the lock clicking solidly home when he let go of the handle.

"Well, yes and no. Yes, Bronwyn is home, and she's fine. No, because we have another threat to worry about. It turns out some bear-like creatures called Urghat are planning a raid or invasion or something."

"Urghat? Yeah, I had to fight a good amount of those in the Crucible. They weren't so bad in small numbers, but if there's an army of them, that could be a problem. I mean, I know I'm kind of out of it, but I don't see a ton of people going out to level and learn combat skills." Morgan followed Olivia down the steps and up the slight slope toward the center of the settlement. The sun was high in the sky, and the moons, Thivia and Galia, were hanging above the eastern horizon. The air was pleasantly cool, and Morgan wondered how long it would be until this world moved from spring into summer.

"Yes, that's an issue. According to Bisset, we have just over three hundred colony personnel actively seeking a combat-oriented class. They've been hunting daily since the barrier came down, and they train with each other each evening. Considering we weren't planning on having anywhere near that many security personnel in the colony, I guess that's pretty good. None of them are beyond level five, though."

"I imagine the wall will help. Do the engineers have anyone working on gates? I haven't looked since my first day here."

"Yeah, we've already got gates in place. The people working the forge were able to make hinges and bolts after just a couple of days of practice. It seems the System is generous with handing out skills to newly integrated beings."

"Oh? Is that confirmed? I noticed I picked up skills pretty quickly when I first started working through the Crucible, but things definitely slowed down until I got my class."

"Not exactly confirmed, but a theory backed by a lot of anecdotes at this point." While Olivia was talking, they began to walk up the hill to the monolith, and a tall, powerful-looking woman came striding down the slope to meet them. "Bron! This is the guy I was telling you about, Morgan Hall."

"Hello," Morgan said, stopping to offer his hand. Bronwyn was a tall woman, maybe six feet. She had a tangled mass of red hair pulled back in a ponytail, and her greenish-yellow eyes stood out brightly from her furrowed brows. She looked like she'd been through a lot recently; scrapes and bruises from old and yellow to new and deep purple covered her arms, neck, and face. She was wearing tightly strapped leather armor with a vest covered in sharp-looking short, black spikes. She took his hand in a firm grip and looked him in the eyes for a long moment.

"Hey, Morgan. I hear you have quite a story to tell? About a dungeon you were in or something?"

"That can wait, Bron," Olivia cut in. "I think we need to tell Morgan about the thing in the cave. I think we need to get that sorted before dealing with the other problem: you know, the bear people."

"Olivia, dammit. I'm going to handle the cave. You are definitely not going back in there." Morgan could hear the strain in Bronwyn's voice, and he decided to keep quiet.

"Bronwyn! A: I'm not planning to go back in there, but B: you shouldn't try to tell me what to do." Olivia scowled and carefully poked a finger at Bronwyn's chest between two spikes.

"Alright. Yeah, I'm sorry. I just can't be worrying about you or other low-levels in there while I fight that thing."

"Hey! I'm up to five now!" Olivia said, mock-defensively.

"Um, ladies, maybe I could be of some help?" Morgan cleared his throat.

"Uh, no. I don't even know you. I don't think I need to be worrying about you while I'm in there either. Thanks, though." Bronwyn started to cross her arms and scowl at Morgan, but she stopped short before she poked herself with her spikes. Her frown deepened, and she ended up putting her fists on her hips like a Wonder Woman pose. Morgan couldn't help smiling.

"Well, why don't you describe this thing to me. Let me be the judge of if I'd be any help or not?" The two women got quiet, exchanging glances, and Olivia held a hand up to her scarred eye.

"It's like a cross between a demon, a spider, and a fucking octopus," Bronwyn spat.

"Oh, Jesus. A fucking Yovashi?" Morgan's eyes grew very dark, and he was suddenly holding his spear. He didn't even realize that he'd put his hand into his pouch.

"You know what this thing is? A Yovashi?" Bronwyn asked him, raising her left eyebrow.

"Yeah, I know what it is. One of those guys almost had me for dinner. They're Energy users, though, and they seem quite intelligent, so I don't know if my experience will help much. I doubt they all behave the same way. Still, I'm going with you; no way I'm letting you fight one of those things alone."

"Intelligent maybe, but goddamn nasty is another way to describe it. It was taunting us, calling us cattle, while it ate our friend in front of us." Bronwyn's voice caught in her throat as she finished her statement.

"Yeah, seriously, you don't want to go in there alone. Let me come with you." Morgan gripped his spear with both hands sideways in front of him, stretching his shoulders back. The leather straps on his breastplate creaked with the strain.

"Well, Olivia says you're supposedly pretty tough and already have your class, right?" Bronwyn's voice had lost a lot of its earlier firmness. She was looking at Morgan appraisingly, eyeing his armor and spear. Olivia nodded and waited for Morgan to respond.

"That's right. I'm up to fourteen now, and I think you'll be glad to have me along. How soon do you want to head out to face this thing?"

"Well, the information I got from the Urghat indicated that they'll be testing our defenses with raids anytime in the next few days. I really would like to have this Yovashi threat dealt with before then. Can we go today? It's about a two-hour hike to the cave."

"Today?" Olivia jumped in. "I think that's a bit hasty! It's already past noon. Let's think on it another day and make some plans."

"How long has it been since you last faced it?" Morgan asked.

"Three days?" Bronwyn asked, counting on her fingers and thinking.

"I've been here three days," Morgan said.

"That's right; it's been four days, Bronwyn."

"Well, as I said, those things are smart. I don't think you should give it all the time in the world to prepare. I think we should go see what's what right now." Morgan gestured with his spear as if he were ready to get started right that moment.

"Yeah, better to rip the band aid off, right? Back in the saddle and all that?" Bronwyn smiled. Olivia didn't smile back; her face had gotten very grave and pale.

"Morgan, please don't let her do anything dumb. Bronwyn, remember what you said to me when we first talked about this?" Bronwyn took on an offended look, but Morgan could see she was putting on a show for Olivia's sake.

"Yeah, I remember, Olivia. Don't worry; we've got this."

BRONWYN

Bronwyn and Morgan were outside the wall and making their way to the trail that led to the Yeksa camp. They'd said their brief goodbyes to Olivia and slipped away before anyone else could bring forward a cause for delay. Bronwyn was glad; she wanted to get this over with as little fanfare as possible. She didn't want to listen to people insisting they come along, and she didn't want to give Arthur or anyone else a chance to debate strategies.

She watched Morgan walking ahead of her on the trail. It was heavily trodden at this point, and he'd just started walking ahead, probably trusting her to let him know if he needed to turn off the path. He was an imposing figure. When Olivia had told her about him and mentioned that he should go with her to the cave, Bronwyn had agreed to talk to him but had expected to find fault with him and shoot down the offer. Unfortunately, or rather, fortunately, depending on how you looked at it, she hadn't been able to deny that he would probably be a boon to her quest. When he'd realized their enemy was a Yovashi, he had bristled, his spear appearing in his hands. Bronwyn had been hard-pressed not to back off when she'd felt the palpable wave of animosity and murderous intent coming from him.

Now, Morgan stalked ahead of her on the trail, following the string of large X marks she'd made in the trees on her previous trips out here. "Hey! It's a few miles hike, but that doesn't mean you shouldn't be careful. We've been attacked by Yeksa and color-wolves out here too," she called out to his back.

"Huh. Color-wolves? They look a lot like wolves but with bright fur, and they have more than one tail?"

"Yeah, that's right. At least some of them; some only had one tail."

"I think those are called boyii. My friend, Issa, told me that. We found some of their corpses in the Crucible." Morgan turned over his shoulder while he spoke, his pale blue eyes glittering in the speckled light coming through the trees. He looked like a fucking CGI supermodel or something, for fuck's sake.

"Have you had your race improved? You seem too, I don't know, too full of color and vigor. You're bigger than life or something."

"I was going to ask you that." Morgan laughed. "Yeah, I got a few upgrades in the Crucible. Seems you did, too?" His smile was infectious, and Bronwyn joined in with her own chuckle.

"Yeah, I did get one upgrade when I rescued the villagers from the Yeksa. It knocked me on my ass, but I've never felt so good in my life."

"It's insane, right? I want to be pissed at the System for kidnapping and manipulating us, but the potential for growth and . . ." He stopped talking when he saw Bronwyn's face fall. "Hey, you alright?"

"It's just I feel guilty." She sighed heavily and shook her head. "I was thinking about how great I feel, and you mentioned the System kidnapping us, and it made me think of the people that have died already. I mean, I didn't know most of them, but I was with some when they died in the cave we're going to, and I just feel like shit that they'll never know that feeling, you know? Like, they'll never get to eat a fucking magical fruit that makes them feel like a new goddamn person."

"Yeah, I get it." Morgan turned and kept walking, but he continued, "I almost died a few times in the Crucible. My friend almost did, too. I know, almost isn't the same as dead, but, yeah, I get how harsh this world can be. The Yovashi we encountered had a few people in its lair, alive, and was eating one of them bit by bit, keeping him alive between snacks." Bronwyn watched his back as he hiked, and she could swear it got darker around him while he spoke.

"So, since we were there, and I ran the fuck away, we've set a lot of guards on the gates, but we haven't risked sending anyone to keep tabs on this guy. I hope he's still there, but the way he was taunting us, I feel like he will be."

"You guys haven't sent people out here in four days?" Morgan stopped and turned to face her.

"Well, not that I know of. I've been away, as you know." Bronwyn shrugged.

"I just ask 'cause there're definitely some tracks on this path that seem fresh to me. I mean, I'm not an expert tracker, but . . ." Bronwyn shoved past him to look at the path ahead of where they'd been. She focused on the scuffs on the trail and used her Tracking skill. No less than ten different tracks came into focus, glowing fairly brightly, all of them labeled as "Human."

"What the fuck? Well, maybe some people have been using this trail for hunting, but Olivia and I warned Arthur to keep people out of this area of the woods." Bronwyn kept her tracking skill active and took the lead up the trail. "Follow me; I can track. I want to see if these turn off at some point." She proceeded along the trail, sweeping her gaze across the tracks occasionally while she watched the woods around them for movement.

They kept walking in silence for a few minutes, but Bronwyn could see that the tracks were at least a few hours old by comparing them to hers and Morgan's, so she started to lower her guard a bit as they went. "What do you think of the settlement? I've been gone a few days, as you know, and I was surprised by how much Olivia and the colonists accomplished. If we can kill this fucker and hustle back, we can visit the new tavern by the pond."

"Now that's positive thinking!" Morgan chuckled. "To be honest, I've been messing around in my tower most of the time since I got here. I got it as a reward in the Crucible, but it came with strings attached; I have to defeat a guardian to access each floor. It's kinda cool, though; there's the spirit of a dragon bound to the tower, and she gives me advice and can identify things." Morgan stopped talking for a moment, shaking his head sheepishly. "I'm rambling. Anyway, the tower is keeping me busy."

"Hah, you aren't rambling. A dragon spirit, huh? Well, I have a little pet creature named Hops that I found in these woods. The Urghat referred to it as a fae. C'mon, Hops; come out and say hi." Bronwyn stopped and spoke into the top of her backpack. Morgan grinned stupidly, watching her. Bronwyn started to flush a little when she realized Hops wasn't going to make an appearance. "He's being shy. I'm not making this up!" She turned and started hiking again.

"I believe you! I've seen weirder shit than that in this world." Morgan followed after Bronwyn, shaking his head with a smile on his face.

"Yeah, well, anyway, the colony is doing well. It's funny how many people are still using tents, though—Olivia and Arthur made sure to create enough housing for everybody before building anything else. I guess with the weather this nice, and with the walls in place, some people prefer having more space than the dorms provide."

"Yeah, I imagine that once they start building more individual homes, there'll be a lot more takers. Personally, I'm excited for the bathhouse that Olivia said was next." Morgan made an exaggerated sniff of his armpit and winced.

"Your tower doesn't have a bath?" Bronwyn laughed.

"Well, sure, but it's on an upper floor, and I haven't made it past the third floor yet," Morgan replied. Bronwyn turned and looked at his face, snorted, and kept walking.

"The System is fucking messed up. It seems like it wants us to be challenged at every turn. I'm not surprised it gave you a reward with a built-in challenge."

"Exactly!" Morgan pounded the butt of his spear into the trail for emphasis. He looked like he was about to say more when Bronwyn heard a thunderous crack, and a tall, green-barked tree directly up the path started falling toward them. Bronwyn dove to the left side of the trail and Morgan to the right, and the huge tree ponderously collapsed between them, bouncing once and then falling still with a heavy thud that shook the ground. Bronwyn rolled to her feet, her fists raised and ready. She heard Morgan yelling from the other side of the tree but couldn't make out his words in the creaking of the branches slapping back and forth as the tree settled. On top of that, she saw several forms moving toward her out of the underbrush.

At first, she almost lowered her guard, recognizing the familiar shape of humans and the loose, pastel clothing most of the colonists wore. Then, as the first got close to her, she saw the dead black orbs where his eyes should be, the rictus scowl on his face, and the way he was reaching forward to grab her. Bronwyn hadn't tried it out yet, but she didn't hesitate to activate her new Stone Fists skill. She felt Energy flash through her pathways to the nodes in her fists, and then her fists grew very heavy and expanded. As her fists grew beyond her gauntlets' capability to contain them, the ensuing explosion took her by surprise. Pieces of metal scaling flew through the air, and the shreds of the leather lining hung from her wrists in tatters. "Fuck!" Bronwyn was both pleased and annoyed. It looked like gauntlets were out for now, but her firsts were like fucking wrecking balls.

They were easily twice their normal size, and she could feel their massively increased weight. At first, she was worried that they'd be too heavy or unwieldy for her to punch quickly with, but those fears were quickly put to rest. She stepped forward and jabbed her right fist into the unguarded face of her first assailant, and, with a loud crack, his head flopped back, and he slumped to the ground. Using her much-improved agility, she danced between the trees and proceeded to lay devastating blows into the other attackers. Never once did any of them make any noise or attempt to speak. They silently pursued her, trying to grab, claw and bite her at every turn. Bronwyn found her Energy was easily up to the task of maintaining her Stone Fists spell, and she didn't let it drop until the last of the zombified colonists was broken and writhing on the ground.

There had been five attackers, two of which were still flailing limply on the ground, too broken to stand, but not dead. The other three had stopped moving when Bronwyn smashed their skulls with a punch. She glanced over the tree and could still hear the sounds of a scuffle. She hoped Morgan could handle himself with these attackers but set off to help him just in case. By the time she made her way around the big tree, he was quietly wiping black ichor off his spear with the shirt of a fallen attacker. He looked up at her and grimly smiled. "These guys are dressed like colonists, but are they human?"

"Yeah, they were. I think the Yovashi did this to them. Last time we fought him, he had dozens of Yeksa that were similarly corrupted in his lair."

"This is a new one to me. What are they? Like zombies?"

"Yeah, just like in the old movies. Or at least it seems like it. How many did you kill?"

"Ugh, four—but now I feel guilty; what if there's a way to cure them?" Morgan straightened and sighed heavily.

"I hadn't thought of that. Jesus. What the fuck were they even doing out here? Goddamn it! C'mon, Morgan. We need to end this thing." Bronwyn skirted the fallen tree and then commenced hiking toward the cave. She noticed that the human tracks she'd been following were much denser here and seemed to go in both directions. "Judging by the tracks, those guys went to the cave and then came back here to ambush us. Hopefully, he doesn't have any more waiting for us."

While they walked, Bronwyn pulled the remaining scraps of her gauntlets off and threw them to the side of the trail. She channeled her Stone Fists skill again and flexed her heavy granite-like hands admiringly. Morgan saw what she was doing and let out a low whistle. "That's pretty cool—built-in weapons? Don't punch me, alright?" Bronwyn let the spell drop and kept walking. She was going to punch something alright, but it wasn't Morgan.

BRONWYN

Bronwyn stood behind the stone outcropping that shielded the entrance to the cave, watching Morgan. He'd insisted that he was good at sneaking and that he'd check things out and come back for her. Currently, he was gliding along the side of the rocky knoll, crouched low and keeping to the shadows. She supposed he did move pretty well for such a big guy. She strained to hear his steps and couldn't make out any noise. Before she knew it, he was slipping into the dark maw of the cave.

The minutes ticked by, and Bronwyn began to fidget. She didn't like waiting. She didn't like letting others take a risk for her. She tried to calm herself, taking deep breaths, but each time she started to relax, she heard Emmet's shriek in her mind. She'd let Emmet scout ahead and look what happened to him. Cursing softly, she started to make her way to the cave entrance quietly. She peered into the dark maw, looking down the sloping tunnel, and couldn't make out any movement or sound. Morgan had told her he'd just look a bit down the tunnel; he wasn't supposed to go that far ahead.

Bronwyn reached into her storage bag and took out the Lightstone that Olivia had given her before leaving. She'd given an identical one to Morgan, saying she'd awarded some guy named Nels some contribution points for creating them. Apparently, he was working toward level eight and was hoping for some kind of Artificer class. The stone was smooth and white, about the size of a plum. It was held in a black iron bracket that had probably been forged in the smithy. The bracket had a ring fastened to it, and a leather thong ran through that. It wasn't pretty craftsmanship, but it worked great when Bronwyn ran a little trickle of Energy into it; suddenly, the smooth white stone lit up like a hundred-watt lightbulb. She looped the leather thong over her head and started walking into the darkness.

She'd only made it about ten feet when she saw her light reflected in Morgan's eyes. He was gliding up the tunnel toward her, effortlessly blending in the shadows. His breastplate winked with a bright reflection of her Lightstone each time he took a step. Bronwyn sighed and got ready to be chastised for not waiting for him. He came to a stop before her, smiling. "Missed me, huh?" Bronwyn didn't reply right away, just mock-punched him and let out a sigh. "Well, don't worry, I don't think anything followed me. I just went down to the first room, the one you told me the Yeksa had been living in. There's nothing there."

"Okay, okay. Another long tunnel from that room leads to the Yovashi lair. No, I'm not letting you sneak ahead anymore. I'm sorry, my nerves can't take it. The guy we let scout before ended up being eaten."

When Bronwyn stopped talking, Morgan looked at her face for a long moment, then he replied, "Alright. I can see your stress. Try to move quietly, just a bit behind me. Step where I step." Morgan turned and advanced with his spear out, silent as a ghost, even in his metal armor. Bronwyn wondered how he had taken charge all of a sudden, but she felt like it would be stupid to argue the point. She waited for him to get about ten feet ahead and then followed as quietly as she could.

They advanced down the tunnel and into the large chamber that had formerly housed the Yeksa. The broken furniture and piles of ratty furs still littered the floor. Bronwyn could see some kind of rodent scurry away from her light. She pointed to the gap in the wall where the tapestry had hung, and Morgan nodded, advancing into the darkness. She followed. The air got noticeably colder as soon as she entered the tunnel. Her bright light exposed every crack in the wall and bit of rubble on the floor for twenty feet.

Morgan stopped and walked back to her, whispering, "How far is it? Should we put the light out?" The idea of going into the Yovashi lair in the darkness again was like a cold hand gripping her heart. She started to respond a couple of times, but each time thought better of what she would say. Morgan saw her struggle and continued, "The fucking thing probably knows we're here anyway. Just keep the light on." Bronwyn scowled, thinking of the Yovashi waiting for them, and nodded, balling her hands into fists.

The two continued, less quietly now, with Morgan in the lead, spear point leading the way. When they passed the site of the undead Yeksa battle, their charred remains stacked along one side of the tunnel, Morgan looked at Bronwyn and raised an eyebrow. She grimly nodded, and they continued. Bronwyn's light didn't leave anything to the imagination, and soon they were advancing on the Yovashi's lair and looking in through the opening.

The pool of blue, icy water was still there, the corpses of various creatures still floating in it. Morgan narrowed his eyes grimly and continued. He was about two paces from entering the chamber when they heard the low, baritone, gurgling laugh, and then the Yovashi spoke, "Oh? Two sweet System slaves have come to pay homage? Why, then, did you slay my new pets? They take me a little effort to create, so I should feel outraged, but instead, I just feel hungry. Come, pets."

Morgan growled and stepped forward into the lair. Bronwyn followed him with the light, summoning her Stone Fists. "Hmm, your scent tastes familiar. Come!" Bronwyn had stepped into the lair, and her light exposed the scene in great detail. The Yovashi was still lurking in the back section of its cave. The dismembered corpses of at least ten humans were arrayed around it like an insane science experiment. Piles of limbs were in one area, several heads in another, and flayed, open torsos dominated the area just before the creature. Its giant black saucer eyes seemed to shrink in the light that Bronwyn brought into the room, and it hissed as it spoke, clearly irritated: "Come."

Bronwyn felt herself moving forward. At first, she wanted to resist the pull, but then her rage came bubbling up, and she decided to go with it. She turned her lurching stumble into a sprint, summoned her improved Stone Warding over her entire body, and barreled into the nightmare creature. Her improved Agility stat paid off immediately. Rather than just seeing a blur and being smashed by his leg, she actually saw it moving and was able to sidestep; at the same time, she brought her Stone Fist around and crashed it into the limb. Chitin cracked and fluid sprayed, and the Yovashi howled in rage. Bronwyn grinned. She circled to the right, and swatted away several more attempts to strike her. Clearly, her levels and focus on agility were what she'd needed to face this enemy.

The Yovashi turned to follow her movement, exposing his side to Morgan. Morgan, however, didn't seem to want to strike yet and was skirting the Yovashi in the opposite direction. Bronwyn had a fleeting fear that he would chicken out, but she couldn't focus on that; the Yovashi was trying to strike her with two different legs at once, and she needed all her attention just to dodge them. She was just getting used to the rhythm and was about to launch an offensive strike when the Yovashi suddenly thrust its shoulders backward, whipping his tentacle appendages toward her. She felt them wrap around her arms and her legs, and though she struggled, they were pulling her in. She knew that the creature's terrible beak was nestled among those tentacles. She panicked, kicking and thrashing and pouring as much Energy as she could into her Stone Warding. She felt the tentacles inexorably pulling her forward; she saw the chitinous beak extend from the shadows, her light glinting off its shiny surface. She saw Morgan, fully ten feet behind the Yovashi, lurking in the shadows. What the fuck was he doing?

One minute she was looking at Morgan, about to yell at him to help her, and the next, he was gone, and a spear, coated in black gore, came exploding out the mouth of the Yovashi's beak. The Yovashi let loose a thunderous discordant screech, writhing back and forth. Its tentacles let go of Bronwyn, and she scrambled backward and up to her feet. Now she could see Morgan. He was standing behind the Yovashi, gripping his spear, grinning madly while a dark, glittering stream of Energy flowed out of the Yovashi, up the spear, and into him. The Yovashi wailed horrifically. Bronwyn smiled grimly and lifted her right fist. She wanted to punch that thing's fucking skull in, but first, she needed to get to it. She commenced pounding his chitinous legs into broken thrashing fragments.

"NO!" Suddenly the Yovashi, broken, bleeding, pale with its loss of Energy and blood, screamed out. One of its tentacles slithered up to its neck, and, for the first time, Bronwyn saw a small black metal disk hanging from a chain there. When the tentacle touched it, it started to emit purple, glowing steam. "I'll return, cattle!" Morgan saw what it was doing and let go of his spear, leaping up to try to grab the pendant from the tentacle. Bronwyn roared and reached for one of the creature's fat tentacles, pulling it toward her, forcing the Yovashi's head down, and she smashed her fist into it, savoring the crunch of bone.

"Got it!" Morgan said, yanking the pendant away from the tentacle as the creature collapsed. His triumphant grin changed, though, as the purple, glittering smoke didn't stop and began to expand around his arm and hand. "Oh fuck," he said as it rapidly engulfed his arm and then his chest. He locked eyes with Bronwyn as the purple haze fully engulfed him, and then he was gone. The smoke spread out and dissipated, and Bronwyn was left standing over the dead Yovashi, Morgan's spear still impaling it. Yellow motes gathered on the corpse and streamed into her.

Congratulations! You have achieved level 11 Stone Pugilist and have gained 3 Strength, 3 Agility, 3 Will, 3 Vitality, and 2 Dexterity.

Congratulations! You have completed a Quest: Explore the cavern from which the Yeksa emerged. Contend with the evil that lies within. Return to the Colony Stone to claim your reward.

"Morgan!" Bronwyn furiously scanned the room, seeing no sign of him among the many corpses and parts of bodies. She grabbed one of the Yovashi's legs and pulled it, making sure Morgan wasn't under it. She knew she wouldn't find him. The way he had looked at her, he knew something was up. Had he died? She didn't think so; if the smoke had been some kind of deadly acid, it would have hurt her, too. The Yovashi had activated that amulet when it realized it was losing; it had said it would return. Did Morgan get teleported somewhere? She knew teleportation was a thing in this world. "It had to be something like that. Fuck, Morgan. I hope you aren't someplace worse than this."

Resignedly, Bronwyn worked to pull Morgan's spear out of the Yovashi. It was damn heavy, and the blade was like a razor. She admired it briefly while she wiped it on a rag and then stuffed it into her storage pouch. She kicked around the corpse, making sure the Yovashi wasn't sitting on any other magical rings or pendants and finding none. She took her bright light to the farthest corner of the cavern and saw a small, polished wood chest. It was about the size of a jewelry box, made from a lovely cherry-colored wood and inlaid with hundreds of runes. It had been placed, presumably by the Yovashi, on a smooth boulder with a flat top. She recognized some of the runes as similar to those on her storage pouch.

She stared at the box for a long time, wondering if she should open it. The Yovashi had known some powerful magic. What if it was trapped or warded or something? She decided to take it back to the colony for Olivia and some of the artificer types to study. She cautiously ensured that there weren't any strings or wires attached to it and then picked it up. She briefly tried to put it into her storage pouch, but some kind of force prevented her. It felt like she was trying to shove a pillow into a keyhole. Looking around, she called, "Morgan!" Hearing no answer, she turned and walked out of the lair.

BRONWYN

Bronwyn jogged out of the cave, loath to be in there any longer than she needed to be. When she came out of the cold dark cavern into the sun, she took a deep breath, some tension running out of her; she knew that she still had a few hours of daylight left and slowed her pace to a walk. She wasn't sure if it was the weight of the confrontation being lifted from her shoulders or if the Yovashi had been sapping the Energy from the land, but everything around her seemed greener and more full of life. Birds flitted happily between the trees, small fuzzy rodents clambered about in the underbrush, and she saw a sizeable beaver-like creature with pastel green fur gnawing on a sapling. Hops even made an appearance, climbing out onto her shoulder. He stood up tall, and his head swiveled about as he took in the forest around him, chirping happily. Bronwyn smiled, looking at her small furry companion and feeling at ease for the first time in a long while.

When she passed the location where she and Morgan had fought the undead colonists, she laid the bodies on the side of the trail, making sure their dark, black pitted eyes were closed. When she got back, she'd tell the guards about them, and hopefully, they'd send some people out with a cart to collect them and bring them home to be buried. The remaining trek back to the colony was pleasant and uneventful. She took her time, admiring the beauty of the forest around her.

When she arrived at the colony's gates, she gave the guards a wave and exchanged some brief pleasantries before telling them about the bodies and heading inside. The settlement was abuzz with activity and looked more and more like a thriving community. Even as the sun faded, people ran about working on some task or another. The smithy billowed out clouds of smoke in the distance as the new smiths practiced their craft. She stood a couple of dozen yards from the gate, her hands on her hips, just taking in the sights. She felt a gentle hand on her shoulder as Olivia walked up from behind and stood beside her.

"Pretty incredible, isn't it? All we've accomplished in just a few days?" Olivia spoke with a sense of wonder in her voice. "I waited here at the gate for you; I was starting to get worried. I almost made Arthur send out a search party.

What . . ." She hesitated for a moment. "Can I ask what happened in the cave, Bron? Are you okay? Morgan isn't with you. Did he make it out, too? Sorry, that's a lot of questions." She smiled nervously and moved to look Bronwyn in the eyes, holding her hand as she spoke.

Bronwyn sighed and then let out a slight chuckle. "You can ask me anything, and yes, I'm okay. In fact, I feel amazing. We killed that Yovashi bastard, but I don't know what happened to Morgan. He got teleported away at the end of the fight, trying to stop the Yovashi from using some kind of amulet. I don't exactly know why, but I feel like he's alright. It's almost like I had a sense of him or something. It's weird."

"That's amazing, you're amazing. I can't believe you two were able to defeat that creature. I know I put on a positive face, but you have no idea how nervous I actually was." She gave Bronwyn a huge smile and laughed. "I'd give you a hug, but I think your armor might impale me!"

Bronwyn laughed with her. "It's probably for the best; I'm sure that I'm absolutely filthy anyway. I've been running around for days without a proper bath." She ran her fingers through her hair and could feel the sweat and grime clinging to it. "Thank God we don't have any mirrors yet; I probably look and smell worse than an Urghat."

"We have a bathhouse!" Olivia practically shouted in excitement. "We raised enough contribution points while you were out in the fields for our latest two buildings, the brewery and the baths! I can lead you there now unless you have something else you need to do first?"

"Well, I need to stop by the Colony Stone, and I have a couple of items I wanted you and the other mage-types to look at. The items can certainly wait, though; a bath sounds goddamn incredible." Bronwyn looked toward Hops on her shoulder. "You could use a bath, too, you little stinker; your face is still mostly purple." She chuckled as she patted him on the head.

"The stone's on the way anyway, so no worries there. I am, however, very interested in these items, but I suppose I can hold my curiosity for a bit." She dragged out the word "suppose" and pouted mockingly, turning toward the center of the colony. "Follow me!"

Bronwyn walked with Olivia to the Settlement Stone and pressed her hand on its smooth cold surface. When the gray screen popped into view, a prompt overlayed all other menu items.

You have completed a Quest: Explore the cavern from which the Yeksa emerged. Contend with the evil that lies within. Claim reward? YES/NO

Bronwyn pressed her thumb into the yes button and found herself surrounded by a swirling white mist that quickly dissipated.

Congratulations! You have been awarded 10,000 Contribution Credits.

"Holy shit, ten thousand credits." Bronwyn looked toward Olivia and chuckled. "Guess I'll have to do some shopping after the bath."

Olivia's eyes widened. "Yeah, for sure! There're all kinds of skills and items you could get with that many credits. Speaking of fancy magic items of dubious origin, weren't there a couple of things you wanted me to look at?"

"Oh! Yes, of course. Here, one second." Bronwyn rooted around in her backpack and pulled out the small gilded chest she took from the Yovashi lair, holding it out toward Olivia. "Don't open that right away. I don't know if it has some magical trap on it. That's why I need you to check it out. There's one more thing, as well." Bronwyn reached into her dimensional pouch and retrieved the tapestry embroidered with runic circles that she had taken from the cave on their first venture. "I don't know why exactly I took this, but I think the runes on it might mean something, and I've been meaning to give it to you to look over. Something else keeps coming up, though, and I forget. And, I mean, it might not be anything at all; it could just be random circles in a pretty pattern or something. I just, well, I don't really know much about magic or any of that stuff. Also, it's um, a little bit wrinkled." Bronwyn's cheeks flushed, and she let out a nervous laugh realizing she was rambling a bit and felt a little embarrassed.

Olivia smiled at her. "Don't worry; I won't flip this open until I've thoroughly inspected it. If this tapestry seems important to you, then I'm sure it must be. It undoubtedly holds all the secrets of the universe!" She winked at Bronwyn and started folding the tapestry into a neat square. "Only teasing, but who knows? All of the magic items we've found so far have runes inscribed on them; these may be just as important. I'm certainly very excited to take them back to study them." She tucked the folded tapestry under her arm and held the small chest in front of her. "Thank you, very much; as soon as I figure anything out about either item, I'll be sure to let you know straight away. Now, are you ready for me to show you the bathhouse?"

"Yes! Definitely! Lead the way!" Bronwyn walked next to Olivia down the road.

Olivia stopped in front of a large, wood-paneled building with a set of double doors. "Well, here it is, the bathhouse of First Landing. There're changing rooms inside and separate bathing areas for men and women. Now, don't get lost in there; it's honestly incredible, and I wasn't sure I would ever leave, but we have an important meeting tomorrow." She put on her mock-serious voice, pointing a finger at Bronwyn.

"Okay, okay. Yes, boss; I promise I won't be late!" Bronwyn raised her hands and laughed.

"Alright, well, I'll see you then, Bron. Have a nice soak." She turned and started to walk down the street toward the permanent housing area.

Bronwyn watched her walk away and called out, "Olivia, wait! What time and where is the meeting tomorrow?"

Olivia grinned and called back, "In the back room of the new tavern! I'll find you beforehand, don't worry."

Bronwyn waved goodbye to Olivia and stepped into the bathhouse. The air inside the changing room was warm, even away from the baths, and she could feel some sweat start to bead on her forehead as she gathered a towel from the wall cubby and shoved all of her armor and clothing into her dimensional pouch. She didn't feel entirely safe leaving it in the open cubbies and decided to take the pouch with her. She'd had her stuff stolen at the gym once and never really felt okay with the trust system after that.

She wrapped the towel around herself and held it against her chest with one hand, her pouch in the other, and Hops on her shoulder. She pushed her way through the curtain into the women's baths and was greeted by a face full of steam and the sounds of dozens of conversations. Looking around her, she saw that the bathhouse was massive, with multiple pools. Even in the somewhat poor visibility, she guesstimated that there were at least a few dozen other people spread out in various pools. She wasn't self-conscious about her body but worried about how people might react to her bringing Hops, so she headed toward one of the least crowded pools with only three other women in it; they were seated close to one another and talked in hushed tones.

Bronwyn folded up her towel and set it on the floor at the edge of the pool, slipping into the warm water. Hops immediately flung himself from her shoulder and landed in the middle of the pool, creating a tiny cannonball splash, and began to zoom through the water. The three women sharing the pool stared in amazement as his turtle shell zipped this way and that. He eventually swam back to Bronwyn and spun in small circles in front of her. "Well, I guess that shell isn't just for show, after all, is it, buddy? I had no idea you liked the water so much! I would've taken you to the pond!" She chuckled, watching the fuzzy little creature dive under the surface like a fish and come back up, shooting a small stream of water out of his mouth.

Bronwyn sank in up to her neck and felt more relaxed than she had since she'd left Earth. She let out a long sigh. "Fuck, I forgot how nice this is." She leaned backward and dunked her head under the warm water. Using her nails, she began to scrape away the dirt, smoke, sweat, blood, berry juice, and God knows what else that was caked to her scalp and hair. After a couple of minutes, she sat back up and was startled to see one of the women had floated across the pool to her.

"Hey there! My name's Akari Yakahira. You must be Bronwyn, right? And is that Hops? He's absolutely adorable." She was smiling broadly and holding out her hand.

Bronwyn was a little caught off guard but reached her hand out to shake. "Uhh, yep. That's me. Nice to meet you, Akari, and, yeah, that's my little buddy."

"I'm so excited to meet you, finally! My father was one of the colonists you saved from the Yeksa! I wanted to thank you. I'm sure it's kinda awkward being ambushed in the bath, but it looks like you could use these; I bought them at the contribution store this morning." She was positively beaming and held out a scrub brush, a small washcloth, and a bar of purple soap. Bronwyn's face fell, and she had a surge of emotion that took her by surprise; conflicting waves of guilt and happiness assailed her. She pushed down her feelings and smiled broadly at the young woman.

"Oh my God! Yeah, of course. I'm just glad I was able to help! Are you sure it's okay if I use these? That would be awesome; I'll give them back as soon as I'm done." She started to reach her hand out toward the brush.

"No need! They're a gift! Take your time and enjoy your bath. I gotta head back to the brewery anyway. I'm sure the crowds are already gathering; you should come check it out when you're done!" With that, she swam back over to her friends, and they all exited the pool.

Bronwyn set herself the task of scrubbing off a week's worth of filth and making a mostly successful attempt at washing out her mane of curly hair. Maybe she would go check out the brewery tonight. She hadn't really done anything relaxing since she'd woken up in the field, and the System started fucking with her life.

⊗ MORGAN ⊘

Morgan knew what was happening as soon as the sparkling purple smoke started to climb up his arm. He could feel the tug of some sort of dimensional magic and knew he was being teleported. He stared at Bronwyn, his brain spasmodically jumping from one thing he should say to another, and before he knew it, the smoke had engulfed him, and he was gone. It was different from the way the Token of Travel had worked. Instead of his vision going wonky and then him instantly arriving in a new place, he felt his mind fill with heavy fog, and then he was engulfed by darkness.

Morgan drifted in a dark void for what could have been a few seconds or a few months. It was a strange sensation—it wasn't like he was sleeping; he felt conscious the whole time, but he couldn't accurately mark the passage of time. He'd find himself thinking about something mundane, like what the next guardian in his tower would be like or whether Bronwyn would get back to the settlement safely. Then he'd have a sensation like a lot of time had passed, but on reflection, he realized he hadn't thought about too much, and it couldn't have taken long at all. It was very confusing, and the only thing he could think of was that whatever space he was moving through was outside of time itself.

As suddenly as the darkness had engulfed him, Morgan's indeterminate voyage through the void came to an end; green lights that seemed blinding to his deprived eyes suddenly blossomed, and he found himself sprawled on a cold stone floor. The air was frigid, much like the deep cave from which he'd teleported. He held very still, allowing his eyes to adjust to the lighting, and looked around, listening with every fiber of his being. He heard a slight bubbling sound coming from off to his right, but nothing else other than his own breathing.

As his eyes adjusted, he realized he was in a smallish room built from stone blocks. The floor he was lying on was carved with intricate symbols, and he could feel the grooves of concentric circles beneath his fingers. He saw that the walls of the room were lined with wooden workbenches, and there were bookshelves above the benches. One large volume, probably six inches thick and bound in something like wood and clasped in gold, was open on a lectern near where he was lying.

Morgan slowly climbed to his feet and saw the rest of the room. The green light was actually quite dim, now that his eyes were adjusted, and came from a sconce in the wall near the door. It held a glowing green ball of glass. The bubbling sound was coming from a large beaker filled with some sort of boiling liquid; a small flame was burning beneath it. Morgan dipped his hand into his pouch and pulled out his backup spear. It wasn't nearly as good as the one he'd left behind, but at least he didn't feel naked anymore. He walked over to the lectern and looked at the open page of the huge book. Script he couldn't read met his eyes, along with diagrams that looked like advanced math to him. Still, the book looked important, so he closed the heavy volume and stowed it into his pouch. Shrugging, he walked over to the shelves above the workbench and touched each book, willing them into his storage pouch. He smiled, constantly amazed by the abilities of the dimensional container. His "sense" of the container's space informed him that he hadn't filled half of it yet, and there was a lot of junk in there he could dump if he needed to make space.

Just as he was getting ready to check out the door, he heard the handle rattling. Quick as a ghost and just as quiet, he slipped into the corner behind where the door would open. He silenced his breathing and waited while the handle turned and the door swung open. Ice filled his veins when the spider-like legs came into the room. Still, he remained motionless, watching. The Yovashi that tapped over to the workbench was a lot smaller than the two that Morgan had met before. This one wasn't naked and bald but rather wore a silky black gown, its tentacles writhing just beneath its hem, and had a long mane of silvery hair. Morgan raised an eyebrow; was this the mate of the one in the cave?

He knew he couldn't wait for the creature to notice the missing books and sound an alarm, so he lowered his spear, activated Hollow Charge and Backstab, and flashed forward, impaling the creature in an upward thrust from its kidney to its heart. The Yovashi thrashed as adrenaline coursed through it, letting out a weak mewling cry, dead before it knew what happened. One of its long legs knocked over the beaker of bubbling fluid, and it rolled onto the bench in a semi-circle, the liquid dripping onto the wood and smoking as it ate through it. Morgan yanked his spear out, holding the twitching body down with his boot. Golden motes coalesced on the creature and flowed into him.

Energy coursing through his pathways, Morgan took a moment to examine the corpse, especially its neck—he was wondering if he'd find another amulet like the one in the cave had been wearing. He came up empty-handed at first, but then he saw a glint on one of the creature's tentacles. With the tip of his spear, he pulled up the hem of the silky black robe and saw that the Yovashi had eight tentacles in total, six were thin and slightly longer, and two were thick, short, and had hooked claws on their ends. One of those thick tentacles was adorned with a silvery ring. Morgan grinned and carefully reached down to slide the ring off the tentacle and over the hard, sharp talon.

The ring was large, too big for his thumb even, but then Morgan had an idea and trickled some Energy into it to form a bond. Instantly, he was aware of a substantial interdimensional space. "Ah, fucking cool, a storage ring?" Morgan slipped the ring onto his right hand, and it shrank to fit his finger perfectly. He examined the items in the ring, finding a wide array of belongings: several bolts of some kind of silky material, dozens of vials filled with a variety of liquids, several more books, more valuable looking than the ones he'd already pilfered, an extremely sharp knife made from a black crystalline material, and ten pouches filled with Energy beads that gave off a dark, smokey blue luster. Whatever this Yovashi had been up to, it had been wealthy.

Morgan contemplated trying to bond with the knife to see if it was magical and perhaps better for sneaking around and stabbing, but he loathed the idea of giving up his reach advantage with the spear. He was also afraid the knife might be dangerous; he thought of how Tiladia had warned him about bonding with the diadem and figured the knife looked like it might have something dark inside it. He decided he'd wait until he made it back to the settlement and have Tiladia take a look at his loot before he tried to use any more of it. Thinking of the settlement, Morgan had a thought and activated his Guardian's Senses, concentrating on Bronwyn. He could feel her strongly, probably only ten or so miles away. She felt like she was off to his left, and, of course, in that direction was solid stone. Morgan would have to get out of this place before getting a sense of the direction.

Before walking over to the door, Morgan took another look at the Yovashi he'd just killed. He realized he'd been avoiding looking at its face, so, to spite himself, he knelt and gripped the sides of its head and turned it, so its face came into view. He felt his suspicions that this was a female of the race were justified. The features of this Yovashi were smaller; the black, saucer eyes were more like large coins and more angular. Still, it had razor-like teeth that extended out of its lower jaw, and even in death, there wasn't a hint of kindness in its expression. Morgan dared himself to feel some sympathy for the dead thing, but he couldn't find any. All he could think of was the horrible things the other Yovashi he'd encountered had been capable of doing. He had never believed that any type of person could be inherently evil, but he was seriously doubtful that he'd ever have a peaceful relationship with the Yovashi.

Morgan went to the door and listened; he thought he could hear some sort of murmuring or distant movement, but he couldn't be sure. Carefully he opened the latch and peered through. A wide hallway, constructed of the same materials as the room he was in, stretched to his left and right. With the door open, he could hear the muffled conversation more clearly, and it seemed to be coming from his left. Leveling his spear, he concentrated on moving silently and prowled in that direction.

He came to a left-hand turn and saw the end of the hallway with a door on either side. He crept up to the doors and was sure the conversation was coming from the door on the right. He padded close to the door and placed an ear to the smooth, polished wood.

"No. Foolish, eggling. Focus on your spirit; use the conduits in your hook palps. Concentrate on corruption." The voice Morgan heard was sibilant and seemed to be issued by several slightly discordant vocal cords. It sent a shiver down his spine. "NO! You are wasting this meat. Don't drive the hooks so deep, and before pulling, you must apply the corruption!" The voice was strident, and Morgan heard a whimper and some sort of commotion or struggle. Curiosity warred with caution, and Morgan couldn't help himself; he carefully depressed the door latch and pushed it open just an inch. He pressed his eye to the crack and looked within the room.

The room was spartan—mostly plain stone, but lovely daylight filtered in through some sort of glass block that made up the top third of the far wall. A rack was situated in the center of the room, and a naked human male hung from the rack. A Yovashi, similarly garbed to the one Morgan had just killed, stood to the left of the rack, and a much smaller Yovashi, also wearing a silky robe, though this one was blue, stood to the right. Both Yovashi had long, white manes. The small Yovashi had its tentacles extended, and the two fat, hooked ones were embedded in the man's stomach. Morgan studied the man's face for signs of life, but he was either comatose or dead.

Morgan's pulse quickened, and he could tell he was subconsciously priming for a fight, but he held himself back. The daylight coming through that wall meant he wasn't far from the surface. He could make a run for it. On the other hand, here was proof that the Yovashi regarded humans as nothing more than "meat"—even training their children to use them as such. Could there ever be any peace between such different peoples? What if the man were still alive? Could Morgan live with himself if he left him here? He'd chosen to be a Hollow Guard for a reason. Could he kill a child, though? Even a Yovashi? As he watched, the adult Yovashi slapped away the hooked tentacles of the juvenile and then said, "Watch, I'll show you again."

Morgan gripped his spear firmly, below the streaks of black blood left behind by the last Yovashi, and steeled himself for combat. He pushed the door open with his foot and prepared to fire off Hollow Charge and Backstab in quick succession again. So far, he'd used the combination of the two skills twice to great effect. The charge seemed nearly to teleport him from one spot to another; he moved so quickly. Even so, his Backstab skill hadn't had any trouble guiding his placement of the spearpoint as he'd collided with his enemy. He hoped his luck would hold as he stepped into the room.

Of course, he wasn't directly behind the bigger Yovashi. He was slightly behind it and to the side. This meant that he was somewhat in front of the smaller one, which meant it could see him as he stepped into the room. Morgan saw its eyes widen, and it lurched backward. The bigger Yovashi said, "Hold still, fool, watch me closely!" Then, Morgan was charging, his spear driving up into the torso of the larger creature. The Yovashi gasped, stumbling forward, black ichor flowing freely from its mouth. Morgan immediately started to channel his Energy Drain ability, and he felt the strange, cold Energy come flowing into him through his spear.

The smaller Yovashi stumbled backward into the corner of the room and curled up into a ball, its big, round eyes staring at Morgan while it whimpered. Morgan's victim was thrashing weakly, and he thought he'd have another quick victory, but then it lurched forward, pulling away from the spear with a sudden burst of strength. Morgan was relentless, though, and he followed it with another stab, ripping another jagged hole in its back. Suddenly, the Yovashi swelled up like it was inhaling, and a colorless wave of force drew into it, jostling Morgan as it passed, and then that same wave of force exploded outward with ten times the power.

Morgan was flung backward by the wave, slamming into the wall. The rack where the human was hanging was blasted away, smashing into the wall with the glass bricks, knocking several loose. The wave of pressure didn't spare the little Yovashi, driving it into the corner where it was huddled, causing some of its legs to twist and snap. The big, wounded Yovashi slowly straightened, ichor pouring out of its wounds and mouth. It turned and, still choking and gasping, regarded Morgan where he struggled to stand up. "Come for vengeance, have you?" It coughed, the discordant sibilance of its voice made even more strange and eerie by the fluid in its throat.

"Your kind picked this fight," Morgan said, back on his feet and stalking toward the Yovashi, spear leveled.

"Our kind? Fool. We didn't come to your world. We don't kneel at the altar of the System." Morgan was taken aback by that statement. There was so much to unpack that he physically stumbled while contemplating a response. Recovering himself, he noticed that the creature's tentacles were moving in a circle, forming a ball of dark Energy. Was it just stalling? He tried to use Hollow Charge to slash at the tentacles, but it was on cooldown. He moved to close the ten-foot gap, and the ball of black Energy surged forth, striking him full in the chest. His breastplate made a hollow clanging sound and bent into him. It felt like an oversized sledgehammer had hit him. The air in his lungs expelled violently, and he stumbled backward, trying to catch his breath. The Yovashi pressed the attack, it was sluggish due to its terrible injuries, but it was on him in a matter of seconds, nonetheless.

Morgan couldn't get his breath, the breastplate's curvature had been reversed, and it was pushing into his diaphragm with incredible pressure. Gasping, he backpedaled, driving his spear at the Yovashi with one hand while he called the only sharp object to hand that was in his storage ring. The black crystal knife appeared in his hand, and he quickly slashed the leather straps on one side of his breastplate, relieving the pressure and allowing him to breathe at last. Taking a deep breath, he refocused his efforts on the fight, only to see that the Yovashi had stopped advancing and was looking at the knife in his hand. Its front legs gave way, and it crumpled in front of Morgan. "Where did you get that knife? You killed her. We're undone!" The Yovashi collapsed to the floor, all the fight taken out of it. Still gasping for breath and worried about possible reinforcements, Morgan didn't hesitate; he stepped forward with the knife and hammered it into the Yovashi's chest.

Dense golden motes, almost as thick as a tangible liquid, flowed out of the Yovashi, streaming together and pouring into Morgan.

*****Congratulations! You have achieved level 15 Hollow Guard and have gained 5 Strength, 5 Will, 4 Vitality, 4 Intelligence, and 3 Agility.*****

*****You have earned the title: Yovashi Bane.*****

That second message took Morgan by surprise. He'd killed a lot more Yeksa and Urghat than Yovashi. Why was he considered a Yovashi Bane? He looked around the room, listening for sounds that someone was coming. He didn't hear anything other than the soft whimpering from the small Yovashi, still huddled in the corner. He walked over and closed the door, and then he went over to where the wooden rack had slammed into the wall. As he got close, he could see that the human was long dead. The body had flopped onto its back, and Morgan could see that the man had been partially flayed and some of his organs were missing. He turned to look at the cringing Yovashi. He sighed heavily and then opened his status screen, pulling up his Feats and Titles page and reading about his new title:

*****Yovashi Bane: You have personally killed a significant percentage of all remaining Yovashi. Your aura has grown heavier and will strike fear and doubt into the minds and hearts of any Yovashi that you encounter. This effect will impact other beings that you encounter to a lesser extent. Those affected by your aura will have a reduced ability to resist your abilities and be more likely to avoid conflict with you.*****

Morgan counted on his fingers to make sure, but this was only the fourth Yovashi he'd killed. A significant percentage of all remaining Yovashi? Apparently, there weren't many of these things. In his mind, that was alright. He put away the black crystal knife and walked toward the whimpering Yovashi with his spearpoint leading the way. "Can you speak?"

"Yes," the creature replied, very softly. Its voice had that sibilant quality, but the discordant notes were less severe, and it was easy for Morgan to understand it.

"You're a child, right?"

"Yes." Its face was turned down, and two long, spider legs were bent in front of it as though to shield it from Morgan.

"Well, look at me. What's your name?" Morgan tried to soften his voice. He still had adrenaline coursing through his veins, but the title message had sobered him up a bit.

"I am Ykleedra. Are you going to kill me, too?" The Yovashi lowered her legs, and Morgan could see her big eyes again, and black streaks ran down her cheeks. Suddenly he felt like shit.

"Look, I'm not going to kill you if you can promise you aren't going to hunt my kind. Do you have more family around here? Did you kill this man over here?"

"I won't hunt your kind, I promise!" Ykleedra gasped, staring at Morgan imploringly.

"Well? What about my other questions?"

"I didn't kill him! Matriarch Tkvanee did that! I only ate what was given to me after. Only my mother is nearby, but you have her knife." Ykleedra broke into a sob as she finished speaking.

"Ah, fuck." Morgan looked around, at a loss for his next step. "Just how much of a kid are you? Can you take care of yourself, or do I need to get you someplace else?"

"Oh, please! Don't make me leave. With Mother and Tkvanee gone, I have to tend the eggs." She spoke quickly, but as she finished, she seemed to realize what she'd said and covered her face with her legs again, shrinking into the corner and breaking into new sobs.

"Um, eggs? How many are we talking about? Are they Yovashi eggs?" Morgan started to get a queasy feeling in his stomach.

"Only three. We don't have eggs easily anymore. Please don't kill us!" Ykleedra started to crawl toward Morgan submissively, imploringly. Morgan felt sick.

"Ykleedra, listen. I killed those other Yovashi because they attacked my kind. More than that, they threatened us and ate our friends. I'm going to let you live here with the eggs, but you have to promise me that you will avoid conflict with people and raise the children that come from those eggs to be peaceful, especially with my kind. Can you do that?"

"Yes, yes! I can do this!" The little Yovashi practically sang the words. Morgan concentrated and found the direction where Bronwyn was with his Guardian Senses skill. He pointed in the direction.

"My people don't live very far away, that way. I'll come to check on you or send someone else, but you have to be friendly. If we find you're resorting to the ways of your elders, I won't be able to stop my people from hunting you all down. Don't eat people! Eat other animals that can't think and speak. Do you understand?" She nodded emphatically, and Morgan sighed, standing up straight. "Are you going to be okay? Do you know how to heal or bind your broken legs?"

"Yes! I will be okay, kind one." She writhed at Morgan's feet, and again he felt like a criminal of some sort.

"My name's Morgan. Stand up. You don't have to debase yourself." She slowly and painfully rose to her feet, favoring two of her legs.

"Thank you, Morgan," she said, ducking her head again. Morgan backed up a step. Even as a juvenile, the Yovashi was a creature from his nightmares, and he just wanted to put some distance between himself and this place.

"Show me the exit, and I'll get out of here."

MORGAN

Ykleedra moved out of the room with surprising adroitness. She held her two wounded legs up and used the other four to move at a steady pace. Morgan noticed that she kept her tentacles held close to her torso, out of sight in her robe. "Ykleedra, why do some Yovashi wear robes and others not?"

"You would have a female roam naked like a savage?" She snorted like the notion was pure insanity.

"Oh, no, I suppose not. Are male Yovashi different from females? Other than the obvious differences, of course!" Ykleedra glanced back in the room, her eyes falling on the dead Yovashi before she spoke.

"Yes. Male Yovashi are consumed by insanity during their coming of age. They're only allowed back at the clutch-home during the conjunction. I only know of my sire, though. Our males grow scarce." She continued into the hall, and Morgan followed.

"What's beyond that door?" Morgan asked, pointing to the door on the opposite wall.

"Our sleeping chambers and the clutch. The exit is down the hallway, past our den and kitchen, then up some stairs. Please, let me go to the eggs now." She spoke softly, her eyes downcast. Morgan was tempted to look through the rest of the dwelling, but he didn't want to keep this tormented child hostage with his presence.

"Yeah, alright, you go that way, and I'll work my way out of here. You're sure there are no other Yovashi here? I don't want to have to kill more of you." Morgan let a little steel enter his voice at the last statement.

"No! There are no more! Just me. Everyone I know is dead." For a moment, her voice exposed her despair, but by the time she finished speaking, she had grown quiet.

"Oh, God, why did I have to ask? How are you going to be able to take care of the eggs? Are you even well enough to get food?"

"I am not helpless. I will heal, and I can feed us. Soon I won't be alone; my siblings will be here. I'm sorry I complained. I am grateful you didn't kill me."

She was staring at the floor again. Despite being viscerally disturbed by the appearance of the Yovashi, Morgan found himself entertaining thoughts of moving her and the eggs to his tower.

"Are you sure, Ykleedra?"

"Yes! Please, may I go?" Her voice rose in pitch, pleading.

"Yes, yes. Alright, go to the eggs." Ykleedra opened the door with her tentacles and then slipped through it. Morgan heard a bolt slide home on the other side of the door. He supposed he didn't blame her; he'd just killed her family. Were they all family? He still wasn't sure about the structure. One thing he knew was that he felt like he'd committed a crime. He wasn't sure why he felt that way—they had been eating a dead human; every Yovashi he'd met had tried to kill and eat him. Were his actions unjustified? Was he being an idiot leaving one of them alive? Not only was he leaving her alive, but also some Yovashi eggs. He thought back to movies he'd watched and books he'd read where a young child saw a criminal murder their parents, and then they spent their whole lives growing strong so they could enact revenge. Was Morgan setting himself up for something like that? Was that just the movies? He supposed it didn't matter; he wasn't going to go through that door and kill that child.

Thinking of the dead human reminded Morgan that he'd left the corpse lying against the wall where the Yovashi's spell had flung it. He walked back over to the badly mutilated corpse and determined that he should bring it back to the colony. Someone might be missing him. He took one of his spare blankets out of his pouch and then rolled the rather light body into it. It seemed it had been largely drained of fluids already. Once he wrapped it up, he stored it in his pouch. The thought of keeping a human corpse in the same container with his food disturbed him, but nothing seemed to spoil in the dimensional container; he wondered if it was an absolute vacuum in there. Maybe it was even outside of time somehow? He had to shake his head, realizing he had absolutely no idea how it worked.

He followed Ykleedra's instructions and passed through the living area, a plain stone room with strangely carved bone figurines lined up along the walls on shelves. The figurines looked like animals and insects. Some of them were familiar to Morgan—shapes of wolves, rodents, wasps, birds. Some weren't, looking more alien and varied from mammalian to serpentine. Morgan thought about scooping them up, but then he thought of Ykleedra and how he'd already stolen all the books in her home, and he left them.

He passed by the kitchen with only a glance—no way was he going to steal food from children, not to mention, he didn't want to know what kind of meat they had stored away. The hallway made a turn, and then the stairs going up came into view. They were spaced a little oddly for his human legs, but he managed to climb them without much trouble. Soon, a large, round door came into view with a glass window fitted in its center. He stepped up to the door and peered out the glass. A smoothly sloping hillside fell away before him, covered in soft blue, feathery grass. A trail lined with smooth, round gravel led away from the door along the hillside to Morgan's right. He couldn't see anything moving, so he pushed the door open and stepped outside.

The air was crisp and warm, the natural sunlight a relief to his deprived eyes. He looked back at the Yovashi dwelling and was surprised to see that it was part of the hillside on which he stood. He could see the shape of the roof jutting out from parts of the hill, also covered in grass. Stone blocks made up some exterior walls, and one wall was lined with glass blocks along the top, cracked and broken. Morgan surmised that that wall led to the room where he'd fought the "matriarch." The grassy hills extended beyond the dwelling into the distance, and Morgan felt an odd incongruity with the idyllic nature of the scene when juxtaposed with his ideas of how the Yovashi would live. He had imagined dark caves lined with thick spiderwebs or a murky, dense forest with hordes of Yovashi and giant spiders in the canopies.

He pondered what Ykleedra had said about male Yovashi going insane when they "came of age." Perhaps that was why the ones Morgan had encountered had lived in veritable charnel pits. Still, the females here had been eating a human. Speaking of which, where had they gotten their hands on a human? Morgan reached out with Guardian's Senses and could feel Bronwyn off to the northwest, maybe ten miles away. He concentrated on Issa and could still feel her, distantly to the southeast. Morgan looked in the direction where he felt Bronwyn and saw that the rolling, grassy hills fell away into a thickly forested slope. He figured that was probably the same forest that bordered the human colony. Could a human have wandered this far afield and run into one of the adult Yovashi that had lived in this dwelling? Or perhaps, even in his insanity, the male from the cave had been bringing them "food?" Morgan realized he wouldn't find the answer unless he went in and interrogated Ykleedra some more, so he decided just to let the mystery go for now.

Before leaving, Morgan took off his breastplate and laid it on the ground, stomping on the metal to try to bend it into the correct curvature. He didn't get it looking perfect, but he hoped it was close enough for the self-repair function to start to work. He put it back on and used some leather scraps to tie the straps he had cut back together. He wasn't sure the leather would self-repair, but he figured he'd give it a chance.

Morgan began the trek toward the human colony, keeping a leisurely pace, using his backup spear as a walking stick. He marveled at how good he felt, physically; he hadn't had a thing to eat or drink or any rest in many hours, but he felt just fine. Out of habit, he pulled a waterskin from his storage pouch and took a long drink. It felt good, but he didn't think he needed it as much as he would have in his pre-System life. Being realistic, he knew he would have been exhausted and wrung out from the activities he'd been through in the last day. Morgan surmised it had to do with his increased store of Energy and his racial improvements. He looked and moved like a professional athlete these days.

Reflecting on how he had improved physically, Morgan started to think about his ability scores and how their improvement had changed him. He used his strength as a baseline for comparison because it seemed like an easy metric to gauge. When he'd first come to this world, the System had said he had a strength of six. Now his strength was forty. He was definitely stronger than before, but there was no way he was nearly seven times stronger. Before he gained any levels, he imagined that he could probably pick up something that weighed around a hundred pounds. There was no way he could pick up a seven hundred-pound object now. He asked the UI for an explanation of strength again:

*****Strength is the measure of your physical power relative to other Energy infused beings.*****

Morgan realized the System used the attribute numbers as a measuring stick to compare all Energy users. He imagined that if you took a billion people and tried to rank their strength on a scale, you'd have someone with a strength of one and someone with a strength of one billion. That didn't mean that the person with the top rank was a billion times stronger than the lowest; it just meant he was stronger than everyone else. Morgan suddenly felt a lot less accomplished by his forty strength. He was probably the strongest human in the settlement, but that didn't mean he could toss people around like ragdolls. Not yet, at least. Thinking about other stats, his understanding of the System's attribute points made even more sense. His intelligence was his highest stat, but he didn't feel like he could crack quantum mechanics theories in his head. Sure, ideas were coming to him more quickly, and he seemed to react better to situations, but he wasn't four times smarter than he'd been; he'd just gotten smarter compared to other people.

Morgan was deep in the woods now. Every so often, he'd pause to get his bearings with Guardian's Senses. He felt like he'd made it about halfway when the sun started to dip into the western horizon, and he debated whether he should push on in the darkness or make a camp. As far as Morgan knew, he'd only been gone from the settlement for a day, though he remembered how the teleportation seemed to be outside of time, and he didn't really know if more time had passed. He decided to push on.

As the shadows lengthened, Morgan debated whether he should use the Lightstone that Olivia had given him. He could hear rustling sounds all around in the woods, and the strange calls of birds and other little animal noises.

Morgan knew he'd be more comfortable with a well-lit path, but he also knew he'd call a lot of attention to himself. He wasn't sure if he should be worried about that, though; he'd only heard of Yeksa and boyii in these woods, other than the Yovashi he and Bronwyn had killed. He decided to just muddle on in the moonlight, even though the dense canopy made the going rather treacherous. He made good progress until the sun finally fully descended, and then he realized the moonlight wasn't going to cut it in the forest; he tripped several times and thunderously rolled through a brittle row of shrubs.

Cursing and rolling to his feet, Morgan dusted himself off and then pulled the Lightstone from his pouch, hanging it around his neck and then channeling some Energy into it. Soft white light bloomed out from his position, casting the tree trunks in stark relief from the shadows that danced behind them as Morgan moved forward. He paused to get his bearings once again, and realized he'd been heading a bit too far north. He turned westward, stomping around a tight copse of trees, and nearly fell into a massive hole. He skidded to a stop and looked around: ancient limestone structures were jutting out of the forest floor here, covered in undergrowth, lichen, and moss. On the other side of the pit, Morgan could see the crumbled walls and foundations of some sort of building.

Morgan lifted his Lightstone from his neck, wrapped it around the tip of his spear, and held it out over the pit, trying to illuminate its depths. He couldn't see the bottom, but about ten feet from the edge, he could see a broken limestone stairway leading down. Moss and lichen covered the steps, but they looked relatively sound. He didn't see any apparent missing stones or cracks. Morgan debated leaving the ruins and continuing on his way, but something about finding ancient ruins on an alien planet in the middle of a forest grabbed his imagination and wouldn't let him leave. He wanted to see what he could find down there. He dug in his pack for his coil of rope, tied it to a nearby tree, and then lowered himself to the top of the ancient stairs.

MORGAN

As Morgan descended the ancient steps, he got the feeling that the structure he was entering was the basement of a square tower. The steps, covered in broken deadwood and moss, were rather treacherous, but he had his Lightstone to reveal pitfalls, and his nimble footing was more than up to the task to make the descent safely. He kept feeling like something was missing, and he realized he missed Issa's company. The absence of her hand on his shoulder and her soft breaths just behind him struck him with a note of melancholy, and he resolved to make finding her village more of a priority in his life.

The descent wasn't overly long, and after just a few winds of the square, exposed foundation, he found himself stepping onto a scree-covered limestone floor, with deadwood, leaves, and rubble making progress difficult. He looked up and saw a patch of the night sky, the big, ringed moon just coming into view. He listened but didn't hear anything stirring in the room, so he started to explore, stepping over the broken stone, rubbing his hands along the mossy walls, tapping suspicious-looking sections of the floor, and shining his light into dark corners.

He was starting to think his exploration would be fruitless, but as he got to one of the darker corners of the base, obscured by the shadow of the steps going up, he found that a rotten, fallen section of a tree was blocking an old, weathered door. He stood to one side of the damp, rotten log and kicked it. Large chunks of bark and rotten wood sloughed off. He kicked it several more times until it was a pile of decayed bark and pulpy wooden dust. With the door fully exposed, Morgan could see that it had a bronze handle that had turned green in the elements. Morgan grabbed the handle, turned it, and pulled. The door didn't budge. He put a foot on the stone next to the door to brace himself and pulled harder. Still, the door didn't move, so he braced himself again and gave the handle a mighty jerk.

The door handle ripped free of the old, swollen wood, and Morgan sprawled backward onto the limestone floor, sliding through moldy leaves and rubble. He cursed, standing up and brushing himself off. The door had swollen with exposure to rain, and now the handle was gone. He wished he'd purchased some sort of prybar or even an axe before heading out. Looking through his storage pouch and the storage ring, he didn't see anything that would work well to bash the door; he'd dropped off most of his spare weapons in the forge. Well, he wasn't going to let an old wooden door end his exploration.

Morgan stood in front of the door, lifted a leg, and kicked it as hard as he could. Morgan's foot smashed one of the old wooden planks in half and continued through into the space beyond. He fell forward and had to pull his leg out of the hole he'd made. He yanked the broken board pieces away from the door and held his light up to the opening. A dusty, empty limestone corridor stretched away from him for a good twenty feet, and then Morgan could see another door. Smiling, Morgan gripped ahold of the next board and yanked. The rotten wood ripped away from the nails holding it to the doorframe. He did the same with the next board and judged the opening wide enough to slip through.

The corridor was musty but dry, and dust was the only debris on the floor. The old door might have been rotten, but it had kept things out. Morgan padded quietly in his leather boots up to the next door. It was similarly designed but hadn't been rotted by rain. The bronze wasn't gleaming, but it wasn't green. Morgan depressed the handle and gave it a gentle pull. The door opened, creaking on its hinges. He shone his light through the gap when it was about a foot wide. The pale light exposed a square limestone vault with what looked like stone sarcophagi lining each wall. Morgan, leery from his experiences in the Crucible, stood still in the doorway for a while, patiently observing the room. Nothing moved, save the shadows that jumped with each involuntary movement of his hand holding the light.

Morgan pulled the door wide and stepped into the chamber. The ceiling was a vaulted limestone dome, and Morgan could see faded paint on the stone. On closer inspection, he realized that only the walls to his left and right held sarcophagi—the far wall was dedicated to an altar with a faded, threadbare tapestry hanging above it. Morgan could just make out the faint outline of a tree and a circle of stars in a night sky. He stepped forward, looking more closely at the tapestry for any more clues about the origin of this ancient space. His boots, though soft, made echoing scuffs in the room. It was deathly silent. He held his light a bit higher and saw that more tapestries hung above each of the six sarcophagi.

They were terribly faded, but Morgan could see that the tapestries each depicted a different person. The first one he studied was a humanoid man with black plated armor. The figure wore a helm that obscured its face, so Morgan couldn't tell what type of person he or she had been. He looked at the next tapestry and saw a woman with pale skin and large eyes. The threads were so faded that, at first, Morgan actually thought it was a tall, thin human woman, but then he noticed the faint outlines of gossamer wings and realized she was a Ghelli. He quickly looked at the various other tapestries and confirmed that they all depicted Ghelli. Some were men, some were women, some wore armor, and some wore silky gowns.

For a brief moment, Morgan contemplated opening up the stone coffins and seeing what sorts of treasures these people might have been buried with. The room was so quiet, and the faces of the Ghelli in the tapestries so serene that Morgan felt like it would be an ugly transgression, though. Perhaps it was because he was still feeling some guilt about how things went at the Yovashi dwelling, but he decided to leave things alone. Morgan quietly walked around the room once more then started making his way to the door. He was about to step through when he noticed a sudden chill in the air. He turned and saw a translucent, ghostly figure standing in front of the altar.

"Hello, Protector. Have you come to pay your respects to the six?" The spirit was tall, thin, and wore plate armor that glinted with a silvery light. Huge, double wings spread out from his upper back, shaped like those on a dragonfly.

"Um, hello. Yes, I'd like to pay my respects, but I regret to say that I don't know who the six are." Morgan felt that honesty might be the best policy when dealing with a spirit.

"No? Has so much time passed? Stranger, I sense the soul of a protector in you, but I'm not familiar with your kind. Tell me, what news have you of the Azure Empire?" The spirit stepped forward, his ghostly greaves making metallic clicks on the limestone floor.

"I'm sorry, sir, but I don't know of the Azure Empire. My people are new to this world." Morgan turned to face the knight fully, stepping closer. He didn't feel any animosity from the spirit; rather, he felt an inexplicable sense of kinship with him.

"Ah, I see it in you now: you're as lost as I am. I know much time has passed since I was interred. Time moves strangely for a spirit though, friend. This much, I'm sure: my kin are gone. I think I remember them moving on, but my mind plays some tricks with me. Are all of your people gone?"

"No. Not all of them. Our numbers are few on this world, though, and we are surrounded by hostility." Morgan wasn't sure what the ghost was getting at, but he did have worries about the humans; there were less than five thousand human souls on this massive hostile world.

"Good that you've chosen to be a protector, then. It is a noble path. You are young, though, just a fledgling. Do you have a strong mentor?"

"I'm afraid not. In fact, I think I'm the strongest among my people." Morgan realized that something about the knight made him want to speak openly for the second time.

"This won't do. What is your name, guardian?"

"Morgan Hall."

"Morgan Hall, will you receive my Legacy? The Legacy of the Azure Paladin?" The spirit stood in front of Morgan, looking down at him, and rested its ghostly hands on Morgan's shoulders as it spoke. Morgan didn't pull away; he wasn't sure he could have if he wanted to. The spirit held his gaze transfixed.

"I, uh, I . . ." Morgan's mouth had gone dry, and his mind spun. It seemed like the spirit was offering him something beneficial, but he didn't know. He didn't know how any of this worked. He decided just to be honest. "I'm sorry, sir; I want to say yes, but I don't exactly know what you're offering me."

"I have no kin, and you require training. I can pass my Legacy to you, serving us both—you will learn some of my skills, and my memory and Legacy will live on through you and your kin." Morgan looked into the spirit's transparent eyes and saw nothing but sincerity in them. He thought about what was being offered and couldn't imagine something called the "Azure Paladin" could be an evil trick. His gut told him to go with it, so he complied.

"Yes, I accept your Legacy, sir." Morgan spoke firmly, and as he finished the word "accept," he started to feel a warm pressure in his shoulders, and then he saw a System message:

You have been offered the Legacy of the Azure Paladin. Accept? YES/NO

Morgan selected the yes option, and then the warm pressure in his shoulders turned into a flood of Energy, and a bright flare of brilliant blue light flashed outward from the Knight. The bright light overwhelmed his vision, and Morgan's sight went dark. He found himself kneeling alone in the vault when he could see again. There wasn't any sign of the spirit, and he had notifications waiting for his attention:

Congratulations! You have gained the feat: Legacy of the Azure Paladin.

You have learned the skill Azure Burst—Basic.

Legacy of the Azure Paladin: You have formed a soul bond with the one known as the Azure Paladin. Periodically, as you gain levels, you'll be offered the opportunity to commune with the Azure Paladin to learn from him.

Azure Burst—Basic: A true paladin wades into the thick of the battle, fearing not the surrounding hordes. Channel your Energy to release a burst of Azure Energy, dealing fire-based damage and blinding enemies that fail to resist your will. Energy Cost: 200, Cooldown: Long.

"Holy shit. Thank you, sir Paladin!" Morgan couldn't feel the spirit's presence anymore, but he thought it was better to show gratitude than not. He stood, debating on whether he wanted to leave right away, and decided against it. Why stumble through the dark when he had this peaceful vault to meditate in? He stepped over to the door, closed it, and then sat down in front of the altar. He took the lotus position and proceeded to work through his Vortex cultivation drill. Over and over, he performed it, and he felt like his Energy gains were higher in this place than when he was sitting in the empty library of his tower. By the time the night was nearly over, he could tell it wouldn't be many more sessions before his Core was ready to level again.

❦ MORGAN ❧

Morgan made his way out of the ancient vault in the early light of the dawn. As he climbed the steps out of the foundation of the crumbling tower, he marveled at the clean, crisp air and the way motes of pollen and dust danced in the rays of the sun peeking through the canopy. Everything was fresh and it matched his mood perfectly; Morgan felt refreshed and inspired by his experience with the spirit of the Azure Paladin. He regretted not questioning the figure before he'd bestowed Morgan with his Legacy. He was curious about who the old spirit had been in life, other than his title. What had been his name? What had become of his civilization? Who were the six, and why were they buried here together? He consoled himself in the knowledge that he'd hopefully have more meetings with the paladin as he gained levels.

Once out of the ruin, Morgan got his bearings with Guardian's Senses and then continued his hike toward the settlement. Throughout the night, while he'd been meditating on his cultivation drill, a portion of Morgan's mind had wandered, still affected by the wonder of what the ancient paladin had done for him. Now, as Morgan walked, he reflected on some decisions he had made: he'd thought about how the paladin had called him a "protector," and he thought about the class he had chosen for himself—a Hollow Guard. He'd thought about the way he'd been forced to sneak around so much and stab creatures in the back to earn victories. Sure, a victory was a victory, but he didn't want the way he'd been thrust into situations by the System to dictate the way he cultivated his own fighting style. He had thought about the description of Azure Blast: "A true paladin wades into the thick of the battle, fearing not the surrounding hordes."

He had spent a long time thinking about his battle with the guardian on the third floor of his tower, the elemental duelist. He hadn't liked feeling outclassed in a face-to-face fight, even if he had won in the end. He felt almost like he had cheated. This thought led him to think about how he'd been able to win against the Yovashi, and in every case, he'd started with a backstab. At the time, he hadn't had a problem with it because the Yovashi were terrifying creatures, and he was happy to slay them in any way that he could. However, did he want to have to rely on subterfuge to win every difficult conflict?

All of these thoughts had run through his mind, but most of all, Morgan had been struck with a pure sense of admiration for the Azure Paladin. He'd come to the, perhaps naive, realization that he wanted to be more like that. Coming to terms with that over the long course of his meditation, Morgan had felt a renewed sense of purpose and, in fact, a cheerful outlook for the day to come. That mood still carried him forward as he veritably galloped through the woods, making short work of his trip to the walls around First Landing.

In the last mile or so of his jaunt through the woods, Morgan encountered no less than three different hunting parties. Two of the groups had let him run right past, unchallenged, but the third had seen him coming and hollered out a greeting; Morgan had yelled back a hello, a little surprised that they hadn't considered him a threat at all. Apparently, there wasn't any fear of him being mistaken for a Yeksa. When he got to the gate, he was pleased to see that there were five guards on duty, and they all were wielding long spears and wearing identical leather armor and shiny, conical helms. He strode up to the group of guards, two of which were playing some sort of dice game in the grass. The other three seemed alert enough, though. "Hey, everyone. I like the uniform. Did you guys get that from the Contribution Store?"

"Woah, hey there. You're Morgan, right?" A tall woman with a long brown braid hanging down behind her metal helm stepped forward.

"You know me?" Morgan stopped in front of the woman, smiling.

"Well, no, but I saw you hanging around the Colony Stone with Olivia and those guys a couple of times. And, you know, when you created a huge fucking tower in there." She gestured over her shoulder toward the wall.

"Ah, yeah, right."

"Also, Bronwyn put the word out to be on the lookout for you. I guess you disappeared or something?"

"Hah, yeah. That was a trip. How long have I been gone, by the way? Just to be sure—in my mind, I've been gone just over a day."

"Hmm. More like a day and a half, I think. Anyway, we got the armor from the Contribution Store, yeah. The council paid for 'em in exchange for a weekly guard rotation. They did the same for a couple of hundred folks."

"Alright, well, I'm gonna head in and look for some hot food." Morgan waved, and the guards waved back, and he walked through the open gate. He was surprised to find that in the time he'd been away, more buildings had gone up. There was a gatehouse now with an attached guard station. While looking at the new structure, he realized he was walking on a cobbled road. He followed the road westward toward the little knoll that was in the center of the colony. On the way, he passed a few tents, but a lot fewer than when he had last been in town. Off to the southwest, he could see the sizeable dormitory-style housing units that the settlers had built over the last week.

As he approached the Colony Stone, he saw that the road ran all the way up to the base of the hill, and off to the right was a long, low building. The building was roofed in clay tiles, and there were a dozen tile-capped vents along the building's roof producing prodigious amounts of steam that wafted into the morning sky. As Morgan walked by the front of the building, he saw that the walls were planked in a wood that reminded him of cedar. Double doors leading into the building were situated on a slightly raised wooden porch. The doors had dark wooden frames with stained windows depicting red-skinned people with bushy white manes bathing in a steamy blue pool. "Oh, hell, yes. Baths?" Morgan stepped up on the deck and pulled the doors open.

He walked into a darkly tiled foyer with pale-blue plaster walls. Shelves filled with white towels lined the far wall. A large wicker basket for dirty towels was in front of the shelves. Morgan didn't see any attendant or anything, so he walked through the door on the left side of the towel shelves; it was marked with an engraved M. He picked up a towel as he walked by. The door opened into a locker room of sorts, though there weren't lockers, just wooden cubbies. Morgan sat at one of the benches and began to get undressed. He'd never been shy, but if he had been, his service in military units had made sure to extinguish that feeling. He kept his storage ring on, but he stuffed the rest of his belongings in one of the cubbies, wrapped the towel around his waist, and exited through the far door.

He stepped into a steamy bathing area much like he'd seen in movies about ancient Greece or Rome. A large, pale-blue pool filled with steaming water dominated the majority of the expansive room. Clay-tiled decking surrounded the pool, with wooden lounge chairs scattered about. Little dishes of soaps were placed along the edge of the pool. Morgan immediately saw that there were five or six men in the bath, lounging quietly. He waved happily, walking over to one of the wooden chairs and taking off his towel. As far as he could tell, the men in the pool were naked, so he figured it would be fine. As he slipped into the hot water, the guys already in the water politely looked away, except for one older fellow who stared at him and said, "Hey, good morning!"

"Ah, good morning!" Morgan splashed hot water over his face and head. "Damn, that feels good! Hey, folks, not to be a jerk or anything, but you might want to get out. This is the first bath I've had since I got to this planet, and I've been in some shit!" Morgan was half laughing while he spoke, but, in his mind, he knew he really *was* filthy. Some of the men soaking nearby started to angle away from him surreptitiously.

"Oh, no worries, pardner. This bathhouse has some neat features due to the power-stones in the back room. As long as we keep 'em charged, they'll pull water through the heater and filter it at the same time."

"Ah, that's cool. I was wondering how all this worked. Energy makes the world go round, I guess." Morgan couldn't help smiling as he vigorously scrubbed himself with one of the little soap bars. It smelled like beeswax. "So, is there an attendant or something?"

"That's right, pardner. I work here. I have to work here for free for a while 'cause the council paid for the bathhouse, but they told me after things get settled, I'll be allowed to start charging a small fee for each person."

"Ah, sounds good to me." Morgan laid back in the water, just floating, letting the heat soak through him. After a while, he heard the sounds of people getting in and getting out, but he kept floating and soaking. It must have been nearly an hour later when he went back to his cubby and got himself dressed. Morgan tossed his used towel in the basket on his way out, making his way up the hill to the Colony Stone. More people were out and about, but the ones he was looking for weren't around; no sign of Olivia, Bronwyn, or any of the other de facto leaders of the colony.

Before wandering the colony to find someone, Morgan decided to do some business with the Contribution Store. He pulled one of the black pouches filled with the blue, smoky Energy beads, looking for the sale prompt. The System was offering him two thousand contribution points for what it called fifty Cold and Rot attuned Energy beads. "Huh, forty apiece, eh?" Morgan didn't even know you could have more than one attunement, let alone attune a bead with more than one.

Morgan slipped the pouch back into his ring for now and pulled out one of the bolts of silky material. It was a dark, midnight blue color, and the way it was tightly wrapped around a central rod, Morgan thought there might be dozens of yards of it. Once again, a green sell bar lit up on the Stone's menu, offering him four thousand contribution points for a bolt of Yovashi Uirgha silk. "Goddamn," he muttered, one by one pulling out the other four bolts and making sure they were the same. They were, meaning he had twenty thousand contribution points worth of silk here. No trade menu appeared when he held the crystal knife up to the stone. Out of curiosity, he tried trading a few of the books he'd pilfered from the Yovashi dwelling, but again, the stone didn't seem interested.

Before he traded away any of his goods, Morgan wanted to see if he could get any of the things he had hoped for when he'd had his epiphany earlier about how to start directing his development more intentionally. He opened up the Contribution Store menu and searched through the categories until he found a "Skills" submenu. He parsed through it until he saw "Weapon Skills." He clicked the menu and saw a massive list populate. Many of the list items were green, but quite a few were red. On the top of the list, highlighted in green, was "Brawling—basic." He scrolled down to the first item highlighted in red: "Firebolt—basic." Experimenting, Morgan tapped the red skill, and a System message popped up:

This skill requires either a qualifying class or an affinity for fire-based Energy.

Understanding flooded his mind as he started to read through the list carefully. Lots of spells were available to him; apparently, they were low-level, generalist spells like "Light," "Find Direction," "Ward Door," and hundreds of others. However, many more powerful spells were barred; evidently, his Hollow Guard class and his vanilla Energy-based Core didn't qualify him. Morgan wasn't after spells right now, though. He clicked the filter button and sorted by melee combat skills, revealing dozens of basic weapon proficiencies. Two were grayed out: "Dagger Mastery—Basic" and "Spear Mastery—Basic." Each of the basic mastery skills cost fifteen hundred contribution points, but Morgan saw one that cost five thousand: "Melee Weapon Mastery—Basic." This one was highlighted a brighter shade of green, and Morgan clicked it to see the description:

Qualifying Class Detected: Melee Weapon Mastery—Basic: You have basic combat capabilities with most common melee weapons. This general combat skill will allow you to advance individual melee weapon skills beyond the Basic level with training and experience.

Morgan pulled out a bolt of silk and a couple of sacks of Energy beads, selling them for nine thousand contribution points, then he purchased the "Melee Weapon Mastery—Basic" skill. Blue and yellow smoke coalesced near his feet and, when it cleared, a small, ornate scroll was sitting there on the ground. Morgan picked it up and opened it, looking intently at the odd, swirling characters moving around on the page. They continued to move more and more quickly and then streamed off the page and into his eyes. The sensation of having the information in that scroll streaming directly into his brain wasn't something Morgan felt he could ever get used to. Just as it seemed that it was almost over, a message flashed in his vision:

Warning: This skill will overwrite the Dagger Mastery—Basic and Spear Mastery—Basic skills. Do you wish to proceed? YES/NO

Morgan selected the yes option, and then another message appeared:

Congratulations! You have learned the skill Melee Weapon Mastery—Basic

Morgan knew he hadn't gained anything other than some options with this procedure, but it was leading in the right direction to fit his plan for himself. He scrolled down the list of combat skills, beyond the basic mastery skills, into more specialized areas. During his meditation in the vault of the Azure Paladin, Morgan had made the decision that he wanted to learn how to fight with a sword. Logically, he knew the spear was a great weapon and that it could outperform swords or other weapons in many circumstances; he didn't intend to throw his spear away or stop using it, even. When he envisioned himself as a guardian or a protector, or even a paladin, he saw himself with a sword, though—he wasn't sure why; for all he knew, it was because of movies he'd watched as a kid or the pulpy fantasy novels he'd read on long patrols with his squad. Mostly, he wanted to do something that was entirely his choice, his idea. It felt like the System had pushed him into the spear, and frankly, he didn't like being pushed into things.

Under the "Sword Skills" category, there were several that interested him. Among the generic-sounding skills like "Broad Slash" and "Riposte" were a couple that really caught his attention. The first was called "Fighting Crane Style—Basic." Morgan selected it and read the description:

Qualifying Class Detected, Qualifying Skill Detected: Fighting Crane Style—Basic: The first step on the mysterious path of the Fighting Crane Swordsmen. This method, recovered from ancient relics, may open the door to great power for the individual capable of recreating this style lost to the ages.

Morgan assumed that his qualifying skill was the new Melee Weapon Mastery. The idea of recovering a lost style appealed to the romantic in him, and Morgan impulsively selected the purchase option. Only after he'd paid did he have a pang of regret, seeing the price tag of four thousand credits. Again, a scroll appeared, and he opened it to learn the new skill. This time, a lot more runes seemed to be crammed onto the parchment, and as they streamed into his eyes, Morgan began to see something more: the scene before him of the Colony Stone and the grassy hillside dotted with people, standing and walking around, faded.

In Morgan's vision, a different sort of meadow took shape. The grass here was green, and corpses littered the ground. Long red swaths of blood streaked the grass, sunlight shimmering in the wetness. A man stood among the bodies, facing off against four other men. They all wore loose clothing—baggy trousers with belted tunics hanging down to mid-thigh. The lone man's clothes were black. His tunic had a shiny silver and blue crane embroidered on the back. He wore a wide-brimmed straw hat and wielded a long, narrow, single-edged sword with a slight curve to it. The men facing him were similarly garbed, but their clothes were a deep red color, and they bore a variety of weapons: one wielded a spear, one a sword and shield, and two had swords similar to the lone man's.

As Morgan watched, the lone swordsman walked toward the other four, his sword held high over his head. They moved to attack him from multiple angles. Morgan saw the men move, and he heard the whistle-whip of a blade moving through the air, but before he could figure out what had happened, the lone swordsman was whipping his sword free of blood and sheathing it. In pieces, the four other men collapsed, looks of shock on their faces. Morgan's heart started beating again, and his vision faded, to be replaced by the familiar presence of the Colony Stone.

Congratulations! You have learned the skill Fighting Crane Style—Basic

MORGAN

It took Morgan a few moments to come back to his senses and grasp what had happened. The endowment of the fighting style seemed to have given him a vision of someone using the style. Was it the founder of the style? Or was it just a random person in the history of the universe that had mastered it? It certainly seemed like that man had been a master; Morgan hadn't even been able to see his sword move. Reflecting on the vision, Morgan couldn't be sure if the men he had seen fighting had been human, but that was the impression he had. How strange, really, to find a skill named after a bird on Earth here! Was this style from Earth? Was it from a world that was like Earth? The possibilities boggled his mind, but when it came down to it, there must be other planets in the universe or, as he'd come to understand it, the multiverse that resembled Earth.

Morgan turned his mind inward and tried to see what he had gained from the scroll. At first, he had a hard time distinguishing what he'd gained from the general Melee Weapons Mastery skill and the Fighting Crane Style. Concentrating on wielding a sword, he instinctively knew how he should hold it, how to thrust, how to parry, what a guard position was. He knew how to keep his center of gravity low while he advanced and how to move his feet without crossing them. Hundreds of little facts like this flooded through his mind, but then he started to see some specifics that had to come from the Fighting Crane Style; he realized he knew a series of five "forms" that were to be performed with a two-handed sword. They had distinctive names: the Crane Forages, the Crane Takes a Minnow, the Crane Defends the Nest, the Crane Advances, and the Crane Flutters Its Wings.

Morgan could picture the forms in his head and how he was supposed to move, but he wasn't so confident that he could pull them off in reality. Deciding he had enough to work with as far as sword work went, he decided to put off buying more weapon skills. Instead, Morgan navigated to the section of the Contribution Store where he could find weapons for sale. He narrowed the filter to swords and was surprised by the extent of weapons on offer. He saw everything from wooden practice swords for two contribution points to iron short swords for ten contribution points to something called Ulnoor's Hunger for three hundred thousand. Morgan messed with the filter to only display two-handed swords, limiting the price to fifteen thousand. This narrowed the list substantially, and he zeroed in on a fine-steel hand-and-a-half sword for eleven thousand points.

He almost bought the sword, but then he thought about the vision in which he'd seen the master of the Fighting Crane Style. He thought about the sword he'd used, and something clicked in his head. Suddenly, he could picture what a typical hand-and-a-half sword looked like: the blade was the right length, but it wasn't usually curved, and it had two edges. Sometimes it was called a bastard sword. Morgan had read fantasy novels and seen plenty of movies, but he was by no means a sword buff. Somehow one of the two skills he'd just acquired had given him a basic knowledge about sword types. Morgan knew that the kind of sword he was looking for was kind of like a two-handed falchion, or even a katana but longer and with a broader blade.

He searched for those types of swords, and none were listed. He was disappointed but reckoned he could make do with the straight sword for now; he'd have to hope he found a weaponsmith or another sword down the road that fit his new style better. Morgan sold another two bolts of silk and two bags of Energy beads and then bought the fine-steel bastard sword.

Morgan picked up the sword. It was strange that the System had types of weapons that were, as far as Morgan knew, invented on Earth. Then again, he'd already given up trying to figure out how the System integrated everything, including their language, into its domain. For all he knew, the System took this sword from the databases on the *Pilgrim-9* or out of one of the colonists' heads. Morgan was pleased to see that it came with a polished, black leather sheath and belt. He tied it around his waist and drew the sword. It looked and felt pretty good in his hands. It wasn't quite as long as the sword the master in his vision had used, and it had two straight edges, but it would do until he found something more appropriate. Morgan could wield it with one hand, but there was plenty of room on the grip for two, and he was pretty sure he'd be able to practice his forms with it.

After sheathing his sword, Morgan scrolled back through the list of spells, hoping to find something that was meant to work with his Vortex Core. Nothing was on the list that indicated any sort of relationship to his Core or that even had anything to do with draining Energy. Most of the spells that weren't highlighted in red were simple utility spells. The spells that looked intriguing to him were universally unusable—all required an affinity with different types of Energy. "This is bullshit," he muttered as he continued to scroll through the list. How had Olivia gotten so many affinities? Even Bronwyn had an affinity if he recalled correctly. Morgan supposed it had to do with their Cores, but he was proud of his Vortex Core, and he didn't want to even consider messing around with it. He was sure there had to be more powerful spells that he could learn that didn't require some sort of affinity; either the Contribution Store had a limited selection, or he didn't know what to look for.

In frustration, he dropped his hand from the stone and decided to save his money for now. He'd work on his sword skills, improving his Core, and gaining levels for now. Hopefully, he'd learn new spells from his class and whatever class refinement he got at level twenty. If nothing else, he could ask Tiladia about it, and hopefully, he'd be heading to see Issa soon, and there might be more options in her town.

That resolved, Morgan stepped away from the Colony Stone and took a good look around. To the East, a crowd was forming outside the new bathhouse. From the angle up by the stone, he could see the new cobbled road that led out to the east gate. He could see that the road continued around the hill in a circle, and he moved around the stone to look north. The cobbled road continued around the hill to pass in front of the smithy. Smoke was billowing from the stacks on the smithy, and through the haze, he could see his tower off toward the northern wall. Morgan continued around the top of the hill, seeing that the cobbled street continued over to the western side of the hill, where the brewery and tavern sat near the little pond. Smoke was also coming from the tavern chimney, and Morgan could see quite a few people down there, hanging around on the deck.

Morgan resolved to check out the tavern, but first he continued his survey, looking out from the southern edge of the hill. The circular road around the grassy hill continued, and it stretched for about a hundred yards toward the south gate; apparently, that was all the council had purchased so far. Most of the population was in the southern direction, where all of the housing had been constructed. He saw groups of people milling around and getting started on whatever they had planned for the day. Morgan didn't see any other new buildings, so he decided to head down to the tavern.

A faint trail was worn in the grass around the Colony Stone and down the hill in various areas. Morgan thought about mentioning to Olivia that they should put some steps and walkways in, but then he figured that was pretty obvious, and they'd probably get around to it. He took a deep breath as he let gravity pull him down the hill, savoring the fresh, crisp air. He felt good. He supposed part of it was the hot bath he'd just had, but another factor was definitely his decision to take charge of his skill development instead of just letting things happen to him. Morgan would never resent the spear he'd used so effectively up to now, and he might come back to it at some point, but he was looking forward to practicing his new sword forms, so much so that he almost skipped the tavern and went straight to his tower.

That was when he smelled the unmistakable scent of bacon and eggs and saw that people were standing around with plates of steaming food, and more people were inside the tavern eating and laughing. The scene called to him on a visceral level, and Morgan pushed his way into the crowd, smiling and greeting everyone he passed. Everyone he passed was friendly, more or less, and when he got to the door, pulling it open, a familiar voice called out, "Morgan! Morgan! Come over here!" Morgan looked into the largely wooden common room of the tavern. He saw that a couple of dozen wooden tables were spread around the large area, and from one of the closer ones, Olivia Bennett was waving animatedly at him.

"Oh, hi, Olivia," Morgan said as he walked up to her table. She pushed against the man sitting next to her, urging him to scoot down and making room for Morgan.

"Morgan! I'm so glad to see you! Bronwyn wasn't sure what happened to you!" She slapped the bench next to her, and Morgan sat down, smiling.

"Ah, yeah, I got teleported. It's kind of a long, sad story, actually. I'll be glad to tell you about it sometime, but right now, how do I get some of that food?" Morgan was eyeing the wooden bowl a man across from him was eating out of. It was filled with scrambled eggs and thick slices of something that looked like ham. Was it possible they had ham? Was there a smoker operating already?

"Oh, one of the bar hands will bring you some; just sit tight! You don't have to pay yet, either. Right now, we're all kinda just pitching in. Once we get things settled, we'll allow the economy to sort itself out, but that was the deal the council made with the tavern keeper; he's providing services for free while we supply him with the building and ingredients. Well, it's not really free—he's getting tons of improvements to his non-combat skills." Olivia was beaming the whole time she spoke, and Morgan was struck by how pretty she was. Her silvery metallic eye glinted, and her blue eye sparkled, and her smile really lit up her face. He felt a slight pang of guilt when his thoughts inevitably turned to Issa, and he cleared his throat, smiling.

"You seem happy. Things going well?"

"Oh yes, the colony is shaping up. We do have the looming threat of the Urghat, but we've taken some good steps in forming a militia, and Bronwyn is working on other preparations for them. Did she tell you about the whole weird thing about her stealing a title from one of their leaders?"

"What? No! That must not have been something she wanted to mention when we were hiking out to that cave, hah."

"Yeah, she's convinced they'll be coming to challenge her for it back. She's tough, but I think we need to use caution." Olivia shrugged, drinking from a wooden cup.

"What is that? Coffee?"

"No! I wish! It's some kind of tea from local herbs. We have a few people that have identified some good edibles in the nearby woods." As she spoke, a tall, thin fellow with stringy hair pulled back in a ponytail placed a bowl of steaming food in front of Morgan. Before Morgan could thank him, he was off to clear a nearby table.

"Goddamn! This is ham! Where's it from?" Morgan was already shoveling some of the food into his mouth.

"There are boar-like creatures in the woods. Our hunters are finding tons of game. Literally!"

"Mmmf, but, mmm, like, is there a smoker here or something?" Morgan tried his best not to spit any food while he spoke.

"Oh! Didn't you see the smoke? The guy, Alec Green, who took the tavern keeper job, built a smoker off the side of the tavern kitchen."

After finishing his meal and promising to meet up with Olivia and some of the council members later, Morgan took his leave and walked toward his tower. As he walked down the grassy slope to the northern edge of the colony, he noticed that his tower wasn't alone anymore. About a hundred feet to the west of it, a sprawling villa-type home had taken shape. It was a rather impressive structure—two stories of whitewashed stone with a low wall encircling a budding garden. Morgan raised an eyebrow, resolving to meet his new neighbors sooner or later, but continued to his home. He hustled up the steps and laid his hand on the door, pulling it open as soon as he heard that tell-tale click of the lock opening.

"Welcome home, Morgan! I can sense you've experienced a lot—has it been a long time since you were home?" Tiladia's lilting, tinkling voice had a note of concern about it.

"Not too long, Tiladia. I'll tell you all about it, and maybe you can help me with some books and potions I found."

MORGAN

Morgan walked through the central stair hall and into the library. Tiladia followed behind, her lights flaring brightly as her misty form swirled around them. Morgan walked over to one of the large study tables in the library and began to unload the items from the ring that he'd taken from the Yovashi female. He started with the Yovashi Uirgha silk bolts, the two he had left, and then he placed down the four heavy, intricate tomes. Next to those, he unloaded the twenty-eight vials and bottles filled with varieties of liquids. Finally, he set the black crystal knife down on the wooden surface. As Tiladia started to flit around the table, her lights flashing inquisitively, he stepped over to a nearby table and unloaded all the books he'd taken from the shelves in the portal room of the Yovashi dwelling. He counted them as he dropped them on the table, coming up with eighteen hefty tomes, thirty-two much smaller books, and the one massive book that had been on the lectern.

Tiladia continued her tinkling perusal of the items on the first table, and Morgan walked over to watch. After a few moments, she paused and said, "That silk is quite dense in Energy. I bet it's very tough. It would be an ideal material to use in crafting robes or other garments." She continued flitting about, and Morgan nodded, packing the silk back into his ring. "I'm sorry, Morgan, I don't know the language that these books are written in. I can spend some time trying to puzzle it out, though. Especially while you are away, I find that time does strange things if I don't have a task. I've told you that before, haven't I? I can say for sure that these four books are all steeped in a dark and cold Energy. Perhaps there are skills or spells outlined within."

"Hmm, yeah, that would be great if you could work on that. Can you, like, turn the pages?" Morgan gestured to her ethereal form.

"Oh, I don't need to; I can just let my consciousness drift down through the pages." She moved over to the knife and began to pulse more rapidly.

"Morgan, there's an intelligent spirit in this knife. A powerful and hungry one. I think you need to be a lot stronger in will before you attempt to bond with it."

"Wow, I was actually right in my caution!" Morgan chuckled and put the knife away in his ring.

"Oh, Morgan, I wouldn't keep it in that dimensional container. Remember what I told you? Spirits hate that feeling. It will be even crabbier and harder to control when you take it out. Perhaps it will even go insane if it hasn't already. You should store it here in the tower."

"Oh shit, that's right." Morgan took the knife out of the ring. "While you're looking at those potions, I'll go put this in the study." Tiladia flared in acknowledgment, and Morgan walked over to the study room with the big desk and the map table. He'd been meaning to ask Tiladia about that map but never got around to it. He walked around the desk and dropped the knife into the same drawer where he'd stashed the diadem. On a whim, he opened all the other drawers to make sure he didn't miss anything in his earlier exploration, but they were all empty, and he couldn't find any sort of secret compartment. Shrugging, he walked back to the library.

"Morgan, these four potions with the swirly yellow liquid are healing draughts. They aren't terribly potent, but they'll undoubtedly speed healing or help to overcome an infection. These three tiny vials with the clear serum in them are concentration potions. If you drink them while performing a difficult task, your chance of success will increase. These five little black bottles contain a powerful sedative. If you were to drink one, you'd be dead to the world for many hours. The rest of these liquids are all ingredients or catalysts for alchemy."

"Thanks, Tiladia!" Morgan swept the potions and vials into his storage ring. "Keep me posted on any progress with the books, okay?"

"Of course, Morgan!"

"Tiladia, is there a broom here? I bought stuff to wash the tile before, but I need to clean the ashes out of the dueling hall."

"Oh, that won't be an issue. The dueling hall has enchantments on the floor and walls to facilitate and speed self-repair and cleaning. The old master used to have some very messy exhibitions in there." Tiladia flared and spun about as she spoke.

"Ah, while I enjoy that convenience, it kinda creeps me out." Morgan shook his head ruefully and began walking to the stairs. Tiladia followed along behind him.

"Morgan, your aura has grown more threatening, and I sense more depth to your combat abilities. Would you like to talk about your journeys?"

"Uh, yeah. I killed some more Yovashi, and it seems there aren't very many of them left in the world, so the System gave me this title that makes me more threatening. Oh, and then I found an ancient paladin's spirit, and he gave me his legacy."

"Quite eventful! I think, with a bit more training, you'll be ready to challenge the next champion."

"That's the goal. I want to clear a couple more floors of this place; then, I have to get serious about finding my way to my friend, Issa. What's on the next floor, anyway, Tiladia?"

"That's the portal hub."

"Portal hub?" Morgan stepped onto the stairs and, after another step, was on the second floor.

"The old master had a hub of portals on the fourth-floor landing. They opened to his other estates and some major cities' libraries."

"Holy shit, that's cool! Are they still active?"

"No, but the keystones to them are probably in the reliquary," Tiladia answered as she followed Morgan onto the third-floor landing and into the dueling hall. Just as she'd predicted, the ashes and burn marks were gone from the springy wooden floor. The hole he'd made in the wall with his spear had also disappeared. Morgan smiled, stepping over to one of the benches and removing his armor, belt, and boots. He stepped out on the floor in his black trousers and shirt; with just his sword in his hands, he began to work through the five forms of the Fighting Crane style.

The first form, the Crane Forages, had him holding the sword low, pointed in front of him, as he slowly advanced, the tip weaving back and forth in a deceptively hypnotic pattern. From there, he transitioned to the Crane takes a Minnow—a powerful thrust that had a slightly downward angle and positioned his side to the target. After that form, he smoothly rolled into the Crane Defends the Nest, a back step, then a side step, with tightly controlled parrying motions. Next, he transitioned into the Crane Advances—sword held high, point forward, solid and deep steps toward the enemy with a low center of gravity. Finally, he practiced the Crane Flutters Its Wings, a sweeping flurry of blows that arced from high to low and then low to high angles.

After a complete set of the five forms, Morgan found it natural to slip back into the first form and start again. He knew he could practice these forms in a different order, but he wanted it to feel like he had perfected them before he began to mix them up, and right now, he was going very slowly, quite a long way short of mastery. In the rhythm of practice and the sweat of honest work, Morgan began to lose track of time, and it was only after hours of training and a rumbling in his stomach that he decided to take a break. His focus had been so complete that he wasn't sure if Tiladia had been there the whole time, but when he went to put on his boots and armor, she was hovering nearby.

"Your movements were a lot more natural-looking at the end there, Morgan."

"Thanks! I wish I had an instructor or a sparring partner."

"I'm sorry I'm not more help in that regard. My form is too incorporeal. I never learned much about swords, in any case. I did my fighting as a dragon with claws and teeth and fire."

"Sounds like you were formidable!" Morgan smiled, pulling his boots on and standing. He shrugged into his breastplate and slipped the sword into his ring; it was just more convenient than having it slapping against his legs while he walked. "Any idea of the time?"

"I'm sorry, no, but I can tell you that you've been practicing for just a bit more than four hours."

"Perfect! Thanks again, Tiladia. Any idea how long it takes to improve a skill past basic with just practice?"

"It depends on many factors—the skill, the person, the practice. Some skills improve much more quickly than others. Some people are more gifted learners. I've seen someone improve their skill in alchemy from basic to improved in one day. Of course, that person was a skilled enchanter with hundreds of points in intelligence."

"Shit. I thought I was doing well with my intelligence." Morgan started walking for the stairs.

"You're young, Morgan! You're doing quite well!" Tiladia flashed brightly, following after. "Have you considered inviting some of your colonist friends to come and spar? It might improve your learning."

"You read my mind, Tiladia." Morgan smiled. "Don't worry, I wasn't fishing for compliments; I know I'm still fresh meat in this world." He bid Tiladia goodbye, then walked downstairs and headed out to meet with Olivia, Arthur, and the others. He was pleased with his progress; he really enjoyed doing the sword forms. Now that he knew such things as styles existed, he figured there were probably some for spears, but he was happy with the sword for now. He felt like he could improve quite a lot just by practicing his forms and then doing some cultivation drills. He kind of wanted to commit the next few days to just that; he just needed to avoid getting wrapped up in something else, though.

It was mid-afternoon as he walked up the slope toward the colony's center. He passed a few people who waved in a friendly manner. Thinking about how the System had subverted their plans to start a colony on a new world, Morgan had to admit that things were going reasonably well so far. Even though he'd been forced to fight for his life and experienced some real horrors, the colonists hadn't lost even fifty people in the couple of weeks they'd been here. From extensive briefings and repetition about risks, he knew that the Pilgrim program had anticipated losses of life up to 30 percent in the first year on a new colony. Of course, they'd had best-case scenarios that were a lot cheerier, but the fact remained that colonizing an unknown planet was a risky business. Morgan shook his head. Here he was, in a good mood from a bath and a hot meal, and he'd already begun forgiving the System. He needed to remember how it was meddling with them on so many levels. Sure, there were benefits, but was a loss of freedom worth it? "Control what you can control, dummy." He chuckled and walked up the hill to the Colony Stone.

He wanted to check one thing in the Contribution Store before finding the others. He put his hand on the smooth surface and called up the menu for weapons. He found and bought wooden training swords of several different types. He searched the menus but didn't find any kind of practice dummy. "Guess I'll have to find a living dummy." He laughed and walked over to the edge of the hill, looking down at the tavern. Olivia had said they'd meet there; apparently, there was a private room off the common area. He walked down the hill, across the cobbled road, over the raised deck, and into the bustling tavern.

The inn was busy but not nearly as busy as it had been in the morning. Morgan figured he was past the lunch rush and too early for dinner. He saw a burly man cleaning the bar with a rag and waved. "Heya, is the council meeting yet?"

"There's a couple of them in there. You want some mead before you go in? It's not fresh brewed; that takes a while. The council bought a few kegs off the Contribution Store, though."

"Well, shit, yeah!" Morgan walked over to the bar and took the proffered mug of mead. He'd never had mead, so he was surprised by the thick sweet taste. "Honey?"

"Yeah, but be careful. It's strong as shit." The man smiled, rubbing his curly brown hair with a hand. "Name's Alec, by the way."

"Nice to meet ya! I'm Morgan." Morgan took another pull of the mead, then smiled, waved, and headed over to the wooden door leading to the private table.

MORGAN

The meeting in the tavern's backroom had been going on for a while now. It started with introductions; Morgan knew Olivia, Arthur, Bronwyn, and vaguely Dr. Kerns. He knew he'd met some of the others but was glad to hear their names again. A lady named Maria Rios represented a large group of craftspeople and citizens, then there were other technicians and engineer types like Rene Bisset, Tanya Delgado, and Morgan's old friend, Boris. All told, nine people sat around the table and discussed everything from the status of the latrines to where they should put the next road to who on the leaderboard deserved the next private home.

Morgan sort of tuned out a lot of the logistical discussions. He figured he was here as a kind of courtesy, because he'd arrived with so much information and had reached a level in the System that others hadn't experienced yet. He was staring into space, thinking about how he might improve his transitions between the various forms of his fighting style when he heard his name and realized Arthur had repeated it. "Hmm? Oh, yes?"

"Uh, yes, we were wondering what your thoughts were in regard to the likelihood of an invasion by these "Urghat" creatures?" Morgan glanced at Bronwyn and saw she'd drawn her eyebrows together in a scowl. Did the council doubt her assessment?

"Well, before you all arrived, Olivia and Bronwyn filled me in on her duel with the big Urghat. I fought a lot of those guys in the Crucible, and they seem like the kind of people who like to fight. My friend, Issa, said that her people were constantly at war with them, the biggest issue being that the Urghat liked to eat her kind. Well, they seem to want to eat everyone they meet, so . . ." Morgan stopped talking as he realized he was rambling a bit, and the faces of the people had grown a bit shocked.

"What the fuck is it with the natives here wanting to eat people? The Yeksa, the Yovashi, the Urghat. Seriously, what the fuck?" Bronwyn let out an explosive sigh.

"Not all the natives are like that. I told you guys about Issa's people, but I met some other races that weren't cannibalistic, too: the Ghelli and the

Cadwalli. Issa mentioned a couple of others that her people were allied with, but I can't think of their names. Sorry, she only mentioned them once."

"So, you think Bronwyn's assessment that we need to prepare for an attack is correct?" Arthur pressed.

"Yeah, of course. We should prepare for anything in this place. I think the wall is a great first step, and it looks like you started arming a militia. Now we need to train and get stronger. The Urghat I fought were not much in the way of Energy users, but they were savage and tough as hell."

"The only one I saw using Energy was the one the System coaxed into dueling me," Bronwyn added.

"What do you mean the System coaxed him?" Maria Rios asked.

"Bron got a quest to fight him, and before they fought, the Urghat told her the System gave him a quest to fight her," Olivia said, suppressing a bemused chuckle.

"That kind of takes the wind out of the theory that we're the protagonists in the System's eyes," Dr. Kerns muttered.

"What? Hah, I could have told you that; we're a drop in the ocean of the individuals that the System is fucking with!" Morgan laughed.

"Alright, everyone, please focus on what we can control. Morgan, may I ask how many people might be able to take shelter in that tower of yours? Olivia mentioned to me that you said it was larger on the inside?" Arthur asked, and everyone quieted down to hear the answer.

"Hmm. Well, I only have access to the first three floors currently. I'd say between the library, and the reception hall, and the two galleries we could stuff a thousand people in. Not comfortably, mind you."

"Well, that's good to know as a last resort. Why can't you access the rest of the tower?"

"Each floor has a guardian I have to fight." Morgan shrugged as if there wasn't anything more to say. A thought occurred to him, and he continued, "You know, I very much want to help out here, but I also want to find a way to my friend's town. I think I might be able to kill two birds with one stone there; as I said, her people are at war with the Urghat. They might be willing to help us out."

"Intriguing . . ." Arthur seemed about to say more, but Olivia cut him off.

"That's a great idea, Morgan. I'd love to meet this friend of yours and her people. Allies are just what we need!" Olivia leaned forward earnestly as she spoke.

"Uh, yeah, I'd planned to spend a few days practicing with my weapon and trying to level my Core, but maybe I should get going? How soon do you think we'll see Urghat raids, Bronwyn?"

"I mean, I've already killed that scouting party about a day's hike north of here. I don't know how fast they can mobilize, but it could be any day. It could be a month. I wish I could say more. Maybe I should scout them out?" Bronwyn drummed her fingers on the table, visibly losing herself in thought. The table grew quiet for a moment while everyone thought about what had been said.

Arthur cleared his throat and spoke first: "I'd like to propose a course of action." He paused to see if anyone objected. "Morgan, I think you should make the journey to the Ardeni village as quickly as possible. I'd like Olivia to travel with you as an ambassador from our Colony. Not that you couldn't represent us, but I think it's better if she accompanies you. Bronwyn, I think you'd be an excellent candidate to scout out the Urghat. You're resilient and have proven your ability to face those foes. However, I must insist, respectfully, that you assign full permissions to the rest of us here, on the council, with the Colony Stone." He cleared his throat again as he finished speaking and looked down at the table, bracing himself for arguments.

"Yeah, that sounds smart," Bronwyn said casually, causing everyone to look up sharply in surprise. "Hah, don't get so freaked out. I'm not a power-hungry monster, you know. I mean, yeah, I want to be powerful, but not politically. You guys are doing a great job running things; I'm happy to just be one voice among many with regard to the colony."

"Just a moment," Dr. Kerns spoke up. "I'm fine with that, but we must all agree that an election is in order as soon as we've stabilized. I like the idea of a council, but the people must have some sort of voice in its composition." Around the table, many people voiced their agreement, and Bronwyn nodded.

"Yeah. I was playing around with the stone's settings this morning, and it, conveniently, has an election system built-in. Members of the colony can vote anonymously at the stone once we set it up."

"That's very convenient, isn't it? I suppose, with millions or billions of worlds under its influence, the System has had time to perfect things. Well, I'm in agreement, and I'm also in agreement with the idea that I should travel with Morgan," Olivia said, looking at Morgan with an eyebrow raised inquisitively.

"Yeah, that's fine with me. It might be a dangerous journey. I don't know the exact route, but it seems she's about a hundred miles southeast of here."

"How the hell do you know that?" Bronwyn asked.

"I got a skill with my class. It lets me feel, roughly, where people I consider allies are." Once again, Morgan shrugged.

"The System is fucking weird." Bronwyn shook her head, smiling ruefully.

"Well, before you all get going your separate ways, come out to the common room and have some soup. I started cooking a big pot of ham and beans early this morning!" Maria stood up, deciding for everyone that enough had been said. Morgan was quick to agree, sliding his chair out, and then it cascaded; everyone walked out to the common room, but Morgan saw that Olivia and Bronwyn lingered at the table. They'd been sitting next to each other and were talking in hushed voices. It seemed like Bronwyn was worried about Olivia. He shook his head; everyone had to find their path in this new world. He'd do his best to protect Olivia, but if he'd learned anything during his time in the Crucible with Issa, it was that he wasn't perfect. He'd lost count of the times Issa had saved his ass.

As he walked out to the common area, he saw Alec behind the bar, and a couple of other people wearing aprons were scrubbing tables and sweeping the floors, apparently getting ready for the dinner rush. Maria walked behind the bar and called out, "Hey, Akari, Tim, help me dish up some of this soup for the council real quick." Alec smiled and kept wiping down the bar, but the other workers hustled back to the kitchen to help Maria.

Morgan was standing around waiting for the food when Bronwyn and Olivia came out of the meeting room. Bronwyn looked around the room, then beelined for Morgan. "Hey, can I talk to you for a sec?"

"Sure," Morgan replied, turning to her. "I can already guess what you're going to say, though. Olivia is . . ."

"I already almost got her killed once," Bronwyn interrupted. "You know that. She's got the scar to prove it."

"Hey, she's a big girl, as I was going to say. She chooses where to go and what risks to take. You can't take the blame for every bad thing that happens."

"Hah, tell that to the colonists that are dead because I went to sleep knowing the barrier was down, like an idiot." Bronwyn shook her head and frowned, grinding her knuckles into a nearby tabletop.

"Look, I'm not going to promise that Olivia, or myself for that matter, won't get into trouble on this trip, but I'll do my damned best to make sure she gets through alright. Okay?" Morgan grabbed her shoulders and shook her a little, making her look into his eyes.

"Alright, Morgan. Thanks. I can't ask more than that." Bronwyn shrugged off his grip and walked out of the tavern, like the weight of the universe was on her shoulders.

"The fuck is going on with her?" Morgan shrugged and walked over to the table where the tavern hands were setting down bowls of bean and pork soup.

"She has a little bit of a self-persecution complex," Olivia said from off to the side.

"Oh, you heard that? Sorry . . ." Morgan winced. Him and his big mouth.

"No, you're right. She's trying really hard to make up for some mistakes she made early on, and I think she's her own worst critic. She'll be alright." Half-heartedly, Olivia smiled, running a hand through her hair and then walking over to the table to eat. Morgan followed her, grabbing a bowl and sitting with the others. No one mentioned Bronwyn's absence, and soon Morgan was lost in the delicious flavor of the soup. At first, he'd thought it sounded more like a stew, considering the main ingredients were beans and ham, but it had a delicious broth—just the right amount of spiciness over the smokey taste of the ham with a slight vinegar aftertaste.

"This is great, Maria! Thank you so much for cooking," Dr. Kerns said, tipping his bowl to his mouth to finish the dregs. Around the table, people echoed his compliment, and Maria smiled proudly.

"Don't thank just me! Alec smoked the pork, and the whole colony contributed to build this tavern with the great kitchen!"

"You're too modest," Alec called from the bar. "That soup elevated my pork by a factor of ten!"

"Morgan, what time do you want to leave in the morning?" Olivia asked from across the table.

"Oh, tomorrow, huh? Yeah, I guess we should get moving. Hmm, let's meet at the south gate a little after dawn? I'll buy some supplies from the Contribution Store on my way."

"Perfect! Thanks for the reminder. I don't have a backpack or boots. These shoes I've been wearing are probably not going to cut it! I've got a few Energy beads I can turn in for credit."

"Hey, you have multiple affinities, right?" Morgan asked, as he pulled one of the pouches of Energy beads out of his ring from the Yovashi dwelling.

"Yeah, that's right," Olivia replied, looking with interest at the pouch that had suddenly appeared in his hand.

"Check these out. They're Energy beads with two different affinities—rot and cold." Morgan handed her the pouch. Olivia opened it and took one of the smokey blue Energy beads out, taking in a sharp breath.

"Amazing! You can put more than one affinity into an Energy bead? I have to try this!" She started to hand the pouch back to Morgan, but he held up his hand.

"Keep it. I have a lot of them. Use it to buy equipment and provisions for the trip. I'll see you at the gate in the morning." Morgan stood up and waved to the table. "Thanks all! Good luck if I don't see you before I leave tomorrow." He left the warm inn with everyone's well wishes following him out. Morgan couldn't help the smile that was spreading on his face; he wasn't sure why he felt good—maybe the sense of community or maybe the prospect of finally getting on the road to see Issa.

OLIVIA

Olivia walked out of the tavern and took a deep breath of the evening air. She closed her eyes and savored the slight chill that tinged the spring twilight. Someone bumped past her to get into the tavern, and she stumbled to the side. "Oh, excuse me!" Her cheeks reddened as she realized she'd been standing in the doorway, but the person who'd bumped her was already gone. "Oh, well!" She smiled at the people standing around on the deck, but no one seemed to be paying attention. Stuffing her hands into the flimsy pockets of the smock-like shirt she was wearing, Olivia hustled down the steps and started making her way to the tent she'd set up all those days ago when she'd started the orientation.

As she got closer to her tent, once a part of a large group but now sitting lonely across a firepit from just two others, a few people called out friendly hellos. She waved good-naturedly and walked up to her firepit. Her tent neighbors weren't home, but there was a good-size stack of logs nearby. She walked over to the pile and grabbed a couple of big logs, dropping them into the pit. She concentrated on the logs and said, "Ignis!" A fiery beam of Energy surged out of her palm and engulfed the logs for a few seconds, and when it faded, they were charred and crackling merrily. She smiled inwardly; she didn't need to say ignis or anything else for that matter; she just had to concentrate on activating her skill, Fiery Burst. She'd learned Latin to help with her research and thought adding a little flair to her magic was fun.

She flipped open her tent flap and sat down near the opening on her blanket. Olivia was tired, but she wanted to mess around with the Energy bead idea Morgan had given her. She paused for a moment and thought about her stats sheet:

Status	
Name:	Olivia Bennet
Race:	Human - Base 1
Class:	–

Level:	6
Core:	Prisma Class - Base 2, Fire, Earth, Water, Air
Energy Affinity:	9.1, Fire 9.6, Earth 9.6, Water 9.6, Air 9.6	Energy:	530/555
Strength:	6	Vitality:	7
Dexterity:	8	Agility:	6
Intelligence:	35	Will:	15
Skills:	System Language Integration - Not Upgradeable, Stealthy Maneuvers - Basic, Prisma Core Cultivation Drill - Basic, Orb Manipulation - Basic, Icy Shards - Basic, Fiery Burst - Basic

She pulled the pouch of beads from her pocket, taking one out to study it again. It was fascinating to her; if she looked closely enough, she could see swirls of smokey-looking particles and tiny flakes of blue crystals. The smoke was always in motion, and the crystals would form and then dissipate in a seemingly endless cycle. The bead felt dense in her fingers, and she could sense the Energy thrumming within. She put it away before she accidentally started drawing the Energy out. She'd done that with the first bead she had created, rendering it useless before she realized what she'd done; the Energy moved so easily for her that she had to be careful. Not many of her colleagues had an affinity as high as she, and she figured that was why.

She tucked her legs up and crossed them before her, placing her forearms against the insides of her knees. She opened her palms, like she was cupping an invisible ball between them, and started to concentrate on moving Energy out through her channels. She began with fire, gently coaxing a thin stream out between her hands and pressing it together with her will. Then, still concentrating on the fire, she sent a parallel stream of earth Energy out and into the tiny seed of an Energy bead between her hands. At first, the differently attuned Energy resisted, falling away from the little ball she was trying to form. She concentrated, pushing with her will, imagining that she could feel the elastic shell of the Energy bead she was trying to create and squeezing it down tight.

Slowly, the fire and earth Energies started to swirl and mingle at the center of the space between Olivia's hands. She continued to feed the two different Energies into the bead, pressing and pressing down with her will. After about an hour, she knew she was on the right track, the bead was taking shape, and she didn't have to push as hard to keep the Energies together. Seeing that her project was becoming stable, Olivia started to channel a third stream of Energy, this time water attuned. Soon, a third, pale blue stream of Energy poured out of her palms and added to the partially condensed bead.

Olivia struggled to get the third Energy stream to mix in with the other two; the water attuned Energy kept drifting off, her will insufficient to force it into the mix with the earth and fire Energies. She huffed and stopped the water stream. Next time, she'd try mixing three in from the start, not adding a third halfway through. Resigned just to create a double affinity bead, Olivia opened up her channels as much as she could for the earth and fire Energy she was pouring forth and managed to finish forming the bead in the next half hour.

The little earth and fire bead she'd created glistened in her palm. Olivia held it up to the night sky and stared into it. Tiny embers winked in and out of existence within the bead, surrounded by minuscule flecks of gold and silver floating in its depths. It was wonderfully beautiful. She'd gotten a lot faster at making Energy beads, and it didn't seem to take any longer to make the dual attuned one. Olivia yawned and thought about going to sleep, but she really wanted to try a triple-attuned bead first. She smiled and got to work.

Olivia's eyes sprang open with a start. What time was it? She sat up and looked out the tent opening and sighed with relief. The sky was turning light, but the sun wasn't out yet. There was no way Morgan could call this dawn; she still had a little time. She crawled around in her tent, piling her few belongings onto her favorite blanket: a journal and tin full of pencils, a sheathed knife, a corked bottle full of water, a few extra sets of the everyday, cheap clothes from the Contribution Store, the tattered banner from the Yovashi cave, and the beautifully ornate little chest that Bronwyn had given her to examine. She really wanted to investigate the chest herself but didn't think it would be fair to take it with her on a journey that might take weeks. She'd take it to Boris Saltzki—he was almost to level seven and had been studying "artificing" ever since the orientation.

Olivia hurried to the little house Boris shared with a few others and knocked on the door. It took a while for anyone to answer, but luckily, a sleepy-eyed Boris opened the door after her third knock. "Boris, I have to run, but I need to give you this chest to check out. Bronwyn got it from a very dangerous creature. Please see if you can determine if it has a trap or anything. After you get it open and study its contents, report to Bronwyn. I'm leaving town for a while."

"Uh, who is this?" Boris blinked blearily and moved his face close to Olivia's. "Olivia?"

"Damnit, Boris!" Olivia had to explain to him twice more what she was asking of him, but he finally woke up enough to acknowledge her request. She ran from Boris's house all the way to the Colony Stone, and she could see that the first rays of the sun were poking above the horizon as she scaled the little hill.

Catching her breath, Olivia slapped her hand on the Colony Stone. She traded the Energy beads Morgan had given her plus the four she'd made before going to bed; the dual-attuned bead, two triple-attuned, and one with all four of her attunements. The store gave her an extra twenty credits for each attunement. She was pretty pleased with that, considering after she'd gotten the hang of it, the beads with four attunements were just as quick to produce. After her sales, she had just over twenty-five hundred credits in the store. She really wanted a magical container like Bronwyn had, so she flipped through the menus to the "containers" category and scrolled down past all the cheap items like sacks, backpacks, barrels, and boxes, and suddenly saw a price jump: Satchel of Spacious Storage—two thousand.

Olivia groaned. She wanted the satchel so much, but it would take all of the money that Morgan had given her. Thinking about it, though, she reasoned Morgan wouldn't want to deal with her lugging around a heavy backpack, would he? She smiled and bought the satchel. After the smoke cleared, she picked it up, a grin spreading from ear to ear. The satchel looked like a messenger bag made from supple leather dyed baby blue. She couldn't have imagined anything better. Olivia hugged the satchel to her chest and then quickly slung it over her shoulder and slapped her hand back on the Colony Stone.

Olivia spent almost all of her remaining credits on food, extra clothes, sturdy boots, a warm cloak, and a tall staff made of a hardwood called Nettlewood. She tossed the rest of her belongings, including her blanket, into her new satchel and then started hustling down the southern road toward the gate. The sky was a pale gray-blue by this point, and she hoped Morgan hadn't left without her. She didn't think he was that type, but the worry still tickled the back of her mind. Sighing, she broke into a trot and then a jog, already glad to have new boots and a satchel to hold all her belongings.

Her worries proved to be unfounded. Morgan was sitting by the side of the gate when she walked up; his eyes were closed, and he was in the lotus position. She was still catching her breath from her jog when he opened his eyes and smoothly stood. "Ready?"

"Good morning!" Olivia straightened up and smiled broadly at him. "Yeah, I'm ready. Were you waiting long?"

"Oh, no. I don't really sleep much anymore, so I did a walk around the walls this morning, and I'd just been sitting here for a little while."

"Well, off we go, then. A grand adventure awaits!" Olivia spoke cheerily and led the way through the gates. As she cleared the tunnel and waved to the guards, she thought about how she'd been so rushed that she hadn't said goodbye to Bronwyn. She glanced over her shoulder at the wall and the gate, almost stopping.

"Everything alright?" Morgan asked, catching a glimpse of her frown.

"Yeah, it's fine. Let's go!" She turned and started walking. Bronwyn had said goodbye at the tavern yesterday. She'd be fine, and a little time to herself was probably just what she needed.

MORGAN

Morgan and Olivia made good time traveling through the southern forest near the colony. Thousands of settlers spending the last week or more foraging and hunting in the woods nearby had created paths and scared away most of the low-level creatures that might pose a threat. That being the case, Morgan set a pretty tough pace, being sure to pause now and then to monitor Olivia's progress. She definitely had a shortage of vitality in comparison to him; he knew it was more than just the stat, but also the way his physical body had been improved through the racial upgrades he'd gotten in the Crucible. Keeping that in mind, when he heard her breathing start to wheeze, he'd pause for a few moments, making a show of taking out a waterskin for a long drink.

Olivia seemed to appreciate the rests, though, to her credit, she never complained about the walking. She kept a cheerful demeanor, and Morgan wondered how much was for show and how much was really her. During one of their breaks, Olivia spoke up: "Hey, you don't seem bothered by my lack of supplies. All I have is this little satchel." She had a grin on her face, and Morgan smiled back.

"Oh, you want me to notice your new magical bag, eh?"

"Haha, you caught me! It's pretty, though, isn't it?" She lifted the baby blue satchel in her hands, showing it off.

"Yeah, it's gorgeous," Morgan said half-mockingly, drawing out the word "gorgeous."

"Okay, okay, maybe not your style, but I love it!" She pulled out a fruit that resembled an orange in shape but had a peel like a banana. She tugged off the tough skin and then split the bright red meat of the fruit in half, offering half to Morgan. He took the offered fruit and sniffed it. It smelled vaguely of citrus, so he bit into it. The flavor exploded in his mouth, like a mix between a strawberry and a lemon, sweet but also a bit sour. It was refreshing, though, so he gobbled his portion.

"Mmm, thanks," he said around his last swallow.

"No problem! We've gotta look out for each other, right?" She winked and started to stretch her thighs by pulling her feet up behind her, one at a time.

"You doing alright? Don't feel like you can't speak up if you want a break. I've already got a class, and it gives me a lot of vitality every level; it's kinda hard for me to tell how tired you might be."

"Yeah, I'm alright. Even though I haven't been working on my vitality, the Energy infusing our bodies sure improves our health. At least, it seems that way to me. Let's keep this pace and see how the day goes." Olivia replied, slapping her hands together. Morgan nodded, and they continued through the woods. By noon, they'd passed out of the territory that hunters and foragers from the colony frequented, and Morgan followed the path of least resistance, winding between clumps of shrubbery and following game paths whenever he could find one.

It felt like they were gradually losing elevation, which made the going easier. Morgan occasionally used his Guardian Senses ability to ensure they were going toward Issa as they hiked. By midafternoon, there was a noticeable difference in the distance to Issa that he "felt." At first, he'd been worried that their southeasterly path would bring them close to the vale where the Yovashi dwelling had been. Morgan, for some reason, dreaded another encounter with the young Yovashi that he'd left alone with a clutch of her mother's eggs.

He grudgingly admitted that he felt some guilt about the whole thing. In fact, that guilt had been part of his reasoning for wanting to solidify his path forward as more of a straightforward fighter. If he were better at fighting and able to face his foes directly, would it have been possible to stand up to those Yovashi in the dwelling and talk to them rather than skulk in the shadows and stab them in the back before they knew he was there? These types of questions tormented him when he let his mind wander back to that place, and he was trying to throw off the foul mood he felt descending when he stepped through a break in the tree line. The sight that confronted him took his breath away, and he heard Olivia gasp softly behind him as she stepped up.

Stretching before them, for as far as Morgan could see, a sea of knee-high purple grass spread forth. Each stalk of purple grass was topped with a bright red flower, about the size of a poppy blossom and similar in shade. The sky was a bit gray with clouds, and the late afternoon sunlight peeking through highlighted the waving sea of red and purple, creating a scene that was almost biblical in its ability to inspire. "Goddamn," Morgan said quietly.

"It's beautiful!" Olivia said, her face flushed with exertion and her words coming between heavy breaths. Morgan looked at her and saw that she was coated with sweat and leaning against a tree trunk, favoring her left foot.

"We should camp here." He reached into his storage ring and brought out the heavy canvas tent he'd bought at the Contribution Store before leaving.

The canvas was dark gray and wrapped around the collapsed wooden tent-poles. He started to unpack it and spent the next few minutes setting it up. Olivia, meanwhile, sat with her back to a tree, pulling off her boots and massaging her feet. She had a few prominent blisters on her heels.

"I'll help in a minute," she said half-heartedly, and Morgan laughed.

"Nah, you're good. Just rest those feet." He paused and took one of the healing potions he'd gotten from the Yovashi dwelling and tossed it to her. "Try rubbing a little of that liquid on your blisters." Then he went back to setting up the tent. It looked like it would hold five people comfortably, so it shouldn't be a problem for him and Olivia.

"Hey, this stuff is great! My blisters are already scabbing over," Olivia called as he started digging a little firepit with the shovel he'd also purchased that morning. Olivia walked over and handed him back the potion, but Morgan held up his hand.

"I've got a few more. Put that in your satchel, there, in case of an emergency."

"Okay, thanks! I'm going to find some dry wood." Olivia walked back into the tree line, scanning the fallen branches for manageable firewood. Morgan stepped a bit farther into the purple and red grassland, pulling his sword from his storage ring. While he waited for Olivia to make the fire, he lost himself in the meditative practice of his forms. He didn't stop until the sky was getting dark, and he noticed the campfire crackling. He stored away his sword and walked back, sitting opposite Olivia. "That was interesting," she said, as she munched on some bread and jam. Morgan wondered where she'd seen jam for sale on the Contribution Store. He suddenly wondered if he'd gone too fast through the menu when he bought his dried meat and mixed nuts with dried fruit.

"Oh, just trying to get better with the sword. I picked up a skill that gave me some kind of fighting style. It's pretty amazing how the System can just plant knowledge in your head. I'm finding that practical use is another matter even with that knowledge. I've already improved a lot with just a few hours of practice."

"Oh, definitely! Also, if you're lucky, you can discover new skills by experimenting. I figured out how to do this by playing with my Energy channels," Olivia replied, as she conjured four different balls of Energy to float above her hand. "The more I play around with them, changing their sizes and patterns, the easier it becomes. I think I'm getting close to increasing my skill level."

Morgan grunted. "Huh, pretty cool." They sat in silence for a while, both of them seeming content to meditate. Morgan, for his part, spent some time practicing his cultivation drill. He'd been at it for a while when Olivia spoke up again:

"Are you cultivating Energy?"

"Yeah, why?"

"I swear, I can feel the Energy moving through the air toward you. That's incredible. I've never sat near someone who cultivated before, so I hadn't ever realized it was a tangible effect. Keep at it; I'm going to do some cultivating also." Morgan didn't reply; he just kept working on pulling Energy in a bit more and a bit faster with each cycle. He lost himself in it and was taken by surprise when a System message appeared.

Congratulations! You have improved your Vortex Core to Base 3.

Morgan stopped meditating, a huge smile on his face. He studied his statistics, trying to see how the new Core level would affect him, but the only change he saw was that he seemed to have gained a full one hundred maximum Energy. He imagined his Core was stronger now, as well, hopefully, able to pull even more Energy at once.

"My Core just leveled," he said across the fire.

"Showoff! Leave some Energy for the rest of us, will you? Hey, speaking of showing off, I managed to make some Energy beads with multiple affinities like the ones you showed me yesterday. I even made one with four."

"No shit? I'd ask you to show me, but my Energy doesn't have any affinity." Morgan stood to stretch. "Well, how about you get some sleep. When you wake, I'll get a few hours. I don't need to sleep as much as I used to." Olivia didn't put up much of an argument and crawled into the tent. She pulled her blankets out of her satchel and wrapped herself up. Morgan noticed her breathing changed after a while, and he surmised she'd drifted into dreams. He stood up, walked away from the fire, and put his back to a tree near the edge of the grassland, watching and listening.

Sometime around midnight, after the fire had burnt down to hot coals, Morgan felt the ground trembling slightly beneath him. He stood up and looked around with wide eyes, trying to see what was causing the sensation. After a moment, the feeling intensified, and then he saw movement out on the plain, hundreds of yards away. A great shadow was crossing on the sea of grass, and at first, Morgan thought it was some sort of gigantic creature, but then he realized it was a herd of something. Morgan couldn't make out the creatures in the dark, but the herd was moving rapidly from northeast to southeast across the plains. He sighed with relief as the mass of creatures kept moving, but then something caught his eye. On the far side of the herd, bobbing lights moved, and he could only guess that people were herding the animals along.

After the shadowy herd of animals moved on and the faint rumble of the ground subsided, Morgan sat back down against the tree and waited for Olivia to wake. Even though she'd gone to sleep fairly early, it was almost dawn when she came crawling out of the tent. Morgan had been tempted to wake her during the early hours after midnight, but he honestly didn't feel very tired. "Hey, good morning. I'm just gonna get a couple of hours of sleep. Then, let's get moving. I saw a herd of something move across the plains in the middle of the night, so keep an eye out in that direction for sure."

"Oh, man"—Olivia yawned—"sorry I slept so much!"

"No worries—you were exhausted." Morgan crawled into the tent and lay down. "Hey, don't let me sleep more than three hours!"

"Alright, don't worry," Olivia replied, fussing with the coals to get the fire going again. Morgan closed his eyes, and it felt like he had just started to fall asleep when he felt someone shaking his foot and heard, "Morgan! It's been around three hours, I think. I need to invent a pocket watch."

They packed up the camp and resumed their journey to the southeast. At first, Morgan debated whether they should stick to the tree cover rather than walk openly through the grassland, but not knowing the area's topography, he didn't want to risk doubling or tripling their journey just to avoid this massive sea of grass. After only thirty minutes of walking through the flowering grass, they came upon the swath of trampled vegetation left behind by the herd of animals Morgan had seen. The trampled grass continued in the exact direction where Morgan could feel Issa.

"We're really out in the open here," Morgan said.

"Yeah, but what can we do? At least we aren't scaling mountains or something; we'll make good time going this way." Olivia shrugged, gesturing toward the sprawling plains in every direction. Morgan nodded, and they kept walking.

After only an hour more of walking, Morgan saw shapes in the distance. They kept moving carefully and trying to stay low in the grass to get a better look, but they'd only made it a few feet when they heard a gruff voice: "You ain't trying to sneak up on our roladii, are ya?"

BRONWYN

Bronwyn stretched her neck and rubbed her temples as she left the tavern. The sun was bright in the clear sky, even this late in the afternoon, and she dearly missed her sunglasses and baseball cap as she attempted to shield her eyes with her hand. She walked down the road toward the Settlement Stone, thinking about the mission she had accepted for the council. She was supposed to start scouting out the Urghat to see where their encampments were, how close to the colony they were, and maybe get a rough estimate of their numbers. She was pretty sure they were somewhere on the other side of the northern plains, but the mountains in the distance were pretty far off, and she would need some supplies if she were going to trek that far.

She walked up the hill toward the stone; it wasn't too crowded at this time of day, and she pressed her hand against its cold surface. She had twelve thousand contribution points to spend but intended to save them up to make more significant purchases down the road. Scrolling through some of the clothing options, she opted to buy a heavy dark blue cloak for twenty points; there had been clouds on the horizon recently, and she didn't want to get caught in a rainstorm without any protection. She also bought some basic parchment and charcoal to make maps and take notes on what she saw. Finally, she bought about two weeks of food, a mix of fresh and dried. She didn't think this trip would take more than a few days, but wanted to be prepared just in case. Altogether, she spent around two hundred points.

Bronwyn tucked her new purchases inside her dimensional pouch, and turned away from the Colony Stone. She looked to the west, where her tent was, and groaned when she saw the bright sun. As she struggled with the glare, she became blissfully aware that her tent was far enough to the west to be in the shadow of the wall, away from the shining orb of death in the sky. She walked down the hill toward her temporary but semi-permanent home, her eyes squinted against the afternoon glare.

When she finally got to her tent, she grabbed a couple of logs from the woodpile and placed them underneath her cooking pot. She quickly had a fire going using some dried grass and her fire starter. She had thought about staying to eat with everyone else at the tavern, but the smell of mead had been thick in the air, and she was doing everything she could to not gag during the meeting. She was bummed about missing out on Maria's cooking, though; it would've been a far sight better than the oatmeal-like gruel she was about to whip up.

Bronwyn had spent very little time honing her cooking talents both on Earth and since arriving on this planet. Her monthly delivery bill for food back home was quite frankly absurd. Her daily meals generally consisted of eggs and a protein shake in the morning. Some kind of meal prep chicken and rice for lunch, and she would order dinner from one of a hundred restaurants in downtown LA.

She was resting her eyes and daydreaming about her favorite taco spot when the acrid smell of burning oatmeal wafted into her face. "Fuck, shit, goddamn, motherfuck!" her long slur of expletives ran together as she lurched forward and pulled the pot off of the fire. She stared down into it and saw a mess of burnt grains caked onto the edges of the pot. She sighed. "This is gonna take forever to clean." She ladled some water into the pot from the barrel she kept by her tent. "Just gonna let you soak for a bit, I guess; I think I'd rather die than scrub anything right now."

Bronwyn sat down in the soft blue grass and leaned back against the log by her fire. She pulled some bread, dried meat, and cheese out of her pouch and made a little sandwich. It was pretty dry without any condiments, but it tasted alright, and she was able to wash it down with some water. When she was done eating, she tossed some water on the fire, took off her boots, and crawled into her tent. She was surprised to find a blissfully snoring Hops laying on his back, his little feet sticking straight up. The sight brought a smile to her face, and she laid down to take just a short nap. Hops, waking briefly when she curled up next to him, made a nest in her long red curls and promptly fell back into a deep slumber.

A few hours later, Bronwyn stretched her arms above her head, waking from her nap. She crawled out of her tent and looked around; the colony's evening activities were in full swing. "Great. Slept so much today, I'll probably be up all night again." Her headache was, thankfully, much improved. Standing up fully, she let out a big yawn. She felt Hops crawl up to her shoulder as she did, reached up to give him a little pat on the head. "What do you say we go for a walk, buddy, stretch our legs and get some fresh air?" She slipped her dark brown leather boots back on and headed down the trail in the direction of the colony center.

Bronwyn walked past dozens of people on the new road; some faces were familiar, others not. However, whether stranger or not, everyone she met eyes with she greeted with a nod or a brief "good evening." Everyone seemed to be in high spirits, and the colony was a buzz of activity around her. It was incredible to think that, just a little over a week ago, they had been hiding in tents, scared of wolves in the forest. With the influx of contribution points from all the colonists, the council had been able to build a new building or two nearly every day. There were many residences, the tavern/brewery, the bathhouse, and the smithy. Many of the roads around the colony had become paved in large cobblestones. The place was beginning to look less like a tent city and more like a small village every day. Bronwyn estimated that there had to be less than a thousand people still staying in their tents; by next week, she doubted there would be any at all. She wasn't sure when she would move into a house of her own. She'd never owned her own house. She went from living on base with her father to renting an apartment when she moved out. She certainly could've afforded a home back on Earth, but it was never really a priority for her.

Bronwyn saw a bright glow in the windows of the smithy, so she stopped and peeked inside as she was going by. She saw a dozen aspiring artificers hammering and heating various metals. Some even looked like they were working on simple blades or linking together chainmail armor. Maybe soon, they'd be able to craft armor and weapons for the colony, and they wouldn't have to rely on the System-controlled shop for all their needs. She wondered if the System took offense to people setting out to make things on their own, did it see them as stealing possible Energy? It didn't matter either way; the colony had to grow and thrive. If it upset the System, they would simply have to deal with the repercussions.

She was rounding the central hill, ready to head back to her tent to do some meditation or cultivation drills, when she heard her name: "Bronwyn!" She looked around, and a big, bearded guy was striding up behind her.

"Yeah?"

"Hey, Bronwyn," he huffed, walking quickly, "wait up a sec!"

"I'm waiting; what is it?" When the large man got closer, Bronwyn could feel Hops retreat from her shoulder back behind her neck, wrapping her hair around himself.

"Oh, hey. I'm Reggie Arnold Gandry-Thule." He reached out a hand, and Bronwyn, wondering what was up with this guy, reached out to shake it. He had a huge hand and a firm grip, but he let go after just a short squeeze. "I'm the top of the leaderboard, you know?"

"Oh, right. I hadn't been paying attention." Bronwyn started to turn, but he reached out to grab her shoulder.

"Hey, wait. I wanted to talk to you about the election."

"What election?"

"You know, for council members."

"Oh, what about it?" Bronwyn didn't even really know what had been said publicly about elections.

"Well, I wanna know when they'll be. The people deserve a voice."

"Oh, they'll be soon, I'm sure. Right now, we have our hands pretty full. You know, imminent Urghat invasion and all."

"Huh? Oh, well, we need to have it soon. The people won't stand for this. We deserve a voice!" He'd clenched his fists, and Bronwyn could see he was holding himself rigid like he was on the verge of losing it.

"Look, I'm not up for an argument right now. I agree that people need a voice. I'll talk to Ballard about it ASAP. Now, I gotta go. Nice to meet you, Reggie." Bronwyn saw his fist unclench a bit, and she turned to walk away.

"You see that you do! I'll be speaking with Ballard, too!" Reggie called after her.

Bronwyn frowned as she walked away from the big man. She wasn't exactly sure what it was, but something about him rubbed her the wrong way. For just a second, when he was clenching his fists, she could swear he was starting to activate some kind of ability; she could feel the Energy around him becoming denser. She didn't find him threatening but was curious if that was his intent. She made a mental note of his name and figured she could ask Arthur about him next time they spoke.

As the night grew darker, she found herself finishing the small circuit she was walking and heading back toward her tent. She inspected her soaking pot when she arrived and saw the still hardened grains caked onto the sides. The situation had barely improved. "Fuck me; I'm just gonna buy a new pot, I think." She mumbled as she prodded at the mess with her finger. "Well, Hops, looks like it's berries for you and dried meat and cheese for me." She produced the spartan meal from her pack and sat down on her log bench, placing ten or so small purplish berries in a pile on the ground.

After the two had finished their snack-dinner, Bronwyn decided to spend a couple of hours working on her Core. She sat on the ground, legs crossed, and placed her hands, palm down, on the dirt and grass. She focused on the deep breathing exercises, feeling the flow of Energy travel out to the palms of her hands, infusing her muscles, and then pulling it back into her Core. Each time she pulled the Energy back, she attempted to gather more from the cold earth below her. She could gradually feel the temperature of the ground rise as the Energy began to suffuse the area, and she siphoned it into herself. Over the course of a couple of hours, she could feel her Core heating as well, not a painful heat like when she created her channels, but like her belly was filling up with warm soup on a cold winter day. It was comforting, and she felt like her Core was trying to expand to hold more and more Energy. She hoped it wouldn't be too long until she managed to upgrade it.

When her Core felt full to bursting, she relaxed and let the Energy slowly bleed out of her. She opened her eyes, stretched, and yawned. Even though she'd slept for most of the day, she was still exhausted. She scooped up an already passed-out Hops and crawled into her tent, quickly falling into a deep sleep.

BRONWYN

It was midmorning when Bronwyn left through the northern gates. She had packed up her belongings, stopped by Olivia's campsite, and found that she'd already left with Morgan. She was a little sad that she didn't get a chance to say goodbye, but she was excited for her. Going to meet a new type of people, essentially making first contact with an alien society, sounded pretty damn exciting. Bronwyn had her task, though; she needed to find out more about these Urghat, where they were, and what kind of numbers they had. She was also hesitantly excited about some plans she had thought of involving her new title of "Underclaw" and what she could maybe do with it. She'd have to find the right opportunity, though. For now, she tightened the straps on her backpack, waved goodbye to the guards, and started jogging out into the open fields.

With all the points she'd invested in agility, her jog was starting to feel more and more like a sprint. She loved the feeling of the wind blowing against her face as she ran, her hair blowing back behind her, though Hops was less of a fan and ducked inside of her backpack whenever she was running. Bronwyn had run plenty back on Earth, but a treadmill in her apartment or the gym didn't stack up to the feeling of pounding over the plains with beautiful vistas all around her.

She had been traveling for quite a while when she came upon the large stone pillar in the field—the site where she had dueled Bloodfang. Bronwyn slowed down as she approached the pillar, looking out for any signs of Urghat. She walked to where she had laid the body of Bloodfang. The two dead boyii hounds were still there, little more than skeletons picked clean by scavengers, but there were no signs of the Urghat pack master or Bloodfang. Someone had retrieved their bodies. She activated her tracking skill and found faint footprints leading away from the site. She followed them for a few meters to the northwest, and a small gray window popped up in her view: Urghat. She smiled at her discovery and began to follow the tracks.

The tracks were difficult to follow in the dense grass of the plains, and she lost them and backtracked a number of times. She followed them for about five miles when she saw a handful of faint smoke trails rising into the sky from behind a large hill. She crouched low in the grass and slowly started making her way up toward a large, half-buried boulder at the apex. She put her back to the stone and peeked her head around it. She saw the ruins of a small village, about a dozen stone buildings surrounding a central square. Twenty to thirty completely dilapidated structures were spread out to the north. Inside the ruins, she saw what had to be close to thirty Urghat going in and out of buildings, cooking at the fires, and practicing combat drills.

She crouched down behind the boulder and started drawing a map of the route she'd taken, a few distinguishing landmarks, and a more detailed drawing of the inside of the encampment. She pulled away from the stone to take one last look at the camp, making sure she had all the details right. She couldn't fight this alone and would need to come back with some help. She tucked her crude map and charcoal into her pouch and began to turn away when she felt the sharp edge of a blade press against her neck.

"Well, well, what do we have here, a li'l spy taking notes?" A harsh raspy voice whispered from behind her, breath hot on the back of her neck. "Wonder if I should kill you here or let the boys get some information out of ya first."

Bronwyn raised her hands in front of her and started to speak, but the knife's pressure immediately disappeared, and she could hear the speaker scrambling backward.

"M-my apologies, Underclaw. Please, please forgive me. I had no idea, I swear it. I have no intention of making a claim." His voice sounded panicked, and when Bronwyn turned around, he dropped the knife, his eyes transfixed on the band around her arm.

"What's your name?" Bronwyn stood at her full height, puffing out her chest and trying to seem as intimidating as possible.

"Umberpaws." He looked down when he spoke and hesitated for a moment before continuing. "Please, I meant no disrespect; I have four cubs at home. I would never mean to challenge an Underclaw. I-I can give you information. You're not Urghat; you must have questions!" The Urghat was practically begging her at this point, his brow furrowed, and his hands clasped together.

"Stand up, Umberpaws. I have no intention of killing in cold blood. However, I do have many questions, and I would appreciate you telling me what you know. For starters, what does it mean to be an Underclaw? Who am I under? Also, why didn't you just kill me while you had that knife to my throat?" Bronwyn led Umberpaws around behind the boulder so that they might talk fully out of sight from the ruins. She sat down and motioned for him to do the same.

Umberpaws followed Bronwyn and sat himself in the grass across from her. He still had a concerned look on his face as his gaze met her eyes for the first time. "To be an Underclaw is an honor and also a threat to one's self-preservation. You have the right to lead any Urghat who would follow you. However, once a day, any Urghat who feels as though he or she is deserving of your station may challenge you to single combat. This combat is always fought to the death. So, anyone who challenges you needs to be sure of winning." He paused for a moment, sighing. "Had I killed you just now, ran my blade across your neck, that armband you wear would have turned to onyx and wrapped around my neck; I would be branded a coward and exiled by my own people. This is also why I swore that I did not wish to challenge you; I would have no hopes of winning a fair fight against the one who bested Bloodfang."

He looked deep into Bronwyn's eyes before continuing. "Yes, we know of you, Blodwyn. Underclaw Bloodfang sent a sparii carrying news of his quest and his impending duel back to camp. Many Urghat will be after your title now; outsiders do not keep it long. If you manage to live, and, more so, if you manage to get other Urghat to follow you, your title will grow in power. What else do you wish to know? I want to help, but I cannot tell you anything that would betray the trust of my own lord."

Bronwyn sat there for a moment, thinking. "You've been very helpful, Umberpaws. There are a couple of questions I'd like to ask. I don't think they are compromising in any way. What would happen to me if I were to walk into that camp down there? You also mentioned convincing other Urghat to follow me; how could an outsider possibly do that?"

Umberpaws scratched at his chin as he pondered the questions. "If you walked into that camp this very instant, I doubt they would do anything. Any of them that challenged you, and mind, it could only be one a day, would be committing suicide. I suppose they would undoubtedly send word of your arrival to the other Underclaw and possibly to Overclaw Spineripper. They would not be openly hostile and would allow you to rest at their camp, I'm sure. If you, however, were to attack the camp and start a conflict, they could all defend themselves honorably without risk of being made outcasts. An Underclaw outsider is a tricky situation and one that happens very, very rarely."

Umberpaws was deep in thought for a moment, his eyes staring off into space. "Tricky situation indeed." He refocused on Bronwyn. "On the question of how you would get Urghat to follow you? I haven't the slightest idea." He let out a barking laugh. "I suppose you prove your worth in battle and try to get them to follow you that way. Though convincing new unsworn warriors to follow you over any other Underclaw would be exceedingly difficult, I would imagine." He shrugged his hairy shoulders and held his hands upward.

Bronwyn chuckled with him. "Hah, I suppose following an outsider would be quite the rebellious choice to make." She held her hand out toward him. "Well, Umberpaws, I thank you for your honesty, even if it was out of some sense of duty or self-preservation. I don't suppose you want to walk into camp with the outsider Underclaw, so why don't we part ways here, and maybe I'll see you down there. If I'm feeling risky, anyway." She laughed again and grinned at the large beast-man in front of her.

Umberpaws bypassed her hand and grasped her forearm, so she did the same. "I hope the Urghat that ends you does it quickly, Underclaw. Thank you again for sparing me; I won't partake in your flesh if you die here." He let go of her arm and nodded one last time before heading down the hill toward the ruins.

Bronwyn waited behind the big, knobby boulder for a while after the Urghat left her. She spent some time reflecting on what she'd learned and how it might affect her mission going forward. If the Urghat really couldn't fight her, except once per day, it almost gave her free reign of the area and the ability simply to walk through all their camps unimpeded. However, her fight with Bloodfang had not been easy, she had barely won in the end, and there were undoubtedly Urghat more fearsome than he. She felt safe, well at least, somewhat safe, entering the camp down the hill from her; Umberpaws had seemed confident that none of the Urghat down there would pose a threat to her, even if one did make a challenge.

She slipped off her backpack and set it down in front of her, pulling the top open wide and peering inside. "You okay, buddy? I know you're not the biggest fan of these guys." She reached down in the pack and scooped Hops up in her hand; he peered up at her, poking his head out of his shell. "I'm gonna be heading down into that camp, but don't worry, I won't let any of them see you. Let's have a little lunch first, though." She set Hops down on her lap and retrieved some dried fruits and cured meats from her pouch. She also handed Hops a small handful of nuts and berries. Hops sat happily in her lap as they ate, the sun high in the sky and the grass soft beneath them.

"You all done eating, cutie?" She smiled at him as he turned around to reveal a blue-stained face and bulging cheeks. Hops finished his mouthful and chirped up at her happily. "You wanna ride in the backpack again or up on my shoulder? I won't let anyone hurt you, either way, I promise." Hops looked like he was thinking about climbing up on her shoulder for a moment, but then he hopped off her lap, diving into the opening of the backpack. Bronwyn chuckled. "No worries, buddy, I understand; they can be pretty scary sometimes." She slung the straps of the backpack over her shoulders and dusted off her pants.

As she turned the corner around the boulder, she noticed a glint in the grass beside her and knelt to examine it. Umberpaws had never retrieved the knife he'd dropped; the blade was made of some sort of stone, perhaps obsidian. The edge was sharper than glass, and golden runes floated inside it like it was filled with liquid. The hilt was made of dark wood and wrapped with white leather. She slipped it into her pouch—maybe she'd meet the wiry Urghat again, and she could return it.

Bronwyn took a deep breath, straightened her shoulders, and walked down the grassy slope to the Urghat camp below.

OLIVIA

Olivia's heart jumped into her throat, and she whirled around, looking for the source of the voice. A rather short, blue-skinned man stood off to her left, about twenty feet away. He held a bow with an arrow on the string but pointed it to the ground. The most striking aspect of his appearance was the shockingly bright orange color of his mohawk and beard. Olivia noticed that Morgan had spotted the man and was edging his way in front of her to face him. At first, she bristled a little; she didn't like people thinking she needed protecting, but then she relaxed, knowing he wasn't trying to be overbearing. Morgan just had that personality.

"Uh, hello," Morgan said. "No, to be honest, we don't know what a roladii is." He shrugged, showing his hands were empty.

"I'm Olivia, and this is my friend, Morgan," Olivia spoke up. "It's nice to meet you, stranger." She preferred to lead new encounters with an offensive of charm.

"Huh, well-met, then. I'm Teric." He relaxed his bow even more and whistled in a strange imitation of a birdcall. Around them, in the grass, five more blue-skinned men stood up, also holding bows. "Forgive our caution, but you are strange to us and are coming from the direction of the Gresh Woods, where Yovashi are rumored to lurk."

"Our people live northwest of here, beyond those woods. We're humans and new to this world. I've met some of your people, though, Teric. In fact, we're journeying to visit a friend of mine; she lives in a village or town called Tarn's Crossing."

"I know of Tarn's Crossing. Roylo, there, is from that place." He gestured to one of the other men who had stood up, and he trotted forward, his long, white ponytail trailing behind him. "What's the name of the friend you are going to visit?" His eyebrows drew together, almost like he anticipated Morgan being unable to answer.

"Her name is Issa. We met in the Crucible." Morgan turned to face Roylo, offering his hand. "I don't know much more about her family or clan, but she told me her father is an Artisan." Roylo, his face vacant of expression at first, suddenly smiled and stepped forward to take Morgan's hand.

"I know of Issa! The little welp has gone to the Crucible? And she's made it out?" When he smiled, his sharp teeth startled Olivia at first, but she saw that they didn't extend past his canines—his dentition was suited to an omnivorous diet.

"That's right!" Morgan smiled. "She and I went through a lot together, and she saved my ass a few times." All of the Ardeni were closing in now, their bows hanging loosely in their hands, their arrows stowed away. Smiles and handshakes were exchanged, and Olivia did her best to remember all of their names: Roylo, Teric, Allender, Beyli, Dranil, and Forn. She found the varied, bright coloration of their hair fascinating but didn't want to make a fool of herself by asking about it.

The Ardeni invited Morgan and Olivia to follow them for the rest of the morning and then join them at camp. It turned out they'd pushed the herd through the night to avoid camping near the Gresh Woods and were planning to continue for a few more hours and then take a day to rest. When they drew near the herd, the first thing Olivia noticed was the smell. The closer they got to the large shapes moving in the distance, the more Olivia started to catch a musty scent that reminded her decidedly of the cages where they'd kept animals for research at her first job with Yang Corp. She started paying more attention to the trampled grass, looking for droppings, and it didn't take long for her to see a scatter of round pellets about the size of golf balls.

"Are those droppings from your roladii?" She asked Forn, who was walking closest to her.

"That's right. They eat the grass as they go and shit it out a bit later." He laughed like he'd said something particularly funny.

"Do you have more herdsmen watching them?" Olivia couldn't help her curiosity.

"Naw, when Teric saw you two coming up behind us, he signaled a wait 'n see. Those lazy birds will just wander and eat 'til we get 'em moving again." He spat a stream of brown saliva into the grass as he spoke. Olivia hoped he had something like tobacco in his mouth and didn't have some sort of an illness. They grew close enough to the herd for Olivia to start making out details about the roladii. They were about the size of a small horse or a big pony, but they only had two sturdy legs. They reminded her of a cross between a monitor lizard and an ostrich, a very colorful ostrich.

As they came closer, Olivia's initial impression refined; the roladii had thick rear legs with sturdy three-toed feet. Their bodies had plumage, but they weren't the bodies of birds, more like fat, round lizards. The bright feathers were more like a mane that surrounded their necks and ran down the center of their backs. She could see that the roladii had small, vestigial forelegs, not unlike the T. rex on Earth. The comparison ended there; these creatures were not at all fearsome, having placid eyes and wide mouths filled with flat teeth.

The Ardeni each started calling out with a high-pitched, quick-paced whistling sound, and some roladii that had been mingling with the rest of the herd ran toward them. Olivia was impressed to see that the five roladii came running to the individual Ardeni like they could tell which was making which whistling sound. She presumed that the sounds must be a bit distinctive. She was standing closest to Forn still, so she got a good look at his roladii—as it came trotting up, she saw that its head was a good seven feet off the ground, but the bulk of its body, below the longish neck, was only at the level of her chest. The musty smell was thick in the air as it leaned down with a huff, eating something out of Forn's hand.

Forn grabbed the leather rein strapped to its head and climbed up on the thin leather saddle fastened around the beast's belly. Olivia looked around and saw that the other Ardeni were similarly mounting up. Teric called out, "You two want to ride with us? You're welcome, but you can just walk behind if you would rather. We'll probably make it to our campground a couple of hours ahead of you."

Olivia looked to Morgan, and he shrugged. She was very curious about what it was like to ride the creatures, but she had to admit to some trepidation. She had never ridden an animal in her life, and these men were total strangers. Still, she wanted to! She looked at Morgan again, held up her thumb, and then said, "Which of you can I ride with?" Forn laughed and held out a hand to her, and she grasped it. His hand was roughly calloused, but he carefully pulled her up behind him after she placed a foot in the stirrup he'd pulled his foot out of. Once she was firmly on the soft leather saddle and had her hand around his waist, he urged the roladii around and gently twitched the reins, making another distinctive whistling sound.

The roladii rumbled forward, taking long easy steps. Its big legs absorbed a lot of the shock, but Olivia still felt it sharply on her tailbone, so she leaned forward a little bit, trying to spread her weight more evenly. She looked around and saw that Morgan was riding behind Roylo; he had a huge smile plastered to his face as they picked up speed and started spreading out around the herd. From the vantage of the saddle, Olivia had a better view of the herd and realized there must be more than a thousand roladii spread out over the grass. They all started to move in the direction the six mounted Ardeni urged them. It was like a slow-motion wave of movement—they all seemed to take the cue from the roladii nearest them and spread the word, and soon the whole herd was bounding over the grass. Olivia laughed with the freeing feeling of the wind blowing through her hair, the beautiful grasslands moving by in a blur. Forn looked back at her and smiled, then urged the roladii to go even faster.

"How far are we going to go?" Olivia shouted over the noise of the rumbling herd after some time had passed. Her butt was getting very sore, and the exhilaration of the ride had worn off a bit.

"Only another ten miles or so. Shouldn't take too long. Here, use the stirrups to stand up a bit, to rest your ass." Forn laughed and took his feet out of the stirrups. Olivia's face reddened a little, but she did as he suggested, sliding her feet into the stirrups and pushing up with her thighs. The pressure on her tailbone was relieved, and she sighed. "Good, now use the rhythm of the roladii, relax your legs when she goes down and push up when she rises; that will help you keep from bouncing on your butt!" He laughed again, somehow immune to the bouncing percussion of the beast's steps, even without the stirrups.

For the next half an hour or so, Olivia practiced what Forn had told her to do. She also took advantage of having him in front of her, using his shoulders to help move herself up and down with the rhythm of the mount's gait. She felt like she was getting the hang of it when Forn whistled and clicked his tongue, causing the beast to slow down. She looked up and saw that the herd had spread out like a V, splitting around a long, thatch and adobe-style brick building. Forn slowed his mount and rode it up to the building while the herd passed it by. The unmounted roladii also were slowing, no longer feeling the pressure of the herders. "This is where we'll spend the next day; it's our mid-drive way station," Forn said, as he slipped out of the saddle. He held a hand up to Olivia, and she took it, sliding stiffly out of the saddle. She stumbled and walked like an old grandma around in a big circle, trying to get her legs to work correctly again. Forn and the others chuckled and gave each other knowing glances.

"Oh, my legs! My ass!" Morgan groaned as he too stumbled around, half crouched over.

"Ugh! I'm glad it's not just me! Even you with your Adonis body can feel it!" Olivia laughed as she slowly straightened her back.

"Everyone feels it after their first roladii ride!" Teric laughed, and the other Ardeni joined in. As Morgan and Olivia walked around, getting the feeling back into their numb body parts, the Ardeni took the tack off their mounts and swatted their butts. The roladii ran off to join the herd, eating grass and milling about.

"Don't you worry your mounts won't come back?" Olivia asked.

"Naw, they know better. They're well tamed." Teric spat a stream of brown juice.

"You chewing tobacco or something?" Morgan asked. Olivia cringed; she had wanted to ask but thought it would be rude.

"Tobacco? Not sure what that is, but I'm chewing yiil weed. You want some?" Teric produced a square, brass-colored tin and held it out to Morgan. Morgan shrugged and took it, popping open the lid. Olivia leaned close to see what it contained and saw a dry, brown, leafy substance. To her admittedly inexperienced eye, it looked like tobacco. Morgan lifted it to his nose and took a sniff, shook his head, and handed the tin to Olivia. She sniffed it and caught a strong whiff of an eye-watering, pungently spicy odor. Holding the tin away from her face, she sneezed violently. Teric laughed heartily and took his container back from her. "Bah, soft!"

"So, this is your campsite?" Morgan asked, looking around.

"Aye, we move the herd up and down the Chebli Sea a few times a year. We like to give the chebli blossoms a chance to bloom and propagate during each growing season, so we alternate where the herds will feed." The Ardeni who spoke was Allender, and it was the first time Olivia had heard him. His voice was mellow, and he spoke in a slow cadence like he was thinking about each word before he said it. Olivia looked at him and marveled at how his bright yellow eyes matched his yellow hair. She looked out over the herd of roladii and took note of their variously colored plumage again.

"It seems that bright colors are pretty common among the inhabitants of your world," she said before she could stop herself.

"Oh, aye, the plants be brightly colored, too. Makes for good hiding, I suppose," Forn said, not at all bothered by her comment.

"Well, let's get camp set up. Morgan, we'll be heading out the day after tomorrow, and you two are welcome to travel with us as far as the Rill Catcher. We'll be moving west from there, but you can follow it east to Tarn's Crossing." Teric gestured to the longhouse as he spoke.

"Is that the name of a river?" Olivia asked, just a little annoyed that Teric was treating Morgan like their leader. Could he tell that Morgan was a higher level than she?

"Oh, aye, biggest river in thousands of miles. What about you, Miss Olivia? You think you can tame a roladii before we leave?" He smiled at her with brown-stained teeth, and Olivia couldn't help but smile back.

◈ MORGAN ◈

Morgan was watching the Ardeni herders as they played a game that was remarkably like horseshoes. They had three stakes in a triangle outside their longhouse, and one Ardeni would stand at each stake, trying to throw loops over the other two. It seemed like there was some allowance for blocking your opponents' rings, but only on certain throws. Morgan tried to figure out the rules for a while, but they also hollered out strange phrases like "Red outside," and it seemed to affect where the others were allowed to throw on the next round. Morgan couldn't figure it out, so he shook his head and wandered around the side of the building where Allender was grilling a large haunch of meat over a stone fire pit.

"Smells good," he said, walking up to the yellow-haired man.

"Oh, aye, roladii good for riding and good for eating," he replied in that slow, measured way of his. He grinned as he spoke, slicing off a bit of meat. He cut it in half, popping one portion in his mouth and handing the other to Morgan. His mouth watering from the odor, Morgan didn't hesitate, following suit. The coppery tang of red meat accentuated by the salty rub the Ardeni had used to season it only served to make Morgan's stomach grumble all the louder.

"Good, but don't you feel bad about eating your mounts?"

"Pshaw, we won't eat our mounts. We eat the older, untrained roladii. Never enough to endanger the herd." Allender looked at Morgan like he was an idiot, but then he took in Morgan's strange appearance, and his countenance softened. "But you wouldn't know that, being new here. You should go join Teric and your companion. Pick a roladii to tame." Morgan looked around, startled.

"Did they start that already? I thought Olivia was napping!"

"Oh, she came out a few minutes ago, said she couldn't sleep, and Teric took her to the herd. They're just a bit south, over that rise." Allender gestured past the other end of the longhouse.

"Alright, thanks," Morgan said as he started walking that way. He was a little annoyed that Teric hadn't called him to join them, but then, he hardly knew these people. Suddenly Morgan had a surge of panic. They really didn't know these people! What if Teric meant some harm to Olivia? He quickened his pace, jogging up the low rise. He could already see some of the herd, and he scanned furiously from right to left, then he heard a high-pitched laugh and saw Olivia. She was sitting in the grass; one of the roladii had its face close to hers, and Morgan could see its big, fat, gray-pink tongue dripping saliva all over her. Teric was standing off to the side, laughing.

Morgan's heart stopped racing, and he felt rather foolish. The Crucible and the System had turned him a bit paranoid, maybe. It seemed like it might still be possible to meet plain-old good people. He strolled up to the duo as Teric helped Olivia to her feet. "Hey, I think that one likes you, Olivia!"

"Oh my God! Teric gave me a treat to feed it, and the bugger really liked it!" Olivia's face was red from laughing.

"Oh aye, they love tuntun root. It's how to make friends with one, and then you just keep being friendly with it, and if you're lucky, the System will give you the basic taming skill."

"Really? Does it take a lot of luck, or does the System eventually give it to pretty much anyone? I'm asking because I can't figure out why I got some skills when I got here, and I didn't get others." Morgan hadn't intended to turn this into a lesson about the System, but the idea of learning "taming" by being friendly with a roladii just got his mind working.

"You folks really are that new to the System? Huh, well, the way the System gives you skills is based on some factors. You definitely learn skills faster when you're below the level to take a class. You also learn skills faster if you feel like you need the skill while trying to do it. You really need to feel it. Do you get me? Some people have an innate aptitude for some skills. No other way to explain it; we're all unique. Hmm, of course, you can learn skills directly by buying skill scrolls and the like." Teric spat another long stream of brown saliva, and, grinning at Olivia, he took out his tin and put some more brown powder in his cheek.

"He already explained it to me, Morgan! Just because you're late to class, you shouldn't make him repeat himself!" Olivia winked at Morgan while speaking, laughing. She was such an upbeat person. The way the scar on her eye crinkled when she laughed was endearing, and Morgan felt happy that she was traveling with him, though sometimes he wondered if that positive energy was a little forced.

"Alright, alright, you coulda warned me that class was starting." Morgan chuckled.

"Ha, okay, students!" Teric played along. "Olivia take that root I gave you and pull that little blue-feathered bugger over by the longhouse, and be sure to talk real nice to it while you give it treats. Try to make it follow you around in circles and start and stop 'fore giving it a treat." He gestured toward the longhouse. "Morgan, let's pick you a bird. Follow me."

"Are they? Birds?" Olivia asked, backing carefully away with the blue-feathered roladii in tow, sniffing at her closed hand.

"Hmm. Nar, but they have feathers! We call 'em birds to be funny sometimes, I guess." Teric shrugged, gesturing for Morgan to follow him. Morgan nodded, following Teric in among the herd. They seemed very placid and not at all skittish.

"How do you tell the males from females?"

"See that guy there? With the little crest of feathers on his head? That's a male; the females have longer feathers on the tail end." Teric spoke in such a way that Morgan wasn't sure if he was messing with him. He looked around, and true, only about half the birds had little crests on their heads, and the ones without it did seem to have longer tail feathers. Morgan shrugged and followed as Teric looked closely at one roladii and then another. Finally, he settled on a fairly large roladii with gray and yellow plumage. "This fella is pretty young still, has lots of running left in him. Big enough for a big guy like you, too." Morgan stepped up to the roladii and started to reach out a hand. "Hold on, now. Let me give you some of these roots. Just give him one nibble at a time, and lead him back over by the longhouse away from the herd." Teric reached into a little sack that Morgan was pretty sure was a dimensional container and pulled out a big handful of tiny cubes of the tuber. He handed it to Morgan. "Keep one piece in your feeding hand and the others closed up in your other hand behind your back."

"This is called tuntun root?" Morgan asked, following Teric's instructions. Teric nodded, and Morgan cautiously held out one little bit of root to the big roladii. Its wide, flat muzzle huffed air out, and it used its big, pudgy tongue to scoop the root out of his palm. Morgan reached behind his back and slipped another little piece of root into his hand, holding it out to the roladii and backing away toward the longhouse. He repeated this process a few times and was almost to the flat area around the longhouse when Teric called out to him.

"Remember what I told Olivia! Make him work for the root!"

"Right, right," Morgan said, smiling. He used the root's scent to get the roladii to bob its head up and down and follow him around in a circle. After that, Morgan held the root close to the ground, so the roladii had to lean down and forward, then he backed up slowly, and the roladii scooted after it, its long neck and chin an inch from the ground. Morgan smiled and gave it the treat. "Good boy!"

The roladii wasn't hostile at all, but it resisted doing anything without a treat to encourage it. Morgan spent the next hour working with it, Teric eventually giving him several large handfuls of tuntun root to keep in his own storage pouch. Morgan was pretty sure he did the same for Olivia. He felt like he was making progress, getting the beast to grunt with pleasure as he scratched its wrinkled gray skin above its eyebrows. Morgan enjoyed looking into the glossy depths of its amber flecked eyes, finding them to be quite expressive. He felt good about the connection he was starting to establish with the beast until Olivia shouted out, "Yes! I got the skill!"

"Really? In one afternoon? Showoff!" He groused. Teric heard him and laughed.

"Well, it happened shortly after I gave him a name. Isn't that right, Blue? Try naming yours, Morgan!"

"Blue? How imaginative!" Morgan led his roladii a bit farther away, so no one else could hear him talking to it. "Let's see; you've got yellow and gray feathers. I'm not going to name you after a color, though; Olivia will say I'm copying her. Hmm, are you fast? Should I call you something like Lightning?" The roladii grunted. Morgan fed it another piece of root, and the roladii gobbled it into its seemingly bottomless gullet. "You sure munch these down, don't you? How about Munch? You like that name?" The roladii grunted, sniffing at his hand. "Good boy, Munch."

Morgan worked with Munch for another hour, and then the herders called them in for the evening meal. Teric gave him and Olivia a long length of rope to keep their roladii-in-training away from the rest of the herd. He said it helped in the process of taming them. Then Morgan and Olivia joined the rest of them sitting on some low wooden benches around the firepit. They ate a satisfying meal of seasoned meat and roasted root vegetables that reminded Morgan of sweet potatoes. The sun was going down, and the orange-red highlights on the sea of purple grass and red chebli blossoms filled Morgan with a calm wonder at the beauty of this world.

"What a beautiful view!" He gestured to the sunset.

"Oh, yes—we tend to take it for granted, being out here all the time," Teric replied, producing a stack of short glasses and a bottle of light-brown liquid. "How about a drink to celebrate our guests?" He asked the group, and all the herders enthusiastically agreed. Teric lined the little glasses up on an empty bench and poured a generous helping of the liquor into each one, then he took his time, handing a glass to each person sitting around the fire. Morgan took his drink and gave it a good sniff. It reminded him distinctly of whiskey, and his mouth started to salivate.

Teric held his glass aloft, and the herders did as well. Morgan and Olivia took the hint and lifted their glasses. Teric said loudly and rhythmically, "Bordu, bordu, bordu," and then the herdsmen, in unison, loudly chanted, "HEY!" Then they all took a deep drink of their liquor, and Morgan, without hesitation, did as well. It burned a little going down, but it was surprisingly smooth. Olivia sputtered a little, but her cheeks were red, and she bore a huge smile.

"Cheers!" Morgan said, and Olivia echoed him. The herdsman looked around at each other, then they all said "cheers" as well, and the whole group downed another drink.

"So, your people are from another world, huh? Tell us the story!" Forn said. Morgan looked at Olivia and shrugged. She smiled and started the tale, talking about Earth and their Arkship and how the System brought them down to the planet. Morgan interjected now and then, and when she was finished, he told the tale of his time in the Crucible, leaving out most everything other than the highlights.

Morgan had a warm buzz going from the glass of liquor Teric had given him, and the camaraderie around the fire made him feel relaxed to the extent that he almost dreaded getting back on the trail. He was glad that the herders would be staying here an extra day. "Hey, Teric, what's that liquor called?"

"Oh, that's cheb-cheb. It's distilled from the seeds of these chebli blossoms. It's a pretty long process, but if you ever visit my ranch, I'll show you how." He smiled and produced another full bottle of the liquor, handing it to Morgan. "For a rainy day." Morgan smiled broadly.

"Thank you, my friend. I wish I had some good Kentucky bourbon to share with you. If I can find something like corn here, I will reverse engineer it. I swear!" Teric smiled as if he knew what Morgan was talking about and sat back, staring up at the stars.

"We're having problems with Urghat near our settlement. That's one of the reasons we're going to visit Morgan's friend. We're hoping to get some help—do you think that's likely?" Olivia spoke up, suddenly serious.

"Depends on what's going on with Tarn's Crossing," Roylo spoke up. "If they have a fight going of their own, they'll be less likely to spare some hunters. They often have conflicts with the Urghat from the Deep Down. If nothing is going on, though, they'll probably send a couple of hundred hunters, if only for the combat experience and Energy gains."

"That would be great!" Morgan chimed in. "We just need some help keeping our foothold secure while we learn the ropes of the System and levels and classes, and . . ." he trailed off, finding it exhausting to list all the things they had to come to grips with.

"More allies are always good," Beyli added in a hushed voice. Morgan realized it was the first time he'd heard the magenta-haired little Ardeni speak.

"Ya, right! Let's drink to that!" Teric walked around with his bottle of cheb-cheb, and Morgan felt the warm glow in his stomach start to expand.

MORGAN

After spending a few more hours drinking and swapping stories, the herders and Morgan and Olivia retired to the longhouse to sleep. The air was warm in the low-ceilinged building because one of the hunters had lit a central hearth earlier in the day. By now, it was down to coals, but plenty of residual heat persisted. Morgan and Olivia were given bunks near the far end of the longhouse, while the herders took positions more near the doors. Morgan had a good buzz going by this point and sort of just fell into his bunk.

He woke to find himself the only occupant of the dim longhouse. The only light was streaming through the opening where the central hearth vented its smoke. He stood, stretching, and was relieved to find he didn't have any sort of a headache or hangover. Apparently, his vitality was good for something! Yawning, Morgan walked out the door on the west side of the building and saw that two of the herders were sitting by the firepit eating something that looked a lot like oatmeal. "Morning."

"Hah, he wakes!" Forn smiled up at him and gestured to a bench. Morgan sat and accepted the bowl of warm mush that Beyli handed him. He used the wooden spoon to take a bite and found that it was a slightly salty mix of grains and milk. It hit the spot, and he wolfed it down.

"Olivia already working with her roladii?"

"Aye, she'll be riding that thing before the day's over. You better get to work, or you'll be bouncing behind one of us again tomorrow!" Forn's grin illustrated his love of teasing.

"Right." Morgan stood up and stretched one more time, taking in the wonderfully crisp, clean air, then wandered over to where he'd staked Munch. He found the roladii nearly at the extent of its rope, quietly munching on some grass. "I definitely gave you the right name, Munch." Morgan grinned and pulled some tuntun root from his pouch. "C'mere, boy!" Munch looked up at his voice and then trotted over to him, snuffing the tuber up into his wide mouth.

Congratulations! You have learned the skill Animal Taming—Basic

"Haha!" Morgan laughed. "I guess I just needed to sleep on it!" He scratched Munch's head affectionately. At first, Morgan thought the skill was just a label for what he'd already learned from Teric, but he found that he understood a few things that he hadn't before. Somehow, he knew how to make little whistles that appealed to the roladii, and he instinctively knew where it would like to have him scratch and how to avoid threatening the creature. "Oh, good boy, this is going to be easy, isn't it?" Morgan slipped him another root slice, then began to work in earnest.

After a couple of hours working with Munch, Morgan could reliably get the roladii to come to him with a whistle, even without a slice of tuntun. He still gave him treats often but reduced the frequency gradually. He ran into Olivia while walking around, getting Munch to follow him, and saw that she had made similar progress. They played a little game where they had their two roladii wait while they walked away, and then they each called their mounts individually with a whistle. Morgan was amazed that the roladii easily distinguished the calls. Munch ignored Olivia completely, and Blue did the same to Morgan.

Teric saw them and called them over to the longhouse. When they walked up, their roladii in tow, he said, "We all pitched in some spare gear to make you two a mismatched set of riding tack. Time to move to the next part of the training!"

"Oh, that's very kind, Teric!" Olivia said.

"Naw, it ain't too kind. This is all on loan to get ya up to the Rill Catcher with us. Unless you got something to trade, I'm afraid we can't let ya keep these buggers." He shrugged, his face indicating he really didn't have a choice. Morgan thought about how he was bonding with Munch and didn't want to have to leave him when they got to the river. He could see Olivia's crestfallen expression, also.

"Well, of course, we shouldn't presume you could give up two valuable animals," Olivia said, though her voice had lost its joyful ring.

"Hold on, now," Morgan said, "of course, we'll pay you for them. What kinda trade are you looking for, friend?"

"Oh, hmm." A twinkle appeared in Teric's eye as he spoke. "Well, since you did the hard work of the training, I'd say twenty Energy beads per mount."

"Oh really? So much?" Morgan was smiling inwardly; he could easily afford the mounts. "Doesn't it take someone nearly a full day's work to make an Energy bead?"

"Well, yes, but that's just the average person. Some people make 'em a lot faster, and, by the way, I'm cutting you a real deal here, friend. I can get that price easy if I run some of these birds to town!" Teric took on an offended expression, but Morgan could see it was just for show.

"Alright, alright. How about attuned beads? Or better yet, double attuned?" Morgan didn't want to alienate him with his haggling.

"Well, well, hmm." Teric stroked his chin. "Ten per mount, and I'll throw in the riding tack!" Morgan held out his hand to shake, and both men smiled as they gripped each others' hands. Olivia looked on with a smile of her own, stroking Blue's feathery neck.

They spent the next hour working with Teric to learn how to attach the harness and reins and saddle the roladii properly. The creatures were so naturally docile, especially with people with the Animal Taming skill, that a bit wasn't necessary. Morgan had been worried that his first attempts to ride the animal would result in lots of bucking and maybe some broken bones. However, the animal only acted skittish for a few moments, and then, when he clicked his tongue and whistled instinctively, the animal calmed down and started responding to his directions.

Once Morgan and Olivia were mounted and moving around, Teric told them to ride a bit farther south where the herd was and get their mounts to drink from a pond there. Morgan was chagrined to think he'd had his mount tied up and busy training for a full day without water, but Teric said it was normal—the animals didn't drink very often, getting much of their water needs from the rich grass. He and Olivia did as they were told, then spent the afternoon riding, trying to get a feel for the proper rhythm of rising in and out of the saddle with the roladii's gait. By the time the evening meal came around, they felt that they'd made some good progress, but their butts were still quite sore.

The group spent the evening much as they did the first night at the lodge, but Teric only gave everyone one glass of his liquor; he said that they'd be riding out early in the morning so that they could cover the eighteen miles to the next watering hole. Morgan and Olivia, both exhausted, collapsed into their bunks, and Morgan felt like he'd just closed his eyes when he heard Teric whistling outside for his mount. He clambered out of his bed and heard Olivia groaning from her bunk. It was still nearly dark inside the building, only a bit of gray light coming in through the exhaust hole.

"Guess he wasn't joking about starting early," Morgan said, looking into the shadows where he knew Olivia was.

"Ugh, no kidding! At least I seem to heal faster in this world. My ass is only slightly sore this morning," Olivia replied, laughing a little.

"Yeah, I actually feel great. Put some points in vitality while you can, by the way. When you get your class, you might not get one that gives you vitality. Just an idea." Morgan stood up and walked outside because Olivia was too busy stretching to reply. In the gray light of dawn, Morgan grabbed a bowl of the porridge, thanked Allender, ate it down, then walked a bit away from the longhouse to call Munch.

The morning went by in a blur, literally and figuratively. The herders kept up a fast pace, and Morgan was so busy enjoying the ride and his greater experience being in the saddle that the hours flew by. They stopped around noon to stretch their legs and eat a snack, which they all provided for themselves. Morgan ate some dried meat and once again looked enviously at Olivia while she built herself an actual sandwich. She smiled at him, offering to share, but he waved her off, saying he wasn't very hungry. He really wasn't, but that sandwich looked good.

They were just finishing up and getting ready to move out when Beyli came riding out of the south whistling in a high-pitched repeating pattern. Teric produced his bow from his pouch and shouted, "Boyii pack! Maybe an alpha!" Morgan looked at Olivia, she nodded, and they urged their mounts to follow Teric. They quickly learned that Teric knew how to push his mount to speeds they couldn't match, and they fell behind. By the time they caught up, Teric was riding in a wide circle around a bunch of brightly colored boyii hounds, at least twenty-five of them.

Morgan could see that the other herders were also riding around, loosing arrows into the pack, using their mounts to direct the pack away from the main herd. Olivia rode off to his left, some icy darts forming over her outstretched hand and shooting off into the pack.

Morgan was at a loss—he didn't have any ranged attacks, and he didn't know how to fight from the saddle. The bulk of the pack was only about a hundred yards away, so he pulled Munch to a stop and slid out of the saddle. Calling his sword to his hand, he ran toward the snarling, yipping pack. He yanked the scabbard off as he ran, stowing it back in his ring, and, before he knew it, the pack was upon him. His presence seemed to ignite some sort of rampage among the animals, most likely because they'd been frustrated by the herders' ability to avoid them while loosing arrows at their packmates. At least eight of the animals, each probably weighing between fifty and a hundred pounds, charged at him.

Morgan lifted his sword into a medium guard position and waited. As the first hounds leaped at his chest and throat, he concentrated and unleashed an Azure Burst. It was the first time he'd ever used the ability, and he was stunned by the effect; a ball of crackling blue Energy exploded out from him, burning the grass to charcoal and flinging the hounds away with their colorful hair ignited like so many torches. They howled in agony before succumbing to their horrible wounds. The explosion had brought silence to the melee; the herders had paused their assault, and the remaining boyii were quietly circling Morgan, their hair raised.

One particularly large boyii, sporting three tails and colored a burnt orange, snarled as it approached him, head low and eyes bright with fury. Morgan slipped into his sword form, the Crane Forages, slowly advancing on the hound with his sword held low, circling. Everyone else seemed to snap out of their trance, and arrows and ice bolts began to rain on the other hounds again.

To Morgan's surprise, the hound didn't jump at him; rather, when it was only five feet away, it raised its head, opened its mouth, and howled. Morgan was taken entirely off guard, and the blast of sound hit him full in the chest and face. It was like being hit by a small car. He was tossed back, flipping feet over head, and landed on the grassy dirt with a painful thud. With the wind knocked out of his lungs, he struggled to rise. He was in the midst of a pushup-like motion when he felt powerful jaws fasten around his shoulder, right where it met his neck. He screamed as the boyii alpha crunched down and started to shake.

As quickly as it had begun, the shaking stopped, and the pressure of the bite fell away. Morgan struggled weakly and suddenly felt someone's hands putting pressure on his neck, and then the hound's jaws were pulled apart, and he could struggle to a sitting position. Blood pumped freely from the deep, jagged punctures in his neck. Olivia and Teric were standing in front of him, looks of concern on their faces. Morgan managed a weak smile; then he pulled one of the healing potions from his ring that he'd gotten from the Yovashi, and he chugged it down.

❧ OLIVIA ❧

Olivia winced as the Energy flowed through her channels to form the Icy Shards spell above her hand. She'd never cast so many in a row before, and she could feel her Energy running low. She couldn't believe Morgan had dismounted and charged into the pack of boyii hounds like that. At first, it had looked like the pack would swarm him, but then he'd simply exploded—a ball of crackling blue fire expanding out from him, scorching the grass in a wide circle and throwing the charging hounds back, their fur ablaze with blue-yellow flames. Olivia and the herders had continued to hurl attacks at the remaining hounds as the big alpha squared off with Morgan. That's when things had gone sideways.

The alpha had let loose a howl that seemed to contain all the rage and agony of its dead packmates. The sound had a physical impact on Morgan, hurling him head over heels, slamming him into the ground. Now, Olivia urged her mount forward, gathering as much Energy as she could into the Icy Shards. The alpha didn't wait for her or for Morgan to get up; instead, it charged forward, grabbing him by the neck and shoulder in its fang-filled jaws. With an alarmed cry, Olivia hurled her spell at the alpha's side, pleased to see the five separate shards all make contact, plunging into its exposed flank. Almost simultaneously, Teric shouted a word she didn't recognize, and two long arrows pierced the hound's other side, right behind its neck.

Between the two attacks, it was clear that something vital in the beast's chest had been destroyed, and it shuddered and collapsed, Morgan still held in its jaws. Olivia jumped out of Blue's saddle as she rode up, swaying a little with dizziness. Teric was already on the ground, trying to pry the boyii's mouth open. She knelt to help, and they managed to free him. Morgan sat up weakly. Blood, flowing and burbling out in little rivulets, began to soak his shirt and armor. Olivia pressed her hands against the worst-looking cuts, right on the side of his neck.

For some damn reason, Morgan smiled and somehow produced a potion directly into his hand. He quaffed it, and Olivia could feel the skin under her hand grow several degrees hotter. Carefully, she let up on the pressure and could see that, while the puncture was still there, it was half as wide as before, and the blood had slowed to a trickle. Olivia spared a glance for the rest of the pack but saw that they were either all dead or on the run, with herders giving chase. She stood up and was surprised as a stream of bright golden Energy motes hit her in the chest. Most of them were coming from the dead alpha, but several thin streams were also flowing from other corpses she'd wounded. She noticed similar streams flowing into Morgan and Teric.

Congratulations! You have achieved level 8 base human and have 10 attribute points to allocate.

She was surprised to see the message indicating she'd gained two levels. She supposed the alpha had been worth a lot of Energy, and she might have been getting close to seven already. "Well, I leveled! Morgan, that was risky! You almost got your head ripped off!" She could see that his wounds had closed further from the Energy, already scabbed over. She smacked him on top of his head.

"Ouch! Yeah, I know; I didn't know about that howl attack." He started to struggle to his feet, and Olivia grabbed his thick arm, hoisting.

"You should always use caution when facing evolved beasts," Teric chimed in, walking over. "They can develop abilities that are quite surprising."

"That's an understatement!" Olivia said, falling back and panting. "Damn, you're heavy, Morgan."

"You're lucky you seem to have high vitality. I've seen alphas bite right through a roladii's leg." Teric started to whistle in a signal that Olivia now knew meant for the other herders to gather. Then he produced a long, sharp skinning knife and set to work on the boyii alpha. "This fur will fetch a good price. Those punctures should be easy to mend." As he started working, Olivia walked away, back toward her roladii. She wasn't squeamish, but she didn't want to smell the hound's innards when he pulled them, steaming from its belly. She noticed that the other herders were moving among the smaller hounds' corpses, and Morgan watched Teric intently.

"Hey, girl," Olivia said, stroking Blue's neck. "Did those bad dogs scare you?" She hopped up into the saddle and rode a little ways toward the rest of the herd. She wanted a little peace to think about her attribute points. Earlier, Morgan had made an interesting point to her. He had indicated that some classes didn't reward points for every attribute. She had never considered that and, thus far, had just been stacking most of her points into intelligence because, in her mind, that was the most important attribute. She had to consider that her viewpoint might be dated and based on her old life back on Earth. She had just seen how vitality had saved Morgan's life. She'd also seen how vitality let him recover more quickly from what she'd considered grueling exercise.

This world was dangerous, and just having a lot of intelligence might not be the best long-term survival plan. She decided to take Morgan's advice and put half her free attribute points into vitality. Thinking about resilience, she decided to put the other half into will; she didn't like the idea that her mental stats had such a wide disparity. She didn't know how it would affect her in the long run, but when she'd seen that beast use a sonic Energy attack on Morgan, it got her thinking: if a wolf could use Energy attacks, what other strange abilities might she encounter? After allocating her points, she looked at her attributes:

Strength:	6	Vitality:	12
Dexterity:	8	Agility:	6
Intelligence:	35	Will:	20

A feeling of well-being suffused her body and mind, and she took a deep breath, letting go of the stress of the battle. She wasn't sure she could feel a measurable difference in herself with that attribute boost, other than the immediate euphoria she always experienced when allocating the points. Still, Olivia could have sworn her back felt straighter, and she had a feeling of sturdiness that was new to her.

It didn't take long for the herders, with Morgan acting as an assistant to finish skinning the boyii hounds, and soon the group was riding with the herd, moving fast to make up lost time. Olivia was proud of her connection to Blue—she and the roladii were beginning to understand each other instinctually. When she wanted him to turn, she no longer had to pull on the reins much at all, just nudging with her knees and giving a slight tug did the job. Conversely, Olivia could tell when he was getting tired or bored or simply wanted to run full tilt for a little while. She wasn't sure how, but it seemed to be a combination of his gait, breathing, and head movements; they all added up to indicate to her something like an emotion the roladii was having.

They stopped that evening at another campground of the Ardeni herders. Olivia could see evidence of recent occupation—lots of roladii prints, trampled grass, and a firepit that still smelled like woodsmoke. "Do other herders use these camps?"

"Oh, aye," Forn said after they'd all sat around the fire pit, watching Allender grill their dinner. "There's gotta be thirty or forty herds out here this time of year. We all keep to different routes to avoid our herds eating the same grass, but the Sea is a big place, lots of room to wander."

"Speaking of big places," Morgan spoke up, "I can tell we're about halfway to Tarn's Crossing. How much farther is it to the Rill Catcher?"

"We'll get there the day after tomorrow," Teric replied. "Then you'll need to follow it southeast 'til you get to the village. It ain't called Tarn's Crossing for nothing—it's situated right on the Rill Catcher and is home to the only bridge for a couple of hundred miles."

"How far is Tarn's from there?" Olivia chimed in.

"Just a bit more than a day's quick ride on a roladii. There are even decent roads for most of the way, 'cause that's a trade route," Roylo answered, kicking his feet out and looking up at the stars with a sigh.

"How often do you guys get to go back home?" Morgan asked.

"Between drives, we usually get a month or so off. Sometimes we visit our homes, then," Teric answered.

"Didn't you find it strange to meet us? People from another planet? I'm sorry; I just had to ask—you all have been so welcoming to us and never once acted like our differences were any sort of problem." Olivia flushed from embarrassment, but the strangeness of the situation had been on her mind a lot lately.

Teric just shrugged, putting some yiil weed into his cheek, then spoke: "It's just our way. We welcome strangers to our hearth until they show they are not friends. Then we fight. You aren't so different, anyway; you just have funny coloring. The roladii like you, so . . ." he shrugged and laughed.

After eating, Teric approached Morgan and asked him to see his sword. He said he hadn't seen one of its design before and seemed impressed by its balance. Morgan asked him if he knew much about sword work, but Teric demurely called himself a novice. Even so, he asked Morgan to spar a bit and produced a couple of broad, wooden practice swords. Olivia watched them for a while but eventually grew bored. She turned away from the spectacle and began creating Energy beads with four attunements. She found the complexity of weaving all four of her affinities gratifying, and she grew ever more confident that it was improving her ability to manipulate and channel Energy.

After Olivia finished her first bead, Dranil gave a low whistle and asked to look at it. "I ain't never seen one with four attunements before. It's beautiful! Look, Beyli, see how the fire motes dance around the little ice flakes?" Beyli leaned close, watching for a while in silence.

"You have a rare gift, Olivia," he said after a time in his low, quiet voice. "I don't think I've met anyone with more than two affinities." Olivia blushed at the attention and tried to make light of it, but his expression remained solemn. She decided, then, to make a four-affinity Energy bead for each of the herders before they parted.

This campsite didn't have a longhouse, so they set up tents. Morgan and Olivia's tent was three times the size of the herders,' and Teric and Roylo didn't even use tents, just laying their bedrolls out under the stars. Olivia slept well at first but woke several times in the night. Each time she awoke, she tossed for a while, unable to go back to sleep. Her mind was full of ideas and thoughts; she wondered what was going on with the colony, and she kept imagining what she'd like to accomplish. She had ideas about redeveloping some of their lost tech and mixing it with Energy use. Could she power motors with Energy? Morgan had already shown her what was, basically, a battery for Energy.

With thoughts of the colony, her mind also wandered to Bronwyn and how she was doing. She missed hanging around with her, even though she was kind of a handful emotionally. She hoped Bronwyn was getting along okay in her scouting mission. She hoped she was letting things go from the past and focusing on the future as they'd talked about. Olivia tried to focus on happy thoughts, and her mind drifted to the first night Bronwyn had come back from the cave, and they'd gotten shitfaced at the tavern. She almost started laughing but caught herself before she woke Morgan.

MORGAN

Morgan, Olivia, and the Ardeni herders crested a long, gradually graded slope a few hours after midday of their third day out from the longhouse, and Morgan saw the Rill Catcher for the first time. A long, blue ribbon filled the nearby horizon, stretching from the southeast then gradually curving to disappear into the forested hills west of the sea of grass that they'd driven the herd up. Morgan could see that the grassy plains with the distinctive red blossoms continued on the far side of the river, but, far to the east, following the river as a guideline, Morgan saw a faint line of blue-green that he hoped was the forest around Tarn's Crossing. "What a view," he said, standing in his stirrups to take in as much as he could.

"Aye, this rise gives a nice vantage," Teric replied. "From here, we'll continue west to Galan Vale. You and Olivia will follow the river a bit south and east. You should pick up a trade route in a few hours; just follow it, and you'll end up in Tarn's Crossing."

"I can't believe we're here already! That river looks amazing; judging from the distance, I'd guess it's bigger than the Mississippi," Olivia said as she rode up on her roladii, Blue. Morgan looked at her and was impressed by how naturally she handled the animal. She'd been first to get the taming skill, and she was miles ahead of him when it came to controlling the beast. Not that Morgan was having trouble with Munch, but he and the mount couldn't seem to intuit each others' intentions the way Olivia and Blue did. Even Teric had commented that he'd rarely seen a herder connect to their mount as quickly as she did.

"Oh well, buddy; we can't all be phenoms," Morgan whispered to Munch, scratching the wrinkly skin on the side of his head. Louder, he said, "Teric, we're forever in your debt." He turned to the others sitting nearby on their mounts. "You and all the others. Truly, thank you all for the hospitality and for teaching us to tame and ride these mounts."

"Yes!" Olivia echoed, turning to face the Ardeni. "Thank you so much! I have a gift for each of you." Olivia reached into her blue satchel and pulled out a handful of sparkling Energy beads. "I made a quad-attuned Energy bead for each of you. Use 'em however you want; spend 'em, keep 'em for good luck, or give 'em to your sweethearts back home." She smiled and handed one of the beads to each of the herders. They each were quiet, with solemn expressions, taking the beads reverently. When Olivia passed the last one to Beyli, he held her hand in his and touched his forehead to her knuckles, almost reverently. She blushed a bit and patted his hands, gently pulling hers back and straightening up. "I'll miss you guys. This trip across the Chebli Sea will always be a fond memory for me."

"Ahem," Morgan cleared his throat, smiling. "Well, I hate goodbyes, so, see you later." He waved one last time and urged Munch into a ground devouring lope down the hill and toward the Rill Catcher. A few moments later, he could hear Olivia riding up behind him, and he looked over his shoulder. The herders were turning, heading back to gather up the herd and move off, and Olivia was tearing over the ground toward him, her hair streaming behind her and a massive smile on her face. "Oh, a race, is it?" He snapped his reins and clicked his tongue, urging Munch into a full sprint.

Morgan laughed as the wind roared in his ears, leaning low over Munch's back. He stood slightly in the stirrups because Munch's back was surging up and down, and Morgan didn't want to have his spine reduced to crumbles. The slope of the grasslands was a gradual decline, which only added to the breakneck speed of their mounts, and it was only a minute or two before they were forced to veer left, to the east, by the steep bank of the Rill Catcher.

The grass was short here and worn completely to dirt in patches, and Morgan thought this must be part of the usual route for trading that Teric had mentioned. He was still laughing and leaning forward when Olivia and Blue burst past him on the left. Man, she had a way with that animal! After another hundred yards or so, Olivia pulled up on the reins, bringing her roladii down to an easy walk, and Morgan caught up to her. "Okay, you win!" Morgan laughed.

"Blue might be small, but he's a good, fast boy!" She was breathing heavily from the effort and excitement and stroking Blue's huffing neck. When Morgan walked Munch up close to her, Blue made a huffing, groaning sound and rubbed his neck along Munch's. "Hah, they like each other!"

"Yeah, thank goodness! Though, I've never seen a roladii be anything other than agreeable." Morgan patted Munch's neck.

"They sure are interesting beasts. I wonder how much our taming skill affects their demeanor?" Olivia asked, and Morgan agreed it was a good question. Things couldn't be taken for granted in this world. Energy and the magic you could do with it changed everything. He looked around as they continued at a steady pace. The Rill Catcher was a big, sedate river at this point. Looking down the steep, rocky bank, he could see its sluggish blue-green water flowing east, and the far bank was at least a couple of hundred yards across. He watched the water for a while, wondering what sorts of fish might lurk in those placid depths, but only saw the occasional bubble or ripple.

"I wonder if we can make it to those trees before dark," Morgan said after they'd walked for a while, letting their mounts get their wind back.

"Maybe. Do you want to, though? I'd almost rather camp in the grassland, in the open, then in another dark forest." Olivia gestured to the sprawling grassland off to her left.

"Yeah, I suppose I would too. Let's just get close, and then we'll set up camp. We should be able to make Tarn's Crossing easily tomorrow." They picked up the pace a bit, urging their mounts into their version of a trot, and fell into an easy silence as they devoured the ground between them and the distant blue-green line of the forest.

Morgan thought about his time with the herders while they rode, his mind drifting to the battle with the boyii pack. His Azure Burst spell had undoubtedly been effective, and Morgan wondered if his Human Champion title had played a part. He looked at the description again:

Human Champion: Transient title. Energy efficacy enhanced 1.5x. More frequent access to System generated Opportunities for Refinement.

Did it mean that his spells or skills that used Energy had 50 percent more power? Or did he have to use 50 percent less power for the same effect? He would need to do more experimenting, he supposed. One thing was for sure—the spell had utterly devastated the hounds that he'd caught in the radius of effect.

His spell aside, he had been disappointed not to get a chance to try out his sword skills in actual combat. Teric had proved to be a passable sparring partner, though, and Morgan had learned a lot about his Crane Style. Namely, it was incomplete; if he just tried to fight anyone with any knowledge of swordplay, there were glaring holes in the style. Morgan had found that he needed to integrate some techniques from his basic melee weapon mastery: parries, various guard positions, ripostes, even his footwork. Once he'd stopped trying to just rely on the Crane Style, he'd started having an easier time with Teric. After hours of practice on two different nights, Morgan felt like his skill was on the cusp of advancing. At least, he hoped it was.

Another thing his sparring with Teric had taught Morgan was that his sword was inadequate for the Fighting Crane Style. It was one thing to practice his forms in a vacuum, swinging at the air, but when he had an actual opponent, it became clear that the blade was just too short and too unwieldy to transition between some of the forms correctly. The worst example of that deficiency was when he transitioned from the Crane Forages to the Crane Defends the Nest. He ended up tangled with Teric if the man pressed at all—the bastard sword's blade just didn't have the right balance, reach, or weight to fit the motions of the "memories" the System had put in his head.

These thoughts occupied his mind while they traveled, and Morgan could see that Olivia was similarly deep in thought. When they'd covered more than half their intended distance, Morgan asked, "It was lucky we found those herders, don't you think?"

"Hmm?" Olivia looked over to him, smiling slightly. "I can't think of a luckier break, to be honest. They were friendly, helped us with directions, and even taught us how to ride. Yeah, I'd say it was a lucky break!"

"Yeah, this world, this System, it's so hard to pin down. While in the Crucible, I was bracing myself to fight for my life all the time against one horror after another. Since then, sure, I've had plenty of fights, but there's been so much beauty and so many encounters with kind, peaceful people and creatures." Morgan shrugged, patting Munch again, and he grunted.

"Well, I have my theories about some of that," Olivia answered. "You know, the System placed us in this area for a reason. It measured us, according to you, before it placed us, even. This world is, by all accounts, immense. Creatures and people have found their niches here, and this is the spot where the System thought we'd fit in the easiest. I imagine there might be places with more danger and greater challenges. Here, we have our problems, but it seems, if we just look for it, we can find help, too."

They continued in silence for a while, each mulled in thought. As they came close enough to the forest line to see the individual trees, Morgan reached out with Guardian Senses again and felt Issa almost directly east and only ten or twenty miles away. The sun was sinking, though, and Morgan agreed with Olivia that traveling through an unfamiliar forest in the dark wasn't the most brilliant move. They moved off the worn section of the plains a bit north into the taller grass and set up their camp. After caring for their mounts, Morgan practiced his forms while Olivia created more Energy beads, and then they both practiced their cultivation drills. Once again, they took turns watching while they slept, and, after an uneventful night, they packed up and continued their journey in the gray light of dawn.

When they entered the forest, Morgan was happy to see that the worn path in the plains continued into the trees, and within a mile, it looked like a proper dirt road. Excitement warred with caution, and Morgan urged Munch into a rolling gait that was his version of a cantor, Olivia easily keeping pace. The trees in these woods were tall and mainly of the same breed: thin, white-barked trunks rising hundreds of feet with wide canopies covered in broad blue-green leaves. The undergrowth was sparse, dead old leaves making up a soft, noise-deadening mulch. Occasionally they'd get a view of the Rill Catcher through the trees on their right, but it was usually a bit too far off to see. However, the sound it made was ever-present, a rushing susurration that almost reminded Morgan of the wind. At one point, he swore he could hear the echoing sounds of someone's shouts coming from the river. He wondered if they were getting close enough to the village for boats to be out and about.

After traveling for another hour, a shape started to come into view down the road. Morgan and Olivia slowed and continued at a walk as it approached. Soon, it became clear that the shape was a tall, narrow wagon being pulled by a team of roladii. The two humans pulled their mounts to the side to allow it to pass.

As it approached, they saw that an Ardeni woman with brilliant lilac-colored hair was driving the team. She pulled on the reins and shouted down from her high, wooden bench, "Well-met travelers! Good intentions from me and mine."

As she spoke, little windows opened high on the sides of the tall wagon, and Morgan could see several more blue faces with bright, colorful eyes peering out. He wasn't sure what the proper response was, but Olivia called out, "Well met! Good intentions from us as well!" She waved, a smile revealing her even, white teeth.

"Good journeys to you, then. Tarn's is peaceful today; you'll make it there by midday."

"Thank you!" Morgan said, and then the woman snapped her reins, and the wagon was trundling past. Morgan looked at Olivia and shrugged.

"C'mon!" she said, urging Blue back into a trot.

MORGAN

More and more traffic started to pass Morgan and Olivia as they drew closer to Tarn's Crossing. People were generally friendly, though a few Ardeni they met refused to acknowledge them, hurrying by as quickly as they could. Not more than two hours of travel after meeting that first woman in the tall wagon, they crested a rise and saw the village, or really, more of a bustling town, sprawled out before them. The road was smooth and gravel-covered here, and it sloped gently into a depression in the forest that had been cleared of all but the largest, tallest trees.

Tarn's Crossing had a high, wooden palisade surrounding most of the village structures, though many farms and even a large inn and stable were outside the walls. Morgan and Olivia could see the Rill Catcher bisecting the town from their vantage, flowing through a gap in the walls and under a vast, arched wooden bridge. The village's grounds, with the checkerboard of farms surrounding it, among the massive, towering trees, made Morgan think of a curated park.

"Gorgeous," Olivia said from next to him.

"Yeah, it really is." He started his mount moving again, and Olivia followed suit, riding next to him.

"Are you nervous?" she asked, a sly smile on her lips.

"Huh, about what?"

"Oh, don't be coy; you've been gnashing at the bit to visit this friend of yours since you got teleported to the colony. Now, you've crossed a hundred miles of wilderness, and you're about to come face to face with her again."

"Well, shit, when you put it like that, I guess maybe I should be nervous!" Morgan looked at Olivia and smiled wryly. "Nah, it'll be fine. I have low expectations; as long as I get to see her again and see she's doing well, I'll be happy."

"Mmhmm." Olivia rolled her eyes. As they got closer to the east-facing gates of the town and the huge inn and stables situated outside the wall, they began to pass more and more people. They received a few sidelong glances, but people were generally friendly. Morgan was about to comment about how nice everyone had been, but then he remembered something, and a slight chill ran down his spine. He called up the menu for his titles and looked at a particular one:

*****Ardeni Friend: Members of the Ardeni race will initially view you with less hostility, feeling a familiarity with you as they would a member of the Ardeni people.*****

"Goddamn it," he muttered.

"What?" Olivia looked at him, slightly alarmed by his change in tone.

"I had completely forgotten about a title I got in the Crucible. I'm afraid it explains why we had such an easy time making friends with all the Ardeni we've met." Morgan explained his title to Olivia.

"Oh, wow. So, you think this somehow has an effect on the temperament of the Ardeni we've run into?"

"Well, it says it does. I hate thinking about how the System can fuck with people's minds. It cheapens everything. I'd thought that Teric and his crew were just really nice guys and that we'd made a good impression on them. Now I have to wonder how much was real and how much was the System charming them for us." Morgan sighed and scratched absently at Munch's shoulder. The beast huffed and let out the low, grunting noise he made when he was happy.

"Well, there's nothing to be done about it. We don't know how big or how insignificant the effect might be. Those herders were nice, and they went out of their way to teach us things. I won't take that away from them."

"Yeah, alright," Morgan said, then turned to wave at some Ardeni standing outside the large, two-story building that had a stylized sign hanging out over its deck. The sign read, "The Catcher's Bed." There was a large stable on the other side of the street where Ardeni youths were busy fetching, grooming, and leading away mounts. Morgan was surprised to see a variety of creatures other than roladii, even something that looked quite similar to a horse. One Ardeni girl led a beast into the stable that looked very much like a stag, the tips of its horns plated in shiny brass. Before he could remark about it, though, they were in front of the gates, and a guard called out, "Well met, traveler. What's your business in Tarn's?"

"Um," Olivia started but then looked to Morgan.

"Right, well, we're from a new community and would like to talk to your elders about establishing trade. Also, I have a friend that lives here that I'm hoping to see." Morgan recalled, vaguely, Issa talking about her "elders," so he hoped that was the right word.

"Oh, hmm, so here on business? Can you afford lodging? We can't have vagrants in the streets." He looked Morgan and Olivia up and down, an eyebrow arched.

"Ahem, yes, we can afford lodging! We've been traveling for more than a week and need to freshen up, but we aren't destitute." Olivia managed to sound both polite and deeply aggrieved by the man's words. He looked a little flustered and then motioned for them to proceed into the town.

"The governor's office is off the main market square near the bridge. On this side of the bridge, just follow this street to the square, then look left, and you'll see Aleroot Road; that's where his office is," he said as they passed through.

The streets were busy but not crowded, and Morgan and Olivia had no trouble making their way down the central thoroughfare. On this street, storefronts dominated the buildings, and they were all of a similar design—tall, narrow wooden buildings with peaked roofs. They passed several clothiers, a jeweler, a cobbler, a fletcher, a bakery, at least two restaurants, and, as they arrived at the square, a large storefront featuring various swords and other weapons in the window. "Busy commerce," Morgan remarked.

"Yeah, I'm a little surprised—it seems like the System would take over a lot of these industries, but perhaps its goods or prices leave something to be desired." Olivia's eyes were fixed on the large Colony, or Town in this case, Stone that rose in the middle of the square, perfectly bisecting the view of the arched bridge on the far side. The Town Stone of Tarn's Crossing was smaller than the stone in First Landing and shone with a deep cobalt blue luster. Looking around the square at the people walking from shop to shop, Morgan realized that he and Olivia weren't the only foreigners in town. He saw several goat-like Cadwalli and some of the tall, willowy Ghelli, though only a few small groups or individuals; there wasn't any question that this was an Ardeni town.

They followed the flow of traffic around the square and out the east end, looking for a building that might be some sort of town hall. True to the gate guard's words, they found a stately building, still crafted from wood but a notch up on the architectural ladder: peaked gables, filigreed columns, stained soffits, and painted siding. A placard hung off a little post near the sidewalk that said "Governor's Offices." Morgan and Olivia tied their mounts to the hitch near the walkway and approached the tall green door. A reversible wooden sign was posted on the door that said plainly "The Governor is in."

Morgan depressed the shiny brass handle and opened the door. He and Olivia stepped into a cozy foyer with plush couches upholstered in a muted minty green. The woodwork was polished to a sheen, and a desk, situated opposite the door, was occupied by a small Ardeni woman with violet eyes and mauve hair. The petite woman smiled at them and said, "Hello, may I help you?"

"Hello, My name is Morgan Hall, and this is Olivia Bennet. We're here as a delegation from our, um, village to try to establish communications and trade. We were hoping to meet with the governor." Morgan stepped forward to the desk, offering his most friendly smile.

"Oh, how exciting! What is the name of your community? I'll just go and let the governor know!" She stood up and moved toward the paneled doorway to her right.

"Oh, it's First Landing," Olivia chimed in.

"Alright, just a moment, please." The woman walked to the door, knocked gently, opened it, and stepped through. Morgan could hear muffled voices, and then the door opened, and the woman stepped back out, holding the door open. "He'll see you now." Morgan looked at Olivia with a raised eyebrow. Everything had gone so smoothly; his paranoia was starting to make him wonder when something terrible was going to happen.

The governor's office was decorated similarly to the foyer: polished wood, comfortable chairs, a big desk. But, in addition to all that, there were rows of bookcases filled with leather-bound volumes. A faded portrait of four Ardeni wearing armor and posing with weapons in various positions dominated the wall behind the governor, hanging between two narrow windows. The governor was the first portly Ardeni that Morgan had noticed. He wasn't obese, but he was undoubtedly rotund. He had a neatly trimmed white beard, bushy white eyebrows, and a thick, wavy head of white hair. He smiled at them, the skin around his deep green eyes crinkling. "Welcome, travelers! Please sit down! Rest your weary bones. Lethia, please bring some tea and some of that wonderful squash bread you made."

"Of course, Governor!" Lethia turned and closed the door behind her as she left. Morgan and Olivia sat in the proffered chairs, a sigh escaping Olivia's lips as she sank into the plush upholstery.

"Thank you, Governor. My name is Morgan Hall, and this is Olivia Bennett. We're representing our village, First Landing." What followed was a long and, to Morgan, bizarre conversation about where First Landing was, where humans came from, what sorts of industries they were proficient at, what their hopes for trade were, and dozens of other topics. They spoke for nearly three hours. Morgan was acutely aware of his inability to answer most of the governor's questions and often had to sit quietly, gratefully watching while Olivia provided detailed answers.

Lethia brought them tea and a deliciously moist, sweet bread that reminded Morgan of banana bread. Over the course of their meeting, she refreshed their teapot twice. As the conversation began to wind down, Olivia finally brought up their main reason for coming here, the Urghat. The governor, who had introduced himself as Holis Gatherton, frowned and tapped his fingers on his desk. "Urghat, you say? From the plains or mountains north of your settlement?" Morgan nodded. "Hmm, yes, I knew there were clans up north there; they could certainly be a problem for you."

"We were hoping we might be able to rely on some aid from your people.

At least, until we managed to establish ourselves and develop some stronger defenses," Olivia pressed.

"Hmm, well, the Deep Down has been quiet these last few years. We do have a lot of hunters anxious to get some fighting in, if for no other reason than to accelerate their leveling. I'll propose an open bounty at our next council meeting. That should get you a few hundred eager hunters up to your area to look for Urghat kills. I'm sure they'd be even more motivated if you offer to add them to your Contribution roster on your Settlement Stone."

"Oh, we can do that?" Olivia asked.

"Certainly. People don't always just live and operate out of the towns where they were born." The governor smiled and stood, dusting some crumbs off his lap. "Now, have you secured lodging?" When Morgan shook his head, he continued, "Here, I'm going to refer you to the Riverfront Inn. Meagan will give you an excellent rate, and her rooms are often raved about by visitors." He pulled a scrap of paper from his desk and scribbled a note on it. He slipped the message in an envelope, impressed it with a heavy brass crimper, and passed it to Morgan. "I'm sorry, but I have another engagement, or I'd love to talk more. Perhaps you can stop by again tomorrow? In any case, our next council meeting is in two days, and I'll bring up the Urghat problem then."

As they were leaving the governor's office, shaking hands one more time, Morgan heard the front door jingle and turned to see who had come in. He saw a familiar face with bright yellow eyes framed by curly yellow hair. In a blur, Issa was grabbing him around the waist and squeezing. "Why didn't you come to see me, first thing! I had to hear about you coming to town from a nosy guard!" She pulled away, slightly, a big smile belying her true feelings, and glanced at Olivia. "Who's this?"

OLIVIA

Olivia watched as Morgan and Issa walked away down the street. They'd agreed to meet up at the inn around dinner time then walk over to Issa's family home for a meal. At first, Olivia had been worried about Issa's reaction to her. She'd had a big smile when she asked who Olivia was, but there was something in Issa's eyes that made Olivia feel like a rabbit being regarded by an owl. She'd warmed up, though, even giving Olivia a welcoming hug when Morgan introduced her as a "good friend." Then she'd walked them to the Riverfront Inn, waiting while Morgan booked their rooms and the stablehands took their mounts. Issa seemed impressed that they had such a connection to their roladii, and Olivia could tell it earned her points with the locals.

Issa said she wanted to show Morgan around and introduce him to her family. She'd invited Olivia, but Olivia didn't want to feel like a third wheel, so she professed her desire to do some honest-to-goodness shopping. The market square they'd passed through twice now really did have a festive atmosphere, and she'd seen so many stores that appealed to her that she wasn't lying when she said so. Morgan had insisted on giving her another pouch of the dual-attuned beads he'd gotten from the Yovashi, even though she'd held up a handful of quad-attuned beads she had made during their travels. He'd just shrugged and said, "Easy come, easy go."

Now, as they walked away, Olivia just smiled at the prospect of getting some tailored clothing and some delicious treats, and who knows what else. Issa was certainly pretty, and she was not shy about her possessiveness toward Morgan; they were walking with her practically hanging off his arm. Issa wore a gorgeous, shimmering blue cloak adorned with golden stitches that created whorls and other designs highlighting runic symbols. Underneath that, she had a shimmering silver shirt that appeared to be made from fantastically lightweight and thin metal. Her leggings were made of some kind of silky, form-fitting black material, and she wore beautifully crafted leather boots and a belt. All in all, it made Olivia feel like a vagrant standing near her. The only article of clothing she felt proud of was her baby blue storage satchel.

Patting her satchel lovingly, Olivia turned toward the market square, which was just across the bridge from their inn, and started walking. Like everything else in Tarn's Crossing, the bridge was constructed of wood. Massive timbers made up the side struts, and smooth planks created the roadway. A raised portion near the rail was meant for pedestrians, and Issa looked out over the railing at the river as she walked over it. The Rill Catcher was deep and mysterious at this point, only about fifty yards across as it went through the town; it was moving faster than when she and Morgan had seen it out by the plains. Most of the buildings along its length had decks or even little piers attached, and Olivia saw many people fishing. It looked like fun, and she wondered if maybe they'd be here long enough for her to give it a try.

Soon she was in the market square, and thoughts of fishing fled from her mind. Thanks to the governor sharing his delicious bread with her and Morgan, Olivia wasn't terribly hungry, but she couldn't help following her nose to a bakery as her first stop. It was a busy shop, so she didn't make any small talk with the baker, just pointed to a pastry that reminded her of a Danish in appearance. The woman handed it to her, and Olivia handed her one of the smokey blue Energy beads that Morgan had given her. The baker looked at it for a moment, then tsked, digging beneath her counter and pulling out a plump leather sack. "Yer gonna use up all me change. Lucky the rush is over." She proceeded to count out a large handful of very small, clear Energy beads.

"I'm sorry, it's all I have," Olivia said, feeling flustered.

"Oh, don't worry, now." The woman said, pouring the handful of tiny beads into her cupped hands. Olivia slipped them into a pocket, then hastily grabbed her pastry and walked out to the square. A few tables were set up around the bakery's entrance, so she sat by herself at a little square table and pulled out one of the tiny, clear beads. It was made from unattuned Energy, that much she could tell, and it was about a quarter the size of a regular Energy bead. So, was it possible to stop the process early? Is that how they made these tiny beads? She figured it made sense—why would someone trade hours of hard work for something like a pastry. There had to be smaller denominations.

While enjoying her pastry, which tasted much like a cheese Danish with a lovely, buttery, flaky texture, she looked around the square, trying to decide where to go first. She saw a shop with dresses in the window, and she wondered if a new dress would be too overboard. It wouldn't be practical for traveling, and it would be obvious she bought it just to go to dinner, so she decided to hold off. Maybe she could find some nicer clothing that was also fit for riding around on a roladii. Deciding just to wander a bit, she brushed off her fingers, swallowed her last bite, and walked toward the next shop in the square.

In the window display, she saw staves. No, not just staves; she also saw wands and beautiful shimmering balls in a rainbow of hues. The door had a sign that read "Wyn's Energy Foci." Olivia felt her heart rate speed up a bit with excitement. She desperately needed an Energy focus, and she didn't even know what it was! Giggling a little to herself, she pulled the door open, and a silvery bell tinkled, announcing her presence to the clerk.

"Welcome, welcome!" Olivia was surprised to see the speaker wasn't an Ardeni. He was one of the tall willowy people with shimmering iridescent wings that Morgan had called Ghelli. She felt guilty for making the comparison, but his wings reminded her of dragonfly wings.

"Oh, hello." She stepped into the shop, noting the faint scent of spices and carefully navigating the narrow aisle between crowded stands and racks. When she made it up to the counter, she saw that the shopkeeper had incense burning in an ornate metal dish, and his attention was on a document he was writing. Olivia took the opportunity to study him, noting his pale green robes and sandy brown hair. When he looked up, she was surprised by how human his eyes looked; somehow, she'd assumed they'd be more alien. He smiled when he saw her and turned the paper he'd been writing on face down.

"Oh, welcome, indeed! One of the humans I've heard so much about, I presume?" He had a deep voice and a charming smile.

"Oh? I hope you're hearing good things! My name is Olivia," she replied, holding out a hand. He took it in a warm but very light clasp.

"Pleased to meet you. My name is Wyn, and as I'm sure you've guessed, this is my shop." He released her hand and gestured around the cluttered store. Olivia realized she was his only customer. "Regarding what I've heard, nothing much, other than the rumors about young Issa's Crucible run and how one of your people became her brave companion!"

"Ah, I see. Is it uncommon for people to have success in the Crucible?"

"Well, let's just say that Issa was more successful than most and much more than people thought she'd be. She even earned a class upgrade and was offered a class that none from our town had ever seen. Her father hosted quite a celebratory bash, from what I hear."

"You didn't go?" Olivia found Wyn's voice almost hypnotic and wanted to encourage the conversation.

"Oh, no. I'm not particularly close to Issa or her father, but in a town this size, gossip travels quickly!" He chuckled, and Olivia smiled at the warmth in his voice. "Well, how may I help you, Olivia of the humans?"

"Well, I'm not really sure. We are new to Energy and its uses, but I saw your items on display and was instantly fascinated. Could you tell me about them?"

"Of course, of course." Wyn gestured to his many racks and shelves once more. "Foci are used to enhance the effect of Energy-based spells. Special foci can even be used to enhance some Energy-based skills or abilities. Additionally, the use of a proper focus can help improve the rate of Energy cultivation."

"How do you know what a 'proper' focus is?" Olivia asked, looking at the incredible array of foci on display.

"Well, some foci work better with different types of Cores, and some are attuned to different Energy types. Do you know if you have an affinity for a certain type of Energy?" For a moment, Olivia wondered if it were a wise idea to be sharing information about her Core and her affinities with everyone she just met. She had to remind herself that she had come here and asked for information, not the other way around.

"Yes, I actually have four affinities: fire, water, air, and earth." She shrugged and smiled as Wyn took a step back.

"You're serious?" When Olivia nodded, he continued, "That's exceedingly uncommon. Do you mind telling me what kind of Core you have?"

"Eh, sure, in for a penny, in for a pound, right?" He looked at her confused, so she continued, "I have a Prisma Class Core."

"Prisma Class? Hmm, one moment." He turned to a bookshelf behind his counter and pulled out a book that reminded Olivia of an antique dictionary she had in her office back on Earth. He set it on the counter with a thump and then began to leaf through the pages, clearly looking for something.

"You haven't heard of it?" She asked, trying to read the book but finding it too hard with how quickly he flipped pages.

"Oh, it rings a bell, and I sell a type of focus that has a very similar name, the Prisma orb. I'm just looking up something about it, one moment." He continued to flip through the book, and then he found the page he was looking for, exclaiming, "Aha! Here we go." Olivia watched as he ran his finger over the page. "Mmhmm, that's right, that's right. Well, I'm afraid a Prisma orb won't work as a perfect focus for you. Theoretically, it could focus any elementally attuned Energy, but when opposing elements are channeled through it in short order, it could explode."

"Opposing elements?"

"Well, yes, such as water and fire. If you were to cast an ice spell, then a fire spell through that orb, you'd have a problem on your hands."

"Oh, I see."

"I was hoping I was wrong—those orbs are powerful foci. I can probably find a more generally attuned orb that will work for you, but it won't have as significant an effect. Unless. . ." He started flipping through the book again. Olivia waited patiently, looking around the shop, noticing that many foci were very dusty. "Oh, yes, this is brilliant. I could, theoretically, create you a focus staff using two different Prisma orbs."

"A staff?"

"Yes, yes, don't worry, it would be an elegant affair. I could mount the two foci on branches of silver or even amber ore, budget depending, running the veins through the length of the staff. You'd be able to channel water and air spells through one orb while casting fire and earth spells through the other. Yes, yes, this would be marvelous. I could use an umbrilak branch—it could easily handle all of your affinities!" Olivia could see the excitement on his face, and she couldn't help being caught up in it.

"Oh, that sounds amazing, but it also sounds expensive." She smiled, but Wyn's face became more serious.

"Hmm, perhaps, perhaps. One moment, please." He reached under his counter and brought up a paper and pencil. He scribbled for a few moments and then looked at Olivia. "Two-hundred standard Energy beads."

"Oh"—Olivia felt her smile falter and knew he saw it as well—"I might be able to scrape close to that amount together, but then I'd be destitute. I'm not sure I need a focus that badly, perhaps after I've accumulated more wealth. Thank you so much for your time, Wyn."

"Oh, oh, wait, wait!" A look of panic crossed his eyes. "Don't go, don't go. I'm sure I can find some discounts. Let's see; I can wave much of my artisan fee, but only on the promise that you'll be a repeat customer and tell your human friends about me!" Olivia nodded eagerly. "Hmm, that quote included an Amber Ore contact pad, but we could use silver. That's always something we could upgrade down the line! Um, well, now that I think about it, you don't need full Prisma orbs mounted on a staff; we could use crystals instead. Hmm, yes." He paused to scribble on his paper for a moment. "Yes, this brings us in at ninety-five standard Energy beads!"

"Well—" Olivia looked at the hopeful expression on his face and the dust on the foci in his shop, and she continued, "I think I can manage that. How many dual-attuned Energy beads would that be?"

"Oh, the simplest of maths, let's see," he said, staring into space, "just shy of thirty-two!"

"That I can do!" Olivia announced, knowing she had forty-nine of those beads that Morgan had given her, plus five or six quad-attuned beads.

"Oh, that's excellent! I'll get to work on it right away and should have it ready within two days. I have all the materials!"

"Thank you, Wyn! Thank you for being so kind and not taking advantage of me," Olivia said, looking him in the eyes, a genuine smile on her face.

"It's my pleasure, Olivia! I think it will be good for my business. Your Core and aptitude with Energy is very uncommon. You should speak with Magister Karn at the mage's guild. He might offer you further guidance."

"There's a mage's guild here?"

"Well, a very small branch office. Magister Karn is the only full member in our town. The Ardeni tend to produce more hunters than mages." Wyn had a sardonic smile on his face, and Olivia wondered if he was subtly taking a jab at the Ardeni.

"Okay, I'll check it out! Thank you again. By the way, could you recommend a ladies' tailor?"

MORGAN

Morgan was happy. He was so happy that he felt guilty about it. He was healthier than he'd ever been; he had new friends, a new world to explore, and even a budding relationship with the most amazing woman he could imagine. Walking over the bridge with Issa holding onto his arm, made him think about how much he'd gained coming to this world. He thought about how much his sister would have loved it. Morgan thought about how many people he'd seen killed fighting for scraps. He thought about other colony ships landing on inhospitable planets and having to scrape a living out of frozen soil. He thought about all of those things, then looked down into Issa's eyes looking up at him, and all he could do was feel lucky.

They had just met with Issa's father, Roald, at his shop. Roald was a strong-looking man who, to Morgan's eyes, didn't seem old enough to have a grown daughter. He had been welcoming and very warm to Morgan, somehow crediting Morgan with his daughter's safe return from the Crucible, even though Morgan insisted they had helped each other equally. Issa had smiled along during the interaction, the impish twinkle in her eyes making Morgan theorize that she'd talked him up a great deal to her father.

Roald apologized for having to work, saying he had a big project to complete for an important client, but insisted they return to the family home for a celebratory dinner.

Before they had left, Morgan noticed that Roald had a few weapons on display and remarked about their quality. Roald informed him that he had a deal with a weaponsmith in town: Roald added enchantments to the weapons and sold them from his shop, splitting the mark-up with the smith. Naturally, this got Morgan's mind working, and he'd asked Issa to take him to visit her father's partner as soon as they left.

Now, as they strolled over the bridge and back to the market square, Morgan smiled at the easy comfort with which he held Issa's hand. "I really missed you. I'm sorry I didn't get here faster," he said, lifting his arm over her shoulders and pulling her close. He inhaled deeply of the clean, spicy scent of whatever she washed her hair with as they left the bridge and walked among the market crowd.

"You made it! That's what's important. I was afraid you'd be across the world and take months or years to get here. I knew you'd come, though! I felt you, I think. Each time you used your skill to sense me? I think I felt you."

"Well, that's one thing the System has done for me that I can't think of any complaints about. You should know, each time I reached out to sense you, everything seemed to be okay for a few minutes." Morgan felt sappy saying it, but so far, being honest with Issa had never done him wrong.

"The shop's this way," Issa said, squeezing his hand and pulling him to the western edge of the market square. They walked in front of storefronts, receiving occasional glances and smiles from the people they passed. A few people called out a greeting to Issa, and she smiled and waved.

"You're pretty popular in this town!"

"Well, there aren't that many people living here, and word spread about my time in the Crucible pretty quickly. Plus, I got offered a class that's unique around here."

"Oh shit! I haven't asked you—what class did you get?" Morgan stopped and pulled Issa around to face him.

"Battle Witch!" She said, grinning fiercely.

"That sounds . . . well, that sounds scary," Morgan said, pushing Issa back to arm's length.

"Hey!" She knocked his hands aside and pushed forward, grabbing him into a hug. "Are you scared of me now?" she asked, nuzzling his chest.

"No, I'm just kidding, but that sounds like a pretty impressive class. Can you tell me about it at all?"

"Sure," she said, pulling back again. "It's an Advanced class like yours. It provides me with abilities to help in close-quarters fighting and spells to enhance myself and my companions in battle."

"So, you're kinda a celebrity because you aren't a hunter or some non-combat class?" Morgan asked, taking a closer look at the expensive-looking clothing and armor that Issa was wearing. Issa took an exaggerated sniff of him as they turned to keep walking.

"By the way, you stink!"

"Hey! I've been on the road! How about you take me someplace to buy some new clothes and get a bath after I talk to the smith?" She nodded, laughing, and pulled him into a faster walk.

The weaponsmith's shop was only a couple of streets off the market square and had a building all to itself. It sat on the corner of two roads; the side facing the north-south street was open and exposed a well-equipped forge. The side of the shop facing the other street was the storefront. Issa led Morgan right past the storefront and back to the forge area. A well-muscled Ardeni man wearing a heavy leather apron was busily hammering away at a bright piece of metal held between the pincers of some heavy tongs.

"Brint!" Issa yelled over the clamor of the hammer, *ping*ing away at the metal.

"Hmm," the man said, holding his hammer in the air and looking around. "Oh, Miss Issa! What brings you?"

"This," Issa said, pulling Morgan over and pointing at him, "is Morgan, the man I went through the Crucible with and someone I care about *very* much. He wants to buy a sword from you."

"Uh, pleased to meet you," Morgan said, his face flushing a little. He reached a hand out to shake. The smith, for his part, smiled broadly within his bushy black beard and put down his tongs and hammer. He made a show of pulling off his leather glove and then shook Morgan's hand with a grip that felt like it could collapse a steel beam. Morgan gamely hung on, gripping with everything he had and thinking about how Brint was the first Ardeni he'd met that didn't have colorful hair.

"Well," he said, letting go of Morgan's hand at last, "seems like you have some potential. What kind of weapon are ya looking for, youngster?"

"I'm looking for a particular kind of sword." Morgan pulled his bastard sword out of his ring. "You see, this sword has a long, double-edged blade, and I want one that is slightly curved and single-edged and a bit longer." He handed the blade to the smith, who took it and waved it around a bit, then tapped the steel with his hammer.

"I know the design. This is a pretty cheap blade, though; who crafted it?"

"Oh, I bought it from the Contribution Store in our settlement."

"Ah, yeah, unless you pay a lot, and I mean a *lot*, of contribution points, you get some pretty shit craftsmanship out of those shops. Anyway, what is this, about thirty-two inches of blade? Sure, the handle is long enough to grip with two hands, but if your style is focused on two-handed weapons, this won't do."

"Yeah, that's what I'm finding out." Morgan shrugged. "Do you have something like what I need?"

"Why'd you change from the spear, Morgan?" Issa asked from next to him.

"Um, it's a long story, but suffice it to say, I felt like the System was leading me around by the nose, so I'm kinda rebelling, I guess." The smith watched him with solemn eyes as Morgan spoke, then slightly nodded.

"Let's go into the shop, and I'll show you my sword room." Brint pulled off his other glove and gestured for Morgan and Issa to follow him through the wooden door to the back of his shop. From there, he led them through a stockroom full of crates and barrels and then up a side hallway. Morgan saw an opening to the storefront off to his right, but the smith kept walking to another sturdy door on the left. He fished a heavy key ring out of his apron pocket and then unlocked the door, pushing it open.

A yellow-white light flared from a hanging fixture as they entered the room. Morgan could see by its brightness and lack of smoke that it was some sort of Energy lamp. He couldn't study it, though, because his eyes were drawn to the walls of the room. Hundreds of swords of all shapes and sizes were exhibited in wooden display cases. Their blades gleamed in the light, sharpened and oiled to protect them from the elements. "My one-handed swords are on this wall. Here in the middle are my greatswords, and on the right, here, are my long-blades and bastard or hand-and-a-half blades." He walked over to the right wall, and Morgan followed.

Morgan's eyes roved over the blades. Some were thick, straight, and obviously very heavy. Some were slender and elegant with two edges. Then his eyes wandered to the right side of the wall where an assortment of single-edged swords hung. One of the blades caught his eye immediately; it reminded him of the swordsman's weapon in his vision. The sword had a long round hilt, wrapped in some sort of light-gray leather. Its blade was significantly wider at the base than a katana and a good twelve inches longer. The pommel was a round ball of steel with what looked like a tiger's eye gem set directly in the middle. Other than that, it was unadorned; even the guard was just a plain steel ring, maybe an inch wider than the hilt.

"That's the one I was thinking of when you described what you needed," the smith said, standing quietly next to Morgan. "Well, go ahead, pick it up."

"Alright." Morgan picked up the sword, noticing the rough sandpapery feel of the leather hilt and its significant heft right away. He stepped back from Brint and Issa and lifted the blade into a high guard. He looked around to make sure he had room, then moved into the Crane Defends the Nest and quickly transitioned to the Crane Flutters Its Wings. The movements felt more ponderous with the big sword, but the *whoosh* and *snap* sound of the blade cutting the air was viscerally gratifying. The forms felt completely different with a proper sword.

"Interesting style," Brint commented as Morgan flicked the blade around and hung it back on the display board.

"I got it from the System, and I hope it wasn't a mistake. It's incomplete, and from the description, I'm going to have to work at finding the rest of it." Morgan grinned. "I kind of like the challenge, though."

"Well, how did the sword feel with it?"

"Perfect." Morgan couldn't hide the eager smile on his face.

"Mmhmm, I was afraid of that." Brint looked at Issa with some trepidation but continued, "That blade is twenty percent Amber Ore. It took me nearly a month to forge. I'd love to give you a sword, seeing as you're special to Issa, but

I can't let this one go for free." He lowered his gaze, not wanting to meet Issa's eyes.

"Oh, I wouldn't expect it for free," Morgan quickly said before Issa could speak up. "Thank you very much for even considering that! I hope I can pay a fair price; what would you ask?"

"Well, if you were a stranger, I'd charge you five-hundred standard Energy beads." He glanced at Issa. "But, I can cut my artisan fee in half for family and friends. Three-hundred for materials and another hundred for my labor." Morgan glanced at Issa and saw that she was frowning, but she didn't say anything. He figured she thought the deal was fair but didn't think he had the money for it. He'd figured out from the Contribution Store that his dual-attuned Energy beads from the Yovashi were worth three times a standard bead. He had five bags of fifty left.

"I can do that. Thank you for the discount, Brint!"

OLIVIA

Olivia held still while the diminutive Ardeni woman measured her for the third time. She was a lovely, older woman who'd been thrilled to show Olivia the many styles of clothing that were popular in the surrounding areas. She had sketchbooks, wonderfully painted in watercolors, that depicted women in everything from dresses to skirts to pants paired with various types of blouses, some with deep, revealing V-necks and others with tightly buttoned collars. Olivia was instantly enamored with the fancy coats that the seamstress had on display—they reminded her of Victorian-era military coats with long tails, shiny buttons, and colorful, ribboned brocade.

She'd asked the woman, Mrs. Ketti, for an estimate on three different outfits. When Olivia showed her the quad-attuned Energy beads, the woman had agreed to trade her three outfits for six beads. Olivia had no idea if that was a reasonable price, but the woman was so sweet that Olivia couldn't imagine Mrs. Ketti'd take advantage of her. Besides, she could make a bead in just a bit over two hours. Olivia figured these quad-attuned beads were worth more than their Contribution Store face value—their rarity seemed to make them rather coveted in and of themselves.

After Mrs. Ketti measured her and Olivia had chosen her favorite fabrics and styles, she told Olivia that she'd have the first outfit sized and ready within two hours, and she'd have to come back for the other two later tomorrow. Olivia decided to use that time to head back to the inn and have a nice soak. She and Morgan had both gotten private rooms, and they'd noticed the oversized brass bathtubs in their rooms with anticipation.

The innkeeper, a woman who had introduced herself as Mrs. Hane, was happy to see Olivia when she came in, just a bit after noon, and asked her if she'd be coming down for dinner. "Oh, no, tonight I have dinner plans, but thank you!"

"You're welcome, dear. Is there anything else I can help you with?"

"I wanted to take a bath and get cleaned up. Is there any trick to getting hot water in the tub?" Olivia hadn't noticed if there was running water or if she'd need to boil water or something.

"Oh, just turn on the faucet, dear. We have a pump and heater in the basement."

"Really? Does Energy power them?" Olivia knew this was possible—the bathhouse they'd just built in First Landing had something similar; in fact, it had three components: a pump for water, a heating element, and a cube that the water passed through that somehow filtered it, all run by power-stones that had to be recharged regularly.

"Aye, lass, all the amenities are here for you. Please enjoy yourself. Let me know if you need aught else. By the way, there are soaps and towels on the stand near the tub."

"Thank you, again," Olivia said, walking up the flight of stairs at the back of the common room. Her room was the third one down the hallway at the top of the stairs, next to Morgan's. She entered, using the little brass key she'd been given earlier that day, and was once again filled with warm happiness at the sight of the comfortable room. The bed was large, something like a queen-size back on Earth, and covered with a fluffy, white down comforter and several plump pillows, also in clean white pillowcases. The floor was polished hardwood, and opposite the bed was a small fireplace, logs set and ready to be lit. The room was bright, sunlight streamed through banked windows on the far wall, and in front of those windows was the large, brass tub. The view from the windows was of the river and the far bank. Olivia could just make out people walking around across the river, between houses, and down on little jetties.

Olivia pulled the sheer curtains, making the view fuzzy, but still allowing in lots of light, then she started the tub running. After a few seconds of hissing and clanking, the brass nozzle began to flow with steaming hot water. She undressed, a little annoyed that she'd have to put on her dirty clothes again but cheered by the thought that her first new outfit would be ready soon.

As she soaked in the tub, after she washed herself with the fragrant beeswax soaps Mrs. Hane had left for her, she concentrated on creating another quad-attuned Energy bead. She only had five, and she'd promised Mrs. Ketti six. By the time Olivia finished the Energy bead, her skin had become wrinkly, and the bath was only lukewarm. Still, the time flew by while she was concentrating on the process, and she exited the bath in a very relaxed and pleasant mood. She dried her hair the best she could with just a towel, then slipped on her old, travel-stained, pajama-like clothing she'd gotten from the Colony Stone back in First Landing.

Grabbing her satchel, Olivia hustled out of the inn, waving to Mrs. Hane on her way, and made a beeline right back to Mrs. Ketti's clothing shop. The tiny silvery tinkle of the bell on the door alerted Mrs. Ketti, who came bustling out of the back room. "Olivia, you're just in time. Lori is just finishing up the brocade hem of your coat. Come in, and we'll see how the pants and shirt fit.

Olivia was pleased to find that Mrs. Ketti sold undergarments that were comfortable and not unlike what she could buy at a boutique back on Earth. She'd had fears of bone-ribbed girdles and scratchy wool garters, but this world, with its Energy enhanced crafting, seemed quite advanced in the clothing department when compared to its medieval weaponry, transport, and architecture. She reasoned that having access to the clothing from other worlds via the Colony Stones must have influenced them in this regard.

A short while later, Olivia exited the shop feeling immeasurably better about her appearance. She still wore her dirty, travel-stained boots, but tucked into them were a pair of deep navy leggings made of a cloth that seemed to be somewhere between silk and cotton. Mrs. Ketti said that the material was very durable and easy to wash. She wore a silky royal blue button-up blouse, and over that was her favorite purchase: a sharp-looking, double-breasted, navy blue coat with shiny brass buttons and a turquoise brocade hem and lining. The lining was silky, but the outside of the jacket was almost felt-like. She loved the way it accentuated her waist and how the coat's tail hung just a bit over her butt. It felt smart, in a faux military manner, and she couldn't help standing up straighter and strutting just a bit as she walked.

Mrs. Ketti had suggested she pick up a pair of knee-high, black riding boots to complete the ensemble and recommended a nearby cobbler. Olivia didn't know how soon boots could be made ready for her, but figured she'd check it out. She walked past a few storefronts, inadvertently admiring her reflection in the glass panes, then stepped into the cobbler's shop. She had to wait a few minutes while the shopkeeper, a young Ardeni man with long orange hair, helped a customer. She browsed the shoes and boots on display, admiring the wide variety, from elegant ladies' slippers to heavy, thick-soled work boots.

"How may I help you, miss?" the man asked, and Olivia realized that his customer had left.

"Oh, hello, I was looking to buy some boots like these," Olivia answered, pointing to a pair of shiny, black leather boots that looked exactly like what Mrs. Ketti had described.

"Alright, those are three standards," the man said.

"How long will it take to make my size?"

"No need, they're artificed. After you bond, they'll match your foot size. That's the only enchantment, though—they won't self-repair or clean." Olivia's mind was boggled at the implications.

"You mean clothing can be enchanted?"

"Naturally." He looked at her askance, perhaps only at that moment noting her strange appearance. "You ain't a Ghelli, are ya? Sorry, I thought you just had your wings folded away."

"No, I'm a human. We're a bit new to your world. Can any clothing be enchanted or 'artificed'?"

"Nah, some material can't hold the Energy. Some material can hold a lot more Energy, though. Them boots could probably also be artificed to self-clean, but that would double the cost." Olivia knew that some of the colonists were learning about artificing, but she'd been so busy that she hadn't spent enough time understanding what exactly they could do. The ideas flooding her mind at the thought of self-resizing boots left her reeling. "You okay, miss?"

"Oh, yes. I'll take them!" Olivia handed one of her remaining dual-attuned Energy beads to the man and then sat down on the nearby bench. The man nodded, making the bead disappear into some container he had on his person, and then grabbed the boots. He gently took her hiking boots off, and Olivia reached down, stowing them into her satchel. After he slipped the boots on, which were at least four sizes too large, he stood up and nodded.

"Now, just bind 'em. Just like ya did your satchel there." Olivia did, and as she trickled her Energy into the boots, they shrank before her eyes, sizing themselves perfectly for her feet.

"Amazing!" Olivia stood and walked around the shop, marveling at how well the boots fit. They had a bit more heel than her other boots, and she felt tall, clean, and elegant. What a difference a bit of shopping and a bath could make! "Do you mind telling me how to find the mage's guild?"

Olivia reckoned she had a couple of hours to kill before she was supposed to meet Issa and Morgan, so she made her way over to the mage's guild. The cobbler had smirked when she'd asked about where it was, but he'd gotten over his initial reaction and told her the guild was on the other side of the bridge, not far from the southern gate of the town. As Olivia made her way through town, she smiled at people, and they generally responded in kind. The town was bustling; everywhere she looked, people were carrying goods, standing around talking and laughing, or calling out their wares. Guards were omnipresent, wearing their telltale mustard tabards with some kind of bird of prey embroidered on the chest. Not so much that it felt like a police state, but enough to feel like help was just a shout away.

When Olivia neared the gate, she noticed that the buildings were a bit more run down on this side of town, and the crowds, while still heavy, were made up of kids playing in alleys and people that looked a bit run down and wearing threadbare clothing. It wasn't hard to find the mage's guild—she called out the question to a group of Ardeni kids playing with a ball, and they pointed her down a side street just a block from the gate. When Olivia turned down the road, she saw a squat wooden building, its stain long dried out, leaving the planks gray. A sign hung above the short deck depicted an eye on a black field with stars around it. The eye had once been painted silver, but most of the paint had flaked away, and the black had faded to dingy charcoal.

Olivia stepped up to the door, pulling it open. The interior was a lot better off than the exterior; the floors were polished hardwood, and plush, comfortable-looking leather couches made a sitting area in front of a stone fireplace. It was too warm to warrant a fire, but the scene was inviting, nonetheless. Off to the left of the sitting area was a desk absolutely buried in books and sheaves of paper. A white-haired, very thin Ardeni man was sitting at the desk, holding a magnifying glass up to a large, faded map. "Hello," Olivia said.

"Hmm? Oh, hello there, miss. What brings you to the mage's guild? I'm sorry, but I can't do any contract work today."

"Oh, no, I'm here to enquire about the mage's guild. I mean, you were referred to me by, um, Mr. Wyn? He owns a shop in town selling foci; are you familiar with it?"

"Ah, yes, yes. Wyn. What a good lad. So, he said you should come here?" The frail-looking man stood, setting his magnifying glass down on the table. Olivia didn't think there was an ounce of fat on the man and very little muscle. He couldn't have been more than five foot four, and his beard was long and unkempt. Something about his eyes made her forget the idea that he was frail, though. When he studied her, she felt he was looking right into her soul with those sharp, mint-green eyes. "Hmm, interesting. May I ask permission to Analyze you? It's a skill I have that will let me get an idea about your potential."

"I suppose I don't mind." Olivia stood up straight, self-consciously, and straightened the lapels of her coat. The man kept staring at her, and then she felt a push, almost like an invisible hand was gently pressing its palm against her forehead. A bit of warmth spread through her skin, and she felt the nudge again, but this time right below her solar plexus. She stepped back, holding her hands to her stomach, suddenly uncomfortable with the idea that he was feeling her with his mind.

"You could feel that?" he arched an eyebrow.

"Yes!" Olivia was blushing and looked over her shoulder toward the door.

"Don't be alarmed! I was simply trying to evaluate your Core. Most people don't have enough Energy affinity to be aware of my probing, at least not most people your level."

"Are you Magister Karn? I think I'd like to make sure I know who you are before you go probing me!" Olivia didn't know why, but she felt a little violated.

"Yes, yes. But who are you? I didn't get a full look, but it seems you have a Core with multiple affinities?"

"My name is Olivia Bennet, and yes, I have four affinities."

"Remarkable! The first I've seen in a long while. Are you able to channel more than one at a time?" Olivia, still annoyed at the invasiveness of his first inspection, wanted to retake the upper hand in this meeting. She used her Orb Manipulation ability and summoned her four elemental balls, channeling a bit of Energy into each of them so that they grew to the size of baseballs and began to spin and orbit one another in a complex pattern.

"Yes, I can channel all four at once." She thought Magister Karn's eyes were going to pop out of his head.

"Impressive! And to think, you're only level eight! Unclassed yet!" He practically capered over to her, staring at the orbs that were circling about her left palm. The fiery orb circled the rocky, earth-toned sphere, and around both, she had an ice orb and a little ball of clouds sparking with tiny lightning bolts spinning. "Miss Olivia, you must attend the Fainhallow Academy!"

"The what now?"

"It's a school for magically gifted people. I don't mean just anyone who can manipulate Energy, but truly gifted, like you." Olivia frowned. She hadn't been called gifted since they had come to this planet, and the word sparked a lot of memories—her parents introducing her to friends and family, her professors talking about her research, her employers doing the same. Magister Karn saw her frown and hurriedly continued, "You don't know what a great opportunity this is! I've had a token of admission to give to a promising student for forty-two *years*! You're the first who I think meets the criteria. Listen, you can't go to the academy if you already have a class, and you have to demonstrate skill on a level similar to what you just did, though I'd have settled for much less! Nobody has been able to do that around here in all my time as the Magister of this branch."

Olivia let her elemental orbs dissipate and wink out of existence. She looked at Magister Karn and could see that he was earnest; he desperately wanted her to go to this school. "Where is this school, and how long would I have to go? I have people depending on me back at my settlement."

"The school is on the Thelican Peninsula. It's a thousand miles from here, but I have a teleportation token for a promising student! Your time there could stretch into the years or decades, depending on your aptitudes and courses of study."

"Out of the question, I'm sorry. We're facing an invasion." Olivia shrugged helplessly. "I'm sorry, I actually quite enjoy school. I'd love to learn more about Energy and magic, too."

"Wait, wait. The next enrollment isn't until the first of Belintide; you have two weeks to decide. Miss Olivia, listen; as I said, you're the first promising student I've met in many, many years. Please take the token. If you don't use it, you can bring it back next time you come to Tarn's Crossing." He hurried over to his desk and pulled open a heavy bottom drawer. He rooted around, pulling out books and notebooks and pencils, and then, finally, a box that looked a lot like the kind of box a fancy watch comes in. He blew the dust off it and then brought it over to Olivia.

"Are you sure? I don't think I'll be able to go to the academy. What if someone else shows up . . ."

"Nonsense! Of course, I'm sure. Take it. You are meant to go!" He cut her off, smiling and looking at her ingratiatingly. She took the proffered box and opened it. Tucked into the maroon felt material within was a silver token embossed with the image of a book.

"Alright, but if I don't use it, I'm sure I'll be back to Tarn's sooner or later."

"Excellent, excellent! You're going to do wonderful things, Miss Olivia!" The diminutive, old wizard looked like he'd gained a new lease on life. He was beaming, his teeth on full display. "Would you like to sit down and talk about the Academy? Perhaps I have some cookies around here." He turned and started moving toward his desk, a searching expression on his face.

"No, no, I'm sorry, Magister, but I have to meet some people. I'm afraid I'll be late." Olivia put the teleportation token into her satchel and turned to the door.

"Very well. I hope you don't mind if I send word to the Academy. I'm sure they'll be excited to hear of your pending arrival. To be honest, I just want to toot my own horn; I have some rivals there who never will believe I've found such a promising student."

"Well, aren't you going to feel embarrassed if I don't go?"

"I might, yes, so I'll just trust that you'll be going! The fates wouldn't be so cruel to an old man." He laughed loudly, and Olivia had a hard time not smiling. She walked to the door and opened it.

"Thank you, Magister. I hope things work out for both of us." Then she stepped outside and hurriedly walked toward the inn; she didn't want to miss dinner with Morgan and Issa.

MORGAN

"Alright, Morgan, I'll come back to meet you and Olivia in an hour," Issa said, squeezing him around the waist. "Unless you want me to come up with you while you bathe?" she growled softly, with an impish grin.

"Uh, hell yes, come up with me!"

"You scoundrel! What do you take me for? We've hardly kissed!" Issa pulled back, slapping him on the shoulder.

"Oh, I should have seen that trap!" Morgan laughed.

She laughed, too, and said, "Well, if you're that eager, at least kiss me now." Morgan was happy to comply, and they shared a moment there, under a willowy tree in the grassy area next to the inn. After a short while, they parted, and Morgan walked, somewhat dazed, up to his room to get cleaned up. His travel-weary bones were happy for the opportunity to bathe, and when he finished, he was even more pleased to put on his new clothes.

After visiting her father's smith, Issa had taken him back toward the inn, but they'd stopped by a bustling tailor's shop. Inside had been no fewer than four tailors who, Issa had said, were all able to enhance their clothing creations with Artisan skills. Morgan hadn't known what to expect of that, but it soon became apparent: after measuring him and selecting some fabric, they'd gone to the back room and come out with tailor-made shirts and pants for him in a matter of minutes. They weren't anything too special: four button-up shirts with loose collars in white, turquoise, rust, and black. The rust and black shirts were made from more sturdy material and meant for daily use during travel or "adventuring."

Issa had talked him out of buying four of the same pants style. Instead, he bought three pairs of black, sturdy pants that reminded him of wool-blend suit pants. He thought they looked nice, but Issa had forced him to buy another pair of slightly lighter material with a barely noticeable design, kind of like paisleys stitched down the outer seams in a dark, shiny thread. Then, of course, she'd talked him into some new boots and a belt, both made from polished black leather.

Morgan slipped on the generic underpants and shirt that he'd bought—basically like handmade boxers and a V-neck T-shirt, then put on his fancy pants, his turquoise shirt, and his dimensional ring. He put his power-stone necklace into the ring with all his other valuable items, leaving only his camping supplies and food and beverages in his pouch. Doing so, he felt okay stashing the pouch under his bed before walking down to the common room to wait for Olivia and Issa.

On his way out, Morgan stopped in front of the empty armoire near the door, opening it to look at himself in the mirror mounted inside. He cut a pretty good figure in his new clothes, and he grinned, but then a thought crossed his mind and the grin faded. Was he being stupid and selfish, wasting his time getting new clothes and touring Issa's village? Shouldn't he be racing back to the colony with help, ready to fight the Urghat? He shook his head, remembering that the Tarn's Crossing council hadn't even met yet. What good would he do racing off before he'd gotten an official answer? Sure, the governor sounded hopeful, saying it was mostly a formality for the council to agree, but he should be here to receive the official reply. On top of that, this whole new world business wasn't temporary. He cared about Issa, and he wanted to meet her people. He wanted to see how she lived. It might be a little selfish, but he was damned if he wasn't going to get cleaned up and have some dinner with her father while he was in town.

He nodded to himself, straightened his collar, and carefully closed the armoire door. He could get killed falling off his roladii or by an alpha boyii. He could get abducted by some horror that made the Yovashi seem like a cuddly rabbit. He needed to grab what pleasure he could while he could because he quite literally didn't know what was coming next in this world. He stepped into the hallway, used the little key Mrs. Hane had given him to lock up after himself, and walked toward the stairs.

As he descended, he could see that the common room was crowded with the dinner rush. Apparently, Mrs. Hane's customers were fans of her cooking because the tables were all busy with people, and some folks were even standing around the hearth drinking from large wooden mugs. The room was warm, and Morgan felt a bit uncomfortable, so he decided to step outside into the evening air to wait. He was surprised when he walked out to see that Olivia was already out there, sitting on a bench next to the walkway that led to the street, talking to Issa. "Oh, am I late?" Both ladies stopped talking, looking toward him, and Issa rushed over to hug him.

"No, we've only been here a couple of minutes," Olivia said, clearing her throat and standing up.

"Let's go!" Issa said, tugging on Morgan's arm and walking toward the street. Morgan followed, but not before he got a look at Olivia and her new clothes.

"Hey, you look nice! I like that coat," Morgan blurted.

"I was just telling her that!" Issa said, squeezing his hand. Olivia flushed, her red cheeks on her pale face easy to spot, even in the dim evening light, and straightened her jacket.

"Oh, thank you. I had an enjoyable day of shopping. I ordered a new staff, too, and it cost most of the Energy beads you gave me. Sorry!" she said, smiling sheepishly.

"No worries, I spent a ton on a new sword, too. I think we're going to need to find a way to make money with our expensive tastes."

"You'll make plenty! After we save your colony from the Urghat, we'll do some real adventuring!" Issa said matter-of-factly.

"Are you coming with us back to First Landing, then?" Olivia asked, walking just a step behind Issa and Morgan. Issa turned back to her and nodded.

"Of course!" She said, picking up the pace and pulling even harder on Morgan's arm. Olivia looked at Morgan, and he shrugged, a grin plastered to his face, while he hurried after Issa. They hustled through the market square, over the bridge, then west past another street full of shops, and up a road that began to wind over a gentle hill. The buildings were more sparse here, obviously homes with larger lots. Soon they came to a brightly lit home, its windows shedding light on the dark grass in the gloom of the evening. "This is it!" Issa announced, leading them up the path and to the front door.

What followed was a night that put their long journey and all their recent tribulations out of their minds. Issa's father was a remarkable cook, and he served them a delicious roast huldii, garnished with a sweet, minty jam. He had a mash of some root vegetable that was remarkably like sweet potatoes. And a delicious cold soup that Morgan thought had a hint of cucumber and pepper flavor. For dessert, Roald served a pie that Olivia swore tasted just like her grandma's pumpkin pie. Roald claimed he didn't know what a pumpkin was.

Sitting around in the den with their bellies swollen and a sweet liquor in their hands, they talked about life in Tarn's Crossing, how happy Roald was to have Issa home, and how he knew they'd soon be leaving. Word had already traveled among the town elders that First Landing had an Urghat problem, and that hunters would be needed to help solidify the new alliance between their peoples. Roald seemed at ease, even though he knew Issa intended to go with Morgan.

"I know she won't let you go off and defend your home alone," Roald said when Morgan brought up the prospect of heading home in a day or two. "I'll level with you, Morgan; Issa is very dear to me; she's my last remaining family! I tried to talk her out of going with you just before she went to pick you up to come to dinner!" He laughed, face flushed a dark shade of reddish-purple with the exertion and drink. "She'd have none of it, though, and I can't argue.

I daresay she's better equipped to face some Urghat out here than the horrors you two lived through in the Crucible."

"Well, she's dear to me, too, so you don't need to worry about me taking her safety lightly."

"Stop talking about me like either of you have any say! I'm a Battle Witch, and I can take care of myself!" Issa growled, her words just a little slurred from the drink. Observing from a couch off to the side, Olivia smiled at Issa, clearly thinking about something that the scene reminded her of. Morgan just held up his hands and sat back, swirling the sweet brandy in his glass.

"Right, daughter, of course," Roald said, shaking his head. "That class! Why couldn't you have chosen an Artisan path? Who will I leave my shop to?"

"Oh, you're ridiculous!" Issa growled.

"Not to interrupt," Olivia said, "but is it possible to do Artisan work like enchanting items without the class? Like if you had a class like Issa's but still wanted to be able to put enchantments on weapons?"

"No, thank you for interrupting!" Issa said, sitting back and taking a long drink from her glass. Roald cleared his throat and nodded.

"Yes, if someone like Issa were interested"—he emphasized *interested* and glared at Issa—"and wanted to study enchanting, she might find an interesting class refinement offered to her at level twenty." Olivia just nodded and smiled.

"Um, speaking of Artificers and enchantment, Father, Morgan bought a sword from Brint. Do you think you could do some work on it before we leave?" Issa's voice had transformed from vexed to syrupy, and Morgan looked at her, startled. She arched an eyebrow at him and pursed her lips. Meanwhile, her father rushed to please her:

"Oh, of course, of course. Morgan, come to my shop first thing; I'll set aside my project for Dran Gorram. He owes me, anyway, and I know he won't mind a little delay."

"That's very kind; thank you, Roald." The conversation continued for a while, but Olivia and Morgan were clearly exhausted, and soon Roald cleared his throat and suggested that their company might want to get some rest. Issa resisted at first but soon relented, walking Morgan and Olivia to the door.

"You're sure you can find your way back to the inn?" Issa asked, still clasped in a goodbye hug with Morgan. After saying her goodbyes, Olivia had wandered away to the end of the path near the road.

"Yes, of course. Will you meet me at your father's shop tomorrow? We can get breakfast after I drop off the sword."

"Yes, that sounds nice." Issa reached up, and Morgan met her halfway, and they shared a brief kiss; then, Morgan let her go and walked out to join Olivia on the road.

"Well, should I phone ahead and let everyone know we need to plan a wedding?" Olivia giggled, as they started back the way they'd come.

"Oh, jeez. Gimme a break; I didn't tease you about your love interest." Morgan almost didn't say it, but it came out before he could stop himself.

"Huh? What love interest?"

"Oh, c'mon; I've seen the way you and Bronwyn look at each other." He figured there was no going back now.

"Oh, really? Well, that's all in your head, mister. Besides, she and I . . ." A low whistle came from an alley on their left, cutting off Olivia's retort. Some shadows had detached from the larger, darker shadow cast by the building and were approaching them.

"What've we here? A couple of huldii fawns left by the herd?" The voice was sneering, nasal, and not at all friendly. Morgan felt a jolt of electricity run down his spine, and he was instantly sober, at least to his mind. He turned toward the four figures slinking toward them. Olivia, for her part, didn't panic; instead, she summoned an orb of fire and let it hover over her palm.

"Quiet now, Kwint. Let me speak." Another voice spoke these words, this one quite a lot deeper and sure of itself. "Which of you two is Morgan? I'd venture to say it's the big one, but I'm unfamiliar with your strange, pale race, so I wouldn't want to assume." Olivia took in a breath, about to speak, but Morgan beat her to it.

"I'm Morgan. Who's asking?" Morgan turned to the figure that spoke, just now coming into the light.

"Ah, good. My name's Swent, and this is my second, Bennic. I'm assuming that skinny lad there is your second?" The Ardeni man came into the light of Olivia's orb, and Morgan could see that he was a stout fellow with coloring similar to Issa's—bright yellow hair and eyes. He wore a scaled hauberk, each scale an intricately forged replica of a leaf. Morgan knew he was trying to get a rise out of him by repeatedly insulting Olivia, and it was working. Still, he managed to rein in his sharp retort. About to reply, he felt Olivia's hand on his wrist, and she spoke:

"That's right; I'm his second. What of it?" Olivia spoke like she knew what the guy meant by "second." Morgan wasn't quite sure what the term meant, but he had a vaguely unpleasant feeling about this whole thing.

"You heard the lad, Bennic." Olivia bristled but didn't say anything, and Morgan didn't trust himself to speak, so he just stood next to her. Meanwhile, Bennic, a thin, pleasant-looking man with mild eyes and a long, red mustache, stepped forward and held out a scroll to Olivia. Olivia took it in her free hand, but, at the same time, she did something to make the fiery orb in her other hand double in size and flare suddenly. Bennic backed away, stumbling over his own feet, and Olivia smirked.

"You have received my challenge. Witness?" Swent said.

"Witnessed!" All three of his companions said in unison, and then they turned on their heels and walked back into the alley. Morgan stood there dumbfounded and only then concluded that he probably was a bit drunk still. He looked to Olivia and saw that she'd opened the scroll and was looking intently at the writing, her brow furrowed.

"What the hell was that about?" Morgan huffed out a breath he didn't realize he'd been holding.

"Well, it looks like you've been challenged to a duel."

"Oh, for fucks sake."

◈ MORGAN ◈

Morgan woke the following day with the gray light of dawn coming through the bay windows of his room. He used the washbasin next to the wardrobe to splash water on his face, banishing the grogginess of his hangover. He hadn't slept well; he'd had a lot of wine with dinner and then too much of that brandy that Roald had served out. He dressed in some of his new pants and the sturdy black shirt he'd bought, keeping his armor stowed in his ring. Sure, he'd been challenged to a duel, but it wasn't until tomorrow, at dawn no less. It seemed like a dream, partly because he'd been drunk, but also because of the strangeness of it all. The idea that Swent had been lurking in the shadows waiting for him to pass by so Swent could challenge him to a duel over some perceived slight to his honor just baffled Morgan.

Olivia had read the challenge and said she'd explain it in the morning, but, in short, it was about Issa. Apparently, Swent felt like Morgan had stolen her from him. The whole thing was irritating to Morgan. He was irritated, most of all, that he had never heard of Swent, not from Issa, not from her father, not from anyone. Morgan tied his pouch to his belt, looked around the room to see that he hadn't left anything behind and then walked down to the common room. There wasn't any sign of Olivia, and he figured he could meet her later. "Mrs. Hane, do you mind letting Olivia know that I've gone out to run some errands, and I'll look for her here around noon?"

"Of course, dear. No breakfast for you?" Mrs. Hane was wiping down a table. Most of the tables were unoccupied at this early hour, but a few people were sitting around eating eggs and sausages, drinking from steaming mugs. It looked good, and Morgan's stomach rumbled.

"I wish I could, but I'm meeting someone soon. Maybe we'll come back this way to eat." He waved and stepped out into the cool morning air. The streets were quiet, only a few early risers out and about. Morgan walked briskly to Issa's father's shop. When he arrived, he was pleased to see the light in the window and smoke coming from the little stack above his wood stove. Morgan pulled the door and entered with the jangling of the bell. Roald was sitting in front of his stove, reading a thin book with illustrations of birds.

"Morgan! Good morning, lad. I hope you slept alright," he said, closing his book and standing. "Issa will be along soon; she wasn't feeling great this morning. I must admit that I teased her quite a lot. Imagine, she's already improved her race twice and still can't hold her liquor as well as I can with no improvements!"

"You probably have me beat, too," Morgan replied, smiling wanly.

"Hah, well, when she comes, you two should get a hearty breakfast; that'll set you straight. Now, let me see this sword my friend Brint has sold you." He walked over to Morgan and waited while Morgan summoned the sword from his storage ring. The smith had sold it to him in a nicely tooled leather sheath with brass-colored metal chape, locket, and suspension rings. He'd told Morgan he could wear it from a belt or on his back, but Morgan found it just as easy and convenient to keep it in his ring. He pulled the sheath off and extended the handle to Roald. "Ah, now that's a beauty," he said, taking the sword and setting the point on the ground. He squatted to run his fingers along the flat of the blade.

"Can you do much with it, you think? I hate to put a deadline on things, but I'll probably need it tomorrow by dawn. It seems I have a duel." Morgan's voice was flat, he wasn't trying to sound irritated, but he felt like someone should have mentioned Swent yesterday.

"What's this now? Who'd you get mixed up with?" He squinted up at Morgan.

"Oh, some fellow named Swent or Swint issued a challenge last night on my way home from your house." Morgan studied Roald's face as he spoke, looking for a reaction, and he wasn't disappointed. Roald's dark-blue skin turned purple, and he growled several words that Morgan didn't quite catch.

"That grott-loving fool!" He stomped around his shop, stopping by the counter to grab a heavy book and fling it against the wall. Pages flapped, and documents he'd had stuffed in the binding fluttered around. "I'm sorry, Morgan. That fool had been courting Issa long before she went to the Crucible, but nothing was ever promised."

"Well, Olivia has the challenge, and I don't know the details, but do I have to fight him?" Roald looked at Morgan sharply, but his scowl softened, and he spoke:

"I almost forgot how new you are to our culture. No, you don't have to fight him; you can back out. You'll lose credibility in this town if you do, as will my family. He believes he has a grievance. Law allows for a duel between peers if there is a perceived slight, regardless of the validity. You have a class and haven't had a refinement, same as Swent, so in the law's eyes, he is your peer." He blew out an exasperated breath, puffing his cheeks, and, just as he was about to continue, the bell rang, and Issa came into the shop.

"Hi!" She was all smiles and hurried over to hug Morgan. He hugged her back, but when she looked at her father and noted the silence, she said, "What's the matter?"

"Swent challenged Morgan to a duel last night." Roald bent to pick up Morgan's sword, which he'd let fall in his tirade.

"What? That idiot!" She pulled away from Morgan and looked at him with a concerned face. "I did not promise myself to him, Morgan! I'll settle this, though. I'll challenge *him* to a duel!"

"You can't cancel a duel with another duel, Issa. The law is explicit. Besides, you're only level ten and have barely just gotten your class. Swent's made a name for himself dueling, and isn't he on the doorstep to level twenty?" Issa growled and kicked over her father's wooden stool.

"He's such a self-important twit! I'm sorry, Morgan. One of the reasons I insisted on going into the Crucible was to get away from his attentions. His family has had a seat on the council for generations, and the governor listens to them far too much. Oh, what a sneaky rat to call you out when I wasn't around!"

"So, will be hard on you and your dad if I don't fight him?" Morgan already knew the answer, but he thought he should sound things out completely.

"Yes, we'll lose face, to the point that if I wanted to stay with you, I'd need to leave. My father could probably stay, but his business would suffer. Honor is important to Ardeni, to the point that it's become less of a boon and more of a burden."

"Hush, Issa; don't talk that way," her father admonished.

"I will not hush! Wait here; I'm going to go and sort this out!" Ignoring her father's protestations, Issa turned and stormed out the door. Morgan looked at Roald, who cursed again while looking at the ground and followed Issa out the door. He saw her walking briskly toward the market square and gave chase. His long legs allowed him to catch up to her as they crossed the northern end of the market and onto the bridge.

"Hold up, Issa. Tell me what's going on! I feel like I stepped into a movie that was halfway over." He reached for her arm, but she pulled away.

"I'm going to talk to Swent. This is nonsense. The law is stupid. He's stupid; this whole thing is stupid. You don't have to fight him, Morgan!"

"Alright, well, let's talk to him then." He fell into step with Issa, and she huffed, upset, and too flummoxed for words. She stomped over the bridge, turned right, and followed three different streets through a residential area until she came to a house that resembled her father's in style and size. She didn't pause but stalked to the door and began pounding on the wood. A short while later, an Ardeni woman with black hair, plump cheeks, and eyes that glittered like flakes of obsidian opened the door with a frown.

"What the ancestors? This better be an emergency!"

"Rua! I need to talk to your brother right now!" Issa leaned forward, her words dripping with venom.

"Oh, you. Issa, you shouldn't be here. You also shouldn't have promised yourself to Swent and then embarrassed him the way you did. It's really effected our family!" Rua backed a step away from Issa and put her hands on her hips. Her face said clearly, "I'm not moving."

"I did not promise myself to him! Rua, you know Swent! Just because he's known me my whole life and assumed with his friends that I was his doesn't make it so! Did you know he challenged Morgan to a duel? As if it's Morgan's fault I didn't want him!" She pointed her thumb at Morgan. Who, feeling very out of place, shrugged sheepishly.

"Hmm, yes, I'm not surprised. You should be more honest, Issa. You and Swent were together a lot in the last few years, and his friends are bearing witness that you two were promised before you went to the Crucible."

"What?" Issa's face was getting darker by the second, and she leaned forward, eyes watery with frustration. "His friends are saying we were promised? Don't you think you'd have heard that from Swent or me? Rua, we were friends!" A choked sob of frustration escaped Issa, and Morgan saw that this wasn't going the way she'd hoped. He reached forward to touch her shoulder, but, again, she shrugged off his touch. "Do you want Swent to die, Rua? Will that help your family save face?" Morgan didn't like the idea of having to kill some ex-lover of Issa's, jilted or not. He finally cleared his throat to speak.

"Speaking for myself, I'd rather come up with a solution to this issue that didn't involve anyone getting killed." Issa glanced back at him, tears brimming in her eyes, and Rua looked up at him and snorted. Had he said the wrong words?

"I'll see if Swent wants to talk to you, Issa, but you need to be honest with your new man." She turned and closed the door. Issa sniffed and turned to Morgan.

"I swear, Morgan. I swear! I did not promise myself to this lying ass! He probably told his friends I did, and this is him trying to save face."

"I believe you, Issa. This whole thing is surreal to me. Like, even if you 'promised' yourself to him, is that some kind of binding contract?"

"No! But, if he's been telling his friends we're promised, and then I came back from the Crucible and didn't give him the time of day, it made him look a fool. Now he thinks he can save face by beating or killing the man I've been telling people about."

"The law says he can do that? Just start a fight with anyone he wants?" Morgan raised an eyebrow.

"Not exactly. He has to have a case that his honor has been sullied. If his friends back up his claims, I can see the law allowing this to go forward. I'm sorry, Morgan! What a mess you walked into when you met me!" Issa's voice was thick with frustration, her eyes welling with unspilled tears. Morgan was about to reply when the door opened a few inches, and Rua pushed her face out.

"He says to go away. He'll see you tomorrow morning on the martial field." She looked at Issa for a long moment, then frowned and said, "I'm sorry, Issa. I want to believe you, but what's done is done. I hope Swent is quick with your new man; I hate it when a duel is cruel and slow." With that, she shut the door, and Morgan heard a lock click home. Morgan put his arm around Issa's shoulders, and this time she didn't try to shrug him off. She leaned into him, and they walked together back to the road and slowly retraced their steps toward Roald's shop.

They were more than halfway back when Morgan finally broke the silence. "Well, I'm not going to let us all be driven out of town by some prick. If he wants to fight, so be it." He shrugged. Issa was silent for a long time, walking under his arm, leaning into his side. Several times he felt her inhale to speak but stop. They were outside Roald's shop when she pulled his arm off her shoulder and turned to look at him. She almost said something when Roald pulled open the door.

"Well? What happened?" He seemed oblivious to the interruption he'd made, and Morgan's lip quirked into a smile. Here was a father that loved his daughter and was full of concern. How nice it must be to have a family!

"Looks like I'll be fighting the guy. He's been lying about his relationship to Issa, I guess." Morgan turned to Roald, pulling Issa under his arm again and grinning like a fool.

"Morgan, he has a fairly unique class for our people; he's a Skirmisher, and he's spent his youth perfecting his combat skills. He's been dueling since he was twelve years old," Roald said, a frown furrowing his brow. "I'd hoped Issa would talk some sense into him."

"Alright, well, is the fight to the death?"

"A combatant can yield, asking for mercy, but their opponent need not be merciful." Roald shook his head, looking down with a deep frown. "Swent is bitter. He knows Issa won't forgive him for this. It's not like she'll take him back, especially now that she has her class. He's doing this to punish her and embarrass me. I wouldn't count on his mercy."

"Huh. Can I use all my skills? Or is this just about weapon skills?"

"No, you can use any skills or spells that you have." Issa nodded knowingly at Morgan while she spoke. "You can beat him, Morgan."

"So, you think you can be done with the sword before dawn?" Morgan looked at Roald and did his best to smile gamely.

"Oh, yes. I have something I've been saving. I can't see how I could go wrong using it on the weapon of a man willing to put his life on the line for my family's honor. You aren't too partial to this agate on the pommel, are you?" Roald was still gripping Morgan's sword, and he lifted it up, point down, to display the orange-yellow stone.

"It looks nice, but no, it's nothing special to me," Morgan replied, reaching out to rub the stone with his thumb. It didn't feel like anything special.

"I have a gem I've spent the last few years working on, off and on, as a pet project. I began it when I received my class refinement at level twenty. I'll replace that agate with it. It's a bit larger, and it isn't as heavy as the metal I'll have to cut away, which will disturb the balance of the sword. Don't worry, though; I know a simple enchantment I can put on the tang to increase the weight proportionate to what we're losing. It will still be perfect. I need to get to work; you kids go and get some food." With that, he stepped back into his shop, waved quickly, and closed the door on them.

"Hey, let's go back to my inn and eat. Mrs. Hane was putting on quite a spread!" Morgan smiled and squeezed his arm around Issa's shoulders, turning with her to walk up the street toward the inn.

"Aren't you worried?" she asked, her yellow brows drawn into a scowl.

"Nah. Come on, we've been through worse."

"I'm so sorry to cause you this trouble, Morgan." Issa tugged out of his arm and turned toward him as they walked. "I'm sure you have a million things to worry about, and now this. I really won't hate you, if you and Olivia want to just leave town tonight."

"Are you fucking kidding me? You better be kidding! I won the galactic lottery by finding you in the first place; I'm not going to let some asshole scare me off. Not to mention, our people need this alliance. Come on, let's not talk about it anymore." With that, he put his arm back over her shoulders, and she grabbed him around the waist, and they made their way back to the inn.

Morgan was surprised to see Olivia already up and sitting at a table with a heaping plate of scrambled eggs and four pieces of buttery toast. She was sipping on a big mug of steaming tea which she set down to wave them over. The room was crowded but not full, and Olivia's table was unoccupied save for her. "Good morning," she brightly said when they walked over.

"Good morning to you!" Issa replied, sitting down across from Olivia. Morgan smiled and sat next to Issa. He'd only just scooted his chair in when a young Ardeni girl, maybe only ten or twelve years old, stepped up to the table.

"Do you two want some breakfast?" She had her green hair pulled into a topknot and wore a dirty apron. Her eyebrow was quirked in a way to suggest she was willing to wait for an answer, but only for a few seconds. Morgan couldn't help smiling at her.

"Well, of course. I'll have what my friend there is having. How about you, Issa?"

"You know I'm hungry!" Issa nodded to the girl, and she left.

"I guess menus aren't a thing here. When I said I wanted breakfast, Mrs. Hane just had her daughter bring me this plate." Olivia shrugged. "It's perfect, though!" She shoved another big forkful of eggs into her mouth. Issa laughed and reached toward her plate.

"Could I have a piece of your toast? I'll pay you back when mine comes." Olivia nodded, her mouth still full.

Morgan watched Issa eat her toast and Olivia shovel in her eggs, and he sat back feeling strangely content. Sure, he had a duel, possibly to the death, waiting for him in the morning, but things were going well, all told. It seemed improbable that he was here with Issa, sitting in a crowded inn, eating breakfast with friends. While still fresh in his mind, the Crucible also seemed to be a million miles and years away. He knew he should be a bit more worried about Swent—apparently, he was something of a professional duelist, and he had four levels on Morgan. Still, Morgan had an advanced class himself, and he had some titles that also gave him strength. He didn't know how big a deal his Human Champion title was, but it seemed to him that his Energy-based abilities having a 50 percent boost in efficacy wasn't something to sneeze at.

Their food came, and everyone got quiet for a few minutes as they all got to work, eating with gusto. After a few minutes, though, Olivia spoke up, "Hey, I'm assuming you guys aren't mentioning it for a reason, but are we good with the whole duel thing happening tomorrow morning?"

"Yeah," Morgan said, looking up from his plate, "we kinda don't have a choice. If we want to have a successful alliance with these people, fleeing from a challenge to my honor would make for a bad precedent."

"Mmhmm, when I read the challenge, I noticed some legal phrasing, and it seemed like Swent might have some legal or customary backing."

"Technically, he does," Issa interjected, "but it was cowardly to ambush you in the middle of the night and make the challenge before anyone could object or at least call him out for his foolishness. Now it's been served and accepted; even if I make a fuss, it will look bad if anyone were to intervene. Though, I swear, Morgan, if he kills you, I will kill him or die. He's made a terrible mistake with this duel." Issa's face had become solemn, and Morgan couldn't help trying to dispel the mood.

"There's some egg on your chin." He laughed, reaching out a hand as though to wipe it away. She hissed and slapped his hand, wiping her face with a napkin.

"No, there wasn't!" Olivia said, a big smile making her eyes crinkle up at the corners. Issa put some egg on her fork, holding it threateningly as if she'd throw it at Morgan.

"Relax, I'm sorry, but I don't want to talk about the duel anymore. It is what it is." Morgan sighed and sipped at his tea. It almost reminded him of coffee, but it was just a bit too watery.

"Well, I have some other news we could talk about!" Olivia said, reaching toward her satchel and producing a polished wooden box like one might keep a ring or watch in. She opened it, revealing a silver coin with a book stamped on it. "The magister at the mage's guild here in town gave me this. It's a teleportation token—he said it would take me to an academy where I can learn more about magic." She snapped the lid closed.

"What? That sounds awesome!" Morgan said.

"Really? I've never heard of anyone from the town going to such a place," Issa added.

"Well, he seemed to be impressed with my Core and the way I can manipulate different Energy affinities at once. He said he'd been holding this token for decades. The thing is, the school starts in a couple of weeks. Also, I can't take a class or get to level ten before I go." Olivia sniffed, pulling her straight black hair back over her shoulders. Morgan could see she had a lot on her mind, and he supposed it was a big decision.

"Any idea how far away the school is? Or how long it will last?"

"Magister Karn said it's on a peninsula a thousand miles away. He said it could last months, years, or decades, depending on my pursuits and success. I don't know how any of it works—will I be able to visit between terms? Will I be able to communicate with the colony at all? I feel excited about the idea of a school to learn more about magic, but I also dread leaving you, Bronwyn, the colony in the lurch."

"Well, you have two weeks," Issa said. "I'd take some time to really think about it. We'll make it back to your settlement by then, and you can talk to your other friends, too." Olivia smiled and nodded at Issa, but Morgan could see the storm cloud behind her eyes. He decided, once again, to change the subject.

"Hey, we've got a full day with nothing to do; what's fun around here, Issa?"

MORGAN

It was still dark out when Morgan heard the knock on his door. He sat up in bed. Having been awake for the last hour or so, staring at the ceiling, he wasn't startled by the sound. He stood up and slipped on his boots—he was already dressed. He went to the door and said, "Who is it?"

"It's Roald. I have your sword." Roald's voice was a gruff whisper. Morgan opened the door, and the older Ardeni walked into the room, a bundle wrapped in black silks held in his arms. "I just finished an hour ago. I took a minute to eat some food then came right over. Take a look at this beauty." He pulled the silk wrappings away from the naked blade, holding it out to Morgan sideways, resting it on his palms.

"Wow, it looks different. I didn't expect this much of a change." Morgan gingerly took the sword from Roald's hands. The most striking change was that the metal, previously steel-colored with a hint of amber when you turned it just right, was now a dark blue-black color, even in the bright orange light of the Energy lantern in Morgan's room. The blade was etched with dozens of runes. They ran from the guard up and around the sides of the shallow fuller. Even the dark metal circle of the guard had runes etched around it. At the bottom of the hilt, the agate pommel stone had been replaced by a much larger black onyx. The onyx was also inscribed with dozens of tiny silvery runes, and it gave off a very faint, smokey black aura.

"The color change is due to the gem—it's bound with the sword now, some of its essence mixing with the metal. You'll need to bond with the sword now for all of the enchantments to benefit you." Roald spoke softly, almost reverently, while he looked at his work. "It's not the greatest weapon I've ever worked on, but it's damn close. That gemstone is my best creation so far."

"Thank you, Roald. I hope I don't let you down today." Morgan held the sword, giving it a couple of practice swings away from Roald. "Should I bond with it now?"

"Yes! No point wasting time." Roald seemed excited, so Morgan stopped goofing around and held the sword still, slowly trickling some Energy into the hilt. He felt his Energy course quickly through the metal tang and spread throughout the blade, including the black opal pommel stone.

*****Umbral Razor: Artificed Weapon. Enchantments: 1. Sharpness—This weapon will maintain its unnaturally sharp edge, recovering from wear and damage over time. 2. Hardness—This weapon has been strengthened by a master Artificer; resistance to shattering is increased by a factor of one thousand. 3. Umbral Eye—This weapon has pseudo awareness and can see a short way into the future. In combat, it will occasionally make its wielder aware of an enemy's strike before it happens.*****

After Morgan read and dismissed the notification, he noticed that the sword didn't feel the same in his hand. He was still aware of his hand on the grip, but it felt far more natural, almost like it was a part of his body. He swung it around, and he felt like he knew exactly where the blade was in relation to objects he was swinging it by. "This is fucking amazing, Roald!"

"It is, isn't it?" Roald's grin spread from ear to ear.

"Can I still store it in my ring? Once, a spirit told me that intelligent items suffered while in dimensional storage items."

"Aye, it's not really intelligent—it doesn't think about things when you aren't fighting, and when you are fighting, it's only looking for what your opponent is going to do next. It's good you know that, though. Intelligent items can be driven mad, languishing within dimensional storage devices." Morgan nodded, making a few more short swings with the sword before stowing it into his ring.

"Thanks again for the enchantments, Roald. They ought to help! Well, I suppose I should get my armor on. I don't think I'll eat breakfast, though." Morgan sat down on the side of the bed and started calling forth his armor, piece by piece, and strapping it on. He donned his vambraces first, then his greaves, and finally his breastplate. The breastplate, while plain, was undoubtedly sturdy. It had long ago finished mending from the damage it received fighting that Yovashi matron. Roald watched him from a wooden chair situated near the hearth. He didn't say anything, probably not wanting to distract Morgan before the fight.

Yesterday, while walking around town with Issa and Olivia, they'd visited the martial field where most duels took place. Standing with a grunt, Morgan went out to the hall and, with Roald trailing, went down to Olivia's door. He knocked lightly, and it opened almost immediately. Olivia was dressed similarly to when she'd gone to dinner the other night. This time, though, she wore black pants, a silky mustard blouse, and another coat much like the blue one she'd had on; this one was dark maroon with a mustard and silver-gilt brocade hem. "You look fancy," Morgan said.

"Hmm? This old thing?" Olivia ran her palms along the lapels of her coat, pulling it snugly on her shoulders.

"Shall we?" Morgan asked, motioning down the hallway. Olivia nodded and fell into step behind him. Roald nodded a greeting to her, and they made their way out, through the dark common room and to the street. They were halfway to the martial field when Issa came jogging up.

"Hey, I just missed you at your inn." She walked up next to Morgan and took his hand in hers.

"Glad you're here," he said, squeezing her hand. They were the first to arrive at the field, a flat open area near the town's southern gate. The sky was still dark—Morgan knew it would be dawn soon; looking out over the distant tree line, he could see the western horizon lightening. Morgan was glad they'd gotten there before Swent and his crew and any observers. He pulled forth his sword, walked out onto the field, away from his companions, and began to practice the forms of his Fighting Crane Style.

He'd never felt so connected and smooth with the forms before. He felt the sword snapping from one position to the next, slicing the air with a satisfying whipping sound. He knew part of it was due to having a proper weapon, but the enchantments that Roald had performed on the sword added up to more than the sum of their parts. Something about the weapon made it more of an extension of his body, and he wondered what hidden attributes it had that resulted in the feeling. He was worried about his low dexterity, though. The faster and more powerful his motions became, the more he struggled to hold the blade precisely right or to turn it in time for the speed and strength of his larger movements. He felt he even had to hold back a little to make sure the minute adjustments of his wrists were set before he completed a swing or thrust. He hoped it wouldn't be a factor in this duel, but he knew he had to find a way to increase his dexterity if he wanted to keep improving his swordwork.

"Morgan," Olivia's voice interrupted his practice and his thoughts, and he looked over to her. She walked closer to him and said, "You should meditate or something now. Don't let Swent get a look at your swordwork." Morgan nodded and stowed his sword. He sat near his friends and began his cultivation drill, losing himself in the flow of Energy. Sometime later, he became aware of low voices and a warm glow behind his eyelids. He finished his cycle and then opened his eyes. A small crowd had gathered around the field, maybe thirty or forty people. He saw Swent and the men who'd been with him the other night on the opposite side. Glancing over the crowd of faces, he saw some looking somber and others joking and smiling. He didn't see Rua, Swent's sister. Was her not being there a condemnation of the duel? Did it matter?

"Are we ready, then?" Morgan asked, standing up.

"Not yet. There's supposed to be an official from the council to oversee the duel. From the chatter, it sounds like the governor himself is on his way," Issa said, resting a hand on Morgan's shoulder. "I wish I could give you some battle magic, but they'd disqualify you."

"I know, don't worry." Morgan patted her hand and then turned to the field, looking at Swent. He noticed Morgan and turned to face him, a smirk on his face. "He sure is cocky."

"Aye, he's a right prick," Roald said, spitting into the flattened grass. Morgan made a mental note not to sit there. He didn't have time to respond because a murmur broke out in the crowd, and then, under the yellow and orange-streaked clouds of sunrise, the governor strode onto the field.

"Alright, let's get on with the proceedings!" He called out. "Duelists and seconds, come forward." Swent walked toward the governor, but before Morgan could take a step, Issa pulled him close and kissed him deeply. Morgan knew part of the passion in that kiss was Issa trying to piss off Swent, but he didn't care.

He pulled her into a tight hug and whispered into her ear, "Don't worry."

"I'm not, you dummy," Issa replied, smiling. Morgan straightened and looked at Olivia. She nodded, reached into her satchel, and suddenly she was holding an impressive staff. It was made out of a long, straight branch of dark wood streaked with bits of lighter grain. A silvery band surrounded the central third of the staff. Long silver rivers ran through the wood up to the staff's top, where they branched off to form casings for two large crystals. The crystals reminded Morgan of prisms because of how the light played through them, but they were smooth and round, almost cylindrical in shape.

"Impressive." Morgan grinned at Olivia, the fluttering in his stomach momentarily forgotten.

"Why, thank you, sir." She gestured to the field, and Morgan's reality came flooding in as they walked together onto the field; he was about to fight a person to the death. Swent and his second stood glowering at them as they approached, and Morgan noted that Swent was wearing a small round shield and held a naked sword that reminded him of a Roman gladius. He decided that he didn't want to get caught unready, so he pulled his sword out of his ring, holding it in a low guard position while they stood, waiting for the governor to speak. Swent scoffed, twirling his gladius in his hand. Morgan couldn't help noticing how his fingers blurred while manipulating the hilt.

"Right then. All parties are present. We have before us a duel to satisfy a grievance. Does the aggrieved party acknowledge that the person here"—he gestured to Morgan—"is the transgressor?"

"Aye." Swent spat on the ground in front of Morgan. Up until now, Morgan hadn't been angry, per se, but that dismissive, rude action did more to boil his blood than all of Swent's posturing or, in fact, the challenge. He felt heat on the back of his neck and let his ill humor pour forth in his aura. More than that, he let the weight of his Yovashi Bane title suffuse it as it spread out from him. The anguish of a defeated race, the horror of realizing he'd been part of it, his self-loathing when he'd spoken to Ykleedra, all were part of that palpable wave. Everyone around him took a step back, the governor's face blanched. Swent struggled to regain face, standing up straight and moving back toward Morgan, but the damage had been done. Morgan just smirked.

"Ahem, yes, Morgan, do you acknowledge that Swent has challenged you to a lawful duel?" The governor's voice took a moment to steady, but he spoke clearly by the end.

"As far as I know. I'm not familiar with your laws." Morgan stared coolly at Swent while he spoke.

"Do any parties present object to the validity of this duel?" the governor called out.

"I do!" Issa yelled. "He had no contract or promise from me. I don't see how he can claim grievance!"

"Is this true, Swent?" Holis, the Governor, asked.

"Of course, not. She swore her hand to me on many occasions, and I have witnesses here. Why my second is one of them. Correct, Bennic?" Bennic, face solemn, nodded. Morgan saw the governor was going to ask more questions, but he could see that Swent and his friends were prepared to spread any lies they needed.

"Governor, I don't want Issa's name dragged through the mud. Let's just get this over with." Holis looked at Morgan for a long moment, and then nodded.

"The duel will commence," he said in a loud voice. "Seconds, clear the field." He backed away, and so did Olivia and Bennic. Soon it was just Morgan and Swent on the field. Morgan was glad that there was a lot of space; he'd been a little worried about having to hold back to protect bystanders. "Combatants, take your guard!" Morgan backed up a step and raised his sword into position for the Crane Defends the Nest. Swent raised his shield and held his gladius in a short guard. "Begin!" Governor Holis shouted.

❦ MORGAN ❦

Swent moved like lightning. He drove forward, his shield held high, and punched his gladius straight at Morgan's stomach in a thrust that was more a blur than a movement. Morgan barely had time to react; he fell back, carving his sword down in a sideways slash. Swent knocked the blade away with the edge of his shield and kept driving. He was too fast for Morgan, and the tip of his gladius pierced Morgan's stomach before he was able to spin sideways and back away while Swent's momentum drove him past. The cut wasn't terrible, but it burned, and blood flowed freely. That bastard had managed to stab him right below his breastplate. Morgan felt a surge of rage and immediately moved into the Crane Flutters Its Wings, rushing forward with all of his agility and whipping his razor-edged sword into a series of diagonal cuts, Swent at their center.

Swent raised his shield and calmly blocked the first attack. Morgan drove the slash through and back in an arch for another and another and one more. The fury of his attack and the longer reach of his blade kept Swent from counter-attacking, but he blocked all the attacks. Deep gashes were left on his shield; the metal partially cut through. He staggered back, surprised by the ferocity of the attack. As Morgan transitioned into a high guard, beginning to advance again, Swent let out a low shout and blurred into motion again. He dashed to Morgan's right side, and Morgan swung his sword down in an attempt to strike him, only to find that Swent wasn't there; he'd somehow faked the movement. As Morgan began to spin, trying to lay eyes on his opponent, he felt a terrible, deep pain in his back and knew that Swent had driven his gladius deep into him.

Morgan cried out in pain but kept his wits; with a shout, he triggered his Azure Burst, and a blue circle of flames erupted out of him, blasting out with the full force of his Energy. The short trampled grass underneath him blackened instantly, and he heard Swent scream. Morgan turned and saw him knocked back by the burst, but he was still standing. His shield was blackened and glowed orange at the edges. His leather leggings were charred, and his face and scalp were blackened with soot, his hair burnt down to a stubble. Swent's eyes were bloodshot, and he had a horrible grimace on his face, but he still spat and growled, "Nice trick, worm. It won't save you." He spat again, trying to hit Morgan, but it fell short.

Morgan was worried that Swent might be right. That stab had grievously injured him. He could feel things were going very badly inside him. Blood still flowed from the gash on his stomach, but it pumped freely out of the horrible, deep stab wound on his lower back. The simple truth was that Swent was faster than he was and seemed to have more melee fighting skills. Morgan's vision was starting to darken on the edges, and he shook his head, trying to focus on Swent's movements. The man was circling him slowly behind his shield with a smile on his face. "I could probably just let you bleed out." Morgan felt a jolt of panic, realizing the truth to that statement; he was bleeding a lot. He contemplated taking out a healing potion but knew it would disqualify him. He needed to do something.

Morgan was thinking of a plan of attack when Swent charged again. This time, Morgan saw him take his first step, and he felt, deep in his mind, a certainty that Swent's attack would come from the left, low and fast. Morgan dropped his sword into low gate guard, angling it over his left leg. He swung it up where he knew Swent's sword would be coming from and just barely managed to parry the attack. Swent backed off, shield high, his eyebrows drawn together in a frown. Morgan silently thanked his sword for the forewarning and formulated a plan of attack.

Swent seemed confident in avoiding attacks, so Morgan let his exhaustion show, lowering his blade into the Crane Forages. To someone who didn't know the forms, it might have looked like he was having trouble lifting the sword, the long blade just inches over the ground, slowly moving side to side. He watched Swent, keeping his sword between them and measuring the countdown on his Azure Burst cooldown. As soon as it felt ready, Morgan used his Hollow Charge, ripping a furrow in the grass as he blasted forward to Swent. As he raced over the ground, he lifted his sword and slipped it into Swent's thigh, easy as sticking a fork in a baked potato. Simultaneously, he fired off another Azure Burst. His sword had plunged deep into the meat of Swent's thigh, and, as his Azure Burst coursed out of him, Morgan saw the surprise on Swent's face as he jerked his shield up.

Impressively, Swent managed to swing his gladius as he was blasted backward, carving a deep slice in Morgan's left shoulder. Morgan kept hold of his sword as Swent was blown back, and he felt the blade rip through the length of Swent's thigh, carving the majority of it away from the bone down to the knee. Meanwhile, the flames from his Azure Burst scalded Swent for the second time; only his upper chest and face were spared, thanks to his quick movement with his shield.

Morgan planted the tip of his sword on the blackened ground and leaned heavily on it. Swent was on his back, moaning faintly, his leg was mangled, and his sword arm was burned into a blackened, misshapen twist of flesh and bone. Morgan walked forward, stepping on the char-covered gladius, and looked down at Swent's writhing form. His vision had narrowed to a tunnel, but he could hear, as if from the depths of an echoing well, Swent's hoarse whisper: "I yield. Mercy." Morgan nodded.

"I grant mercy," he said, looking to where the governor was hovering, wondering if he should approach. The governor nodded, walking over. Morgan, still seeing dimly and feeling like he was in a room where someone was slowly turning the dimmer down, felt himself fall back onto his butt. He sat there in the grass for a moment, and then he felt soft hands on his neck and cheek and even softer kisses on his face. Then someone was tipping a bottle into his mouth, and he drank the syrupy liquid, feeling the warmth spread out from his throat, down through his body. Suddenly things were brighter, and he could hear individual sounds again.

"He's alright, just lost a lot of blood," said a gruff voice.

"Swent ain't gonna make it," a panicky young man was saying. "He ain't drinking, and I poured the potion on his leg, but nothing happened. Oh, ancestors, he's moting up. He's dead." Morgan was just realizing what was happening and had reached up to clasp Issa's hand when he felt a surge of Energy slam into him.

*****Congratulations! You have achieved level 16 Hollow Guard and have gained 5 Strength, 5 Will, 4 Vitality, 4 Intelligence, and 3 Agility. You have learned the skill Sword Mastery—Improved.*****

It seemed mercy hadn't been enough for Swent. Morgan was pleased to see that his sword mastery had improved; it seemed that life or death training was the most effective. While he sat there in a pool of his blood, listening to the voices around him talking about the fight and Swent and how it was a shame he'd insisted on the duel, Morgan looked at his status sheet, focusing on his attributes and skills:

Energy Affinity:	9.2	Energy:	812/1188
Strength:	45	Vitality:	44 (46)
Dexterity:	8	Agility:	33
Intelligence:	52	Will:	45

Titles & Feats:	Human Champion, First Hollow Guard, Ardeni Friend, Mark of Loyalty, Yovashi Bane, Legacy of the Azure Paladin	
Skills:	• System Language Integration - Not Upgradeable • Animal Taming - Basic • Stealthy Maneuvers - Basic • Melee Weapon Mastery - Basic • Fighting Crane Style - Basic • Sword Mastery - Improved • Vortex Core Cultivation Drill - Basic	• Backstab - Basic • Energy Drain - Improved • Guard Ally - Basic • Hollow Charge - Basic • Azure Burst - Basic

Yes, dexterity was becoming a real problem. Morgan knew that if he hadn't had Azure Burst, he would have tried an Energy Drain on Swent. Without those two trump cards, Swent would have picked him apart. He just didn't have the speed and skill he needed to stand toe to toe with skillful melee fighters. Or ranged ones, for that matter, he thought, fatalistically. "Nothing to do for it, but keep practicing, trying to improve."

"What was that?" Issa asked softly, pressing her forehead against his.

"Uh, nothing, just rambling." Morgan managed a weak smile and gave her a quick kiss, and then he struggled to his feet. He was feeling much better after the potion Olivia had given him to drink and the influx of Energy from Swent. His lower-left back was still stiff and sore, and he knew Swent must have punctured several organs. Morgan silently thanked his high vitality, for he was sure he would have bled out in the time it took for his Azure Burst to come off cooldown. Still, he could have used Energy Drain. Maybe he should have used Energy Drain. Why hadn't he? He chalked it up to blood loss and tunnel vision—he'd been so focused on blasting Swent again with Azure Burst, he'd nearly made a fatal mistake. What he needed was to have more practice fights—he needed all of his abilities to be reflexive, not something he needed to plan out in the middle of a battle.

Morgan looked down at Swent's corpse. He looked pathetic, almost—small, twisted, soot-covered, his eyes still wide open with his neck arched, almost like he'd died trying to pull in one last breath. Morgan didn't feel sad for Swent, but he didn't feel proud looking down at him. Nor did he feel any better when he saw an older Ardeni woman openly weeping into the chest of a stoic-looking, stern-faced man that closely resembled Swent. Morgan accidentally made eye contact with him, and the hate smoldering in those orbs was palpable. Morgan held his eyes steady for a moment, then turned and walked off the field with Issa. Olivia and Roald followed close behind.

"Well, did it work?" Roald asked, after they'd walked clear of the watching crowd.

"What?" Morgan glanced back.

"The sword, you brute, did the sword work?"

"Oh, yeah, I think so. It saved me from at least one more puncture."

"Can you describe it?" Roald was grinning, and he hustled up to walk next to Morgan. Morgan stopped walking and thought about what Roald wanted to know.

"Well, it was almost like I just knew where Swent was going to attack. I didn't feel it coming from the sword or anything, but I have to assume that's where it came from because that guy moved too fast for me to follow."

"Excellent, excellent, just like I theorized! This enchantment will make me a fortune in the right market."

"Oh, uh, do you want the opal back?"

"No, no. It's bound to that blade now. It's a gift, anyway; wouldn't be very honorable to ask for it back!" Roald clapped Morgan on the shoulder. Morgan nodded, clasping Roald's shoulder for a moment, and then turned to keep walking toward the inn.

"Are you going to suffer any repercussions from Swent dying?" Morgan asked, looking at Roald and Issa.

"His father was already a problem for me, so I don't think so. He's lost face because of this; many of the gathered people thought the duel was a mistake and a misuse of our Honor Code. Word will spread about how you tried to grant mercy. Swent asking for mercy when he issued the challenge also looks bad for his clan. I don't think we'll need to worry about his influence on the council." Roald shook his head, a frown on his face.

"Clan? That's the first I've heard you mention clans. What about you and Issa? Do you have a clan?" Olivia asked.

"Aye, us that live in towns don't live by clan rules as much as the Ardeni in more wild regions. We do have an extended clan, though none that live here with us." Again, it was Roald who answered. Morgan looked at Issa and saw that she was looking ahead, not really listening. Her face looked very sober.

"You alright?" Morgan asked, giving Issa a little nudge. Was she upset about Swent dying? She had known him most of her life, after all, even if he was an asshole.

"Hmm? Oh yeah, other than the fact that you almost died a few minutes ago? I knew Swent was dangerous, but I thought you'd have an easier time. It scared me, Morgan."

"Yeah, it scared me, too!" Morgan laughed lightly, giving her another little push on the shoulder.

"I'm serious! You need to get stronger. We need to get stronger! I don't want to watch you get killed." Her voice had risen, and Olivia and Roald stopped chatting about clans and stared.

"Hey," Morgan said, putting his arm on Issa's shoulders, pulling her into his side while they walked, "I don't intend to stop trying to improve. I know this place is dangerous; that's one thing the Crucible showed me. It's tempting to get complacent when riding around with a herd of roladii or hanging around a picturesque town with my girlfriend, but I know danger is lurking out there. C'mon, chin up; I'm still kicking."

"Girlfriend?" Issa's mouth quirked up in a smile.

"That's your takeaway from what I just said?" He laughed. "I would say yes, you're my girlfriend, you nut. Considering what we've been through? Considering how much I care about you?"

"Hmm, I like the term, I think, but I'll be calling you my mate," she replied, grabbing Morgan by the sides of his breastplate and pulling him down for a kiss.

"Oh my god, get a room," Olivia said. Roald, standing beside her, nodded, holding a hand over his eyes.

OLIVIA

Olivia was glad to be back in the saddle again. She hadn't spent much time visiting Blue during their short stay in Tarn's Crossing, and she'd missed him. More than that, she was glad to have that whole duel business behind them and to be making quick progress back toward First Landing. They left the day after the duel, and Olivia could see that Morgan and Issa were glad to be going as well. Something about that event had soured their experience. Morgan was glum in the evening, and it was Roald that suggested they get a head start heading back to the colony ahead of most of the Hunters who'd be coming to aid in the upcoming conflict. Olivia liked Tarn's Crossing, but some time away for memories and tempers to fade would be good for all of them.

They'd been riding hard for three days, just stopping to eat and sleep a few hours each night. Issa had her own roladii named Gopp, and she had proven to be quite an accomplished rider. Gopp had a different disposition than the roladii Olivia had experienced so far; he was crabby and snapped at the other mounts if they got too close to him. Issa laughed at his antics, though, saying he was an old grouch that her father had purchased when she was a little girl. Still, Gopp had no trouble keeping pace, and they were moving a lot faster than they had with the herd. Already they were halfway through the plains, following the trampled grass that Teric's herd had left in their wake.

Each night, they took turns sleeping, and Olivia felt that Issa and Morgan were giving her extra sleep time. She didn't know if it was just because they'd both improved their race and had higher levels than she, therefore needed less sleep, or if they wanted to sneak some extra time together. In either case, Olivia was glad to get nearly a full night's sleep at each camp.

Now, on their fourth day, the roladii rapidly devoured the miles of grassland between them and the Gresh Woods that bordered the meadow where the colony was situated. Morgan was confident they'd get to the woods by nightfall, and Olivia couldn't argue; he was able to use his ability to sense allies to feel the distance. Her mind wandered back to the duel and how Morgan had almost bled to death before finishing the fight. He was significantly stronger than she was, and it drove home the point that she needed to improve herself and her magic if she wanted to survive the harsh realities of this world. Tarn's Crossing and the Ardeni had an honor code that wouldn't let someone like Swent challenge someone like her, but that didn't hold true for all the peoples of this world.

Her thought process brought Olivia to the usual, frustrating conclusion: she couldn't improve any more if she wanted to go to the academy, and she wanted to go. The more she thought about it, the more she knew that she would probably choose to use the teleportation token. It was just too much of an opportunity to pass up. She knew she would do well; she always did well in school, and Olivia had already proven that she had extraordinary aptitude with Energy. Doing well at the school would undoubtedly pay dividends when it came to gaining knowledge that could benefit the colony. It would be selfish not to go; her cynical side laughed at her roundabout way of talking herself into doing something she wanted to do.

Morgan was proved correct; they arrived at the edge of the woods just as the sun was starting to dip below the western horizon. They ended up camping at the same spot where they had first laid eyes on the Chebli Sea. They cared for their animals and then sat around the fire, sharing a meal that Issa prepared in an iron pot that she produced from one of her storage bags. The dish consisted of chunks of flavorful meat in a grain mixture with roasted vegetables. The seasoning was fairly spicy, but Olivia enjoyed it.

"This is good, Issa," she said around a mouthful.

"Thanks! It was my mother's recipe. My father roasted the meat and vegetables before we left and made me pack enough to feed a small army."

"Do you miss him?" Morgan asked.

"A little, but I'm used to being apart from him. He travels a lot for his business, delivering projects, visiting other masters, procuring materials; you get the idea."

"How far behind us do you think the Hunters will be? You really don't think they'll have any trouble finding the colony?" Olivia asked for what was probably the fourth or fifth time since leaving Tarn's.

"Not far, and no, they won't struggle to find us. Morgan gave good directions, and they can track. Every Hunter has that skill. Stop worrying, Olivia! Things will work out!" Issa smiled and tossed a twig at Olivia.

"Alright, alright"—Olivia laughed—"I can't help it. I'm anxious to make sure things are going well for the colony because I'm feeling more and more sure that I want to use this teleportation token." Olivia gestured to her satchel, where the token was stowed.

"You're sure?" Morgan asked.

"Yeah, it just seems like it's too much of an opportunity to let go. I'm stressing about it because I'm afraid I'll have to leave in the middle of a crisis. I have to use the token before the first of Belintide, which I think is just a bit more than a week away."

"That's right," Issa said, looking into space and counting on her fingers.

"Also, I don't know if it would be smart to show up on the last possible day. I mean, I never went off to school on the first day of classes; I always got there early for orientation or to find my dorm or to buy books. You know what I mean?"

"Yeah, sure, I get it," Morgan said. "You don't have to stress, Olivia; we're going to be okay while you're gone. I think you should check things out when we get back, and talk to the people you need to talk to, and then you should go. You'll feel better if you don't wait until the last minute."

They talked for a while longer, enjoying the warmth of the fire and the prospect of finishing their journey the next day. Morgan shared some grain alcohol that Issa's father, Roald, had given him the morning they left, so it was with a warm, pleasant buzz that Olivia snuggled into her blankets that evening.

Olivia woke with a start sometime later. She wasn't sure what had woken her, so she lay still, listening to the darkness. After a moment, she heard a voice. She listened closely, and she was fairly sure it was Morgan's voice. Then she heard a high-pitched, raspy voice say something, and the strangeness of it, brought Olivia fully awake. The fire had died down, and so, she summoned her fire-attuned Energy orb. She made it as small as possible, like a little marble of fire, and it illuminated the interior of the tent. Olivia saw Issa's wavy yellow hair poking out of her blankets, but there was no sign of Morgan. She crawled toward the tent flap and poked her head out as quietly as possible.

In the cool night air, under the light of the sister moons, as Issa called them, Olivia could see Morgan standing a ways off to her left, facing into the forest. She could very faintly hear him speaking, but she couldn't see who he was talking to. She slowly climbed out of the tent and stood, walking softly on the grass toward him. As she drew within twenty feet or so, she caught sight of the other person, and her heart nearly stopped. Without warning, memories of the Yovashi cave came to her mind—a terrible beak surrounded by tentacles chomping down on Emmet's corpse, a deep mocking laugh, being thrown like a ragdoll into the wall. Suddenly her scarred eye throbbed, and she stumbled, taking a knee in the grass.

"Wait, Ykleedra, I'll be right back," she could hear Morgan say. Then she heard his footsteps and felt his hand on her shoulder. "Are you okay? Don't worry, Olivia; she's not like the other Yovashi." He squatted before her and put his other hand on her other shoulder. "Hey, look at me. It's alright."

"I. I, um, I'm sorry about that. How do you know that creature? Morgan, you know what they're like!" Olivia shook her head, banishing the memories that kept rushing up in her mind. Shakily, she stood up, noticing that Morgan didn't let go of her, keeping himself between her and the Yovashi.

"She's a female. They're different—they can reason better than the males. I know her because I murdered her family after getting teleported out of the Yovashi lair. Listen, she came to me for help. When I left her, she told me she would try to help her mother's eggs hatch. Well, it didn't work—she thinks the eggs are dead. She found our tracks from our earlier passage and has been waiting and watching for us."

"Oh God, Morgan. A Yovashi? What does she want from you?" Olivia tried again to suppress her shudder. She hadn't realized how much emotion she'd buried about that experience in the cave.

"Well, I think she wants to come with us. She's all alone. There aren't any other Yovashi around—they're almost wiped out as a species."

"Truly?" The idea that the creature was almost the last of its kind softened Olivia's viewpoint.

"Yes, truly, and she's only a child, Olivia."

"Well, let me meet her, then." Olivia started walking toward the creature lurking in the trees, and Morgan hurried to walk in front of her.

"Ykleedra, this is a friend, Olivia." The creature came forward out of the shadows, and Olivia could see that it really was a lot smaller than the one in the cave. Even on its long spider-like legs, it wasn't as tall as Morgan. Most surprising was the fact that it was wearing a silky gown, its tentacles tucked up under it. Olivia saw that its small face was framed with long, silvery-white hair, and the creature's eyes, like bottomless dark pits, swallowing light, were smaller and slightly angular when compared to the enormous saucers on the devil that had lived in the cave.

"Hello, Ykleedra. Morgan tells me that you're all alone?" Olivia looked into those dark eyes, and for the first time, she thought she could see emotion—they squinted slightly, and it seemed almost like a spark flitted through the darkness.

"Yes, Mistress. I am alone. I sought Morgan because he told me to if I needed help." The girl's—Olivia determined at that moment to stop calling her a creature—voice was tremulous, strange, and full of sorrow. When she said the word "alone," Olivia felt like her heart would tear.

"Oh, dear, Ykleedra. I'm sorry I was so frightened when I saw you. I've had bad experiences with another Yovashi."

"I'm sorry, Mistress. The madness is a curse on our kind but only affects our males. I am no threat to you."

"Well," another voice spoke up from behind Olivia, "bring her over to the camp. No sense keeping her skulking out here in the woods." Olivia turned and saw Issa stepping out from behind a tree.

"Uh, yeah. Alright. Ykleedra, come on over to our camp. You're safe with us; that's Issa who just spoke, and she's not one to invite someone to her camp and then hurt them. Right, Issa?" Morgan stared pointedly at Issa, and Olivia cringed at the glare she gave him.

"Of course, but this seems like a big secret to have kept to yourself!" Issa said, turning with a huff back toward the camp. Olivia made eye contact with Morgan, and he winced, shrugging. Ykleedra, hesitant at first, then with more confidence, walked out of the woods, onto the grassland, and followed them to their camp.

BRONWYN

Bronwyn couldn't help the nerves she felt as she strode down the hill toward the Urghat camp. She made sure the Underclaw ring on her bicep was in plain view and did her best to appear nonchalant. She was a good hundred yards from the first tents when the shout went out among the Urghat, and they started to crowd out of the camp toward her. Most of them had weapons displayed, and Bronwyn felt the pressure of their stares as they moved toward her. She'd never seen so many Urghat at once, and it was interesting to note their variety. Some were much taller than she, and some were the size of a smallish human. The small ones were more wiry and looked almost like they were built for speed.

"You're not welcome here, slayer!" One of the Urghat yelled. Another, larger Urghat with black fur and a white stripe down the center of his face shoved him and growled.

"Don't give this softling the credit of a name like slayer!" He stepped forward from the rest of the Urghat and spat through his tusks in Bronwyn's direction. "You think you can come among us because you managed to trick the newest Underclaw?"

"I think I can walk wherever I want. Do you have a problem with that?" Bronwyn was really hoping that Umberpaws hadn't lied to her about how this whole Underclaw business worked.

"I can feel your title, hairless one, and no one has challenged you this day. I will right that wrong! I challenge you! Come, face me. You won't trick me like you did Bloodfang!" He brandished his large, hooked axe and stomped toward her. The rest of the Urghat howled and cheered, spreading out into a loose circle around Bronwyn and the aggressive challenger.

"Very well, state your name, so people will know what to call my first victim!" Bronwyn felt her blood start to pump, almost like she was about to step into an important match back home. She knew this was more serious, but she couldn't feel worried for some reason. She raised her fists and began to walk toward the Urghat.

"I am Goreblade, and soon, I will be an Underclaw!" He shouted, roaring into the sky, shaking his axe up and down in a pumping motion while the rest of the Urghat roared their agreement. Bronwyn circled the Urghat, summoning her Stone Fists and waiting for him to make a move. As soon as she saw him flex his thigh like he would leap toward her, she cast Fetters of Stone on him, watching as his eyes widened in surprise. She ran forward while he was off-balance, blocked his clumsy swing with one stone fist, and smashed the other into his ribs. A satisfying crunch rewarded her.

When she'd deflected his axe, it had flung his arm back, windmilling, and he nearly fell backward. Bronwyn took advantage of his off-balanced stance and circled around him. She jumped onto his back, locking her legs around his waist, and grabbed his hairy neck in a chokehold. She arched her back and pulled against his throat with all her strength. Goreblade flailed his arms and fell backward toward her, his feet still trapped; he fell on top of her. Bronwyn didn't let go, using every point of her prodigious strength to crush his neck. Goreblade thrashed and bucked for several seconds, but then he fell still. She knew she'd blocked the blood flow to his brain, but he might not be dead, so she kept up the pressure until motes began to form around his body.

*****Congratulations! Your title, Underclaw, has been upgraded to Underclaw 2: + 1 additional strength and vitality.*****

Bronwyn threw the body of Goreblade to the side and hopped to her feet. "This fool just made me stronger. I'll be glad to fight any others if you want to issue the challenge come morning." The boisterous Urghat had calmed down and now stood, looking anywhere but into her eyes. Muttered curses and insults were the extent of their hostilities, though, and they began to move away from her, back to their camp. A couple of Urghat didn't walk away. One was small and wiry, and the other was large and wide. They came up to the body and stood quietly. "Did you want something?" Bronwyn scowled at them.

"We are waiting for you to finish your looting rights before we take the body," the smaller of the Urghat said. Bronwyn nodded and looked down at the corpse. She supposed his axe might be valuable, but the rest of his gear was just worn leather and hide armor. She saw that he had a pouch, though, and she figured it might be a dimensional container, so she bent to take it off his belt. She could see the telltale runes as she untied it and knew that she'd been correct. She held onto it for now, and after she stowed the Urghat's axe into her own pouch, she nodded to the two others.

After they'd pulled the body away, Bronwyn took a minute to look through Goreblade's pouch. There was an ample supply of dried meats and even three paper-wrapped smoked fish. Another bag stored within was filled with hundreds of tiny Energy beads. Other than a cask of strong, clear liquor, that was all that she felt was worth keeping. She dumped a few wolf corpses on the ground along with some old blankets. She called out, "Anyone who wants this stuff can have it." Then she walked farther into the camp.

Bronwyn spent the evening observing the Urghat and slept fitfully in her own blankets, off in the grass about a hundred feet from their tents. She made sure to wake before dawn, packing up her supplies and walking back into the Urghat camp. During the evening, she'd watched them cooking and laughing, picking up snippets of conversation about how this Underclaw or that warrior would teach the scrawny human a lesson. She also heard them talking about attacking the colony, but they never mentioned when or how many Urghat would be involved. When she tried to question them about anything, the Urghat, almost universally, had ignored her. The few who hadn't ignored her offered her insults instead.

As the sun began to rise, Bronwyn walked toward the center of their camp and shouted, "Any takers on today's challenge? I only have room for one!" She didn't know why she was taunting them, but something about the way they talked about fighting and joked about watching her get killed and ravaged irritated her and made her want to see them back down. None of the Urghat met her eyes, and they went about breaking camp, preparing to move.

"Where are you going? She asked one of the Urghat that was packing a tent nearby."

"Don't worry about it, hairless welp." Bronwyn knew that these creatures respected strength, and she wondered if she'd lost some respect by allowing them to insult her all night. She summoned stone to her fist and walked up behind the Urghat that had just spoken, smacking him with an open palm in the back of the head. He fell forward like she'd hit him with a hammer. He lay, groaning, on the ground but didn't move to get back up.

Bronwyn looked to the Urghat helping him pack, his eyes wide and his mouth open. "Same question to you."

"Um, I'm sorry, Underclaw, what was the question?"

"Where are you going?" Bronwyn growled.

"We, um, we're moving the camp, half a day to the east."

"See how easy that was?" Bronwyn walked away from the cluster of tents, pulled her map from her pouch, and noted where the camp was moving. The Urghat were almost packed, and some of them were starting to walk to the east, clearly not following any sort of formal marching order. Bronwyn walked to one of the stragglers and said, "Hey, where's another Urghat camp near here?"

"What?" he asked, turning around and flinching when he saw how close she was.

"Where's the nearest Urghat camp? Don't make me repeat myself again."

"That way"—he pointed to the northwest—"about a day's hike." Bronwyn nodded and motioned for him to get moving. She watched them walk away for a few minutes, and then she turned and jogged in the direction the Urghat had pointed.

Bronwyn alternately walked and ran for several hours, making good time over the primarily flat plains. Shortly after noon, she crested a short rise and saw the camp in the distance. This camp had twice as many tents as the previous one and seemed to look a bit more permanent. There were simple fortifications—trenches dug and dirt mounded in berms on the far side. She could see Urghat on patrol, walking the perimeter, talking and laughing. She walked purposefully toward a gap in the trench.

Her experience went similarly at this camp as it did the one before. Insults gave way to threats, gave way to a challenge, and, again, the challenger made a good example to keep the others more in line. Bronwyn's title gained another rank, and she started to appreciate the potential if she kept getting in fights like this.

After she beat the challenger, a short but very wide, orange-furred Urghat wielding a spiked club, the mood at the camp went from raucous to subdued. Many of the Urghat cast sidelong glances at her as she walked around, counting tents, supplies, and enemies. There were sixty-five Urghat at this camp. As she walked around, poking her head into tents and receiving withering stares from the occupants, she came upon one of the smaller wiry Urghat scribbling onto a large parchment. His fur had once been black, but it had gone mostly gray, leading Bronwyn to surmise that he was old for his kind.

"What are you working on?" She asked, as she poked her head into his tent.

"A map, Underclaw. Tell me, are you here to join us? Are you embracing your title and turning upon your kind?"

"No. I'm here to convince you to stop fighting with my kind." She ducked into his tent, as he hadn't protested yet about her intrusion.

"That's a fool's dream. We are Urghat. We fight." Bronwyn didn't say anything, but she looked at his map, noting a depiction of mountains at the top of the page, a forest at the bottom, and many notations in between.

"Is that a map of these plains?"

"You're wise, Underclaw. This is a map of these plains. I use it to help guide our hunting parties and messengers to other clans." He waved his hand over the page, drying the ink of a notation.

"Is this a clan, then? Here at this camp? Do all of the Urghat clans camp separately?"

"For the most part, yes. We tend to get in fights when too close to our distant kin for any length of time."

"Well, I think I'm going to need to take that map. Or, I could copy it, I suppose." Bronwyn gestured to the table the Urghat was writing on and continued, "I'll just copy it here if you don't mind."

"I do mind, but I'm not in a position to challenge you. I will have to tell others that you've done this, though." He sighed heavily and stood up, moving away from the table. Bronwyn nodded, pulled out her mapping supplies, and began to copy his detailed map of the region. It had notations for dozens of different ruins, little circles for the different clan camps, including the names of the clan leaders.

"Are these clan leaders all Underclaws?" she asked while writing.

"No. Underclaws are part of the Ur-clan. They, you, serve under the Overclaw and have authority over normal clan leaders."

"I do, do I? So, if I order you all to act, you will have to listen?"

"No, it's not so simple. You haven't been accepted. Thanks to the ring on your arm, you have authority that protects you from murder, but until the Overclaw accepts you, your commands will have no weight."

"Mmhmm, makes sense. Okay, what's your name?"

"Bonechew." As he spoke, Bronwyn finished the last notes on the map and began to roll it up when a notification surprised her:

Congratulations! You have learned the skill Cartography—Basic.

"Alright, thanks, Bonechew." Bronwyn tucked the new map into her pouch. She wondered how the new skill would help. Would she be able to draw faster or more accurately? She'd have to do some experimentation, but she wanted to eat something and get some sleep for now.

BRONWYN

Bronwyn woke to the sound of stomping feet and the raspy voices of many Urghat around her. The sun was just starting to rise, and as she looked around in the morning light, she realized Urghat had surrounded her sleeping area; they had formed a circle around her and were waiting patiently. A sense of dread crept down her spine, and she scooped up the still sleeping Hops, depositing him in her backpack before she stood.

"It'll be alright, buddy; they can't hurt us," she said in a hushed voice.

Bronwyn stood up and stretched, rolling out her shoulders and staring out into the crowd. "Little early to be killing Urghat; you're sure this is what you want?" She called out, not shouting but loud enough for all of them to hear.

The crowd fell silent as she spoke, and she began to worry the Urghat had overcome their fear of exile and would swarm her. Then, they parted, and a huge figure strode through their ranks toward her. He was clad in plate armor and carried a massive maul over his right shoulder. He stopped as he entered the circle and dropped the head of his maul onto the ground. The Urghat removed his helmet, a long silver-colored mane spilling out, and held it under his arm as he addressed her: "My name is Ironhide, and I intended to challenge the one known as Bloodfang. You now possess his title, so my challenge is to you instead. I hold no resentment for your actions, nor do I care that you are not Urghat. I simply wish to rise in rank. All I ask is that we fight fairly." He slid the helmet back down over his head and gripped his maul with two hands. "Are you ready, Underclaw?"

Bronwyn bounced back and forth on the balls of her feet and shook out her arms to get the blood flowing through her body. This Urghat reminded her of Bloodfang; he was much more civil and matter of fact than the other Urghat she'd fought duels against. She bowed her head to him and said, "Alright. I'm ready when you are." She raised her fists and beckoned him forward.

Ironhide held his maul low, its head trailing behind him as he ducked his head and charged forward at her. Bronwyn attempted to cast Fetters of Stone on him as he ran, but his immense strength shattered the stone around his legs as it formed. He barely even seemed to notice. Bronwyn growled in frustration and channeled her Stone Fists, keeping her eyes trained on the head of his hammer. Just as he got into range, he heaved the hammer toward her in a large sweeping strike, the air distorted by its force. The Urghat was not fast for all his strength, and Bronwyn jumped backward, the end of the maul missing her by an entire foot. Ironhide arced his swing upward at the end of its path with a tremendous roar and attempted to bring the hammer down onto her skull.

Bronwyn channeled a massive amount of Energy into her strike as she lunged toward the Urghat. Before he could bring his hammer down, her punch connected with his chest plate, the impact of her Stone Fists against his metal armor echoed like a car crash as it crumpled inward. Ironhide dropped his hammer and fell backward, the concave shape of his armor only allowing him the shallowest of breaths as it pressed into him. Bronwyn leaped onto him, sitting on his chest and pinning his left arm to the ground with her knee. She ripped off his helmet and pulled Umberpaws's dagger out of her pouch, holding it to his neck.

"What happens if I don't kill you?" Bronwyn stared into the Urghat's panic-filled, dark purple eyes as he struggled to breathe.

Ironhide couldn't speak between gasping breaths, but another Urghat near the edge of the circle answered for him: "He'll be marked and exiled; neither his clan nor any other would speak to or share food with him again."

"Gah! This doesn't feel right! Why would you challenge someone without knowing their power?" Bronwyn pressed the blade into Ironhide's throat, a droplet of blood welling up at the tip. "You're a fool for challenging me." Bronwyn could see the fear etched into his face. "But you don't deserve to die. You speak and fight with more honor than any of these bastards around us. If I let you live, none would take you in, no other Underclaw, no other clan. However, swear your life to me, and I'll make sure you become stronger than any of them."

Ironhide took as deep a breath as he could manage, and, with a raspy, barely audible voice, he said, "I . . . swear. . . ."

Bronwyn pulled the knife from his throat and slid it down the side of his armor, slicing the leather bindings, allowing him to pull the armor off and take a deep breath. The circle of Urghat slowly broke apart with muttered curses and a few spitting at their feet. Bronwyn ignored them and reached a hand down toward Ironhide, helping him to his feet. She smiled down at him as he clasped his large fur-covered hand around her wrist. "Welcome to my band, and, uh, sorry about the armor. I'm sure we can get you something better, though."

Ironhide stood, removed the rest of his ruined chest piece, and then took the armor off his right arm. A blackened band of fur was slowly etching its way around his bicep. "A small price to pay for my life, I suppose. I thank you for your mercy, Underclaw." Ironhide looked away from his arm and made eye contact with Bronwyn. "Now, I wish to know of this new clan, these new people, that I have pledged my life to."

Bronwyn spent the better part of the day exchanging information with Ironhide; she taught him about the humans, and he told her stories about the Urghat. When the sun was low in the sky, they decided it would be best to stay at that camp for one more night. Bronwyn had explained that she wanted to explore more of the Urghat camps detailed on her new map, and Ironhide seemed to know information about many of them already. He only asked that they avoid the camp of Earbite's clan, his former home, and she agreed.

In the morning, Bronwyn was a little surprised to find that another of the Urghat from the camp wanted to challenge her. Ironhide scoffed and said, "Why would you challenge? You couldn't even best me." The extremely rotund, black-furred Urghat spat on the ground and grunted, brandishing the cleaver-like axe that he held in both hands. Bronwyn fought him, easily overcoming his clumsy attacks, but he refused to yield. The victory once again improved Bronwyn's Underclaw rank and even gave her a level.

Over the next two weeks, the trio of Bronwyn, Ironhide, and Hops made their way through many of the Urghat camps on her map. At most, at least one Urghat challenged Bronwyn, and she was able to force three of them to yield and swear fealty. With her slowly growing band of followers, she made her way ever northward, deeper into Urghat territory.

Ironhide urged her to avoid entering the northernmost camps, saying they should just scout them from afar. They were home to the most fearsome Underclaws and their followers, Urghat that Bronwyn may not be able to defeat should they challenge her. From a distance, Bronwyn tried to estimate their number. These northern camps were more like fortresses; they held easily a hundred Urghat, possibly more. The largest of them was home to the Overclaw himself. Bronwyn felt half tempted to stride in and see who this legendary leader of the Urghat was, but her followers convinced her it would be a suicide mission, so she settled for taking stock of his holdings from a distance.

The Overclaw's fortress was surrounded by a veritable city of tents and semi-permanent structures constructed from raw timber and clay. Her band camped about two miles away from the sprawling compound. She was watching this camp one evening, counting a column of Urghat that was moving off to the southwest when Heartseeker, a female Urghat that had sworn loyalty to her, came running up with her long spear held ready and her rust-colored brows furrowed with concern. "Underclaw, a challenger approaches. I know not how he knew of our location."

"Alright, where are the others?"

"Watching them approach."

"Them?"

"Yes, he has two retainers with him." Heartseeker shrugged as if to emphasize that the situation was beyond her control. Bronwyn smiled at her; the lanky Urghat had grown on her over the last week, displaying a casual disregard for consequences that was almost inspiring. She hiked down from the small knoll from which she'd been watching the massive camp and followed Heartseeker around a small copse of scrub-like trees where she could observe a trio of Urghat walking out of the northern foothills.

Bronwyn stepped out of the underbrush and stood with her arms crossed about a hundred feet from the leader. He was a wiry Urghat with black fur, a patch over his left eye, and long tusks protruding from his bottom jaw. She called out, "Who approaches my camp? Name yourself and your intentions."

In a deep gravelly voice filled with resentment, the Urghat responded, "My name is Goretusk, and I come to claim your head." He reached one of his hands out toward each of his companions, two smaller Urghat that looked to be children or, at most, adolescents. They were similar in features with bright white fur and red eyes. The one on the right was a female, who placed the handle of a long whip in his hand. The boy on the left fumbled with his dimensional pouch, and Goretusk slapped him across the face. "Hurry, you worthless twit!" The boy Urghat winced in pain but managed to pull a wicked-looking kukri out of his pouch and handed it to Goretusk before stepping back. The Urghat snapped his whip and grinned. "Are you ready to die, Underclaw?"

Bronwyn scowled at how Goretusk treated his subordinates and summoned her Stone Armor and Stone Fists. "Come on, then."

Goretusk inched toward Bronwyn, slowly circling and closing the distance. Bronwyn couldn't tell exactly how long his whip was, but she knew she had to close the distance before he could get in any free blows. She braced herself, with her arms covering her head and charged, rushing headlong toward the Urghat. She was twenty feet away when his whip cracked out toward her, it was faster than she could even see, and the next thing Bronwyn knew, she was tumbling forward, the whip wrapped around her ankles. She rolled across the ground and landed on her back. Goretusk was immediately upon her; he lunged down, dropping to one knee, slicing his kukri down at her neck. Bronwyn rolled to the side just in time, the blade sinking into the soft grass.

Goretusk scrambled forward and sat on Bronwyn's stomach. Bronwyn grabbed his wrists as he attempted to force the blade down into her neck. She strained with all her might to stop the advancing edge. She spat blood into Goretusk's good eye and wrenched herself to the side, allowing the blade to plunge into the earth just an inch from her face. Her hands free, she reached upward and grabbed each of his tusks with her stone fists and wrenched downward, ripping one from his jaw and snapping the other in half. He screamed out in pain, reaching up at his face and stepping up and away from her. Bronwyn used his blade to cut the whip away from her feet and rolled to stand before him. Goretusk's face was a bloody mess as he stumbled toward her, and it wasn't long before her flurry of blows smashed through his feeble guard. She landed a few good hits to his head before he slumped down, and golden motes started to form around his body.

Bronwyn slumped to her knees, catching her breath as the motes flooded into her.

Congratulations! You have achieved level 14 Stone Pugilist and have gained 6 Strength, 9 Agility, 9 Will, 9 Vitality, and 6 Dexterity.

Congratulations! Your title, Underclaw, has been upgraded to Underclaw 10: +8 additional strength and vitality.

The two young Urghat ran up and fell to their knees at the corpse of Goretusk. The boy spoke up with silent tears falling from his eyes: "Y-you killed him, you actually won." He looked toward his companion, a smile breaking out across his face. "We're finally free; he can't hurt us anymore!" He rushed to her side and embraced her, burying his face in her neck, his chest shuddering with each breath.

The girl spoke in a somber tone: "But where will we go, brother? He killed Da, we have no home to go back to, he burnt it all . . ." her voice trailed off as she stared blankly at the corpse.

Bronwyn watched the two for a silent moment; they were obviously twins. "Are you putting on this show for me? I know you don't know me or have any reason to trust me, but if you're truly alone, we'd take you in." She beckoned toward the woods, and Ironhide, Heartseeker, Shadoweye, and Fangripper came out to stand behind her.

The boy looked up at her and then back to his sister. "What do you think, Fur? You heard what Goretusk said at the other camp, this Underclaw's been beating everyone that challenges her, and she even shows them mercy, sometimes. I'm sure you'd be safe, even with the, uh, well you know, and . . ." He trailed off, looking back at Bronwyn. "I'm not a warrior yet, but I want to be. Could you train me?"

Bronwyn laughed. "Well, if not me, I'm sure at least one of us could." She threw her thumb back toward her band of Urghat.

The boy practically beamed with excitement. "Well, whaddya say, Fur, can we join 'em?"

The girl took a deep breath and smiled, looking at Bronwyn and her ragtag group. "Guess it can't be worse than this scumbag." She kicked at Goretusk's body.

"Yes!" The boy pulled his sister into a side hug and stood in front of Bronwyn. "I'm Bright-tooth, and this is my sister Soft-fur, but you can call me Bright, and she likes to go by Fur!"

His excitement was contagious, and Bronwyn couldn't help but smile. "Well, welcome to the family, Bright, and you, too, Fur, we're glad to have you both!"

Later that day, another Urghat rode furiously out of the Urghat encampment toward the low foothills where Bronwyn and her band had made camp. Heartseeker saw him coming long before he was a threat and said, "Guts is riding out on one of the raskii."

"Shit, Guts?" Ironhide said.

"Who's that?" Bronwyn asked.

"It's the Overclaw's son. He'll be looking for you to challenge."

"Well, bad news for him; I'm all outta challenge slots for the day, and we're heading out tonight." Bronwyn chose to wait in the open for the big Urghat. It took him a while to pick up their tracks, but after half an hour or so, he rode into the little hollow where she waited. He was riding on a pony-size lizard, and its baleful eyes and flicking tongue made Bronwyn even more nervous than the three-hundred-pound Urghat sitting on its back. Guts had reddish-brown fur, wore heavy iron-ring armor, and sported three long tusks in his wide, frowning mouth. "Bah, you've already had a challenge today," were his greeting words.

"Yeah, sorry to disappoint."

"You're lucky. I'd follow you until dawn, but I have an important task to complete." His calm voice suddenly changed, and he screamed into the copse of wiry trees where her followers were lurking, "I'll rip each and every one of your traitor heads off after I finish with your worthless, soft Underclaw!" His orange-red eyes went bloodshot with his scream, and saliva sprayed from his mouth. He growled one last time and spat on the ground between him and Bronwyn, then he wheeled his hissing mount and rode away.

Bronwyn watched the sprawling Urghat tent city for the rest of the afternoon, trying to get a count of the Urghat living there. She estimated at least a few thousand regular occupants, including the warriors and their families. Feeling like she'd seen enough, she and her band of Urghat packed up their things and started the long trek back toward the human colony. Something had changed in the weeks that she'd been out in the plains; she wasn't sure if the Urghat could sense the level of her title or if the word of her previous fights had spread, but none of the Urghat they passed on the way back to the colony challenged her.

On the day she and her band closed in on the colony, only a few miles out, the sun was beginning to set. They made camp in the woods to the east; Bronwyn wasn't sure if she should bring them all into the settlement while the Urghat threatened active war. The colonists might not take kindly to Urghat in their midst. In the morning, she charged them with scouting the plains and taking note of any Urghat movements close by, then she headed into First Landing, alone, to give her report.

MORGAN

Morgan turned to his party and motioned for them all to stop. They'd made good time through the forest that morning, even though Ykleedra was unmounted. She had a natural knack for moving through the woods, and her long legs made it easy for her to surmount obstacles that were a bit of a challenge for the roladii. That being the case, it was only mid-morning when Morgan caught a glimpse of the colony wall through some trees in the distance. He knew they were coming in from the southeast and that if they continued on their current course, they'd arrive at the west gate in a matter of minutes. Morgan patted Munch's shoulder while he waited for the others to pull up close. "Listen," he said as they gathered, "I'm going to lead Ykleedra through the woods and bring her in through the north gate. There's less traffic up there, and my tower is close by. That way, she won't have to deal with as many people freaking out about her. I'm assuming you'll come with me, Issa? Olivia, are you good with that? Or do you wanna head to the west gate here by yourself?"

"I'm fine with that; let's just go together," Olivia replied gamely. Issa just nodded, smiling. They changed their course to more of a northerly one and continued. Now and then, Morgan heard the sounds of people. He could hear yells, the sounds of cracking timber, and even the *ping*ing sound a hammer makes when it's pounding on stone or metal.

"Sounds busy," he remarked to no one in particular.

"Yeah, lots of activity." Olivia nodded. Just then, a thunderous bang rang out from the direction of the colony. "That sounded like an explosive!"

"It sure fucking did. Let's pick up the pace!" Morgan gave Munch a bit of a kick, and they all rumbled through the light underbrush, moving parallel to the eastern wall of the colony. Soon they were near the edge of the woods, and Morgan could see the northern plains through the trees. He turned west and continued to urge Munch to move quickly through the trees until they burst through the tree line into the meadow about a half mile from the northeast corner of the wall. They moved quickly over the open area, and as they got nearer the wall, Morgan saw two men rolling a long black barrel affixed to wooden wheels. "Holy shit! Is that a cannon on the top of the wall?"

"It looks like it!" Olivia said, with a big smile on her face. "I knew Boris was working on a mold for cannon barrels, and it's not like black powder is hard to mix. Arthur had people scouring the foothills for caves with potassium nitrate. They must have found some. Or could they have figured out a way to cause explosions with Energy? Think of the possibilities, Morgan!" They hurried along the northern wall to the gate and were greeted by two guards, leveling flint-lock blunderbusses at them. Behind them stood two more guards with spears pointing their way.

"Woah, don't shoot! We're friends!" Morgan pulled up his roladii about thirty feet from the guards, and the others followed suit. Ykleedra hunched behind Morgan and his mount. "Umm, Olivia, can you go forward and talk to them? I don't want to leave Ykleedra." Olivia nodded and walked her mount forward toward the guards.

The guards had lowered their guns slightly when Morgan called out, and they relaxed entirely as they got a good look at Olivia. Morgan could hear her speaking to them, but the words were indistinct. After a few moments, the guards backed up and waved for Morgan and the others to advance. They watched warily, eyes wide, as Ykleedra gamboled forward on her spidery legs, but to their credit, they didn't point their guns or say anything inflammatory. Morgan looked down at them from Munch's back. "Flint-locks? What's the story with those?"

"One of the Artificers that works in the forge got his Class—he got some ability that lets him shape simple metals like iron. He's been making barrels for cannons and guns like this. I'd be scared to shoot a gun with an iron barrel, but some other guy has an ability that hardens the metal. It holds up to the black powder pretty well." The guard shrugged and held the rifle out for Morgan to look at.

"Not rifled, I take it?" Morgan asked, gesturing to the blunderbuss the guard held on his shoulder.

"Nah, it isn't accurate past a couple of dozen paces, but they say they're working on it!"

"Any action from the Urghat, yet?" Olivia asked.

"Lots of encounters in the plains. We don't send people out there anymore, but we've also had some encounters in the woods. Bronwyn returned recently with maps of their camps and even a count on their numbers. She thinks the first real attack is going to be soon." The guard sniffed loudly, looking to the north with a frown.

"Where'd you get them mounts? Is that one of the Ardeni? We heard you were going to get help from them." The other guard stepped forward a little as she asked her questions. She was vaguely familiar to Morgan, and he realized he'd spoken to her before by the Colony Stone when he'd been shopping for goods.

"Yeah, this is Issa, and she's a friend. Her people are sending Hunters to help fight the Urghat. This is Ykleedra," he said, pointing to the Yovashi. "I need to get her to my tower. She's uncomfortable out here in the light around so many strangers. I'll be glad to tell you all about the mounts another time." The guards all backed up and waved them through the open gate. Issa waved at them as they passed, saying hello, and the guards, giving Morgan a small surge of pride for his people, cheerfully greeted her in turn.

The first thing Morgan noticed was that a gatehouse had been added with a guard station attached. He counted at least five other guards hanging around the gates, all armed with spears. Looking over his shoulder, he saw several guards within sight on top of the wall also, and they had muskets slung over their shoulders. He wondered how effective the weapons would be against the Urghat. They hadn't seemed to be particularly powerful in the Crucible, and he didn't remember any of them having especially strong defensive skills. He figured the muskets would probably prove quite helpful in a potential conflict with the creatures. According to Olivia, the System had warned the people here not to become reliant on technology because, in the long run, powerful Energy users would shrug off their tech-based defenses. Still, Morgan didn't see that being a problem with Urghat. Besides, he felt like it was good to explore all avenues—he didn't trust the System's assessment that tech would be useless in the face of an Energy-rich environment.

The party rode their mounts slowly, waving to the guards, up the cobbled road toward Morgan's tower. The road was new, and it went in a straight line up the gentle slope toward the hill where the Colony Stone rose like a dark gray finger. They could see many more people moving around up there and several new buildings. Morgan's tower was off to the left, though, so they rode into the grass toward it. Once again, Morgan noticed the large villa that had been constructed near his tower, and he wondered who lived in it. "Hey, Olivia, who lives in that villa?"

"Oh, we bought that as a reward and incentive for the leaderboard. Some guy named Reggie. Kind of a weird guy but very enthusiastic about earning points for the colony. He lives there with some of his friends."

"That tower is yours? The one from the Crucible?" Issa asked.

"Yeah, there it is! Unfortunately, we can only access up to the third floor. I still need to deal with the guardians higher than that."

"Oh? You didn't tell me about that. What's the deal with the guardians?"

"I don't know. I guess the guy who built the tower put a guardian on each floor. I have to fight each guardian by myself to access the rooms on that level. There are eight floors."

"We can't help you?"

"No, the stairs are magical—if you take a couple of steps on them, you arrive at the next floor. They'll separate me from anyone trying to help me." Issa huffed at that explanation. Soon they were in front of the short set of steps leading to the tower door, and Morgan and Issa tied their roladii to the railing with long lengths of rope, giving them room to forage for grass. "I guess I'll need to build a stable."

"I'm going to go find Bronwyn and Arthur and tell them about our trip," Olivia said, turning her roladii toward the center of the settlement. "Come find us after you get Ykleedra settled—I'm sure the council will want to hear from Issa."

"Alright, we will." Morgan climbed the steps and motioned for Ykleedra and Issa to follow. Olivia watched them for a moment, then nodded and rode off. Morgan put his hand on the door handle, and a loud click reverberated, indicating the lock had disengaged. He pulled open the door and held it for Issa and Ykleedra. Ykleedra scurried in, happy to move out of the bright sunlight. Issa smiled at him and also walked in, and Morgan followed. They'd only managed a handful of steps into the foyer when Ykleedra hissed and scurried back, scrunching herself into a ball of angular limbs behind Morgan. A tinkling flashing of lights indicated that Tiladia had made an appearance, and her voice soon followed.

"Morgan, welcome home. I see you've brought company!" Ykleedra shivered from behind Morgan, clearly distressed by the appearance and sound of the spirit. Issa just smiled, looking at Morgan with an arched eyebrow.

"Yeah, Tiladia, thank you. This is Issa, and this is Ykleedra," he said, gesturing to them. "They're guests and should be allowed to come and go. Can you make it so that they can open the front door?"

"Of course, Morgan. It is done," Tiladia's voice replied with a melodic cascade of harmonic tinkling sounds.

"Ykleedra, it's okay. Tiladia is a friend; she's a spirit bound to this tower." Slowly, Ykleedra peered out from around Morgan, and then she scurried past the glowing misty form of Tiladia into the central hall of the tower. Tiladia flashed slightly and seemed to rotate, almost as if she watched the Yovashi pass by.

"It's good to meet you, Mistress Issa," she said after a brief pause.

"And you, Tiladia. Please just call me Issa."

"Come on, I'll show you around," Morgan said, taking Issa's hand and walking forward. "The only real problem is that I haven't cleared the floor where the bedrooms are. What floor is that again, Tiladia? The fifth?"

"Yes, Morgan. I've taken the liberty of closely examining you. I think you stand a good chance versus the fourth level guardian now, but attempting the fifth would be quite risky." Morgan frowned at Tiladia.

"Hey, what the hell? What if I were trying to impress my guests? It's not very helpful for my home's spirit to announce my capabilities."

"Oh, don't worry," Issa said, squeezing his hand, "I think you're impressive!" She had a wicked grin on her face.

"That's not the point, and besides, I know you're teasing now."

"Feeling sensitive?" Issa's grin only widened.

"I'm sorry, Lord Morgan!" Tiladia's chime sounded slightly discordant and high-pitched with concern.

"Oh, relax, you two. It's fine. I have no secrets from Issa, Tiladia, but for future reference, please don't advertise my strength to anyone who comes into this tower." Morgan led Issa around the first floor, finding Ykleedra skulking around in the darkened kitchen. They managed to coax her into following them around for the rest of the tour. He explained to them that he'd been sleeping in the library on one of the couches and was about to lead them out to go up the stairs to the second floor when he saw Ykleedra standing near the table where he'd stacked the Yovashi books. "Oh, hey, yeah, those books are from your home, Ykleedra. I'm sorry, but when I took them, I considered your kind to be my enemies."

"I'm glad they aren't lost. My mother often spoke to me about how important they are, and I had to study this one"—she pointed at one of the thinner books—"almost every day."

"So, you can read them?"

"Some, but I've never been allowed to look in most of them."

"I was making some progress with the language, Morgan, but knowing that Ykleedra can read some of it will make things much faster." Morgan jumped slightly. He didn't realize Tiladia had come up behind him. Ykleedra also cringed, shrinking down, but she didn't flee this time.

"What do you say, Ykleedra? Can you help Tiladia to learn the language?" Morgan could see Ykleedra visibly steel herself and stand up straighter, then she nodded.

"I will do my best to help your spirit, Morgan. Thank you for bringing me here to your home."

MORGAN

Morgan spent the next few minutes showing Issa and Ykleedra around the tower, at least the parts he had access to. Both of his guests were impressed when they saw the atrium, but Ykleedra scurried into the thick foliage with a squeal of delight. Morgan could hear her moving through the hedges and trees, and though he had spent a lot of time cutting back the overgrowth, there was a lot of shadow-dappled space for her to explore. After a time, she returned and asked, "Morgan, is that bright sun always there?"

"No, Tiladia says it follows a day-night schedule."

"I'd like to stay in here for now, if you don't mind. There are even fruits for me to eat, though I wouldn't mind some small animals or meat if you get a chance to bring me some."

"Um, yeah, you can stay in here, but not all the time, Ykleedra. It's important that you have company. If I'm not home, spend time with Tiladia, and after you're more comfortable, I'd like to introduce you to more colonists."

"As you say, Morgan. Thank you!" With that, the young Yovashi scuttled back into the shadowy depths of the atrium.

"Well, Issa, are you ready to go and meet a bunch more humans?"

"Yes, but Morgan, I think it would be nice if you could clear the way to your bedrooms sooner rather than later." She smiled coyly, and Morgan didn't have to use his imagination to wonder what she was thinking. They'd definitely grown closer since he found his way to Tarn's Crossing. Plenty of hugging and kissing had taken place, but neither of them had pushed things farther than that. Part of it was that they'd never been really alone; all the way back to the colony, Olivia had been with them, and Morgan felt awkward enough trying to put the moves on Issa, not knowing her cultural norms, he certainly didn't want to add making Olivia uncomfortable to the mix. He could take a hint, though.

"Yeah, I'll make that a priority. After we meet with the council, let's come back here, and I'll see what the deal is with the fourth guardian." Issa grinned, took his hand in hers, and led the way back down the stairs.

It was a short walk from his tower to the cobbled road that led to the center of town. Morgan walked confidently. He wasn't wearing his armor, but he was wearing some of his new clothes, and he knew they were quite a step up from the simple outfits most of the colonists purchased from the Contribution Store. Issa walked beside him, holding his hand, and garnered even more stares than Morgan had when he'd first come back to the colony. Many people shouted out greetings, and they waved and replied. Morgan didn't remember people ever being this friendly to him in his old life, but he had to consider that things were different. He stood out like a professional athlete would if they walked around in a small town. Issa was strikingly beautiful, at least in his mind, but even if he were biased, there was no denying her blue skin and bright yellow eyes.

In any case, they'd drawn a small crowd by the time they reached the cluster of buildings near the Colony Stone hill. On this side of the hill, Morgan recognized the smithy, but there was another large workshop next to it, and an open-air market had taken shape on the other side. Several stalls were set up, and Morgan could see people perusing the wares of the fledgling artisans and other entrepreneurs. "Things are starting to take shape around here."

"This is new to you?" Issa asked.

"Yeah, there weren't as many buildings and roads and stuff when we left." Morgan gestured around. "Let's take a right around the hill; the tavern where the council meets is over there." They walked along the road that curved around the hill, and Morgan noticed that a set of stone steps had been built into the hillside, creating an easy pathway up to the Colony Stone. When they came around the hill, and the tavern and pond behind it came into view, Morgan was surprised to see a crowd of around fifty people standing and sitting on the hillside looking toward and listening to a large, red-haired man. He looked vaguely familiar to Morgan, but he couldn't quite pinpoint how he knew him.

"The time for waiting is over. This supposed Urghat army that will invade 'any moment' may never come. Meanwhile, we have unelected people making every important decision for our community. What have they done to earn that authority? Most of them aren't even on the leaderboard anymore. I've been at the top of the leaderboard since almost the beginning. Even after being awarded my home, I've worked to improve this community. You know I have your best interests at heart! How many of you have eaten food that I've hunted? Had homes built from wood that I've gathered? Been saved because I killed dangerous beasts? Shouldn't someone like me be helping to make decisions about the colony's future?" Each time the big man made a point, he hammered a fist into the palm of his other hand. Several audience members responded with affirmative exclamations, backing up his claims. By the time he finished speaking, the whole crowd seemed agitated, and Morgan could hear echoes of his speech in their conversations.

"That seems like trouble," he said quietly to Issa.

"Who is that?"

"I don't know, to be honest. I think he might be the guy that owns the big house near my tower." Morgan gripped Issa's hand more tightly and led her past the crowd to the tavern. He couldn't help noticing the large, red-bearded man turn and watch him as he walked by. Morgan returned his stare until he had to turn to open the door. The inside of the tavern had an entirely different mood. People sat around talking, drinking from mugs, smiling, and laughing. Morgan saw Alec behind the bar and called out, "Hey Alec, is the council meeting yet?"

"They are, but hey, who's your friend?" Alec's grin was infectious, and Morgan walked over to the bar with Issa in tow.

"This is Issa—she's an Ardeni. They're going to be helping us with the Urghat." He noticed a slight frown on Issa's face, and he continued, "Um, she's my girlfriend, too." He was dimly aware of the absolutely ridiculous fact that his face flushed a little. How could a grown man who'd been battling for his life over and over again suffer from such a juvenile response? He glanced down at Issa and saw that his words had brought the smile back to her face.

"Pleased to meet you, sir. I'd love to try some of your wares. Could you suggest a drink?" Thankfully, Alec had eyes only for Issa and her exotic appearance, so he left Morgan alone. He turned around and filled a mug from a tapped cask on the counter behind him.

"This is a honey mead that I think is quite delicious. I wish I could take credit for it, but our own homebrews are still fermenting. Still, it's a cut above the cheap stuff available on the Contribution Store."

"I, uh, I'll take one too, Alec," Morgan said, finally having found his voice. Alec handed him a mug, and Morgan took a deep drink. The mead was sweet, but it had a solid kick to it. Morgan cleared his throat and said, "Hey, what's with the dude outside riling everyone up?"

"That's Reggie, um, Gandry-Thule, I think it is. He's been bugging the council to hold elections for a couple of weeks now. He's starting to get a lot of people to agree with him. Arthur told me they're thinking of going ahead with an election soon because of the pressure that guy is stirring up."

"Huh. Alright, well, let's go meet the council, Issa."

"It was nice to meet you, Alec," Issa said, following Morgan to the door leading to the back room. Morgan opened it and walked into a lively conversation. Everyone stopped talking, though, when he came in, staring as he and Issa walked over to the table. Not everyone was present; Morgan saw Bronwyn, Olivia, Arthur, Dr. Kerns, Maria Rios, and Tanya Delgado.

"Hey all, this is Issa. She's here ahead of the other Ardeni Hunters to help with the Urghat." Morgan gestured to Issa. She smiled pleasantly and waved. "Maybe you all could take a minute to introduce yourselves?" Morgan pulled out a chair for Issa and sat down next to her while Arthur spoke.

"Of course. Olivia has been filling us in about your journey—it sounds like a great success! I'm Arthur Ballard, Issa. I was selected to lead this colony back on our home world, but the System made our preparations moot. Still, I'm doing my best to help coordinate things here." Morgan relaxed and drank his mead while the rest of the council members introduced themselves to Issa. They all had additional comments or questions for her, and Morgan could see that they were fascinated by her. He supposed it made sense; this was the first meeting they'd had with a friendly, conversant non-human.

After introductions, the conversation drifted to preparations for war, including a report from Tanya Delgado about the new cannons they had mounted strategically along the wall. Morgan was interested to hear about their iron supply—it seemed that some of the colonists had gotten Quests to find ore in the hills east of the forest. That was where they'd found caves with plenty of naturally occurring sulfur and potassium nitrate, in addition to the iron veins the System had sent them to find. Several dozen colonists had started mining the iron ore for rewards and had gained non-combat Skills that sped up the process remarkably, so much so that the smelter had been running nonstop for almost two weeks. The iron, combined with the ingots that came with the smithy, proved to be sufficient for creating several hundred blunderbuss and musket barrels as well as five cannons on each side of the colony.

"Considering the relatively low level of most colonists, I think it's great that you're working on black powder and projectile weapons, but I think we might have a smarter way of melding our technology with Energy," Olivia chimed in as Tanya wrapped up her report.

"What do you mean?" Tanya asked.

"Well, barrels and lead balls are great, but the black powder is messy, slow to load, and proven to be unreliable. What if we were able to use Energy as a power source? What if we could create power-stones and attach them to an Artificed barrel?"

"Hmm." Tanya drummed her fingers on the table. "We don't know how to make power-stones. The ones we have came with the buildings we purchased. It would take a lot of experimentation."

"Well, it's an idea, and yes, we should do some experimenting," Arthur interjected, "but I want us to focus on what we can do for now. Keep making the black powder. Also, now that we've purchased the Alchemy shop, I think the priority should be making a smokeless powder variant."

The discussion continued in that vein for a while, but when that topic died down, Dr. Kern spoke up with a question that interested Morgan: "Issa, do you mind if I ask you a few questions about your racial anatomy? I assume some of your people might be injured in the fighting that seems to be imminent, and I'd be interested in knowing the best way to treat you."

"Um, is this really the best place to talk to her about her anatomy?" Bronwyn spoke up from the far corner where she'd sat, mostly quiet, for the entire meeting. Dr. Kerns's face reddened slightly, and Bronwyn snorted.

"Oh, of course, I'm sorry. The scientist in me got out of hand. Perhaps I could meet with you later, Issa?"

"That's fine with me. Maybe you could come to Morgan's tower sometime this evening?"

"Very good, thank you." Dr. Kerns smiled and nodded.

"One final matter," Arthur said. "Like we've discussed ad nauseam over the last week, we're going to have to have an election. Bronwyn, can you set it up on the stone?"

"Yeah, I looked at it when I gave all of you permissions. It's simple to set up, but it's permanent—once we put in the candidates and everyone votes at the Colony Stone, the changeover will happen automatically."

"I think it's safe to assume that at least some of us already acting as council members will win a spot, even if it's just based on name recognition. That being said, if we want to avoid some kind of riot or mutiny, we're going to have to go ahead with it. I'm accosted by more people every day, and the mood is getting downright hostile out there," Maria Rios added.

"Yeah, Issa and I heard that Reggie guy giving a speech outside the tavern just now." Morgan gestured toward the door behind him with his thumb.

"Alright, I move that we hold an election in three days for nine council positions," Arthur said, a dour expression on his face.

"I second," Maria said.

"Any objections?" Arthur looked around the table. No one was smiling, but no one spoke up.

"It's settled then. Please set up the election, Bronwyn."

"I will." Bronwyn nodded, then caught Morgan's eye and said, "Hey, Morgan, before you go, I have something of yours. Remember that spear you left in the Yovashi cave?"

OLIVIA

Olivia stood by, watching while Bronwyn set up the election on the Colony Stone. A few other people were around, but it was surprisingly quiet for the middle of the day. It seemed like most of the colonists had fallen into a routine of sorts. Some people had duties they needed to fulfill, like a guard rotation or working in one of the council-purchased buildings. Others were keeping themselves busy working on earning points on the leaderboard or improving their new System-granted skills.

While Bronwyn stared into space, her brow furrowed, Olivia walked over to the north edge of the hilltop. There was a walkway around the stone now, and it led to four separate sets of steps leading down from the hill in each cardinal direction. The walkway was similar to the cobbled streets in the colony—rectangular brick-like pavers laid in a perfect grid, so close together that no mortar was necessary. Standing above the northern set of steps, Olivia could see the smithy and the new general workshop next to it. Further on, she could see Morgan's tower where, presumably, he was looking into gaining access to the next level.

Arthur had sent runners to all the gates, spreading the word that more Ardeni might arrive at any time and that they were to be treated as allies. Maria Rios had taken over the militia organization, and now there was a schedule that maintained one hundred guards on the wall in four different shifts. Combined with the new black powder weapons, it went a long way toward making the colony seem like a safe haven, ready to meet the threats of this new world.

"Hey, come here for a minute," Bronwyn called from behind her. Olivia turned back to the Colony Stone and walked around to where Bronwyn was standing. She still had a hand on the stone, but she looked at Olivia. "So, I have everything set up for the election—I just have to hit the confirm button. It's set to allow anyone to nominate themselves for a council position. Each colonist can vote for nine different members; people with the top nine vote counts will win and be automatically granted privileges with the Colony Stone. I have it scheduled for dawn in three days. Does that sound right?"

"Yes, but what sort of privileges? Can you set it so that a majority quorum needs to be present for large expenditures of System Credits or changes to the colony structure?"

"See, I knew it was a good idea bringing you along." Bronwyn laughed, and her eyes went glassy as she perused the menus some more. "Yeah, I guess it's kinda crazy that all of us acting council members have full access right now. Smart to have a failsafe. Hmm, yep, there it is. Okay, I set it!"

"Let's hope there isn't an entirely new council right before the Urghat attack."

"Well, that's the problem—we don't know when they'll attack. They're definitely on a war footing and have a couple of thousand warriors in camps out on the plains, but none of the Urghat I questioned knew when the order to attack would come. The Overclaw keeps his plans to himself, it seems."

"It's so weird that you have that Underclaw title. They just let you walk among them?" Oliva ran a finger along the band on Bronwyn's bicep.

"Yeah, it's weird, alright. I had to fight off a few zealous challengers while I was out there, but they're only allowed to challenge me once per day. That rule saved my ass, I think. I'd just beaten a fairly weak challenger when a fucking huge Urghat named Guts rode into the camp on a giant lizard. He was furious that he couldn't challenge me until the next day. He went off on a tirade because he couldn't stick around—apparently, he was on an important task for the Overclaw."

"You think he would have beaten you?" Olivia asked quietly.

"I don't know for sure, but he wasn't just big; he had a lot of power. I could feel his aura."

"Well, I'm glad you didn't run into him again before returning. Speaking of power, I need to talk to you about something; can we go back to the tavern?"

"Uh, sure. Let's go." Bronwyn started walking down the hill, Olivia beside her. As they descended the steps, she asked, "What's it about?" Her voice was soft, and she looked nervous.

"Well, I got an opportunity, but I want to run it by you. Let's get a drink and sit down; then I'll go over it." Bronwyn nodded at Olivia's words, and they stepped into the crowded tavern, finding a space at the end of the bar where they could squeeze in for service. Alec gave them both a mug without asking, and Olivia leaned close to Bronwyn, speaking under the loud hum of conversations. "I got offered a spot in an academy for magic."

"What?" Bronwyn raised an eyebrow, took a big drink of her ale, then continued, "Really? A school for magic? Where is it?"

"That's the thing; it's really far away." She pulled the box with the teleportation token out of her satchel and showed it to Bronwyn. "This will take me there, and I have to go in the next few days. I guess the new term is starting soon."

"Really? Um, well, are you sure it's safe? Do you trust this token? How do you know it's not some kind of weird trap?" Bronwyn's brows had furrowed, and Olivia could see that she wasn't really excited about the news.

"I do trust it. The old wizard that gave it to me seemed very genuine, and the people of Tarn's Crossing all seemed to think he was legitimate. I want to do this, Bron, but I'm worried about the colony. I'm worried about you." Olivia reached a hand out to rest on Bronwyn's on the bar top. Bronwyn looked at her hand, then she looked right into Olivia's eyes.

"Hey, we're going to be fine. We have the walls. We have guards; we have guns. I know a lot more about the Urghat now. Shit, we have the Ardeni coming to help, thanks to you. We'll be fine. I'll be fine. It's not like you're leaving for good, right? Maybe you get vacations and shit. Besides, I'm sure I'll have to leave again to deal with this Urghat title." She sighed heavily and turned her hand over so she could grasp Olivia's. She squeezed it. "You're important, you know? Your desires count. You want to go, and it makes sense; you're the most talented human on this world, but even if you weren't, you should be allowed to pursue things that are interesting to you." Bronwyn's face turned a little red, perhaps because she'd said so many words at once, and she hid behind her mug while she took another long pull of the warm, bitter ale.

"I love you, Bron. Do you know that? I don't know why, you moody knucklehead, but I do! You better keep yourself safe and out of trouble while I'm gone!" Olivia leaned forward, kissed Bronwyn's cheek, and pulled her into a hug. Bronwyn's mug clattered against the bar while she tried to hug Olivia back. She smelled like dry grass and berries, and Olivia loved it. She squeezed her tighter, and Bronwyn sniffed; Olivia could tell she was on the verge of crying.

"You dummy. You're the one that better keep safe! Don't let those teachers talk you into doing anything crazy. If any other students give you shit, you better let them know about me . . ." she trailed off, sniffing again. They held each other for a long moment, and then they sat together, finishing their drinks. They talked about each other's journeys; Olivia had Bronwyn laughing about how awkwardly Morgan had behaved around Issa and her father, and Bronwyn regaled her with tales of Urghat camps and duels. The hours stretched into the night, and before Olivia knew it, she was hugging Bronwyn goodnight and walking to her dark, lonely tent.

Olivia woke the following day with a slight headache, although it wasn't nearly as bad as she'd feared it would be when she'd sprawled into her blankets in the middle of the night. She ate a pastry that she'd purchased in Tarn's Crossing, washing it down with some very watery wine. After her stomach was satisfied, she summoned her new staff from her satchel and examined it:

Stave of Prisma Foci: This focus item has been enchanted by a** journeyman Artificer. Using two focus crystals to keep opposing elements apart, it is capable of focusing elementally attuned Energy, greatly enhancing the efficacy of the Energy used.

The staff was a lovely piece of craftsmanship. The wood it was made from was smooth and dense—Olivia couldn't see any grain or pores. It was a sleek, nearly black length of wood with white streaks along its length. The silver band in the middle of the staff was wide enough for her to grasp with both hands, and it seemed to automatically channel her Energy to the correct Prisma crystal on the top of the staff. Fire and earth-attuned Energy went to one crystal, and water and air-attuned Energy went to the other. She'd tried out her Icey Shards and Fiery Burst spells, and they were significantly more potent with the staff. It took her a second or two to send her Energy through the staff, though, and she didn't know if that was normal or if it just meant she needed practice using a focus item.

Olivia had taken the staff out because she wanted to try something. When she'd woken in the early light of dawn, she'd lain in her blankets thinking; she often did her best thinking right upon waking. Sometimes, it felt like she thought of a solution in her dream and put the thoughts together while she lay in bed. In this case, she'd wondered what would happen if she channeled a complementing Energy affinity into her staff while she cast one of her spells.

She stood with her staff in her hands, pointing the end with the silver-ensconced Prisma crystals toward the grass, and she channeled her Icy Shards spell. Her ice attuned Energy surged into the staff, and after a second's lag, a half dozen razor-sharp icicles about the size of a person's finger formed in the air above her staff. She released them, and they shot into the grass with heavy staccato thuds. Olivia nodded to herself, then repeated the process, this time channeling air-attuned Energy alongside her water-attuned Energy for the Icy Shards spell. She could feel the different streams of Energy exit her hands, passing into the staff. A moment later, like before, the shards materialized, but this time, Olivia could see a current of electricity sparking and warping around each shard, almost like a tesla coil. She released the spell, sending the shards thudding into the grass, and Olivia could hear and see the electricity discharge a short way into the damp turf.

*****Congratulations! You have learned the spell Stunning Ice Shards—Basic.*****

Olivia laughed with glee. She'd been right! It wasn't just a matter of whim, whether the System gave you a new spell or skill. It was different from the animal taming skill, also. There had seemed to be some chance involved with learning that skill, but here, she just used the correct combination of Energy affinities, and she'd unlocked a new spell. Her mind raced with possibilities. She was thinking of her next experiment when she realized motes of Energy were coalescing in the air above the ground where she'd sent her spell. A moment later, they surged into her. She felt a rush, like when Energy came to her from a defeated monster. "What the hell?"

Was the System rewarding her for innovating with her magic? If that were the case, she'd have to be careful; she didn't want to level before leaving for the academy.

MORGAN

Morgan stopped before he stepped onto the stairs leading to the fourth floor. He'd asked Issa to wait for him back on the first floor and assumed that Ykleedra was still in the atrium. He was alone for the moment, and he wanted to gather his thoughts. Was he rushing this encounter for sex? He almost laughed at the idea, but the concern was valid. Issa had said he should hurry up and clear the fifth floor to open up the bedrooms, but she'd been at least partially joking around. He figured if they really wanted privacy, they could use any of the other rooms that had a door. No, Morgan wasn't rushing this particular fight; he'd been planning on attempting the fourth guardian ever since he'd learned the Azure Burst spell, and since then, he'd improved his swordwork and gotten a fantastic new sword.

Morgan nodded to himself, gripped the hilt of his sword in two hands, held it in a guard position, and mounted the stairs. His third step brought him to the landing of the fourth floor. The landing here was different from any others; no doors were leading away, and the room around the stairs was larger. A warm yellow-orange light suffused the space, seemingly emanating from the smooth plaster ceiling itself. Large black and white tiles made up the flooring, laid in a checkerboard pattern. From his vantage, Morgan could only see about half the room, but along the wall, about twenty feet from the stairs, he saw three ornately carved stone archways that seemed to be placed against the dark iron-like material of the tower walls. In other words, they led nowhere.

The archways were the size of a large door, wide enough for two people to walk through shoulder to shoulder and around eight feet high at their peaks. Morgan cautiously stepped away from the stairs and slowly turned, taking in the rest of the room. He could see that another three similarly carved archways lined the other half of the room. He had almost turned in a complete circle when he noticed movement and an accompanying sound: the grinding *clang* of a heavy metal foot stepping on the tile. Morgan slowly circled to his right, sidestepping around the central stairway. As he moved, he saw the dark shadow come forth from beside one of the stone archways—it looked like a thin man with four arms, but its movements were jerky and strange, and it rattled and clanged as it moved. "What is this? A robot?"

As he muttered the question, the being's head swiveled quickly toward him, and Morgan saw the glowing, angular red eyes illuminating matte black sockets and cheekbones. As he cleared the stairwell and squared off with the thing, Morgan could see that it was essentially an iron skeleton, complete with orange oxidation stains. "Oh, great." He looked at his sword, wondering how well the enchanted blade would hold up against a metal enemy. The skeleton's four arms moved suddenly, swiveling at the elbows and reaching toward its back. Each of its hands seemed to grab something, then they jerked outward into a wide stance, a rusty, iron short sword extending from each hand.

About twenty feet separated Morgan and the iron skeleton, and Morgan decided to take the initiative. He activated his Hollow Charge ability, aiming to the skeleton's left and swinging his sword in a powerful sideways slash, using his arms, his entire core, and the momentum of his charge to power the attack. The skeleton reacted swiftly, faster than Morgan probably could have countered if he weren't under the effect of his charge ability. Still, it wasn't fast enough—two of its swords hit Morgan's blade and were shattered by the impact. Amid bits of flying iron, Morgan's sword cleaved on as he flashed past the skeleton, and he felt the concussion of his sword slamming into the iron monster's ribs deep in the bones of his wrists. He held his sword perfectly, though, and used his momentum and strength to power through the slash, ripping a furrow an inch deep into the iron ribs and sending the skeleton crashing back into the tower wall. Morgan immediately dropped his blade into the Crane Forages, moving toward the skeleton while its limbs flailed, and it struggled to gain its footing.

As he got close, he lunged into the Crane Takes a Minnow, trying to stab the sword between the ribs of the lurching, flailing creature as it scrambled to its feet. Midway through his attack, the skeleton moved, and Morgan corrected his angle of attack, but his larger movements were too fast for him to adjust the grip and angle of his blade, and he growled with frustration as it skidded along the iron pelvis of the construct. He was bringing his sword around, about to launch into the Crane Flutters Its Wings, when the skeleton got its feet underneath it and burst into motion. Its eyes flared a brighter shade of red, and it stood up tall, swinging its two remaining swords in a flurry of blows and grasping and clawing with its two empty hands.

It was all Morgan could do to parry two heavy slashes, but a clawing iron hand grabbed him around the vambrace of his left arm, pulling him off balance. Morgan swung his arms in a tight circle to break the grip, but a sword skidded over his breastplate, and another punched into his thigh while he was doing that. He grunted in pain and activated Azure Burst. Crackling blue flames erupted from his center, flaring out in a circle and blasting the skeleton away to crash into the iron wall once again. Morgan realized it had left its sword in his thigh, so he pulled it out and stowed it in his ring.

Grimacing and limping, he walked to the skeleton, which seemed to be stunned. The light in its eyes had dimmed, and its limbs were twitching slightly. As he approached, the skeleton moved its head to look directly at him, and then the eyes started to regain their luster. Morgan brought his blade up to his style's form of a high guard, the Crane Advances, and approached. He was wary because the iron skeleton hadn't made a move to stand, and its eyes continued to increase in brightness. Morgan was contemplating how he might try to finish the unmoving thing when its eyes suddenly flared so brightly that Morgan had to turn away. He had time to blink once, and then a beam of red fire lanced into his chest.

Morgan used every ounce of his agility to leap to the side, rolling away from the beam, but the skeleton merely had to track him with its eyes. The scorching red beam melted a runnel into his breastplate, and when he rolled, it scorched down, ripping through his enchanted girdle and scorching the flesh of his side and hip into a blistered, blackened mess. The pain and impact of the scorching blast knocked him to the ground. Thankfully, the beam sputtered at that point, and Morgan had a momentary reprieve. He could hear the skeleton clanking and scrabbling against the tile, trying to stand, and he knew he had to do the same. He did his best to ignore the white-hot pain of his side and pushed himself up to his knee, then to his feet.

Morgan limped toward the skeleton, which had just regained its footing. Its eyes were dimmed to a faint red luminosity, but otherwise, it seemed largely unharmed. Morgan was aching, and he felt stiff and slow, but he knew he had to do something. The skeleton must be a creature that was dependent on Energy to function, so he did what he did best: he activated Hollow Charge again, thrusting with his sword, trying to gain purchase between the skeleton's ribs. Again, his charge was too fast for the skeleton to avoid, so his strike hit home; he felt his blade slide between the skeleton's ribs, and he immediately activated Energy Drain.

He felt red-hot Energy flood through his sword, into his hands, and through his pathways to his Core. He urged his Core to spin ever faster, pulling the Energy in with all his might. The skeleton's thrashing slowed, and the light in its eyes dimmed to just a faint glimmer. Morgan, meanwhile, felt his flesh regenerating from the stolen Energy and raised his knee, slamming the heel of his boot into the skeleton's pelvis and sending its weakly thrashing frame off his sword and sprawling to the ground. The skeleton laboriously rose to its hands and knees, and Morgan approached it from behind. He unleashed a flurry of blows with the Crane Flutters Its Wings, each mighty angular cleave aimed at its head and neck.

His dark blade carved shadowy arcs through the air, clanging and ripping into the skeleton's skull and neck. With his fourth blow, he felt the edge of his blade bite deeply into the spine of the construct. He wrenched the buried sword down, dragging the skeleton to the floor, then he stomped on the back of the blade, forcing it through the final portion of the metal vertebrae, shattering the brittle, rusty bone. The skeleton's head rolled free, the fire in its eyes wholly gone, and its frame collapsed in an ungainly heap.

Large, dense motes of Energy built up around the downed enemy and poured forth into Morgan. He felt his fatigue wash away, and the residual pain of his wounds faded to just a faint ache.

Congratulations! You have achieved level 17 Hollow Guard and have gained 5 Strength, 5 Will, 4 Vitality, 4 Intelligence, and 3 Agility.

He pulled the remnants of his girdle off and dropped it, looking to where his flesh had been seared when the skeleton had tried to immolate him. His skin was pink and tender, but he didn't bear any terrible scars. He sat down on the hard tile, sighing. These fights weren't getting any easier, and he was worried about his attribute points. He pulled up his status sheet to look at his attributes.

Strength:	50	Vitality:	48
Dexterity:	8	Agility:	36
Intelligence:	56	Will:	50

His dexterity deficit was becoming more and more pronounced. Even before this level, he'd had trouble with his agility and strength being too much for his fine motor skills to cope with. He either had to hope for a class refinement at twenty that allowed him to gain dexterity, or he needed to find another way to improve it. He would rather get started improving it now—he'd theoretically have sixty-five strength at level twenty and still only have eight dexterity. It was already hard to manage his body when he went full out; he didn't want to hold himself back constantly.

"Congratulations, Morgan! You've gained mastery of the fourth floor!" Tiladia's chime-like voice startled him out of his reverie, and Morgan stood up with a grunt.

"Thanks, Tiladia."

"Morgan!" Issa's voice came from the other side of the stairwell.

"I'm here! All's good." He started walking around to her, but she beat him to it, practically running around the stairs to grab him into a bear hug.

"I hate that this tower makes you fight alone!" she said into his chest. Morgan laughed softly and hugged her back.

"It's alright, I'm not really hurt, but I lost my old Urghat girdle from the Crucible. Also, I don't think I should try the next guardian until I do something about my dexterity. I had to slow down my attacks in order to aim and maneuver my sword properly." Issa looked at Morgan's scorched and parted girdle; then, she traced a finger along the melted runnel on his breastplate and down his side, where his shirt had been burned away. She slipped her hand into the burnt cloth and gently rubbed the pink skin where his burn had healed. Morgan felt himself responding to the warm, gentle caress, and he pulled back, clearing his throat.

"Do I want to know how bad this was before you healed it with your Energy Drain?" She asked, arching an eyebrow.

"Nah, it wasn't a big deal," he said, taking her hand in his and walking over to one of the imposing, stone archways. "Tiladia, tell me more about these portals."

MORGAN

"It still doesn't feel right; it's like the forms from my style are just fancy, sometimes inefficient versions of standard sword fighting moves." Morgan wiped the sweat from his forehead and stretched, shaking out his wrists in frustration. Issa had parried all of his attacks and, using her Haste ability, given him a few good thwacks with her wooden practice sword.

"I agree, they don't seem exactly spectacular. Do they consume a lot of Energy?" Issa stretched while she spoke, pulling one leg up behind her and rotating her hip. Morgan was dumbstruck on two fronts—one, she looked incredibly sexy in her tight-fitting practice outfit, and two, what the fuck did she mean about his styles consuming Energy?

"Uh, what do you mean?"

"When you perform the forms from your style, are you infusing Energy into the movements?" She stopped stretching and looked at him quizzically.

"No. Goddamn it, I always feel like I'm playing catch up. Is that how all martial styles work?"

"I don't know about all of them. Think about it, though, if you have a combat style with forms designed to utilize a person's full potential, and it was developed by a master swordsman who used Energy . . ." she trailed off, seeing that Morgan was connecting the dots.

"Of course, they would use Energy. Dammit. So, when I learned the style, any idea why I didn't learn that simple fact?"

"I don't know! I don't have a special style. Maybe it was expected that you'd have a master to guide you?"

"Right, well, do you have any idea how one should go about infusing Energy into a form?" Morgan hefted the large wooden practice sword he'd gotten from one of the artisans in the craft hall. He'd made it to look like Morgan's sword and even put a minor enchantment on it to make it harder than regular wood. After a couple of hours of practice, the wood was still almost unmarred.

"You remember when Swent attacked you, and you thought he was coming on one side, but he struck you on another? That wasn't a spell or anything—that was him using a special style. Before I knew what an idiot he was, I used to practice with him. He talked about channeling Energy into the movement. I remember him saying how hard it was at first but that it became second nature. I bet, with your high affinity, it will come easily."

"Huh, alright, let me see here," Morgan said, thinking about his forms. He turned away from Issa, down the length of his dueling hall, and concentrated on his Crane Flutters Its Wings form. He very slowly, very intentionally brought his blade into the first movement while trying to channel Energy into his arms and then into his sword. When he felt the Energy flow along his pathways and out of his hands, he launched into the form, swinging the sword, stepping forward, and trying to push Energy into it the whole time. He felt *something* happening, but he could tell it wasn't quite right. Still, his sword moved more quickly through the air, even the wooden blade making a snapping hissing sound as it moved through the motions. Issa clapped from behind him.

"That looked different! I think you're on the right path!" she called.

Morgan checked his Energy stat: 1310/1320. He had used some Energy, but not much. "It felt different, but it felt off, somehow. Like my arms were moving ahead of my body, out of sync."

"When you learned the form, did you learn just to move your arms, or did you learn to use your whole body? Don't just send Energy into your arms!" That was a good point, Morgan conceded silently. He readied himself again. This time he sent a surge of Energy not only to his arms and into the sword but also through the pathways in his lower extremities. Energy thrumming in his body, he performed the Crane Flutters Its Wings. He moved forward in a blur, the strikes of his sword snapping down in a diagonal slash and up and around to reset before slashing the other way. The wooden sword shrieked through the air, and Morgan swore he could see a wave of Energy rippling off it as it arced through the four powerful slashes.

He found himself ten feet from where he began the attack, and when Morgan looked back over his shoulder, he saw Issa standing quietly with wide eyes. "Don't practice that one on me!" she said when they made eye contact. Morgan smiled and rechecked his Energy stat: 1213/1320. So, accounting for some passive regeneration, the attack used around a hundred Energy.

"That sure would have made my last couple of fights easier!"

"It's my pleasure to instruct you, novice." Issa laughed and hurried toward him. Morgan laughed, too, leaning over to kiss her when she got close enough.

"You're a great teacher. Now, let me see if I can try this with my other forms." Issa nodded and moved to the side, sitting on one of the wooden benches to watch.

Morgan started with the Crane Forages. This time, when he held the sword low, his center of gravity low, and his feet carefully walking forward, he infused all of his movements with Energy, and the form clicked for him. He practically glided over the ground, his steps as light as feathers and his movement smooth, like water rippling over a polished stone. He felt the potential Energy in his blade, ready to snap up and parry or snap forward in a lightning thrust. This form was meant for hunting a quarry, and now that he had felt it with Energy, Morgan understood it much more thoroughly. He found that while he performed that form, moving around, and poised to strike, he consumed around five Energy per second. As he gained in power, he knew that drain would be trivial, but for now, he would have to be careful not to overuse it.

The Crane Advances and the Crane Defends the Nest were both guard positions. The former, a high guard with an advancing movement component, the latter, a close guard that allowed for movement in any direction. Morgan was stunned to find that when he channeled Energy into these forms, he not only moved more smoothly, but an actual shield of Energy extended around his sword blade. When he had Issa try to strike him, he found it trivial to block her attacks because the surface area of his parries was much greater. Even if he missed her strike with his blade, the extended Energy shield knocked her sword aside. The Crane Advances was the cheaper of the two, probably because it wasn't meant as an active defense, but more of a preparatory one—it consumed ten Energy a second, roughly. The Crane Defends the Nest, though immensely effective at blocking even a flurry of Issa's Hasted attacks, was costly—in just five seconds of defending, he burned through over a hundred Energy.

Finally, Morgan practiced infusing Energy into the Crane Takes a Minnow. When he'd practiced the form without Energy, he'd taken it to be a rather tricky downward angled thrust meant to catch an opponent by surprise, striking at their lower extremities. When he infused his movements with Energy and performed the stutter step and lunge, his sword moved so quickly that he swore he heard it split the air. What's more, even though his thrust ended with his blade angled to the side and the point a good foot from the ground, the floor of his dueling hall split as though the blade continued past the point of his sword. He looked at his status sheet and saw that he'd burned around fifty Energy with the attack. "Well, I sure feel better about my Fighting Crane Style now. Thank God I asked you to practice with me today."

"The forms look much, much better, Morgan! Still, we should practice more until it's second nature for you to use them. You want it to be like a reflex, not a conscious thought." She whipped her wooden rapier around and continued, "At least, that's what my instructor told me when I was learning the rapier."

They practiced for another hour or so, and then Issa said she needed a break; it was late in the evening, and they'd had a very long day. Morgan showed Issa where he'd been sleeping, and she insisted that he push a couch close to the one he liked so that they could sleep next to each other. "I wish I had cleared the fifth floor—Tiladia says there are some nice bedrooms on that level."

"Well, we don't really need a bedroom, do we? We've spent nights sleeping on stone floors and other nights under the stars. Some comfortable couches are nothing to complain about." Issa sat on the edge of her couch and yawned.

"I wanted to head into the colony for some quick shopping; I want to see if there's anything in there that can help with my dexterity deficit."

"I'm sure your Contribution Store has attribute boosting items, but I bet they're costly. Once your council gets things set up with the Urghat bounty, there might be a way for you to earn a bunch of points." She yawned again and laid back. Morgan pulled a blanket up over her and kissed her softly. "Mmm, that's sure to give me sweet dreams."

"I'll be back soon. In the meantime, Tiladia will let you know if there's anything worth waking up for. Sleep well." Morgan kissed her one more time on her warm, soft eyebrow resulting in more quiet, sleepy murmurs; then he walked out to the central hall.

"Are you heading out, Morgan?" Tiladia's tinkling voice asked. Morgan saw her floating near the stairs and walked over.

"Yeah. Hey, Tiladia, I need to improve my dexterity, and I'm going to explore some options in town. I wish Vormendion hadn't disabled his teleportation portals. Imagine what I could find in his other homes or the great libraries he had linked." Tiladia had explained the portals to Morgan after his victory against the fourth guardian. They were still functional, but he needed their anchor stones which were in the reliquary on the eighth floor. Once he had the anchor stones, he could place them wherever he wanted and create a link to the portal in his tower. Vormendion broke all the links to his old portal destinations by returning the anchor stones to the tower.

"True, Lord Vormendion had one portal anchored in the city of Hazard's End. It's said that anything and everything could be found for sale there."

"Well, that's a story for another day. I want to head out before everyone's asleep. Talk to you soon, Tiladia." With that, Morgan turned and walked to the door.

"Wait! One moment, Morgan," Tiladia called after him.

"Yes?" He stopped and turned to her.

"I was watching you practice with Issa for a while. I've reevaluated your combat prowess based on your apprehension of the process by which you imbue Energy into your sword forms. I think it's highly likely that you would be able to best the fifth guardian."

"Hmm. Well, that's good news. Still, I want to see if I can improve a bit more before taking it on. Thanks, Tiladia." Morgan walked out of the tower and strode over the grass to the road, following it to the Colony Stone hill. He felt good knowing that Tiladia thought he could defeat the fifth guardian now. She tended toward caution, so he must seem significantly stronger now that he could use those forms properly. He wanted to spend some time practicing them, though, until they felt more fluid and natural in the heat of combat.

Soon, he was climbing the steps leading to the stone, surprised by how many people were still out and about. He didn't know what time it was, but it had to be several hours past sundown. He stepped to the stone and was surprised to have a prompt pop up before he could access the usual menus:

*****Morgan Hall, do you wish to enter your name for possible election to the First Landing Ruling Council? YES/NO*****

Morgan wanted to select the "NO" option, but in the last meeting, everyone present had agreed to run, just to try to ensure some continuity in policy. He selected the affirmative option and was rewarded with a message that he was one of forty-three candidates so far and the election would be live in just about two and a half days. Then he spent nearly half an hour searching through various Contribution Store options and ended up somewhat unsatisfied. He found a rare, Energy-rich fruit that was described as "potentially increasing dexterity by up to five points," but it cost 105,000 contribution points. To make a dent in his deficit, he'd need to be very rich, or he'd have to find another solution.

He found a temporary stopgap, though, a potion that gave a short-term boost to dexterity that he could drink before battles. It only cost fifty points per potion, and it gave a ten-point boost to the attribute for up to five minutes. Morgan bought five of the potions, and then he walked down the hill to the artisan workshop where he'd gotten his practice sword earlier in the day. The structure was next to the smithy and at least twice its size. It was built in a manner to accommodate as many craftspeople as possible. Large, rolling barn-style doors opened on each of the four walls, and within there were several dozen workbenches. Other crafting paraphernalia was placed around the workshop, from stacks of wood to tool racks, to barrels filled with tanned hides and forged metal.

There were still ten or more people working on projects at this hour, and Morgan scanned their faces, hoping to see a familiar one. It seemed to be his lucky night because he spotted Boris Saltzki leaning over and looking through a monocle at a piece of shiny metal that he appeared to be engraving. He walked over to the workbench and cleared his throat. "Hey, Boris. How's it going?"

"Huh? Oh, hey Morgan!" Boris sat up and set his monocle down next to a set of intricate engraving tools.

"Good to see you! I've heard you're really taking to this Artificing business."

"Yeah, I am! I'm already level thirteen. The System rewards Energy for innovation, and I've figured a lot of shit out. I was the first Artificer in the colony to get a class—Enchanter."

"Oh? I thought Artificer was a class?"

"I think it can be, but it's also a general term that refers to lots of different Energy-based crafts." Boris shrugged.

"Well, I wish I could say I just stopped by to say hi, but I have an ulterior motive." Morgan smiled, leaning one elbow on Boris's workbench.

"Ah, yeah, I'm not surprised. Lots of stuff going on, eh? Well, let me have it. What do you need from me?" Boris smiled back at him, and Morgan noticed how his friend had changed for the first time. He had a thin beard covering most of his face, which was new, but Morgan could see that he looked healthier. His skin had a healthy glow, and his eyes were bright. He looked better than when they'd been back on Earth, that was certain. Back then, Boris had been undernourished, haggard, and ready to get the hell off the planet.

"You know, Boris, you're looking good. I think this world agrees with you."

"Oh, jeez, you don't have to butter me up. Just spit it out!" He laughed, shrugging off the compliment.

"Alright, alright. Well, I have a problem. I have really high strength and agility, but my dexterity is low. I'm starting to struggle to control my movements in combat when I go all out. Is there any way to enchant items to boost an attribute?" Boris's eyes lit up even more as Morgan spoke, and Morgan could see that he'd come to the right guy, even before he responded.

"Hell yes, there's a way! I learned a rune enchantment for each of the attributes. Well, technically, the System gave me three of them when I got my class, but I figured out the others. That got me two levels, by the way! I can put a dexterity enchantment on any suitably strong material that will grant anywhere from one to five dexterity to the person wearing the item."

"What's a suitably strong material? Can I wear more than one? Do they stack?" Morgan couldn't hide his excitement.

"Some materials can't hold an enchantment, so they won't work. Most metals can hold at least a weak enchantment. You can wear more than one, and they'll stack, but there is a caveat—enchantments like this need a clear path to your Core, and if you have more than one using the same path, they will conflict. You could safely have one on each limb and your head or neck—as long as you have pathways to your Core in those areas. Do you have extensive pathways?"

"How big of an item does it have to be? Could jewelry work? Like rings and a necklace?"

"The smaller the item, the better the material needs to be." Boris shrugged as he spoke, his fingers drumming on the workbench. "Don't you have some armor I could enchant?"

"Oh, hey, I do. It already has some minor enchantments, though, for self-repair and resizing."

"Let me see it—I have a skill that lets me analyze potential in materials." Morgan nodded and pulled his vambraces, greaves, and breastplate out, setting them on the workbench. Boris picked up his monocle and slowly scanned over each item. "This is essentially a bronze alloy—not the best material in the world, and I'd recommend you try to upgrade soon, but I think I can work with it. The pieces are quite large, so the different enchantments have room. The self-repair enchantment takes up a lot of the material's potential because it has to connect to every part of it, but I can pick a corner to bend the lines around to fit the dex rune in."

"So, with these five items, I could get up to twenty-five more dexterity?"

"Yeah, but I'm never that lucky in my enchantments. I'd bank on getting something more like ten or fifteen. Worst case, though, you'll only get a five-point boost."

"Well, can I get you to do it? I can pay. . . ." Boris cut Morgan off, shaking his head.

"Nah, brother, we're all working together right now. Let's just say you owe me one. Plus, I'll get some practice in! Leave these with me, and I'll have it ready for you sometime tomorrow."

"Alright, definitely; I owe ya. If I come across any cool enchanting items or information, I'll bring it your way. Thanks, Boris!" Morgan clapped him on the shoulder, and Boris smiled, giving him a mock punch in the arm. Morgan walked out of the workshop and contemplated going by the tavern for a drink, but decided he should get some sleep. He turned back toward the north and the dark silhouette of his tower. He'd have to check in on Ykleedra and make sure she wasn't hungry, then he was going to crawl into his blankets and sleep for a solid ten hours.

MORGAN

Issa pulled the straps tight on Morgan's breastplate, and he pulled up his status sheet to see the change in his dexterity. There it was, he had eight Dexterity, but in parenthesis, it said twenty-five. "Yes! Boris was as good as his word. Between the five armor pieces, I have an additional seventeen dexterity."

"That's quite good, considering he's only recently gotten his Enchanter class. He must have real talent." Issa backed up a step and examined Morgan. "Why don't you have a helmet yet? If you get smashed in the head, you'll be just as dead as an unleveled novice would be." She came forward and gently scratched the side of his head with her nails. "I'd rather you didn't get your skull caved in."

"Well, you make a convincing argument. Let's stop by the Contribution Store on the way back to the tower." They were standing in a grassy area next to the artisan workshop. Having spent the morning sparring, they'd come into the colony to have a meal at the tavern and pick up Morgan's armor. Issa clasped his hand, and they walked together up the steps to the Colony Stone.

Morgan didn't take a lot of time to shop around. He wanted to save his contribution points up for something good, so he just bought the helmet that was obviously made to be part of a set with the breastplate that he'd purchased weeks ago. The helmet had the same bronze-colored metal with a soft fur lining. It covered the top of his head, extending down past his ears with a metal spar that hung down the bridge of his nose. When he tried to slip it on, it was too small, so he held it onto his head with a hand and sent a trickle of Energy into it to bond. He felt it slowly expand and slip onto his head, resting snugly in place.

"Alright, let's go back to the tower, and I'll try my hand at that fifth guardian. I feel kinda funny messing around with these challenges when the colony is getting ready for war, but I don't know what else I can do, and, besides, it's helping me improve my fighting." They started walking down the hill toward Morgan's tower.

"As long as you aren't rushing, I think it's a smart thing to do. You gain access to more of the tower's secrets, and, as you said, fighting practice is always good. You're sure you can trust Tiladia and her assessment of your chances?"

"Yeah, you should have seen when I first met her; she tried to give me some extra information about one of the guardians and the binding that Vormendion put her under tortured her for it. I think she has good intentions when it comes to me."

"Hmm, alright." They walked hand in hand to the tower. A few people shouted out greetings, and Morgan recognized one of them as the guy who first spoke to him when he arrived in First Landing. He thought hard about his name and thought it was Nels, but he wasn't sure, so he just waved.

Morgan thought he could feel a difference from his boosted dexterity already. It was hard to put the difference into exact terms, but he just felt more in control of his body. Boris had been pretty excited about his results; of the five enchantments, he'd managed one perfect five, a four, two threes, and a two. Morgan was just happy that there hadn't been any ones. He considered having Boris enchant the helmet, also, but he didn't want to wait for it right now. As he was musing about his equipment and enchantments, they arrived at the tower and entered. "Well, no sense delaying. I'll be done soon, I hope, and Tiladia will let you know when you can come up the stairs." A tinkling affirmation accompanied his words.

"Alright, luck to you. I wish I could give you a spell to boost you, but Tiladia told me that it will be canceled by the enchantment on the stairs."

"Yeah, I guess Vormendion didn't want some runt to kill his guardians because a powerful mage boosted them. Speaking of boosts"—Morgan pulled a dexterity potion out of his ring—"nothing says I can't boost myself when I get in there!" He grinned and kissed Issa. Potion in one hand, sword in the other, he stepped onto the stairway. He concentrated on going to the fifth floor, and the stairs seemed to know his intentions; he took six steps, and then he came out on a landing he wasn't familiar with. Not knowing what to expect, he quickly quaffed the potion and slipped the empty bottle into his ring.

He felt a little surge of warmth from the center of his being, and he stepped into the bright yellow light of the room surrounding the stairwell. Corridors led away in each of the cardinal directions. The flooring was hardwood, the walls paneled in wooden wainscoting with plaster above. Sconces lined the walls in the landing as well as down each hallway. They gave off a warm yellow-white light and were not flame-based—rather, a small mote of glowing Energy sat in the globes atop each sconce.

The ceiling was impressively high—twelve feet or more. The hallways led away through tall smooth archways, and Morgan could see at least four doorways down the hallway in front of him. "Am I going to have to hunt this guardian out? Or will it come to me?" He said aloud, partially because he hoped the guardian was listening. He only had five minutes of his extra dexterity boost, so he wanted to get down to business. He turned, figuring he'd look down each hallway to start his search, but as he began to walk, he heard a susurration come from behind him, like someone dragging a heavy beaded coat over the floor.

Morgan leaped to the side, not knowing what to expect, and he felt the passage of something large and heavy pulling the air into a breeze as it narrowly missed where he'd been standing. Morgan turned toward where the thing had gone and saw the tail of some massive serpent-like creature slipping around the side of the stairwell. He immediately dropped into the Crane Forages, pushing Energy into his body and moving nimbly after the creature. He glided over the floor, his sword out and ready.

He'd just made the stairwell corner when the creature tore out of the shadows, striking at him again. Morgan's sword was ready, rising like lightning; he twisted the edge and sidestepped as he slashed upward. A spray of warm mist told him he'd struck true. Morgan fell into the Crane Defends the Nest and backpedaled, wanting to see more clearly what he'd only caught glimpses of so far.

As he moved backward, Morgan saw that he was, indeed, fighting a giant snake. It was a snake like nothing he'd ever seen, though. It had scales, but at least 30 percent of its scales were colorful gemstones. The creature was a good thirty feet from nose to tail. It was in the process of turning around, leaving a long smear of blood where it moved. Morgan had given it a deep gash about a third way down its left side. When it turned to face him, Morgan, for the first time, saw its eyes and the malevolence that lay within them. They were black, angular pools of darkness with just a tiny circle of red at their center. Intelligence oozed from them, and Morgan knew the serpent was contemplating its next move.

Morgan didn't want to let it get off its heels, so to speak, so he used Hollow Charge, and while he was ripping over the ten feet between them, he primed the Crane Flutters Its Wings. He arrived in a blur, ripping and slicing with his sword, more like flashes of light than dark steel cutting the air, and the serpent hissed and tried to back away from the onslaught. However, Morgan's forward momentum was prodigious, and it couldn't get away. Each of his four slices cut the creature like a plasma torch, sending scales, gems, and blood splashing out over the landing. Morgan's sword didn't hesitate on the scales of the creature. When he hit a gem, it blocked his blade, but only enough to send it sliding to off the side and into scales, where it sliced smoothly through.

The creature hissed loudly at the end of his flurry and its body convulsed, its tail lashing at Morgan. Morgan had time to bring his blade up, but the tail hit him like a small truck—he felt his sword slice deeply into it, snagging on a bone, and the muscular ribbon of flesh smashed into his chest, knocking him back against the wall. The impact knocked the wind from his lungs, but he managed to keep from falling to the floor, catching himself on one knee. His sword was gone—ripped from his hands by the thrashing serpent.

Morgan watched the snake trying to gather itself for another attack, but it was clearly gravely wounded. He'd sheared large chunks of flesh from its neck, and he'd even cleaved a triangular piece of its upper jaw and snout away. Blood poured prodigiously from the colossal creature. Morgan could see his sword sticking out of a massive cut two-thirds of the way down the creature's tail. The tail hung limply below his sword; he'd severed some vital nerve. Morgan pulled his black spear from his ring, feeling glad that Bronwyn had recovered it for him from the Yovashi. He leveled it at the snake and slowly circled to his left, waiting to see what it would do.

For once, time was on Morgan's side—the gem-studded serpent was bleeding out before his eyes, and he felt like he could afford to be patient. The snake tracked him with its eyes, its bloody tongue flicking in and out of the gap where Morgan had sheared away part of its mouth. He began to worry that his opponent might have some regeneration ability, so he used Hollow Charge again, aiming to drive his spear into the creature's eye. He flashed over the bloody, wooden floor, and his aim was true, but as he got within just a foot of the snake, he felt a hot spray cover him from face to waistline. Still, he couldn't slow down, and his spear hit the snake dead in the eye, driving the entire length of the blade into the beast's skull. It flopped once and then lay still.

Morgan had time to smile in victory before he was struck with horrifying pain. His vision went dark as his eyes erupted in fire, and then the rest of his body registered the pain. He felt like his face was melting. He screamed in a hoarse voice, and as he inhaled to scream again, the air he pulled into his lungs tasted like chlorine gas. Darkness threatened to engulf him, but he knew that he'd be dead in seconds if he lost consciousness. Morgan didn't waste any time, calling forth one of his Botner's Elixirs of Superior Mending from his ring and pouring it into the space where he knew his mouth was but felt like a burning hole of agony.

The pain wracking his body stopped instantly, and he felt like he'd been dipped in a numbing fluid. He collapsed to the gory floor and writhed his way away from the snake, sliding on his back. He still couldn't see, but he didn't know if he was lying in a pool of whatever had sprayed him, so he wanted to get away from it. He felt a surge of Energy pour into him, more than he'd ever felt at one time.

*****Congratulations! You have achieved level 18 Hollow Guard and have gained 5 Strength, 5 Will, 4 Vitality, 4 Intelligence, and 3 Agility.*****

Morgan felt tingling sensations spreading through his skin, starting from the deep sockets of his eyes, and then he was engulfed by an empty, sinking feeling; his awareness of his body and surroundings slipped away, and his vision cleared. The scene that resolved around him was a coolly lit stone vault lined with large stone sarcophagi. "Well, it looks like you've been working hard to improve yourself, but not without some great risks." Morgan recognized the voice of the Azure Paladin. "Still, you survived and have gained the levels required for us to meet. It's time I imparted some more of my heritage to you."

✧ MORGAN ✦

Morgan groaned and sat up. He didn't know why he was groaning—his body felt perfectly fine, and he could see that he was uninjured and his clothes undamaged. "Is this real? Did I get teleported here, or are we talking in my head or something?"

"Hmm, are we in your head or mine? What an interesting question." The Azure Paladin replied, moving to stand closer to Morgan. "On your feet, novice, stand at attention when Gareth Tohlemay, Defender of the Blue Deep, addresses you!" Morgan scrambled to his feet and stood straight-backed before the silvery figure. He could hear a hint of amusement in the paladin's voice, but he still wanted to show respect to the knight. Once again, he found himself impressed by the Azure Paladin's appearance. He stood straight as a birch tree, easily seven feet tall, encased in shining, silvery armor that was ornate yet very functional. Most impressive were the enormous, iridescent wings that stood out from the paladin's back.

"Yes, sir," Morgan replied, finding himself reverting to his basic training days.

"Very good, very good. Now give me a report; how have you done with my first gift?"

"The Azure Burst? I've used it in several combat situations, and it has saved my hide more than once."

"Mmhmm, excellent. Yes, we wouldn't be talking together now if you hadn't vanquished some foes. I sense something else about you. You've taken up the sword?"

"Yes, I wanted to make sure I was walking my own path and not one the System had steered me toward. I chose the sword because of a fondness I've had for heroic sword users in the literature that I've read."

"Good, good. Free thought is essential. Never be a puppet. Even to me and my legacy—I am here to guide and teach you, not to control you."

"I learned part of an ancient sword style—the Fighting Crane. Have you heard of it? From what I understand, much of it was lost."

"It sounds familiar, but I can't be sure. I may be able to give you a lead, though: not terribly far from my resting place, through the forest to the west, and up in the Orangerock Hills, a master swordsman once dwelled. He built a keep there, where he taught his disciples. If the keep still stands and his order still exists, you will find the knowledge of many sword styles and forms."

"Thank you, sir." Morgan knew the odds of the swordmaster still being there were slim to none—it seemed that a very long time had passed since the Azure Paladin had lived. Morgan didn't even know if he was native to this world or if his presence here resulted from the System combining worlds. He decided to stop guessing about it and just ask his teacher: "Sir, you mentioned an Azure Empire the last time we met, and it seems like a long time has passed since you lived. I was under the impression that the System and Energy have only been in this world for a couple of hundred years. Are you from this world?"

"Hah. Yes, I am from this world, and no, the System did not bring Energy. True, the Energy is much richer now than in my day, but some masters, like myself, learned ways to gather it and use it. When the System came, I was dimly aware of what it did. With the flood of Energy entering our part of the universe, the System rode the tide. It pushed other worlds together with ours—a feat I cannot comprehend. Now I feel the Energy around me, richer by a million-fold than when I was alive. You should have an easy time finding the power to use my legacy's abilities."

"I was wondering . . ." Morgan started, but the paladin held up a hand.

"I'm sorry, Morgan, our time grows short. I want to impart another lesson upon you while there is still time." Morgan nodded, and Gareth Tohlemay, the Azure Paladin, placed his hands on Morgan's shoulders. Gareth's eyes, set deeply under a shadowy brow, stared down into Morgan's and began to flare with a blue light. Morgan stared into his eyes, and he felt something kindle deep in his eye sockets. At first, it was a warm, tingling sensation, but then his vision flared blue, and the warm tingling escalated to searing pain. Morgan opened his mouth to scream, but just as he inhaled, the pain subsided, and his vision returned.

Congratulations! You have learned the spell Azure Sight—Basic.

Azure Sight—Basic: A paladin's foes cannot hide in shadows of deception. This skill will enable you to pierce even the darkest gloom and see through minor illusions. As your mastery of this skill advances, you will learn to see the truth of beings and items around you. Energy Cost: 50 per minute while active.

Morgan began to thank the paladin, but his vision turned dark, and he felt a sinking sensation like he was falling from a great height. After a while, the falling feeling went away, and he just floated in darkness. As he began to wonder what was going on, he slipped into one dream after another. He dreamt about being back in his first childhood home. His sister read a *Winnie the Pooh* book to him as they lay snuggled on a long couch.

Then Morgan dreamt about eating in the mess hall during his first tour with the Huron militia. He was in basic, or at least the militia's version of basic, but it was strange because Issa was there with him. They were laughing about the quality of the oatmeal. In the dream, Morgan looked around and saw some of his old buddies, but then his eyes fell on Mark Tennet, and he remembered seeing Mark take a sniper round in the forehead while they were clearing a shopping plaza near Old Detroit. That caused him to wake, his heart racing and breathing heavily. "Shh, you're okay." Issa's voice said softly from beside him.

"Ugh," Morgan grunted, trying to sit up. He was under a blanket and lying on a soft bed. The room was nearly dark, but he could make out a high ceiling, posts at the foot of the bed, some kind of dark armoire-shaped shadow against the wall, and an arched window with open shutters revealing a night sky filled with stars. "Where am I?"

"You're in one of the bedrooms in your tower." Issa's voice was sleepy sounding. He heard a rustle in the sheets and felt her warm hand slide onto his bare chest. Morgan sighed and let himself sink back down into the warm, soft embrace of the bed and closed his eyes. This time he slept very deeply, and if he dreamt, he didn't remember it.

The room was bright when Morgan woke for the second time, daylight streaming in through the large, arched window. He could see now that he was in a big, four-post bed under a thick, white down comforter. His head rested on a similarly soft pillow. He looked around and saw that the room matched the rest of the fifth floor in construction—hardwood floors, wooden wainscotting, and plaster walls and ceiling. A dark mahogany-looking armoire sat on the wall at the foot of the bed, and a narrow, arched doorway led into what looked like a private bathroom; Morgan could see the lower half of a large porcelain tub from his vantage.

Movement and a soft sigh beside him brought his attention to his more immediate surroundings, and he realized Issa's curly, golden hair was splayed out on the pillow next to his. That's when he realized he was naked. "Hey," he said, pushing gently at Issa's shoulder. She sighed again and rose up on one elbow, her hair falling away from her face. "Did you take advantage of me?"

"Of course!" She grinned and leaned forward, kissing him.

"That's not fair! I didn't even get to enjoy it!"

"Oh yes, you did! You just don't remember!" She laughed softly, resting her head on his chest. As she snuggled closer to him, Morgan realized she was naked, also.

"Hey, I was just joking before, but now I'm not! What happened?"

"Nothing yet, silly. You were unconscious. You had some horrible wounds from that gem snake's venom. I saw your empty tincture bottle, though, and I could see the acid had stopped eating your flesh, and the tincture plus the Energy from the snake were slowly restoring you. I pulled you in here, pulled off your ruined clothes and armor, and have been snuggling you ever since."

"Alright, thanks, but, um, you're kinda killing me here, you know, pressing your naked body against mine."

"Well, do something about it, then!" Issa slid a leg over him, straddling him, and that was all the permission Morgan needed.

It was a couple of hours later when he finally found the will to extract himself from the bed and Issa's embrace. He sat up and looked around the room. "How is there a window here? I didn't see windows at this level on the tower."

"Mm, I don't know. I think it's the glass. It looks clear from here, but it just looks like the tower wall on the outside. Maybe." Her reply was sleepy sounding, and Morgan wondered how much rest she'd actually gotten while he lay unconscious. She'd played it off, but maybe she'd been more worried than she let on.

"Hey, you can get some sleep if you're still tired. I'm gonna try out this bathtub. By the way, I'm glad it all worked out."

"All what worked out?" she asked, opening her eyes and looking at him.

"You know. Our parts—they were compatible." He laughed, and she threw a pillow at him.

"You're lucky they were because I was worried about your strange species!" She growled and rolled over, turning her back to him.

Morgan found his pitted helmet and breastplate and the remains of his shirt piled in a heap in the bathroom. His vambraces were also scarred but seemed functional, though the self-repair had clearly met its match. The only armor pieces that were unscathed were his greaves. He sighed, putting his greaves into his ring and the remains of his other gear into his pouch, then he examined the tub. It had a tap, and warm water flowed out when he turned it on. "Hell, yes. Thank you, Vormendion."

An hour later, Morgan quietly left the bedroom and returned to the scene of his battle. He was surveying the horrible mess of blood, bits of flesh, a stinking corpse, and spatters of acid when a tinkling sound heralded Tiladia's arrival. "Morgan, I'm glad you were victorious, and I'm glad you suffered no lasting harm from the gem snake's venom."

"Thanks, Tiladia. Yeah, I thought I was going to have a relatively easy victory, and then it sprayed me. I'm glad I had a strong healing elixir." Morgan pulled his sword and spear from the snake's corpse, wiping them on a scrap of his ruined shirt, and then he stowed them in his ring. He looked at the corpse of the enormous serpent—it was about a foot in diameter at its widest point and at least thirty feet long from nose to tail. "What's the deal with these gems, Tiladia? Should I try to salvage them?"

"Yes, Morgan. That serpent was ancient; they only grow a gem every few years, and I count at least three hundred gems. They're treasured by Artificers, as they are excellent for storing and conducting Energy."

"Huh, well, thanks again, Vormendion!" Morgan spent the next two hours slicing the gems out of the snake's corpse and stowing them in his ring. In all, he came away with 327 of the precious stones. Then he spent another hour cleaning up the mess. He dropped the corpse and scraps of flesh and his ruined gear down a shaft that Tiladia said led to the incinerator. When he was finished mopping up the mess, Morgan asked Tiladia about the damage to the wood from the snake's venom.

"The tower will slowly repair itself. It might take months, though. Only the dueling hall has enchantments to repair itself quickly." Tiladia flashed and tinkled as she spun around the landing, surveying the damage.

"Alright. Well, Issa is still asleep, I think, so please let her know I'm heading out to the colony to see what's new and check into getting some new armor."

"I will do so. Also, Morgan, you should know that I put your odds against the sixth guardian at roughly fifty percent."

"Heh, okay, thanks." Morgan hurried down the steps, stopping by the atrium to check in on Ykleedra. The Yovashi girl seemed to be in good spirits, having made a little den for herself among the denser foliage in the atrium's grove. She'd been eating fruit from some of the trees, and Morgan gave her some of the better-preserved meats he had in his ring. Promising to check in on her later with fresher meat, he walked down the stairs and out into the afternoon sun.

MORGAN

All in all, Morgan was in an excellent mood. He'd slept well, things were going great with Issa, and despite his encounter with the snake's acid, he'd managed to conquer it. As he walked through the grass toward the colony's central hub, he even caught himself whistling a little tune. He wore his nice white shirt tucked into his sturdy tailored pants, the sun was warm on his face, and things just seemed good. "Careful, you're going to jinx things," he muttered to himself, smiling ruefully. The town center was bustling, and Morgan had to count on his fingers for a minute to make sure it wasn't election day, but he was pretty sure it was tomorrow. People were just busy, he guessed.

He was about to climb the steps up to the Colony Stone when Morgan caught sight of Bronwyn and Olivia standing over near the artisan hall, talking to each other. He walked toward them, waving, and called out, "Hey, how're things going?"

"Hi, Morgan," Olivia said as he walked up. "Things are good but hectic; Bronwyn just heard from some of her followers that the Urghat are on the move. We think they'll get here tonight."

"You have 'followers?'" Morgan asked, raising an eyebrow at Bronwyn.

"Hah, yeah. While I was scouting the plains, I fought a few duels and earned the respect of a few Urghat. I didn't want to bring them into the colony while there's a war going on, but they made a camp in the woods a bit to the east. I've had them watching the plains for the Urghat invasion."

"Huh, well, that's interesting. So, they're turning against their own kind to help us?"

"No. It's hard to explain; they aren't helping us, they're helping me. They have a fascinating system of leadership that basically revolves around the idea that the toughest should be the leaders. I killed one of their leaders and got his title, allowing me to start earning respect among their kind. I'm still not officially recognized because their big leader hasn't accepted me, so these few Urghat who follow me are essentially making themselves outcasts, banking on me winning official acceptance among their people. In other words, they hope we'll win so that the leaders who are against me will be conquered. That would clear the path for me to be accepted and get them back in the good graces of their clans." Bronwyn trailed off, and Morgan smiled.

"That's the most I've heard you say since I met you."

"Yeah, I'm pretty invested in the topic." Bronwyn shrugged.

"Well, I got my armor wrecked, so I'm heading up to buy some new stuff. By the way, I managed to open the floor of my tower that has bedrooms. I think I have sixteen guest rooms, well, fifteen since Issa and I are using one, so if you ladies are still sleeping in tents, you're welcome to stay with me."

"Uh"—Olivia looked at Bronwyn, then back at Morgan—"yeah, that would be great. I'm going to leave soon for the academy, but I'd love to have a bed to sleep in for a change."

"Yeah, that would be cool. Thanks, Morgan. Oh, hey, you need armor?" Bronwyn reached toward the storage pouch on her belt and started producing pieces of heavy, dark-colored armor made from thick, overlapping metal scales. "I got this off the Underclaw I killed to get my title. It's too heavy for my fighting style, but you're a big guy; maybe it will work for you?"

"Shit, that's some cool looking armor. It has little golden runes in it, too. Do you know what they do?"

"No, I didn't try bonding with it. Since you're giving me a place to live, I'll let you have it." She smiled and punched Morgan on the arm.

"Hah, no worries. I really do have a lot of room, but let's not go inviting the whole colony, okay? I mean, I think Arthur seems like a good guy, but I'd rather not have him as a roomie, you know what I mean?" Morgan asked. Bronwyn and Olivia gave each other a knowing look and burst into laughter.

"We know exactly what you mean," Olivia said.

"Anyway, when I get back, I'll tell Tiladia to let you two have permission to use the door and the stairs. She's the spirit I was telling you about, Olivia."

"Right, okay. Thanks again, Morgan. We're going to head over to the wall to check on preparations." Morgan nodded as they started to walk away. He was kneeling in the grass, checking out the armor. It consisted of a heavy shirt of scales and full vambraces and greaves attached via dark leather straps. He'd have much better coverage than his old armor; he just hoped that he'd be able to get Boris to add dexterity enchantments to it. He trickled some Energy into the shirt, attempting to bond with it:

*****Axe Breaker Scale: Artificed Armor. Enchantments: 1. Self-repair—This armor will utilize ambient Energy to recover from wear and damage over time. 2. Perfect Layering—A master Artificer has enchanted this armor to fit the user perfectly and provide maximum protection versus slashing attacks.*****

"Not too shabby," he said to himself, as he collected the armor and went to look for Boris. He was not surprised to find him working at the same workbench where he'd been before. Boris was inscribing a bracelet that looked to be made of gold, and Morgan waited quietly, not wanting to make him mess up. It took the Enchanter five good minutes before he looked up and smiled at Morgan.

"Thanks for waiting."

"No worries. I have a problem and need a favor, but I think I can make it worth your while this time."

"Oh?"

"Yeah, I got in a fight with something that spat acid on most of my armor, wrecking it. I got some new armor from Bronwyn, but I need that dexterity enchantment again." Boris began to groan, so Morgan continued, "Hold on, hold on; check these out." Morgan pulled five gems from the guardian snake's corpse out of his ring and set them on the workbench. Boris sniffed, putting his monocle to his eye and staring at one of the gems for a long time.

"These are incredible, Morgan. I've been looking for just something like this to use as an Energy battery in enchanted items. I think they're worth a lot, and I'd feel guilty taking them for what will probably just be an hour or two of work."

"Don't even think about it. I have more where that came from, too. Here." He put his new armor on the workbench. "Do you know if anyone is up to making steel items at the forge yet? I want a new helmet, but I don't want a bronze one from the Contribution Store."

"Yeah, there's a guy making steel armor. Tell you what, give me another of these gems, and I'll get him to make you a helmet. He owes me." Morgan nodded happily, producing another gem and setting it on Boris's workbench.

"Do the different colors on the gems do anything?" Morgan asked, noting that the one he'd just handed Boris was blue while the others he'd given him were all orange and red.

"I don't think so, but I have a lot of learning to do. I'll let you know what I find out." Morgan nodded and turned to leave. "I should have your armor ready by tonight or in the morning at the latest. Hang on a second," Boris said, leaning over the scale armor Morgan had set on his workbench. "This isn't steel. It's very dense, and I recognize some of the runes; this is a set. I've been trying to learn about enchanting sets; this'll be great for me to study!"

"Glad to hear it. I'll come back later this evening or in the morning. Thanks, Boris." Morgan was happy to see his old friend so passionate about his work. He supposed he might benefit from learning more about crafting in general, but he just had so much on his plate right now. Speaking of things on his plate, he remembered he'd promised Ykleedra some fresh meat.

He worked his way over to the tanning yard and storage facility the colonists had built while he and Olivia were away. It was in the southwest corner of the settlement, and as Morgan rounded the hill and started walking along the southern road, he was surprised to see how many houses had been built since he'd last walked that way. There had to be more than a hundred small homes now, new rows laid out past the big dormitory-style buildings. There were decidedly fewer tents out in the field these days.

He turned to the left, following the new cobbled path that led to the tannery, and braced himself for the smell. As he got close enough to see the structure, he noticed that it consisted of a large, open-air deck with a peaked ramada-like roof attached to a warehouse-style building. The smell from the butcher yard under the ramada was about what he'd expected, but he didn't smell the awful telltale stench of the tannery. He walked up to one of the butchering tables and spoke to the large woman cleaning a deer-like carcass. "Hello, I'm new to how this works, but I'd like to purchase some meat."

"Oh? Well, I earn credits for cleaning the meat, but I don't sell it. There's a shop just inside the tannery warehouse." She gestured to a set of open double doors where the ramada met the large wooden structure.

"So, there is a tannery in there? Why can't I smell it?"

"They bought the building from the System. It has some air purifiers that run on Energy—regular fans that pull air over the hides and up through vents, and the air going through those vents comes out smelling clean. I don't know how it works, but I'm sure as hell glad." She shrugged her meaty shoulders and smiled. "Name's Anise, by the way."

"Nice to meet you, Anise. I'm Morgan." She nodded, staring at him, and he felt a bit awkward in the silence. "Um, I've got a lot of errands to run, but I'll catch you around." Morgan waved and walked over to the building, stepping through the doors. The room he walked into was clearly just the public-facing side of the operation. A counter ran along one side of the room where a couple of clerks talked to customers. Morgan waited for his turn, and when the young woman with long red pigtails called him over, he approached the counter. "Hello, is this where I go to buy some meat?"

"Sure, but the council has issued a policy that we agreed to in exchange for the building—until, after the Urghat conflict, we give a half-pound of fresh meat to any colonist per day. As long as supplies are good."

"Supplies are good, I take it?"

"Oh yeah, the plains and forests are teeming with wildlife. The hunters claim they ain't putting a dent in it."

"How do you keep track?"

"Oh, one of the Artificers came up with a simple device." She pointed at a black slate with a few dozen runes carved into it. "You just touch this, run a little Energy into it, and it will flash this orange gem at the top if you're cleared for an allowance and this white gem if you already got some." Morgan hadn't noticed the two gems at first, but now he saw what she was pointing at.

"Huh, neat. So, it resets each day?"

"Guess so!" She shrugged, smiling.

"Alright, well, what if I want to buy more than my allotment?"

"One Energy bead per pound." Morgan knew the price was highway robbery compared to what food cost in Tarn's Crossing. Still, he had plenty of beads and didn't feel like bickering. He slapped five of his double-attuned beads on the counter.

"I'll take fifteen pounds. Those are double attuned beads—worth three times a normal one at the Colony Stone."

"Mmhmm." She scooped up the beads and walked through a swinging door. She returned with three large packages wrapped in brown paper a few moments later. "Here you go, hon. See you soon."

"Thanks," Morgan replied, stuffing the meat packages into his belt pouch. He waved and walked out of the meatpacking and tanning warehouse and through the slaughter yard under the ramada, noticing how the raised deck had grates under the workbenches for blood to drain through. Briefly, he wondered where the blood ended up, but he was off the deck and onto the grass, and his thoughts turned to happier things. He wanted to get back to the tower to give Ykleedra some food and check on Issa.

Morgan had walked most of the way to his tower, with just the empty grass slope between him and the door, when he heard the sound of a distant horn. He'd, of course, heard war horns in movies and VR, so he recognized the sound, but it was still eerie. Beyond his tower, he saw people scurrying around on the top of the wall, so he started jogging that way. He'd made it about halfway when several more horns took up the call, and then the drums started. Deep thunderous drum beats rolled over the plains and into the colony. As he ran the rest of the way to the earthen steps leading up to the rampart, the drumbeats continued, punctuated with occasional, long blasts of those war horns.

When he got to the top of the ramparts, the sun was halfway down to the western horizon, and heavy clouds had rolled in, casting long shadows beneath a dark, orange-red sky, leading to a foreboding feeling as he looked out over the plains. The drums and horns continued as he watched hundreds, then thousands of distant figures form lines about a mile out from the wall. He watched for several minutes, noting that the invaders weren't attacking just yet—they were setting up tents and lighting fires. He was going to turn and find someone to talk to when he felt a hand grasp his. He looked down and saw that Issa had come to stand beside him, wearing her silvery armor and a helmet with a ring of long fangs mounted around the brow that he'd never seen before.

"It looks like it's about to begin," she said, a deep frown furrowing her brow.

OLIVIA

"This is absurd!" Arthur Ballard fumed, slamming his fist on the table. "The day after a foreign army lays siege to our community, we are going to hold an election?"

"Look, I only did what you all asked me to do," Bronwyn said, her voice carefully flat but a dangerous spark in her eyes. Olivia thought about interjecting, but she wanted to hear more of what everyone else was thinking. They'd called an emergency council meeting after the Urghat set up their siege lines, and everyone was there, crowded around the table, including Morgan and Issa.

"There's no way you can cancel or postpone the election?" Maria asked, an eyebrow arched.

"No, dammit. The fucking System asked me three times if I was sure and warned me that once set in motion, the election and consequent handover of powers couldn't be stopped." She sighed and slumped down in her chair, blowing a few wild tangles of red hair out of her face. Olivia wanted to reach out to her, to let her know she understood her frustration, but she feared it would only irritate her in her current mood.

"How many of the Urghat are there?" Brian Stafford asked, his voice quiet with resignation.

"We're not entirely sure, but some of the Ardeni Hunters ventured into the grasslands to try to get a good count. They think it's somewhere between twenty-five hundred and three thousand," Arthur replied dourly.

"How many of my people have registered at the stone?" Issa asked.

"As of a few hours ago, nearly two hundred. I'd hoped for more." Arthur looked at Issa, his eyes revealing an almost hidden accusation.

"Easy, Arthur. There are more on the way, and, regardless, any help is better than none, right?" Morgan stared, his eyes expressionless, at Arthur while he spoke.

"Yes, yes. Of course."

"Well, we outnumber them, then!" Maria said almost cheerfully.

"Except these Urghat are all combat veterans. They don't bring their young or old or their few non-combat oriented classes to war." Bronwyn drummed her fingers on the table while she spoke, clearly preoccupied.

"Something you want to say, Bronwyn?" Dr. Kerns spoke up for the first time.

"I'm just wondering how this is going to go down. Urghat aren't patient. I don't see them doing a prolonged siege. I hope our black powder weapons are enough to throw off their first attack and put some doubt in their hearts, then I was thinking I need to challenge their leaders." She turned her drumming fingers into a fist and clenched it, her knuckles turning white.

"What? I don't think so, Bron. You're going to fight all their leaders? You have any idea how strong their Chief or whatever is?" Olivia finally gave in and reached out a hand, grabbing onto Bronwyn's wrist, almost like she wanted to hold her in place.

"He's called an Overclaw, and, no, I don't. I only know he had to be tough enough to survive challenges from any other Urghat." She shrugged.

"Well, let's not get ahead of ourselves," Morgan said smoothly. "We'll cross that bridge when we get there, but just know: if it comes to fighting leaders, Issa and I will be helping."

"Maybe. As you said, we'll have to see how things shake out." Bronwyn sat back and patted Olivia's hand. Her hands were big and calloused but warm, and Olivia knew Bronwyn was trying hard to be agreeable here in this meeting, so she gave her wrist another squeeze then pulled her hand back.

"Well, let's agree on a course of action. One, we can't do anything about the election except hope that we all win. Two, we need to keep as many muskets on the wall as possible and have the cannons manned at all times. Three, we need to start thinking about what we'll do if they do try a prolonged siege. We've done a good job outfitting guards for rotations. We have almost a thousand militia outfitted with armor and spears, and we have almost half that number with muskets and blunderbusses." Olivia ticked off her talking points on her fingers as she spoke, but Morgan cleared his throat and spoke.

"Don't put all your guns on the wall. Have a few up there, patrolling and watching, but have the rest in ready positions at the bottom of the rampart stairs. You don't want the Urghat to see how many we've got before they attack."

"Yes, that makes sense," Maria said. Somehow, she'd taken charge of the militia in addition to her duties with the crafts folk.

"We don't know how sophisticated they are. They might all just charge the north wall, or they might try multiple attack angles. We need to be ready on every wall," Olivia continued.

"The Hunters will be ready to help. Most of them have exceptional skill with bows. You should also get your citizens ready to fight, even if they didn't sign up for the militia. If they breach the wall, the Urghat won't care." Issa looked gravely around the table, measuring their response to her words. "I'm serious. Urghat will kill and eat everyone; they don't leave people alone if they throw down their arms." The table grew quiet at her words.

The engineers spoke a bit more about the logistics of supplying ammo and powder to the cannons on the walls and about how they'd mounted large, Energy-powered lamps on posts a hundred yards out from the walls at fifty-yard intervals. Hopefully, it meant that there would be no sneak attacks in the middle of the night. As the meeting broke up, Morgan said he had some armor to pick up, and he and Issa left. The rest of the council went to manage their business, and Olivia turned to Bronwyn. "I'm going to go pack up my tent and bring it to Morgan's tower."

"Yeah, I'll do the same, but I want to talk to my Urghat scouts first. I want to get their take on this invasion force—whether they'll attack at night, if they seem prepared for a long siege, stuff like that."

"Alright, I'll see you later, then." Olivia smiled; she knew everyone was stressed, and she wanted to try to keep a positive outlook. She left the tavern, walked past the milling crowd outside, and meandered over to her lonely campsite. She was glad for her satchel—she didn't have to pack up everything thoroughly. She could just toss things in, even her unfolded blankets and the little box where she kept her water bottles and snacks. She'd pretty much stopped using her tent for storage once she'd gotten her satchel and left on her trip with Morgan. Still, there were some odds and ends that she didn't want to lose: extra clothes, empty sketchbooks, extra charcoal pencils, some particularly smooth rocks that she'd collected while walking around the colony, and her tent itself.

After gathering her personal belongings, she walked a short distance into the grass near her tent, where she'd staked Blue to a long rope, giving him plenty of room to roam and forage. He snuffled her pleasantly when she approached, and she gave him some pats and scratches. "Good boy. I'm going to bring you over with your friends, okay? Follow me."

She took one more look around the empty patch of grass she'd called home since arriving in this world, then she made the walk through the evening darkness to Morgan's tower. Most of the way was over cobbled roads, but when she turned off to go across the grass to his tower, the night was quite dark, and the grass hushed her steps. She felt very alone all of a sudden, and she had to look around to see the lights and movement in the distance to put herself at ease. "Quiet out here, isn't it?" She jumped at the sound, looking to where the voice came from off to her left on the dark grassy slope leading to the tower, and she had to squint to realize there was a darker shape lying in the grass.

"Who's there?"

"Oh, you know me, Ms. Bennet. Reggie Arnold Gandry-Thule—soon to be Councilman Reggie Arnold Gandry-Thule." His voice was severe, and it struck Olivia as almost funny how he could say his name like that, twice in a row, without realizing how pompous he sounded.

"Jesus, you startled me. Why are you laying out here in the dark?"

"Best way to see the stars, and my home is just over there." A vague movement in the shadows might have been him pointing at the sprawling villa about a hundred yards west of Morgan's tower.

"Oh, that's right. Well, nice to see you. I'm heading in. Big day tomorrow!" Olivia started walking.

"After tomorrow, you won't be able to dismiss me so easily." His voice was soft, and Olivia wasn't even sure he'd meant to speak out loud, almost like he was talking to himself.

"Right, well, good luck." She picked up her pace, thoroughly weirded out by the guy. When she got to the steps leading up to the tower door, she tied Blue's lead to the iron railing near Morgan and Issa's mounts. Blue trotted over next to Munch, and they rubbed their shoulders together with low grunting noises. Issa's roladii stayed alone, off to the side, eating grass.

Olivia turned back to the steps and took them two at a time, putting her hand on the door's handle, pulling. Nothing happened. She might as well have been trying to open a bank vault. "Fuck," she said softly. Just then, a loud *click* sounded from within the door, and it pulled open smoothly. Olivia hurriedly stepped inside and pulled the door closed. Another audible click informed her the lock had driven home.

"Welcome, Lady Olivia," said a tinkling voice, almost musical in quality. Olivia spun around and saw the soft blinking white lights and misty, amorphous form of Morgan's spirit friend.

"Hello, Tiladia; thank you for opening the door for me."

"It was my pleasure. I simply had to confirm your identity, but you'll be able to access the tower without my help in the future. Morgan left me instructions to allow you entry and to show you to a bedroom." Olivia followed Tiladia to the elegant metal staircase and began to climb it. She was surprised that after six or so steps, she came out on a hardwood landing that had hallways leading off it in each of the cardinal directions. Just one of those hallways would seemingly be long enough to stretch the width of the tower as seen from the outside.

"The tower really is bigger on the inside than the outside, isn't it?" She asked the floating, blinking form hovering nearby.

"Oh, yes. Quite a lot so. We're currently on the fifth floor, the highest available to you. If you want to visit the lower floors, just have a destination in mind while you traverse the stairs."

"Wow, that's cool." Olivia looked around, admiring the well-lit vaulted ceilings and the beautiful woodwork. She saw that the area around the stairs was discolored and worn.

"This is where Morgan fought the guardian. Some of its acids damaged the flooring, but it will repair over time. Morgan and Issa have a room down this hallway, but I'll show you the rooms I've chosen for you and Bronwyn if you'll follow me." Tiladia flashed and swirled, then slowly moved off down the lefthand hallway. Olivia followed, noting that the hallway had four doors, and Tiladia stopped at the far left door. "I've chosen this suite for you and the one across the hall for Bronwyn."

"Well, thank you." Olivia touched the door handle, and, after a slight hesitation, it clicked unlocked, and she pulled it open. The room was large with a small sitting area in front of a marble hearth, a sizeable white-washed armoire on one wall, a huge window, pale green curtains pulled open to the starry sky, and a big four-poster bed, also white-washed, with lush, inviting green pillows and a comforter. A small doorway led away on the wall opposite the window, presumably to a bathroom. Olivia walked over to the hearth, resting her hand on the back of a comfortable-looking, pale yellow upholstered chair. "The room is beautiful, Tiladia."

"I hope you'll be comfortable. The old master of the tower used to put important guests in this wing. Facilities are through that door behind you. You'll find running water in the toilet and hot water for the bath."

"Thank you again, Tiladia! I'm quite tired, and I know tomorrow will be crazy, so I'll turn in. Have a good night." Tiladia tinkled in response and then floated away down the hallway. Olivia closed the door, and then she went into the bathroom. It was tiled in a warm light brown tile that made her think of a Mediterranean villa. A counter tiled with light blue squares held a washbasin to her right, a toilet to her left, and a large porcelain tub straight ahead. Another window opened out to the night stars near the tub.

The toilet was interesting—It appeared to be made from bronze and porcelain and had a constant stream of water flowing through it. The tub had one faucet, and when Olivia turned the knob, steaming water immediately flowed forth. "Lovely," she said softly with a smile. After unpacking and laying out a clean outfit, Olivia took a bath; then, she slipped into the soft sheets of her bed. She didn't know how to turn the lights off, but she found that after she'd lain in bed for a few minutes, they began to dim, and then the room was dark, only the soft light of moons and stars pushing back the shadows. She slept well, not waking throughout the night, and would have slept longer if not for the notification that interrupted her sleep with a soft chime and a message:

*****Voting for the Council of First Landing is now open.*****

⚡ MORGAN ⚡

"I saw some of my kinfolk camping near the east wall. If you don't mind, Morgan, I'm going to go and say hello." Issa gestured vaguely to the east, and Morgan nodded.

"All right. I'll catch up with you in a few hours at the tower?"

"That sounds good." She smiled, stood on her tiptoes, and Morgan got the hint, leaning down to kiss her. Before he could say any more, she'd spun and moved briskly down the road. He sighed, watching her go, and could almost forget there was an invading army outside the walls.

He shook his head and walked quickly toward the artisan hall. He'd gotten caught up with the activity surrounding the arrival of the Urghat horde and hadn't had a chance to stop by to see Boris about his armor. Now it was well into the evening, but he figured he'd be there still—everyone was awake, moving around with a frenetic energy that gave away the stress caused by the impending clash. The Urghat had continued with their drums and horns for hours but had finally given it a rest about an hour ago. Morgan was glad; anxiety levels were high enough without that going on all night. He didn't want to count his chickens before they hatched, though. Who knew what the beast-men had planned?

He found Boris busy with another man and waited to the side, leaning against his workbench while he finished scribing some runes on a necklace. The middle-aged bald man took the necklace, handing a small pouch to Boris. "Thanks, mate. She's gonna love it!"

"Glad to help, Harald," Boris replied, shaking the little pouch, producing the telltale sound of Energy beads clicking together. The man, Harald apparently, walked away with a smile, and Boris turned to Morgan. "I was starting to wonder if you forgot about your armor. I think you might need it soon, judging by all that racket earlier."

"Oh, I didn't forget; I just got busy. I noticed you ditched the council meeting."

"Bah, they had enough people in there. I don't think I would've gotten a word in. Besides, these projects are important for the war effort."

"Yeah, you're probably right. It wasn't like we accomplished a whole lot—everything's been in motion for days now. Anyway, how'd it go with my armor?"

"Oh man, really well. That metal holds enchantments a lot better than bronze or even steel. There was still some randomness involved, but I managed to get you a total of twenty-one dexterity. On top of that, I enchanted you a helmet with self-repair and resizing capabilities." He pulled over a large leather bag covered with pyrographed runes. He reached a hand in and started to pull out Morgan's armor. Morgan was pleased to see the helmet was a dark steel-gray that looked good with the rest of his armor. He knew it was silly to worry about armor matching, but he couldn't help the thought.

He picked up the helmet, noticing it was lined with something like rabbit fur, and slipped it over his head. It was loose, but he held a finger against it, sending some Energy to bond with the item, and it instantly shrank to fit his head snugly. He liked that the helmet had a built-in visor and nose guard but had big enough holes for him to see clearly through. The sides covered his ears but had venting to allow sounds through. "Perfect, Boris. Tell your friend I send my compliments."

"I will; now get the rest of this off my workbench. I have a ton of shit to get done." He chuckled to lighten the blow of his words, and Morgan laughed, hurriedly stowing away his armor in his ring. He waved to Boris, then made his way along the northern road to the wall and the guardhouse near the gate; he wanted to get another look at the Urghat situation. When he approached, he saw that there were hundreds of spear-wielding colonists milling around the earthen stairs leading to the ramparts and sitting near cookfires and tents that were spread out all along the base of the wall.

"Heyo, Morgan," a familiar voice called, and he saw that it was one of the guards that had greeted him on his return from Tarn's Crossing.

"Oh, hey. Um, sorry, but I don't recall—did you give me your name?"

"Nah, I don't think so. Name's Raul Lopez. Well, what do you think about this invasion? You think they'll make a run at the walls? None of us can see any siege equipment out there, but I suppose that doesn't mean there isn't any."

"Yeah, I really don't know. Anything, literally, seems to be possible with Energy, though I don't think the Urghat are particularly adept at Energy use. I hate to say it, but I think we'll have to wait and see." Morgan clapped Raul on the shoulder and then climbed the stairs leading to the ramparts. There were at least a hundred militia with muskets around the stairs and on them, leaning against the railings, talking and joking with each other as they waited for the next shoe to drop. When he reached the top, Morgan looked out over the northern plains, and now that it was fully dark, he could see the Urghat had set up hundreds of large fires. They didn't seem to have any sort of order to them, though—nothing like the camps of Roman armies he'd seen in movies with orderly rows and fortifications. "I really hope they're underestimating us," he muttered.

"Yeah, me, too." Bronwyn had come up beside him, also looking out over the Urghat army. "My Urghat friends tell me that, before they left to follow me, the talk around the camps was that we were soft, weak, and easy pickings. When I asked them if they had siege towers or weapons like catapults, they didn't have a clue what I was talking about. I asked them how they'd get through our walls, and they said, 'ladders and through the gate.'" She sighed heavily, slapping the thick, earthen crenelation with her open palm.

"Well, that makes me feel better. We might have an easier time than even I had hoped."

"Hah, you know the System and this world—nothing is ever quite as it seems."

"Too true. Hey, I'm going to go turn in; have you been to my tower yet? Did Tiladia give you a room?"

"Nah, not yet, but I'll follow you. I'm all packed up." She slapped the pouch hanging from her belt.

"These dimensional containers are pretty amazing, aren't they?"

"Yeah, almost don't know how I functioned back on Earth without one!" They both laughed and started down the steps. Once again, people waved and said hello, and, it seemed to Morgan, Bronwyn was given a lot of deference. He was dimly aware of her career back on Earth in the VR gaming arenas, but he really hadn't spent a lot of time watching the Leagues. Still, he had heard her name, and it seemed a lot of the militia on duty knew her from her past or from her exploits here on their new world.

When they arrived at his tower, he noticed that Olivia's roladii had joined his and Issa's. "Looks like Olivia is already here." He gestured to her mount, and Bronwyn nodded.

"Those mounts are something else. They seem so friendly; are they hard to acquire?"

"Olivia didn't tell you about it?"

"Oh, I'm sure she did, but we drank enough to make the whole conversation fuzzy." She laughed again.

"Ah, gotcha. Well, no, they aren't hard to come by; in fact, maybe we can get together some resources and make a trade run to Tarn's Crossing to buy some herd stock. You know—after we deal with the bloodthirsty invaders at our doorstep."

"Hah, sounds good." Bronwyn followed him up the steps, and Morgan was about to put his hand on the handle, but he stopped.

"You try to open it. I want to see how Tiladia deals with you since I told her you were coming." Bronwyn nodded and reached for the handle, tugging at it. It didn't move, and Bronwyn started to say something, but then a loud *click* sounded from the door, and she pulled it open. Morgan nodded, and they both went into the foyer. Tiladia's silvery lights and mist greeted them, and Morgan said, "Hi, Tiladia. I'm glad you were able to tell it was Bronwyn trying to open the door. Is Olivia in here already?"

"Yes, Morgan. Hello, Lady Bronwyn." Her lights flashed as she bobbed up and down slightly.

"Hi, Tiladia. Morgan's told me a lot about you. Please just call me Bronwyn."

"Oh? Morgan has been talking a lot about me? How exciting to be the topic of discussion in a new world!"

"You aren't from this world?" Bronwyn stepped forward, peering into Tiladia's misty form.

"No! I don't even know what world this is! I am from Aradnue—an immense world with towering mountains and abyssal canyons! There, we dragons soar the skies and make roosts in the heights. Or, at least we used to; I'm not sure anymore. I feel like I've been away for a very, very long time." Her lights dimmed in a way that Morgan was starting to recognize as her being introspective.

"Ahem, Tiladia, would you please show Bronwyn to her room?"

"Of course, Morgan. Please follow me, Bronwyn." Her lights swirled in a semicircle, and she floated toward the stairs.

"Okay. 'Night, Morgan." Bronwyn reached out and squeezed his shoulder as she walked by, following Tiladia onto the stairway.

"'Night," he called after her. Morgan waited for them to disappear from sight on the stairs, then he climbed to the second floor and walked into the atrium. "Ykleedra?" He called, not loudly. He heard rustling a moment later, and the juvenile Yovashi peered out between two fern-like plants.

"Yes, Morgan?"

"Are you doing okay? Getting enough to eat? Not too lonely?"

"Oh, yes, Morgan. Between the meat you brought me and the fruit in this garden, I'll have plenty of food for some time, and Tiladia keeps me company when she's not busy with you."

"Oh, really?"

"Yes, she tells me when no one is around, and I go to the library with her to work on those books from my mother's laboratory."

"Ah, well, that's part of the reason I wanted to talk to you. My friend Bronwyn is staying in the tower now, and she hasn't met you. She's had a bad experience with Yovashi in the past, so I want to make sure I introduce you two before you run into her. Do you mind staying out of her sight until then?"

"I will, Morgan. Thank you for your consideration."

"Okay, I'll make sure to do it soon so you aren't cooped up too long. I'm going to get some sleep now, so have a good night. I'll talk to you tomorrow."

"Good night, Morgan." Despite her words, Morgan felt like he could hear a distinct note of sadness in her voice. Feelings of guilt started to surge in his mind, but he pushed them down, going to the stairs and climbing to the fifth floor. When he arrived on the landing, he found Tiladia waiting for him.

"Morgan, is there anything else you'd like me to do before you retire?"

"No, but I wanted to ask you to be sure that Bronwyn doesn't run into Ykleedra before I have a chance to introduce them."

"I will do so."

"Thanks, Tiladia. Is Issa here?"

"Yes, she returned shortly before you." Tiladia flashed and moved up and down slightly. Morgan nodded and walked past her, up the hallway, and into the suite that Issa had claimed for them. He still hadn't looked at all the bedrooms, but Issa had told him that they were all nice, though some were slightly larger and more elaborately decorated than others. She said some had fireplaces and bigger windows than the bedroom she'd first dragged him into, but he didn't want to move. Soon enough, he'd unlock the level with the master suite, and until then, the room they were sharing was plenty comfortable.

When he opened the door, he found Issa sitting in her practice clothing in a cultivation pose in front of the window. She didn't look up, so he decided to join her, sitting a few feet behind her and running through his cultivation drill. He managed two complete cycles by the time she stirred and rose, and then they both agreed to get some sleep. The next day would be a busy one—an election and possibly an assault from the Urghat were on the menu.

BRONWYN

Bronwyn woke up with the System alert about voting in her face. She groaned, swiping it away, and rolled out of her bed. She went into the bathroom and washed her face, used the toilet, and then got dressed in a set of clean clothes, strapping on her spiked armor over them. After pulling on her boots, she went into the hallway and knocked on Olivia's door. There wasn't an answer, but a soft tinkling sound heralded the arrival of Morgan's tower spirit, Tiladia.

"Olivia, Morgan, and Issa are downstairs. Morgan asked me to tell you that they only recently came down, don't worry, and are waiting for you to head into town for breakfast and to vote," Tiladia said, as Bronwyn turned to face her amorphous form.

"Alright, thanks." Bronwyn hustled down the hallway, stepped onto the staircase, and found herself on the first floor in just a few steps. Morgan, Issa, and Olivia stood near the front hall talking when she walked up. "Morning, all."

"Hey, we were going to go vote and then get some breakfast. Sorry, my kitchens aren't up and running yet." Morgan chuckled as though he'd made a good joke.

"C'mon, Bron. Might be our last chance to get breakfast together. I have to use this teleportation token soon, or it's going to burn a hole in my pocket." Olivia reached out and jostled her shoulder with a wry grin.

"You're trying to hide your nervousness with bravado! Think I don't see that by now? Hah, of course, I'll have breakfast with you." Bronwyn reached out and put her arm over Olivia's slight shoulders, tugging her into a side hug as they walked toward the door. Morgan looked at Issa, and she just grinned, displaying way too many sharp teeth, and they followed her and Olivia outside.

When they got to the Colony Stone, a line had formed leading all the way down the hill toward the tavern, and they decided to get in line before it got even longer. Luckily the voting process was quick and discreet—as many people as could squeeze around the stone to place a hand upon it could vote at once, and there was no way of knowing who they voted for. After about a twenty-minute wait, they all got their chance, and Bronwyn voted for all the current members of the temporary council, including herself and Olivia. When she finished, the interface informed her that 18 percent of the populace had voted and that the poll would close when either 100 percent had voted or at midnight, whichever came first.

When they walked down the hill to the tavern, they found all the tables full and a large crowd milling around outside, waiting to get in. "We need another tavern," she said grumpily. Issa had the idea of having a picnic breakfast, and they walked a ways out behind the tavern, throwing down a few blankets. They sat and ate surprisingly delicious fare entirely provided by Olivia and Issa. Apparently, the two of them had similar ideas about using their dimensional storage to its fullest. Bronwyn always felt weird about storing fresh food in her pouch, but it really did seem to preserve the freshness. She wondered if the space in there was a complete vacuum or something. In any case, they ate buttery pastries, sausages, and fruit, washing everything down with spicy mulled wine that Issa warmed on an ingenious little camp stove she produced from her pouch.

They were sitting around, enjoying the late spring morning when the alarm rang out. A loud, clanging bell began to ring from the north and was shortly followed by the more distant rumble of drums and the blaring of horns. "They're fucking attacking!" Bronwyn jumped up and began to run toward the northern wall; Morgan and Issa were close behind.

"I'll catch up!" Olivia called, but Bronwyn only had eyes and ears for the coming battle. She sprinted all out and was surprised to see Morgan and Issa keeping pace. She briefly wondered what level they were now but refocused on the distant wall and the frenetic movements of the people at the base. She could see that the militia was flooding up the four sets of stairs to the ramparts, so she angled herself toward the least crowded stair in the northwestern corner of the wall. As she drew close, she leaped up to the first landing, pulling herself over the railing, and hurried among the militia up the stairs and onto the ramparts.

She rushed toward the center of the wall while she looked out over the northern plains. The Urghat were charging. They were still half a kilometer out, but they were moving fast. Most of them were tearing over the ground on foot, but she could see a few hundred of those huge lizards in the back. Bronwyn passed several militia members with red flags on spears, and she knew they were the Fire Sergeants that Maria and Tanya had appointed to call shots. As she passed them, she heard them shouting to the hundred or so militia under their command things like "Steady! Check your powder! Cannons, clear your caps!" Mixed among the musketeers were dozens of the blue-skinned Ardeni with a variety of different types of bows. She saw one with a short, bone-colored bow that was glowing a faint red, thrumming with Energy. Another had a huge multi-layered recurve bow. None of them seemed agitated, and Bronwyn was impressed by their nerve. She, herself, was already trembling with adrenaline.

Bronwyn wanted to be above the gate when the Urghat came. She wanted to see firsthand how they would try to break it and be there to help repel them if they did. By the time she made it to the center of the wall, over five hundred musketeers and Ardeni were lined up behind the ramparts, with as many spear-wielding militia members standing behind them. Bronwyn knew that the other half of the spear troops were being held in reserve near the colony's center in case the Urghat tried to breach from a different direction. As she contemplated the charging Urghat, seeing that they were only a couple of hundred yards out now, she heard the first fire order echo down the line: "Cannons! Fire!" She realized there were ranging flags planted out on the field and silently applauded the militia's foresight. Huge booms thundered through the air, vibrating the wall, and massive clouds of smoke billowed out and up from the ten cannons.

"Reload! Scattershot!" The Fire Sergeants screamed. Meanwhile, plumes of ripped turf and soil erupted among the ranks of charging Urghat, sending dozens of the burly warriors tumbling through the air. The roar of the cannons and the shock of the impacts sent a ripple through the charging line, and they faltered slightly, but growling shouts echoed over the fields, and the charge resumed. "Steady! Muskets and Blunderbusses! Ready!" Bronwyn watched, fascinated, barely noticing that Morgan and Issa arrived to stand next to her. The Urghat were less than a hundred yards away now. "Muskets and cannons! Fire!" Once again, the cry echoed down the wall, caught up by the different Fire Sergeants, and the muskets and cannons responded, a ripping blasting avalanche of explosions that rolled out from the center of the wall. All the smoke momentarily blinded Bronwyn, but as it drifted away on the breeze, she saw the carnage. "Reload! Cannons! Scattershot! Blunderbusses, ready!" The Urghat line had faltered; dozens, maybe hundreds, of the beast-men were down. Some were writhing around, some were turning to crawl or limp backward, but horns blared, and the lizard riders charged forward, roaring exhortations that Bronwyn couldn't make out, and the Urghat charge resumed.

"Steady! All guns ready!" The Fire Sergeants called the command down the line. The Urghat were less than fifty yards away, and suddenly they stopped, and as if by magic, which it probably was, ladders, shields, and a long wooden, log-shaped ram appeared among their number. "All guns, fire!" Again, the thunder rippled out from the center of the wall; this time, the blunderbusses added their concussion and smoke, and the silence that followed the blast was surreal.

As the smoke cleared, a hesitant cheer rose up among the militia on the wall, and Morgan, his eyes strangely glowing blue, said, "Jesus Christ." A moment later, Bronwyn could see the field and saw that most of the Urghat were running back the way they'd come, their ladders and ram dropped. As the cheer gained momentum and the militia began to celebrate, Bronwyn looked upon the carnage in the field. Hundreds of Urghat lay unmoving, and dozens more flailed and twitched or crawled around in agony. She couldn't muster any pride or happiness about this victory, and that bothered her almost as much as the scene before her.

"They have felt your defenses, so their next plan may be different," Issa said quietly. As she spoke, Bronwyn noticed that arrows were still flying from the wall, sinking into the writhing Urghat, ending their misery and snuffing out any hope that the Urghat might reclaim their wounded. A few zealous musket shots sounded out along the wall, followed by exhortations from the Fire Sergeants.

Bronwyn turned and walked away, down the stairs and back toward the town center. She doubted there'd be another attack that day if the Urghat didn't disperse altogether. She didn't know why, but she was in a foul mood. She reasoned that she should be happy; the Urghat had no noble intentions where the humans were concerned, and the militia had driven them back handily. Perhaps it was just the slaughter that bothered her; perhaps it was that she'd come to know a few Urghat fairly well and seen that they were people, not just monsters. The more she thought about it, the more she realized she was pissed that the Urghat leaders had sat back on their giant lizards and sent the regular Urghat into the meat grinder. In any case, she wanted to be alone, so she went back to Morgan's tower and, after greeting Tiladia, went up to her room.

Bronwyn took off her armor, throwing it on top of the linen chest at the foot of her bed, and stripped off her clothes. She walked into the little bathroom and started the tap running for the tub. She felt guilty soaking in a warm bath while people nearby were being eaten by carrion birds, but she tried to put that out of her mind. She just wanted to soak and not think about problems for a little while. The warm water relaxed her muscles, and she used the soap that the girl had given her in the bathhouse all those days ago to wash her body and hair. She felt a little sad that she couldn't remember her name. Didn't she say she worked at the tavern? Bronwyn resolved to go there and reintroduce herself. She laughed at the thought of using regular soap in her hair, but it was different these days. It didn't tangle as much, and it seemed to have a luster that wouldn't quit. "Perks of upgrading your race, I guess." As she spoke to herself, she idly wondered where Hops was. She hadn't seen him since sometime yesterday when she'd gone out to check on her Urghat followers. Hopefully, he was safe in the woods and nowhere near the conflict.

She'd slept like shit the last few days, so she wasn't surprised that she dozed off while soaking in the tub. When she woke, the water was tepid, almost cool, and she was contemplating getting out and finding Olivia when a System announcement appeared in her vision:

The election of the First Landing Council has been completed. Your new Council is listed below:	
1	Arthur Ballard
2	Reggie Arnold Gandry-Thule
3	Maria Rios
4	Olivia Bennet
5	Bronwyn Tallow
6	Tanya Delgado
7	Alec Green
8	Anthony Kerns
9	Morgan Hall

Bronwyn was glad to see that most of the old council had been re-elected. However, there were two changes: she didn't know the Reggie guy, and she knew that Alec was the bartender at the tavern. She liked Alec and figured he'd do a good job. All in all, it seemed like it could have been a lot worse.

⚔ MORGAN ⚔

Morgan walked out of the council meeting with a burgeoning headache. He couldn't believe that one guy could cause so much dissension. Every single topic had to be explained three times, and every single time, Reggie acted like he still didn't understand or agree with what was going on. He didn't like the way roads were being planned. He didn't like the way the militia was being operated. He didn't like the planned expansion of buildings. Each debate ended with someone frustrated and motioning to table discussion, someone else seconding it, and Reggie acting pissed off. He was grateful that Issa had decided to go and spar with some of the hunters from her town because he would have been embarrassed to have her at this meeting.

The strangest part had been when Reggie started talking about how they needed someone on the council to take a leadership role, a president of sorts. His voice had gotten very strange, kind of echoing around the chamber, and Morgan had looked at him with his Azure Sight, noticing big swirls of Energy pulsing up out of Reggie's Core and out like tendrils toward the council members. "What the fuck are you doing?" he'd asked, causing Reggie to break his speech pattern and stare at Morgan with wide eyes.

"What do you mean?"

"You're casting some sort of spell."

"No, it's just a speech amplification ability—it lets me come across more clearly."

"Don't use it around me," Morgan had said with finality, and the other council members had agreed—no Energy abilities or spells during meetings.

Now, it was early evening on election day; the council members had gone their separate ways to take care of various tasks, and Morgan was free for the night. Nobody expected another attack from the Urghat—they'd been quiet all afternoon—no drums, no horns, and little movement out among their tents. The consensus among the Ardeni Hunters was that they were licking their wounds and trying to brainstorm a new way to attack. Morgan stretched in the cool spring night, taking a deep breath of the fresh air. The battle hadn't really been a battle, and he hoped the Urghat would get the hint and just leave. There were a lot of things he wanted to do in this new world and sitting through a prolonged siege wasn't one of them. He turned toward his tower, which he was finally starting to think of as a home, and hoped he'd find Issa there waiting for him.

Reggie stepped out of the tavern with a frown. These assholes didn't want to give him the time of day. Every time he tried to explain that they were being dumbasses, someone argued with him, and one ass kisser after another would agree with the dipshit resisting him. It was like they had a little fucking club, and they'd all agreed ahead of time to make sure he didn't fit in. Still, he'd won the election, and sooner or later, they'd have to start listening to him.

When he thought about the election, he, of course, started thinking about Thun. Talk about an asshole! Thun had been bugging him for weeks to get the damn election going, and he'd finally put enough pressure on these assholes to make it happen. He walked over to one of the benches the old council had put up around the Colony Stone hill and sat down. He reached into his fur-lined vest and pulled out the little leather book, no larger than the palm of his hand that Thun had given him. He opened it to the last message that had appeared there just after the election had finalized: "At midnight, make sure there is a breach in the western wall."

Reggie groaned and once again scoured his brain for a way to get out of this damn contract. The problem was, each time he really thought about not doing what Thun wanted, he started to feel a queasy sensation in the center of his gut, and his fingers and toes began to go white and numb. It was the damnedest thing. Even now, he felt a little roiling in his belly, and his fingers were starting to go cool. He knew if he kept thinking about how to disobey Thun, the feeling would spread. Once, he'd really tried to push it, and he'd found himself rolling on the ground like his guts were going to come up, and his arms and legs were so numb and weak that he was afraid he wouldn't be able to stand up. He'd given in, swearing aloud to follow Thun's orders, and the sickness had slowly faded.

Reggie walked up to the Colony Stone and put his hand on it. He navigated the menus to the leadership tab and accessed the building menu. The walls were listed, and he could see where he could highlight portions of the wall and select things like "upgrade" or "remove." When he tried to click on those buttons, a message popped up saying he'd need "council consensus," whatever the fuck that meant. "Goddammit." He played around, selecting all the parts of the wall, trying to find a loophole, and finally struck gold. When he highlighted just the gate, there were the usual, yellow-highlighted buttons for upgrading or removing the gate, but another one was highlighted in green: "Open." He pulled out his little book and scribbled Thun a message.

* * *

Ironhide grunted. "They're moving into woods on the west side. They're up to something." He'd been out scouting, unable to sleep in the aftermath of the thunderous destruction of the Urghat charge earlier in the day. It had shaken him, and he was sure the other Urghat felt the same. If it weren't for Spineripper and the Underclaws enforcing their will, he was confident the Urghat horde would have dispersed after that thrashing. "You should sneak closer, see what you can find out." He nudged Heartseeker with his foot, urging the Scout to crawl out of her blankets.

"Why? The humans seem able to defend themselves. Besides, if I get too close, the Ur-clan will kill me, and so will the humans, unless our Underclaw is there to hold them back."

"Bah, you can move in the shadows better than any of them. Just go see what's happening." He nudged her again, and she swatted at his foot, but she got up. She looked around the camp, snorting at the sleeping forms of the twins and nodding at the others sitting around the coals of their earlier fire. Then she pulled her black hood up over her rust-colored fur and slipped into the shadows between the trees.

Heartseeker inched through the underbrush, crawling on her belly. The woods were swarming with Urghat. How could the humans not smell them? She'd worked her way to the edge of the woods and was slinking along the tree line toward the western gate of the human town. All the way, she passed by Urghat that were hunkered down or moving closer; her improved stealth was making fools of them. When she got to the area of the tree line that was adjacent to the human's gate, she began to hear the guttural chanting that she knew to be the Ur-clan shamans. They were working some kind of spell.

She looked through the low scrub she was hiding under toward the gate and saw that the humans had several guards directly above the gate and more patrolling nearby. Heartseeker frowned, wondering what the shamans could be up to. Then she felt a cold, slightly nauseating wave of Energy flow over her, and she watched, wide-eyed, as the guards above the gate slumped down without a word. Almost like they'd been knocked unconscious by an invisible force. Just then, the gates, with an audible creak, parted and opened.

Suddenly the trees and brush around her erupted with movement, and the shadowy forms of hundreds of Urghat began to stream across the open field between the trees and the wall, slinking quietly toward the open gate. Heartseeker knew it wasn't smart, at least not when it came to her own safety, but she pulled her bow from her storage pack and fitted it with an arrow. She channeled her Fireshot skill and launched a flaming, crackling arrow high into the air over the gate, where it burst into a small shower of embers. Then she turned and ran into the forest like a Yovashi was on her heels. She'd done what she could; hopefully, Bronwyn's people saw her warning.

Olivia was sitting near the Colony Stone, contemplating her next day. According to Issa, the first of Belintide was in three days. Did she want to arrive early or right on the deadline? If she wanted to be early, she was running out of days. If she left tomorrow, should she just go without any goodbyes? She liked goodbyes, unlike a lot of people, but she didn't want to make others uncomfortable. Bronwyn was not good at goodbyes. Morgan would probably be fine, and the other council members would just bug her to get back as soon as possible. "What is that?" she wondered aloud as a streak of fire shot up near the western gate, bursting into a shower of sparks, kind of like a firework.

Only when the bell started clanging did she put two and two together. The Urghat! They were doing something at the west gate. She heard shouts and saw militia sprinting from their temporary encampment at the base of the hill toward the gate. Olivia stood up and moved to the slope's edge, straining her eyes to see what was going on. The militia was charging toward the gate, but they only had spears; she knew the black powder troops would be running toward the alarm bell, but it would take them several minutes. Meanwhile, down the straight mile of road, she could see forms streaming through the gate, and then she heard a roar that shook her bones. It was reminiscent of the Urghat roars she'd heard earlier, but its volume and ferocity were more like what she'd imagine would come from a cave bear's mouth. The Urghat were through the gate.

Olivia turned and ran northward toward Morgan's tower. She ran toward his tower across the grass in a diagonal pattern, trying to make the shortest trip possible. It was dark, clouds obscuring the moons, and she was glad the meadow between the artisan buildings and Morgan's tower was relatively flat with little to trip on. She was running so hard that her breath was coming in short gasps by the time she was halfway there. The cool night air stung her eyes, causing tears to stream out the corners. As she reached the last downward slope toward the tower, she began to pick up speed thanks to gravity, but something suddenly caught against her foot, and she fell, tumbling head over heels in the grass.

Bruised and winded, she struggled to her hands and knees when a rough voice came from behind her: "Where do you think you're going, bitch?" Olivia whirled around, still on the ground, scooting backward on her butt, trying to see who had spoken. A large shadow was stalking toward her. Olivia summoned a fiery sphere into her hand, and the shadow shrank back in surprise, and she saw that it was Reggie.

"You motherfucker, why'd you trip me?"

"Because I don't need you stirring up trouble." Reggie had recovered from his surprise at the bright fiery orb and started stalking toward her again. Olivia didn't like the flat look in his eyes or the way his hands clenched and unclenched. She didn't bother speaking again; she just channeled Energy into her Stunning Ice Shards spell and pointed at Reggie.

"Suspendisse glacies!" Four crackling icy shards shot out toward Reggie, striking him dead center of mass. The shards punched through his clothes, sinking into his flesh about an inch, and his body convulsed; he flopped on the ground like he'd been hit by a 50,000-volt taser. Olivia didn't waste time, jumping to her feet and limp-running to the tower. She grabbed the handle, felt it unlock, and stepped inside.

"Morgan! Morgan, please awaken," Tiladia's chiming voice broke through Morgan's dream, and he startled awake. Issa was stirring beside him as well.

"Hmm, what is it?" He sat up and saw that Tiladia was moving around agitatedly, her lights blinking in a frenetic pattern.

"Morgan, Olivia has come with dire news—she says that your colony is under attack, invaders have breached the walls. They need your help!" She practically bounced as she spoke, her cloud of mist and lights flashing and spinning in short circles. Morgan felt a surge of adrenaline and jumped out of bed. He summoned his clothes and armor from his ring and began dressing.

"Issa, please help me with my armor; we have to get out there!" She was sitting up, already pulling on her pants and boots on the other side of the bed.

"I will. One minute, let me get dressed." She continued pulling on her clothes, and Morgan looked at Tiladia.

"Go make sure Bronwyn knows. Thanks for the message, Tiladia." He watched as she flew to the door and seemed to sink through the wood. He'd never seen her traverse a door before, and it was startling to see how she did it. He had his clothes and scale cuirass on by the time Issa came around the bed to help him strap on his greaves and vambraces. He slammed his helmet onto his head, tightened the strap under his chin, and jogged out of his room and down the stairs, Issa hot on his heels.

They found Olivia sitting on one of the foyer benches, wrapping a bandage around one of her knees. "Bronwyn already ran out; please go help her. I'll come do what I can. Also, watch out for Reggie—he attacked me on my way to warn you."

"What the fuck? Reggie, the new council member?"

"Yep. Please hurry!" Morgan nodded, and he and Issa stepped out. Even on the steps of his tower, they could hear the sounds of conflict: screams, roars, clashing metal, and the percussion of black powder guns splitting the air.

"Wait," Issa said, reaching a hand to rest on his shoulder. He felt warmth suffuse his body, but different from her Haste spell. "This will allow you to move much faster than normal, but not nearly as fast as Haste. Still, it will last for as long as I channel it. Go! I'll be close behind." Morgan didn't need to be told twice; his legs felt like they had static electricity running through them, and it almost felt like a release when he started sprinting toward the sounds of combat.

When he crested the low rise where the meadow leveled out toward the center of the colony grounds, he saw true chaos, as wild as any battlefield he'd ever seen back during the conflicts. Clouds of smoke filled the air, illuminated by dozens of different types of lights—fires, torches, lanterns, and floating orbs that colonists had summoned, some blue, some white, some yellow or red. Amid the fog-like smoke, pitched battles were being waged, and the results of those battles were everywhere; corpses and parts of corpses littered the cobblestone street. He saw musket-wielding militia members shoot and run to reload. He saw huge Urghat with metal armor barrel into them, hewing away at their poorly armored bodies with massive, crude weapons. Above it all were the screams and roars. He almost faltered, for lack of direction, trying to decide where he could help the most.

Morgan's decision was made for him as a pack of Urghat broke from around the bathhouse toward him, snarling and charging his way. Morgan had a brief moment of panic when he realized his hands were empty, but then he took a deep breath and centered himself, summoning his sword from his ring. He charged into the group of four burly beast-men and unleashed an Azure Burst. Their bodies engulfed in crackling blue flames, they fell away from him. Morgan followed up with quick slashes to the ones that still writhed, quickly dispatching them. He was looking for his next target when a roar, much louder than any of the others, sounded from near the Colony Stone.

Morgan ran toward the sound, and he came upon another pitched battle, stunned to see a semi-circle of Urghat watching the fight. Bronwyn was holding her own against two very large Urghat, both wearing heavy armor and wielding massive, jagged axes. Also watching, standing on the slope of the Colony Stone's hill, was an even larger Urghat. While Morgan looked at him, he roared again, stomping his feet and waving a huge, curved sword in the air. He wore thick, plated armor, painted red and black, and his fur-covered head was topped with a red-gold crown.

Morgan started toward him and was about fifty feet away when two musket-wielding militia appeared at the top of the hill. They both fired point-blank into the back of the huge Urghat, and he didn't even flinch. He turned, took two strides, and then bisected the men with his gargantuan saber. Morgan felt bile rise in his throat as the top halves of the men fell away and their entrails spilled out down the hillside. He choked it down and felt his disgust quickly give way to rage. "Hey, asshole. Try that on me!"

The Urghat turned toward him, and Morgan saw that the irises of his huge eyes were red and seemed to glow from within. His lips curved in a grin over his single, long, lower tusk. When he spoke, his voice was deep and thick with saliva, rolling out of him like a stone dragging through a rocky riverbed: "You challenge Spineripper? Come, fool. I'll dispatch you then share a meal of Blodwyn with my son and Underclaw." He whipped his saber through the air, sending a spray of blood toward Morgan, and then he charged like a bull down the hill, and Morgan could feel the earth move with each of his strides.

⚭ MORGAN ⚭

Morgan didn't intend to take the Urghat leader's charge head-on. He moved into the Crane Defends the Nest, channeling Energy into his limbs. When the massive brute came roaring into range, swinging his six-foot-long saber, Morgan glided backward and to the side fluidly, like a ribbon blowing ahead of a breeze. He swung his own sword in an upward angled parry, using the Urghat's momentum to fuel his movement away. The Overclaw roared in frustration and fury, and the volume and rage in the sound had a palpable effect. Morgan could feel a lethargic weight enter his limbs as if he should just drop his weapon and fall to his knees. He focused on his earlier rage at the sight of the militia members getting slaughtered, and with a genuine effort of will, he shook off the feeling.

"Morgan!" He spared a quick glance for Issa, who had run up to the scene and was looking at him expectantly, her rapier in hand.

"Help Bronwyn!" He would have appreciated an assist against the Overclaw, but Bronwyn had been fighting a defensive battle, barely keeping the two large Urghat at bay. Issa nodded and ran back into the smoke, making her way around the edge of the hill toward the sounds of the other battle. In the bare seconds it took to convey his message to Issa, Spineripper had turned and was moving toward him again. This time he moved more slowly, a low rumbling growl rolling out of his grimacing maw.

"You fight like a bug. I will water the grass with your juices." As he spoke, Morgan could see the Urghat's chest start to heave, and then he took a huge breath. Morgan didn't need a degree in Urghat studies to know he was about to scream another roar at him, so he decided not to stand in front of him. He activated Hollow Charge, angling his movement to the left side of the Urghat and aiming a sideways slash at the spot where the Spineripper's breastplate met some kind of chain armor over his stomach.

Morgan had fought fast enemies before, and he was prepared to have his attack thwarted by some mystical ability or speed, but he was pleasantly surprised that, as he flashed forward, the Urghat seemed to be moving in molasses.

He could see the Urghat start to swing toward him, but Morgan knew the attack would be far too slow. He tore over the grass, and his razor-edged sword connected with the Overclaw's stomach with devastating force, parting the links of chain armor like they were made of plastic and ripping a deep furrow in the Overclaw's belly and side. Morgan continued moving forward at the end of his charge, narrowly avoiding the backswing of the Urghat's attempt to cleave him in half.

Spineripper roared again, but this time it had little effect on Morgan. He simply shrugged off the lethargic effect and continued to circle his enemy, sword held in a low guard, waiting to see what he would do. As he moved, sidestepping, he was startled to see that another circle of Urghat was forming around him and Spineripper. Some of the onlookers held shields and were rhythmically pounding their weapons against them. Slowly, a crowd of stunned-looking Humans was gathering on the hillside. They had weapons ready and looked shell-shocked, but they were warily watching the Urghat, who, in turn, were watching Morgan and Spineripper. Morgan wanted to marvel at the strange scene, but Spineripper had other plans for his attention, swinging long, heavy cleaves at him. With his large deficit in strength and reach, Morgan was forced to move backward, lightly parrying Spineripper's cleaves at their apex. He knew if he tried to meet one of those saber strikes mid-swing, he'd run the risk of having his sword ripped from his hands.

Morgan had to arc his backpedalling in a semi-circle to avoid running into the surrounding ring of Urghat. Still, he didn't have much trouble avoiding Spineripper's deadly but slow and predictable swings. After dodging another flurry of blows that seemed to rip the air and tore into the turf, Morgan launched his own barrage, slipping into the Crane Flutters Its Wings. With his form fueled by Energy, Morgan brought his sword down and across in a series of cuts that parted the air in glowing shockwaves. The Overclaw was too slow to parry the first blow, which slid along his right vambrace and tore into his arm at the elbow joint. The Urghat blocked Morgan's second slash with his bracer, roaring and jerking his arm upward. Morgan was moving forward with Energy-fueled speed, trying to angle to the Urghat's side. At the same time, he swung, and his next two terrible slashes connected with Spineripper's side and then, finally, carved a deep furrow down his meaty back, slicing through chain armor.

Spineripper stumbled forward, dropping his sword and panting, bloody saliva dripping from his huge mouth. Morgan, for a moment, thought the fight was over, but then a red glow suffused the Urghat's entire body, and he arched his back, roaring into the sky with such volume that the onlookers fell back, some dropping to their knees. Morgan didn't know what was happening, but he wanted to stop it, so he charged toward Spineripper's back, aiming to impale his blade into his kidney. Just as the tip of his sword bit into the Urghat, a flash of red Energy billowed forth from the Overclaw, catching Morgan up in its passage, sending him sprawling into the grass.

Morgan looked up from the ground, somewhat dazed, to see Spineripper slowly turn toward him. He seemed taller, lankier, and his clawed hands had elongated with foot-long razor-edged talons nearly dragging on the ground. Spineripper's eyes had become red, fiery orbs, and he laughed in a gurgling roar, striding toward Morgan with renewed vigor and speed.

Issa hurried through the smoke and carnage, following the sounds of combat. She was surprised to find Urghat, not fighting but rather pressed into a crowd, jockeying for a better view of, what Issa presumed, was Bronwyn's battle. They seemed to be ignoring her, and Issa made her way around the crowd, trying to find an opening to get closer. She was shocked to see some other Ardeni and humans also gathering. It seemed that some sort of mutual agreement to stop fighting while the duels took place had been met. Issa knew that Urghat valued individual combat, and Ardeni would recognize a duel when they saw one, but she was surprised the humans had stopped fighting and shooting. Maybe the shock of the combat and the hundreds of deaths had taken the taste for blood out of their mouths, at least while the Urghat stayed their hands.

She found a section of the circle mostly made up of Ardeni and humans, and she began to push her way through. Not many Ardeni had any size on her, not since she'd upgraded her race in the Crucible, and they deferred to her when they saw who she was. The humans didn't fight much against her either as she pushed through, and soon she was standing on the edge of the ring and could see Bronwyn struggling against the two burly, heavily armored Urghat.

Bronwyn was on the defensive, clearly faster than either Urghat, but unable to push her advantage in speed because each time she tried to attack one of them, the other would start to flank her. She was constantly on her back foot, forced to block and dodge. Bronwyn's fists were huge and seemed to be harder than armor as she smacked their weapons aside. Issa looked at the crowd, and, using her Battle Chant voice, she yelled, "How is this a duel? Two versus one? Have Urghat no honor?" Her voice ripped through the sounds of the melee and over the clamor of the crowd, and the Urghat quieted, looking in her direction. One of the big Urghat fighting Bronwyn backed off a step and also looked at her.

"Bah, this false Underclaw stands with our enemy, and it was she that challenged us!"

"Still, there are two of you! Why not take turns? Do you fear to fight her alone?" As she spoke, Issa watched Bronwyn and saw her glance her way, clearly glad for the short respite. She seemed able to easily avoid the attacks of the single opponent still pressing her.

"Quiet, wench! We'll deal with you when we're done with this false Underclaw!" The Urghat turned and began to move back toward Bronwyn.

"What's your name, beast, that I might know what to call the fool that just challenged me?" The Urghat stopped in its tracks and looked at Issa, a malevolent glare entering its eyes. "You all heard him, right? Here he fights an unfair duel, and he challenged me when I called him out. Shall I not enter the fray?" The Ardeni and Humans started to stamp their feet and shout their agreement. The Urghat, not wanting to look afraid, also started to bang their shields.

"Alright, blue bitch! Come and fight Carnage, first Underclaw of Spineripper. Come, be meat under my axe!" He whipped his massive cleaver-like axe back and forth, evoking snapping, whooshing sounds where it parted the air. Issa only smiled and activated Haste, gliding like a beam of light over the ground to stand shoulder to shoulder with Bronwyn.

"Welcome to the fun," Bronwyn said with a sideways glance.

"My pleasure, now, get ready." Issa, holding her rapier out toward the two Urghat coming toward them menacingly, placed her left hand on Bronwyn's shoulder and channeled a fresh Haste into her. Bronwyn's eyes widened, and then she burst forward in a blur, slapping her opponent's sword aside and unleashing a flurry of devastating punches into his stomach and groin. He tried to react, but it was like watching a honeysipper attack a buldorii. Even with her haste, she wasn't immune to damage, and the other Urghat was finally within range to pose a threat, so Issa darted forward, engaging him with a series of feints and jabs. His clumsy swings with his giant cleaver were easy to dodge, and Issa dodged sideways, forcing him to turn away from Bronwyn and her foe. Then she began a true Battle Chant, her voice becoming loud and discordant, raising the hackles of all who witnessed its eerie sound. Her yellow-gold eyes started to change to deep violet, and a black mist spread into the air around her. She poured her Energy into it and started to feel the strength flow into her limbs, and she knew Bronwyn could feel it also. Conversely, the Urghat's eyes widened, and his swings became even slower.

Issa slowly backed up, maintaining her barrage of thrusts and feints. As she created distance between herself and Bronwyn, she could see, behind the Urghat's back, Bronwyn begin to take apart her opponent. Her fists landed with loud wet crunches as she circled the sword-wielding Urghat. Issa could see that Bronwyn's strikes were destroying the creature even through his plate armor. Issa turned her full attention to her enemy and gave him a wicked smile as her disturbing chant continued to lay a heavy pall over the combat ring. Then, the moment she'd waited for came as her Haste spell came off cooldown again, and she erupted into action.

Issa flashed around the side of the Urghat, burying her rapier into his side and back. Over and over, she stabbed him. He struggled to turn, but Issa just kept circling him, easily twice as fast as he was. Her Haste spell was at the improved level, and she could keep it running for a full ten seconds. In that time, she stabbed the Urghat Underclaw twelve times. Issa backed off when she felt the telltale lengthening of her breaths and pounding of her heart, watching the Urghat slowly realize that it was dying.

She looked over to see Bronwyn standing over the broken corpse of her enemy. Then she saw that the circle was dispersing, and, with dirty looks for each other, the different peoples were moving toward the only remaining sounds of combat—Morgan was still fighting the Overclaw. Motes of Energy were flowing toward her and Bronwyn as she heard a screaming roar that threatened to stop her heart. Bronwyn looked at her, eyes wide, and shouted, "Let's go!"

Morgan scrambled to his feet as Spineripper charged. He'd just managed to plant his back foot and bring his sword up when the brute was upon him. No longer swinging one giant blade, the Overclaw came at him, swinging both taloned hands. The flurry of strikes was too much for Morgan to keep up with; he managed to parry the first couple of strikes but soon found himself backpedaling, desperately trying to keep his blade between himself and those slicing claws. Before he could fall into the Crane Defends the Nest, one of those sets of talons got around his guard and raked across his chest and stomach. Morgan was stunned to see his armor hold up; the heavy metal scales were scored but not cut through. Then he activated his defensive form, and his blade was suddenly able to parry far more slashes. He waved his sword back and forth almost with no effort, repelling the frenzied, slashing attacks.

Spineripper grew more and more frustrated, finally giving up all semblance of strategy or thought, and simply rushed Morgan, barreling into him and pulling him to the ground. Morgan knew he couldn't survive long pinned beneath the gnashing clawing Urghat that had to weigh close to five hundred pounds. Even as he fell backward, he began to channel Azure Burst, and when his back hit the turf and he felt the Urghat's weight begin to settle on him, he unleashed it. Blue light filled his vision as the force of the spell erupted out of him, directed by the ground beneath him. The full force roared upward into the massive Urghat, ripping him away from Morgan and into the air. Morgan rolled to the side, onto one knee, and then stood, taking stock of the aftermath.

Spineripper was rolling in the grass about twenty feet from him; the circle of onlookers had turned into a massive crowd. Urghat swarmed one side, out toward the gate, and the colonists and Ardeni made up the other half, spread out for hundreds of feet and all the way up the side of the Colony Stone hillside. Morgan didn't know how they'd come to agree to stop fighting and mutually watch the combat, but he was glad—as long as they weren't fighting, more people weren't dying. He turned back to Spineripper and saw that he'd stopped rolling and begun to get to his feet. He moved in a jerking, faltering manner, and when he turned to regard him, Morgan could see why: much of his face was burned away, down to the bone, but the baleful red eyes persisted, and though Morgan was sure he'd burned him elsewhere, the beast's armor obscured the damage.

Spineripper let out another terrible roar, the flesh around his jaws parting while he screamed into the air. The crowd grew quieter, backing up a step, but the cry no longer had any effect on Morgan, and he used Hollow Charge to close the distance, unleashing another Crane Flutters Its Wings. The sudden attack, during his howl, caught Spineripper off guard, and he belatedly brought his claws up to block Morgan's series of cleaves. It turned out the lengthening of Spineripper's limbs during his transformation was a double-edged sword: his arms were no longer fully encased in his plate armor. Morgan used his heightened dexterity to make minute adjustments to the trajectory of his blade, aiming for the gaps. His first two cleaves sparked against talons or armor, but his third one bit through flesh and bone, rendering Spineripper's left arm useless. Morgan yanked his blade free and pulled back, interrupting his combo.

Spineripper howled again and turned, rampaging back toward the circle of Urghat, swinging his good arm against their shields. Morgan could only guess what Spineripper was thinking—was he trying to flee? Was he driven mad by pain and rage? In any case, the Urghat didn't break but held their shields up, forcing the weakened Overclaw to turn back toward Morgan. Morgan, for his part, dropped his blade into the Crane Forages, sliding over the ground toward the beast-man. Spineripper's mad eyes darted around, looking from one edge of the circle to the other, then he roared and, like a rabid grizzly bear, charged at Morgan again. Morgan was ready, his footwork perfect, and his sword like liquid lightning as it rose to slip, point-first, over the top lip of the Urghat's breastplate into his neck. Morgan rode the charge, backing up enough to avoid the frenzied claw attack. Then he sidestepped, twisted his sword, and yanked it to the side, cutting through half of the Urghat's neck. Blood fountained from the wound, and the titan collapsed with a ground-shaking *thud*.

With hoots and howls, the horde of Urghat, as one, turned and started to flee, streaming through the gate and into the night. The colonists and the Ardeni cheered, firing bows and muskets after the fleeing horde. Morgan felt a warm hand slip into his, and he looked down to see Issa smiling up at him. Another hand clapped him on the back, and Bronwyn said, "Nice fucking fight! I think we broke their Ur-clan. I don't think we'll have trouble from them for a very long time." Morgan was about to respond when a massive torrent of Energy transfixed him.

Congratulations! You have achieved level 20 Hollow Guard and have gained 10 Strength, 10 Will, 8 Vitality, 8 Intelligence, and 6 Agility.

Level 20 Class refinement. Class refinement is permanent. Human Energy cultivators will next be offered a Class refinement selection at level 30. To view your options and make your selection, access the menu through your status page.

"Did you level? Bronwyn and I did!" Issa's voice was thick with excitement and emotion.

"Yeah, twice, in fact."

"How's that fair?" Bronwyn laughed, but Morgan's reply was drowned out by the cheering jostling crowd as they closed in around the trio. Musket shots continued in the distance, and Morgan almost felt sorry for the fleeing Urghat, but then, they had come here to eat everyone, so he didn't allow his sympathy to venture too far.

MORGAN

Morgan watched as Bronwyn pulled the metal ring off the Overclaw's bicep. "I'll hold onto this and the one from that Carnage bastard that Issa killed. I need to talk to my followers about them. You know, how many Underclaws there are, how one becomes an Overclaw, whether I should destroy these or what."

"Sure, makes sense." Morgan knelt by the huge Overclaw's corpse and pulled the red-gold crown off his blood-matted, furry head. The crown was heavy and unnaturally cold as he slipped it into his storage ring. Before going over the rest of Spineripper's gear, he looked around, almost feeling guilty for stripping the corpse. Most of the crowd had dispersed, and bodies were being pulled away—the Urghat corpses to the field outside the wall to burn on a pyre and the dead colonists to a plot of land outside the south gate. The engineers had decided that a cemetery would be best placed in that direction because it was downslope from the colony. He sighed and knelt to start unstrapping the black, rune-covered armor from the Urghat.

"Morgan"—Olivia walked up, her face flushed with exertion—"everyone's talking about your battle. Yours too, Bronwyn."

"We were just two among many that fought tonight. How many colonists paid with their lives for that fucking asshole's treachery?" Bronwyn spat on the ground.

"Well, it's lucky that you were here to fight their leaders—it cut the invasion off at the knees. You, too, Issa. Thank you for helping Bronwyn."

"You're welcome," Issa said, walking up to the three of them, dragging the massive scimitar that Spineripper had dropped when he went through his transformation. Morgan chuckled and reached out a hand, and Issa pulled the sword's handle up to him. He hefted the sword, but it took two hands and felt too unwieldy for him. He lowered it to better look at the weapon; its hilt was some kind of polished wood, but it didn't feel slippery. The guard and pommel were red tinted steel, adorned with runes, and the blade was a wide, curved affair with a baleful red glint. It seemed like a truly powerful weapon, but he'd have to revisit it when he'd gained more strength. For now, he added it to his ring's inventory.

"Help me get this armor off this guy," he said to Issa, and she grunted in disgust but knelt to help. "Any sign of Reggie?" Morgan asked Olivia, reminded of the traitor by Bronwyn's comment.

"No, but Arthur, a few others, and I removed him from the council at the Colony Stone."

"Well, that's good at least. Hopefully, he winds up as Urghat food." Issa grunted, pulling on the leather straps of the Overclaw's breastplate. Soon they had all the armor removed from the dead warlord, and Morgan put it into his storage pouch.

"I got two sets of heavy armor off the other guys that Issa and I killed. I don't think they're better than what you have, Morgan, so I'll probably trade it to the smiths here for some labor credits. You don't want it, do you, Issa?" Bronwyn asked.

"No, thank you. I don't do well with armor that weighs twice what I do!"

"Well, they each had storage pouches, too. Here's the one off your guy." Bronwyn tossed a rune-inscribed leather pouch to Issa. "Hopefully, it has some good stuff. My guy's only had a few dozen Energy beads, a bunch of meat, some camping supplies, and some leather and fur clothes."

"Thank you, Bronwyn."

"This Overclaw didn't even have a pouch or ring or anything." Morgan sighed. "You supposed he had a designated lackey to hold his gear?"

"Probably. One of the Urghat that challenged me on the plains had some little Urghat helpers that carried his stuff." Bronwyn shrugged.

"Ah, well, I suppose we should help clean up. Then I'm going to sleep like the dead. I have a class refinement waiting for me, and I want to tackle it with a fresh head in the morning."

"Hah, in the morning? It's already here." Issa pointed to the east, where the sky was beginning to lighten.

"Oh, dammit." The four of them got to work, helping the colonists drag corpses out of the colony. Someone had the idea to use storage containers, which made the job go a lot faster, though it weirded Morgan out, popping corpses in and out of his storage bag. The pyre to burn the Urghat was easily accomplished by the various people who knew fire magic but digging the two hundred and eighty graves for the dead colonists was a much bigger task. A few colonists had some skill with earth magic, though throwing stone darts was different than digging holes. With experimentation, one colonist discovered a spell that raised large clumps of soil out of the ground, and he taught it to several others. With their help and nearly everyone in the colony pitching in and taking a turn with the shovels, it was done in a few hours.

Arthur Ballard spoke to the assembled colonists, commemorating the battle, honoring the dead, and noting that their sacrifices helped bring about the end of the first real threat they'd faced as a people on this new world. "Let me remind everyone here: our challenges have only just begun, and true fortitude will be required to make this world our home. We've forged an alliance with the people of Tarn's Crossing that has been tempered in blood, and we've shown the hostile entities in these parts that we aren't going anywhere. Now, in honor of our fallen comrades, let this day, the 34th day of Hondine, be ever known as a First Landing holiday. It is a day of victory and defiance in the face of evil."

More people spoke after Arthur—Maria Rios, Dr. Kerns, and even Olivia. Morgan and Issa listened, holding hands, and for the first time in a long while, he didn't feel like he had a threat hanging over his head.

Morgan looked through his options one more time:

Class refinement option 1: Hollow Swordsman—Advanced. You have embraced the way of the sword and seek to master its nuances. You use your unique abilities to siphon the Energy of your foes while dominating them with speed and martial prowess. Class attributes: Agility, Dexterity, Strength, Vitality, and Will.

Class refinement option 2: Hollow Weapon Master—Advanced. The right tool for the right job, and you have all the tools. The weapons of war are yours to choose from. You learn to manipulate Energy to weaken your foes while controlling the battlefield with your wide array of martial skills. Class attributes: Strength, Agility, and Dexterity.

Class refinement option 3: Hollow Bulwark—Advanced. Standing in the path of danger is your hallmark. You begin to learn how to absorb damage and recover from blows that would defeat a lesser being. Class attributes: Vitality, Strength, and Will.

Class refinement option 4: Vortex Duelist—Epic. More than strength, and more than low cunning, you value skill and the rule of single combat. With consummate adroitness and unparalleled mastery of Energy, you seek to face your foes in open, honorable combat. Class attributes: Intelligence, Agility, Will, and Dexterity.

Class refinement option 5: No Refinement—You are pleased with the path on which you find yourself and choose to continue until your next refinement option.

As soon as he and Issa had come back to the tower, bathed, and put on clean clothes, he'd sat down in front of the window in their bedroom and started going over his options. He'd already described his choices to Issa, and before going to sleep, she had given him her take: an Epic class at level twenty was rare and valuable but not something he should automatically choose. Epic classes gave more stats and more powerful skills, but they also took longer to level and might force him down a narrower development path than he wanted. She'd learned that the higher level a person got, the more likely they'd see Advanced and higher classes, so if he had the option at twenty, there was a good chance he'd see an Epic class at thirty. All in all, her advice had been to focus on the class descriptions and stats. She had suggested paying particular attention to the order in which those stats were listed while he decided; he shouldn't only focus on the label of "Epic" or "Advanced."

The truth was that Morgan liked the sounds of all of the classes. The idea of becoming a true swordmaster appealed to him on a visceral level that called forth memories of fantasy novels he'd read when he was younger. Being a master of all weapons was similarly appealing, and Morgan liked the versatility it promised. Then there was the Bulwark class—shrugging off damage meant for those he cared about was what had pointed him to the path he was currently on. Wouldn't it be great to maximize those abilities? But the Vortex Duelist—that class just sounded badass. He knew he couldn't voice that line of reason to Issa or someone else; it sounded like something a middle schooler would say, but he couldn't deny his feelings.

More than his feelings, though, Morgan was considering the name and description of the class. It reminded him of the Vortex Mage class he'd been offered at level ten, seeming to focus on his specific Core type, but this time it incorporated some melee abilities and attributes. He definitely needed the dexterity, but he also liked the idea of continuing to increase his intelligence and, thereby, his spellcasting ability. None of the other refinement options included intelligence.

The most significant factor, though, was the line about him not valuing low cunning; was the System listening to him? Was it learning from his choices and tailoring this class to him? He'd certainly agonized over his decision to switch from the spear to the sword and avoid killing people with surprise attacks—at least where possible. Much of that had been silent introspection, though—he'd only made a few offhand comments to Olivia while traveling and to Issa when she asked. Was the System that much in his head, or was it just a coincidence?

Morgan felt like more deliberation would only lead to more questions and more doubt. He opened his status screen, moved to the class refinement page, and selected the Vortex Duelist.

Congratulations! You have made your first class refinement: Vortex Duelist. Class skill gained: Energy Drain—Advanced. Class skill gained: Circle of Combat—Improved.

Congratulations! World-first Vortex Duelist! Feat awarded.

Morgan couldn't help the smile that came to his lips as he felt a warm rush of knowledge pour, seemingly out of the air, into his head. By the time it stopped, he was lying back on the rug he'd been sitting on, and he had to struggle to sit up. His head was foggy, and his mouth was dry, and he briefly wondered how long he'd been out of it. He called up the description for his new skills and title:

Energy Drain—Advanced: Prerequisite: Vortex Class Core. You are able to sense the flows of Energy within beings near you and forcefully pull it forth with the strength of your Core. Energy drawn in this manner will help to restore your health and vitality and greatly weaken your target(s). Beings with a stronger Core may resist you. Energy cost: 150 per target being, Cooldown: Medium.

Circle of Combat—Improved: Prerequisite: Vortex Class Core. You expend some Energy to create a void barrier around you and an opponent. Attempts to breach the barrier from within or without will require Energy and Will in opposition to your own. The barrier will persist until you run out of Energy or either you or your opponent is defeated. Energy cost: 500 + maintenance to resist breaches, Cooldown: Long.

First Vortex Duelist: Feat granted: Void Pocket—You have access to an extradimensional space that persists as long as you allow Energy to sustain it. The size of the space is proportional to the amount of Energy you dedicate to it.

When Morgan read the description of the Advanced Energy Drain, he had to reread it a few times and then search out the knowledge the System had put into his head to make sure he was right: he could now reach out and pull raw Energy from multiple enemies at once, and he didn't need to be touching them. "That's a game-changer," he muttered as he read through the other descriptions. The circle was another spell with big implications. Presumably, he could isolate an enemy and force them to fight him one on one, even amid their allies. The whole battle would have been different if the Urghat hadn't been keen on watching a duel. Now, Morgan could force the duel if such a thing came up again.

Finally, Morgan activated his Void Pocket ability, channeling a bare trickle of Energy into it. The space wasn't visible, but he could feel it. He reached out to it with his mind and saw that with just five Energy devoted to maintaining the space, it was the size of a large box, around eight square feet. To double that size took fifteen Energy. Morgan let the space wink out of existence for now. It would indeed be valuable to have a dimensional container that no one could remove from him, but he wondered what would happen to his things if he ran out of Energy somehow. He'd have to do some experimentation. As he sat there, thinking about this new class and the abilities he'd gained, he realized that the light coming through the window was growing brighter, and he groaned. He'd missed his chance for any sleep; he and Issa were going to meet Olivia and Bronwyn in just a couple of hours.

He took one last look at his status sheet before he had to get moving:

Status			
Name:	Morgan Hall		
Race:	Human - Base 4		
Class:	Vortex Duelist - Epic		
Level:	20		
Core:	Vortex Class - Base 3		
Energy Affinity:	9.2	Energy:	1764/1764
Strength:	65	Vitality:	60
Dexterity:	8 (30)	Agility:	45
Intelligence:	68	Will:	65
Points Available:	0		
Titles & Feats:	Human Champion, First Hollow Guard, Ardeni Friend, Mark of Loyalty, Yovashi Bane, Legacy of the Azure Paladin, First Vortex Duelist		
Skills:	• System Language Integration - Not Upgradeable • Animal Taming - Basic • Stealthy Maneuvers - Basic • Melee Weapon Mastery - Basic • Fighting Crane Style - Basic • Sword Mastery - Improved • Vortex Core Cultivation Drill - Basic	• Backstab - Basic • Energy Drain - Advanced • Circle of Combat - Improved • Guard Ally - Basic • Hollow Charge - Improved • Azure Burst - Basic • Azure Sight - Basic	

Olivia smiled to herself as she listened to Morgan talk about his new class. Bronwyn was asking him a lot of questions and seemed excited by the prospect of a class refinement. Of the four of them, Olivia was the only one without a class, and she was also excited, but right now, she was content just to listen and enjoy the company. They'd met downstairs in Morgan's tower and then walked to the tavern together. It was early, and after a hard enough day that most of the colony was still asleep, they didn't have any trouble getting a table. Olivia had wanted to meet early, and the fact that her friends hadn't argued was one of the reasons she was smiling. It felt nice to have friends that felt like family. She'd left behind everyone in her life who cared about her, and one of her fears about the journey had been that she wouldn't be able to make connections with the other colonists.

"Thank you so much for seeing me off, you guys," she said, interrupting Morgan's description of how he hoped one of his new skills worked. They all stopped talking and looked at her, and Bronwyn reached an arm around her neck, pulling her into a side-hug.

"You're crazy for wanting to go so early, but if you think we'd let you go without a goodbye, you're even crazier!"

"Nah, I get it," Morgan said. "The school starts in two days, and we don't know what time it is there. It's like a thousand miles from Tarn's Crossing, right? Also, what if the teleportation isn't instant?"

"Exactly!" Olivia said, beaming at Morgan. Issa reached a hand down to her pouch and brought up a small package wrapped in bright yellow silk.

"A going away gift." Her smile was wide and warm as she passed the package to Olivia.

"Oh, you didn't have to do that." Olivia carefully untied the pale green ribbon and let the silk fall away from the smooth wooden box. The box was polished and light in color, like maple. She carefully lifted the lid, and it swung open on tiny brass hinges. Inside were dozens of brightly colored little pencils. Every color she could imagine was represented. "Oh, they're beautiful!"

"Who knows what kind of classes you'll have to take at this school. Maybe they'll make you draw things, so I thought it would be good to have some colors!" Issa's eyes were wide and bright in her earnestness, and Olivia suddenly felt glad that they were friends. She stood up and walked around the table to hug her. She was warm, and her bright yellow hair smelled like vanilla.

"Thank you again, and please tell me what you washed your hair with; it smells amazing!"

"Oh? Really? Here!" Issa pulled a small brown bottle from her pouch and passed it to Olivia. "It's a mix of some essential oils—I just put a little behind my ears." She glanced around the table and started to blush, her light blue cheeks turning a reddish-purple color. Olivia smiled and took the little bottle.

"Thank you!"

"Oh, geez." Bronwyn sighed. "I'm such a dope. I didn't bring a gift."

"Yeah, me either," Morgan said, rubbing a hand over his head.

"Oh, hush! I don't need any presents. Besides, I'll just expect even better homecoming presents from you two! If they ever let me come home, that is . . ." She trailed off, some of her bravado seeping away.

"Of course, they will," Issa said. "Magister Karn wouldn't send you someplace sinister, don't worry!"

"I suppose not." Olivia mustered another smile. They spent another thirty minutes or so speculating about what the academy would be like, then they talked about all their plans and the plans for the colony. Finally, out of topics, Olivia stood up. "I'm going to get going. Don't make a big deal; just give me a quick hug, then I'm going to use this token." She held up the silvery coin-shaped token. Issa was first to comply, standing up and giving Olivia another squeeze, then she stepped away. Morgan followed suit, and Olivia was surprised at just how big he was; she could barely reach her arms around his chest, and it was like hugging a tree trunk. He stood off to the side with Issa, and then Bronwyn came over and hugged her.

While still large and strong, Bronwyn was softer than Morgan, and she held Olivia more fiercely. Olivia could feel tears coming into her eyes, and she blinked rapidly, shoving her face into Bronwyn's thick red hair. Finally, Bronwyn stepped back, holding her at arm's length, and Olivia could see she wasn't the only one fighting tears. She forced a smile, then said, "I'll be back before you know it. Stay safe!"

Bronwyn started to speak, but her voice betrayed her, and she pulled Olivia close again, squeezing her. Finally, she muttered softly in Olivia's ear, "Remember what I said about anyone messing with you!" Bronwyn sniffed and backed up a step. Olivia sent a trickle of Energy into her teleportation token, and the world went dark.

Reggie ran. He ran, and he ran. He'd been running all night, and when the sun came up, he was still running. As soon as he'd recovered from that bitch's spell, he'd left out the south gate, and he hadn't stopped running since. He'd turned a bit to the west in the dark; he could tell by the sunrise, and he found himself in some foothills leading up from the thick woods surrounding the colony. He figured they were the hills where some colonists had found caves with black powder ingredients and iron.

He was exhausted, and he started to look for a place to rest. An hour or so after dawn, he saw a dark spot on a hillside, and he started clambering up the scree toward it. Hands bloodied from the effort, he finally pulled himself into the narrow cave. Inside, the cave floor had a steep downward angle, and he carefully started climbing in. He had just gotten his feet out of the open when he felt the ground crumble a bit under his hands, and he began to slide, head-first, down the rough slope. He cried out in alarm, but just as suddenly as his slide had started, it stopped, and he found himself wedged tightly into a dark tunnel.

Panic entered Reggie's mind as he tried to inch forward or backward, and he found he couldn't move. He writhed side to side but barely managed to turn an inch in either direction and when he did so, he only seemed to wedge himself tighter. He screamed, suddenly without a rational thought in his mind, and jerked his body in every direction he could think of. It was fruitless, and he soon found himself completely exhausted and stuck tighter than ever. He racked his brain for any sort of solution, but nothing came to him, and after more fruitless grunting and struggling, he finally passed out in exhaustion.

A tickling at his outstretched fingertips woke him. "Is someone down there? Help!" His words croaked out of his dry throat, and then suddenly, the tickling became a searing pain as something bit into his flesh. He screamed again, his vocal cords straining at his panicked agony. More bites on his hands raised the register of his scream several octaves, and then something tickled his beard hairs, and a savage bite ripped away his lower lip.

Distantly, Thun felt his connection to the human, Reggie, fade away. It didn't concern him; the fool had served his purpose, allowing him to do a favor for the Overclaw in exchange for the shrike's heart. His mouth watered at the thought of the artifact; every cell in his body yearned for him to consume it. "Soon enough, soon enough," he whispered to himself as he made his way through the pass. First, he had to cross the mountain, then he had to traverse the frost grove, and then, only after he'd gotten the Lady's blessing would he eat the heart and push his race to the next tier. Perhaps in a few years, he'd make his way back south to see what the humans had accomplished with their victory. Their tenacity and cleverness had impressed him; might be he'd find a much better student in their midst.

ABOUT THE AUTHOR

Plum Parrot is the pen name of author Miles Gallup, who grew up in Southern Arizona and spent much of his youth wandering around the Sonoran Desert, hunting imaginary monsters and building forts. He studied creative writing at the University of Arizona and, for a number of years, attempted to teach middle schoolers to love literature and write their own stories. If he's not out enjoying the beach, you can find Gallup writing, reading his favorite authors, or playing *D&D* with friends and family.

DISCOVER
STORIES UNBOUND

PodiumAudio.com

www.ingramcontent.com/pod-product-compliance
Ingram Content Group UK Ltd.
Pitfield, Milton Keynes, MK11 3LW, UK
UKHW041304180426
11947UKWH00009B/663